Helen Hollick lives in north-east London on the edge of Epping Forest with her husband, adult daughter and a variety of pets, which include several horses, cats and two dogs. She has two major interests: Roman / Saxon Britain and the Golden Age of Piracy – the early eighteenth century.

Her particular pleasure is researching the facts behind the small glimpses of history and bringing the characters behind those facts to full and glorious life. She has an Honours Diploma in Early Medieval History, and may one day, if ever she finds the time between writing and helping her daughter with her career as a semi-professional show jumper, go on to obtain her full degree.

For up-to-date information you are invited to visit:
Main Website: www.helenhollick.net
Muse and Views Blog: www.helenhollick.blogspot.com
Picture Diary: www.helenhollicksdiarydates.blogspot.com

GW00361253

Praise for Helen Hollick's novels

"If only all historical fiction could be this good"
Historical Novels Review

"Hollick joggles a cast of characters and a bloody, tangled plot with great skill"
Publishers Weekly

"A wonderful book ... breathes new life into an ancient legend. Compelling, convincing and unforgettable"
Sharon Penman

"Most impressive"
The Lady

"Uniquely compelling ... bound to have a lasting and resounding impact on Arthurian literature"
Books Magazine

"Helen Hollick joins the ranks of Rosemary Sutcliff, Mary Stewart and Marion Bradley with this splendid novel"
Pendragon Magazine

"Weaves together fact, legend and inspired imagination to create a world so real we can breathe the smoke of its fires and revel in the Romano-British lust for life, love and honour"
Historical Novel Review

"An epic re-telling of the Norman Conquest"
The Lady

"Everything we want in a grand pirate adventure ... A Terrific read"
James L. Nelson

"In the sexiest pirate contest, Cpt Jesamiah Acorne gives Johnny Depp's Jack Sparrow a run for his money"
Sharon Penman

The Kingmaking

Book One of the
Pendragon's Banner Trilogy

Helen Hollick

First published in the UK in 1994 by William Heinemann ISBN 043400068X
Second Edition published in the UK in 1995 by Arrow ISBN 0099416239
Third Edition published in the UK in 2006 by Discovered Authors ISBN 9781905108268

This paperback edition published by CallioPan
an imprint of CallioPress

37 Great Russell Street, London WC1B 3PP, United Kingdom
555 Fifth Avenue N.E. Suite 343, Saint Petersburg, Florida 33701, USA
www.calliopress.com

ISBN 978-0-85778-034-8

Cover Design by Cathy Helms
www.avalongraphics.org

A CIP catalogue record for this book is available from
the British Library.

Available from CallioPress Online, all major online retailers
and available to order through your local bookshop.
Visit www.calliopress.com to buy our books
or email sales@calliopress.com

Printed and bound in the UK by The Callio Press Limited
Printed and bound in the USA by Entelyx International Inc.

For Sharon Penman
with my love and gratitude

Acknowledgements

My acknowledgements for this edition of The Kingmaking remain virtually unaltered. I wrote The Kingmaking some years ago and have therefore welcomed this given chance, with this new edition, to add a final, more experienced polish. I remain indebted to so many: the efficient and welcoming staff at Higham Hill Public Library, Walthamstow; Charles Evans-Gunther and Fred and Marilyn Stedman-Jones for their encouragement and support.

My sincere thanks go to the entire team at CallioPress – especially Michaela who has worked so hard and enthusiastically and to Cathy Helms for the superb new covers. My appreciation to Anne for taking the time to pose as Gwenhwyfar, and to Ashley for her support and ideas. I must also repeat my gratitude to my original editor at William Heinemann, Lynne Drew, who guided me through the first confusing muddle of becoming an author; and say thank you to my previous agent Mic Cheetham.

To my special friends, Hazel and Derek – although sadly Hazel is no longer with us, she is very much missed – to Mal for his belief in me and to Sharon Penman for her support and encouragement, Elizabeth Chadwick for the same and Bernard Cornwell for providing his wonderful quote. I was flattered that he remembered meeting me – thank you. Writing is a solitary occupation, true friends are especially needed. Also, a thank you to Richard Cope for his knowledge of birds; Sue and Geoff for showing me the very beautiful area of Wales near Valle Crucis Abbey; Joan Bryant, and her late husband Bill, who taught me so much about horses; and Doris Hawkins and Joan Allen, both lovely ladies. It is often the little things that help the most. To my Mum and sister Margaret for being there. My only regret is that my Dad is not alive to share the pleasures of success.

Finally, and most important, I thank my husband Ron and daughter Kathy who have never complained at my involvement in my work, nor minded the long journeys to visit remote sites for research. Ron has supported me through some difficult years of writing.

Helen Hollick, 2010

Britain circa AD 455

Place Names

Agealesthrep	*Aylesford, Kent*
Caer Arfon	*Caernarvon*
Caer Dydd	*Cardiff*
Caer Gloui	*Gloucester*
Caer Leon	*Caerleon*
Camulodunum	*Colchester*
Cantii	*Kent*
Ceredigion	*Area around Cardigan Bay*
Crae Ford	*Crayford, Kent*
Dubris	*Dover*
Dumnonia	*Devon and Cornwall*
Dun Pelidr	*Traprain Law*
Durobrivae	*Rochester*
Durovernum	*Canterbury*
Eboracum	*York*
Eryri	*Snowdonia*
Gaul	*France*
Hafren	*River Severn*
Hibernia	*Ireland*
Iceni Way	*Ickneild Way*
Less Britain	*Brittany*
Ligre	*River Loire*
Londinium	*London*
Mon	*Anglesey*
Portus Adumi	*Portchester castle, Portsmouth*
Rutupiae	*Richborough*
Summer Land	*Somerset*
Tamesis	*River Thames*
Tanatus	*Thanet*
Vectis	*Isle of Wight*
Venta Bulgarium	*Winchester*
Yns Witrin	*Glastonbury Tor*
Yr Wyddfa	*Mount Snowdon*

People

Scotti	*Migrated from Ireland to modern Western Scotland*
Angles/Saxons/Jutes	*Anglo-Saxons, English, or Saex*
Picti	*Tribespeople from Caledonia, Eastern Scotland*
British	*Celts/Welsh*
Hibernian	*Irish*

Pronunciation

a basic guide to the rough pronunciation to some of the Welsh names

Abloyc	*ab-loy-c*
Bedwyr	*bed-oo-ear*
Cei	*kay*
Cunedda	*kin-eth-a*
Cymraes	*cum-rice*
Dogmail	*dog-my-1*
Dunaut	*din-eye-t*
Enniaun	*en-nee-eyen*
Gorlois	*gor-loys*
Gwenhwyfar	*gwen-hwee-var*
Gwynllyw	*gwin-(h)lee-oo*
Iawn	*yown*
Llacheu	*(h)lak-eye*
Melwas	*mel-oo-as*
Meriaun	*merry-eyen*
Morgause	*mor-gice*
Rumaun	*rim-eyen*
Typiaunan	*typ-ee-eye-nan*
Uthr	*oo-tha*
Ygrainne	*ig-rine-ya*

Circa AD 450

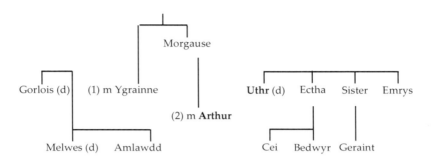

Morgause

Gorlois (d)   (1) m Ygrainne   Uthr (d)   Ectha   Sister   Emrys

(2) m **Arthur**

Melwes (d)   Amlawdd   Cei   Bedwyr   Geraint

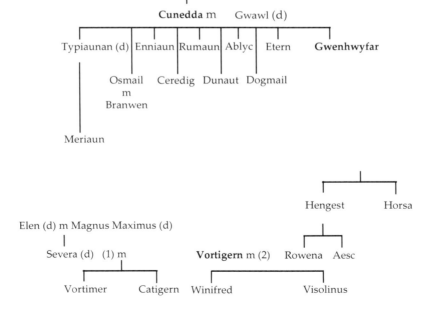

Cunedda m   Gwawl (d)

Typiaunan (d)   Enniaun   Rumaun   Ablyc   Etern   **Gwenhwyfar**

Osmail   Ceredig   Dunaut   Dogmail
m
Branwen

Meriaun

Hengest   Horsa

Elen (d) m Magnus Maximus (d)

Severa (d)   (1) m   **Vortigern** m (2)   Rowena   Aesc

Vortimer   Catigern   Winifred   Visolinus

MAY 450

§ I

He was ten and five years of age and, for the first time in his life, experiencing the exhilaration of the open sea and, for this short while, the novelty of leisure. The boy, with a grin fixed as wide as a new moon, folded his arms on the rail and leaned forward to watch the churn of foam boiling about the ship's bows. Salt spray spattered his face, tingling against skin that bore the faintest trace of manhood about the upper lip and chin. The sharp, sea-tang smell burst up his nostrils like a cast spear to his brain and hammered behind his eye-sockets. He tossed his head high, back, bracing his body with his hands against the leap and plunge of the deck and laughed with the pure energy of unequalled pleasure.

His eye sought the furl of the Dragon Banner flying proud from the masthead. He twisted his body to see it better – a snake-like tubular shape, curling and writhing with a life of its own. Streamers shrieked with the passing of the wind, and the head flashed gold in a display of fire sparked by the caught rays of the sun. Ah, but it was good to be out in the open! Out on the sea, heading for Britain with Uthr Pendragon's war host!

A sister ship, the same as this great war-beast save that she flew no dragon, plunged into the cleft of a tossing wave, thrust herself forward, gallantly keeping pace. The boy waved to men on board, grinning the wider to receive a brief flung acknowledgement.

Then he saw Morgause watching him, standing as straight and stiff as the single mast.

A fine-bred lady, Morgause, with the figure of a goddess and the vanity of an empress. She held her cloak tight around her shoulders, her slender fingers clasping a rose-coloured silk veil that held her sun-gold hair in place against the ripping wind.

If the ship was the perfection of sail then she, to look upon, was surely the perfection of woman. Venus, Uthr called her in the intimacy of their lovers' bed. Perfection to the naked eye, often marred when examined close by a flaw within – hers the arrogance and cruelty that came with high ambition.

The boy's pleasure faded as fast as a tossed stone sinks below the surface of a calm pond. Why did the Lord Uthr need bring her? Why her and not his wife – although she could be as bad, with her constant praying to God and perpetual muttered litanies. An invading army was no place for a woman, not even for the mistress of the man who considered himself to be Britain's rightful king.'

Her eyes, cold, calculating, ice blue eyes, bore into him; evil eyes that never smiled except at the indulgence of her own twisted pleasures. His right hand was behind his back; he made the protective sign against evil, knew she was aware he made that sign. Strange, from tales he had always assumed witches to be ugly, dark creatures, not having the beautiful fair skin of Morgause.

He tried again to feel the joy of the ship but the excitement had faded, lost under this shadow of her foreboding. Instead, the lad ducked below deck and made his way to where Uthr's soldiers squatted playing dice or board and counter games. He was safe from her down here – she would not come where the men lodged – although it was so much better to be out there, in the air and sunlight...

Lord Uthr, called the Pendragon, approached Morgause from behind and wrapped his great oak-branch arms around her slender waist. She stiffened and pulled away from him, not caring at this moment for intimacy.

'You ought not let the boy do as he pleases, Uthr,' she said. 'Give him leave to take holiday and he will be fit for nought when it comes to returning to duties.'

Uthr laughed, a deep bear-growl rumble. 'He's just a lad. Leave him.'

Morgause made no answer. She had no intention of letting the boy run wild, unchecked and undisciplined. Why Uthr had brought him she had no idea. He was nurtured as foster son by Uthr's brother – but a war host was no place for a boy who, in truth, was no more than the bastard brat of a long-dead servant girl. Uthr found the boy to his liking; but to her mind he was a lazy, rough-edged, insolent whelp who needed regular beating to remind him of his place. Common gossip favoured the foster father, Ectha, as the brat's unknown sire – although there had been some who had whispered of it being Uthr himself. He had the more likely reputation, would once have rutted with any whore available. A smile slithered across Morgause's lips, so carefully painted with vegetable dye.

Not now. Now, he lay only with Morgause, youngest sister to his God-possessed wife.

'They say, below decks,' Uthr said, nibbling at her ear – she attempted to brush him aside – 'I have brought you with the intention of finding you a suitable husband.' He ignored her flailing hand. 'Shall I do that, my pretty one? When I have lopped the tyrant Vortigern's head from his noble shoulders and placed myself as King of all Britain, shall I wed you to some noble lord?' He swivelled her around, aimed a large wet kiss at her lips, smudging the red colouring. 'Or shall I set aside my wife Ygrainne and wed you myself? Queen Morgause. It has a nice ring!'

She would have felt pleased had she known him to be serious. But Uthr was always jesting, always making fun of her aspirations. Curtly she answered, 'My lord will do with me as he may please,'

'Ha!' Uthr laughed again. 'At this moment it pleases me to stand here on this swaying deck and kiss you.' He glanced around. 'It would please me even more had I a tankard of wine in my free hand! Where's the boy got to?'

Morgause said nothing, glanced instead at the wake foaming behind the speeding ship. Happen Providence would supply a discreet chance to tip the brat overboard before they reached Britain?

Instead, Fortuna followed the boy. Showing herself in the guise of squalling rain and a blustering westerly wind, she came stamping over the horizon with the dawn. Uthr's soldiers, land men not seafarers, huddled below deck groaning as their stomachs heaved up to their throats. The Less Britain sailors scurried regardless, taking a reef into the square sail and jibing close to the wind. Thunder was brewing, would be upon them before mid-morning. For the boy, the storm was thrilling. To his delight, he found himself and Uthr the only passengers braving the deck.

Weather-seasoned sailors grinned at him as they scuttled about, great waves of spray soaking their clothes to the skin, the wind beating in their faces and snarling through the Dragon Banner overhead. Uthr ruffled the lad's hair, sharing his wild exhilaration.

'Is a battle like this?' the boy asked, eyes wide as a silver salver, salt-encrusted hands gripping the ropes along the rails. 'Is it as exciting?'

Uthr laughed, making a hasty grab at his cloak that swirled in a gust of mauling wind. 'Aye, lad. Danger breeds a sharpness that courses through your blood as hot as a man's lust for a beautiful woman.' He watched fascinated as lightning lit the blue-black sky from horizon to horizon. 'Always,' he shouted through the following roar of thunder, 'be aware. Keep your head, your sense. When you throw a spear, throw your soul with it. Let your sword be one with your arm.' He made accompanying gestures, casting an imaginary spear, cleaving the air with a sword. 'Keep tight control, boy. You will feel fear; fear pumps your blood the faster, but let not the fright touch your face. Keep it close, tucked well behind the shield of calm expression.' He put his arm around the lad's shoulders and declared with a gusted laugh, 'The same applies to handling women.' He grinned. 'The secret there, lad, is to let them think they hold control!'

Involuntarily, the boy glanced astern at the timbered cabin that was, for this voyage, Uthr and Morgause's. Uthr must have seen, for he too looked.

'You are right to fear that one, for she's a woman who seeks what dangles beyond her reach. I have her tamed, but Morgause can scratch as dangerous as a cornered wild cat.'

The boy ducked his head, chewed his lip. Aye, did he not know it!

Thunder bellowed overhead. Uthr made to stride away but paused, waving his hand in the direction of the shuttered cabin. 'She's no sea-maiden, my prized whore. You will see no more of her these next days, not until we make harbour.' He winked and strode for'ard to speak with the captain.

And he was right. Not even when the first haze of the Gwynedd coastline came into view, nor as the shore grew larger, with detail coming clear, did Morgause show herself.

The boy stood on deck, spellbound as the great ship, with her following sister, swung landward. Gwynedd – where the Lion Lord Cunedda ruled. Where valleys nestled green and lush, and mountains heaved upwards to caress the sky. He had heard much of Gwynedd, and found this first view of peaks plunging like an eagle's swoop towards a plain that, by contrast, lay as flat as the sea, not disappointing.

The two ships swept into the straits between the mainland and the Isle of Mon. A lively wind, the tail end of the storm, danced across the sea chasing a galloping herd of white-crested waves that pranced to meet the nearing shore.

A movement there! Two dark specks against the spring vegetation of green, yellow, white and pink. The boy squinted his eyes, attempting to make out clearer shapes. Two riders – not adult, for they lacked height and build – were urging their horses to a fast pace. A chestnut and a smaller, black-coated hill pony.

The oars lifted then dipped to kiss the white foam. The sail dropped and the ship, tossing her prow like a mare held over-long curbed and kicking high her heels, leapt for the harbour sheltering beneath the imposing fortress that was Caer Arfon.

§ II

Heels drumming, the two children urged their ponies into a gallop, the flat land along this seaward stretch allowing the pace faster. The boy, better mounted, was forging ahead on his chestnut gelding, enjoying the reckless speed.

'Etern, wait!' Gwenhwyfar shouted, pleading. She saw her brother disappear into a gully but her words were snatched by the teasing wind; she doubted he had heard. Relief brought a smile when she found him waiting impatiently, his excited horse tossing flecks of foam, hooves fidgeting. The boy's eyes were darting from her approach to the haze of sea, and the sprawl of buildings beside the estuary. He wanted to get back.

At ten and four, Etern was the elder by two summers. He had his sister's copper-gold hair and expressive green eyes, but was taller by a full head and shoulders. He frowned at her an impatiently shouted, 'Kick him on, make him earn his keep!'

'He's going as fast as he can!' Gwenhwyfar hurled a retort sharp with ruffled anger. Reaching her brother she hauled at the iron-tough mouth of her sweating pony, noticed, with a twinge of envy, how the handsome Aquila was barely damp. One dark stain on his neck, a slight quiver to his deep chest, nothing more.

'That pony's too fat for his own good,' Etern observed with critical disapproval. 'About time Da gave you something decent to ride.' Instantly, he regretted the barbed sarcasm. He smiled an apology, smoothing his sister's puckering temper with 'Still, I suppose he does well for his age, but you are growing out of him. Look, your feet are almost to the ground!' He laughed suddenly, impatience swinging to humour.

23

Gwenhwyfar laughed with him, her mouth wide, head tossing, seeing with her brother the absurdity of her lengthening body astride this short-legged, barrel-bellied pony. Fondly, she patted his neck her palm slapping on the wetness that was beginning to steam. 'He has served me well enough.'

'He cannot carry you forever though – would he not make a pony for brother Osmail's son now? The lad will soon see his third summer – time he was riding.'

Gwenhwyfar snorted disdain; brother Osmail was not a favourite of hers, and even less so his fastidiously intolerant wife. 'If Branwen has her way he will be fit for nought save women's work or the priesthood.' Pulling on the reins and giving a thumping kick with her heel, she brought her stubborn pony away from the grass he was eagerly snatching at and persuaded him to walk on.

Etern grimaced, echoing his sister's distaste for the boy's prospects, and nudged Aquila to follow.

For some yards they rode in silence, the horses picking their way through the dull tangle of last season's heather and the fresh colours of mayflowers. The wind brought a sharp tang of the sea to mingle with the smell of warm earth and sweet-scented, sun-speckled plants. Overhead, a flight of gulls, one with a fish flapping from his beak, wheeled shrieking and squabbling. Etern brought Aquila up to the pony's side, rode companionably with his sister.

'What possessed our brother to wed a woman such as Branwen?' A question Gwenhwyfar was often heard to ask, particularly after some fresh outburst of disagreement with her sister-by-law. 'Were there not milder-tempered maids to choose from?'

Aquila was beginning to dance, becoming bored with the sedate pace. He blew through his nostrils and tossed his head, his mane brushing Etern's face. The boy shortened the reins, intending to curb the impatience, managing only to increase the bend to the horse's neck and the jog in his step. 'Osmail seems happy to have a son born, another on the way and a plump woman to keep him warm at night.'

The wind lifted the loose hair always escaping from Gwenhwyfar's braids. She gave Etern a look that could have scorched the may blossom brown. 'There are enough plump women around Caer Arfon to keep an entire legion warm! No need to wed such a dragon!'

Aquila leapt sideways at some imagined fright. When Etern had enticed him back on to the sheep-track they were following Gwenhwyfar added, with a wicked grin, 'And Branwen is not plump, she's as fat as Da's best breeding sow.' She pushed her pony into an ambling trot. 'Come, brother, Splinter has his wind; those two ships will have docked by now.'

Traders' ships were becoming a rarity along this coast. The chequered sails of the Saex sea wolves, aye, or the earth red of the pirates from Hibernia; both a menace to trader or traveller. But sleek, powerful craft like those two fighting the heavy swell of the straits and a bruising westerly wind were uncommon enough to set brother and sister hastening home. Coming down from the hills, the eager canter had increased to a furious gallop, Etern pointing ahead, shouting excitedly, 'It's the Pendragon, Gwen! I can see the Dragon Banner!'

'Uthr Pendragon,' he whooped, his voice crying back into the mountains and hurling towards the afternoon sky.

Gwenhwyfar held her counsel, but as they approached the incline leading up to the stronghold's outer defences she faltered an opinion. It may be his banner, but need he be aboard?'

Her brother blew a crude noise through his lips. 'Of course he's aboard! The Dragon flies only above its lord!' He swivelled to face her, his expression animated. 'Think on it! Uthr Pendragon at Caer Arfon!'

A tale told often around the hearth fires, of the time when, soon, Uthr the Pendragon, the exiled High Lord of all Britain, would raise his war host and come to claim his rightful place as supreme king. A tale of hope fashioned by old harpers and young soldiers. Tales were tales, along with the legends of past gods and heroes; Gwenhwyfar had long since learnt such tales were not always to be believed.

They trotted through the open gateway between ditch and palisade fencing and entered the bustle of the settlement that crowded against the towering turf walls of the stronghold, Cunedda's fortress of Caer Arfon. Within a few strides, Gwenhwyfar believed her brother right.

A festive mood bubbled, tripping over dwelling-place threshold and market-seller's stalls, spilling like heady wine into alley and street. People were jostling, laughing and dancing; making merry as they will when spirits are lifted to the stars, with the promise of hope against the oppression of a tyrant's rule. For even here, under the protection of their beloved Lion Lord, the despised king, Vortigern, cast his greedy shadow.

The ponies clattered through the cobbled archway into the sanctuary of the stronghold proper, their ears pricking as they neared the stables and the promise of corn. Here, within the imposing walls, turreted and top-fenced, swelled the normal bustle of a powerful lord's domain. Kennels for hunting dogs, barns for gathered grain, roundhouse dwelling places for servants and slaves; a latrine and bathhouse. Smoking cooking pits near the kitchen place; the well, and the impressive structure that was Cunedda's Hall, with, beyond, the family apartments, stone built, lime-washed and roofed with slate.

With the horses settled, brother and sister ran, slowing only to slip past the open kitchen door from where a shrill voice could be heard scolding some unfortunate.

'Branwen!' Gwenhwyfar mouthed, exchanging a wary glance with her brother. Safe, they hared for the Hall, heart of the Caer and of Gwynedd.

A crowd pushed to enter at the wide-open oak doors. Men mostly, warriors already gathering for Cunedda's spring hosting, but with a few women of the settlement elbowing their way through. A tumult of noise poured from within.

Etern cocked his head to listen at a side door. He pushed it open and crept through, his sister close as a shadow behind him. The vast building was bursting with excited people. Merchants, Eldermen, a handful of headmen who had ridden hard when the two ships were first sighted.

A bear-pawed hand thumped down on Gwenhwyfar's shoulder and spun her around. She looked up, startled, met with an elder brother's heavy frown. With a none too gentle shake Enniaun growled, 'I wondered how long before you two bobbed up.' He eyed Gwenhwyfar's appearance. 'You been fighting a battle?' He poked a finger at a particularly large stain on her tunic. 'Would it not be polite for our father's two youngest to have washed and changed before entering his Hall?' He twirled Gwenhwyfar round, studying an even larger grass stain on the seat of her bracae. 'God's truth! The pair of you are dirtier than midden slaves!'

Brushing ineffectually at the offending mark on her chest, Gwenhwyfar smiled innocently. 'We were in a hurry. No one will notice us if we stay at the back.'

'I will notice – and have no doubt Da will.'

Gwenhwyfar exchanged a wry glance with Etern. Enniaun was right, of course. Dismally they slouched out again and stood dejected for a moment, heads and shoulders slumped. 'We could creep in through the servants' door from the kitchens,' Gwenhwyfar suggested.

Etern shrugged. 'Da would still see us – or worse, Branwen. Best do as Enniaun says. Just wash the bits that show, put on a clean tunic and comb your hair. Meet you back here!' He said the last quickly, off and running towards the boys' place before he had finished.

Gwenhwyfar envied him those quarters. No twittering chatter from an array of cousins for him! Nor, she reflected as she trotted into the girls' chamber, a mess of discarded garments strewn over floor and cot.

Grumbling to herself she flung someone's crumpled tunic from her bed and kicked her own dusty boots beneath. Stuffing her tunic into the chest of soiled garments destined for the laundry slaves, she washed from a pitcher of cold water and tugged a comb through her tangled hair, cursing her misfortune at being born a girl.

After nine brothers she was the only daughter. In a sheltered recess of her heart, Gwenhwyfar sometimes wondered whether her mother might have survived the birth of the last delivered had she borne a tenth son. Making a face in the hand-held bronze mirror, she studied herself. A squarish chin, nose a little too long, mouth rather too wide, lips too thin. She did not consider herself pretty, did not particularly care whether she was or not. Gwenhwyfar thought, behaved, more like a boy than a girl; learning to run, fight and ride as was the old way for British-born women. The old way, before the Romans came with their tidy ideas. She could handle a weapon, sword or spear, as competently as Etern; could plan an ambush with unrivalled cunning – much to the annoyance of family and servants who often fell foul of her mischief.

She stuck her tongue out at her slightly distorted image in the polished metal, put the mirror down and again attacked her hair with the comb. Her personal bane, this! Cunedda refused to allow her to wear her hair short. He suffered her in boys' clothing – discreetly admired her courage and determination, but wailed, 'Leave something to remind us occasionally that you will be woman-grown one day!'

Hastily she rebraided its thick mass, her fingers flying in and out, then struggled into a fresh tunic. Glancing at her bed, which she shared with Ceridwen, Cunedda's youngest niece, she grinned. All was tidy. The others would be in for a scolding from Branwen when she saw the state of the place! Gwenhwyfar laughed wickedly and skittered back to Etern, leaping up a short flight of wooden steps to where he waited.

'What took you so long?'

'This damn mane of mine, it takes ages to braid – one day I'm going to defy Da and hack it off!'

Eyes widening, Etern stared in horror. 'You would not dare!'

Restraining a smile, Gwenhwyfar retorted, 'Would I not?' For a wild heartbeat Etern believed her!

A second time Enniaun appraised them, nodded his satisfaction. 'You will pass.' Then, 'Do you not have female garments, Gwenhwyfar –more suitable than boys' bracae for an occasion such as this, hm?'

Her eyes grew round with indignation. Those were words more suited to the dragon Branwen, not a beloved elder brother! 'I wear a gown on the Lord's day! Is that not enough?' she answered.

Etern giggled. 'Only because our Holy Father told Da one Sabbath you looked more like a street slave! Da was livid, I recall.'

Gwenhwyfar grinned back at him. She had reluctantly agreed to wear more suitable clothing in the chapel, not to pacify Branwen who grumbled the girl ought always dress as befitted her sex, nor for the priest, but because her Da had been embarrassed in public by a man he regarded as a pompous ass.

'You will find space over there. Go quietly, mind.' Enniaun smiled to himself as the children wormed their way through to where he had indicated. Etern on the threshold of manhood, a fine boy, and Gwenhwyfar, so like her mother. The same vivacious face, sparkling eyes and trilling laugh. The same iron will.

Enniaun was close past Etern's age when Gwenhwyfar was given life and their mother's taken. To the end of his days he would never forget seeing his Da crumpled with tear-stained face, rocking a pitifully crying baby, nor his choking words. 'Aye, little one, I miss your Mam too.' He turned his attention away from his sister, squatting hunkered on her heels, chin cupped in hand, eyes intent upon Uthr – a man so often heard of yet barely remembered by the elder brothers; never seen by the younger ones.

None in this Hall failed to share her excitement. Cunedda's people loved Uthr, and what he stood for – freedom, revenge. They were a proud people, with long, long memories. Under Uthr and Cunedda they had once fought Vortigern and lost. Defeated and shamed Cunedda had surrendered to the King, who claimed the North in forfeit. Giving instead, in gracious compassion, a shabby, forgotten corner of Britain, racked by poverty and plague, and violated by sea pirates. Vortigern intended the giving as an insult. Cunedda had no choice but to accept, and had come with his loyal people to this struggling, dismal corner of valleys and mountains with a heavy heart and bitter pain. Finding a dejected settlement loosely propped beside the remains of a Roman fortress, he turned that heaviness to determination, pain into optimism. He created pride and wealth in place of squalor and shame, hope in place of resignation. The passing years saw the raiders set to flight, the ruins rebuilt and hearts raised as high as the mountains of Eryri. Demand, encourage, bully and praise; the Lion gave might and wisdom, received back from his new land of Gwynedd loyalty and profound respect. Cunedda won enough of both to choose his own friends – and to blow dust in the face of those who objected. But none forgot Uthr, the rightful king; and none forgot Vortigern, sitting safe within his guarded estates and comfortable strongholds in the wealthy south and west.

Cunedda's people – once the proud Votadini, now the even prouder people of Gwynedd – cherished their memories. Of a war begun and lost; of Vortigern hiring the Saxons to fight against them, and the resulting blood and death and sorrow. Memories that whistled on a summer dawn, of sons slaughtered and women taken; or on a frosted winter's night, of hearth fires grown cold and dwelling places lying derelict. Dun Pelidr, the ancient fortress rising like a whale hump from a sea of flat land, fallen empty and dark, Cunedda's fortress where he had governed, as had his father, and his father before him. Dun Pelidr where rotted the butchered bones of Cunedda's eldest son.

Ah, in Gwynedd Vortigern's cruelties were well remembered! It had taken time to reforge strength, to rebuild all that had been lost, but they had it all now, all and more. By moving Cunedda to Gwynedd, Vortigern had intended him to sink into oblivion, but the King had judged wrong, and now Uthr was back from exile!

Accompanied by his three sons an Elderman came before Uthr, bowed and exchanged a brief word before finding seating. The Hall was filling. Soon there would be standing room only; then the porch would crowd with men, and latecomers would need wait outside, the speeches relayed by those who could hear. Glancing round, Gwenhwyfar recognised many of those already seated or waiting to greet the Pendragon and Cunedda; many, she did not know. That one, from the emblem on his shoulder, must be from north Dyfed, and the one seated beside him. Several to the left had come from across the Straits, from the sea wolf plagued Isle of Mon. Word must have flown fast and well guarded ahead of Uthr's coming, for so many notables to be so quickly gathered in this chieftain's hall!

Her attention wandering, Gwenhwyfar gazed fondly about her: at the smoke blackened beams arching under the read-thatch roof, carrying the carved heads and faces of protective and watchful spirits; at the fresh-painted white daub walls, hung with bright tapestries and splendid skins, lined with ranks of spears, swords and shields. Her brothers sat clustered in a group, chattering among themselves, their faces eager and animated. Ceredig, kind natured and easy to talk to, the next born after Enniaun. He was stockier than the others and not so tall, though like many of them he carried the same bush of red hair as their Da. With a wife and three young daughters he was awaiting an opportunity to claim his own land. Seated at the fore of the group were the twins Rumaun and Dunaut, as like as two spears made from the same shaft, both tall and exceptionally handsome, both with wives and young children. Rumaun was bending forward, telling a no doubt lewd tale to Meriaun, only born child of dead Typiaunan. Next to him, Abloyc, legs spread, hands behind his head, thrust himself back laughing. By the turn of summer Abloyc was to wed a chieftain's lass from Dyfed, a blue-eyed, vivacious girl. Gwenhwyfar had met her several times and liked her. And then sleek Dogmail, smiling at a passing serving lass. His bed companion? You never knew with Dogmail exactly who his latest love would be. He loved them all, he said, all women. Osmail was not there. Gwenhwyfar scanned the crowded Hall. Ah, there he was, seated beside an Elderman from the small coastal stronghold of Conwy. Engrossed in serious conversation, judging by the concentrated frown on his face. She turned her attention back to Uthr. A bull-muscled man, richly dressed in a combination of Roman and Brythonic fighting gear, as were most of the fighting men. But Uthr eclipsed all others as the sun would outshine an evening star.

Gwenhwyfar shivered, excitement tingling along her spine. Sa, tales are not true? As she glanced across the Hall indignation flushed across her cheeks, glowered in her eyes. What insolence! Among the Pendragon's personal guard sat a boy hunkered on his heels, openly staring at her with a lopsided grin. Gwenhwyfar turned to Etern, intending to exclaim at the impertinence, but her mouth dropped open as she saw her brother nod and grin back at the boy. Of all the...! She decided to ignore the both of them.

Uthr's purple cloak, spun of the finest wool, was fastened at his left shoulder with a brooch the size of a man's clenched fist. Around his throat he wore a torque of twisted gold shaped like a dragon – a great serpent beast with ruby eyes and gaping jaws, its gold scales winking in the dancing light of the torches. A royal torque, a king's insignia – and Uthr wore it like a king determined on absolute power.

All the while, though she directed her mind to the Pendragon, Gwenhwyfar could feel eyes on her. Eyes belonging to a boy with hair cut ridiculously short in the Roman style, and a nose too long and straight for a face with an etched laugh that could only be described as shameless. Gwenhwyfar tossed a braid behind her shoulder and lifted her chin higher.

Cunedda was coming to his feet, striding forward a step, and holding his arms high to silence the rumble of talk.

Gwenhwyfar shuffled her body around so as to turn her back on the boy.

'Lord Uthr!' Cunedda's voice boomed up to the roof, shuddering the dust from settled corners to swirl a while among the hearth fire smoke curling around the cobwebbed rafters. 'First I speak words of welcome, as custom and honour demands. I say to you, for myself and my people,' he gestured with spread hands at the intent assembly, 'welcome to Gwynedd and to my Hall. Welcome, as my foster brother, unseen for over many years and truly missed.' He grinned at Uthr, then said in a lower tone, 'Despite your tendency to get us both into serious trouble!'

Laughter rippled, and a few handclaps joined enthusiastically by Uthr himself. Stories of these two men's youthful exploits were popular hearth tales, told for the most part with good humour and much laughter. For some, though, they were useful to be spread as malicious gossip. Cunedda might be well respected, but Uthr had left many enemies along his trail.

The lord of Gwynedd let quiet settle before stepping up to the man he had waited so long to receive. He clasped Uthr's arm in recognition of friendship; Uthr stood, returning the gesture. Before the cheering crowd, the two embraced, holding each other close, not heeding their ready tears.

Stepping back, reluctant to relinquish the embrace of friendship Cunedda spoke directly to Uthr, but pitched his trembling voice so all might hear. 'And welcome, double welcome, as rightful King of all Britain!'

As one the assembly leapt to its feet, roaring agreement, hands waving or striking the air, heads back, mouths wide, feet stamping. Gwenhwyfar stamped and yelled with them. Through each season of her twelve years of life her brothers and father had spoken with admiration for this man, Uthr Pendragon. Barely a moon waned without someone bringing up the question of when he would raise an army and come against the tyrant Vortigern. And now it was happening! Uthr was actually here in her Da's Hall! Here he stood, as large as a bear, as imposing as a dragon, ready to renew his war on Vortigern!

The Pendragon held his arms high, humbly acknowledging the acclaim. Deep, dark eyes, set in the earth brown face of an outdoor man, gazed solemnly over those standing before him cheering and shouting.

Gwenhwyfar wondered if Uthr had noticed herself and Etern, knew them to be Cunedda's youngest born. As the thought came the Pendragon's piercing gaze fell upon her. She flushed pink, but summoned enough courage to return his scrutiny.

Unexpectedly, she met something other than stern power. Kindness shone there, and laughter. She smiled a half-shy girl's greeting. Uthr's mouth twitched in response and Gwenhwyfar found it impossible to control the laugh that burst from her as he winked.

The boy must have seen it too, for when Gwenhwyfar turned her head she caught him grinning straight at her. With immense difficulty, she repressed the childish urge to stick her tongue out at the mongrel whelp.

§ III

Couring wine for guests and Gwynedd's warriors was one of the few women's tasks Gwenhwyfar quite enjoyed. To make her way round benches that groaned under the weight of so many, to slide nimbly between the jostling arms of animated revellers without spilling a drop of her Da's most precious wine, carried a pleasing benefit. You could take a while to fill a tankard or goblet, and listen to interesting talk. Men with the drink in them seemed to forget the wine-bearer had ears! Gwenhwyfar learnt much of the comings and goings beyond Caer Arfon by that innocent pouring of wine!

Four suns had set since Uthr's arrival, followed by three heat hazed days busy from dawn's first light to the fall of dusk – aye, and beyond, into damp scented, sound heightened darkness, that carried the clang, clang of the swordsmith's hammer as far as the sleeping hills. By day, horses were brought up from the pasture for the fitting and checking of harness and hooves. Men were drilled, the echoing tramp, tramp of their feet mingling with their shouted war cries. Other men busy with leather and metalwork; a constant bustle of making and mending, and among it all the cheery leave-taking of messengers, swift-bound for allied lords of Dyfed and Gwent. And all the time there came the steady arrival of Cunedda's warriors called by the great boom and boom of the war horns sounding along the wind from ridge to ridge that first sunset, summoning shepherds, mountain or valley dwellers. Fathers and sons, headmen with their shield-bearers – the fighting men of Gwynedd coming eager to fulfil their service of the war spear.

The hill from the Caer, rising in an incline beyond the Stone Ground to where the tumbled stones and timber of the old Roman fortress of

Segontium had once stood, was clustered with tents and campfires. Uthr's men alongside Gwynedd's, and those from beyond the Dovey river. Men who welcomed Cunedda's strong hand against the sea wolves, proud to offer their spears alongside his own. Aiee! This would be a hosting to stir a tale-teller's harp for many a winter's night to come!

The noise of excited talk and merry laughter swirled and buffeted against the high rafters, mingling with the dark waft of hearth smoke. Carrying a new-filled jug on her hip, Gwenhwyfar made her way along the row of benches to where her brothers sat with her father, and Lord Uthr. She poured for the Pendragon, listening to the conversation of the moment – talk of Vortigern's two grown sons by his first wife, a woman long since cold in her grave.

She moved with casual slowness to her father, shifting the weight of the heavy jug and pouring carefully. So-o, Vortigern and Catigern were becoming more outspoken against the second-taken wife? Gwenhwyfar knew much of her. Rowena, daughter to the Saxon warlord Hengest. The marriage had caused outrage some ten and eight years past, culminating in that brief flurried war of Cunedda's unsuccessful rebellion, and Uthr's simultaneous attempt to take the throne. Cunedda had lost his eldest son and his northern stronghold, and Uthr too, had lost his vast holding of land and had fled into exile. Many good men had died through Vortigern's wanting of that Saex bitch! How he had paraded his victory, rubbing the sting of salt into the raw wound and neatly sidestepping remaining criticism by declaring his marriage a treaty of alliance.

'He says,' said Cunedda, talking of Vortigern to Uthr, 'he still regards Rowena as a hostage for peace.'

Uthr barked a shout of laughter. 'And treats her as such? My arse he does! That lecherous toad married her because he was hard for her. Mind, Hengest is a crafty bastard. *You want to bed my daughter? Certainly, Vortigern, but not without a bride price of a claim to British land!*'

Uthr emptied his goblet in one long draught. Wiping his mouth with the back of his hand he crooked a finger at Gwenhwyfar, who was serving her eldest brother, and held out the empty vessel for her to refill. To Cunedda, he added, 'That Saex pirate knew what he was about when he paraded a ten and six year old beauty before a man known for his whoring. I hear she's pregnant again?'

Gwenhwyfar filled one brother's goblet, moved to another. That also was common knowledge. The Queen's birthing would be within the month, the sixth born, and all who despised the King and his bitch hoped for it to be the fifth to die. One child only had survived, a daughter who had the fair skin and sharp temper of her mother.

From a nearby corner someone called her, holding his goblet high. There was still wine in her jug but she walked deliberately past and made her way towards the women's side, where she filled a goblet for herself and sat. She flicked a glance at the one who had hailed her, Etern, her youngest brother, seated cross-legged on the floor among the boys of the Caer. Let someone else serve him, him and that boy! For these three days she had seen nought of Etern so taken with the insolent whelp was he! Well, she, Gwenhwyfar, would have no tangle with him!

Spirits soared and voices grew loud with the laughter of full bellies and good wine. Again it was Gwenhwyfar's turn to take round the wine, and again she found herself pouring for the Pendragon.

He nodded his thanks, grinned broadly at her and said to Cunedda, 'Your daughter will one day make a fine match for some aspiring princeling. Have you plans for betrothal?'

Feeling her face grow pink Gwenhwyfar held her jug steady as she poured. Her Da, though, had been distracted by some shout of laughter along the table and so no answer came. It was not her place, a woman and a child at that, to pass comment but Gwenhwyfar was never one for bowing to convention.

'My lord, I have no intention of being married off to some unlanded, unblooded upstart who wishes to use me for his own ambition!'

Attention caught, Cunedda flashed his daughter a frown of disapproval, but Uthr sat back in his chair and roared amusement.

He thumped the Lion on the shoulder and declared, 'Your lass, my friend, and no mistake! She has your wit – temper too no doubt.' He chuckled again, reached out to hold Gwenhwyfar's chin in his cupped hand and scanned her face. 'Aye, but I can see her mother's beauty shadowed beneath this childhood awkwardness.' He released her, said with a decisive nod, 'You'd do well for a king's wife, girl. I full agree – aim high!' He reached his arm behind her, playfully patted her backside with his palm.

'I will wed none but the highest, my lord!'

'Queen, eh?' Uthr chuckled. 'Even you, at your age, could do a better job than the present one!' More laughter, echoed by others at table and those within hearing.

Cunedda nodded quick agreement and made attempt to turn the conversation but Uthr, his humorous eyes lingering on Gwenhwyfar, pursued the thing. 'I give you a promise, lass.' He raised his wine and said in a louder voice, 'When I have parted Vortigern's head from his shoulders I shall bear you in mind should I need a new wife as queen!'

To Gwenhwyfar's extreme annoyance Etern and the boy joined with the answering shout of hilarity. Passing their corner the boys called for her to leave the wine. Saying nothing she thumped the jug on the table, stepping deliberately on what she thought was her brother's toe. No matter that it was the boy who yelped.

He looked up at her, brown eyes meeting her green. Taking hold of her arm with his fingers he said, with no hiding of the laughter in his voice, 'I am grown quite tall and have yet more growing before I finish. Would I be high enough for you?' His laughter broke with a splutter as he collapsed against Etern, whose arms came about the boy's shoulders, their amusement exploding into joint hilarity.

Gwenhwyfar glared distastefully at the both of them.

'You behave like half-witted mooncalves!' earned herself more laughter.

She turned away abruptly. Arthur had entered Gwenhwyfar's life, and she hated him.

§ IV

Lady Morgause was in a boiling temper. The meat, she considered, had been raw on one side, blackened on the other, and the wine sour. The Hall was draughty and full of choking hearth and torch smoke; loud with men's drunken laughter and the cloying stench of male sweat. She had a headache as thick as beeswax. And that girl had dared flaunt herself before the Pendragon! His eyes had roamed to her all evening, followed her as she left to seek her bedchamber with the rest of that gaggle of girls. Ah, and Morgause knew only too well Uthr's gleam of interest, that curving smile of his!

The iron-rimmed heels of her boots click-clicked on the path in step with her anger, her lips pressed tight, body rigid, as she stormed along the rough-laid path. She hissed an embellished oath as her cloak snagged on a nail protruding from a leaning fence, jerked the material free with impatient fingers, cursing again at the sound of ripping. There was little light out here. A flaring torch set here and there, a shaft of pale, flickering yellow from the open doorway of some hovel of a dwelling place, There was no moon, the faint silver of midnight starlight not quite enough to illuminate the way to the latrines. Not that light was needed; the stink provided guidance enough.

She entered the dim-lit, square-built chamber, her nose wrinkling as the smell of human waste assailed her nostrils. Seating herself at the nearest accommodation she emptied her bladder quickly, with held breath, and would have run for the fresh air had dignity ever permitted Morgause to run.

She was used to the luxury of a Roman villa; light, airy rooms, tiled flooring and paved courtyards. Hot water in the bathhouse – not the tepid, brownish slush that filled Cunedda's excuse for a bathing pool – and latrines cleaned twice daily. She snorted derisively. Small comfort that there was a bathhouse and latrines in this squalid apology for a nobleman's residence! By the name of the Goddess, it was hard to believe civilisation had ever touched this backward place!

As she stepped outside, her sight was momentarily lost in the darkness. She walked forward impatiently and collided with someone running for the door. A flurry of arms, a swirl of hair and a gasped apology Then the dim rush lighting from within the latrines flared briefly as the door opened and closed. Silence. Morgause stood, her breath not yet recovered from the foul stench. That wretched girl again! For a moment she almost made to follow the child with the intention of delivering a severe reprimand. Her hand went to push the door but she had no wish to re-enter the place without desperate need, and even less of a wish to stand hovering here, outside.

Turning back along the path, she swung right to skirt the Hall and strode towards the chamber allotted Uthr, her thoughts dwelling on Cunedda's daughter. Gwenhwyfar. A child on the edge of womanhood, a maiden. A pretty enough thing, though her legs and arms were too long, her body not yet full rounded but with enough promise to excite a man who took an interest in young girls. Morgause caught the swirl of her cloak as a freshening sea wind flapped at its length, and cast the folds across her shoulder. Uthr had made that remark in jest about marriage with the girl, but with Uthr who knew which was jest and which seed to take root? Morgause had long since learnt not to trust Uthr's seemingly idle remarks.

There was a light in his chamber, spreading in a narrow, spilt pool through the open door. Morgause hesitated. Was her lord already come from the Hall? Not yet, surely? A moment since he was still drinking deep with Cunedda, though many were seeking their sleeping furs or already lay snoring where the drink left them. With her mind half diverted by the irritating reflection of Gwenhwyfar, and that disturbing look of lust in Uthr's eye, Morgause entered the chamber.

There was a clatter, a gasp of indrawn breath. The boy Arthur was crouched beside a clothing chest set at the foot of the bed, his hand hovering inside, fingers clasped around a small scroll of parchment. Immediately Morgause was across the room, reaching out, roughly grabbing at him.

'What do you do here? How dare you pry into my lord Uthr's things!' She twisted Arthur's arm behind his back, brought him to his feet and shook him as a dog would shake a caught rat.

Fear and panic had ripped across Arthur's face at her unexpected entrance, his heartbeat leaping, breath catching. All was masked now, controlled, sealed tight behind a shield wall of defiance. He would not let this witch see his fear of her! She would like it if he showed how scared he was of her slapping hand and evil temper.

'I am not prying!' he defended, attempting to squirm away, to free his arm. 'Lord Uthr bade me fetch something.'

'You lie!' Morgause snatched at the parchment. He jerked aside, but not quickly enough. She had it, a sneer of triumph in her pinched nostrils and slit eyes. She moved from him a pace, but did not let go his arm, her grip tightening, claw like nails biting into the flesh beneath his woollen tunic. Arthur would have cried out but he knew to hide that also. Bite hard on your lip, or dig your own nails into the palm to divert the pain she inflicted, keep it hidden.

She was attempting to unroll the thing one handed, not succeeding. Impatient, she hissed, 'What is in here?'

Truthfully, 'I know not. Lord Uthr bade me fetch it.' To add conviction, 'It is for Lord Cunedda to see.'

Morgause waved the scroll before his nose, her face coming close to his, both hands now on his arms, shaking, shaking. 'You lie. You were stealing it! For some purpose of your own, you were thieving from Uthr!'

The defiance came easier now. He was not lying – no need to pretend, to think fast or fabricate untruths. 'Why would I do that? Why should I steal from the man I love?' A mistake! Arthur saw it as he spoke, realised her anger had turned ugly.

Morgause's eyes narrowed. Her hand drew back, the gemstones in her many rings flashing in the subdued light, the gold and amber and jet bracelets tinkling and jangling at her wrist. Then the palm swept forward. Two stinging blows fell sharply across Arthur's cheek, leaving streaks of white that began to redden, would show the blue-black of bruising by morning. There would have come a third.

'Why indeed?' a man's voice drawled. 'What use, woman, would a letter from my saintly youngest brother, Emrys, have for this boy?' Uthr stood in the doorway, leaning casually against the frame, his great bulk blotting out the darkness beyond, his hand resting lightly on the pommel of his sword.

She had not heard him come up behind her. Morgause spun to face him, not letting the boy go. 'I caught him going through your things. It is not the first time he has stolen or lied.'

Uthr pushed himself from his leaning position, strolled a little unsteadily into the chamber and towards a wine flagon, where he poured for himself. 'You too have stolen, my lovely, aye, and lied on occasion.' He raised his goblet in mock salute, said with a light chuckle and an amused smile, 'Did you not steal me from my wife? And do you not, even after all

these years, still lie to her about it?' Then, with the severity of command,
'Let the boy go. He tells the truth.'

Reluctant, lips pouting, Morgause released her hold. Uthr jerked his
head at Arthur. 'Take the parchment to Cunedda – you will find him in
his own chamber – then return here.' He winked, almost as a conspirator
would 'I may have further need of your legs, lad.'

There was triumph in Arthur's bold, eye-to-eye look as with a flourish,
he took the scroll from Morgause's hand. He bowed his head at Uthr and
left, his step jaunty. Beyond the door, he leapt into the air, striking his
fist above his head, into the darkness. Sweet pleasure to have won over
her! Sweet, rare-tasted pleasure! He cared little whether she heard his
accompanying war yell of triumph.

Uthr said nothing more. He set his baldric and sword aside, unclasped
his cloak, peeled off his leather tunic, belched and took a further draught
of wine.

Morgause, too, said nothing. She stood, fists clenched, willing Uthr
to say something more, something she could answer. There was much
she would say! Of that girl, Gwenhwyfar – what was she to Uthr, had he
intentions there? Of the brat Arthur – *whose son was he?* Why had he been
brought here? When was Uthr to set his wife aside and take Morgause in
her stead! She waited, willing an argument. Still Uthr said nothing.

He sat on the bed, busied himself with plumping the pillows, fiddling
with the furs, inspecting the clean linen. He raised one eyebrow in her
direction. The glow from the few bee's wax candles fell soft, flattering on
her skin, ringing her sun yellow hair like a golden coronet. Her breasts
beneath the expensive silk of her robe rose and fell with the quick panting
of her angered breath. Holding his goblet he moved slowly, almost casually,
and encircled her body with his arm. He kissed her, not gently, but with a
roughness that came from the certain knowledge of possession.

'You ought not frown, my beauty, you will get wrinkles around your
eyes.' He ran his thumb under her chin, down her neck, his fingers slipped
briefly beneath her bodice. Then he placed a swift kiss on her lips and
swung away, back to stretch out on the bed, his goblet still in his hand.

'I'm tired, Morgause. Go to your own bed this night.' He waved his free
hand in the vague direction of the door and closed his eyes.

Morgause took three deep breaths. Very calm, but with ice hatred, she
said, 'So, I am to be dismissed like a common whore who is no longer
needed?'

Uthr laughed. 'Common, my lovely? *Na*, you were never common.'
Morgause did not miss the fact that he had not denied the word 'whore',
and had used the past tense.

She stalked to the door, sweeping her cloak around her high and
wide, knocking the flagon of wine from the table sending it spinning and

clattering to the floor. 'I hope your new maiden gives you a dose of the cock-pox!' she flung at him, and banged out through the door.

Uthr yawned. It had been a long day of greeting old friends and new, of good food and wine. He closed his eyes, sighed with tiredness – opened them again with a start. What new maid? He lifted himself on his elbow, peering curiously at the closed door in half a mind to call Morgause back. *Na*, leave it. He settled himself more comfortable, lying atop the furs, booted feet stretched the length of the bed. Ah, Morgause was so easy to bait into a flurry. Always had been jealous, that one, not like her eldest sister, his wife. Ygrainne was the placid one. He yawned again, felt the warm glow of approaching, welcomed sleep. How different sisters could be! The one meek, shut away for hours praying to her God, world weary with the shouldered burden of others' problems and troubles – and Morgause, a blaze of temper that crashed through all reasonable sense, with no thought beyond herself. The one a wife who would not be a wife; the other who could never fill her place. Happen he ought to seek a third party, another female who would be somewhere atween the two minds. His drowsing thoughts drifted to think of Cunedda's daughter. Her pretty face, her tilted, defiant chin. Now there was a maid who could be moulded into obedience without losing her spirit.

When Arthur returned he found Uthr sleeping, the empty goblet still in his hand. Gently he took it and covered the man he loved above life itself against the night cold. Then he found a sleeping fur for himself and, protective of his lord, curled on the floor before the door.

§ V

Gwenhwyfar woke in as irritable a mood as the one she had fostered on seeking her bed, only now she had the added discomfort of a headache. Probably a residue from the wine she had drunk last night – the children were only to have watered ale, but sampling what the adults drank often proved too tempting an opportunity to miss. She lay a moment, snuggled in the comfortable warmth of her bed, her cousin Ceridwen's back jammed close, the gentle rhythm of her sleeping breath rising and falling. Gwenhwyfar listened to the babble of birds greeting the day and watched, in a dreamy half sleep, as the shaft of light trooping through the single small window, crept down the opposite wall and lengthened its march across the floor. She ought to get up. Branwen would come bustling in soon, banging the door, thumping the beds, tutting and squawking at the girls' laziness. She glanced across at the other beds. No one else was up, then.

Damn that boy, it was his fault she had this headache! His fault her mood was as sour as the taste in her mouth. Under her breath she swore a particularly obscene word that she had heard one of her elder brothers use. Did she have to wake with him on her mind! She repeated the word. And she had dreamt of him – curse him. Did he not even respect the privacy of sleep? Was it not enough to have sat laughing at her last night; to have taken Etern?

Forgetting Ceridwen still slept she plunged from the bed, grabbed her clothing and dressed. She would find them both, give them a piece of her mind. She chuckled then – aye, and see how their heads throbbed this fine morning! Order her about, eh? Well, they had asked for wine and they had got it – Da's best fermentation, strong enough to blow the scalp off a seasoned warrior's head! She laughed again. The headache was lifting, her mood swinging into something more pleasurable.

Whistling, she ambled to the door, and ran slap into Branwen.

'Look where you go, child, and stop that noise; it is not a sound to befit a woman.' She stamped into the room, pulling bed covers off the sleeping girls – daughters of Gwynedd's Elders, of Cunedda's elite warrior guard and a variety of kindred, some older than Gwenhwyfar, some, like Ceridwen, younger.

'Gwenhwyfar!' Her back to the door, Branwen lumbered around, the bulk of pregnancy making movement slow and cumbersome.

Gwenhwyfar was almost out of the door; she paused in midstride, looked back with a sweet, innocent smile on her face, murderous words in her head. 'Aye, Branwen?'

'Where are you off to? There is much to be done this morning – you will help me.'

'But I...' Gwenhwyfar ceased her protests; it was never profitable to argue with her brother's wife. Etern and Arthur would have to wait – happen their pounding heads would last long enough to be showing discomfort later.

Those two spoken words were enough to draw a frown from Branwen, accompanied by, 'One day, young maid, you will become headwoman to a household.' Her raised finger wagged with her scolding. 'Come that day, you will need to know your duties.' Branwen waddled through the door, motioning for Gwenhwyfar to follow. 'The dear Lord knows how I try to impress this fact upon you!'

The morning dragged. A bright, sun-splendid morning with the birds busy about their nests and young, and the sky a perfect cloudless blue.

The storerooms were deliciously cool. An arrayed army of pots and jars: preserves ranked along rows of shelves and upon the floor; dried fruits, spices and herbs; honey for sweetening and for adding to the ink used for the writing of ledgers and communications. Amphorae of oil for cooking and lighting. Salt, barrels of it. Further in, steps down to cooler, darker, slate lined cellars where meat, smoked or salted, hung from low beams, and beyond, in a smaller chamber, cheeses made from cow's, goat's and sheep's milk. Produce from the herds that grew fat from Gwynedd's ample grazing.

Branwen poked and peered, tutting often. A heady, potent scent clung to where the barrels of wine and ale were stored, a smell of last summer's end, when the fruit had been gathered and pressed in the great vats behind the granaries. The jugs of apple and pear and wild flower wines were in plentiful supply, so too the barrels of ale, but the fine imported wine drew a burst of exclaimed dismay, the vaulted ceiling echoing her clicking tongue.

Branwen wagged her head. 'We will need to keep close watch on these – I pray Lord Uthr will not stay long.' She clicked her tongue again.

Behind the safe shadows of the smoking torch she held Gwenhwyfar grinned. There was enough wine in here to quench the thirst of two full Roman legions! Branwen did fuss so.

Then out from the stores and across the hard-packed earth of the courtyard heading for the little dark room where gathered herbs were dried and ground for cooking and healing and, beyond, to the linen chests, a particular pride of Branwen's. Few households could boast such fine-woven bedlinen!

Gwenhwyfar trotted at the woman's heels, her eyes drifting to the rise of hills beyond the Caer's turf and timber walling, only half listening to Branwen's list of chiding, so often had she heard the same round of complaints.

'Your father should send you for fostering where this disagreeable side to your nature would be whipped from you.'

Dutifully Gwenhwyfar agreed. Do the tasks, nod your head. Quicker to see the thing through than start a battle of words.

There were steps up to the linen stores. Branwen tripped on the last, falling forward heavily with a startled cry. No matter how irritating she was, Gwenhwyfar would wish the woman no harm, for the sake of the child she carried if for little else. She put out her hand, concerned, offering help. 'You ought to rest more with the babe so close to birthing.'

Branwen heaved her bulk upright. Shaken, she replied, 'Rest? Where would I find time to rest?' Fumbling with her girdle keys she unlocked the door and a waft of lavender scented, sun-bleached linen leapt out at them. 'I expect to birth this child while sorting out some incompetent's mistake.' Branwen moved inside, her fingers lovingly touching the laundered items, selected what was needed and motioned for Gwenhwyfar to carry them. Rest? With the men preparing for war and such a large household to be responsible for – she peered narrow-eyed at Gwenhwyfar – and with this child who preferred the run of the hills and a sweating pony to educate into taking women's work seriously? Branwen sighed. It was the Lord's will that a woman should work to atone the sins of Eve. Rest? Rest!

Uthr's assigned chamber was close to Cunedda's own rooms built at an angle to the rear of the Hall. His room was empty, found to be muddled with armour, maps and discarded clothing. A man's chamber. Bed furs lay in a heap, a wine flagon lay on its side on the floor, its contents long since soaked into the hard-stamped earth. More tutting from Branwen. She called for servants and muttering disapproval at the thoughtlessness of men, moved on to inspect the women's quarters, and to the chamber assigned to Lady Morgause.

Apprehension fluttered within Gwenhwyfar as she followed like a puppy in her sister-by-law's squat shadow. She was well aware who she had collided with last night at the latrines. Aware this lady was not someone to treat lightly. Her temper had been heard throughout the stronghold and was etched in the cold beauty of her face for all to see. Gwenhwyfar was no timid girl, but, oh, did she need to accompany Branwen beyond this particular threshold?

Morgause lay languishing on her bed. She barely bothered a glance at Branwen as she entered, but her brows rose fractionally as Gwenhwyfar came forward to place fresh linen for a servant to remake the bed. The girl risked a quick discreet look at the woman, her eyes darting away as they met with a dark expression of disapproval. She knew Morgause would say something, some disparaging remark.

And it came, silky smooth, laced with the sharpened edge of a dagger blade. 'Gwenhwyfar. The maid who holds no respect for elders, who does not watch where she is going and who thinks she can hold a man's attention by prattling silly nonsense!'

Frowning, Gwenhwyfar returned Morgause's stare. Whatever was she on about? 'I apologised for my clumsiness, my lady. I was in desperate need to hurry.' She lifted her shoulders in a slight shrug. 'For the rest, I know not what you mean.'

Morgause smiled. Gwenhwyfar noticed how that smile went no further than the lips, no trace of it touching her smooth cheek or blue eyes. A chiselled smile that could have belonged to a marble statue. If becoming a woman meant bustling tetchily from storeroom to storeroom, or lying a-bed while the sun rose high, making ambiguous, sarcastic comments, then *na*, Gwenhwyfar did not look forward to womanhood!

Branwen had cast a hard, disapproving glance at the girl, but to Gwenhwyfar's relief, said nothing. Branwen chided her many faults for her own good, but loyalty to your own came before courtesy to this immoral, painted woman. Politely, Branwen asked if the lady had all she required.

Morgause stretched, arching her slender body, and lazily rose from the bed, unconcerned at her nakedness. She was beautiful, and she knew it. Walking like a sleek cat across the room she slid smoothly into a robe, seated herself on a stool and motioned for the slave to begin on her hair.

'I would prefer quarters closer to my lord Uthr's.' Morgause swept her lashes low and blinked several times, staring meaningfully at Branwen. 'We are an inconvenient distance apart.'

'Our unmarried women's chambers are all away from the men's.' Branwen's reply was stiff.

Morgause waved her hand. 'No matter. Distance increases desire.' She glanced at Branwen's rigid stance and sober dress, her eyes lingering on the woman's advanced pregnancy. 'I see you keep close to your man!'

Branwen tightened her lips, affronted. 'The servants are instructed to bring all you need.' She turned on her heels to leave.

Morgause waited until Branwen was almost through the door. 'There is something…'

Branwen paused.

'The boy Arthur has orders to attend me. He has not made an appearance this day.'

'I will instruct the servants to find him.'

Seizing her chance Gwenhwyfar said eagerly, 'Shall I go look for him?'

Morgause spread one of her dazzling smiles that sparked nothing of friendliness. 'Do so.'

Tossing an impish grin at Branwen Gwenhwyfar skipped off before her brother's wife could countermand the order. She searched the Caer and made cursory enquiries through the bustling settlement, to discover the boy Arthur was nowhere to be found.

Nor, for that matter, was her brother Etern. Damn them both! No, damn Arthur; it was he who had captivated Etern!

By early afternoon she gave up the search and, instead, headed for her special private place, a sanctuary of quiet where she could think or dream. She fleetingly wondered whether she ought to report back to Morgause, but decided against the idea. It was Arthur, after all, who was in trouble with the woman, not herself. Sitting with her long legs twined around the sturdy bough of a large old tree at the far side of the orchard, she thought over the morning, wondering where Etern had got to and who Arthur was, beyond the scant information she had already gleaned. And then there was Morgause to consider.

Morgause, how different from Branwen! Gwenhwyfar giggled to herself, stretched her arms above her head and settled her back more comfortably against the sturdy old trunk. Uthr's mistress epitomised all Branwen detested. What fun! She would tell Etern of this morning's encounter. How he would laugh! Morgause with no shame, Branwen bristling with disgust! The Christian priest lay behind Branwen's fastidiousness, of course. Gwenhwyfar thought him a sanctimonious fool. Once, she had asked her Da why he tolerated the man. Cunedda had replied that it was politic to accept the Christian faith.

'Jesu Christ poses no threat to Gwynedd or to me. He's as welcome to my hospitality and acknowledgement as any who bring peace and prosperity.'

'All very well,' Gwenhwyfar thought now, closing her eyes against the dance of dappled sunlight. 'The Christ might be welcome, but need we suffer Branwen's morals?'

45

Voices. Two people talking beyond the wall in the confined space of the herb garden. Morgause's shrill of laughter and an answering deep throated chortle. Uthr. Gwenhwyfar's eyes snapped open: she sat hastily forward, grabbing at a branch to steady herself; the bough swayed, settled.

They had stopped not far from the overhang of her tree. Looking down through the glossy spring foliage, she could see them, standing close together against the sun warmed wall.

'Is it not pleasant here, Morgause? I said you would enjoy Gwynedd.'

'No, it is not.' A whine crept into her correct Latin – not for her the soldiers' clipped accent or the common British tongue. 'I have barely seen you, Uthr.' Then impatience. 'And the boy has disappeared.'

Gwenhwyfar chewed her fingernails. Should she make herself known? It was wrong to listen to private conversation, but...

Morgause was talking. 'Arthur is becoming more disobedient as each day passes! He is at an age, Uthr, when he thinks he can rule the roost, but I tell you...'

The man sighed, interrupted, and peeping through the leaves Gwenhwyfar could see him stroking Morgause's slender arm.

'He's high spirited.'

'He is a self willed, spoilt brat.'

From her hidden place Gwenhwyfar nodded her head in vigorous agreement with Morgause's sharp response. Aye to that!

Uthr was standing very close to his mistress; his hand had slid around her waist. 'Leave the lad be, it is his first time away from the estate.'

'I do not know what possessed you to bring him.'

'I like him.'

'Huh!'

They fell silent. Gwenhwyfar peeped again. Uthr's head was very close to Morgause. He kissed her, his hand sliding up to caress her breast. Irritably, Morgause pushed him away but did not step aside. 'Not here, not where Cunedda's people may see.'

'What? Becoming modest of a sudden?'

She ignored the sarcasm. 'You ordered the boy to ensure I had all I needed.'

Uthr tried again to kiss her but she jerked her head away. 'The boy is a lazy good-for-nothing. I will thrash his backside when I catch up with him.'

Uthr chuckled. 'For punishment or pleasure?'

Morgause laughed, a false, forced sound. 'My lord, what thoughts you have!'

Uthr laughed with her, but there was a rumbling growl beneath the flat humour. 'I know your ways, Morgause, and have a distaste for them. I am fond of the lad. Leave him alone.'

The laughter quite gone, and jealousy rising, Morgause sneered, 'Fond of him? Do I not know it!' She swirled some few paces away. 'Why did you bring him? Because you could not bear to be parted from him? Because you could choose which one of us warmed your bed at night – choosing him last night!'

Gwenhwyfar's grip almost slipped, so far out was she leaning. Uthr had stormed forward, his hand slapping a resonant blow across Morgause's cheek.

'You have a twisted mind, woman!'

'An open one! Why else are you so taken with a servant's by-blow? Why else did you persuade your brother to foster him?'

'The fostering was Ectha's decision, and I'm fond of the lad because he has the making of a good soldier.'

Changing tack, Morgause began fiddling with the lacings of Uthr's tunic. 'As I have the making of a good wife?'

'For someone, possibly.'

'For you?' She was cuddling close.

'I already have a wife.'

Morgause flounced away. 'A wife? You call that God-kneeling, virgin-breed a wife?'

'She is a good woman.' Uthr re-laced the ties. 'As for the boy, I brought him because he needs the experience. Ectha's eldest own-born son, Cei, would also have come had he not been stupid enough to break his leg. Satisfied? Or do you need further explanation?'

He put his hands on Morgause's shoulders. She twitched, indicating she did not want his touch. 'I say again: the boy came because I like him. Ygrainne is my wife; I happen still to like her. What do you want?' The last, to a servant hovering uncertain on the far side of the garden.

'Forgive me, Lord Cunedda sends for you. Urgent word comes from the South.'

Uthr nodded curtly and waved the man away. He turned back to Morgause. 'You, I love.' He kissed her forehead and, without a backward glance, swung away across the garden.

After a while Morgause also left, walking away with quick, angry steps.

§ VI

Gwenhwyfar released her breath in a long, slow exhalation. She was an honest girl, with a dislike of lies and deceits; it was wrong to listen to others' conversation, but if Uthr and Morgause had intended secrecy why talk in the public space of a garden? They had spoken of nothing of great importance, no confidences or intrigue. She chewed her lip, considering, her fingers toying with a braid of hair. Best to keep quiet. No one knew she had been in this tree, after all. Squinting through the green canopy at the floating blue sky, Gwenhwyfar checked the orchard. Two goats solemnly chewed the cud away to the left, geese were preening beneath the shade of a favourite tree, but no people. No one to ask awkward questions needing evasive answers. This heat was becoming oppressive, too close and stifling. She slithered from her bough and, swinging to the ground, strolled across the orchard for the Caer's western gate. She would go to the paddock, catch Splinter and ride to the hills. It would be cooler there, more of a breeze. She might even paddle her feet in a stream, or swim in the pool beneath the waterfall.

Coming round the granary building she stopped short, her jaunty, whistled tune catching in mid note. Leaping back, Gwenhwyfar flattened herself against the roughness of the lime-washed wall, drew breath before tilting her head to peep round the corner.

Morgause was standing in the path of Arthur and Etern, whose horses were slithering to a startled halt. A flourish of spite panted through Gwenhwyfar. She watched, a satisfied smile creeping across her lips, as Morgause marched up to the two boys. Good, Arthur was to have a telling off!

His horse shied at the woman's sudden movement and shouting voice, colliding with Aquila, who bounded forward tossing his head and snorting.

'Take care, my lady! The horses are edgy for want of exercise!' Etern's rebuke was taut but polite. Morgause ignored him.

She took hold of Arthur's bridle. 'Where have you been all morning?'

Suppressing anger and acute embarrassment, Arthur replied with curt civility, 'Etern and I were first with Lord Uthr. We went then, at his suggestion, to speak with Lord Cunedda. He has commanded Etern to show me the horse runs.' The boy looked at her scornfully. 'Would you rather I ignore either of my lords for your benefit, lady?'

Uthr had lied! Morgause caught her breath, her fingers clamping tighter around the bridle straps. He had known of Arthur's whereabouts! He had known! The bastard had lied to her, shielding the boy. In a voice filled with hatred she spat out, 'Do not think, boy, you will be permitted to run wild here in Gwynedd. I shall see to it that you do not.'

She swished her skirts as she strode away, making the horses snort again, dancing in agitation. Etern stared after her, mouth slightly open.

Soothing his mount, Arthur said low to the woman's departing back, 'I bet you will, you bitch.' He brought his hand up in an obscene gesture.

Etern looked across at him, said mildly, 'I take it you do not much like Lady Morgause.'

Arthur laughed, breaking the tension. He squeezed his horse forward. '*Na*, not much. The only person to like her is Uthr!'

For Gwenhwyfar, that small moment of pleasure for Arthur's discomfort had passed. She did not like him, but disliked Morgause even more. The woman had a cloak of evil clinging to her, a darkness that made your flesh crawl and the hairs on the back of your neck prickle. A pulse of sympathy for Arthur flickered briefly. It must be unpleasant to be constantly under that woman's command. Gwenhwyfar slid from her hiding place and ran forward waving her arm to attract attention. It would take only a moment to catch Splinter – she would ride with the boys.

'Etern! Hie, brother!'

The horses were trotting, eager to be away. Etern glanced over his shoulder, saw his sister and called, 'Later! I am too busy for you now!' And he was gone, riding through the entrance tunnel running beneath the twin watchtowers.

Gwenhwyfar felt numb, stunned. She stood staring in disbelief, her arms hanging at her sides, her head empty of thought, incapable of movement. She and her brother had always done everything together. Always. *'Too busy for you'* hammered and hammered at her. Etern, her beloved brother. Too busy.

Fighting back tears, she walked into the stables, not certain where she was going, what she was doing, just doing it by habit. She lifted her pony's bridle from its peg and went from the Caer down to the paddock. Splinter was a friendly pony, easy to catch; he allowed her to slip reins over his head, put the bit in his mouth and fasten straps in place. Not until she was mounted on his warm, bare back and cantering up the valley towards the gentler slopes of the higher hills did she let the tears come. In her misery, Gwenhwyfar urged the pony faster, let him have his head, his sturdy legs stretching forward, mane and tail streaming her own hair coming loose from its braiding. The wind whistled in her ears; whipped away falling tears.

A ground-nesting bird shrilled alarm and scrambled into hasty flight, its whirring wings beating up from the grass almost beneath the pony's unshod feet. Splinter leapt to one side, squealing with surprise Gwenhwyfar was thrown. Instinctively, she tucked in her head and rolled with the landing. Winded but unhurt, she lay still, her head burrowed into the crook of her arm. Then the ache took hold of her; sobs shook her body as she cried, her tears soaking into the grass that was already browning from the days of baking sun. The heartbreak of loneliness and betrayal stabbed and stabbed as her body heaved and choked out there on the wind-kissed hills, where the birds fluttered and chirped as if no wrong could ever be done to the world.

It was a long while before the grief was all spilled, before her body stopped its shuddering and the tears were cried dry. She lay broken and damaged, fragile among the warm heather and coarse grass, with the heat of the afternoon beating down on her back.

Soft whiskers from an inquisitive muzzle snuffed at her ear, rousing her. Stiffly, she sat up, head and eyes aching, throat dry and swollen. She fondled the pony, rubbing his broad forehead, pulling at his shaggy forelock. At least he was a friend. Wearily, Gwenhwyfar stood, found her legs were shaking. Stretching her hand to the reins, she leant against the pony's broad belly, patted and fussed over him a while longer.

There was a chill to the coming of evening, a whisper of rain heralding the clouds massing distant on the sea's horizon. A storm would grow with nightfall and the turn of the tide.

The girl made her way to a stream and drank, letting the cold, sweet taste trickle down her hot throat. She washed her face, patting handfuls of soothing water on red, sore eyes, then sat a while, hunched on the bank, watching the tumble of water as it rushed by, chattering and busy, down the hillside to join the slower flowing river and beyond that, the sparkle of the sea. A thought of Etern came to her. They had shared everything from the day she felt old enough to leave the security of her nurse's holding hand – probably afore that also, though she could remember nothing before her third summer. She knew he must leave her soon, for he was close to becoming a man, and men could not take time to ride and play with girls. But not yet, not this summer!

Unsure what to do next, aware that anger was replacing hurt, she rebraided her hair and dabbed vaguely at grass-stained knees. Vaulting on to the pony's back she turned his head and jogged slowly home.

Evening had taken full hold by the time she made her way into the stable yard. The place was busy; many of the men had passed the day hunting, returning in high spirits with some fine buck and a variety of small game. Bustling slaves took charge of their weary horses, walking them around to dry the lathered sweat, or brushing matted coats. There was the noise and laughter of shared excitement, tossed jests and mock insults from the men of Cunedda's Hall, men eager to share their day, to relive the pleasure of the chase.

Gwenhwyfar led Splinter into a quiet stall at the far end of the stable block and began rubbing down his coat with a twist of hay. It was still thick and shaggy from the winter, great tufts coming out in dusty handfuls as she groomed. His chest, neck, and belly were quite damp with sweat.

Her father insisted a rider be taught to tend a horse in addition to ride it. *'You cannot learn much of a horse by putting your backside on it. Know your mount. Know every hair on its body, then he will know you, and serve you well.'* Gwenhwyfar enjoyed the work. The regular strokes, the steady, relaxing chewing as Splinter tore at hay in the rack before him. Turbulent emotions subsided, jangled thoughts ebbing into a dream-like trance with the rhythm of her grooming and the drowsing warmth and smell of horse and stable.

Lost in her work, she disregarded two mounts being led into nearby stalls. Standing on the off side, bending to scrub at an obstinate stain, Gwenhwyfar was unaware of who led them. A laugh that was becoming unwelcomingly familiar attracted her attention.

'That scruff at the end there is surely not your Da's?' Gwenhwyfar's jaw set, her muscles freezing rigid. She remained taut, waiting for her brother's reply.

'*Na*, that's my sister's pony.'

Again a laugh. 'I would have thought even a sister could have done better!'

Somehow, Gwenhwyfar held her rising temper in check. Surely Etern would answer in her defence? She waited, but he only chuckled.

Arthur then asked, 'Would this be the same sister who served at table last night?'

'Gwenhwyfar's my only sister. Aye, it was she who made a fool of herself in front of Uthr.'

Gwenhwyfar bit her lip. Why say that?

'She had spirit,' Arthur countered.

'Who needs your approval!' Gwenhwyfar mentally thrust a retort.

Arthur giggled, a stupid, childish sound, Gwenhwyfar thought. 'The one sister, eh? Just as well it was nine boys and one girl, not vice versa! Nine girls... whooof!'

Etern responded with another laugh. 'Aye, one can be trouble enough at times.' He meant it, it was no amused jest.

Arthur was moving to the other side of his horse, attending to sweat patches left beneath the saddle. He had no experience of girls. His foster father had two born sons who, with himself, were the only children of the household. There were the servants' daughters, of course, and a few slave girls working in the kitchens, but beyond superficial contact Arthur had little to do with any of them. Gwenhwyfar had brought round the wine at table; he assumed all girls and women were set to serve, had no personal experience to suppose otherwise of Cunedda's daughter. He observed quite innocently, 'I doubt her trailing skirts bother you over much.'

Gwenhwyfar's temper erupted in a howl of rage. She sprang from behind her pony, causing him to start backward in alarm, all the hurt and anguish exploding behind her as she shouted, 'I may be an unworthy girl to your insolent eyes, but I'll have you know I am high born of Gwynedd. I will not listen further to such insult! Splinter has served me with more loyalty than some I can name.' Here she flicked a hand contemptuously in Etern's direction. 'I am proud of my pony!'

Arthur stared, greatly amused at the furious whirl of hair and arms before him. He pointed at Splinter. 'You are proud of that moth-chewed tuft of dune grass?' He rested a hand lightly on his own horse's sleek rump. 'I know Gwynedd's famous for horseflesh – I assumed for riding not eating!' He grinned, expecting laughter from Etern. The other boy remained silent, recognising his sister's dangerous mood.

Arthur mistook the silence and teased further. 'Tell me then, daughter of Gwynedd, do you ride this apology for a mount, or is he intended as a hearthrug?'

'Happen,' Gwenhwyfar retorted with dignity, 'it is fortunate I am a girl. It seems the bastard-born boys of Less Britain do not have manners bred into them!'

Moving with quick steps, Etern came from behind his horse. 'That's no way to speak to a guest!'

Her answer was almost a snarl. First he had not wanted her, now he sided with this dung-heap of a boy! 'He speaks disrespectfully to the daughter of his host!' To Arthur she snapped, 'You will observe, bastard boy, I do not trail at my brother's heels, nor' – indicating her bracae – 'do I wear skirts!'

'Gwenhwyfar! Enough!' Etern glared at her, his own anger rising at this show of rudeness to his new friend. He lifted his hands in expressive despair. 'Forgive her, Arthur, she is upset.'

Arthur gave a single nod of his head. What was there to forgive? Being snarled at, called a bastard? He was used to it. Everyone back home spoke to him so, save his foster father, Lord Uthr, and his young foster brother Bedwyr, who was too little to know anything anyway. He liked this girl; she was not like the servants, grubby drudges who poked fun, or whined or giggled and chattered. She reminded him of a wild cat he had once found caught in a snare. How it had spat and clawed and fought for freedom, even though a paw was almost severed! He turned, intending to fetch hay for his horse, waved his hand in a dismissive gesture. 'There is nought to forgive, my friend. She's only a girl.'

Furious, Gwenhwyfar reached for the nearest item to hand, which happened to be a bucket of water. She swung the thing up, hurling the contents at Arthur.

Etern stood speechless – as did Branwen.

Guessing Gwenhwyfar would not be far from the stables, Branwen had come in search of the irritating child, entering the building just as the water dowsed its victim.

'Master Arthur!' she screeched, rushing forward to dab ineffectually at the dripping boy. To Gwenhwyfar, 'You wicked child! You heathen demon!' Branwen glared at her, furious. 'I will see you whipped raw for this!' She flapped her hand at Etern. 'Run for a cloak, a blanket, anything to turn a chill from the boy.'

'Thank you for your concern.' Arthur smiled politely, dropping the British tongue to speak in precise, correct Latin. 'I have come to no harm, it was an accident. Gwenhwyfar was emptying the bucket and I walked in the way.' He removed Branwen's hand that was patting rather personally at his wet bracae.

At that moment, Gwenhwyfar hated him more than ever. How dare he make excuses for her?

'It was no accident, as well you know!' she yelled. 'I threw it deliberate and aimed well. Could as easily do it again.' She whirled and seized a second bucket from the next stall, hurled the water. Prepared, Arthur ducked aside, and the full force sluiced over Branwen.

She stood speechless. Water dripped from her hair, soaked

through her gown, spread in a puddle at her feet. Her mouth opened and closed once or twice, then her face puckered and turned a deep shade of puce. Without a word, she strode forward and clamped a hand around Gwenhwyfar's wrist. The girl made no sound as she was dragged forward and borne away, too proud to cry out at the twisting pain of that vicious grip.

Besides, there seemed little point in saying anything. What was there to say?

§ VII

Where are you taking me?' Picking at the fingers around her wrist, Gwenhwyfar attempted to pull Branwen to a halt. This path from the stable yard was rough shale and gravel, a narrow way, pocked by foot worn hollows. Gwenhwyfar stumbled and fell forward, a stab of pain shooting up her left arm as she tried to save herself. Branwen hauled her upright and ploughed forward, a trireme under full oar.

'To your father,' she replied curtly.

Few things frightened Gwenhwyfar. In weapon practice she could stand firm against a thrusting spear or sword blade; she was capable of mastering a wilful horse or outfacing a snarling dog. Not for her, the shriek of panic when a spider scuttled across the floor or a mouse ventured bold into a room. Punishment she could endure, but to face Cunedda's displeasure, witness his disappointment? Fool girl, what had she done!

'My wrist hurts. Please stop.' She was close to tears, her hand throbbing, the fingers already swelling.

There was no turning Branwen when her mind was set. 'It is time your father saw the wickedness that lies within you child.'

Sweeping up to Cunedda's private chambers, Branwen barely paused to seek admittance.

The Lion Lord of Gwynedd stood at a table studying a spread of maps and papers, his head bent to see clearer, fingers moving across the yellowish parchment. Grouped around the table were his sons and eldest grandson – and, pointing at some particular note of interest, Uthr. Cunedda glanced up at the unexpected entrance and frowned. Uthr withdrew his finger from the map, dark eyebrows raised in enquiry. Heads turning. Surprise, puzzlement and a flutter of amusement. A slight pause from both sides, men and woman.

Cunedda: 'What means this interruption?'

Osmail: 'Branwen? What do you here?'

At the front of the cluttered table, Abloyc, Rumaun and Dunaut, drew aside to allow the woman access, their grins widening as they noticed her wet and spoiled clothing.

'Gods!' Cunedda barked. 'My maps!' He snatched the precious articles from threatening drips of water, tutting and barely listening as Branwen launched into the telling of her grievance.

Uthr tactfully busied himself with the view from the unshuttered window, choking back laughter at the account of Arthur's dowsing.

Abloyc, however, always one for merriment, gave a great bellow of delight, echoed by his brothers and nephew. Even Osmail permitted himself a smile, which faded rapidly under a sour look from his wife.

'Why bother me with this childish prank?' Cunedda snapped, with no sign of amusement. 'Is it not your duty to settle household matters?' Then, annoyed, 'By the Goddess, woman, we plan a war campaign here!'

Folding her arms, Branwen stood in a posture of defiant determination. 'And I plan to put end to the devilment within your daughter. She is deceitful and rude, becoming quite unmanageable.'

'I have not found her so.' Cunedda stood behind his table, matching the defiance:

Ceredig, leaning against the wall, interrupted. 'Mischievous I would agree to, even impudent, but not the words you use, sister-by-law.' He winked surreptitiously at Gwenhwyfar.

Smiling back at him, Gwenhwyfar felt more at ease. Catching that slight gleam, Osmail frowned reproof.

Spreading her skirt Branwen shook the sopping material, and picked disconsolately at her bodice and bedraggled hair. 'Look at me! I am soaked through, my gown is ruined and the servants are laughing behind my back. How can I maintain discipline within the Caer while this girl runs wild?' A thin wail entered her voice. 'I may take a chill from this. I tell you, Lord Cunedda, I will have her hide if harm comes to the child I carry!'

Straightening from where he had been leaning over the maps, Cunedda folded his arms, said drily, 'Happen you ought to have changed your garments before coming here.'

'I judged it best to bring this wicked deed direct to you.'

Cunedda sighed, exchanged a brief glance of mutual resignation with Enniaun and crooked his finger at Gwenhwyfar. 'Come here, child. Why?'

Gwenhwyfar answered without fear, to the point. 'Because the boy was rude to me.'

A smile threatened Cunedda's composure. His sons were snorting, holding laughter in check. They had gathered in a semicircle behind him, interested in this digression from serious discussion. Only Osmail stood apart, and Uthr, who remained beside the window.

Pointing towards Branwen, Cunedda asked, 'And was your sister-by-law rude also?'

Again a direct reply. 'She stepped in the way as I aimed a second bucket.'

Uthr's laughter mingled with the rise of chuckles and Cunedda found he dared not look at any one of them for fear he would lose his hard held restraint. Curse the lass, the little vixen! With forced severity he queried, 'You are, I assume, sorry for what happened?'

Standing spear-straight before him, Gwenhwyfar debated a truthful answer. She would not lie to her father. 'For wetting Branwen I am.' She paused. 'Not for Arthur, save I'm sorry I missed him that second time.'

Again Uthr spluttered, smothering the sound with a strangled cough. Enniaun, Abloyc and the twins were laughing outright. Ceredig's shoulders were shaking, a hand covering his face, spluttering noises coming from between the fingers.

Branwen raised her arms in despair, ignoring these fool men. 'Gwenhwyfar has disgraced our laws of hospitality, disgraced Gwynedd!'

'Oh, come, that is exaggeration!'

'A prank cannot be construed as anything more than high spirits.' The laughter was abating, indignation creeping in as Branwen made more out of this than necessary.

Ill at ease, Cunedda shuffled a few papers. He agreed with his sons, but then Gwenhwyfar was running leeward to the acceptable of late.

Osmail came forward. It rankled that his brothers always sided against Branwen and himself, made their jests and snide little comments at their expense. Branwen ran this Caer. She was an efficient head woman, a good mother. They forgot that. Forgot where they would be without her.

'My wife has suffered gross humiliation, Father.' He indicated her appearance. 'Insolence cannot be tolerated.'

'In my experience, the occasional dose of humility causes no harm,' Cunedda observed. 'Be that as it may, such behaviour will not do, my daughter. You are confined to the Caer for one week.' He hooked a stool from beneath the table and sat down, turning his full attention back to his maps. The matter was settled.

'You are not serious!' Branwen's shrilled protest jarred through the room. The flat of her hand banged on the table, her other hand shooting out to jerk the girl nearer. 'She deserves a public thrashing for this outrage, not mere confinement!'

The last shreds of laughter vanished, hostility snaking to the fore instead. Instinctively, the brothers gathered behind their father, Osmail in turn taking a step nearer to Branwen on their side of the table. Each side drew themselves up, frowns creasing deeper. Battle positions, second nature to a fighting man.

Thrusting the stool aside, Cunedda came sharp to his feet. 'No child of mine receives public reprimand!' One had, once. Typiaunan. Butchered before the gloating eyes of Vortigern's hired Saex.

'She needs a thrashing, and a thrashing she will get!' That was Osmail., defying his father, his brothers.

Shocked gasps. Osmail turning against their lord? Even Branwen took a small, hesitant step away from her husband, then recovered to move even closer, standing shoulder to shoulder with him.

'Too long have your eyes been turned against discipline,' she said.

Cunedda had no time for Branwen. A woman in your bed to while away a summer night, or to snuggle against when the winter winds and snows raged, was one thing. But Branwen's incessant bad tempers – why his son kept her, he could not understand.

He regarded Osmail through slit eyes, looked at him for perhaps the first time in many years. Always a disappointment, Osmail. A clumsy child, dropping things, tripping over something, a molehill, his own sword. Spewing or swooning at the merest hint of blood, unable to handle a sword efficiently. Grizzling when a younger brother bested him on the practice ground. Cunedda had despaired of the lad as a child, rejected him as a man grown. He ought have gone into the Christian priesthood.

He turned his attention back to Branwen. 'I have more important matters to attend than household squabbles.' He raised a hand against the flood of answer and frowned at Gwenhwyfar. 'You put me in an awkward position, daughter!'

Chewing her lip, Gwenhwyfar hung her head. For, that, she was sorry.

Striding to the front of the table, swearing beneath his breath, Cunedda unbuckled his belt. 'Off with your tunic, girl, let's see this thing ended.'

'Da, this is not warranted...' Abloyc had come round the table on the other side, his hand extended.

Ceredig with Dogmail, appalled, joined him. 'A whipping is no punishment for a child's prank!'

Osmail stepped in their path. 'One such prank, happen not, but how many more need we endure from this devilish girl?' He glowered at

Cunedda. 'You whipped us often enough as boys.'

'Never for something so trivial!' countered Rumaun.

'Trivial! You call deliberately soaking my wife trivial!' Osmail bunched his fists, rage reddening his face, his anger all the more potent for knowing that his brothers were right. Branwen was overreacting in this silly nonsense, yet he had to declare for her, back her. He had not the chance of escaping her sour temper during the next few weeks as they had! 'How dare you belittle her status!'

'Belittle her? God's teeth, she has welded her supremacy so tight, it would be easier to shift Yr Wyddfa a mile nearer the sea!'

Cunedda raised his hand for silence. 'There is no time for argument, we have more pressing matters to discuss. Gwenhwyfar!'

She stood quite silent, staring steadily into Uthr Pendragon's eyes as the strap whistled through the air five times to strike across her back. It was Uthr who kept the cry from reaching beyond her throat, not her silent watching brothers. Their mixture of sympathy and indignation would have unstoppered that tight control, but not with Uthr there. She would not disgrace her father before such a man by crying out, so she looked at Uthr and kept the pain from showing in her face and voice. When it was finished, her shoulders burnt like fire and her wrist throbbed sporadic drumbeats of pain, but the cry was jammed firm in her chest.

'Satisfied, Branwen? Now be gone.' Cunedda swept his hand meaningfully towards the door. He felt anger and revulsion at himself for being pushed into administering a punishment he knew to be unjust, cursed the circumstances that left him no time to argue this dispute.

Bobbing a brief obeisance, clumsy in sodden skirts and advanced pregnancy, Branwen began to chivvy Gwenhwyfar out of the room, waited for someone to show the courtesy of opening the door. Abloyc was the nearest. Casually he leant against the wall and folded his arms, his expressive eyes daring her to make comment.

Branwen regarded her husband, a disdainful glance that ordered him to intervene. Resentment flashed across Osmail's soul. Before all his brothers she put him down, trod him into the dirt. He came forward and opened the door, saying with pent-up malice, 'One day, woman, you will push me over this hurdle of restraint!'

Branwen snapped, 'You have not the wit or the courage to even approach it, Osmail.'

'A bitch wife and a coward husband.' It was Dogmail who sneered, who said the words that they all thought.

Osmail turned, bunched his fist and hit him.

Dogmail fell backwards, sprawling across the table, sending maps and papers flying, his nose spouting blood.

'Jesu Christ!' Several brothers murmured the same incredulous expletive, standing gaping, mouths open, eyes wide. 'Jesu!'

Osmail flexed his knuckles, felt the soreness and bruising swelling already. He said nothing, but stumped out the door, flinging it wider open as Gwenhwyfar darted back in and skidded to a halt, her own expression registering disbelief.

With no word he pushed past, shouldering Branwen aside also. She called after him for an explanation, but he stumped on, shoulders hunched, rage boiling. He had never hit another man in temper before. Never hit a brother. A brother, by God, a dear brother! And that woman, that nagging, managing, arrogant... He slammed the outer door, crossed the courtyard and disappeared into the smithy. There would be work to do. Best stay out of her way a while, she'd not be over pleased at all this.

Inside Cunedda's chamber all stayed still and quiet, exchanging glances, unspoken thoughts. Gwenhwyfar's eyes were enquiring, darting from one face to the other.

Dogmail dabbed at his nose, his head tipped back. 'Well well,' he chuckled, 'Osmail! Who'd have thought it!'

'What now, child?' rasped Cunedda, seeing Gwenhwyfar. 'Am I still confined within the Caer?'

The question eased any remaining aggression; back came the familiar laughter. Enniaun and Ceredig bent to retrieve papers, Abloyc was fetching a stool from across the room, Uthr approached the table. 'Fearless your daughter, my friend!' he said with a grin.

Cunedda laughed, tension easing from hunched, tired shoulders. 'She has the audacity of a vixen!' He ruffled Gwenhwyfar's unruly hair. '*Na*, lass, you have taken your punishment' – wagging a solemn finger – 'but no more scrapes this day, eh?' He waved her away out of the door, and turned to his maps.

§ VIII

Beyond the closed door, Branwen shook Gwenhwyfar, scolding her impudence. Despite the punishment she had achieved little. It was not enough, nowhere near enough. Taking firm hold, Branwen pulled the girl out of Cunedda's apartments and across a rear courtyard. Well, a lesson would be taught, a lesson to be remembered! To the Caer's chapel she took her, entering its dim interior by a side door.

'Does she intend me to beg God's forgiveness then?' Gwenhwyfar thought, defiance coursing at the idea. Never!

A square-cut stone altar dominated the little building, a single lamp upon it remaining always alight. Gwenhwyfar bobbed a reverence before it, deciding it best to comply with whatever crazed idea Branwen carried in her head – for now. Sometimes it was easier to swim with the current rather than fight against it. There was always a shallow pool somewhere ahead.

Branwen passed by the altar however, crossing instead to the far side of the chapel, and only then, as she tugged open the door to a rarely used storeroom, did Gwenhwyfar begin to feel the first stirring of alarm.

The priest, she remembered, was not at Caer Arfon. He had ridden out the day of Uthr's arrival to attend some arranged meeting of holy men. The chapel was likely to be barely used for some weeks, save by a devout few.

Briefly Gwenhwyfar wondered if his absence was more than coincidental, the thought instantly forgotten as Branwen pushed her into the darkness beyond the door.

'You will stay here until I decide to release you. In God's sight you can dwell upon your wickedness.' With satisfaction, Branwen slammed the door shut and pushed its bolt home.

Gwenhwyfar listened to the disappearing tap, tap of footsteps on the stone floor. The place was cold and rather damp. High to one side, a small ventilation brick through which the last rays of remaining daylight cast shafts of eerie half light. She sank to the floor and sat there dismally for a while, then bitter tears burst from her. She sobbed; it had been an awful day! A beating, her swollen wrist throbbing and throbbing, both pains of little consequence beside the loss of her brother's loyalty, that was unbearable! Her heart broke. Etern needed the companionship of a boy near his own age. This boy Arthur was foster kin to an acknowledged hero; naturally her brother would feel drawn to him. He needed no younger sister trotting at heel when the call of nearing manhood came.

For the first time in her life, Gwenhwyfar understood the sorrow of loneliness and rejection. It came hard to a child who had been close companion to one brother and under constant nurture from the others. Creeping miserably to a corner she felt a cloak hanging from a hook on the wall. Pulling it about her, seeking comfort from its small warmth, she sobbed more tears.

The sound of a man urinating against the stonework of the chapel wall woke her. She sat up with a start, unaware she had slept, disorientated at first by the dark and the chill. Did he not realise his blasphemy? Happen he cared as little for the Christ God as she did. No doubt he had mistaken his way to the latrine, or had not bothered seeking it.

She wondered whether to call out. As she hesitated the man belched and stumbled back towards voices that rose and fell from the direction of the Hall. The chance had passed – would she have taken it? To shout for help would be an admission of defeat, a blow to her pride. Hunched beneath the thin cloak she sat listening to the distant rumble of thunder and the muted roar of a wild surf. How long had she slept? She felt uncomfortable, the growing urge to urinate becoming unbearable.

Had she seen a bowl of some sort on that shelf? Body and fingers stiff from cold Gwenhwyfar fumbled in the dark, knocked something over sending it crashing to the floor. The bowl. She choked back a sob, scrunched over the debris to an opposite corner and relieved herself, disconcerted as her urine splashed on the slate floor.

Even with her lack of conviction for the Christian faith she felt ashamed at defiling holy territory. She thought of the man earlier, outside. He had probably been too deep in his wine to have noticed where and what he did.

Returning to the corner where the cloak lay Gwenhwyfar huddled into its scant warmth, doubting sleep would return. The sound of scraping bolts; she had dozed then. Heavy headed and swollen eyed, she felt suddenly aware of shivering cold and gnawing hunger.

Branwen stood in the doorway, a flickering torch in her hand. Saying nothing she set down a pitcher of water and a platter of food. The door closed, and Branwen went away.

Numbed fingers felt for the food, tears pricking Gwenhwyfar's eyes once again as she almost knocked the pitcher over. She drank great gulps of the cool, sweet water, easing her tight throat then poured some over the hot swelling of her wrist. The pain eased slightly but came back almost at once. Frugally, she chewed the barley bread and goat's cheese; she had no idea how long Branwen intended to keep her locked away, or when the next meal would come. At the thought, she regretted drinking the water so thirstily.

For a while the darkness held no fear, nor the discomfort, though the hard floor did little to ease her hurts. But the isolation quickly became intolerable. Never before had Gwenhwyfar been entirely alone during the night hours. There had always been her nurse, or Ceridwen and the other girls; or a brother, or her Da. Always someone else's back to snuggle against, to feel safe beside.

Glaring flashes of light penetrated the blackness, followed by long, rolling booms of thunder. It must be late; sounds from the Hall had ceased. The Caer slept beneath the growling storm.

Never had Gwenhwyfar faced darkness totally alone.

Another great roar of thunder. The girls would be cowering in their beds, blankets over heads, giving little screams and moans. Gwenhwyfar would normally scoff at their silliness – but it was different alone, vulnerable, exposed. A muffled rustling stirred close by. Mice or rats? In the dark, the pattering movements sounded menacing, unfriendly. Gwenhwyfar's heart pounded; she pulled the cloak tighter around her, sitting wide eyed, shivering, as rain drummed outside and the storm swept over the bay and echoed around the mountains. She covered her ears with her hands, and found herself praying to whatever God was listening for the dawn to come, soon.

As it did, eventually. Daylight brought welcome sounds: fowl scratching nearby; birdsong and distant movement, some activity. Muffled calls of male voices, the snorting and stamping of horses.

The sun strode high overhead when Branwen returned. Gwenhwyfar stood firm in the centre of her cell to face her. 'My father will have something to say when he hears of this outrage!'

As she set down fresh water, food and a chamber pot Branwen's laugh was low but victorious. 'That will not be for some while. They rode out this morning, off to war. Laughing and joking as if they were riding to some holiday! Fool men, glorying in death and destruction!'

Gwenhwyfar swayed, unbelieving. Her father and brothers off to war at Uthr's side? Gone? Without a word of parting?

'You lie!' she shrieked, running forward. 'My Da and brothers would never leave without bidding farewell.'

Branwen barred the door with her own body, holding the girl at arm's distance. 'You think not? A search was made for you, my dear, but you could not be found. It was assumed you were in hiding, ashamed at your conduct. The search was not over thorough.'

'You lie!' Distraught, Gwenhwyfar threw herself at Branwen, fists beating and feet kicking. 'I heard no call to march!'

Branwen gave Gwenhwyfar a push that sent her hurtling to the floor. 'Did you not? How would you know? The hearing of such is a man's affair, not for a woman or child. There was a messenger last afternoon, I believe, some while before your disgraceful escapade, something about King Vortigern heading into Powys.' She shut the door, wearing a thin, straight smile of satisfaction.

Stunned, cradling fresh pain from her injured wrist, Gwenhwyfar listened as Branwen walked away. She remembered the messenger who had arrived while Uthr talked with Morgause in the garden, who spoke of urgent news which had sent Uthr hurrying to her Da. And the bustle that morning. Horses, men laughing and shouting. The army marching!

§ IX

Etern sighed and kicked the wooden palisade with the toe of his boot; to emphasise his angry frustration, kicked again. He turned to gaze at the hills, watched as colour flicked from dark to brilliant to dark again, cloud shadows chasing each other as if playing some frenzied children's game.

'I tell you, Arthur, Gwenhwyfar would not take herself off after a punishment.'

Arthur was leaning over the wooden parapet, peering down at the clustered settlement with its huddle of round and rectangular houses, its market stalls, taverns and other buildings that made up a thriving place where people lived and earned an honest, or not so honest, living. A busy place, even with the men gone off to war. Directly below, a blacksmith hammered at a bent wheel rim outside his forge. Arthur watched, fascinated, as the man's muscles rippled across naked shoulders, strength pushing a piston arm up and down.

'Aye,' he said at length, 'your sister's different from other girls.' As an afterthought said, 'Wears bracae, has excellent aim – a fine temper too, eh?'

Etern grinned at his friend's attempt to cheer him. He liked Arthur. He had some quality about him, a daring attitude that promised excitement, danger and adventure. Why his sister had taken such a dislike to the lad, he could not understand. He missed Gwenhwyfar, her bright chatter, her mischief, but he enjoyed Arthur's company. Somehow, the two had not come together.

Arthur had a way of telling tales as good as any harper. He had told Etern of foreign lands, of Rome and Greece and India. Tales of strange beasts, long and striped or tall and spotted, elephants, lions, hairy apes. Of war and heroes, battles lost and battles won. Etern had learnt more these past days from Arthur, than from all those lectures droned by a succession of tutors. Arthur brought the past alive; his enthusiasm inspired Etern, who listened, thirsting for more. Gwenhwyfar would love to hear those tales – if only she would set aside her ridiculous animosity!

'My sister would not hide.' Etern frowned into the glare of the afternoon sun. The storm of last night was quite gone, leaving the world washed and fresh, the air cooler and lighter. 'No reasonable explanation would account for her missing the departure this morning. Gwenhwyfar finds it hard to accept she will never ride to battle – but that doesn't stop her wishing for it!' Etern chuckled. 'She glories in my father's campaigns – and is as excited at Uthr's war host as you and I. To miss our standard flying high beside the Dragon as our men march to war?' He shook his head, then swung round to grip the fencing. 'Never!' He strode a few paces along the walkway, his fingers skittering along the top of the palisade. From up here on the high turf wall there was a commanding view across the plain that slid on one side into a wave tossed sea and, on the other, raised up to meet the mountains that clustered, like a king's guard, around the Snow Mountain, Yr Wyddfa.

Etern stopped his walking and frowned across at the purple haze that was the island of Mon. The Romans had stormed across those wind whipped straits once long, long ago, to put an end to the Druids who had made their sacred place there. Aiee! There had been blood shed that night! When the wind blew just right, you could hear the screams of the spirits that haunted the groves and the shadows. Women priests had fought and died there – women among the men, fighting for what they believed in, useless against the strength and power of the Roman Eagles. They were gone now, the Druid priests, save for one or two crazy men who clung like limpets to the way things had been then, way, way back. The worship of the old gods and goddesses was remembered, of course, but as habit, something that was always done. Who thought twice about touching sacred wood, or offering the gods a pinch of spilt salt? The Christ had altered all that. The Old Ways were changing, the new, striding forward to acceptance.

Women went with the war host in those days, the days before Rome came to sweep the Old Ways into the midden heap and introduce the new, masculine way of things. Gwenhwyfar maintained that Rome was frightened of a woman's potential capability. She was probably right.

The memory of the past was strong today. The past, swirling and mingling with the present, spreading like a flare of torchlight, bright pathed into the future. Caer Arfon, built from the ruins of Segontium, and Cunedda, both already legend. Cunedda's wisdom and strength, the Caer's four timbered corner towers, turf wall and wooden palisade. Beyond the settlement, another defensive wall set atop a soaring rampart and plunging ditch.

'Not built to keep the enemy out,' Cunedda had laughed once, with his youngest born, *'but to keep you two horrors in!'*

Cunedda might never return. His sons might never again stand and look to the beauty of the hills or across a tossing sea to Mon. War was bravery and excitement, but war was also death.

'Gwenhwyfar knows the reality behind the glory,' Etern said quietly. 'Some of those who passed under that arch over there will never return through it.' His eyes pierced Arthur's. 'We are a close family. We do not ride to battle without bidding farewell. Never would my sister have failed our father. Never against her will.'

Arthur believed him. It was not a jest when he had said Gwenhwyfar was different from other girls. Oh, not different in the obvious sense. The serving girls back home, those drabs who toiled to fetch and carry, to clean and cook, were menials, workers, nothings. Gwenhwyfar was noble born, but there was something about her aside class and family connection. Pride? Character? Whatever, he wanted to know her, befriend her. There was a lot, he thought, to the real knowing of a girl like Gwenhwyfar. That was it, though – she was still a girl, a child, but one day soon she would be a woman grown. Arthur felt a quick sense of pleasure at the thought. He shrugged, unsure how to answer Etern without sounding condescending.

'The few girls I know seem a mewling lot to me. Quick to seek their mothers' skirts.'

Etern's sharp glare of reprimand told Arthur he had not then spoken tactfully.

'You forget – we have no mother's skirt. Gwenhwyfar may seem a tiresome girl-child to you, but I assure you, she is not.' Etern's voice was shaking – with anger or emotion, Arthur was uncertain. 'We have had it rough, living along this coast. Da and my brothers have fought long and hard to make Gwynedd the land it now is. Vortigern knew what he was doing when he took Da's northern lands and forced him to come here! Uthr had the soft side – exile to a wealthy, comfortable villa in the sun!' He rushed on, barely pausing for breath, arms waving, animated, pacing up and down. 'Da's founding more than a place where we live and rule. He is founding a dynasty. Gwynedd is destined to become powerful, a land that nurtures princes and fathers of kings.' Then he paused, with an earnest, pleading look at his companion. 'Gwenhwyfar has grown with me, Arthur, learning from the first days we toddled together. She's a girl thrust into the violence of a man's world. She carries double the burden, for she needs to prove herself as strong and capable as her brothers.' The frown slid from Etern's face and was replaced by a broad smile. 'Although I grant her pranks can be pretty childish at times!'

'Like throwing water over people?' Arthur laughed with Etern. The two fell silent, brooding their own thoughts.

Below, the smith had finished the wheel, had returned inside his forge. A billow of steam and smoke hissed and curled from the open doorway, showing he was busy about some other matter.

'So,' Arthur said, pushing himself away from the palisade and straightening his tunic. 'If your sister's not moping or hiding in shame then she must be detained somewhere. Against her will.'

Leaping forward, his face suddenly pale, Etern grasped Arthur by the shoulders. 'Could she be lying hurt somewhere?' He swung his head left and right as if he might suddenly see her. 'Happen she's fallen, or become trapped or…'

'Hold hard! Would she not have been found, either in the search this morning or since? Use your brain! Who was most affected by yesterday's piffling incident?'

Etern calmed down and dropped his hands. 'Yourself and Branwen.'

'Aye, and who has been parading around with the smug look of a cat who has found the cream?'

'Branwen.'

Arthur nodded, then leant back against the palisade once more, his arm draping along the top. 'I would surmise that Branwen has some knowledge of your sister's disappearance.'

'What are you suggesting?' Etern's frown deepened. This hinted at a malice he felt reluctant to meet head on.

Looking away, Arthur studied the mist-swathed heights of Yr Wyddfa, beautiful against the cloud-patched blue sky. He had never seen mountains such as these. Quietly, to the hills he asked, 'Have you ever been locked away as punishment?'

Etern shook his head and came to stand beside Arthur. 'We are whipped, confined to quarters, or something. Why?'

A little laugh, forced in its humour. 'Oh, suffice it to say I am familiar with such things.' Arthur chewed his lip, his nails digging into the wood. 'I clash often with Uthr's mistress.' He jerked his shoulders in a shrug of indifference. 'Branwen reminds me over much of Morgause, that's all.'

The other boy guffawed, his head tossing back, delighted. 'Hardly! They are as different as queen and peasant!'

Arthur snorted. 'Which one the queen?' Then, serious again, *Na*, I did not mean like that.'

Etern's frown returned as he thought on Arthur's insinuation. Was he suggesting Branwen would go against Cunedda's authority? That she would... The suggestion was ridiculous! He flicked a hand dismissively. 'You talk nonsense.'

For some moments Arthur continued gazing towards the hills, not seeing the shadows that now clung to the slopes, damping down the vivid colours, making the heights seem brooding and oppressive. Dark thoughts of black places and slamming doors chased through his mind, of her laughter and his heart thudding, thudding. 'Do I? You lead a good life here, Etern of Gwynedd. Your father is an honourable lord. You say you know the realities. Do you? What do you truly know of hatred and malice? Out there,' Arthur gestured towards the horizon, 'out there, men die bloody deaths. There is no law, only an instinct to survive. Men take that instinct home to their womenfolk who become dulled by sickening reality. For that, the children suffer, because we are the poor sods who cannot fight back.' He stopped abruptly. Morgause knew Uthr would never set aside his wife and take her instead. She knew the reality and took that knowing out on the one who could say or do nothing against her. Cei and Bedwyr were Ectha's own born, privileged, special, protected. But he, Arthur, was only a bastard foster child, at the witch's whim and mercy. He finished with one word, spoken so softly that Etern barely heard: 'Yet.'

Arthur was adept at rapid swings of mood. The cloud lifted from his face as the real cloud shadow lifted from the mountains. He strode purposefully for the descending steps, waving Etern to follow, calling cheerily, 'Come on then. If Branwen has your sister shut in somewhere, we have to find her and let her out.'

Etern trotted to catch up with him. 'Swords and spears! Have you any idea of the size of this Caer? Then there's the settlement, beyond that the old fortress. It could take days!'

Arthur was running down the wooden steps; he jumped the last three. 'I doubt Branwen would go where the men were billeted. The settlement, happen, but I'll wager your sister is within these walls. Aside, what else is there to do this afternoon?'

As dusk approached, they were on the verge of calling a halt. Squatting on the sheltered top floor of the north-east watchtower, Etern shared the barley bread begged from the kitchens, while Arthur recounted some lurid ghost tale. His gleeful cackles and eerie moans adding some impressive embellishments.

A sudden flap of wings. Etern leapt to his feet, heart bumping. A creature summoned by the story! *Na*, only a bird taking startled flight. Hand on thumping chest he glowered reproach at Arthur's crowed amusement, then peered negligently through the narrow slit in the wall that gave little light but served well for ventilation. Suddenly he waved Arthur's laughter to silence. 'Look! Over there, entering the chapel – Branwen!'

Arthur was on his feet, pushing Etern aside and squinnying through the opening. 'Where?'

Losing interest, Etern returned to his bread. Branwen was always praying in the chapel.

'Now why,' Arthur said thoughtfully, 'would she be going to the chapel this time of the evening? Surely she ought to be supervising the Hall – it will be time for gathering soon.'

'Why, indeed?' Etern's reply was grim. Crowding behind the small aperture, they waited, watching. Branwen reappeared, glanced around and made her way back to the kitchens, unaware of her two observers.

Releasing his breath slowly Etern slid his back down the wall and hunkered down on his heels. 'In all truth I thought we were on a fool's errand, though to follow it at least passed the day.' He flicked a glance up at Arthur, who stood watching him reflectively. 'It seems I owe you an apology.'

Rather gloomily, Arthur squatted beside him, replied, 'Branwen's close to dropping her child; happen it's a whim of hers to be alone – or something.' He shrugged. Plenty of the young women at home disappeared to secluded sites for a short while; admitted, they usually reappeared dishevelled, pink faced and hugging a secret pleasure. But surely a woman heavy with child would hardly be slipping away to meet her secret lover?

They waited a moment, each nurturing his own thoughts. 'You had best fetch Osmail, Etern. I will go on ahead, over there.' Arthur jerked his thumb in the direction of the chapel.

'She will be mortified if you find her in such a situation. You fetch my brother,' Etern protested.

Equally emphatically Arthur countered with, 'Where do I look? Where do I find one busy man among buildings I do not know? Go, Etern, don't argue.'

Arthur gave the boy a firm push towards the south stairway, then ran to the north steps leading down beside the low orchard wall that met with the chapel and the door that, moments before, Branwen had pulled shut.

His enthusiasm waned as he approached the door, disappeared altogether as he reached tentatively out to push it open.

Inside, one lamp burnt upon the altar, throwing grotesque shadows leaping and flickering against the walls. There was a smell of stale incense, beeswax, and a mustiness Arthur found peculiar to all places of worship, Christian or otherwise.

Standing two paces beyond the threshold he allowed his eyes to grow used to the dim light, then began picking out the familiar cross shape of a Christian building. An unobtrusive door caught his attention. He walked to a recess, his steps sounding loud and unwelcome in this silent place, took a candle and lit it from the burning lamp. Hesitant, he went up to that door.

His hand hovering over the bolt, he did not know what to expect, though he was certain he had the right place. He convinced himself the trembling of his hands was due to the fear of finding a girl's dead body, but the truth taunted him. The close confines of dark crowding walls made his palms sticky and his throat taste sour. Shut in; silence. Cannot get out, cannot get out. He took a breath and drew the bolt.

The candle cast a long, wavering shadow over a rumpled blanket to one side. The room smelt strongly of must and human waste. Apprehensive, Arthur took a pace forward. A movement from the shadows on his left made him whirl round and drop the candle. It fizzed out as a pitcher crashed over him, spewing water.

'Blood of Mithras!' he gasped, water and surprise taking away his breath. 'Are you so damned determined to drown me?'

Gwenhwyfar stood speechless. The faint light from the single lamp barely illuminated her hands, covering her open mouth. Slowly she raised them in a gesture of apologetic helplessness. 'I thought you were Branwen come back.' As if that explained everything!

'Aye, well.' Arthur brushed at his wet shoulders. 'As you can see, I am not.' He shook his head, scraping water from dripping hair. 'Your brother is fetching Osmail.' Then, 'Are you all right? You're shivering.'

Without waiting for an answer, he fetched the blanket and draped it around her shoulders.

Gwenhwyfar felt flustered. Mixed feelings coursed through her: embarrassment, guilt, relief. She cradled her wrist, it hurt abominably. Without protest, she let Arthur lead her to the light and seat himself close beside her, but not touching, on the altar steps.

'I suppose we had best wait in here for the others,' he said. They sat and waited. The silence within the chapel grew, the shadows darkening, advancing nearer.

Arthur was trembling, his teeth chattering slightly.

Gwenhwyfar had to say something, some words to explain, to ease the shame. 'I am sorry. It smelt in there.' Gwenhwyfar hung her head. 'There was no utensil to use. I had to use the corner.'

'The stink clings, doesn't it?' He spoke simply, as if he really did know, really did understand. 'It's getting darker in here.' He launched himself to his feet, went with rapid steps to the side door and thrust it open as far back as it would go. Daylight was fading fast into a purple and red sky that promised another day of sun on the morrow.

He crossed to the main doors, intending to let in more light, and worried the handles. They were unyielding, locked.

'It's dreadful when you are alone in the dark,' Gwenhwyfar said quietly, pulling the blanket closer against the numbing cold.

Again, Arthur answered, 'I know.' He returned to squat at her side, uneasily, watching the encroaching darkness.

She was unsure what more to say to him. Finally, 'Are you all right?'

He was fiddling with a battered gold ring on his left hand and staring into the looming shadows. 'When I was younger, not so long past, Morgause used to lock me up.' He faltered, licked dry lips. 'She would shut me in a place no more than a hole where there was no slit of light, nothing. It was like being inside a sealed tomb.' He twirled the ring on his finger, round and around. 'I never knew when she might decide to let me out. Each time I believed she might never come back, might leave me there to die, huddled alone in the dark.'

'Why would she do such a thing?' Gwenhwyfar was appalled, could not, even after her own experience, comprehend such cruelty.

Arthur had no answer. He had asked himself the question many times, but had never found an explanation. Jealousy, hatred, just the pleasure of creating pain and fear – who knew with Morgause?

'Did your foster father, or Lady Ygrainne, never stop her?' In a family that knew each other's secrets, each other's fears and delights, Gwenhwyfar found it incomprehensible that such a wickedness could take place uncensored.

For Arthur, it was very different. 'Ectha is frightened of her, Uthr besotted by her, and Ygrainne has no time for her, or me – hates me more than Morgause does. Lady Ygrainne spends her life with God. Morgause runs the household.' He was sweating profusely now, beads of perspiration standing out on his forehead, trickling from his armpits and down his back. His breathing was becoming rapid. The walls were closing in, falling in, the roof pushing, pressing; the blackness engulfing, chewing him up, gorging itself on his fear.

Urgently he said, 'Would you mind if we went outside?' Not waiting for an answer, he bolted for the open door.

Gwenhwyfar followed more sedately, her blanket trailing. Arthur stood with his back against the wall, eyes shut tight, taking great gulps of the cool, sweet air. She put a tentative hand on his arm.

'I was terrified last night,' she admitted. 'I was so alone; I wanted someone, anyone to come, but...' Her voice had changed, defiance mustering. She looked directly at him. His eyes were open now, looking back at her. 'I'm not sorry for what I did, Arthur!'

Managing a weak laugh he said, 'I am – I was wrong. Etern was frantic with worry about you.' He put his hand over hers, held it. Her fingers were cold; he closed his own around them to bring more warmth. 'So was I.'

'I'm surprised my brother has even remembered I exist,' Gwenhwyfar said bitterly.

'What?' Arthur pushed himself from the wall. 'Bull's Blood, he talks of no one but you! *Gwenhwyfar this, Gwenhwyfar that*, or, *My sister found this trail, this bathing place*, this whatever. He says your father thinks of you as a true Cymraes, not someone watered by Roman wine!'

Gwenhwyfar shrugged, flattered, but not ready to show her pleasure. 'I am of Gwynedd, not Rome.'

'Bravely spoken, my *Cymraes fach*, my little British woman!' Arthur was feeling better

His confidence was returning now the threat of those squeezing walls was gone. He still had hold of her hand. It pleased him to feel her closeness, her fingers in his own. 'Etern is like a lost sheep without you, Gwenhwyfar. That's not healthy for a boy of his age!' He added the last with muffled laughter.

Gwenhwyfar smiled at him, her eyes crinkling. She remembered her hand, and shyly withdrew it. She liked him! He made her laugh.

With mock sincerity Arthur said, 'I grant you are an exceptional girl, Gwenhwyfar, but a man needs other men.'

'A man needs a woman to comfort him through the night and to give him sons.' Gwenhwyfar's retort came with a knowing grin.

'Aye, well.' Arthur grinned back, unable to counter her argument. He still trembled slightly, but the violent fear had dwindled. Darkness seemed less terrible when shared with someone else.

'Am I forgiven my bad conduct?' he asked. He knelt before her, desperately wanting her friendship, needing her approval.

'Forgive me, lady. I offer my humble body as your friend and my sword as your servant.' Earnestly he looked up into the dim outline of her pale face, seeking her eyes, red-rimmed but with the sparkle fast returning.

Gwenhwyfar giggled. She could see now why Etern had been so captivated. Arthur had a vitality that swept you along with his enthusiasm and wild ideas. And suddenly, she realised his long nose and short-cropped hair were not ugly at all; in fact he was rather handsome, in a rough, rugged sort of way.

She took his proffered hand and laughed. 'I forgive you and I accept your sword. Will you defend me to your death, from dragons and demons?'

'Dragons and demons certainly. Branwen and Morgause *na*!'

Gwenhwyfar roared with laughter, then caught her breath as movement jarred the swollen wrist.

'What's wrong? Are you hurt?' Arthur was on his feet, showing immediate concern.

'My wrist. I fell – it's nothing.'

'Nothing be damned! I can see the swelling even in this poor light. Hie!' He waved attracting the attention of the two people approaching. 'Here come your brothers!' Arthur ran forward, gesturing wildly as he explained the situation, urging Etern, who was anxiously herding Osmail, to hurry.

The big man looked displeased at what he was sure would turn out to be a boy's prank. Etern had babbled something about Branwen locking Gwenhwyfar in? What nonsense!

But as he came upon his sister, saw her pain and distress, his irritation became profound anger.

Branwen had done this? His wife, the mother of his children had deliberately and callously done this?

He squatted before Gwenhwyfar and examined her wrist, asked a few direct questions. After brushing aside her tears with one finger, he lifted her and strode back across the orchard tight-lipped, his expression grim.

Branwen had committed this disgrace. Aye, well, it would be her last! Push him to the limit, to that hurdle of endurance? He was over it, by God, over and spurring fast for manumission!

Etern exchanged a wry look with Arthur as Osmail walked away. 'I have never seen my brother look so angry. By God!' He laughed suddenly. 'Am I glad not to be in Branwen's boots this evening!'

Together the boys ambled across the orchard heading for the glow of torchlight streaming from the open doors of the Hall. The sound of tables being set up and women chattering drifted into the darkening stillness beneath the trees. A heavy dew had fallen, leaving a trail of silvered marks where the boys walked.

'Your sister,' Arthur said, placing an arm around Etern's shoulders, 'I like her.'

Removing his arm, he pushed his hands through his bracae belt and whistling, walked on ahead into the comforting welcome of Cunedda's Hall.

§ X

Early afternoon. Etern poked his head round the door and grinned broadly. Gwenhwyfar, sitting cross-legged on the floor, tossed two wooden dice in the air and neatly caught them in her right hand. She grinned back at her brother.

'You are supposed to be in bed,' Etern chided. 'Alone?' he added, searching the chamber with his eyes.

'They,' and Gwenhwyfar gave a little toss of her head indicating the beds that belonged to the other girls who shared this chamber, 'have grown bored with gossip of Branwen's disgrace, and as my injury is not fatal they have decided to leave me and follow more interesting pursuits.'

For most of the morning the girls had fussed around Gwenhwyfar, excited and curious, making a nuisance of themselves with their wittering and twittering – plumping pillows, tut-tutting and overemphasising sympathy which was as shallow as a dried-up river ford. All this Gwenhwyfar suffered for the few scraps of information among the nonsense. Branwen had been ordered to her apartments by her outraged husband – and with the army's departure Morgause had apparently raged and stormed at not being allowed to accompany Uthr. Gwenhwyfar had attempted to pursue this line of conversation, but those silly lily-brained creatures had gone off at a tangent about hairstyles and face paint.

Few women went with the menfolk to war these days – not decent women anyway. The patched whore wagons trundled after any hosting, making their way as best they could along the rutted, disintegrating roads, but women no longer joined in the fighting – as Cunedda had been at pains to point out to his daughter many times. Some British women still learnt to handle weapons to defend themselves and their children according to the old ways, yet Morgause was no traditionalist; she was Roman bred and born.

Gwenhwyfar rolled the dice to the floor and smiled triumphantly. 'Venus!' She glanced up. 'Are you coming in, or are you a doorstop?'

Etern ambled over and sat cross-legged next to her. 'Four counts of six in a row?' he queried, claiming the dice and beginning to shake them vigorously in his closed fist. 'You cheated.'

'I did not! I scored Venus fair. What would be the point of cheating myself?'

Throwing a total of five, Etern handed the dice to his sister. 'Best of three throws?'

She nodded agreement and played her turn, then gave him the dice. Casually she asked, 'Not with your friend today?'

'Who, Arthur? *Na*, he has been claimed by Morgause.' Etern wrinkled his nose in disgust at his low score. 'You know, Gwen, I don't much like the woman.' He shivered, as if a chill had crept down his spine.

As Gwenhwyfar tossed her last throw she said, 'Neither does Arthur.'

Spreading his hands, Etern admitted defeat. '*Canis* to me, lowest score. Another go?'

'*Na*, I have had enough of dice.' Gwenhwyfar stretched lazily and, climbing to her feet wandered to the window. The chamber was on the first floor, built above storage rooms, its single square window overlooking a courtyard and, to the far right, a vegetable garden. It was all very well to be ordered to spend a day in bed, but it was so boring! She felt fine, beyond a dull throb in her wrist, would rather be out doing things.

'Osmail was with me earlier,' she said, watching three slaves tending the young spring growth. 'Do you suppose he minds being left behind?' Then, as if on the same topic, 'Cabbage for supper by the look of it.'

Etern, coming to stand behind her, laughed. 'Remember the time too much salt was put in for the cooking? Aye, I think he minds, but one of our brothers must stay to watch over Gwynedd.'

'He has never professed to like the killing of men, our brother. All that Christian talk of love and turning the other cheek! Da despairs of Osmail, you know. He's the eldest and has no stomach for war.' She had been leaning on the sill, looking out and down at the small empty courtyard below. 'What does Morgause want with Arthur?'

Etern shook his head doubtfully. 'She expects him to run errands for her, entertain her, I don't know. Why ask me?'

'Don't get cross.'

Glowering at his sister's rebuke, Etern shuffled away from the window and plonked himself on the bed. 'I'm bored,' he admitted with a heavy sigh. 'Da and the others away, you confined in here, Arthur with her.' He nodded in the vague direction of Morgause's chamber.

Still at the window, Gwenhwyfar knelt on the floor and shuffled herself into a more comfortable position. Morgause's chamber was just visible, away across the vegetable plot and a little to the right. Gwenhwyfar fiddled with the bandage around her wrist, chewed her lips, watched a worm seeking blackbird hopping in the wake of the gardening slaves. 'Why, I wonder, are her shutters closed?'

Lying back across the bed, Etern stretched his arms. 'Whose shutters?'

'Surely the woman is not sleeping at this time of day?'

'What woman?' Etern sat up, irritated by the obtuse dialogue.

'Morgause.'

Her brother lost interest. 'Oh, her.' He began lifting and bending his legs in some elaborate thigh exercise.

Folding her arms across the sill Gwenhwyfar rested her chin on her hands, mindful of the injury. She whistled a few bars of a tune plaguing her mind. Suddenly sat up straight and turned abruptly towards her brother. 'I thought you said Arthur was with her?'

'What is this?' Etern demanded. 'I am not his keeper.'

Gwenhwyfar feigned indifference. She got up and moved vaguely around the room, touching this, tidying that. An uneasy feeling niggled, like an itch you could not reach.

Heading for the door, Etern stated, 'I have a few things to see to. Call back later, shall I?'

Nodding at the other beds, Gwenhwyfar answered, 'If the boneheads have not returned.'

As his retreating laugh faded she began dressing, awkward with the limited use of one hand. There was no logical reason for suspicion, no cause to doubt yet her unease was becoming more insistent. All those things Arthur had said yesterday. Those confidences spoken, she was certain, through the need to ride the fear. It was the things he had not said that worried her. He was vulnerable to Morgause's spiteful whims when not protected by the Pendragon's presence – and Uthr had gone.

Gwenhwyfar slipped quietly from her chamber, down the back stairs and across the courtyard, her leather sandals making barely a sound as she padded along the raised walkway running the length of the other wing. She stopped outside Morgause's room and listened at the door. Shutters, firmly closed, blocked any view inside. She could hear voices within: Morgause's penetrating lilt and Arthur's sullen responses.

This wing was a single storey construction of timber and stone. Living chambers were ranged along the ground floor, with the limited space beneath the low eaves of the slate roof seldom used, for access was difficult and headroom low.

Jogging to the rear, Gwenhwyfar clambered up the ladder and with difficulty lifted the trapdoor at its head. The thing was heavy, reluctant to move and hard to push with the use of only one hand. She found the need to climb higher, brace her shoulders against the unyielding door and heave. It fell back with a startling thump, scattering a cloud of choking dust and musty straw. For a moment Gwenhwyfar balanced on the top rung, coughing, and blinking her eyes. She sneezed, took a breath, and carefully pulled herself up into the diffused light of the cavern beyond. Several slates were missing, and in places holes had worn through the plaster below the eaves, convenient for a number of nesting birds. Gwenhwyfar's ears caught the fluffing and flurry of feathers as brooding mothers squatted over their young, anxious at this unexpected intrusion. She could see their tiny heads and bright black eyes peeping nervously over nest rims at her, keeping so still. Feet pattered away from the broad shaft of light the open trapdoor let in, a squeaking of protest as mice scuttled to safety.

The place was empty save for a tumbled heap of wooden crates, several piles of discarded sacking, a few cracked amphorae and what looked like a battered saddle. Squirming through the layers of dust and sticky cobwebs, Gwenhwyfar crawled along to the far end that would be the ceiling of Morgause's chamber. She had to keep her weight on the timber rafters, for the plaster between crumbled most fearfully when she put hand or knee on it. In places, the fragile stuff had already worn, and she caught tantalising glimpses into the chambers below; for a moment, she was tempted to turn about and investigate the opposite far end, to spy down on where Branwen had apparently shut herself. She heard Arthur's voice, a sharp, 'No!' With renewed determination she scurried forward.

The roof here sloped sharply down to the walls, and the narrow space was piled with collected dust and heaps of old leaves that had blown in through gaps in the tiling. Gwenhwyfar found she had to stretch out flat. Several small holes afforded a limited view of the chamber below. Spreading her weight along the rafters, she put her eye to the nearest and squinted down.

Morgause was talking in her low, singsong voice, husky and heavily slurred with over much wine. To her disgust, Gwenhwyfar could see nothing save the worn pattern of the rather crudely laid mosaic floor. She made to shift position, saw to her horror a puff of plaster collapse and scatter downwards in a fluttering shower. The rafter beneath her right knee creaked, sounding as loud as thunder to her ears. Heart thumping, she lay rigid, not daring to move.

'You do want to please me, do you not, boy?' Morgause was saying in her precise Latin. 'Is that not why Uthr brought you, so you might please me?'

'You know damn well why he brought me. I am almost a man grown, I need the experience.'

The woman laughed, a low, casual chuckle. Gwenhwyfar heard the sound of wine being poured, a jug clinking against a glass. Morgause's sickly sweet answer: 'Experience, yes.' The sound of movement, a rustling of silk garments and soft leather slippers. Morgause came into view briefly, carrying a second goblet, which she handed to Arthur somewhere beyond Gwenhwyfar's sight.

'It is time you became a man, boy.' Morgause walked again beneath Gwenhwyfar's spyhole, carrying one goblet. Arthur must have taken the one offered.

The question was unexpected, floating upwards with the sun swirled flitterings of dust: 'Do you find me beautiful?' There came no answer. 'Or are you too much Uthr's boy?' Morgause's wine-smooth voice changed to a harsh rasp as she commanded, 'Come here!'

Arthur did not move. He was standing pressed tight against the wall: it felt safer to have something solid at his back. He shook his head defiantly, wondering if he could make a run for the door. Three, four paces, draw back the bolt. He gulped the wine; it was strong but it steadied his quivering nerves – though he must not drink over much.

'You would do well to obey me, boy, to answer me.' Morgause sprang forward. Arthur yelped, an involuntary sound as her hand caught viciously at his arm. He dropped the goblet, the fine blue glass shattering.

Pinning him against the wall, Morgause pressed her body close, the thin silk of her flame coloured gown sharply outlining the curves of her body beneath. She smelt of strong perfume, a rich, spiced scent. Her breath bore a hint of chewed mint clouded by red wine. There was no denying Morgause was beautiful. Arthur swallowed, his eyes drifting towards the inviting swell of her breasts. He knew nothing of women, but his body was on the verge of wanting to know, that confusing time suspended halfway between boy and man.

With a curving smile she saw him looking, interested but indecisive. She adjusted her clothing, loosened the shoulder brooch, letting the folds of the bodice slip slightly. 'These breasts should be suckling Uthr's son, but I have borne him only girl brats. Three – did you know that?' She moved a fraction away, the better to read his blank expression. 'No, you could not. I was discreet with their bearing – remember my visits to kindred?'

He remembered well. Those glorious months of freedom from torment!

'I exposed them,' she said with a small, careless gesture, drifting, to Arthur's small sigh of relief, further away. 'I have no use for girls.' She spun to face him, that soft seductive smile back again. 'Do you wish to bed with me, Arthur?' She swayed her body, lithe and supple, so very sensuous. 'Ygrainne bore Uthr two dead girls after the first boy died – did you know that also? Ah, I see you did not.' Her smile was arrogant, all knowing. 'There is no maleness in Uthr's seed.'

Arthur felt hot, and a little sick. The sweat trickled down his back. His throat dry as he stammered in a high, cracked voice, 'Uthr had that one son!'

Morgause spread her arms, her head lolling back with a scornful laugh. 'His son? The thing died because it was not his!'

Both of them were out of sight now and Gwenhwyfar squirmed forward, seeking another hole. That rafter creaked again, and another fragile cascade of dust spiralled down. She cursed under her breath.

Arthur's hissed response to Morgause's slander was shocked. 'Lady Ygrainne would not do such a thing!' For all his dislike of her, he knew Ygrainne to be an honest woman. She would not kill a child or deceive her lord husband. Not now, not then. Morgause was standing so close, her breasts large beneath the loosely fitting bodice. He had never seen her naked. Arthur's heart was racing, his breathing coming shallow and fast. Curse the bitch! He hated her, wanted her dead, gone, anything. Wanted so much to reach out and touch.

Morgause knew, was goading him deliberately, her teasing subtle but intense. 'Ygrainne has not always been such a blessed woman. She rutted with Uthr while still another man's wife.' She ran her fingers lightly over his cheek, across his mouth, feeling the slight prickle of hair above his lip.

Arthur jerked his head aside, attempted to squirm away. She grabbed at him, pushing him harder against the wall.

To her fury, Gwenhwyfar, her teeth jammed into her bottom lip, could still not see anything, yet she dared not move.

'Everyone knows Ygrainne's first husband was a brute twice her age, and a heel-hound of Vortigern's at that.' Arthur's voice was rising in pitch, panic beginning. 'None gave her blame when she divorced the bastard and took Uthr as husband.' He tried again to free himself, added with bravado, 'Save you.'

Morgause's lips were on his, her fingers searching beneath his tunic for the lacings of his bracae. Arthur kicked, hard. She screeched, her hand lashing out to strike him. Again and again her hand beat at his face;

Arthur crumpled, covered his head with his arms. She used her fists and her feet, hitting and kicking at him.

Gwenhwyfar began to squirm backward. She must do something to stop this, fetch someone.

Then the fury ceased as abruptly as it began. Morgause squatted, held Arthur's bloodied face tight between her pinching fingers. 'Why is Uthr so fond of you?' Her angered features were distorted and grotesque, like some foul spirit's mask. 'You are his boy lover!'

The room was spinning, blood dribbled from a split lip, sparks and flashes shot before his eyes, but Arthur answered, furious at the insult to his lord. 'Your mind is tangled in a weed garden of jealousy! You think because I love Uthr there must be something sordid, something obscene, because that is what you are, a foul minded bitch! You cannot bear Uthr giving affection to anyone but yourself, can you?'

Her palm cracked sharply against his cheek. This time he did not flinch or try to hide away. He looked straight at her, let her hit him. 'I'm not afraid of you,' he said, though his voice shook. He was, desperately afraid, but anger had seized hold of him. 'You are jealous of me,' he taunted, 'jealous because Uthr thinks more of me, a bastard son of a serving girl, than of you, his ageing whore!'

Morgause drew a sharp breath and flashed back, 'Then you do bed with him!'

Arthur laughed. 'You poor slut. You have so little idea of what love can really be – no idea of respect and admiration, pride and hope.'

Her fist caught him a savage blow to the temple; he fell forward stunned, but the blows still came.

Gwenhwyfar did not know what to do. What could she do? She moved back quickly, not wanting to see more, or hear. That loose rafter creaked and groaned, then gave way. She screamed as the ceiling caved in.

Rafters, plaster and dust cascaded down. Nesting birds took sudden flight, whirring wings and squawking alarm. Gwenhwyfar landed in a heap and sprawl among the cloud of debris, coughing and spluttering. The training of weapon handling and riding saved her from injury, for she rolled with the fall and was instantly on her feet, winded and covered in grime, but unharmed.

Arthur was crouched down his hand cradling bruised ribs. He wiped at blood trickling from his nose then reached forward tentatively to the sprawled form of Morgause. She lay on her back, one arm flung at a weird angle, dark blood oozing from a deep cut on her forehead.

'Oh, Mithras!' He spoke through a slow exhaled breath. 'She's dead.' He was uncertain whether to feel relief or what. There would be a deal of explaining to do over this.

'Nonsense!' Gwenhwyfar was recovering her wits. She pointed at the steady rise and fall of the woman's breathing. 'We had best be from here. Now.' She stepped to the door and opened it a little way. 'Now, Arthur! Come on!'

He rose unsteadily to his feet; the room was spinning, his head ached, his face felt puffed and bruised. Gwenhwyfar grabbed at his hand, pulled him out of the door and quickly round the corner. The first comers were entering the courtyard seeking the cause of the noise.

Running, Gwenhwyfar took sanctuary within the nearest granary. A babble of voices and alarm filtered from outside with, once, the commanding voice of Osmail demanding explanation.

Beyond the stillness and quiet of the granary the noise passed by, gradually dwindling. Gwenhwyfar brushed dirt and cobwebs from hair and clothing, wrinkled her nose at her grimed hands, guessed her face to be a similar colour. She fiddled with a tear to the shoulder of her tunic. She would need to wash herself and get this mended afore anyone asked questions.

Arthur had seated himself on a grain sack his shoulders hunched, head resting between his hands. With thoughts shrivelling his insides he suddenly felt sick. Morgause. Words and implications. Implying he was bedmate to his beloved lord, her hands on his body, mouth covering his. He tumbled forward spewing out the disgust.

Concerned, Gwenhwyfar hunkered beside him, one hand resting lightly on his back waiting for the violent shaking to cease, though her own body had not settled.

Embarrassed, Arthur stood, wiping at his mouth, disconcerted to find his legs were having difficulty supporting him.

Tactful, Gwenhwyfar retreated a few paces, squatting down on her heels. 'Best get the thing out of you.' A slight smile. 'I have been long enough with Etern to know how a stomach reacts to distasteful things.' The smile broadened. 'My brother's guts are as unpredictable as a sea wind on a summer day!'

Arthur attempted to return the smile, said with an over lightness that did little to hide his discomfort, 'Who need know of this?'

'Of what?' Gwenhwyfar had ambled to the door, was peeping out. Love of the Gods, but her wrist ached! People had drifted away about their business; all seemed quiet. 'There's nothing for anyone to know. Some rafters gave way – it has been expected. We're not allowed up there, Da knows the timber's rotten.' She turned suddenly to grin at him. 'And I am unwilling to broadcast disobeyed orders!' She shrugged. 'No one save Morgause knew you were in there.' She threw the door wide, stepped out into the sunshine. 'And she certainly did not see me!' She cocked her head on one side, looking back into the muted shadows within the great building. Colour was returning to Arthur's ashen face, blotched by the blood and bruising. 'I would suggest you had a fall from a horse, or a fight with some low born in the settlement. None will query it.'

She walked away, but returned a few seconds later with the need to say one thing more. Arthur had not moved.

In the doorway she was silhouetted black against the brightness. 'There are things that sometimes you wish others not to know, but between friends a secret can be as binding as the blood-tie of kinship. And the keeping can last as long.'

JUNE 450

§ XI

The boys, stripped to the waist, were turning new scythed hay, making idle, breathless conversation as they tossed the sweet smelling, drying grass. Arthur's bruising was a faint memory of shaded yellow against sun tanned bronze skin; gone was that weary look of watchfulness and unease, replaced by relaxed laughter and happy contentment. His hair was longer, the close-cropped Roman style beginning to grow, with a slight curl, down his neck and flop across his forehead. Arthur enjoyed this work; it was hard but that was nothing to shy away from. Among friends and with the freedom to enjoy oneself, who noticed the soreness of sunburn or aching back and shoulders at the end of a long day? Lord and slave alike were out in the meadows for this haymaking. Animal feed must be gathered whether the menfolk were away or no, and the grain harvest would soon follow. Winter did not forget to call for the sake of a war hosting!

June had begun cool and cloudy with a wind that blew steadily from the sea, but as the month neared the longest day the wind veered and the sun blazed. If the rains held off these next weeks, it would be a good harvest. Wheat and barley were fast ripening, the green corn spreading wide smiles of rich gold.

Gwenhwyfar straightened, one hand easing her back, the other pushing the wide brimmed straw-plaited hat from her forehead. Etern tossed his pitchfork, turning another few yards of hay to dry the underside. Arthur, working along the opposite side, looked up and regarded Gwenhwyfar, leaning now on her fork.

'If you're intending to stop work, lass, you could employ your rest by bringing us a skin of water!'

'I'll do better,' she answered, happily compliant. Digging the prongs of the fork into the sun baked soil, she unknotted the girdle that hitched her skirt to above her knees, letting the material fall full length. There were some advantages in being a girl after all! How much cooler to feel the swirl of thin-woven cloth around your legs, rather than the tight cling of bracae. 'I'll fetch food and wine. It's time we rested – look, others are going off to the shade.' She wiped at the sweat on her neck and face with the back of her hand.

Sitting beneath a chestnut tree, legs outstretched, spine secure against the broad trunk, Arthur remarked, 'It's hot for the hosting. They'd not be able to get away from this noon heat if engaged in battle.'

'Would you notice the sun, I wonder,' Etern said through a mouthful of goat's cheese, 'in the midst of fighting?'

'Happen not.'

Passing along the skin of watered wine, Gwenhwyfar folded her arms behind her head and looked up into the bluest of blue skies. A few great puffs of cloud floated lazily, a shriek of swifts darted past. She closed her eyes, let the drone of bees and hum of grasshoppers float by as peaceful as a meandering river. The air was full of lazy summer scents, mingling with the salt tang of the sea. 'We must hear soon,' she pondered, 'surely?'

Neither Etern nor Arthur made immediate answer. One or other of them proclaimed the same thing almost every day: 'We must hear soon.' But nothing came, no word of the hosting. Good news, or bad.

'When I become War Lord,' Arthur announced, 'I'll set up efficient lines of communication.'

Eyes snapping open, Gwenhwyfar chuckled, not unkindly. 'Oh ho, so you are planning on the honour of War Lord? A high ambition for a fatherless servant's brat!'

Good-natured, Arthur lifted his shoulder then let it fall. 'We've all got to harbour some plan. There'd be no point of expectation and hope otherwise.'

Gwenhwyfar settled herself again, lying prone amid the swathe of uncut grass, chuckled drowsily. 'Dream on, lad, for that's all that desire can lead to – more dreams!'

Arthur sat forward and absently picked up a stick, prodding a hole in the ground between his legs. 'I'd have a fair chance if Uthr were my sire, but...' He sighed, rammed the stick too hard, snapping it in half.

'But Ectha is your foster father, and he has two sons of his own besides being as timid as a doe in fawn.'

Arthur grinned at Gwenhwyfar's plain spoken accuracy. 'Aye, it'll be working the estate or serving as junior officer in some petty lord's hosting for me.' He reclaimed the longer part of his broken stick, and twiddled it between his fingers. 'I want to be part of a great army, want to lead – I've ideas to improve efficiency!' He tossed the stick aside. 'Happen I'll have a chance when Uthr becomes king.'

Kindly, laying her fingers lightly on his arm, Gwenhwyfar remarked, 'That could be any day now.'

Etern had stretched himself full length in the shade and closed his eyes to doze in this brief respite from work and sun. He opened one eye, squinted through the dappled brightness at his sister. Something had happened atween these two, some great event had twined them together as firm as stitching in leather harness. Neither had said what and, for all his questioning, he had gleaned no hint. He closed his eye again. It had something to do with that foul woman Morgause and the day the ceiling had collapsed into her chamber. He smiled at the recollection. It was not funny, of course, but there had been much secret pleasure throughout the Caer these past weeks. Bad tempered Morgause confined to her bed with the pain of a fractured arm and dizzying headaches; Branwen similarly out the way from lingering disgrace and the birthing of her second born son. Were it not for the worry of the hosting, life would be almost perfect!

'What for me?' Gwenhwyfar said idly. 'I have no particular dreams,' she beamed at Arthur, 'beyond owning one of Da's best horses!'

Etern, without moving, added to her, 'You, Gwen, will marry a lord in a strategic alliance. Your offspring will unite Gwynedd and whatever noble line this man comes from, making the strongest and most formidable family in the country!' He spoke carelessly, meaning no offence, stating fact. Alliances were for the female born to bring to the male line.

Gwenhwyfar, however, leapt to her feet, her fists bunching. 'If that's all you hope for me, brother, then you had best think again!' She stamped her foot. 'I will not be bargained out for breeding, not for all the "strategic alliances" on offer!'

Etern sat up open mouthed, staggered at the unexpected explosion. Now what had he said!

'If I marry,' his sister declared, 'I will only wed with the strongest leader, a man who will unite Britain and drive out our enemies!' Her green eyes flashed with sparks of tawny gold; she tossed her head, the sunlight catching on those loose wisps of hair that would never be tamed, setting the colour glowing with vibrant reds and golds. 'I mean it, this is no idle boast.'

Etern exchanged a glance with his friend, who shrugged sympathy.

Arthur was thinking how pretty Gwenhwyfar was. A child still, with only the subtle hints of womanhood touching her face and figure, but it was there, the beauty, waiting to open like a flower from its budding. Morgause was beautiful, but she was like the ice and snow that set a dull winter's day bright with cold exhilaration. Gwenhwyfar's beauty would be softer, more like the gold and russets and warmth of a sunlit autumn day, with all its toss of wind swirled leaves and crackling orange flamed fires. Aye, and have the touch of frost that nipped your fingers of a morning and caught your breath sharp in your lungs!

'Vortigern's sons are already married,' he said lightly, pushing an unexpected, alarmingly erotic thought aside. 'Happen you are thinking of wedding one of their sons? Or the sons of Vortigern's sister are favoured, though the eldest, Gorlois, was unlucky in marriage.' His caustic laugh was derisive. 'He could not keep a wife – losing the first to God's kingdom, and the second to Uthr.'

Etern chuckled, echoing Arthur's irony. The story of how the young Ygrainne met and fell in love with Uthr was well known, had almost become legend. The consequent fighting, heightened by Uthr's feud with Vortigern, was made all the more violent through Gorlois's desire for revenge against the man who had stolen his wife. Gorlois lost both wife and life, though Vortigern eventually won the victory of the warring.

Arthur buffeted his friend's shoulder with his fist. 'There are always his two brothers to consider. Melwas or Amlawdd would serve.'

Gwenhwyfar made a crude, insulting noise through her lips. 'Both fat-bellied toads.' She laughed, the sour temper evaporating as suddenly as it had come. 'Vortigern is about to fall, his obnoxious kindred along with him.'

'Aye, happen even now Uthr has removed his head and is marching in victory!' Etern scrambled to his feet, slicing through the air with an imaginary sword. 'There will be a new line of sons for Britain.'

Reluctant to quell this enthusiasm, Gwenhwyfar still felt impelled to interrupt. 'What line, brother? Uthr has no sons. He would have to divorce Ygrainne and take a new wife.' She chattered on with Etern, discussing possibilities. There was no shortage of noble born ladies, and then Uthr's two surviving brothers had issue: Ectha two boys, and Emrys, the youngest brother, an infant son.

Gwenhwyfar tossed a question at Arthur, unaware he had taken no part in this conversation. He sat quiet, shoulders hunched, systematically shredding a grass stalk. There was no place for him in the line of descendants. He was a bastard, unacknowledged. That Ectha had probably sired him was as nothing. He found it difficult to believe that Ectha, a quiet family man who still shed tears at the long ago death of his beloved wife could have, would have, so casually rutted with Ygrainne's serving maid.

'Would Uthr dare take Morgause as wife?' Gwenhwyfar repeated.

He glanced up, eyes flickering between Etern and Gwenhwyfar, not quite at them. 'She would like that, has been hoping for such a thing for some while. A mistress is one thing, but marriage?' He spread his hands, indicating the difference. 'The bitch likes to think – for us all to think – that Uthr loves her, but I believe he does not.'

Leaning forward hugging her knees, Gwenhwyfar asked with keen interest, 'What makes you say so?'

Arthur threw aside a piece of the broken stalk. 'Little things, like – oh, I don't know – he says things about her, lewd or coarse remarks, laughs with the men about her.' He glanced again at Gwenhwyfar. 'It seems to me, a man will say what he likes about his whore, but he keeps private the woman he loves.'

Bats were flitting through the deepening blue of twilight as the outer defences of the settlement loomed ahead. The three had seized the chance to ride, heading for the glow of a brilliant red sunset Racing their horses until they were blown, they turned and ambled home as the first stars brightened against the darkening night sky.

As they clattered under the inner archway into the stronghold old Marc, the gatekeeper, stepped forward and caught Aquila's bridle causing the horse to skitter in alarm. Etern, almost unseated, shouted in quick anger; 'Take care!'

Marc, his old, wrinkled face ashen grey stroked the horse's damp neck, calming him. 'My apologies, young master, I had no intention of

alarming you.' He spoke to Etern but his gaze drifted towards the lad Arthur, who rode on Aquila's off side.

'There be news. I have orders to tell you, and young Master Arthur here, to go direct to Lord Osmail.'

Etern exchanged a swift glance with his friend and his sister. Good news? Bad?

Longing to go with them, disappointed that she had not been included, Gwenhwyfar slid from Splinter's back and ran to the boys' horses.

'I will see to these,' she said, taking their bridles; 'go quickly.'

Etern nodded his thanks and gave her shoulder a brief squeeze as he dismounted, aware of the effort the offer had taken. As their hurried footsteps echoed away, Gwenhwyfar turned to Marc. 'What news?'

His hand still resting on Aquila's neck, the old soldier regarded Cunedda's only daughter with sad eyes. Her mother's gaze looked back at him. She touched his hand, felt a faint tremor beneath the twisted old knuckles. 'What is it? Tell me.'

'Bad,' he said at length. 'Terrible bad. The messenger's horse was on its last legs, ridden almost to death.' He swallowed hard, seeing again the sight of the foundering horse, not an hour since, plunging through this same archway and staggering on the cobbles beyond, falling.

Tears slipped from Marc's short-sighted old eyes.

'They say,' he said, 'that Uthr be dead.'

§ XII

Cunedda returned to Caer Arfon in grief. Behind him came no elated army marching proud beneath flying banners; no blaring of war horns or rousing marching songs. Instead, a weary, blood grimed rabble, tottering to its knees, grateful for a place to rest and a chance to weep for the many dead. Tears fell from the eyes of a standard-bearer who defiantly carried the Dragon, tattered and stained with Uthr's own spilt blood.

Uthr's men and the men of Gwynedd, heads bowed, shoulders hunched, nursing disbelief and sorrow. The men of the Pendragon following wearily behind their lord's friend, hearts and spirits empty and lost. Defeated men, uncaring what happened to them, with no further cause to fight and no cherished lord for whom to lay down their lives.

Many a man marching that last, endless mile regretted missing death on the battlefield. The lucky ones had gone ahead with their beloved lord.

The people, mostly women, of the settlement stood watching as the host returned, lining the broad main thoroughfare or clustered at the gateways. A mother here, a wife there shouted their joy, welcoming a son or husband home; many, too many, threw their hands over their eyes and let loose their grief as they learnt their own would come home no more.

Others waited, silent, watching, remembering – as the straggle of wounded men limped or were carried past, bloodied, grey-faced men leaning on spears or friends, bundled into carts, draped over tired horses –remembering that other time of defeat, when Vortigern's hired Saex had come tramping in the wake of Cunedda's host. Remembering too, what he had ordered done.

Beyond the cries of relief or sorrow, they stood fearful. Cunedda's stallion trailed his head, a front hoof stumbled on a sun baked rut. His rider automatically gathered the reins and collected the animal's balance. He heard the uneasy quiet, could see plain the nudging panic. His people remembered well the revenge of Vortigern. Cunedda entered his stronghold, dismounted and standing for a moment with one hand on his stallion's weary neck gave orders for seeing to the men's well-being. He stroked his hand along his horse's crest. Horses too had been lost, noble animals that gave courage without question. Few sights were more sickening than a horse with its belly slit open struggling to stand, not understanding why it could not. He saw Gwenhwyfar waiting before the open doors of the Hall.

Gone was the untidy urchin with dirt-smudged nose, ripped tunic and scraped knees. Her hair, shining copper-gold in the sunlight was neatly braided and looped. She wore a robe of palest green, the colour of spring and eternal life. In her hand, the chalice of welcome. A faint smile flickered to her father and brothers, thankful at least for their safe return. Cunedda stepped forward, sipped the red wine, handed the drinking vessel on to the son beside him.

Enniaun was the last to drink. He touched his lips to the red liquid and then spilt the rest on the threshold. 'In honour and remembrance of those not with us,' he murmured. 'May the blood of their killers one day stain as this wine stains.'

They stood, heads bowed, grouped around the spreading red puddle, watching as it soaked into the wooden boards of the steps, seeing again the blood of the battlefield.

'Welcome home, my father and brothers.' Gwenhwyfar stammered over the words, her throat aching with sorrow. She wanted to cry, great gulping sobs, but held back her tears for the sake of her father and for the memory of Uthr, the Pendragon. She looked into Cunedda's grave eyes, saw the emptiness of grief there and spoke the words that pressed on the mind of every man and woman: 'Da, will Vortigern come?'

Briefly Cunedda cradled his daughter's chin in his cupped hand. 'Who knows, lass? Probably. I would, if I were he.' He forced a crooked smile for her and suddenly pulled her close, holding her so tight she thought she would be crushed. Then his eye fell on Arthur, waiting with Etern a few steps within the Hall.

The two days of waiting for the hosting's return had been two days of bitter tears and lonely desperation for the lad. His eyes were red rimmed, puffy and sore, his cheeks drawn hollows of wretched misery. Arthur had loved Uthr, loved him as he would never love Ectha, the man who fostered him, who might be his sire. It was Uthr who had given the boy his first sword, who had taught Arthur to fight, to use spear and shield, to ride, to hunt. Uthr who had taught him all he knew of battle and war, for Uthr had favoured Arthur, had never objected to the lad's constant questioning, his eagerness to learn. Arthur had never seen anything unusual in the attention, had assumed his lord was pleased to teach someone so enthusiastic – until Morgause had soured the dream, until she had planted seeds of doubt and disgust. Had Uthr tolerated a boy trotting constant at heel because he intended one day to use him in his bed? Now Arthur would never know.

The Lion Lord released Gwenhwyfar and walked up to the boy, placed a hand on his shoulder. 'Come with me, lad, there is much to tell.'

Arthur went with Cunedda. He would be sent home, back to Less Britain, back to dull Ectha and the banality of the estate. Gone were the hopes of an army life, shattered the dreams of becoming War Lord. Not now, not without Uthr. Cunedda led him through the silent Hall, past servants who stood uncertain of the future, through to his private chambers beyond.

Gwenhwyfar watched them go, stood staring blankly at that shut wooden door, feeling Arthur's sorrow as if it were her own pain. So many dreams left in ruins. So much blood spilt, and more yet to come. A tear dribbled down her cheek. Arthur had wanted so much, and one sword blade had taken it from him. Still she looked at that door. The death of one man – affecting, now, the lives of so many.

A hand settled softly on her shoulder. Surprised, she gasped, and turned around, her heart thundering. It was Osmail. Of all her brothers, Osmail offering comfort?

He stroked a finger around her face. 'We'll be safe enough, lass,' he said, a tenderness in his voice that she had never heard there before.

She smiled at him, at his own sad eyes, but he turned from her and walked away, that brief offer of love fading. All the same, she heard the thought he spoke aloud.

'I wish to God I had been there with the others.'

Now that Cunedda had departed, a trill of conversation rippled, as if they were all released from a hag's binding spell. Slaves darted to pour wine and serve food for hungry men; wounded were ushered to medical aid, comfort and rest. The war host, for better or worse, was home.

§ XIII

Ceredig climbed the steps to the rampart walk with a heart as heavy as his tired feet. The night seemed very still, almost at peace. The cloud-dabbed sky was pocked with stars, and a crisp mountain smell, mingling with the sharp tang of sea, threatened rain. Reaching the top, he turned sunwise along the walkway, nodding acknowledgement as the night watch snapped to attention. They had doubled the guard, though this night they would not be needed. Come tomorrow, and tomorrow...

The settlement, spreading below the rampart, gave the impression of normality; a light came and went in a doorway, a child cried. A man's voice called good night. The darkness cloaked an uneasy waiting.

Padding footsteps behind him, a light touch on his arm. A face, pale in the starlight, with eyes wide and anxious.

'You ought to be abed, little sister,' Ceredig said, then shrugged noncommittally as she begged to walk his rounds with him. All the same, he shortened his long stride to match her slower pace.

They stopped to speak here and there with the sentries, exchanging a jest, sharing the grief of loss, enquiring after a bandaged wound.

Halfway along the eastern walkway Ceredig halted to stand before the palisade, looking out and beyond to the mountains, their familiar outline black against the dark sky. Companionably, Gwenhwyfar leant beside him, her elbows just about reaching the top of the wooden fencing. She folded her arms there, rested her chin, gazed with her brother into the night.

A hunting owl called, her mate answering. A dog-fox barked. All the normal sounds of night. Stars twinkled, clouds sailed by overhead. Normal. Save that Vortigern would be somewhere out there beyond Eryri.

A star trail fell across the sky, glimmered a while, faded.

'An omen sent for the Red Dragon of Uthr or the White of Vortigern's Saex?' Ceredig wondered aloud, shifting his weight to the left leg that seemed not to ache so much as the right.

Gwenhwyfar shrugged. 'Without the Sight of a Myrddin, who can say?'

'Tck, those old Druids. What knew they, beyond mumbled charms and drug-induced prophecies?' Ceredig followed the Christian faith, though not as devoutly blinkered as his eldest brother.

They fell silent again, each sharing silent company with their own thoughts. The Druids, the ancient priesthood, were gone, their power destroyed by the might of Rome, replaced by the growing persuasion of Christ. Even those who clung to the old gods had abandoned the Druid influence.

'I wonder why stars fall as omens?' Gwenhwyfar mused.

'The problem with omens, sister, is that interpretation depends on which view you look from.' Ceredig altered position to lean his shoulders against the fencing, looked down into the torch-lit courtyard below. Men were moving about, loading wagons, tending horses, seeing to armour and weapons. They would move out on the morrow to defend the passes, barricade the ways through the mountains. Vortigern would not find it easy to march into Gwynedd.

'We see a star's portent one way, sister; Vortigern's rabble another.'

'Da said once that stars fall when a person dies or a child is born, marking a sorrow or greeting.'

Ceredig made no reply. The whole sky would need to fall to mark this great sorrow.

Gwenhwyfar had not been able to sleep. This restless unease that swaddled the Caer pressed on her mind, setting her tossing and pitching in her bed. In the end, she had risen, dressed, and gone to find solace. The mountains always called when fear or sorrow battled against her heart. It was too dark to ride to their protective comfort, but the rampart walk gave a good view of their slumbering presence, so up she had come, softly up the steps to greet her friends. Had seen Ceredig walking his rounds.

Into the stillness she asked, as she had her father, 'Will he come – Vortigern?'

Footfalls behind her, two men approaching. Gwenhwyfar whirled, her hand flying instinctively to the dagger in her tunic belt. She laughed in relief at the sight of another brother and her cousin.

'Who knows with Vortigern?' Enniaun said, coming up to lean his broad hands on the palisade.

Meriaun, shorter by a handspan and thinner, breathed in the night air, said as he exhaled, 'He will have to come up the passes, or go the long way around the coast.' Both their faces were shadowed with lines of apprehension, and a tiredness that went deeper than a lack of sleep. 'Either way, he will lose many men.'

The three men leaned together along the fencing, staring outwards. Ceredig gripped the wood between large, strong hands. Enniaun seemed more at ease, though it was the careworn relaxation of an experienced warrior. Worry about tomorrow when it comes, take today for what it offers. Difficult to set worry aside, but possible, with practice.

Meriaun stood next to Gwenhwyfar, his hand fiddle, fiddling with the rounded pommel of his sword. A babe newly born when Cunedda left the north, Meriaun had grown from boy to man beneath Gwynedd's sheltering mountains, had never known the desolation up beyond the Wall; nor his father. He knew the terror Vortigern aroused, though, and the hatred he had for him. His fingers tightened, the knuckles white against the iron. He thought, *Let Vortigern come! Let him and I will kill him, here beneath the watching eye of Yr Wyddfa!*

Enniaun spoke his thoughts aloud. 'Vortigern goes as the impulse takes him. Our King is no brave hearted seeker of blood. He prefers his comfort, the warmth and luxury of a palace, not the mud and slush of a tent and an army on the march. Is he satisfied with Uthr's death? Will he be content with the taking of a few hostages and the payment of a heavy fine? Or will he want a greater revenge – as he did at Dun Pelidr? Either way, Gwynedd will not escape lightly.'

'Who is to secure the passes?' Ceredig asked. He had missed the orders, feeling the need to walk these ramparts.

'Dogmail the Beris pass; Dunaut and Rumaun head down to the Tremadog coast; myself, Aber Glaslyn ready to fall back towards the Black Ford if necessary; and Abloyc up to secure Llyn Ogwen. It ought to be enough, with men watching the northern coastal road.'

'Safe. But for the sea.'

'Even Vortigern's Saex cannot whistle up boats from nowhere!'

Silence drifted again. The mountains ringed Caer Arfon as securely as this palisade protected the Caer; but no defence was sure. Wood burnt. Passes could be breached.

'I am thinking there are two ways of approaching our passes,' Ceredig said into the quiet, waving a hand out to the dark, waiting mountains. 'With wisdom or foolishness.' He patted his sister's shoulder and made ready to resume his rounds. 'Go to bed, sweetheart, there is nothing to be done until morning.' He walked some yards, stopped and turned to face his kin, hand tight around the pommel of his sword. His voice was calm, but had a fierceness born of the certain knowledge that the deaths might not yet be ended. 'I dislike Vortigern, but I freely admit he is not the fool.'

§ XIV

In the encampment set within the crumbling stone walls of the old Roman fort, Uthr's men sat weary and uncertain beside their night fires, talking softly or dozing fitfully. Some nursed wounds that throbbed and ached; most cradled their weapons, sword or spear close at hand, ready. Waiting. Bewildered, confused and bereft, each man wrapped in his own thoughts of loss and shattered hope. Leaderless men in a foreign territory, with the fear of Vortigern at their backs.

Cunedda needed to put an end to this black mood before it got out of hand. Men afraid could so easily follow a mistaken path. He needed calm, and new heart. Come dawn's first light, word to rally before the Caer's Sacred Stone had spread through the camp, and rumour surged with a force like that of the Hafren's bore tide.

Uthr's men broke their fast with barley bread and porridge, sharing conclusions reached during the interminable night. What had Cunedda in mind? Each held an idea as they assembled beside the men of Gwynedd before the hallowed Stone, the symbol of a warrior's strength and the chieftain's right of leadership. The whetstone, with its spiral carvings and score marks from many a warrior's blade had come with Cunedda from the North. An ancient thing this Stone, given, it was said, by the gods to the first of the Votadini. It was here, with a hand upon this sacred, carved rock that loyalty was vowed, promises exchanged and oaths sworn; here that Cunedda had proclaimed Gwynedd as his own. It was before such stones, in the time before and before the coming of the Romans, that kings were made.

The Kingmaking

Muttered theories passed back and forth from soldier to soldier, group to group. Emotion was running high, with anger directed at Vortigern. Talk ceased as Cunedda, Lion Lord of Gwynedd, and his family approached. Standard-bearers carrying the two banners of the Lion and the Red Dragon took up positions on either side of the Stone. A ragged cheer broke out as the first stirring of a morning wind lifted the Dragon. Gwenhwyfar sensed the pride her father's men felt in her family. She had chosen to dress resplendently for Uthr – a gown the colour of a summer's green-blue sea, and a plaid cloak draped almost to her ankles and fastened by two huge gold and garnet brooches. Her hair hung loose, and at her throat, glinted a torque of twisted gold.

They stood beside the Stone, before the men, to honour the passing of a noble lord. How Gwenhwyfar wished it could have been to honour his victory! The waiting men looked on with mingled hope and doubt as Cunedda took a single step forward and raised his hands for silence.

'Friends! I grieve with you for the loss of our beloved Pendragon. As children he and I grew together at my father's stronghold; as men we fought our enemies – aye, and each other over a pretty girl!' Chuckles, a few cheers; the tension had eased. 'It grieves me to realise never again will that valiant lord thunder his battle cry.' Cunedda's voice cracked; for a moment he could not speak, so great was his sorrow. Somehow he managed to go on. 'I say to you, Uthr is not gone! His spirit remains among us. With us, his hopes, ambitions and dreams live on. He wished a Pendragon to sit on the throne of all Britain. Ha!' He barked the word, startling the few murmurs into stillness. 'Do I hear some of you muttering that now this will not be?'

Cunedda paused, stared fiercely at the sea of faces. His stern gaze blazed out from beneath his bush of red hair, quelling dissent. The Lion would be heard!

'This banner' – he touched the Dragon reverently – 'symbolises all we believe in, binds us together as one, and the Dragon is ours!'

An uncertain cheer drifted into the damp morning air, then a gruff voice rose clear above the others: 'What good a banner if the name it leads be empty?'

The thin cheering died, fading to nods and mutterings of agreement.

Gwenhwyfar knew her father's ways, realised he was playing with these men, preparing them. But for what? She glanced from Etern's blank expression, along her brothers' frowns. Did they follow their father's thoughts? Arthur stood impassive to one side beyond Cunedda, pale-faced and oddly lost, a little uncomfortable. It would be hard for him with no one to stand between him and Morgause. Would the woman take herself away now her lord was dead? Gwenhwyfar caught a fluttered glimpse to

97

the edge of the crowd, of Morgause's bright clothing, imagined she heard the loud jangle of bangles and necklace. *Sa*, she had come to listen then.

As they had snatched a hasty dawn meal, Etern had confided to his sister the opinion that the Pendragon's Banner was expected to pass into Gwynedd's keeping, with one of the sons taking it as his own. It seemed plausible. Had Uthr named Cunedda as heir, or was it to pass to Osmail, the eldest brother? Surely not to Osmail, who disliked war, who professed to putting love to God before the killing of men?

Enniaun then, a red-haired giant, taller by half a hand span than their father. Or Ceredig. Kind Ceredig, whose soft eyes could fill with sad tears at the telling of a harper's tale; Rumaun and Dunaut the twins, alike as two seeds. Abloyc, the humorous – always laughing, rarely serious save for occasions like this. Meriaun, the grandson; or Dogmail, at eight and ten a handsome man, loved by all the women, servant or high born. He doubted he would marry – *'Over many beauties to choose from!'* Etern? Impatient for manhood.

And Arthur. Gwenhwyfar wondered about Arthur. Traces of his tears were still visible. What future had he to face now?

Cunedda allowed the rumble of voices to circulate, to swell, then interrupted, his powerful voice carrying. 'The name of Pendragon is not finished! Uthr's murder by a Saex-loving tyrant is not the end. Were we not all impatient to topple Vortigern from power? Uthr tried once and was forced into exile, to wait. This second time, we have rocked the foundations. Vortigern will fall, but we have to wait again, wait to put the final boot to his backside. We are not defeated. This is a new beginning, my friends, a new beginning!'

'How so?' The man who had questioned earlier spoke a second time. He had a loud, carrying voice that quickly attracted attention. Thrusting forward, he touched the mask of his wolfskin cloak in a gesture of respect, but for all that, stood defiant before Cunedda. 'How can it be a beginning when the body of the lord we have served – some of us for many a year – lies mangled in Vortigern's hands? We cannot serve a memory, Cunedda!'

A ripple of assent.

'What is your name, soldier?' Cunedda asked in a kindly voice.

'Waiting,' thought Gwenhwyfar. *'He's waiting like a cat watching its prey, judging the right moment to unleash his claws and pounce.'*

'Mabon. I served Lord Uthr for nigh on twenty year, from when I was still but a whelp green behind the ears; I fled with him from Dumnonia,' he swept an arm behind him, indicating other men, 'as did many of us here.'

Cunedda pulled at his moustache, one hand cradling his bent elbow. 'It was a Mabon, I recall, who raised the alarm that night when Vortigern's paid men came to murder Uthr in his bed.'

'It was.'

'You?'

'Aye, me.' The veteran straightened his shoulders, his pride shining through a battle-grimed scowl.

Cunedda nodded at the man. 'For your loyal service, I will recommend you for an honour, Mabon.'

'With respect, Sir,' Mabon replied, 'I thank you, but to whom will you give such recommendation? We,' again he swept his callused hand towards the men, 'have no lord.'

Direct into Cunedda's hands. 'That,' the Lion snapped, eyes blazing in triumph, 'is where you are wrong!'

Dissent grumbled louder, each man talking rapidly to the man at his shoulder, heads shaking, a few fists being raised.

Cunedda boomed out, 'Do you, Mabon, recollect Lady Ygrainne's condition when you found an urgent need to flee that night?'

'As if it were yesterday,' Mabon answered forthright. 'We were all concerned for my lady, heavy with child as she was.'

Cunedda beckoned Mabon forward. 'Come out here, man, so all may see and hear. Recount the tale to those who do not know.'

Hesitant at first Mabon began to talk. He could not see the point of all this, but Cunedda must have his reasons.

'After the defeat, Uthr fled into his own secure lands of Dumnonia. He knew it would be only a matter of time afore Vortigern and the followers of the slain Gorlois made an attempt on his life. For some months we managed, our people were loyal, looking to Uthr and his new lady with affection. But there is always the risk of traitors. The attack came at a bad time – rough seas and foul weather.'

The man was settling to his tale, confidence growing. 'Lady Ygrainne had no choice but to take ship with us. It was she Gorlois' kin wanted dead, for her insult in leaving that lecherous bastard.' He spat, nodded apology at Cunedda and, as the nearest female present, Gwenhwyfar. 'The sea crossing was bad, bad enough for a fit man let alone a woman close to her time.' Mabon shook his head. 'She was delivered of a son soon after we disembarked in Less Britain. The child lived a day, no longer.' He shook his head more vigorously at the enormity of the loss. 'Uthr's only true born son. There have been no more.'

Silence, save for the rustle of a spirited wind rising with the incoming tide. They all knew the tale but this time the recounting hit harder, rubbing salt into an open wound. No heir to carry the Dragon. No son to follow Uthr's dream and title.

Cunedda tugged at his moustache. 'Were there not two women with child on that ship?'

Mabon frowned, startled, uncertain how the lord of Gwynedd came to know such small detail. 'Aye, my lord.' He spoke slowly, thinking what to say. 'Caromy, my lady's maid, carried a child. She birthed a boy during the crossing.' Mabon pursed his lips. 'Poor lass had a bad time of it.' He glanced sideways at Arthur, who stared back at him.

The story concluded lamely, a few beads of sweat standing out on Mabon's brow beneath the snarling head of the wolf cloak as Arthur's eyes continued to bore into the man.

'At first, tongues wagged that the child was Uthr's doing.' He spread his hands. 'He liked his women. Then Ectha took the boy in formal foster, so it was considered his had been the,' he coughed, 'indiscretion.'

Pushing further Cunedda probed for more information. 'And this son of Caromy's?' He smoothed his moustache with the tip of his index finger. 'How did he fare?'

Mabon's resigned glance flickered between Arthur and Cunedda. 'Ah, 'tis the shame of it, with all respect to the lad here.' He nodded in apology to Arthur. 'Caromy's child was a sickly thing, but 'twas the one that lived.' He sighed, pointed to Arthur, 'As you see, he thrived.'

'The mother?'

'Took sick, died.'

Throughout the telling Arthur's expression remained impassive, almost bored. Gwenhwyfar, following the exchange of words and glances felt herself teetering on the brink of excitement. She had not missed that familiar twitch about her father's lips; he was enjoying himself. For a heartbeat, she felt she knew what was to come, then it was gone like a seed lost to the wind. She waited, holding her breath.

Cunedda's voice suddenly roared like the creature he was named for. Many jumped; Gwenhwyfar almost squeaked. 'I can add to the telling!'

His listeners shuffled in anticipation, eyes and ears riveted, locked on to Cunedda's muscular bulk. He placed a hand on Arthur's shoulder, brought the boy forward, then with apparent carelessness rested his other hand lightly on the Stone.

'Mahon has identified this lad to you as Arthur. I can tell you now of something I have held safe unto me these many years.'

Gwenhwyfar took hold of Etern's arm, a thrill of anticipation streaking through her. She had known, deep down, where these things rested, unspoken and unheeded!

Excited talk, muttered questions. From the back, a few shouts. Raising the hand resting on Arthur's shoulder, Cunedda paused, waiting for complete silence to fall.

The incoming sea shuffled against the shore, and a gentle salt wind hissed from the hills. Two screeching gulls wheeled overhead.

To the misted blue of the new day, Cunedda boomed, 'It was not the son of Uthr and Ygrainne who died, but Caromy's!'

The hand went back to Arthur; the other still touched the sacred Stone. He let the murmur rumble, heard the rise of hope begin to dawn as the men around him realised what was to come.

He went on, speaking fast. 'The babes were exchanged, a deception to shield Uthr's firstborn from Vortigern's spite. Only four of us knew the truth of it: Uthr and Ygrainne, Caromy, and myself.' Cunedda nodded grimly. 'Now you know it. And by all the gods that ever were or ever shall be, Vortigern too shall know soon enough!'

The muttering had grown louder, men pushing closer, faces that a moment before were grey and lost coming alive, eager.

With ringing triumph Cunedda finished his speech. 'There is another Pendragon – still young, I grant, we need wait for him to come of age. We, Uthr and I, had hoped we would not need to reveal him until he was ready, but that was not to be.' Cunedda chivvied Arthur before him and shouted above the rising excitement, his voice ringing out almost to the watching mountains. 'Here, before the hallowed sanctity of our Stone, I give you your next king! I give you the Pendragon – Arthur!'

He stepped back leaving Arthur to stand alone as a great clamour rose up into the sky. The lad smiled now, the pain and sorrow fading with that great roar of acclaim. Cunedda was wrong: five had known Uthr had his heir. Arthur had known, all these years in his dreams and thoughts, he had known Uthr to be his father. Why else had he loved the man so, and the man been so fond of a lad? He grinned, broadly, triumphantly, at the pride in Cunedda's face, the unexpected pleasure on those of his sons. Arthur winked boyishly at the exultant Gwenhwyfar.

Unexpected, Cunedda knelt before the lad, offering his sword as a token of his loyalty. Few heard the words he spoke, above that tumult of approval raised by those watching men. It did not matter, all knew the oath of allegiance.

'To you, Lord, I give my sword and shield, my heart and soul. To you, Lord, I give my life, to command as you will.'

Arthur could not hide his consternation at so great a man kneeling at a boy's feet. With shaking fingers, he touched Cunedda's offered sword then, impulsively, he raised the man and embraced him as a friend.

It if were possible, the roar increased. Men of Gwynedd yelled their delight at seeing their lord accepted by the new Pendragon, and men of Uthr, heartsore and bruised, shouted and cheered, relieved to have their anxiety and uncertainty so splendidly lifted.

One by one the sons of Gwynedd stepped forward to follow their father's example. Etern too knelt.

'I am not yet come to manhood, I cannot swear oath to you. But this I can swear, Arthur, when the time comes you will not be wanting for a more loyal sword, for mine shall be yours, whenever you have need of it.'

Arthur choked, almost unable to speak. He clasped his friend's arm and stammered, 'Then I shall indeed be blessed with a greater fortune than I deserve!'

As Etern stepped aside, Gwenhwyfar, with head high, strode forward. The sun burst through a low covering of misty cloud, making her hair and jewels sparkle with dazzling brilliance. She knelt solemnly before Arthur, her grace and hint of woman's beauty showing clearly through the lankiness of her child's body, catching every watcher's attention.

The noise abated. No woman took the oath of loyalty. What was this girl-child about?

She held Arthur's eyes and her voice, young though it was, carried clear and bold.

'I too am of the blood of Gwynedd. Were I born male I would swear my oath, but I am woman-born. I have no shield or sword.'

Arthur took her hands in his. Like a fool he felt a sudden urge to weep. Looking down at her earnest face, his dark eyes seeing deep into the hidden secrets of her tawny flecked green, he realised how much he wanted her for his own.

Tremulously Gwenhwyfar said, 'I have something else to give, Lord.' Her heart was hammering. 'When I am woman-grown I shall have a greater gift to pledge. I offer you, my Lord, Arthur Pendragon, to use how you choose, my unborn sons!'

The family behind, ranged behind the Stone, roared delight and approval along with the excited host. Cunedda almost burst with pride as he shouted with the rest of them. Aye, his only daughter was as fine a woman as the one he had taken in marriage! Had he not always known it would be so?

Arthur gripped Gwenhwyfar's hands and raised her to her feet. He spoke quietly, words for her alone, not trusting the emotion to lie easy. 'I accept your pledge, my Cymraes fach – only, before you take him, ensure your future husband agrees also!'

Gwenhwyfar tossed her head, a little annoyed. 'I told you: I will not wed with any but the best.'

Arthur grinned, suddenly confident, emboldened. 'Would you consider a Pendragon the best?'

The men of the war host were jostling forward, eager to take the oath. Gwenhwyfar found herself swept aside, her answer lost to Arthur's ears.

'I will not bear my sons to anyone less.'

§ XV

Morgause was leaving. She had informed Cunedda curtly last evening of her intention, demanding suitable escort and horses. He had not attempted to dissuade her.

She had stationed herself apart from the knot of women gathered on the far side of the Stone Ground, her expression as granite hard as the Stone itself. Watching the elated men swarm around Arthur her fists clenched, the nails digging into the flesh of her palms. All the words and oaths and curses that were ever sworn, swirled in her throat ready to spew from between clenched teeth. It all made sense now! Uthr's excuses, the evasive replies. That was why he was so fond of the boy. That was why he had refused to divorce Ygrainne! Bastard. Lying, deceitful bastard! '*The Goddess rot your bones, Uthr Pendragon!* '

Her maid approached warily, sensing the mood. She whispered, indicating a group of waiting men and horses. Morgause walked to them with quick, angry steps, mounted the mare held for her and prepared to ride out, then changed her mind. With rough hands and kicking heels she forced her mare through the tightly packed men, and halted before Arthur. For a long moment Morgause said nothing, just stared at the boy with malevolent hatred.

Arthur returned the look, unflinching, triumph sparking behind his dark eyes, this unexpected knowledge of identity provided a greater courage than he knew he possessed. 'You are leaving us?' he said coolly in the neat, precise Latin she always used, added with a sarcastic smile, 'You will not be missed.'

The mare, uneasy at the press of men, swung away suddenly, eyes rolling, head lowered and rear hooves lashing out. There came shouts of alarm, men darting backwards, jumping aside. Morgause yanked hard at the horse's bit, hauling her back. 'You may have discovered you are no bastard, but I tell you this, your father certainly was!' She spat at Arthur and dug her heels into her mount, causing the mare to leap forward with a squeal of protest.

Several men fell beneath the plunging horse; one screamed as a thrashing hoof crashed on his leg, smashing the bone. Others crouched, arms protecting heads, or scrambled to safety. The instant reaction was rage. Hands reached out to stop her, grabbing at the bridle, countering her double insult. Morgause slashed faces, hands, heads with her riding whip, glaring and snarling like a savage cat.

Dabbing at the spittle, Arthur wiped it, repugnant, from his cheek. 'Let the bitch go,' he commanded in the men's British tongue. 'We shall be well rid of her.'

He strode quickly to the injured man, laid a sympathetic hand on his shoulder, ordered, 'Send someone for a stretcher, see this man's well tended.'

Morgause was galloping, driving the mare hard. Arthur stood and watched her leave. He ought to feel elated, joyful, at the very least relieved. Morgause was gone, gone from his life. No more of her slaps and tortures. No more of her venomous tongue and sharp sarcasm.

If only he could be certain. Certain that she really had gone from him. For good. But nothing was ever a certainty where that witch woman was concerned.

JULY 450

§ XVI

The grain harvest was ruined. Persistent rain worked through garments, soaking uncomfortable to the skin and aching into the joints of old bones and new-healing wounds. That glorious month of June had rumbled into a July, that brought a torrent of wind-driven hail from the west with all the fury of an angered boar. Had Vortigern used some dark power in the sending of that storm?

Within the one night oats, wheat and barley that had stood proud and golden, lay sodden and blackened. Fortunate that Gwynedd was not reliant on the growing of crops for survival; they had their sheep and cattle; the wild deer, fowl and boar. The sea to fish. But the grain was needed for the horses, for the baking of bread, and for the staple poor man's diet of porridge.

When Arthur had taken up the title of Pendragon there came a flourish of exuberance and optimism which filled the next few days – even though Cunedda had ordered the lad home to safety in Less Britain.

Gwenhwyfar missed him. Missed his laughter and jaunty teasing. His friendship. Theirs had developed into a special liking, something that went beyond the sharing of seemingly endless summer days. Gwenhwyfar was a girl-child, but a girl on the brink of womanhood. With the coming of Arthur, she had felt as though she were walking in the wild foam of the surf – neither a girl on the firm, golden sand, nor a woman grown, in the open swell of the sea. She walked somewhere between, neither one nor yet the other, she could only look back to where the innocence of childhood romped, and ahead to the unknown future.

'Do not forget me!' he had called, as his ship slipped its moorings and the tide bore him away, that first night after his proclaiming.

'Never!' she had shouted back, standing on toe-tip to watch until the darkness took him. She would not forget Arthur. None would forget the vibrant boy who carried their dreams and their hopes of freedom. But nor could they forget Vortigern.

For a few days they shrugged off the threat of his coming, mocking his incompetence, carolling lewd songs and passing even cruder jests at the King's expense. False bravado. With the coming of that storm, hope and gaiety fled Caer Arfon.

A depression settled clinging like the grey swathing mist of low cloud that shrouded the brooding mountains. Even the sea rolled flat and grey.

Vortigern had come as far as Llyn Tegid and set up camp, entrenching himself and his stinking Saex mercenaries beside the river that fed the lake. Envoys began passing back and forth, riding dismally through the torrential rain. Cunedda's proud messengers, Vortigern's haughty emissary. A skirmish of words. The King demanding Cunedda surrender his sword and pay homage unconditionally; Cunedda playing for time with excuses and delays – seeking sanctuary from the inevitable.

How long, though, would Vortigern wait?

His patience would ebb, the relay of verbal procrastination eventually run its course. A few days; a week; ten days – twelve. It was to be the Lion Lord's homage to the king or battle. Cunedda wanted no further bloodshed, but Vortigern was not a man to trust, and his terms of surrender would not sit easy. One week turned slowly into two. Time had ended. So must the waiting.

Enniaun stirred more heat to the hearth, sending sparks and flames spitting high as he tossed wood to the reluctant blaze. The kindling was damp, more smoke than heat curling into the privacy of Cunedda's chamber. He shifted his brother Ceredig's boot aside and reseated himself within the circle around the hearth.

'To my mind,' Osmail said, shuffling his cloak tighter about his shoulders, 'it is naught but insanity for you to ride alone into Vortigern's encampment, Da.'

With a snort of contempt, Cunedda hurled back, 'Then I am insane.' He raised a finger, pointed it at his eldest son.

'The moment I agree to ride out of my gates I hand my pride to Vortigern. Pride I can afford to lose, it's a thing easily restored. The life of a son is not.'

Ceredig shifted his weight from a cramped ankle. 'He would not dare harm any of us, Da. If we must humble Gwynedd before his army, then let us do so together. All of us.'

'Aaghh!' Cunedda swarmed to his feet and stormed from the circle. 'Must I tell you this again? Have you all lost your hearing and wits?'

He stalked up to Ceredig and bent so as to speak directly to his face. 'I have no choice but to submit without condition. I do have a choice as to who accompanies me. I take for escort thirty of my guard. No sons.' His finger pointed at each face, looking back at him with mixed expression as he repeated, 'No sons. Never again will I be forced to witness the cold-minded butchering of my own flesh and blood.'

It was useless to argue further, but Enniaun made one last attempt. He spoke softly edging away from the rash heat of the argument that had been tossed back and forth around the hearth this past hour or more. 'It was different then, Da, as well you know.'

'How? How was it different?' Cunedda stormed around the circle and jerked Enniaun roughly to his feet. 'You know all about it, eh? You remember the taking and the killing at Dun Pelidr, do you boy?'

Enniaun hung his head, his fingers fiddling with the hilt of his dagger, teeth biting his lower lip. He remembered.

The fighting men had stumbled and dragged themselves up the steep sides of the Dun weeping and bloodied. Knowing the bodies of their kinsmen had been left to the crows and the indecencies of Vortigern's hired Saex. For five nights and days they held out before the Saex managed to fire the wooden palisade. Even then, Cunedda's proud people clung to freedom for another half day, choking in the acrid smoke that blackened and invaded their crumbling fortress home. Held long enough for the wife of the eldest son to give safe birthing to their first child. Then Cunedda surrendered, opening the gates for the King to enter and take what he would, never dreaming the price of rebellion would be enforced evacuation – and the execution of that beloved eldest son.

Lifting his head, Enniaun gazed into his father's eyes. Remember? How could any forget the gathering of their belongings and being herded through those soot blackened, body-strewn, mud and blood-churned streets of Dun Pelidr? Forget the jeers and taunts of Saex barbarians and king's men. Forget the rise of vomit as the family and people of Cunedda walked proud beneath the still smouldering gateway and saw, hanging there by the entrails, the hacked body of Typiaunan, Cunedda's son.

He swallowed, made to reach a hand towards his father, hesitated. Said instead, 'I remember, Da. We all, save Etern and Gwen who were not then born, remember.'

Meriaun, that grandson born while the flames leapt high and the end was approaching, came to his feet, his hands spread. 'I was a babe little more than a day born when the tribe left our old homeland. Smuggled from the Dun as a serving woman's child.' His voice too, choked, and the tears trickled unashamed. 'I knew only my grandsire's wife as Mother. The woman who birthed me chose to accompany her torn and mutilated lord into the next world. It was a brave love that gave her courage to drain her own blood from her veins.'

Cunedda stood slumped, seeing again that terrible time. Slowly he shook his head. 'And you ask me to take one or all of you into Vortigern's camp?'

He straightened, tilted his chin, defiant. 'I go alone. If the King needs blood then he can have my old bones, not yours.' He strode for the door, his decision final, halted as Osmail, still seated cross-legged before the hearth, said, 'I am coming with you, Father. It matters not, my life. I am no warrior. Gwynedd needs me not.' He looked up, an expression of pleading in his eyes. '*Just this once, Da, acknowledge me. Think of* me *as the eldest, not dead Typiaunan.*'

A stirring and shuffling as the brothers and Meriaun turned to stare at him. Osmail? Osmail offering this?

'Vortigern will demand a hostage to ensure future peace,' he added. 'Happen I can serve better thus than mouldering useless here.' Still he held his father's eyes. 'I ask only that you take care of my wife and sons.'

For a fleeting moment Cunedda hovered on agreement. How much better to have at least the support of one son! He looked quickly away from Osmail's eye lest he see the truth, spoke as quickly. 'No one comes with me save my chosen guard.' He left the chamber shutting the door firmly behind him. What use Osmail? What use his woman's stomach, his clumsy handling of weapons?

Stiff, stretching cramped muscles, the family of Gwynedd rose from the hearth, followed their father through the door back into the Hall. Only Osmail remained seated before the sulky flames, tossing bits of broken twig into the fire. Hurting that no one, not brother, nephew or father had denied his acknowledgement of failure.

An hour after cockcrow Cunedda rode from his stronghold of Caer Arfon. A chill spray of mud splattered the horses' legs as they rode down from the Caer. Steadying his stallion from a jogging trot, Cunedda looked back at the gateway aware it might be his last look, willing to accept it so for the lives of his sons and the peace of Gwynedd.

No good this remembering of the past! He urged his horse into a canter. Uthr had lost that war too, and Cunedda had lost everything including dignity. Vortigern had enjoyed humbling him, seeing him near destroyed; enjoyed the added insult of granting a dark, mountainous corner where starving peasants lived in rancid poverty, and raiding pirates plundered what little remained.

Gwynedd. Cunedda smiled grimly. Vortigern had played a wrong move! Gwynedd had rebuilt Cunedda's pride twofold, and what could be regained once, could be gained a second time. *Na*, Cunedda would not sacrifice Gwynedd or his sons to Vortigern. An easy price to pay, a bent knee and a few spoken words of homage. He set his face for Llyn Tegid, riding at a steady canter.

§ XVII

Three days he was gone. Three days of waiting in the hushed Caer, where at any moment the war horns of the King's hired Saex were expected to boom and crash through the passes and heights of the mountains. Three days of discomfort for Cunedda's escort, squatting, huddled beneath sodden cloaks, beside hissing campfires and glaring across the river at Vortigern's encampment.

And then Cunedda brought his men home to Caer Arfon one mid-afternoon when a weak sun struggled to break through grey cloud pressing as chill as unsmelted iron. His expression was inscrutable; only his hands, clutching the reins, showed his great anger. Speaking not one word to those waiting to bid him welcome, he stormed into his Hall, issuing curt orders to stand all men down.

'Vortigern will not be making reprisal?' Etern asked, following, with his family and retainers.

Cunedda made no answer, went direct to his own chamber where he slammed the door behind him and bellowed for wine.

The evening gathering was a morose and dispirited meal with no singing, no laughter. One table called for the harper to tell a tale, but his heart was not in it, the chosen narrative a woeful story of lost love. Cunedda sat picking at his food, glancing often at his daughter. She caught his eye once and flashed him her most brilliant smile. He managed a smile back then busied himself with his pork. *'How can I tell her? How do I tell what I have done to save Gwynedd?'*

110

The talk across the tables came in hushed voices. Few of the hosting had yet disbanded. They would drift away on the morrow at first light, tramping back to their homesteads and families, back to salvage what they could from the ruins of the harvest. Eyes flitted again and again to the red-haired lord at his table. On every lip, the same question. At what cost, this surrender?

Uncertainty and disquiet swirled with the woodsmoke, as choking and blinding. Belatedly, Cunedda realised he had made a mistake; he must say something, some few words to dispel this black mood. Those watching him were like whipped dogs, squirming low on their bellies, reluctant to approach the master for fear of further reprimand. Men and women, his people, were entitled to some explanation as part payment for unquestioning loyalty. But the great Cunedda was at a loss. What to say? How much to say? All of it, some?

Again he stole a glance at his beloved Gwenhwyfar, deep in earnest conversation with Etern. The pair missed young Arthur; it had been good, that friendship, and for Gwenhwyfar something more than friendship? Cunedda had been pleased at that discovery. A short lived pleasure that, now.

He pulled absently at his moustache. Do I tell her? Do I share this misery or carry it alone, for as long as I need keep silence? He exhaled slowly, coming to a decision. *Na*, let the lass hold the innocence and happiness of childhood while she might. It would be stolen from her soon enough. No need to sign for silence; Cunedda rising to his feet and clearing his throat settled the hushed conversation immediately.

'I have little to tell.' He stood with the tips of his spread fingers resting lightly on the table. 'I reached a personal agreement with the King. It is not to my liking, but for the sake of Gwynedd I accepted the conditions.'

He laid his hands flat, the wood smooth and cool beneath his sweating palms. 'We took a gamble and lost. Vortigern has claimed a high payment of corn, cattle and horses and such, for Gwynedd's surrender. He will take many of our young men also, to swell his British army. All that can be met,' Winter would come hard this year, and the next. Happen the next too. Cunedda flicked his cloak, preparing to sit, then paused. 'As to the other part of the settlement, that is for me to bear alone.'

Low talk began again; wine was poured, food eaten. Cunedda plucked meat from a bone. His family knew not to question further.

Abruptly Cunedda pushed back his chair, strode into the centre of the Hall and cast the bone into the blazing hearth fire; burning fat spat from the flames. Anger brewed like fermenting fruit in his belly.

'There is one thing you need know!'

Faces turned expectantly towards him. Some sat with tankards half raised, others with meat or bread poised in their fingers. One man paused, bending to retrieve his dagger from the floor where it had fallen.

His voice like the great boom of the war horns Cunedda cried, 'Uthr was betrayed – we were betrayed!' The words were as deadly as a viper's venom. 'Betrayed, by one who teaches love and peace. Vortigern knew where to find Uthr Pendragon!'

They had taken great care to hide this knowledge, to conceal their direction, changing course and changing it again. That Vortigern would know of Uthr's coming, and the war host was to be expected. Spies in Less Britain and the King's Saex pirates keeping close watch to the southern channel would ensure accurate intelligence. But Vortigern could never have been certain where the Pendragon was headed – Gwynedd, Dyfed, or home to Dumnonia? He gathered his army, made ready to march where and when needed, but would not have known so soon. Not so soon!

'One among us rode hard to tell Vortigern, to give him the edge in choosing the place to give battle.' Cunedda paused, then roared his great anger, 'It seems our holy priest did not approve our plans to overthrow tyranny!'

The response was immediate. A few protesting cries in defence of a holy man, hastily smothered as most let their anger go.

Cunedda raised his hands, shouted against the din. 'I knew Vortigern's spies; knew them and fed them enough tit-bits to keep their bellies well fed, ensured they were safe detained when the time was ripe. But one, one I overlooked.' His eyes narrowed as he looked around the incredulous faces. With a sudden hatred he said, 'There was no meeting of holy men, only the meeting of one turd to another. It was a man of God who caused Uthr's death!'

This, Cunedda knew, was stretching the truth. Vortigern would have come soon enough anyway; Uthr could as easily have been slain in battle without a spy's tattling. Except the advantage had gone to Vortigern, allowing him to anticipate and outmanoeuvre the uprising before it was fully fledged.

Branwen came to her feet, outraged. She detested this backwater and its heathen people. Her only solace had become her faith in God and she had a sudden, alarming vision of that too being snatched from her.

'The father is a good man!' she cried, taking several quick steps to stand before Cunedda. 'He is a man of God and answerable to Him only. You have no right to make such a vile accusation!'

Cunedda turned on her. 'Enough of your tongue! If it were not for my son you would have been thrown beyond my walls afore now! I have ordered the stoning of better women than you!' He was standing before her now, one hand raised, finger pointing. 'Your Christianity, lady, means betrayal and murder!'

Someone echoed agreement, cursing the priest and his God. Another spat upon the poxed Christian religion. Voices began to rise, the curses more volatile. It needed little for frustrated, bewildered and defeated men to reach for a revenge closer to home. Someone took up a torch, another cried for action. They rose as one and left the Hall, hands grasping more torches, the ululation of anger and defiance rising like the blood lust of the hunt.

The cheering swelled as the fire took hold of the squat chapel, the laughter rising with the flames licking up the walls, eating hungrily at the roof.

Branwen sat slumped in a heap by the hearth, weeping bitter tears at the roar and crackle of destruction. What was left to her now? Her church was gone!

Osmail stood helpless, torn between his faith and his father. His mouth worked but spilt no sound.

The three were the only occupants of the Hall; even the servants had run outside to witness the bright glare of burning. Cunedda was seated again, drinking deep draughts from his tankard. A small taste of revenge this, but as sweet as comb from the hive. He was aware his son followed the Christian religion with devoted passion. Aware, but suddenly, unreasonably, resentful.

His wife had loved Christ, and Christ had taken her from him. Damn Christ, all curses on the Christian God!

Brutally he said, 'You may weep, woman. Shed your tears for a traitor whose action will bring more bitterness to this family than any pagan devil ever would.'

Osmail knelt to comfort Branwen, then looked for a moment at his father who sat swilling wine, seeming to enjoy the frenzy outside. Osmail, who could never say the right words, do the right thing. Osmail, who believed in the love of God above all else. Osmail, who had at last discovered what it meant, how it felt, to be master.

He stood up and walked slowly over to his father. His throat felt dry, his heart pounded but this thing was for him to do, this last hurdle set for him to leap. 'I shall leave on the morrow. My sons shall not be raised where God is not welcome.'

'God is more than welcome. His traitorous servants are not.'

'In my way, I am a servant of God,' Osmail said. 'Am I then a traitor?' He paused, willing his father to say something more, plead for him to stay. Nothing. No word.

'I will take Branwen to a holy house, somewhere that will appreciate generous funding.' He did not add, *'Where I and my wife will be welcome; where I will be useful.'* He had gone to Branwen's side. She looked up at him, her eyes full of wonderment. Was this her husband speaking? Was it Osmail saying these words she had prayed one day to hear? He helped her to her feet and she threaded her arm through his; went proud beside him as they walked from the Hall.

Only once did Osmail feel an urge to look back, to look one last time at his father. But he did not. To look back would be to admit weakness. And he could not risk losing this sudden-found, unexpected courage.

§ XVIII

The first pink fingers of dawn were creeping across the paling night sky as Cunedda rode out alone, eyes hollow and red rimmed from lack of sleep, desperate to outrun the wallowing despair. He urged his stallion into a mad gallop along the sea-wet sand, and the wind clawed at his cloak, stinging his face like arrows. The horse stretched its body, the firm, taut muscles rippling, strong legs pounding, crested neck extended his small pointed ears flat back and nostrils flaring. His tail arched, spreading like a banner. Distance was swallowed beneath his speed.

Cunedda let him run; let him go until he slowed of his own accord, head tossing, flecks of foam flying. The horse eased to a crab canter, slowed to a bouncing trot and finally down to a blowing walk. Cunedda brought him to a halt and slid, defeated, from the saddle to stand in the swirl of the incoming sea.

Not since his wife's death had grief torn so pitilessly at his heart.

The ugly submission to Vortigern weighed unbearable. Conscience wrestled with pride of leadership. Was he right to put Gwynedd before his children? Yet all of Gwynedd, all the people – rich, poor, Eldermen, farmer, peasant, servant and slave – were they not all his children? Anger at the unjustness followed the outpouring of sorrow. The Dragon Banner flew for the new Pendragon. Like Uthr, this one would be back to fight openly or with more subtle means. Either way, the Red Dragon survived to claw its way to the throne. Vortigern knew this now, knew he had still to watch the shadows.

Cunedda laughed, a roar of desperate grief, remembering Vortigern's expression on learning of Arthur's existence – no further sense in hiding the truth. He had told the King outright, after kneeling in public homage and agreeing wholesale to Vortigern's terms. It had been most pleasant to see the King's sardonic smile of triumph wiped instant away.

The brief glow of pleasure faded. The tide swirled around Cunedda's boots, climbing up the beach. Because of Arthur's perilous position, ungrown and untried, he had no choice but to accept Vortigern's demands. No choice.

A single gull swept low with a harsh, mournful cry. Cunedda crumpled to his knees, slammed his fists into the surf and raged at the bird.

'By all the power I hold, and all the gods that ever were or will be, I shall see to it that the claws of the Dragon rake deep for this, Vortigern!'

APRIL 451

§ XIX

They were trying out some of Uthr's best wine, stored for special occasions. What could be more special than an unexpected visit to the estate in Less Britain by Cunedda of Gwynedd! Besides, as Arthur pointed out, breaking the wax seal on an amphora of Vintage Greek, it would not keep forever.

They drank companionably, the young man and the elder, admiring the red glow of a sinking sun and exchanging talk of brave men and braver deeds. A cool, pleasant evening for early April. Spring had come early, bringing mild nights and sunny days, a promise of a fair summer. Cunedda had risked the sea voyage, for he had need to talk with Arthur, the kind of conversation that could not be well written on wax tablet or scrolled parchment, or conveyed by messenger. This was for him alone to say, but now that he was here the saying was not going to be so easy.

Arthur cut himself a chunk of soft goat cheese and said, almost flippantly, 'So what brings the lord of Gwynedd to my mother's estate?' He lifted his goblet, a rare, fine glass of the palest green, and saluted his companion. 'This wine is the best, but it does not warrant such a hazardous journey.'

Cunedda loosed a brief smile. 'Nor such a short stay. I remain but the one night; raiders are hovering off Gwynedd's shores. My sons are capable, but I do not like to leave her too long.'

Arthur chuckled. 'You make your land sound like a wayward mistress!'

Cunedda gave another small smile. Arthur would find out for himself one day, the gods willing. Held land was more than a mistress – was whore, wife, daughter, mother, all of those, with all their tempers and loves and smiles and sorrows.

Arthur's eyes had a question, one eye half closed, the other eyebrow raised. 'Why have you come?'

Clearing his throat – this would not be well met – Cunedda placed the tips of his fingers together. 'I will be open with you, lad, no shuffling around the arena exchanging feints.'

Arthur nodded.

'I suggest, Arthur, you offer your sword to Vortigern.'

A moment's silence – nothing moving, no sound, no breath – then the fine glass flew from the table shattering into tiny pieces as it hit the floor. Arthur's chair toppled backwards as he exploded to his feet in a torrent of abusive language, some words new even to Cunedda's ears.

Waiting for the violent diatribe to subside Cunedda sat patiently; the reaction had not been unexpected. Calmly he continued, 'Come summer you will be seven and ten years of age, a man grown, the son of a war lord. Yet you sit here, idling away your time picking grapes and pressing wine!'

Arthur had been about to add further disparaging remarks, but Cunedda slammed the flat of his hand on the table, his expression fierce. 'What do you intend, boy? To be a vine grower or a soldier?' Allowing him no time to reply, he went on, 'You need experience of war, of leading men. How are you to gain it here?'

His pride stung, Arthur countered, 'I serve with the local militia. A month back we sent scurrying a party of Saex who were attempting to set up a settlement to the south!'

Cunedda sipped his wine. 'Sit down. Let us talk of men's business like men.'

Glowering, Arthur sat.

'I have heard you train hard with the militia, that you do well.'

Gruff. 'You have sharp ears then.'

'Would you rather I left you to rot?' The rebuke was sharp, to the point. Cunedda refilled his glass, handed it to Arthur, who took it and drank. With sympathy the lord of Gwynedd took a breath and continued. 'Where will you gain experience of war if not in Britain with Vortigern's British men?'

Arthur stared into the fading red glow in the western sky, his lips pouting. Where, indeed?

'Without experience, Arthur, men will laugh when you come to claim what is yours. Aside,' Cunedda spread a hand, 'if we do not soon drive out these Saex, there will be nothing left for you to claim.'

Arthur answered, 'I thought of approaching the King of Gaul, he and Uthr were friends. I have met with his son several times, we are of similar age,' but he spoke with only half a heart. He did not, in all truth, really wish to fight to save some other king's land. Though he was reluctant to admit it, at least fighting for Vortigern would, indirectly, mean fighting for himself.

Reading Arthur accurately Cunedda offered, 'Working for your own ends would give you more of an advantage.'

The hot reply was defiant, anger and resentment rising again. 'Not if I need bow before Vortigern!'

'You do not have to bow before him.' Cunedda could be so damned persuasive, particularly when he spoke calmly, placidly, somehow making Arthur's raging seem like childish temper.

'Gather those men who once followed your father, and their sons, all who would follow the Dragon.' Cunedda was leaning forward, eager, excited. 'Offer their swords, under yours, to Vortigern. Gain time. Get to know the ways of war, and the hills and valleys of Britain; the marshes, the coast. The people. Let them get to know *you*.' His smile for future planning crinkled to his eyes. 'Befriend the tyrant, tell him the disagreement was between him and the father you did not know. Make him believe you are content with holding these estates, you want nothing more. Offer what you can, bribe where you can. Sit, listen, watch and learn.'

Petulant, reluctant to acknowledge Cunedda might be right, Arthur rasped, 'And what if Vortigern will not accept me and takes a dagger to my back at the first opportunity?' He slammed his fist on the table. 'Damn it, I am the Pendragon! He will not trust one of that title for a single handspan!'

'Of course he will not – no more than he trusts me – yet we get along reasonably well, if warily.' Draining his goblet, Cunedda laid his hand on Arthur's arm. 'Vortigern will take you and, providing you step carefully, he will tolerate you.'

'Why? Tell me that. Why will he?' Arthur slumped back in his chair, arms folded, bottom lip thrust out. Stupid idea. Might as well fall on his own sword and make an end of it rather than offer himself to that murdering bastard.

'Why? Because Vortigern would prefer to keep you where he can see you. Where he can be certain you are not raising an army against him. Also, he's a desperate man. He has few British officers with a talent for soldiering. Even he has no wish to turn his entire army over to the Saxons!'

'Are you listening to yourself, Cunedda? You seriously expect me to fight under that – that toad who murdered my father!'

'Aye.'

There was no point in saying anything further, for that was precisely what Cunedda was expecting. They argued some more, Arthur offering protests, Cunedda countering with adequate answers. Both knew Cunedda spoke sense, that Arthur had no choice. He needed experience, he needed to learn, and neither would come his way here in Less Britain.

'I would willingly have you with me, lad,' Cunedda sighed, as a final thrust, 'but were you to join with me I'd have more Saex in my mountains than there are blades of grass. Vortigern would never permit it.'

Mid-afternoon the next day, a trading ship lifted her oars and glided downriver making for the estuary. Aboard her, Cunedda, heading home, and by the turn of the month another ship carried Arthur, his cousin and foster brother Cei, and sixty seasoned swordsmen to Britain and mercenary service under the tyrant King, Vortigern.

APRIL 453

§ XX

Councillors drifted from the dilapidated basilica of Londinium in knots of twos and threes; huddled groups talking softly to one another, exchanging muted grievances, mostly against the King.

Arthur sighed exaggeratedly and tipped his stool back on its rear legs. 'There's only one thing I dread more than a full meeting of Council.'

Seated beside him, arms folded on the table, Cei looked with lazy enquiry at his foster brother and cousin, asked, 'And what might that be?'

Arthur stood, scraping the stool over the cracked flooring. He stretched cramped muscles, reaching his arms up towards the equally cracked ceiling and yawned. 'The next meeting!' He grinned and thumped his friend between the shoulder blades. 'What a damned waste of time! There are days when I regret my decision to throw my soul in with Vortigern.' He walked a few paces, flung his arm in the direction of the open door, declared with passion, 'We ought to be out there, Cei, fighting these sea wolves who come to steal our cattle and land, not sitting here muttering about it!'

Cei nodded agreement, opened his mouth to reply, found another voice cut him short.

'Aye, but try telling our beloved King!' Arthur spun round with a yelp of delight and clasped the newcomer's hand in greeting, jerking the arm up and down as if it were some rusted old water pump.

'Cunedda! You have come!' He motioned a thumb over his shoulder. 'You have just missed the first pointless discussion.'

Cunedda's hands were clasping Arthur's arms in firm greeting. 'If only I had ridden faster!' They all three laughed at his open sarcasm.

'The Saex sit easy on their backsides and wait for us to talk ourselves into old age and beyond,' said Cei sardonically, draining his ale tankard and setting it down on the table.

'All possibilities need exploring before action is committed.' Cunedda so perfectly mimicked Vortigern's much uttered phrase, even to the slight slurring of the Latin, a legacy of a sword wound to his left jaw.

'Meaning,' Arthur translated through the ensuing laughter, 'let us not rush into anything that's likely to cost over much from my treasury!' He gripped the older man's hand tighter. 'Ah, Cunedda, it's good to see you!' His smile broadened. 'I was not keen on persuading this Council into seeing sense on my own!'

''Tis as good to see you again, boy.' Placing his hand on Arthur's shoulder, Cunedda studied the young man before him. 'You are taller than your father, though much like him.' He approved of what he saw. A confident young man with an alert eagerness and self-assurance. Different colouring from Uthr, who had had quite black hair, Arthur's being more brown with a slight curl, but the same family trait of a long, prominent nose and that same piercing eye.

A leader of men, Uthr, superb in a fight but never one for patience or tact, too often a raging bull. At eighteen, it was too early to tell whether the same leadership qualities were strong in this lad. Cunedda frowned, his brows creasing into a deeper, more penetrating search of Arthur's animated face. Something simmered beneath the surface of those brown eyes beaming back at him, something ready to spill out when the heat was raised. This Pendragon possessed a more profound shrewdness than Uthr ever had, a sparkle that would rise to brilliance with the catch of sunlight.

Cunedda was reminded of an uncut diamond he had once seen. A thing of great value, he had been told, though for his life he could not understand why. A rough-hewn, rather dull, almost ugly object. And then the same stone after the jewelsmith had been at it; a gem so exquisite, so perfect, there were no words to describe the beauty that flashed and blazed within its cut and polished facets. Arthur reminded him of that diamond: rough-edged, unpolished, but beneath those disguising layers, ah, beneath!

Suddenly remembering his manners, Arthur indicated Cei, jolting Cunedda from his scrutiny. 'You remember Cei, eldest son of Ectha my uncle and foster father? He is a second right arm to me.'

'We met briefly when I visited Less Britain.'

'Everything about it was brief, as I recall,' Arthur growled. A pause, recollections of that unexpected visit. And the consequences.

'So,' Cunedda said, 'Vortigern has not put a dagger in your back? He accepted you, as I predicted he would.'

Arthur's lip and nose wrinkled in distaste. '*Na*, no dagger. We have, shall we say, an uneasy understanding.' He laughed suddenly. 'You leave my back alone and I'll leave yours alone!'

As the slight moment of tension slipped past, Cunedda nodded and grasped Cei's hand, pleased to meet the young man again. 'I have heard tell of your exploits with Arthur, they reach even as far as my distant mountains of Gwynedd!'

Cei's laugh was a deep-throated chuckle of wry amusement. 'The blame for those lay firmly with Arthur; he's the planner I merely follow orders! Though one or two of his schemes have turned out well.'

Arthur interrupted with a snort of indignation. 'Well? They are brilliant, man!'

Cei raised his eyebrows, unabashed. 'All? What about last September – Glas Dhue?'

Rubbing his clean-shaven chin, Arthur grimaced then casually placed an arm around Cunedda's shoulders, steering the older man aside. 'How's your brood? Are your sons with you?'

Cunedda roared his delight. 'No need to turn the subject! I heard of Glas Dhue also! A brilliant – what – failure?'

Arthur scowled, then smiled good humouredly, appreciating the jest at his expense. 'Had it not been for that sudden deluge turning firm ground into marsh, we would have sent fifty Saex into oblivion.'

Understanding the frustrations of an unexpected change in the weather, Cunedda nodded. 'You cannot win all the time, lad; learn by your mistakes, take defeat positively. Your father had his share of failure,' he added sombrely, then smiled swiftly. It was well to turn the subject on occasion. 'Three of my offspring are with me.' He glanced at the few remaining men and said softly, 'There's much to talk upon, in private.' He glanced meaningfully at those last men who were noting with interest this friendly exchange between Lion and Dragon.

Few had forgotten where Gwynedd's loyalty lay.

Louder, for the benefit of curious ears, Cunedda remarked, 'We attend Vortigern's welcoming entertainment this evening. Will you join me, Arthur? Cei also, of course.'

Thanking him for the invitation, Cei made his apologies, pleading an alternative engagement.

Arthur leered. 'With that well-endowed widow, no doubt?' he slapped Cei's shoulder. 'Vortigern's feasting would be more rewarding!'

Countering swiftly, Cei retorted, 'The King cannot offer such large,' made a suggestive motion with his hands, 'ripe fruit!'

Laughing together the three men pushed their way through the crowded exit out into the open forum, where they took their leave, followed by more than a few speculative glances.

Vortigern's palace had seen better days when it had been the residence of the Roman Governor of Britain. Years of neglect had traded its opulence for cracked walls and peeling plaster. Rugs and spread furs hid fragmenting mosaic floors; the hypocaust heating was blocked and useless. Still, who noticed crumbling walls and the occasional hole in the ceiling when good wine flowed and excellent food was served?

They were all there, Vortigern and his kin: his sons by his first wife; the second wife, Rowena, with her father, Hengest the Saxon, and his son; the daughter born to Rowena and Vortigern, the Princess Winifred. The King's guests were the Elders and leaders of the governing territories of Britain who made up the Grand Council, some of whom had brought their wives and families, sons, brothers and uncles, as well as officers of the King's army and bodyguard, British and Saxon. A hotch-potch of nobility and rough chieftains, intent on clawing their way from tribal landholding to the prospect of eventual petty kingship.

Arthur ate with enthusiasm: army food was nothing special, the slop served in Londinium taverns as bad, and it was not often Vortigern opened his purse to pay for an extravagance such as this!

'How is your mother?' Enniaun asked politely, finishing the last of a fine roast fowl.

'I have no idea.' Arthur selected more meat and bit into it hungrily.

'You do not keep contact with her then?'

With mouth full Arthur replied, 'To what end? We never liked each other. My father's death and my coming to manhood did not alter that.'

Etern, a man grown now with a moustache as red as his father's, said with a hint of reproach, 'She is your mother.'

His voice indifferent, Arthur answered, 'Childbearing does not make a woman a mother.'

'But surely, after all these years, now you are acknowledged as...'

Arthur cut off Etern's persistent questions quite philosophically. 'In childhood I meant nothing to Lady Ygrainne, I mean nothing to her now.' His plate empty, he chose a meat filled pastry shaped in the form of a sucking pig. As a boy his life had been endorsed by periods of intense misery – the shame at being labelled bastard, the whisperings of speculation. And Morgause. Release came through Uthr's death. Arthur had understood his father's need to stay silent; Ygrainne's too, but not her coolness. It was not within him to forgive her for abandoning him to Morgause.

'You blame me for my father's death, don't you?' Arthur had asked Ygrainne before he left to serve in Vortigern's army. She had answered quite frankly; 'It was because of you I lost him.'

He had assumed she meant Uthr's death; only much later did he realise she meant Uthr's turning to Morgause.

124

Pulling at his moustache Cunedda said thoughtfully, 'She and your father were very much in love when Uthr took her from Gorlois.'

Arthur gave a bark of scornful laughter, scattering golden pastry crumbs from his lips. 'Nonsense! He wanted her wealth and her dead father's estate. Fighting Gorlois was an excuse to hit at Vortigern, fanning the flames of a war that was already brewing. Uthr would have done anything to further his bid for the kingdom. As would I.' Another trait inherited from his father, cynicism.

Servants were bringing in the next course, the guests applauding the spectacular arrangements of boar and hare and swan, borne high on silver platters so huge they needed two men to carry them.

When eating had again commenced, Enniaun asked the Pendragon, his voice lowered, 'And how is service with our King?'

The reply was succinct. 'Oh, wonderful! He's a most uninspiring man.'

Etern guffawed. 'That must keep alive a desire to knock his head from his shoulders!' They laughed, then sobered on remembering their whereabouts.

'Vortigern treats you well, I hear, almost like one of his own brood?' Enniaun wiped boar meat juice from his dish with a hunk of wheat bread and nodded at Vortigern's two sullen sons seated at the high table. It was noticeable that they both ignored their father, their manner towards his Saxon wife verging on rudeness.

'Oh aye.' Arthur stabbed at a portion of hare, busied himself with picking the meat from the bone, kept his expression guarded. 'We fight and snarl at each other like whelps over a tossed bone.'

Flicking a finger in Hengest's direction, Etern commented, 'I'm not impressed by his choice of company.'

Arthur scowled towards the high table, at the huge Saxon, a great bull-muscled man with arms like oak trees, thighs as sturdy as a ship's mast, and privy tackle, it was said, as penetrating as a well shot javelin. Unfortunately the Princess Winifred noticed his expression – and he looked hastily away. Like her mother, that one, a second arrogant and self-opinionated sow. Pretty, though, as her mother had once been, with flaxen hair and fair skin. But a temper like a rutting bear. He chewed at his meat, throwing a quick smile at the young woman sitting beside the princess. Her face came alive at that smile, eyes and mouth smiling back.

Arthur had come late to the banquet, hurrying and breathless, delayed by the need to tend an injury to his favourite horse. Entering as the guests were summoned to table, he had stood stunned at the sight of Gwenhwyfar waiting with her father and two brothers. He had not expected her to be with Cunedda, was unprepared to see her, a woman grown and so different from the girl he remembered. She had been as flustered as himself, her cheeks flushing pink as he kissed her hand; then their rather awkward embrace, as if greeting a stranger. A pity she was seated as Vortigern's guest, companion to the royal piglet, Winifred. He dare not glance often in her direction for fear of shifting this persistent throb beneath his bracae to something more noticeable on his face. Why? With other women he made much of his desire, had discovered they found the attention most flattering. With Gwenhwyfar, such crudity seemed obscene. She was beautiful and pure, a maiden to be respected, treated with honour. But by the Blood of the Bull, how he wanted to leap up from this table, cross the room in three strides and kiss her! Not a polite kiss of greeting either, but a slow, lingering kiss that would last for days and take all breath from the world!

Enniaun was remarking, 'Vortigern seems well at ease among those who wear a flaxen mane and carry a Saex sword.'

'Jesu's love,' Etern spat beneath his breath, 'when will we be rid of him and these pox-ridden Saex! It is time you became king, Arthur!'

Taking a while to drain his goblet, Arthur wiped his mouth and shifted to a more comfortable position. The food might be good, but these benches were damned hard on the backside! 'I am in the King's service, Etern, I command men of his cavalry. Such talk could soon see me kicking on the wrong end of a rope.'

About to say more, Etern found Cunedda's stern gaze on him. Not here, boy, not now.

'Aside,' Arthur said, setting his goblet down carefully. 'Vortimer's the eldest son. When Vortigern dies, he takes up the royal torque, not I.'

'Pig-swill!'

Laughing to himself, Arthur thought of his earlier analogies: Rowena the sow, Winifred the plump little piglet. Aye, pig-swill. Patiently, he waved aside Etern's derision. 'I support Vortimer, he's as much against the King as are we. We cannot afford to fight among ourselves; if we do, we may as well stand back and invite Hengest in. He waits for a squabble in the front gate so he may creep in at the back.' With a leisurely shrug, 'Vortigern cannot live forever. Things will change when his eldest son comes to power.'

'True enough,' replied Enniaun, emphasising his point by flapping his eating dagger, 'but Vortimer himself is no spring cockerel – he could journey to the next world before his father.'

'Or,' added Etern, 'Vortigern's wife could yet bear a son.'

They glanced furtively at Rowena, again heavy with child. A beautiful woman once but the years of constant pregnancies that ended in miscarriage or stillbirth had not been kind. None save her own people and the King much liked her.

A brooding silence descended on Cunedda's table, their individual thoughts broken by Etern. 'Even if she did, who would want to follow a half Saex brat?'

His brother laughed, the humour cut short by Arthur's unexpectedly curt response. 'Hengest and the Saex would.'

Servants cleared away used dishes, removing uneaten food. Conversation turned to lighter matters. Several times Cunedda noticed Arthur looking at his daughter. Vortigern had expressed the wish to have Gwenhwyfar sit at table with his family – how could Cunedda refuse? He gulped a mouthful of strong wine, gestured to a slave to pour more. How did a lord refuse Vortigern the King without risking the loss of land and people?

Cunedda had known Uthr well, had run with him as a cub, fought with him, pursued women with him. Now he recognised that same look in his son's eyes, knew Arthur took after his father in more than a love of soldiering and a similarity of features. Women seemed drawn to a Pendragon as water was drawn downhill. How pleased he had been those summers past to discover his Gwenhwyfar had formed a friendship with Arthur – Gods, how pleased! He remembered how Uthr had first met with Ygrainne, then wed to another, and had wanted her. 'Nonsense,' Arthur had said when he had spoken of Uthr's love for her, but Uthr had started a war because of Ygrainne. The aim was to claim the kingship, but it started because of his desire for Ygrainne.

Ah, Uthr had loved Ygrainne, always, Ygrainne, and only Ygrainne. The others, all the others, had only fulfilled a passing need. Another thought, that again made Cunedda drain his wine. What if Vortigern were also to read Arthur's glances towards the girl? He should not have brought her to Londinium! He rolled his goblet between his hands, staring into the empty cup. A burst of laughter from the assembled company caused him to look up. How does a snared lord ignore a summons from the King?

'*Do not harbour dreams for my daughter, Arthur,*' Cunedda thought with anguish. '*She cannot be yours.*'

It was late when Vortigern at last withdrew. Rowena had retired earlier, taking the ladies with her. Reluctantly, Gwenhwyfar had left the banqueting hall with them, casting a pleading look at her father, who had responded with a gesture of helplessness. She had endured the princess's insults and snide remarks all evening, had swallowed her pride and her temper though her palm itched to slap the horrid girl's fat cheeks. They were almost the same age, no more than half a year between them, but that was their only similarity.

'Do you ride?' the princess had enquired.

'Aye,' Gwenhwyfar had replied, to which Winifred had answered scornfully, 'Mother says horse riding bows your legs. I will only travel by litter.' Such was the conversation for most of the evening.

To her relief Gwenhwyfar discovered she was not obliged to accompany the ladies to the Queen's rooms, but was free to return to her own quarters where poor Ceridwen lay abed with a feverish headache. She entered the semi-darkened room quietly, whirled a few joyful paces and danced from the door to bed.

Ceridwen sat up, her eyes bleary. The journey from Gwynedd had been exhausting – mentally, because of the excitement, as well as physically.

'You sound happy. The banquet was good then?'

Gwenhwyfar did a few more twirls before plonking herself on Ceridwen's bed. The goose feather mattress bounced up and down. 'It was awful! The food was far too rich and I had to sit next to the Princess, a spoilt madam if ever I met one!'

Ceridwen frowned. Her head ached, her stomach still churned; had she missed something here? 'May I ask then,' she said timorously, 'why you are so gay?' She twitched Gwenhwyfar's neat hair. 'You have met someone! A lad.' She sat up eagerly. 'Who? What's he like?'

Gwenhwyfar was off the bed, hugging herself as she skipped away across the room, deliberately teasing. When the fluttering excitement became too much she ran back to Ceridwen and hugged her. 'Arthur's here! Arthur the Pendragon. I assumed he would be on campaign or something, but no, he's here!' She lay back across the bed, arms flung wide, gazing up at the cracks on the ceiling. 'Oh, Ceridwen, he has grown so tall, so...' she released her breath in a whoosh, 'so wonderful!'

Ceridwen said nothing, snuggled into the warmth of her bed. It was only April, quite chilly at night, and this great echoing palace seemed rather musty and damp.

'Oh,' she said, feigning indifference, 'you're in love. I thought something exciting had happened.'

Despite the girl's headache, Gwenhwyfar thumped her with a pillow.

Winifred lingered before seeking her bed. She detested her father's banquets – boring occasions for boring old men with boring conversations. She paused, her comb halfway down the tress of her unbound hair. She combed her own hair; the slaves were too clumsy, they pulled. One or two presentable young men this evening, but country clods, sons of over-ambitious petty lords. She would not waste time with such dismal prospects.

Winifred sighed, set the comb down, walked aimlessly towards the bed. Arthur, now, he was no dung-shoveller, he was the Pendragon, wealthy, in command of her father's cavalry. She twitched back the bed furs, slid beneath the smooth linen of the sheets. He was not exactly the most handsome young man, though, was he?

Snuffing out the lamp beside the bed, Winifred settled herself to sleep, lying with her arms crooked behind her head, thinking. Arthur Pendragon was the most presumptuous, impertinent, discourteous lout in all her father's army. She had paid him no heed before this night – but it interested her, this interaction between him and that rustic bred girl from wherever it was.

And there was nothing Winifred liked better than destroying a lovers' intrigue.

§ XXI

Cunedda selected an olive and studied it for a moment, wondering for how much longer such succulent fruits would be obtainable. Leather, glass, metal, cloth, everything of quality was disappearing, becoming more difficult to get hold of. Cheap stuff – now that was readily available, shoddy goods, badly made, poorly crafted – ah, it was all going, gathering speed, rumbling away downhill.

This chamber, a fair sized room, overlooked the palace gardens, attractive in the moonlight but revealed by day to be a mess of cracked paths, weed-choked flower beds and straggling, unkempt shrubs. Cunedda stood by a table, his two sons sprawling on couches, draped like discarded clothing.

'Your inspired use of cavalry, Arthur,' he said, moving to the nearest couch and cuffing Etern's boots from the cushions before sitting down, 'is earning you quite a reputation.'

Arthur, perched on the edge of a stool, picked with the tip of his dagger at a morsel of meat caught between his teeth. 'Most of my boyhood was spent with a good friend, an old soldier whose farm borders the estate. Gaius served in a Roman cavalry unit. I learned much from him.' Warming to his subject, he expatiated. 'I have tried to develop more than the basic tactics and skills within the limits of my own command.' He frowned, busy with placing the dagger back in its sheath. 'But in all skirmishes not under my sole command we are held back. My fine mounted men are used for reconnaissance or harrying the enemy when he's already in flight!' Contemptuously he sliced the air with his outstretched hand. 'You,

Sir,' he said, looking straight at Cunedda, 'use your horses with more intelligence, as the tribal British have always done.'

'Indeed, some of Rome's best cavalrymen were British, and our ponies crossed with the better of Rome's imported mounts have proved more than their worth as war mounts.' Cunedda sighed, nudged Etern further along the couch, stretched himself comfortably. He had drunk too much wine at that banquet; now it was swilling around in his belly with an over-indulgence of food, and the day's ride atop that. By the Gods, but he was tired. 'Vortigern, like so many others, prefers infantry. Horses cost more to keep.'

Arthur waved the Lion's words aside. 'I know all that.' His smile was a lop-sided grin, his right eye half shut and left eyebrow cocked, giving him a penetrating, self assured expression that seemed to bore into Cunedda. 'None the less, you have continued breeding good horses, Cunedda. You know there's more to using a horse than just placing your arse on its back to get from alpha to beta.'

Cunedda swallowed down a belch and regarded the lad, undaunted by that off-putting gaze. Cautiously, 'A cavalryman knows more than how to lullump along clutching at mane and saddle, aye.'

'A good cavalryman is a horseman. Men under my command are all horsemen. They, Vortigern's mules,' he jabbed a finger towards the window, 'grunt and mumble, refusing to listen to any suggestions I attempt to put forward. The high ranking commanders of the army – I include Vortigern's sons here – argue that we have fought well enough with infantry for centuries so why change now?' He had his dagger out again, was twirling it between his fingers. 'Fah! They see no further than day's end!'

Containing his amusement, Cunedda could almost see his old friend Uthr sitting before him, bellowing some tirade against whatever near-sighted stupidity had enraged him on this occasion.

Arthur was still talking. 'Vortigern originally hired Hengest and his rabble because we do not have the men to furnish an effective army of infantry – Mithras, Rome could call on the entire Empire to swell ranks, but what have we? One stagnating little island, surrounded by water that every day brings yet another keel-load of Saex! How can we ever match the skill of Rome? Not with men on foot, for sure.' Eagerly he swept on, Enniaun and Etern giving nods or murmurs of agreement. 'Look at the success of Attila's Huns, who fight, eat, sleep – even copulate, so I've heard tell – on horseback.'

Enniaun said sharply, 'You sound as though you admire that Scourge of God!'

'As a commander and horseman, aye, I do.'

Etern almost shared Arthur's view. 'Attila was not infallible, though. Gaul defeated his dunghill mob.'

'Not so,' Arthur replied, leaning forward to rest his elbows on his knees. 'Attila was halted.' He stressed the word, 'Halted, not defeated. He turned round and went for Rome itself instead.' He cupped his chin thoughtfully in his hand. 'I wonder if our problems would have been less had he not died so prematurely – if he had continued into Gaul, and beyond.'

Faces turned to look at him in astonishment. Arthur grinned, confident of his argument. 'Would so many Saex have been eager to leave their kindred with Attila's sword coming daily closer to their throats?'

'On the dexter side,' Enniaun said drily, 'happen the Saex took to their keels because of Attila!'

'I heard,' Etern said, a well padded cushion held close against his chest as if it were a companionable woman, 'that Attila's remains were buried with three coffins containing all his wealth. One of gold, one of silver, one of iron.'

'Aye,' Arthur agreed, with a wistful sigh of slight envy, 'I heard the same. His funeral songs were sung by squadrons of his men riding round and around his body, which lay beneath a silken draped pavilion.' He whistled between his teeth. 'That must have been a sight worth the watching.'

They fell silent for a while, lost in their own thoughts. Etern stood up and fetched more wine. He took the jug round, pouring for his brother and Arthur. 'Think you this suggestion of Council to try another appeal for help to Gaul will be of use to us? Da says it will not.'

'I am in agreement with him.' Arthur wrinkled his upper lip. 'Attila's gone, but his hordes remain, and despite my admiration for his horsemanship, Enniaun, I am afeared of what his rabble almost succeeded in doing! *Na*, Gaul has too many of her own problems. We are abandoned to our fate. 'Tis a pity that some of these fusty Councillors cannot see Rome has gone from Britain for ever and will not be returning, not now.' He snorted, shaking his head. These older men were so blind – aye, and not only the older men! Uthr's own youngest brother, Emrys, claimed Rome would govern Britain again, and the Emperor would come swinging up the road from Dubris demanding to know what fool had let the country fall into such decay. 'If we do not soon stop all this sitting around a council chamber endlessly talking instead of doing, there will be nothing worth coming back to anyway!'

Cunedda had been listening through the drowsy fug of wine to the exchange of talk. He said cautiously, 'They are men, Arthur, who cannot perceive life outside the dominance of Rome. Others – influential, wealthy men – have tasted freedom from Imperial taxation and would not want a return of those binding restrictions.

Which is why Vortigern maintains such strong support. I do not want Rome, but then, I do not want Vortigern as an alternative. In my view we have exchanged one tyranny for another.'

Enniaun sipped his wine. This was fine stuff, Vortigern's best. 'Let them write their appeal. They may be right: when the unrest settles the Legions might be back. Although,' he raised his goblet towards Arthur in salute, 'I agree with you, lad.'

'If we got ourselves organised there would be no need to seek help!' Arthur bounced to his feet, fists waving. 'We can do it alone, drive out the Saex and make peace between neighbouring tribes!' Arthur slammed the arm of a couch with his fist. Damn it, he knew he was right, but how to make others see?

Cunedda sipped his wine reflectively. It was time for bed, but this talk was becoming interesting. He let a smile touch his mouth.

Seeing it, Arthur said, not without bitterness, 'You too laugh at me then?'

'On the contrary. Continue.'

For a moment Arthur was doubtful. His belly was full of men sniggering behind his back – and to his face. He would not have his father's friend also making mockery of his ideas. But then, those others were as useless as cracked pots; Cunedda was different, a man of wisdom and sense, a man who knew how it felt to be backed into a corner with only a broken sword for defence. He lifted a foot onto a stool and rested his arm across his thigh.

'I believe a strong, well-drilled cavalry force could tip the balance of survival in our favour.' Now he had started Arthur became eager to share his hopes, his plans. 'Attila usually fought with three wings, left, right and centre, crashing forward at a gallop.' He moved his hand ahead of him, but was interrupted by Enniaun.

'How many do you mean by *strong*?'

'Three alae comprising five hundred men each. Small enough to move fast and efficient. Large enough to be effective.'

Enniaun half smiled. 'Speaking kindly, lad, it is no surprise men laugh! That may not sound so many until you add on remounts and shield bearers and...'

Undeterred, Arthur would not allow him to finish. He had heard the arguments too many times before. 'Disciplined cavalry, under able commanders, moving fast to where they are needed, when needed. Used not as a reserve or for scouting or carrying packs and men to battle, but as a main, elite force. Coming down on the enemy from the centre and the wings together. '

'No infantry?'

'Aye, infantry, and archers, where needed, local militia who know the land.' As he talked, Arthur had straightened, setting his goblet down on a table to move freely about the room, gesturing with his arms. 'Normally it is the cavalry who back the foot. With my way of thinking I would reverse it. Cavalry swinging in here, militia with bows and javelins here.' Carried away, his arm sent a potted plant crashing to the floor.

Cunedda bit his lip, strangling a roar of laughter. He stood, retrieved the broken top half of the stem, looked at it with grave concern. 'Aye, well, I imagine the thing needed pruning.' He managed to stammer the words before the effort of restraint evaded him and he doubled up in laughter.

Enniaun, laughing also, bent to retrieve the bottom half. 'Curb your enthusiasm, Arthur,' he grinned, 'else we will be answerable to Vortigern for wrecking his apartment!'

Red-faced, stammering apologies, Arthur found his stool and sat down.

The laughter died, Cunedda dozed as lighter conversation gradually drifted to more mundane matters. Wine was poured and drunk as the young men exchanged notes on the virtues of women.

Cunedda sat quiet, drifting from sleep to thought and back to sleep. They needed time, a thing they never had! Time for Arthur to mature. Time for the elders and the British army to realise the great potential of this young Pendragon. Talk diminished momentarily, and Cunedda jerking awake asked, as if an hour had not elapsed, 'This use of cavalry, Arthur. Is it all formed of your own ideas?'

'A compilation of my veteran friend, Attila's history, and what I have read – the works of both Arrian and Xenophon on horsemanship are most informative.' Arthur shrugged. How to put the vivid images of his dreams into words? To face an enemy with a disciplined and united cavalry. An almighty, unstoppable force pounding down, forward... ah! 'I have discussed the thing with Cei; between us we have thrashed out the problems.' He paused and said with an impudent grin, 'Or rather, I have put the ideas and Cei has pointed out the pitfalls.'

Pulling at his moustache Cunedda asked, 'And what conclusions, Pendragon, have you reached regarding mounts for this wondrous cavalry? Until men like my father's father began cross-breeding fine horses, Rome imported its stock from Arabia. We do not have the ships or the funds to do that.' He deliberately cultivated a blank expression, talked in a flat tone. As if he could not guess the answer!

Arthur beamed. 'Your best horses are descended from those same desert bred Roman imports. Strong, swift, surefooted and stout-hearted warriors' mounts that do well, even on poor pasturing and in a bad winter.' Arthur's grin broadened, showing straight, even teeth, white against his wind tanned skin. 'I would come to Gwynedd.' He lifted his hands. 'Where else?'

Cunedda maintained his impassive expression; the muzziness of drink had cleared, that short sleep reviving his flagging energy. He barked, 'You are talking thousands of horses, boy! Remounts, as my son said, and remounts and remounts. Horses die, horses fall sick. Mares need the seasons to breed, to drop and suckle their foals.'

The Pendragon's buoyant confidence wavered. He chewed the corner of his bottom lip. Then, softly, 'I know.' He felt deflated, beaten. What nonsense was this? These men who would not listen were commanders, seasoned warriors, experienced with shield and sword, veterans of battle. They would not listen because he talked nonsense, a boy's prattling.

Cunedda took his time to drink a last cup of wine. When it was emptied he placed the goblet carefully beside him on the table and folded his arms across his belly, that still felt full.

'Are you so easily defeated then, boy?' he boomed, causing Arthur's dropping head to jolt upright, eyes wide, lips apart. 'Your father stopped at nothing to gain what he wanted. Aye, he had to wait and wait again, but he never hung his head in defeat! Never. Even as that last sword slashed into his body he fought on, fought on his knees and kept fighting until the blood had all run from him!'

Angered at the unjustness of the taunt, Arthur thrust back with, 'Na, he stopped at nothing to get his way! He wrecked my mother's life and my childhood. Because of his ambition you were forced to kneel before Vortigern in homage – twice. And for what, in the end? His death!'

Cunedda sucked in his breath, reeling at Arthur's attack – which struck all the harder, for he spoke the right of it. He pointed a finger, the golden lion's head of his ring seeming to leap at Arthur. 'You do not ask the impossible. My great-grandsire ran four, happen five times the stock you need – the highlands were adequate then, of course. We were granted overlordship of the Votadini because of our horses.' Cunedda shrugged, setting aside the pang of memory for those high hills and sweeping moors. He grinned, his face suddenly young. 'I see no reason why Gwynedd could not do the same for you.'

Arthur felt a sudden, soaring elation; he sprang to his feet and strode over to Cunedda, demanded, 'My idea is not so stupid? This thing could succeed?'

Etern interrupted, coming also to his feet, caught up in the excitement. 'We have good stallions and mares but it would take a while and a while to breed on such a scale again!'

Enniaun was behind him. 'The initial outlay, then the supply for future years. It would only take one fight to go bad, and close on all the horses would need replacing.

'*Na*, my son, with careful management it can be done.' Cunedda, pulling, as ever when thinking, at his moustache was making rapid calculations, taking into account the yearlings and foals to be dropped this year. Then there were the two and three year old colts. Sales had been low for some while – the failing economy and unsettled times made men wary of paying out for extravagances. Who needed a fine-bred horse when oxen were more suited to pulling wagon or plough? 'If I can be sure the Hibernian sea wolves have begun to understand my coastline is not for them, then I will be free to breed – and train – uninterrupted. Horses are not broken to carry a rider in battle overnight. It takes months, years.'

He slapped his knee with the palm of his hand, and rose to embrace Arthur. 'Aye, lad, I can breed you such a cavalry! Once you were up and leaping, you could raise additional stock elsewhere!' He offered his hand to Arthur, who took it warmly, returning the Lion's strong grip. Had it all been as easy as that?

Seating himself again Cunedda leant back against the comfort of his couch and crossed his legs at the knee. 'If, of course, you can come up with some equally brilliant method of payment. I do not breed horses for nought. I am wealthy, boy,' Cunedda thrust his grim, determined face at Arthur, 'and intend to stay so!'

There was always the sting in the tail. Uneasily Arthur drew back a little, Etern and Enniaun on either side of him, waiting. He wiped a hand nervously over his mouth, found to his annoyance he was sweating. 'I have thought of that also.'

Cunedda waited.

The words were unexpectedly difficult to spit out. Why? It was a natural enough proposition, was it not? A common way of settling business. Words tumbled from Arthur's mouth like a stream at winter snow-melt.

'When I become king, I intend to raise taxes from my father's lands that shall then be returned to me, and from the fat merchants of the South. In the main it's they who demand the protection, so they must contribute towards the cost.' That part was easy; this next made his tongue stick to the roof of his mouth. 'Initially, I would accept the horses as a marriage portion with your daughter.'

Cunedda's heart jolted, seemed to stop then began pounding wildly. He felt sick, the surge of rich food and sweet wine rising almost into his mouth. Fool! Damned blind, idiotic fool! Why had he not anticipated the obvious? What was he to say? How could he answer?

He studied the expectant faces of his two sons. They were nodding and smiling, agreeable to the idea, Etern even patting Arthur between the shoulders, especially pleased.

Cunedda stood. His bones ached; the tiredness had returned with a vengeance. He walked slowly across to the window, opened the casement, stood looking out at the river mist that lay over the dark gardens. Somewhere an owl screeched, its cry mournful in the darkness of early morning.

The pleased laughter behind him subsided. Why did he not answer?

He had known this day would come. These months, these years, he had known he must one day reveal the second part of that dirt-encrusted, enforced submission to Vortigern. He should have told of it then, but it had hurt too deeply. The buying of freedom by the binding of another. It hurt as much now, more, but it had to come out. He faced the room. Turned to his sons and Arthur.

'You cannot. Gwenhwyfar is already pledged.'

§ XXII

Stillness. No word, no murmur. Then, like hounds released from the leash to the strong scent of a stag the two brothers protested, shouting together, questioning, expressing outrage.

'Who to?'

'When?'

'Why?'

Nothing from Arthur. Oblivious to the surge of anger around him, he remained quiet, numbed, cheated.

The possibility had never occurred to him. She had never been far from his mind; always, since that night of childhood parting, he had assumed she would be his, one day. Gwenhwyfar had been special to him even then. She was his, damn it. His!

This evening, he had been so certain she still felt the same, that she had not changed. The long legs, awkward body and freckled, usually grimed face were now just a memory. In their place, copper-gold hair, tamed though not altogether obedient, framing a perfect face, with gold-flecked emerald eyes that had flashed with pleasure whenever their gaze met across the banqueting hall. He wanted to hold her, take her for his own. To talk and laugh with her, share that special closeness they had found on the hills of Gwynedd. Arthur had always intended to come back for her. For her, not for the horses... that idea had come later.

His throat felt dry, choked. With a shaking hand he reached for wine, hoped no one noticed the spillage as he lifted it to his lips. Mithras, he had been so sure of her! Had he been deceived then, by those innocent green eyes? She was devoted to another. Who? Whoever it was, he would kill him before he laid a finger to Gwenhwyfar!

'What means this, Father?' Etern demanded. His elder brother, with a calm that did not fool anyone added in a low voice, 'You said nought of this.'

'Must I then discuss my plans with you?' snapped Cunedda. Enniaun was his favourite son, the eldest since Osmail had left Gwynedd. Cunedda had never raised his voice to him before.

'This must spoil your plans, Arthur,' Etern remarked wryly. 'I trust you were not considering marriage with our sister on the grounds of gaining Gwynedd's horses alone. Happen you would do better to wed one of our mares.'

Cunedda remained by the window. Tears were brimming in his eyes as he held his hands, palm open in attempted apology, out to Arthur. 'The horses are yours when you need them, lad. Payment can be negotiated later.' He added, well intentioned, 'There are plenty of wealthy young women ripe for the picking.'

'But Da,' Etern entreated, 'Gwenhwyfar loves Arthur!' He looked pleadingly from his father to the Pendragon. 'I know how much she loves you.'

Arthur shrugged as if he did not much care. 'Love?' he said off-handedly. 'What has love to do with marriage? Happen you speak right, Cunedda.' He grunted a single rasp of laughter. 'I ought wed with Vortigern's daughter. Her dowry would buy ten times the number of horses I need.' His jesting was flat and unconvincing. He walked to the table, refilled his goblet and raised it to his lips, to mask the stabbing hurt.

The one comfort, if it could be so described, this seemed not to be of Gwenhwyfar's doing.

Etern glared fiercely at his father. 'Why have you not spoken of this? How could you betray my sister? Does she know of it?' He snorted. 'I assume not, she would never have agreed!'

Cunedda rubbed his hands together; the palms were damp, sticky. 'She does not know. I bargained hard for Vortigern's agreement that for the time being none save he and myself were to know. He was willing to have it so, a shared knowing between the two of us alone.' Cunedda spat. 'The King must leave his options open. For the sake of an alliance, there might have come a more urgent need to mate his nephew elsewhere.'

An explosion of fury, like ill-set pottery within a kiln.

'What?'

'Vortigern's nephew? Melwas!'

'You agreed to wed my sister with that murdering braggart!'

'That slime-trailed, hag-spawned bastard!' Arthur hurled a couch over as he darted at Cunedda, taking hold of the older man by the loose folds of his tunic. 'Melwas?' He hissed. 'She's to marry Melwas? Are you serious? Are you the prime madman of all Britain?'

Etern was at his side, just as livid, made no movement to loose Arthur's clamped fingers. 'Melwas is an evil, malignant snake!'

Enniaun, a pace behind, said, 'He's hand in fist with Saex scum!'

Melwas, the second son of Vortigern's sister; brother to Gorlois, erstwhile husband of Uthr's wife Ygrainne. Melwas, captain of the King's personal guard. Melwas, who had lied and cheated and murdered his way to power, wealth and a trusted position at the King's side. If the Pendragon had enemies, then Melwas was chief among them.

Softly, his words all the more menacing, Arthur said, 'I shall never allow Gwenhwyfar to wed the likes of him.'

When the time came for the telling, Cunedda had expected trouble from his sons, but he was unprepared for Arthur's passionate outburst.

Guilt at the enforced bargain heightening his reaction, he thrust Arthur's hand aside, then crossed to the table and upended it, scattering dishes and goblets and wine flagons on the floor. His shout of rage filled the room. 'Do you think I want to see her wed to such a twisted creature?' His foot kicked at a wine jug, sending it spinning across the room, red wine spewing like spattered blood. 'And you.' He pointed at Arthur, his finger quivering. 'Who are you to tell me what I can or cannot do with my daughter?'

He met the hostile gaze and held it, his breath coming fast, uneven, rasping in his throat. He groaned, passed a hand over his eyes, bent to right the table, replace the debris of tableware in order to occupy his hands, then said, 'It is no easy thing to ride as lord to people who look to you for their safety and well being. Decisions must be made – decisions that are sometimes difficult but must, all the same, be taken.'

His back to them, Cunedda the Lion Lord of Gwynedd buried his head in his hands, his shoulders hunched and shaking. His sons knew he was weeping. 'What could I do when Vortigern demanded it?' he asked simply as he lifted his grey face. 'What choice had I – Gwynedd or Gwenhwyfar?'

'You bargained our sister for land!' Etern cried. 'What kind of greed is this!'

Cunedda aimed a stinging blow at his youngest son's cheek. He held the palm before his own eyes, staring at the redness, shocked that he could strike so easily. 'See how Vortigern sets a son against his father.' He let his hands drop useless to his side. 'Defeat carries a price, son. For Uthr it was death. For us, it would have been the end of Gwynedd. Nor our death, not mine or yours, but Gwynedd's – her women, her children, her cattle, her crops. He gave me the choice, you see. Gwenhwyfar for Melwas or Gwynedd for Hengest and his Saex, to do with as they will. Is it greed, Etern, to sacrifice one for the many?' Eyes pleading for understanding he added, 'I could not lose my land. Not a second time.'

Silence. What was there to say?

Etern tried one last protest. 'We are strong. Stronger than when we were at Dun Pelidr. We have friends, many warriors on our side. How could he take our land and give it to the Saex? He could not, not now.' He faltered. 'Could he?'

Cunedda placed his two hands on Etern's shoulders and drew the lad to him in a tight embrace. 'He did before, when he sent the Saex to destroy me. They did their job well. But most of them left after the burning and the butchering, left the north to its ghosts. With Gwynedd, it would be a death within life, for they would remain, make her their slave.'

Arthur, shoulders slumped, offered his hand in submission and acceptance. Cunedda took it and patted the lad's arm.

Enniaun, subdued, with nothing more to say, retrieved goblets. Etern fetched fresh wine and passed the flagon round. They seated themselves, dwelt a while on the warm taste of rich red wine.

'I hoped, prayed, Vortigern would die – Gwenhwyfar even...' Cunedda broke off, appalled at his own thoughts. *Na*, not that! Anything to save his daughter from this monstrous betrothal, anything, but not that!

'Or Melwas.' Etern spoke with calm menace. 'Accidents can happen.'

His father shook his head. 'Think you that has not occurred to me? *Na*, I would not have murder on our hands; the revenge of the blood feud can soak through generations, can kill more innocents than a ravaging plague.' He shook his head again. 'For Melwas's death the King would take all my sons.'

There was a longer silence, each thinking his own bitter thoughts.

At last Enniaun spoke. 'My sister will not take kindly to this. Happen, when Melwas is let in on it, he may not want such a fire tempered woman.' Empty laughter. It was a poor jest.

Enniaun added, 'You ought have kept her safe in Gwynedd, Da, not brought her here.'

Cunedda toyed with his goblet. 'Do you think Vortigern needs my words at this Council? Does he truly need the few men we have brought, to fulfil our annual service within his army? I was ordered here for those things, and to bring Gwenhwyfar for Melwas.'

Etern sneered, pointed an accusing finger. 'So you jump to do as he bids!'

141

Dropping the goblet, Cunedda pressed his fingers to his temples. His head throbbed, hooves pounding his brain. Would they not understand? 'Aye, I do as the King bids, boy. It took every trick and ounce of experience I had to retain Gwynedd after Uthr's wasted rebellion. I grovelled at Vortigern's feet, begged forgiveness, pleaded for Gwynedd to be spared. I have kept that humility and knelt cowed before his every word. To keep Gwynedd safe I will do anything, even give my daughter in marriage. As,' he raised his head silently and looked eye to eye at Arthur, 'as the Pendragon would do anything to gain his kingdom.'

Arthur returned the challenge. He had swallowed his pride to come to Britain and serve under Vortigern, had bitten back anger, ignored whispered insults, followed idiotic orders, for the sake of waiting. Waiting for the time when he was old enough and experienced enough to raise his own host, to cut like sharpened iron through Vortigern's stinking skull! He nodded once, curtly. 'Aye. I would do anything.'

Enniaun emptied his goblet and refilled it. He drank another gulp, said, 'Our mountains protect us, but we could not defend ourselves from Vortigern's unleashed Saxons if he decided to cede our territory to them. For how long could we withstand a siege, an assault from north, south, east and west?'

Reluctantly Etern nodded agreement. 'Gwynedd is defensible, but not impregnable.'

'I might add,' heads spun round at the sound of Arthur's tired voice, 'were Gwenhwyfar to wed another her life would be in danger. Vortigern and Melwas are both malevolent men.'

He trailed wearily to the door. 'Defy Vortigern and his nephew in this and she would spend the rest of her life watching shadows.'

Etern extended a hand to Arthur. 'Do not leave us, there is much to talk of.'

Arthur shook his head. He steadied his breath, passed a hand over his cheeks, nose and mouth, then forced a smile. 'Happy endings are for lovers in harpers' tales.' He left, calling for a slave to fetch his cloak.

'Happen the wind will change,' Etern said.

His brother and father looked at him. He lifted his hands, let them fall. 'Something may yet be awaiting to release us from this snare.'

'After all these years? I doubt it.'

§ XXIII

Whistling a jaunty tune Cei sauntered through the empty streets, savouring the delights he had discovered during the evening. He chuckled to himself, recalling Arthur's teasing about his relationship with a rich widow. Aye, she was not young, but what did age matter compared to experience? He fingered the ruby ring on his finger, given impulsively when she had entreated him to stay the rest of the night. He had refused, having learnt from past mistakes not to linger too soon. Women had a habit of construing much from very little. He had left with promises to return another evening – happen he would at that. The streets were dark, and a dog barked somewhere. Cei yawned, ready for his own bed; it must be close on the third hour of the morning.

Someone hailed him, the voice loud in the night time silence, a guttural accent, Friesian. Curious, Cei strolled across the cobbled road, avoiding piles of dung. He nodded a greeting. 'You're open late, taverner!'

The man was agitated, fingering the grubby apron covering his ample middle. 'You are Lord Cei? I recognise you, you drink here with other officers.'

Cei nodded again, amiably. 'You serve good wine and hot food.'

The man was pleased at that, but his smile of thanks faded with the return of unease. 'I wish to close, it is so late, but I do not know what I should do with him.' He pointed a stubby finger at a cavalry officer lying slumped across a table in the shadows beyond the open door.

Annoyed that one of the men should drink so heavily as to reach this state, Cei said harshly, 'I'd toss him in the street if I were you. Let the sewer muck sober him.' He made to move on. As the man said, it was late.

The taverner stepped hastily in his path and shook his head, embarrassed.

With a short, exasperated sigh, Cei strode over to the drunkard. As he was about to shake the man's shoulder, he broke into a chuckle. Ah no, the poor tavern keeper could not give this one to the street! Roused by Cei's persistent nudging, Arthur staggered unsteadily to his feet.

'He has drunk most of my best wine.' The Friesian was hovering, put out by all this inconvenience.

Cei felt in his belt pouch and produced a small, battered coin. 'For your trouble,' he said, placing a supportive arm around Arthur's waist.

It was only a short journey to the palace but, hampered as he was by the almost dead weight of his companion, it took Cei a while to reach their assigned rooms, where, laughing, he waved Arthur's sleepy servant aside. 'Go back to your bed, I shall tend your master.' He seated Arthur on the bed and pulled off his boots. 'An enjoyable evening, I assume. Trust you to spoil it by getting yourself over full of wine.'

'I talked to them of the horses, Cei.' Arthur's words were slurred. 'Cunedda agrees with me. Think on it – he agrees!' He laughed with pleasure and fell backwards across the bed.

Cei frowned. 'Is that why you are so drunk? Filled your belly to toast the hooves? Well, 'tis a good enough reason.' Cei began to unbuckle the tunic, but Arthur, clumsily sitting up, stayed his hand.

'Why am I such a fool? My head has been so filled with dreams of cavalry that I never stopped to consider other details of life. My life. Hers.'

'What are you rambling about, man? You have drunk more than I thought!'

'You would not believe a dowsing with a water bucket could create so much feeling, would you? She's a woman grown now and,' Arthur paused, eyes as blurred as his speech, 'and I love her.' He grabbed at Cei's shoulders, pulling him close. Cei wrinkled his nose at the stink of wine.

'She makes me laugh, Cei, makes me feel I could take on Vortigern and his damned Saex friends single handed!' Arthur waved a hand expressively, then toppled sideways. He looked blankly up at Cei, not seeing him, filled only with a sense of emptiness, of great loss. 'All that, and I can't have her.'

'Who? Cannot have who? Ah, you are talking daft!'

Suddenly Arthur was asleep where he lay, lost in a swirling world of heavy wine, where hooves drummed and the dragon streamed before them. Swords clashed and glistened in sunlight. Sweat and blood, men fighting. Mingled, in the strange way of dreams, with a girl's shout of defiance drifting into laughter. Her face floating above the Pendragon's banner. An angry young girl, copper hair tumbling, face grubby, a bucket of swilling water in her hand; changing, shifting to a woman grown, serene and beautiful. Gwenhwyfar.

§ XXIV

Gwenhwyfar did not particularly like shopping; the noise and the bustle around the stalls and crowded, smelly streets held no appeal. She was not a frivolous young woman, and usually took minor interest in the acquisition of jewels or cloth and coloured ribbons. It therefore came as some surprise to her cousin Ceridwen when Gwenhwyfar enthusiastically agreed to go to the market with her – all the more so when she seemed to be enjoying herself.

The market of Londinium was, of course, far larger than their few street stalls at Caer Arfon. So many traders, so much to choose from! Pots and pans of glass or clay, fine gems, polished beads; materials for gown or cloak, silks and wools, every kind of weave in reds and blues and greens – a rainbow of colour. Spices and herbs, cooked food, raw food; shellfish, meat, gape-eyed sea fish, river fish, pasties and pies, sausages and cakes. Wine and ale. The girls ambled with the flow of the crowd, giggling together or prodding and poking, curious about some item, asking the price, wrinkling their noses at the telling. Too high!

Gwenhwyfar had bought ribbons – green, to match her eyes – Ceridwen, a fine bracelet crafted in jet and gold. They were making their way along the wider of the streets to a little tavern to take a tankard of wine and a pastry, when Gwenhwyfar squeaked, grabbed Ceridwen's arm and pointed some distance ahead, through the milling of the Londinium crowd.

Arthur coming towards them, strolling beside the man Cei, his red cloak swinging, his dark head bobbing above the crush of shoppers and

146

traders. He stopped, pointing to a stall; Gwenhwyfar lost sight of him, then spotted him again behind a trundled handcart. Impulsively, she called out, standing on toe-tip, waving to catch his attention. Twice only had she seen him these past five days since the banquet, both times at a distance making it impossible to speak. He could not have heard or seen her this time either, for he turned without acknowledgement and disappeared down a narrow side street.

'Whatever are you doing?' said a contemptuous female voice, directly behind Gwenhwyfar. 'Jumping up and down as if you have fleas in your undergarments!'

Gwenhwyfar whirled embarrassed, and found herself looking into the disdainful face of the Princess Winifred. She stammered, 'I thought I saw someone I knew.' Bear's breath! Why did she have to justify herself?

Winifred poked with a slender bejewelled finger at some saffron material on a stall near by, then peered haughtily along the crowded street. 'Well, she has gone now, dear, whoever she was.'

Condescending bitch. Gwenhwyfar would have enjoyed saying that aloud. Best not, keep smiling. To her dismay Winifred linked arms and began walking with her; people melting aside with barely concealed scowls to allow them through. Winifred and her mother were tolerated but not liked, save by the merchants, who were falling over themselves to show their wares.

Gwenhwyfar twisted her neck to look down the side street into which Arthur had passed. He had gone; the street was empty except for a woman with three squawking children, and a one-legged beggar. She did not notice Winifred also looking, for she too had seen Arthur, realised whose attention Gwenhwyfar had been attempting to catch. A smile slid across her mouth. Oh, he had gone – what a shame.

Until the night of the banquet she had not paid much mind to the Pendragon, had tried to avoid him. Her father detested 'that boy' as he called him, and her cousin Melwas seized every opportunity to be as nasty as possible to Arthur. Some kin feud between them, to do with Arthur's father Uthr and Melwas's elder brother Gorlois. Silly, why dwell on the doings of men grown cold in their graves? However, days that would otherwise have been extremely boring, often proved most amusing whenever Melwas and the Pendragon were both at court, though such occasions were rare.

Melwas was not here at present, was away about the King's private business. He was expected back soon. Winifred hoped so: these tedious days of Council needed livening up.

The sneering attitude of father and cousin, both highly influential in Winifred's upbringing, had caused her own low opinion of Arthur. With that long nose and perpetual scowl he was not a handsome young man, but Gwenhwyfar's attraction to him had caused her to look again and see for the first time the character beneath his unprepossessing appearance. Discovering unexpectedly that Arthur had a possibility of being a most exciting man.

Resigned to her unwanted companion, Gwenhwyfar walked with Winifred, feigning polite interest in her purchases, answering yes or no to irritatingly personal questions. She would see him again, happen on the morrow, the Sabbath.

And she did.

Vortigern's Christian church was a splendid building, richly decorated and furnished to show his devotion to the faith. Everything about the King was deception. All attending the Council were expected at the bishop's special service. Chance put Gwenhwyfar opposite Arthur. Her heart raced as she took her place on the women's side and saw him standing there, tall and impressive, very bored.

Once, Gwenhwyfar raised her eyes to venture a glance across at him; she looked away again quickly, a blush heating her cheeks as she saw him watching her. She stood after that with head lowered, telling herself not to act like a moonstruck child. But how the thrill of his nearness made her tingle! Only a few feet away, she could practically hear his voice, smell him, touch him!

Winifred also enjoyed the service. For the same reasons as Gwenhwyfar.

There was an undignified rush from the church, Vortigern's Council, many of them non Christians, retreating, eager for the pure air and sunshine. Eager, too, for the entertainment laid on for their benefit at Vortigern's expense. There were to be games of skill and challenge, displays by gymnasts and riders, then, later, feasting and dancing. The King was keen to keep his Council sweet. The congenial air of festival rarely failed.

Gwenhwyfar found herself swept forward with the crush, away from Arthur, was annoyed to see that Winifred had managed to waylay him. She did not see him again until the mounted displays.

His cavalry gave a daring exhibition of equestrian skills: throwing spears and fighting a mock battle; leaping on and off their horses at varying speeds and picking up articles from the ground at a gallop. One rider seemed to slip, went down under the horse's belly beneath the pounding feet, emerged on the other side, pulling himself back into the saddle, grinning. A horseman's trick! Arthur took the salute, resplendent in parade armour. Gwenhwyfar clapped and cheered, proud of him and his men.

And then the feasting, the banqueting hall filled with men and women, loud talk and much laughter. To her disgust, Gwenhwyfar found herself seated with the unwed women. Winifred, with her sickly sweet smile, beckoned her to sit beside her, welcomed her to the table. Why the princess was going out of her way to give this impression of friendship, Gwenhwyfar had not yet decided. It was so obviously false.

As usual for Winifred, she monopolised the conversation throughout the evening, whispering, not so quietly, various uncomplimentary remarks about her father's guests. Gwenhwyfar paid her scant attention beyond the demand of politeness, concentrating on her food and the entertainment – until Winifred said, 'Ah, Lord Arthur has at last joined my father's captains, he can never arrive on time!' She giggled, coyly covering her mouth. 'Did you see how he barely took his eye off me in church this morning?'

The others – silly creatures Gwenhwyfar thought them – giggled. One said, 'Happen he has design on you, Princess. After all, you and he are a most eligible pair!'

Fury, most of it born of jealousy, swept over Gwenhwyfar like a surge tide. She announced without thinking, 'It was hard to miss you. That gown you wore was bright enough to eclipse the sun!'

A hush fell over the girls.

Winifred looked at her with steel eyes. 'Were you by chance speaking to me?'

Gwenhwyfar covered a stammer, said quickly with a glowing smile, 'How could even a blind man have missed your beauty?' She cringed in self disgust at her enforced ingratiation. That was close! You did not cross Winifred, any more than you would taunt a basking adder!

The Princess extended her hand and patted Gwenhwyfar maternally, as if sharing some great secret. 'Arthur has a liking for a pretty face. Mine, I have noticed, he likes in particular.' To the others, 'I would not object to him taking a liking to more than just my face!'

They tittered, simpering at Winifred's humour. Gwenhwyfar held a fixed smile, and with difficulty, her tongue still. Arthur, she hoped, would have preference for a better woman than Vortigern's Saex bitch.

It was herself he had watched, she was sure. But then, was she? The flicker of doubt, once planted, grew rapidly, refusing to be uprooted. Winifred had wealth and status. Na, Arthur would not be swayed by those. It was she, Gwenhwyfar, he wanted They were pledged albeit a childhood promise, but made, all the same, with sincerity. He had not sought her out, though – had, now she thought of it, avoided her.

Winifred sipped wine, her expression smug. She had been right, then, the rustic girl Gwenhwyfar was indeed infatuated with Arthur. Were the feelings returned? She must find out. The Pendragon was suddenly more than a passing interest. Winifred wanted him for her own – and Winifred was used to getting what she wanted.

Soon the dancing began. Young men warmed to the women's side and whisked chosen partners off to whirl the haze of food and drink from their heads. A knot of ambitious hopefuls clustered around the princess, who flashed her blue eyes at the flattery, making an elaborate game of choosing. She was ten and five years of age, ripe for betrothal, and this might be the only chance for many a chieftain's son to obtain a royal torque.

A shadow fell over the clustered group. Standing to one side, Gwenhwyfar looked up into Arthur's hawk eyes. He held her gaze briefly, then, coming to a decision, smiled warmly and walked towards her.

'You watched the display this afternoon?' he asked, making a surety of opening a conversation.

'Aye,' Gwenhwyfar murmured as she bobbed a slight greeting; 'your men are most impressive.'

Motioning her admirers aside, Winifred bustled forward and laid her hand on Arthur's arm, her smile dazzling. 'It was superb, my Lord! You rode so… manfully.' Her blue eyes flicked up and down his body as she threaded her arm tight through his. 'Let us dance,' she said, leading him to join the whirl of laughing men and women. She glanced back at Gwenhwyfar with a victorious toss of her head.

Gwenhwyfar's body was shaking, her throat tight as if someone were steadily pressing two thumbs on her windpipe. The bitch. The fatherless tavern slut. The...

A voice, Ceridwen's, remote and distant. 'Gwenhwyfar? Are you all right?'

Gwenhwyfar ignored her cousin's concern. For agonising minutes she stood rigid, fists clenched, watching as Arthur responded to Winifred's blatant flirting. His hands around her waist, he was laughing, his eyes never leaving the generous swell of her bosom under the thin silk garment that did little to conceal the delights beneath.

After much stamping and laughter the dance came to a breathless end, the dancers breaking apart, dizzy from the pounding rhythm.

Gwenhwyfar seethed as Winifred demurely whispered something into Arthur's ear, watched helpless as he nodded and guided her out to the terrace, disappearing into the darkness of the gardens beyond.

Unable to hold back the tears of anger and hurt disappointment, Gwenhwyfar turned and fled.

150

§ XXV

It was quite late before the sounds of revelry began to fade away. Midnight had passed before the stragglers took their leave and those staying at the palace had staggered to their beds. Winifred sat stiff and silent, allowing her maidservant to undress her. If the girl noticed her mistress's disarranged hair or the bruising to her neck, she made no comment. She dismissed the girl, but did not go immediate to bed, sat naked before her mirror inspecting the marks on her white skin, lowering the polished bronze to examine the reflection of her breasts. Suddenly, she hurled the thing from her, smashing it against the far wall. Damn! Damn him and his insolence!

In a few months she would be ten and six, the age her mother had lured Vortigern to the marriage bed. If Rowena could do it, then so could her daughter. She would not be spurned by some – some boy! Going to her bed, Winifred drew the covers close around her skin. The feel of his hands on her breasts, his breath and lips on her neck, had been so very good. She pounded the pillow. Why then had he turned away from her and walked away? He had wanted her, that was plain – but he had walked away!

Whatever did that Gwynedd girl see in him? An arrogant, self-opinionated, ugly son of a rebel! Winifred drew up her knees, hugging them close. It had been so easy to lure Arthur into the seclusion of the palace gardens. She had backed away, of course, as he went to kiss her but then an unfortunate slip of the hand had caught her bodice on one of her rings. Naturally, he had helped her release it.

Why had he suddenly swung away, left her alone, her breasts exposed, and so very humiliated? She lay a long while, tossing, unable to get comfortable, unable to sleep. Her body felt hot, aching. She had enjoyed Arthur's touch, had wanted more. Still wanted more.

Her father disliked Arthur because he feared him – feared him because the Pendragon was a threat. Vortigern rarely made political mistakes, and never the same one twice over. He had let Uthr out of his sight; the son must be close watched. An idea germinated. What if Arthur were to be even more closely watched?

Winifred sat up, hugging her pillow to her chest. There had been talk again lately between her parents on the subject of her marriage. The arranged betrothal, some months past, she had put an end to. If they seriously thought she was going to some crusted old veteran's bed, then they had best think again! Winifred shivered with distaste, recalling the slimy feel of his dribbling mouth, and his rough, gnarled hands. A pity the poor old fool had suffered that seizure of the stomach! He ought never have eaten fruit before retiring. Winifred sniggered. Who would have thought that one small drip of poison on a single fruit could create such interesting, and rewarding, results!

Her idea was growing, becoming more appealing. This latest talk was something about a chieftain of her grandsire's. What – wed one of Hengest's Jutes and live in a midden-hut Grubenhauser? Ah, no, not when the Pendragon was on offer!

She slid from the bed, wrapped a light cloak around her and padded from the chamber, her bare feet making no sound on the tiled floor. What better way for her father to keep Arthur under observation? As son-by-law he would be chained as firm as a tethered bull! And poor Gwenhwyfar! Winifred tossed back her head. Poor Gwenhwyfar, her lover lost to the Princess Winifred!

Arthur stirred, roused by the thin shaft of light as the door quietly opened and closed. He mumbled, moving restlessly in his sleep. Winifred held her breath. He must not wake! She clutched her cloak tighter around her throat, though it was not the chill of night that scuttled over her naked flesh. She stood a while, her breath coming fast between parted lips, her eyes fixed on the dark shape asleep in the bed.

In her own chamber, this had all seemed so easy! She slid the cloak from her shoulders, let it fall to the floor with a gentle swish. For a few heartbeats she almost retreated back to the soft, safe glow of the corridor beyond the door. The reality of doing, more daunting than she thought. Doubts came, followed rapidly by conviction. Rowena had ensnared Vortigern by the use of her body – and Winifred was every inch her mother's daughter.

Letting go the cloak she padded across the floor. Arthur lay face down, his back uncovered, one arm flung carelessly above his head. His dark hair, curling slightly and long enough to touch his broad shoulders, spread in a tangle across the pillow.

Winifred resisted the temptation to run a finger down his spine. She had been kissed and fondled by young men, but had never allowed them to go over-far. It amused her to encourage their manhood to rise and then push them from her, leaving them frustrated and rejected. As Arthur had rejected her. No one spurned Winifred. No one!

Deftly, she twitched back the covers and slid her body next to his. He stirred, stretched his arm to her, encircling her waist, pulling her closer, mumbling in dazed pleasure as her warmth touched him. Lazily he opened his eyes, lingering over the sensation, half unconscious, of soft flesh beneath his touch – then sat upright as realisation slammed him awake.

'Blood of Mithras!' he swore, recognising her. 'What in the Bull's name are you playing at?'

Sweetly, 'I am not playing, my Lord.'

'If your father discovers you have been here he will flay me alive!'

'I don't doubt it!' she thought, said confidently, 'He will not discover it; no one saw me come.' She walked her fingers down the dark hairs of his chest and across his flat stomach. 'You have a fine body; you ought use it, not deny its need. Do you not think the same of mine?'

Irritably, he brushed her hand aside and rolled off the bed. 'Get out, Winifred, before...'

'Before what?' She stretched the length of the rumpled sheets, her thighs and breasts glistening in the dim lamplight, ran a fingernail seductively from her throat to the soft patch of pale hair that curled enticingly between her legs.

Arthur swallowed, at a loss, unsure what to do.

'You wanted me earlier,' Winifred persisted, her voice silky. She beckoned, more sure of herself now, enjoying this new game. 'You all but stripped me naked to touch me in the privacy of the gardens.'

'I was drunk, but still knew when to call a halt.' Arthur ran his hand through his hair. He could not bring himself to look away from her slender, so enticing body.

'Then are you no longer drunk?' she purred, raising herself on one elbow. 'I am, with desire for you.'

Arthur swung away, punching the air with a clenched fist. 'You are a maiden – and more to the point, Vortigern's daughter.'

'A maiden?' She had expected that, had used the same excuse herself on occasion when men became too insistent. 'What makes you so sure?'

She watched him from beneath lowered lashes, recognised the hesitation and pushed on. 'I was betrothed not so long since. He was a dear man – older, but experienced, and very, very good to me.' She flicked her eyes at him, pouted seductively. 'How were we to know he would die before we could legalise our union in the marriage bed?'

She rose slowly in one fluid movement, crossed to Arthur and touched him intimately, a butterfly touch. She smiled. 'It would seem you are interested after all.' She took his hand, kissed the palm and placed it on her breast. 'There – round and smooth, awaiting your attention.' Her arms encircled Arthur's waist, lips brushing his, and as her body pressed against him his response became undeniable.

With a low moan Arthur lifted her, his mouth covering hers, and carried her to the bed. Her body, young and new, responded delightfully to his lovemaking and at her urging he probed into her, her legs twining around him, drawing him in. She cried out, moaning with pleasure.

He froze. She had lied to him, the bitch! Astride her, he stared in disbelief, stunned that he had fallen so easily for her trickery.

Winifred moaned again impatiently, shifting beneath his body, the movement fuelling his need. Angrily he thrust harder, taking her maidenhood as savagely as he could.

Spent, panting, he rolled from her, horrified. 'Mithras, get you from here, back to your bed. Say nought of this!'

'Must I go so soon?' She stretched her aching legs. 'Can we not have more?' The afterglow of passion still lingered with a delicious throbbing. It had felt so good; why had she denied herself such pleasure for so long?

'That once should never have occurred. If your father...'

Winifred sat up slowly and leant back against the pillows. 'Finds out? He would only hear of it from you, or me. You would not tell him – and I?' She slid down into the bed. 'Will I ever have need to tell him?'

Cynically, 'No doubt you could find some reason.'

'My father wishes me to marry. I will wed, but one of my own choosing.'

Arthur laughed. 'There are many who would willingly take a girl's maidenhood, but not so many who would accept used goods as wife – save those eager for a fat dowry to compensate.' He smiled at a private jest. He could use such a gift... but he was not yet that desperate.

Winifred's next words dispersed the private humour. 'Or if a man and woman pledge themselves by the giving and taking of a first time.' She was finding it difficult to steady her voice. She had been so certain she could win him – as her mother had won Vortigern; only, these things were not quite as easy as she had expected. 'I will make you a good wife, Arthur.' She stood up and moved towards him, resting her hands on his chest. 'In time, an even better queen.'

154

'I do not want a half Saex bitch as wife. Or queen.'

She hit him then, the palm of her hand slapping hard against his cheek.

'You bastard.'

Arthur's expression remained impassive, inscrutable. He nodded once, with a thin, set smile, one eye half shut in that insolent way of his. 'That's right.'

Furious, she clawed his cheek with her nails, leaving bloody scratch marks. 'No one,' she breathed through flaring nostrils, 'shall dare talk to me, Vortigern's daughter, the Princess Winifred, in that manner.'

Arthur shrugged his shoulders, indifferent, ambled to where his clothes lay, pulled on his bracae.

'Princess? I assumed you were whoring this night.'

'My father shall hear of this!' she cried furiously. 'He shall know how you forced me here, took me against my will!'

Arthur turned slowly to face her. Was this a bluff? Would she be capable of crying rape convincingly enough? He studied her a moment. Winifred was indeed a beautiful creature; aye, but the beauty was all to the surface. Beneath that soft, enticing skin oozed putrid black poison. She was capable of lying, more than capable.

'You forget one thing, Princess.' Arthur rested his backside on the edge of a table and folded his arms. 'Your father has never trusted me. He has me watched at all hours, in all places.'

The Pendragon twitched his eyebrow higher. 'All places. We were followed into the garden' – he pursed his lips – 'and a guard keeps constant watch over this chamber. Ah, Winifred.' He spread his hands, palm uppermost. 'Did you then, forget the spies?'

'You lie!'

'If you say so!'

Winifred snatched up her cloak, flung it around herself. With a proud tilt of her head and the quirk of a triumphant smile, said, 'Spies can be bribed to tell the story the way it might have been.'

Arthur ambled to the bed, sat down, lounged back on his elbow. The self assured smile broadening, he nodded in agreement. 'That they can.'

Digesting his words, Winifred returned his direct gaze, her anger confronting his relaxed amusement. Striding towards the door, she threatened, 'You will take me as wife, Pendragon, or,' she opened the door, 'or I shall personally see to it you will not, shall we say, keep the equipment necessary for any other marriage.'

She stalked out, slamming the door shut behind her.

Arthur lay back on the bed, let his breath go slowly, stared up at the high ceiling. Two abandoned cobwebs were draped in the far corner, thick with dust. To the left, a patch of brown damp stained the yellowing plaster. A crack zigzagged from the centre almost to the wall. A crack, like the crooked scar running across Vortigern's cheek.

After a while Arthur got up and sluiced cold water over his face and hair. He felt dirty and disgusted with himself. How could he have been so easily lured into this? What sickened his stomach was the knowledge that in the garden he had wanted her. He had been eager to leave that crowded room that pressed in on him, making him feel hot and trapped, had willingly walked her away to the cool shadows outside. Winifred was a beautiful young woman, her perfume pleasant, her skin soft and her response to his first, exploring kisses encouraging.

What had excited him about her? He detested her and her family. He had lain with many women, barely remembered the first, taken with fumbling ineptitude. Ygrainne, his mother, had been furious to discover he had attended the pagan ceremony of celebrating the successful harvest. Would have been more furious had she discovered with whom he had come to manhood. A whore Uthr had once favoured, a woman three times his age with three and thirty times his experience.

Unexpectedly, that first time came back to him as he stood with his head bowed over the basin of water in his chamber. She had caught his hand in hers, whirled him around the blazing bonfire, her great, pendulous breasts bouncing beneath her loose tunic. He had reached out tentatively to touch one, wondering what the pulpy flesh would feel like. She had laughed, scooped him up like a toddler in her arms and whisked him away into the bushes where, in the dark, other couples grunted. It had all happened so fast. He found himself lying naked atop her gross bulk mouthing at her breast like a calf at some swollen udder. He had not enjoyed the experience. Revulsion at her vast bulk and haggard age hit him the next morning, the remembrance that his father had taken her when she was young and pretty making the act somehow obscene. He had avoided women for days afterwards.

The next had been a slave tending the goat herds some weeks later. Cei and he had been riding, had stopped to cool the horses, noticed the woman and two girls. Cei had grinned, swung off his horse and sauntered up to the woman. In a moment he was back with the girls while the woman returned to her goats, pleased with the more than adequate payment. Cei had taken his girl, there by the side of the track, with no more thought than a dog mounting a bitch. Arthur had followed his example, rather than look foolish in front of his elder cousin. The girl had been young, a maiden, her breasts new formed. He had been clumsy, hurting her; the blood that came frightened him, and her. More spots of blood stood out on her lip where she had bitten to stop herself from crying out. Some months later he caught sight of her again, labouring beneath a heavy basket of kindling, her belly swollen.

He wondered now, incongruously, what the child had been. Had he a daughter or son?

How many since?

He did not much like women. Women lied and cheated, set their little traps to lure you in, then, bang, bolted the door, leaving you shut in the dark to sweat and tremble, screaming to be let out. He reached to pour more water but his hands were shaking. He dropped the jug, bent to retrieve it and came face to nipple with one of the figures on the mosaic floor. He had not noticed the naked women before – seductive, suggestive, weaving a web of enchantment around their victim.

Arthur's stomach heaved. Wine and self-loathing spewed from him. 'Shit,' he muttered. 'Holy, bloody shit!'

§ XXVI

The first light of dawn touched the eastern skyline as Gwenhwyfar opened her eyes. She had not slept well, had dozed fitfully and tossed about, dreams drifting and ebbing; strange dreams of unknown faces and far-off exotic places. Her head aching, she slid from the bed. One or two birds were starting to sing outside, their happy chirrups incongruous against her misery. It would probably be a bright sunny day too. Lashing rain and dramatic thunder would suit her mood better. Gwenhwyfar dressed and let herself out of the room. She would walk in the gardens.

She turned right outside the chamber, then left and left again. *Na*, that was wrong, she did not recognise this corridor. Damn the place! You could get lost in here, starve to death before anyone found you! Imagine stumbling for days through this maze of passages to be found, tongue hanging out, eyes bulging, gasping for water. She laughed, caught her breath suddenly listening intently.

Footsteps walking fast – another corridor crossed this one a few yards ahead. Two men marched by, their boots rapping on the stone floor, swords and body armour jingling. One was Cei, Arthur's cousin, the other her brother Enniaun. Their steps halted as they banged on a door.

Curiosity getting the better of her, Gwenhwyfar ran forward to peep around the corner. If there had been an answer to their knocking, she could not have heard it. The men entered, then 'Jesu Christ, Arthur! What's wrong? Are you ill?' After Cei's exclamation and the sound of steps running quickly into the room, the door was firm shut and she heard nothing more.

Hesitantly, she slipped forward and pressed her ear against the wood. Muffled voices interspersed with an occasional florid oath, then her brother's voice. She could not catch the conversation, but it was obvious the three inside were arguing Enniaun was hurling a string of curses – followed by an equally embellished retaliation from Arthur, then a crash.

Gwenhwyfar leapt back from the door in alarm, glancing quickly up and down the deserted corridor, expecting guards to come running or the door to be flung wide. Nothing happened. No one came.

Were they fighting? Cautiously, she wedged her ear tight against the door. Their voices were a low murmur, with the occasional word spoken louder. Words like 'irresponsible', and 'damn fool!' with, intriguingly, 'What if her father discovers...' and 'Worse, what if there comes a child?' Footsteps coming towards the door!

Heart pounding, Gwenhwyfar swung away seeking a hiding place. Too late to run back up the corridor and round the corner – she would be heard if not seen! A door opposite stood open, with darkness beyond. Ducking round the doorpost, she ran in and set her back flat against the wall, breathing hard, heart thumping.

Outside, someone walked quickly away.

What was that other noise? A grunting, laboured sound. Gwenhwyfar's eyes were becoming used to the semi dark; the shutters at the small windows were not quite closed, dimly lighting the small room. It was bare of furniture and tapestries; nothing save a tankard on the floor and a tipped jug. A few feet away was a mound covered by a blanket which moved slightly. Warily, Gwenhwyfar stepped forward. She peered at the bewhiskered face of some unknown man who lay on his back, mouth open, snoring gently and stinking of strong ale.

Footsteps again. She tiptoed back to the door in time to see Enniaun re-enter Arthur's chamber carrying what looked like a water jug. No good to stay hidden here. That man, drunk though he was, could wake at any moment. Gwenhwyfar slipped out, along the corridor, noticed an entrance ahead leading into a secluded garden courtyard. Best to go out there. Arthur's door opened, she hesitated. Enniaun stepped out and instantly caught sight of her.

'What in the name of God are you doing here?' He strode towards his sister, wearing a frown of disapproval. 'What are you about, girl?'

Smiling a greeting, Gwenhwyfar explained half truthfully, 'I woke early, brother. As it seems to promise a fair day, I thought to watch the sun rise.'

Enniaun's face softened, and he patted her shoulder absently as he used to do when she was a child. In British, he said, 'I understand, lass. We are all feeling the need for Gwynedd.'

Startled, Gwenhwyfar's eyes fluttered to his. Until that moment she had not realised that they had exchanged their native British tongue for formal Latin.

Suddenly, unbidden, she longed for the mountains and green valleys of Gwynedd. For the wild sea, hurrying streams and lazy rivers. Enniaun was right: she did feel that special longing, that inner something that went deeper than mere homesickness. 'I want to go home,' she said.

'We all do, but it cannot be, not yet. I leave immediate with Da and Etern and our men to go north. The Saex have pushed across the frontier and have run riot near Camulodunum.' He did not add the rest, that farmsteads had been burnt to the ground, villas looted, the men slaughtered and the women and children taken for pleasure or slaves. There were several wealthy estates in that area, and many of their owners were here at Council. Only one had brought his family.

To conceal the words unspoken, Enniaun confided, 'Da is bound to serve his given days with Vortigern's army – he thought to take advantage of this opportunity to ride beneath the Pendragon's command. We,' he indicated Cei, who had come from Arthur's chamber at the sound of voices, 'came to rouse him.'

As he spoke, Enniaun turned, Arthur was emerging from his room dressed in undertunic and bracae, his eyes tired-bruised, his face pinched, grey and unshaven. Four angry scratches stood out on his cheek. The blood was fresh, barely congealed. Only an animal's claws or a woman's nails could cause such a wound. Gwenhwyfar's quick mind considered it unlikely that he had suddenly developed a fondness for a pet cat.

A thrust of vindictive resentment stabbed at her – serve him damned right! If he will have a woman with him for the night – changing, within a heartbeat to a plunge of pity. He looked so haggard and lonely.

Arthur spread his hands. 'I heard you talking, Enniaun. Forgive my appearance, Lady Gwenhwyfar, I thought someone I have no wish to see had come.' He shrugged, and added as if it would explain everything, 'I have not slept well.'

'*Na*?' said Gwenhwyfar in a tone that questioned the excuse. 'I find the most effective method of dealing with mares that ride the night is to turn over and ignore them.'

Arthur raised an eyebrow and nodded ruefully. 'If I ever find myself in a similar situation again, I shall remember your advice.'

Enniaun glanced shrewdly at his sister, more aware than Arthur of her way of thinking. Something did not quite ring true about her air of innocence. Bushy eyebrows drawing together he wagged a warning finger at her. 'We do not want unsavoury rumours spreading, Gwenhwyfar.'

Was her brother referring to Arthur's woman or this Saex trouble? Both?

'Vortigern wishes us to delay, discuss tactics before we ride to teach these Saex a lesson.' Unaware that Gwenhwyfar might be alerted to that other reason, Arthur was talking about the uprising. 'But Vortimer has decided to leave now. It's more prudent to head north before too many Saex learn of our coming.'

'The Queen does not rise until well after the sun,' Gwenhwyfar replied with straight innocence.

'That, young lady,' Arthur replied, grinning, 'could be considered a treasonable statement!' He winked. 'But well said!' He began to walk back into his chamber. 'I must dress, we are delaying over long.'

'Arthur!' On impulse, Gwenhwyfar ran forward to pluck at his sleeve. He was a tall man, standing two fingers above six feet, his height as imposing as his direct gaze. The crown of Gwenhwyfar's head barely reached his chest. She looked up at him. 'There's a man, drunk, in the room opposite yours.' She pointed. 'He looks as though he may be one of Vortigern's Saex.' She felt suddenly foolish. Why would Arthur want to know where a drunken heathen lay? She dropped her eyes, looking at her neat Roman shoes, and said with a stammer, 'I thought you might need to know.'

He laughed, a single snort, and putting a finger under her chin tilted her face up. Almost kissed her. 'I know. He serves the King, but he also spies for the Queen.' Arthur chuckled, happy to share a secret. 'He was well pleased with a jug of strong ale to keep his solitary watch company.' He grinned. 'Given by one of my men.' He glanced at Enniaun and Cei. 'Keeping these spies occupied is costing me a fortune!'

Arthur took Gwenhwyfar's fingers in his hand and rubbed his sword-callused touch over her softness. Her skin was cold, but her answering grip, firm and steady. 'My thanks for your concern.'

Her answer was a radiant smile. She wanted to ask whether it was the princess he preferred; wanted to say that she loved him, said only, 'Take care while you are gone.'

The need to hold Gwenhwyfar in his arms and keep her close became almost too great for Arthur to bear. She was not like the others – no traps or deceit from Gwenhwyfar, no pretty smiles hiding malicious intent. Her earnest green eyes were gazing up at him, trusting and loving. He wanted to say so much to her, but how could he? What would be the point in saying that he loved her? It would only bring her more pain.

He forced a less potent, a more brotherly smile. 'Aye, my Cymraes fach, I always do.' He whirled away before he lost all sense and committed some other stupid deed. He had made one mistake that would send far-reaching ripples into the future months this ill-starred night already. There must not be another.

MAY 453

§ XXVII

The attack was swift, unexpected, all the more startling because Arthur was lost in thought, pacing the new-cleared floor of a thirty foot-deep defensive earthwork. The madness of the past two weeks had been fraught with chaos. The desperate ride north to Camulodunum, the assessing of damage . . . Men attacked, killed. Homesteads and farms burnt. A frenzy of bloody skirmishes.

Vortigern had not heeded warnings, left matters too late, and the Angli had swung together to unite their strength in a bid for independent supremacy. In a frenzy of bloodlust, they moved swiftly towards the gentle ridge that shouldered between the flat marshlands and dense woodlands of what had once been the territory of Queen Boudica's proud people, the Iceni. One satisfaction for Arthur, he – and others of his thinking – had been arguing for months that this would happen soon. It had needed only one man to rise into a position of power, one man to fire the young warriors and set the blood pulsing in the old. Icel was such a man – an English princeling seeking himself a kingdom.

English, Angli – how Vortigern stuck obstinately to the correct use of title! His wife and her kin were Jutes, this Icel an Anglian, and the settlers sprawling along the coast down towards Londinium were Saxons –'Saex' being the popular word used by the British for the lot of them. A loose, derisive play on the term for a foreigner and for the Saxon short bladed sword.

Arthur bent to retrieve a lump of flint from the wall of the ditch, tugged at it, surprised at how firm the nodule was lodged. He pulled again, the thing coming free suddenly, showering him in a mist of chalk dust. He sneezed, wiped whitened fingers on his bracae that were already white-coated. The damned stuff was so dry, hard baked by the early heat and lack of spring rain. It got everywhere – in your boots, your hair, even inside your undergarments. The men had stripped off their tunics and were working bare skinned under the scorching sun.

He tossed the chunk of rock onto the pile of debris. This earthwork had lain abandoned for centuries, disused since the days when the Iceni lost the need for man-made boundaries to the supremacy of Rome. He sneezed again, cursed. It was a damn awful job clearing this scrub-choked, twenty-foot-wide ditch. And a waste of energy. The construction was wrongly sited for their purpose, with the rampart on the north side. It had been built as a gateway straddling the ancient Iceni Way. Built against an enemy coming from the south-west, not one firm entrenched to the north-east!

He turned to face the towering bank, shielding his eyes against the glare of new-cut chalk. All day had they been digging, all day in this insufferable heat, with no shade – and, with thirty men working, only a few handful of yards yet completed! Mithras' Blood, it would take months to reopen the entire seven mile length!

Winifred had not tattled to her father, nor her mother – he was certain of that. Could he trust Cei and Enniaun to remain silent? He had been indiscreet in telling them the truth of that night, but then, what use making excuses for the state they had found him in?

He had best go up to check the sentries in a moment, ensure they were not drowsing.

As for Vortigern's Saex spies, Arthur had handled them easily enough for months now, ensuring only harmless information filtered back to the King. Or Queen. That she had the upper hand at court was undeniable. It would be the queen who was the more likely to find out about him and Winifred. *Na*, it was safe kept. The girl could not betray him without betraying herself, and she had the more to lose. He laughed, walked along to the uncleared area ahead, where straggling bushes grew rampant and wild flowers clustered in brilliant profusion. Which was the greater? For her to have lost her virginity, or for him to lose his balls were her parents to find out? He pointed at a path of tufted grass along the lower slope, shouted a reprimand at the man who had missed its clearing, received a returned scowl of silent annoyance. The men thought as he did.

Ah, forget that night. It was a thing done – badly done, aye, but finished with.

Arthur plucked a yellow flower, idly wondering whether it had a name. Gwenhwyfar would know. She knew about plants and herbs. He tore the petals off one by one – Winifred, Gwenhwyfar, Winifred, Gwenhwyfar – threw the thing testily aside. Forget her, forget Gwenhwyfar. She was lost to him.

As the first flickering, swift moving shadows topped the bank and began slithering fast down, with the startled cries of sweating, digging men and the whish and thud of spears brutally destroying or maiming, Arthur had a fleeting, incongruous thought, Forget Gwenhwyfar? How?

He had his sword out, was rushing to meet a Saex, full clad in war gear. They came together, Arthur's weapon parried by the Anglian's shorter blade. Arthur had no shield. He leapt aside from the returning thrust and yelled for help. Ducking low, Etern ran along the ditch, Enniaun hard at his heels, with the intention of giving aid to the men. But the Anglian Saex were swarming down the bank and coming up from the cover of uncleared undergrowth. Mithras, they were everywhere!

The three and twenty survivors of Arthur's work force tried to run for the weapons they had laid aside, found it useless, used instead the picks and shovels to hand.

A Saex sword hissed along Arthur's left arm, leaving a trail of oozing blood. Three more men fell, a fourth, a fifth. The virgin white chalk was turning a sickly, red tinged pink. Etern was down. No time to think, just fight. Use strength and muscle, cunning and wit. The Bull! From where did they come?

Enniaun saw Etern fall, sliced his sword through the nearest Saex abdomen and turned to aid his brother; saw, as he lunged forward, Arthur fall to his knees. He was a big man, Enniaun, tall and powerfully built with broad shoulders, his bush of red hair this day tied back in a thong against the heat. His voice echoed along the sun baked, bloodied ditch, an anguished, howled cry. Head down, shoulders hunched, he burst through the press of fighting men, uncertain where to help first. His much-loved brother or the more politically important Pendragon? A decision to be made as he ran, no time to think. Instinct.

Etern lay motionless. Arthur, still on his knees, was grappling a Saex with his hands, his sword lost. Another Saex was standing over Etern, axe raised to strike off the lad's head. One was coming at Arthur from behind... Enniaun shouted urgent warning to the Pendragon, caught hold of a spear as it whistled overhead, and flung the thing at the man about to mutilate Etern. Enniaun guessed his brother to be dead, so still was he lying. He took a step towards Arthur, saw him rise and swing his held opponent round, using him as a shield. A Saex short sword aimed at Arthur plunged into the wrong back. He was all right, up again, fighting. Relieved for that at least, Enniaun straddled his brother's body, swinging left and right with his sword, slicing through air and bone, whatever came within reach of the blade's vicious bite. Stories would be told later, around the Anglian hearth fires, of a red-haired giant among the British who killed with a magical, shining sword that spat blood.

For a moment Arthur held on to the dead Saex, manoeuvring behind him, gaining time to reach for a weapon. His fingers clenched, mercifully, round his own sword; he shoved the cumbersome body into his attacker and drove his blade deep into the entangled man, withdrew it and turned to face a new opponent. Something hit him from behind with a sharp thump to the back of the head, the butt of a spear knocking sense and awareness from him. He sprawled forward, the turmoil and shouting a haze of dizzy unreality.

Enniaun cried out, yelled for Arthur to get up, stepped forward intending to shield the Pendragon, felt a blow to his shoulder, saw a fountain of blood and felt a curious numbness down his right arm. He stopped, looking in amazement at a spear tip that had passed clean through the flesh of his shoulder and was protruding obscenely from his tunic. Enniaun gaped at the slimy redness on the metal, not quite believing the oddity of having a spear sticking through his own body. The weirdest thing, it did not hurt, not much anyway.

There came more noise, shouting from the top of the bank, the bloodlust cries of battle, shadows and forms moving, darting. Enniaun saw nothing of it; he crumpled against the wall of red spattered white chalk, felt and saw nothing more. Arthur, too, saw nothing of the frenzied activity, heard nought, save a wheezing breath in his own throat accompanied by a swirl of brightness fizzing behind his eyes. He was aware of someone standing over him, beginning to strip him of tunic and boots. His fingers moved, stiff, slow, closed around the smooth, hard surface of a rock, a lump of flint. He had it in his hand, brought his arm up, slowly, so slowly from the thump-thumping in his head, the burn of torn flesh along his arm. Up, lift up. The rock was so heavy, so damned heavy. He came up with it, hand pounding into the head of the thieving Saex squatting over him. A dull crunch, a muted gasp. Blood. Blood everywhere.

Curious, Arthur sat, staring at the flint in his hand, at the yellow and brown mixing of colour, at the exposed, cold and dark interior of the stone. At the razor-sharp edge that had sliced, as sharp as any honed sword, through the face of the Saex. There was hardly anything left of the man's features, the eye and jaw gone. Spinning and whirling sensations brought vomit to Arthur's throat. He dropped the flint, lay down and closed his eyes, vaguely aware the battle cries were no longer of the Saex, but British. That the Saex were fleeing along the ditch, scrabbling up the steep bank. Idly he wondered if Icel himself had taken part in the fighting.

A chill breeze woke him. His body was hot; sweat and the stink of blood and vomit assailed his nostrils. He opened his eyes, grimaced at the mess spewed down his chest and legs, grimaced, hoping it wasn't all his own contribution. Surely some of the blood came from a Saex?

'So you've decided to wake at last?'

Arthur looked up bleary-eyed, saw Etern squatting before him.

He said nothing, stared puzzled, one eye half shut, the other eyebrow raised. Looking sideways, he saw Enniaun lying there as grimed as himself, eyes closed but breathing steady. Back to Etern.

'I had hoped,' he said, mouth dry, rasping as if it were full of chalk dust, 'the next world would at least have a decent bathhouse. It seems not.'

Etern laughed and playfully ruffled Arthur's chalk-matted hair. 'We need wait and see. Not for us the knowing this time, my friend.'

A gruffer voice, ahead and above. 'You will wish you were in the other world, lad, when I finish with you.' Etern drew his mouth down in a warning expression; Arthur forced his throbbing head up and saw Cunedda silhouetted against the evening sun. He stood, legs spread, fists bunched against his hips, stern and angry. Very angry.

'It came unexpected,' Arthur said, without much conviction. A poor excuse and he knew it. Knew also he deserved the merciless tongue-lashing Cunedda launched into. There was, could be, no excuse for the danger he had placed his men in, for failing to supervise the sentries – paid for by their murder as they dozed in the shade of their own propped-up shields. For the carelessness of having no weapons to hand... the list went on and on.

Arthur sat listening, taking each verbal blow with a mounting sense of shame. He had been lax, careless. Men lay dead through his indifference to safety. He had not wanted this job of ditch clearing, had fussed and grumbled, and disregarded all the rules. You did not strip off your armour so close to enemy territory. You did not post a few idle sentries as sole guard along the ridge. You did not heap your weapons yards away. If Cunedda had not happened by on routine patrol... aye, well. A lesson in command learnt. A bitter, sharp lesson that had resulted in the death of over half his men, a jagged wound along his arm, Enniaun alive but wounded, and Etern with a lump to the back of his head the size of a hen's egg.

Oh, they would talk and laugh about the near disaster later. Arthur's first and last mistake. Etern's life saved by being struck unconscious, and Enniaun's shoulder that for the rest of his life ached whenever a cold easterly wind blew. But there was no laughter at this moment on Cunedda's outraged face, or in his harsh voice.

Nor was there laughter for Arthur, who when Cunedda walked angrily away hauled himself to his feet to supervise the burying of the dead; men under his command. Men he had not commanded well enough, who, through his negligence, had died.

It would not happen again.

Only one good thing came out of it all – the clearing of the earthwork was abandoned.

The Anglians later reused the fortification. Its construction attributed to their skills. Forgotten, as the years and the years passed, were the others who had come and gone, before the settling of the Anglo-Saxons.

§ XXVIII

Glancing through the open window at the sudden shrill of a blackbird, Gwenhwyfar drove her sewing needle into her finger. 'Damn the thing!' She flung the material to the floor and sucked at welling blood. She detested sewing. Her stitches never seemed to come out neat or even, the needle was always unthreading or the thread snagging and knotting.

'Is it so surprising the Pendragon grew tired of you and turned to me? You have the breeding of a sow, Gwenhwyfar of Gwynedd.' Winifred sat working at an elegant tapestry, tossed her insult without bothering to glance up.

Gwenhwyfar hurled an ill-tempered response. 'Better a well bred sow than a half breed runt!'

Four other young women in the room paused from their work, needles hovering in mid stitch, expressions appalled. No one spoke to the Princess like that and got away with it.

'You insolent bitch!' Winifred shrieked, her own sewing tumbling to the floor in her indignation.

'Bitch? It is not I who fill that description!'

'How dare you!' Springing to her feet, Winifred crossed the small chamber in three quick strides to slap Gwenhwyfar across the cheek.

With squeaks of alarm the others drew back, holding their sewing to their breasts as if the flimsy material formed some sort of shield. Ceridwen alone came forward, her hand extended in appeal.

Gwenhwyfar too was standing, a dagger, which normally hung discreetly from her waist, in her hand, its tip pricking at Winifred's throat.

168

With breathing controlled, her body loose, shoulders bent slightly forward and arms flexed Gwenhwyfar was ready for action; ready to fight, defend, or kill.

Frightened, Winifred had the sense to move a pace back, a little scream escaping her. 'She threatens me! Threatens to kill me! Treason! This is treason – you are all witnesses to it!'

With a laugh, Gwenhwyfar lowered her weapon, sheathed it and turned away in disgust. 'You are pathetic, Winifred. A spoilt, conceited, half breed baggage! Arthur loves me – we are pledged. If you think he feels anything more than a passing fancy to fondle your teats, then you are also a fool.'

It was enough to tip the fear into fury. Rushing at her, arms whirling, Winifred took Gwenhwyfar by surprise. She staggered trying to fend off the flailing fists, but Winifred caught hold of her hair, twisted a hank round her hand and pulled while her feet kicked at shin and calf.

'Stop! Oh, stop!' Ceridwen fluttered around the locked pair, tugging vainly at Gwenhwyfar, trying to pull Winifred off, to stop the fight.

The Princess, unschooled in fighting, was pummelling anyhow with fist and toe, with no balance to her body or designed co-ordination. Gwenhwyfar, though, had always enjoyed the training for warfare, and had learnt well. Winifred had winded her; she let her blows come, caught her breath, then dropped suddenly to one knee. Winifred lost her balance and toppled forward with a shrill cry. Gwenhwyfar had no need to follow through, for Winifred lay gasping like a landed fish.

Guards and servants were running in.

'What is the meaning of this riot?' One commanding voice carried clear above the turmoil, which subsided abruptly as the queen swept into the chamber. Rowena stood a moment on the threshold surveying the whimpering heap that was her daughter, and Gwenhwyfar on one knee breathing hard. 'Is this how women of Gwynedd behave? What is happening here?'

Nervously, Ceridwen bobbed a curtsy. 'There was a difference of opinion, my lady.'

Rowena addressed Winifred sharply. 'Stop that noise, you cannot be so badly injured.'

'Mother,' Winifred made no attempt to rise, 'she threatened me with her dagger, attacked me.'

'You probably deserved it. Is this true, Gwenhwyfar? You hold a weapon?'

Undeterred by the queen's austere tone, Gwenhwyfar answered boldly, 'I carry a dagger. Who does not?'

Rowena regarded her with a steady blue gaze. She was a small woman, standing shorter than Gwenhwyfar by a few inches. She was ageing also, no longer the sixteen-year-old beauty who had captured Vortigern. The beauty now was painted on, and the silky blonde hair had paled into streaked silver-grey. She had no figure, for the child she carried swelled her stomach to a great bulge, a thing Vortigern seemed to admire. In the hopes that this time, at last, his wife carried a boy that would live? All these years, and still Winifred the only living child!

Defiant against the hard scrutiny, Gwenhwyfar added, It was my mother's weapon. I have carried it since childhood.'

'Then you will carry it no more. Give it here.' Rowena held out her hand, the fingers puffy and misshapen from pregnancy. 'Quickly, girl. I am no common stall-holder to stand here arguing.'

Reluctantly Gwenhwyfar gave her the dagger.

'You will go to your own chamber. Remain there until I say otherwise.'

Winifred scowled at her mother. 'Is that all the punishment she…'

Rowena rounded on her. 'Be silent!'

Petulant, the princess obeyed.

The Queen surveyed the chamber, with an expression as if they all carried some foul disease. Then, 'Daughter, come with me,' and she swept out, the heavy scent of her perfume lingering in her wake. Winifred, struggling unsteady to her feet, trotted obediently to heel.

Rowena said nothing more of the matter until later in the afternoon. She sat stitching an altar cloth by the light of a western window, patiently fashioning neat little stitches that steadily expanded this section of the Christ's crucifixion. It was incongruous, she reflected, that this Roman breed called her father's Jutes barbarian and savage, yet they thought nothing of this slow, tortured form of death. She sat back, easing a pain in her lower spine. How many weeks more to carry this wretched child? *Please God, let it be a living son, and let this be the last!* She pointed with her needle at her work and enquired of her daughter, 'What think you of it, girl?'

'Is it difficult to work such small stitching?'

Rowena sighed in annoyance. 'How like your father you are, always answering one question with another.' She picked at a piece of fluff with her nail. 'You were arguing with Cunedda's daughter. What about?'

Winifred found a sudden need to attend to her spindle. 'No important matter, a misunderstanding.'

'I see. Over what?'

Winifred struggled to sound indifferent. 'A man.'

'A man?' Rowena persisted, honey-sweet. 'Which man?'

'Oh, no man in particular.'

'It would not, by chance, be the Pendragon?'

Winifred dropped the spindle and stooped quickly to retrieve the spoilt wool. She forced a laugh. 'The Pendragon? Why him?'

Did her mother know of that night? Those spies he had talked of... she was certain he had lied about them, for if her father had been told, he would not have remained silent on the matter. And yet he and the Pendragon went away, were north of here, fighting the Angli folk.

Rowena said scathingly, 'The entire palace watched as you danced together at the feasting, my girl. And many tongues were set wagging when you both retired to the seclusion of the gardens.'

Winifred blushed. 'I needed air; the wine and heat...'

Rowena regarded her daughter with a stem eye. 'I have no objection to your walking in the gardens with the Pendragon, child. As long as it is only *walking* that you do.'

Feigning shock, Winifred exclaimed, 'Mother! What more is there to do in a garden?'

Returning to her tapestry, Rowena sewed some half-dozen stitches. 'If you are that naive, child, then it is time we talked of betrothal. There is a chieftain, loyal to my father, who would suit well.'

Winifred felt suddenly afraid. God, no! She lowered her eyes. 'You have the wisdom I do not yet possess.'

Suddenly, like a striking snake, Rowena was on her feet and moving across the room as if she were a lithe girl, not a woman heavy with child. Her palm smacked across her daughter's face. 'You stupid girl!'

Winifred squeaked, tried to draw back. 'Why? What is it I have done?'

Rowena mimicked her. "What is it I have done?" Do you think you can entice the Pendragon by letting him mouth at you as though you were some tavern-slut? No, do not deny it – you were watched! Your father and I have men constantly following Arthur – he cannot be trusted. I am ashamed of you, do you hear? Ashamed!' She paced around the room, agitated. 'At least, thank God, that is all you allowed him. Stupid, stupid girl, he could have taken matters further!' Rowena stood over her daughter like some goddess of darkness.

'And now this! Brawling like some street brat. You deserve a whipping for your behaviour!'

At that Winifred protested. 'I deserve a whipping? What of that Gwynedd bitch who dared insult me! What of her?'

Rowena waved her hand dismissively. 'She is of no consequence. It is you I am concerned with.' She returned to her stool, but did not pick up her needle.

Winifred came to stand behind her mother. 'Did you know the Pendragon is in love with her?'

'Is he?' Rowena kept her voice neutral. This she was not aware of. 'And how do you know?'

Winifred folded her hands before her. 'From the way he looks at her, and she at him.' She laid her fingers briefly on her mother's shoulder, emphasising her point. 'Gwenhwyfar said they were pledged.' She moved away to the window so her mother should not see her scheming smile.

'Nonsense!' Rowena began stitching: the blue here needed particular care. But was it nonsense? *Ja*, she had noticed Arthur watching Gwenhwyfar, had taken it for a man's lusting. How strong would that make the Pendragon and Cunedda of Gwynedd? Too strong, dangerously so. Such a betrothal must never be allowed. She unpicked the last stitch, having formed it crooked. But wait – had not her husband said something recently about Gwenhwyfar being a possibility for Melwas? She began sewing, calm again. She must raise that idea again as soon as possible. And find a more suited wife for the Pendragon. She sighed. It would be so much easier to have the awful young man disposed of, but Vortigern had expressly said not. 'Too many would use the memory of his name. *Na*, my beloved, with his incredible talent for rubbing people the wrong way, it will only be a matter of time before he makes himself more enemies than friends. There will be few willing to follow him.'

'Might not such a pledge cause a troublesome alliance against my father?' Winifred enquired innocently from her window seat. 'What if it is not nonsense? What if Cunedda has agreed a match? My father could be placed in great danger should the Pendragon be allowed such a kin alliance.'

Rowena peered at her stitching; the thread had knotted. Patiently she unravelled it. 'She spoke idle fancy.'

'Happen she did, but what if it was not?' Winifred hurried on. She must seize this opportunity to press her point, catch her mother's interest. Woden's breath! If she were to marry this chieftain of her grandsire's and be found on the wedding night not to be... She swallowed a hard lump. What did they do to women who went to the marriage bed no longer maiden? 'It would be more prudent for Arthur to betroth a woman of my father's choosing; someone with whom he could be watched more easily.'

'I would assume your father has already thought of that.'

Winifred ducked her head, feigning modesty. 'The Pendragon is an arrogant, toad-spawned dog-turd, but for my father I would wed with him.'

Rowena continued sewing, a small smile touching the corners of her mouth. This sudden idea would have nothing to do with that episode in the palace gardens, by chance? Thank the God her husband's spies always reported to her first whenever her daughter was concerned! Vortigern would have had the girl flayed if he knew half the things she did! Foolish rosebud! That was no way to catch a man. You must dig a hole, hide the net, lure him forward and let him fall headlong in; not allow him to see the trap dangling!

At least the Pendragon had held the sense not to pluck this particular flower! There were one or two young men who had taken liberties with her daughter. She, the queen, had found it necessary to dispose of them without fuss. It was time the child was wed. But to the Pendragon?

Rowena never had discovered which girl Arthur had taken to his bed on that feasting night. There had been one – her servants had told of a virgin's blood on the sheets and the cling of perfume. Rowena liked to know all that went on – curse that drunken fool set to watch the Pendragon's chamber! She had not made him suffer enough for his neglect; slitting his throat had been over-quick, punishment ought have been longer drawn out. She smiled, amused. Mayhap the Romans had the right attitude to punishment after all! Then another thought, alarming. Could the girl have been Gwenhwyfar? No, unlikely.

The Pendragon for Winifred? The queen was warming to the idea. Vortigern was ageing, her father Hengest not yet in a safe position to make a bid for power, and he too was ageing. This child she bore, what if that too died or was a girl? *Ja*, there could be possibilities if Winifred were to wed Arthur. It was good to have a choice of roads to reach the same destination.

She said, 'I will speak to your father about it.'

Considering it prudent not to press the matter, Winifred asked permission to retire. She turned back at the door.

'That dagger, Gwenhwyfar's. Can I have it?'

Rowena pointed vaguely to a table on the far side of the room. 'It is over there. Take the thing – I have no use for it.'

Well pleased with herself, Winifred found the dagger and holding it clasped in both hands, left the room. *'Spurn me, Pendragon? I told you, I always get my way. And as for you, Gwenhwyfar...'*

She held the dagger to the light, admiring its fine craftsmanship, and walked along the corridor with a triumphant swagger. 'You can be flower maiden at our wedding!'

JULY 453

§ XXIX

Vortimer was the King's eldest son by his first marriage, his brother Catigern two years younger. Father and sons hated the sight of each other. Leaning across the wooden table, Vortimer offered his guest more wine, though he was already quite drunk.

Arthur accepted, holding his tankard out a little unsteadily. This endless patrolling, the pretence at keeping the Saex behind a hypothetical border sickened him. The fighting these last weeks had been sporadic –skirmishes only, nothing substantial. Icel had entrenched himself this far south, and here he would stay.

At least Icel was contained to the western edge of this great bulge of flat fenlands; but there would be no hope of salvation, of retrieving what was lost, unless Vortigern gave orders for a combined force to march against him – and that he would never do. The King had not the funds, nor the guts, to unite his own British. Too easily could such a hosting turn against him. The mood Arthur was in this night, it would not take much to encourage him to lead that force either! Good men had died in these pointless skirmishes, too many men to name. Their faces swam before Arthur's blurred vision; he raised his tankard in salute, drank in their memory.

'When are we going to drive this scum back to the sea where it washed in from?' he demanded venomously, crashing his drained tankard down.

Again, saying nothing, Vortimer filled the tankard. With the passing of the years he was losing patience. Would his father never die, leave the way open for his son to salvage what he could without resorting to taking the throne by force? Vortimer's dark hair had long since turned grizzled and his eyes wore a permanent rim of red around sunken hollows. He was no longer a young man, fit and full of enthusiasm. 'We cannot attack as you advocate, Arthur, we have not the men.' How often had he made that self-same reply to Arthur, to his brother. To himself.

For answer Arthur made a crude noise through his lips. 'And the King does not intend to muster enough British men.'

'My brother, we are here for a matter of importance,' said Catigern impatiently. 'Is it not time we discussed that, not this same, endless quest?' Like Arthur, he took little pleasure in pointless action. Allowing the Pendragon to drink himself senseless this night seemed yet another waste of time. 'We have talked around every other subject imaginable. Our matter must be raised now, brother.' He looked meaningfully towards Arthur, who had the glazed look of one ready to sleep off excess liquor.

'What matter?' Arthur rose unsteadily to his feet, looking from one brother to the other. 'Whatever, it must wait – I am for my bed.' The room spun, and clumsily, with a surprised, distracted expression, Arthur sat down again.

'A thing of some delicacy,' began Vortimer, uncertain how to broach the subject. He liked Arthur, admired him as a soldier and as a friend, though their ideas on warfare were very different. He had been amazed when the raw youth presented himself at court for duty with the army. Amazed but pleased, for Arthur was a useful man to have at your shoulder.

Vortimer took a breath and decided to tackle the problem head on. 'From our spies we know much of our father's planning – and the bitch's scheming.'

Belching, Arthur examined the flagons of wine, seeming surprised that all were nigh on empty.

'Will you listen, man!' Vortimer thumped the tabletop in frustration.

Catigern shook his head. 'We should have talked of this earlier; he is too damned drunk now to listen!'

'I am not drunk, just bloody tired!' Arthur's words slurred together, he spoke part truth: it had been a long day in the saddle, with nothing to show for it come evening.

Standing behind the Pendragon, leaning over his shoulder, Catigern spoke urgently, with more force. 'We have received word that Rowena is to arrange Winifred's marriage.'

Arthur tapped a rhythmical beat on the table with his fingers, grinning inanely. 'Well, good for her.' He turned his head to face Catigern. 'Do I know the unlucky bastard?'

Catigern put a hand to his head and groaned. 'Will you be serious!'

His brother added, 'Vortigern's daughter is to marry with a Jute chieftain – a thegn, I think the word is. One of Hengest's sworn men.'

Arthur sat grinning happily. 'Then we might be rid of her? Hooray for that!'

'God's truth! *Na*, we shall not be rid of her. There will be yet more Saex settling their feet over the door sill.' Vortimer, across the table from Catigern, leaned closer to Arthur like a spider lurking hidden from a hovering fly. 'Unless Rowena's babe is a boy, Winifred is the only child of the union. On Vortigern's death the Saex – her mother, her grandsire and, if this marriage goes ahead, her husband – will claim all on her behalf. Do you not see? That Saex rabble will claim the British throne!'

'Then we had best hope for a boy to oust the princess. Mind, even then the brat will be half Saex won't it.' Arthur said..

'Or we can arrange some alternative marriage, Arthur, give Vortigern a better offer. One it would be impolitic for him to refuse. One that would cut Winifred off from her Saex kindred.'

The craving for sleep taking hold, Arthur nodded slow agreement, wagged a ponderous finger. 'Good idea. Who do you have in mind?'

Catigern let out the line, dangling the bait lower. 'There is one man who could use Winifred's parentage to his own advantage and benefit from a handsome dowry.'

Vortimer added, 'My brother and I are no longer young men. We may not live to see the day when our father falls. A sorry fact, but it must be faced head on.'

Catigern again: 'If any man aside from ourselves is to take the kingdom, we would like that man to be you, Arthur. You have a claim through Uthr.'

'You could add to that claim by wedding a wealthy heiress.'

They stared solemn, at Arthur. He looked back, one to the other, a sickening horror creeping over him.

'You are not serious! Oh *na*!' He was on his feet, backing away, hands upraised. 'Blood of the Bull, after all your ravings against Rowena you have the nerve to foist her bloody daughter on me? Are you out of your minds? Think again. No. Good night to you.'

He strode to the door and flung it open. Vortimer said with quiet menace, 'If you refuse this, Arthur, then you are no friend or,' he paused for emphasis, 'ally.'

Arthur rounded on him, the blur of drink quite gone. 'Do you think I fear you, Vortimer? You cannot threaten me. I have allied myself with you because it suits my purpose. My purpose, not yours. I could as easily stand with others.'

'And end up like your father?' Catigern cut in. 'Hacked to pieces on the battlefield?' This was going badly. Pausing for breath, he continued, treading softer, 'This has been no light matter for us either. You – we – have no choice, you must see that!'

'Which one of you thought up the stinking idea?' Arthur glared at the two men.

Catigern hooked a stool forward with a foot. 'It was suggested to us. We have thought upon it some days now.'

Arthur sneered. 'Suggested? By whom?'

Trying to evade the question, Vortimer said lightly, 'No one of importance.'

'By whom?'

'Damn it, Arthur! We had word that Rowena is to arrange a marriage for her daughter. She has suggested two possibilities to her husband. This Saex thegn or... '

'Or?'

'You.'

Arthur laughed, punched the wall with his fist, bellowed, 'And you, like the two fools you are, have neatly pushed me into her snare!'

'Nonsense!'

'It is a good arrangement!'

'Good?' Arthur stamped back to the table. 'Who for? Me? Rowena and Vortigern? Winifred?' He kicked a stool aside, sending it half way across the room. No one made a move to retrieve it.

Vortimer challenged; 'Have you another in mind then? A woman who could bring you as much as Winifred?'

Arthur opened his mouth to answer, closed it again. Defeated, he leant on the table, head bowed.

'Well, have you?' Catigern repeated his brother's question.

The Pendragon looked up and said quickly, stubbornly, 'As it happens, aye, I have.'

He gave a long, slow sigh. He fetched the stool, righted it and sat down, toying with an empty tankard. His palms were sweating. 'Na, there is no one. Not now.'

Strange, he had not thought of Gwenhwyfar these past weeks. Death, often only a spear's length away, allowed no time for thinking. His mind slid back to the memory of her. Mithras, he still wanted her for his own, but he could not have her. What was it he had said to Cunedda about obtaining the wealth to buy his horses – that he might as well marry with Winifred? He groaned and put his head in his hands. It had been a jest, but the listening gods had obviously taken it seriously.

'Get it done quickly then. Before I change my mind. Only I tell you this,' he stood up, the stool's legs scraping on the stone floor, 'I will take her as wife in name. Nothing more.'

Relieved that the matter had worked out easier than he had expected, Vortimer put a hand on Arthur's shoulder. 'We ask nothing more.'

Catigern rubbed his hands together. 'At least,' he said with forced jocularity, 'you will have a virgin bride.'

Arthur stared at him for some moments before bursting into laughter.

As he left the room Vortimer and his brother exchanged puzzled glances. To what reason the laughter, they had no idea.

AUGUST 453

§ XXX

Camulodunum wine was of poor quality, but Arthur cared little about the taste; it was the effect he chased, and the stuff packed enough punch to remain hammering in his head this sun shining day. He was wallowing in a temperamental mood, ready to growl at anyone who crossed his path. Already by mid morning he had argued with Cei over some minor matter, had found his dog limping from a cut paw, and now faced an audience with Vortigern to receive orders that would probably conflict with common sense. The rest of the day did not bode well.

The town was untouched by the Anglian uprising, though its inhabitants remained badly shaken, demanding protection and assurances of future safety. Life in this damp, wind-swept corner, such as it was, was slowly returning to normal – or as normal as it could be with the King in residence and his daughter about to join him.

For Vortigern, each conflict was a greater headache. His British army awaited payment, and Hengest's Jute mercenaries also sought payment for their services, their demands growing daily louder. To pay them Vortigern needed to collect taxes, and those same men who demanded protection consistently avoided the paying of taxes – so the army grumbled, Hengest grumbled and the civilians grumbled. God's eyes, the thing went round and round in a never-ending circle!

Every way he turned, he encountered problems. Problems with the economy, and with the threat of rebellion. The thing was spiralling out of control, like a dropped spindle twisting and jerking, knotting the thread, spoiling the wool. More and more men were coming to join Hengest, settling land that was not theirs for the taking. The British were openly quarrelling with each other and with himself, their king – and the Pendragon was gleefully stirring the dissent. Damn him to hell!

Melwas, now, he trusted implicitly, for his nephew was ambitious but not greedy. Vortigern had made it clear that he would do well out of loyal service to his king. The Summer Land, which had once been Uthr's, was now under Melwas's governorship, and he had the recent given promise of a prized bride. Another trouble: the Pendragon and Melwas fought like cat and dog, their bickering growing louder with each setting sun. Vortigern groaned. He wanted this interview as little as the Pendragon.

It was unfortunate that at the door of Vortigern's chamber Arthur encountered Melwas. The Pendragon stood his ground before the narrow doorway, in no mood for politeness.

Melwas had few good traits. A sour life had left its mark on his sallow, pockmarked skin and scowling features. He had few enjoyments, save women and fighting.

Disdainfully he looked Arthur up and down, his nostrils wrinkling as if the man gave off some foul odour.

'So you're back,' Arthur said cynically. 'Some people are well content to be given the comfortable tasks while the rest of us are left with the men's work.'

Melwas stood squarely before the door. 'You ought to thank me, Pendragon – I have this very hour delivered your future wife to her father.' He thrust his face closer. 'There are none, save myself, the King would entrust with her safekeeping.'

Arthur laughed. 'Happen he can trust you for escort, but it seems he trusts me more in the longer term as her husband!'

Melwas jeered. 'Trust you? This marriage tethers you.' He raised his arm to push Arthur aside. 'Out of my way, Pendragon; I have work to see to while you dally over the niceties of wedding plans.'

'Dare to raise a hand to me, whore-son, and I will remove it from your arm.' Arthur spoke soft, almost casually, his voice the more menacing for its total lack of venom. All he needed was an excuse, and this fat-bellied toad would be lying dead.

They loathed each other, these two men. The one corpulent, loose-jowled and with the strength and stamina of a bull; the other tall and lean with dark hair curling almost to his shoulders, and dark hawk eyes that missed nothing. Each more than ready to kill the other.

It was Melwas's instinctive desire to draw his sword and butcher this arrogant whelp here and now, get the thing finished, but something made him hesitate, some warning that Arthur's words were no idle boast. He did not want a fight on Arthur's terms, so he said, 'I doubt our king would appreciate blood spilt on his threshold. Let me pass.' He pushed Arthur aside and walked away.

Their paths had crossed only a few times these recent months. As fate often wove the way of things, they were to meet as many times in as many days. Outside Vortigern's chamber as Arthur was entering, then the following day, after yet another lecture from Vortigern on not harassing the more peaceful English settlers to the east of Icel's taken boundaries.

By early afternoon Arthur's mood was far worse than the one of the morning. His head throbbed, his body felt strained and taut.

Cei was not sympathetic. 'You never learn. Stay away from the drink, and its after effects will stay away from you.' He had laughed at Arthur's coarse reply.

The horses were waiting, the men ready for afternoon patrol. Flies were irritating the animals, who were stamping hooves, kicking at their tender bellies, and tossing their heads. The heat, after the cold earlier in the month, had come back with a vengeance.

Eira, Arthur's grey stallion, matched his master's temper, laying his ears back and snapping at Cei's chestnut. 'Another worthless patrol to while away what remains of a wasted day,' Arthur complained as he gave the signal for his men to move off. He touched Eira's flank lightly with his heel and the stallion leapt forward, eager to be away from the hovering insects. Arthur restrained him with a firm hand on the rein, keeping him at a dancing walk, head tossing against the bit. The twin towered arched exit loomed ahead; a group of mounted officers burst from the right at a canter, intending to reach the narrow gate first.

Arthur swore as Eira shied, hurtling with a squeal to the left and colliding with Cei, whose stallion reared. Eira bounded forward, his head down, bucking. Somehow Arthur managed to get his hand up and bring him to a halt, head snaking, nostrils snorting.

Melwas sat his mount watching, amused. 'That horse will kill someone before the year is out,' adding in an aside to another officer, 'with any luck, its rider.'

Arthur glared, ready to reply with some colourful oath. Cei urged his chestnut forward, caught Arthur's arm. 'Leave it. You know he goads on purpose. It would not be seemly to fight here.' He nodded over his shoulder, back to where Vortigern had appeared, watching from a window.

Wheeling Eira to rejoin his turma, Arthur said, 'Let the King's favourite ride through first – we need the air cleared of this stench.'

Melwas caught the faint chuckle of amusement from Arthur's men, though he had not heard the words.

Sweeping a hand forward with elaborate politeness, Arthur indicated the other man should proceed. The instant Melwas had his back to him, made an obscene gesture. His men laughed.

Their paths crossed again within the span of another two days.

The patrols, as Arthur had predicted, were proving a waste of time. Ride in fast, burn the Saex in their hovels, that was the answer; not this senseless riding round and round chasing shadows. Then there were at least two British villas worth checking. Arthur and his men had found the owner of one a week since, footsore, bleeding and near death. He had stumbled through the darkness avoiding the rowdy groups of Saex and made his way south to the British. He died an hour after reaching sanctuary, having told of how his family had been dragged from their hiding place and slaughtered; he had escaped because he was busy burying his massed wealth. 'Out in the field beyond the granary wall I put it!' He coughed, spitting flecks of blood. Silver salvers, gold, jewels... Arthur had laid the man to rest. Happen he'd get the chance to go looking for it one day.

Hot and sweating, grimy and dry-throated returning from patrol, Arthur made his way to the bathhouse with Cei. The place was crowded with like minded men thankful to cleanse their bodies of the day's work and heat. A storm was brewing, they agreed, though the black clouds were not yet visible. Come nightfall rain and thunder would be upon them. What was drearier – riding patrol in dusty heat or lashing rain?

The bathhouse provided an opportunity to relax, to talk with friends and take life at an easier pace for a while. Arthur dozed in the steam of the hot room, let the dirt trickle from him with the opening of pores and sweating skin. Rousing himself, he plunged into the pool of the frigidarium, its coldness taking his breath away. He swam energetically, ignoring the scream of protest from his hot skin, the water sluicing away tiredness with the grime. He swam another width then heaved himself from the pool with a grunt of satisfaction. Taking a towel from a slave he rubbed himself vigorously until his body tingled refreshingly clean. Casting the towel down, he made for the changing rooms, waving a greeting to Cei, still reclining in the steam room and embarking on what promised to be an easy win at dice.

Whistling some soldier's tune Arthur reached for his clothes. A sudden thump in the small of his back sent him reeling, gasping for air. His hands struggled for a hold, but he fell, his head striking sharply against the corner of the wooden bench. Men crowded round, lifting him from the floor. As their faces and the room spun before his eyes, Arthur focused on one in particular. Melwas.

The man feigned a concerned expression, asked if Arthur was all right, said something about the effect of strong wine.

Pushing the helpers aside, Arthur scrambled to his feet. 'You punched me, you bastard whore son!'

Melwas raised his hands in innocent surprise. 'I have just this moment entered the building!'

Another voice. 'You lie, Melwas. I saw you.'

The room fell silent, eyes turning to the speaker who stepped forward from the entrance. Etern pushed his way through the crowd to face Vortigern's nephew, the favoured one.

'So Gwynedd has pulled out already, eh?' Melwas sneered. 'Had enough? Can't take hard work?'

Etern folded his arms and leant against a pillar, nodded a greeting to Arthur. 'On the contrary, we have cleared our allotted area to the north; all is settled, quiet and under control. We have served our required time and now return to Londinium to collect my sister and cousin before going home.'

A smirk. 'Gwenhwyfar will not be leaving Londinium.'

'Will she not? We shall see.' Etern shifted his weight to the other leg, his gaze never leaving Melwas's face. 'I followed you in,' he said. 'I watched as you passed behind Arthur. Saw your fist strike him.'

Melwas turned a blotched, angry pink, his eyes narrowed, lips thin and colourless. 'I would expect you to side with the Pendragon, Etern of Gwynedd,' he snarled. 'Traitors' dung clings.'

Arthur lunged forward, but someone grabbed his arm and hauled him back. Melwas was facing Etern, who stood relaxed, casual, arms still folded, wearing an easy smile.

'You regard us from Gwynedd as traitors then, Melwas?'

'The whole warren is infested with them! It needs smoking, every last one cleansed from its lair, the Pendragon here along with the rest.' Melwas flung a hand in Arthur's direction, but directed his accusation at Etern.

Shrugging off the arm that held him, Arthur stepped forward to stand beside Cunedda's son. 'Even Gwenhwyfar?' he asked, his voice so low only those nearest caught the words.

Melwas leered. 'The moment I have her in my bed she will be too busy satisfying my needs to draw breath for Gwynedd. With her belly full, she will have no time for thoughts.'

Etern smiled lazily. 'I should think my sister will have something to say on that score.'

'Your sister will not be permitted her say. She is mine for bedding and breeding.'

Arthur could listen to no more. 'You bastard!' He flung the words as his fist came up, striking Melwas on the jaw.

Staggering, Melwas recovered his balance and brought a dagger to hand, bearing down on Arthur, who belatedly realised his lack of clothing and weapon. He leapt back, arching his unprotected body away from the swooping blade.

It all happened so swiftly. Etern lunged forward, grabbing at the sleeve of Melwas's tunic, dragging him to one side, away from Arthur. Melwas roared with anger and swung in the direction he was pulled, stabbing with the blade.

Etern clung to the woven cloth, stubbornly refusing to let go as he sank to his knees, aware of some dull ache in his chest. He coughed, spewing blood from his mouth, and fell slowly forward, ripping the tunic with his hand.

They stood stunned, frozen in disbelief as the life flowed from Etern, spreading in a grotesque dark puddle across the mosaic tiles.

Melwas clutched his cloak to him, away from the blood. He took in the hostile silence, dropped the dagger, sending it clattering to the floor. He fled, leaping over the sprawled body, running for the door. No one followed.

Arthur bent to Etern, turned him over, wiped the frothy blood from his blue-tinged lips, closed the eyes that stared in questioning surprise. He felt nothing, only a solid wedge of loss, a knot of desperate bereavement.

Tears spilt unchecked from his eyes, though whether he wept for Etern or Gwenhwyfar he would never know.

§ XXXI

The purple malevolence of storm darkness was gathering in the
northern sky, louring down into the western night-cluster of violent
red sunset-tinged cloud. Sitting alone in her chamber, Gwenhwyfar
aimlessly combed out the tangles in her hair, watching fascinated as the
storm loomed closer above the reds and greys of Londinium's jumbled
rooftops. A streak of lightning ripped across the blackness, followed by
the boom of thunder. She sighed: there would not be much sleep if that
was going to be trumpeting all night. Turning at a sound in the doorway,
she smiled a greeting as Ceridwen entered. 'Any news?'

The girl dropped the packages she was clutching on a couch and
ran her hand through wind tousled hair. Drops of water spattering the
shoulders of her cloak scattered as she removed it and shook away the
damp. 'It's starting to rain, I got back just in time.' She sat down and began
to remove her boots, replacing them with softer house shoes. She leant
forward, selected one of the packages and tossed it to Gwenhwyfar. 'A
present.'

Catching it and eagerly unwrapping the folded cloth, Gwenhwyfar
said, 'You ought not go treating other people, my lass, but thank you all
the same.' She discovered a new comb, fine carved from elephant ivory,
and held it beside her old one with its broken teeth. 'This,' she said,
moving across to give Ceridwen a kiss of thanks, 'I needed!'

A twelvemonth younger than Gwenhwyfar, Ceridwen was a slight girl
with fine features and a fragility of build that belied her strength. She
had been a happy child, though timid, and was now a contented young

woman eager to please and serve her cousin as friend and companion. She displayed her other purchases: a roll of silk and a small wooden bird, carved so delicately that it seemed it might fly away if released from her hand.

Admiring the things, Gwenhwyfar asked again, 'And is there any news?'

Ceridwen ignored the question; instead she fetched her own comb and stood to tend her damp, ruffled hair. Gwenhwyfar playfully pushed her towards the bed, tickling her ribs. 'Tell me, you wretch!'

Laughing, Ceridwen fended her cousin off, calling pax. 'You did not want to know of the Queen yesterday when I told you she was in labour.'

'That was yesterday,' Gwenhwyfar retorted.

Eager for the chance at her own teasing, Ceridwen adjusted her rumpled clothing and sat forward on the edge of the bed.

'You ought have come shopping with me, the market was full of the news.'

Exasperated, Gwenhwyfar threatened more tickling. 'If you don't tell me...'

Ceridwen laughed. 'Apparently she's well after the birthing.'

Gwenhwyfar buffeted her cousin with a pillow. 'I don't give a Picti curse for the queen! The babe, Ceridwen, the babe?'

'Oh, the babe!' Ceridwen feigned deliberate misunderstanding. 'You are interested in babies of a sudden!'

The pillow thwacked harder, amid a splutter of giggles from Ceridwen and a burst of feathers as the thing split. Giving in, she announced, 'The Queen gave birth some hours past to a fine healthy boy!'

'What!' Gwenhwyfar leapt to her feet, a swirl of feathers drifting around her like a blizzard. 'A boy! Good God!'

'I thought you would be pleased,' Ceridwen said sarcastically, drawing her knees up to her chest.

Gwenhwyfar strolled to the window, hands joined, fingers on lips. After all these years the King's Saex wife had given him a living son! The window rattled with a gust of storm wind, the fragile glass quivering. Another flash of lightning, illuminating the lurid sky, and a crash of thunder. Outside, in the bedraggled gardens, the trees and bushes tossed under the assault of wind and rain. A slate from the roof tumbled past this first-floor window and crashed to the ground. Another gust caught the casement, the frail wood shuddering. Gwenhwyfar put her hand on the catch, intending to pull it more firmly shut. Lightning lit the British patrol guard struggling along the outer wall-walk that surrounded the palace, his hooded cloak pulled tight around his ears, the rain lashing his back. What did he think of this babe, then? The same thoughts that ran through Gwenhwyfar's mind, that must be in the minds of all who hated Vortigern? That a half breed Saex son might become king?

The wind gusted again, sending a swirl of leaves and twigs high into the sky, caught with a thud of anger at the window, ripping the catch from the rotten frame. The casement swung wide, two panes of glass shattering. Rain and the ice bite of the gale howled like a charging war host into the room.

Gwenhwyfar swore as the catch ripped her hand and the sharp edges of glass splintered.

Glancing up startled, Ceridwen saw Gwenhwyfar's hair blown in a great wild mass, the faded tapestries lifting from the walls; heard the wind rush through the room, the cry of the storm as it invaded the warmth and safety, breaching the defences. Gwenhwyfar gasped as blood dripped from her hand. Ceridwen jumped from the bed and, grabbing a cloth, made to wrap it round the jagged oozing gash running across her cousin's palm.

Gwenhwyfar stared at the blood drip, dripping on the tiles at her feet. The wind moaned in her ears; the room was spinning, her head swimming with the noise and whirl of confusion. She sank to the floor, her skin chalk white, lips tinged blue.

Running to the door Ceridwen shouted for help, ran back to Gwenhwyfar, frightened. Gwenhwyfar never fainted, never acted so strange. She patted her cousin's cold, clammy cheeks, calling her name.

Trembling, Gwenhwyfar responded, her senses floating in a misty profusion of semi reality. She clutched at the younger girl, mouthed something, the words refusing to come, spinning and spinning around in her head, catching in her dry throat. There was blood on the floor, running down her arm, staining tiles and gown, smeared across Ceridwen's cheek. Gwenhwyfar screamed, a long, unending howl of grief, she had seen Death revealed beneath his leering mask.

She was being lifted, carried. Voices, people clustering and flustering. Her head and hand throbbed. Her body ached. 'Please go away.' Did they? Or did she drift into the darkness of that other world, where reality becomes nothing and dreams leapt alive?

Thunder grumbled and the wind rattled at firmly closed shutters. Shadows from the two lamps leapt and danced, stirred by creeping draughts. Gwenhwyfar woke, felt a weight heavy at her feet that shifted as she moved. Ceridwen, sprawled asleep across the end of the bed. What had happened? For an anxious moment, Gwenhwyfar could not recall.

Ceridwen sat up, stiff from the awkward angle that she had slept in. Her hand tingled as it came to life. 'Gwen? I have been so worried.'

Fumbling for her cousin's hand, Gwenhwyfar drew her close with an urgent need to hold tight to something solid. Tears flowed, softly at first, then uncontrollably.

'Gwen, what's wrong?' Ceridwen felt more frightened than ever she remembered. This was not like Gwenhwyfar. Gwenhwyfar was strong, nothing frightened Gwenhwyfar. Gwenhwyfar never cried. Ceridwen shuffled up the bed, gathered her cousin close, rocking her as if she were an infant. 'Please, tell me what's wrong.'

Gwenhwyfar gulped, steadied her breath and gathered her confused thoughts. 'I saw blood.' Her teeth wouldn't stop chattering.

Ceridwen shook her head, not understanding. 'But you are not afeared of blood, even your own.'

Hugging herself, Gwenhwyfar tried to control the shaking, the great trembling that shuddered through her cold body. 'Not my blood!' Her eyes were staring, frightened and shocked. 'I saw a man's blood spreading on a tiled floor.'

Ceridwen's eyes were puzzled. 'Which man? Who? A brother, your father?'

Arthur? The thought roared like a charging boar into Gwenhwyfar's mind. Not Arthur! Please, not Arthur! Aloud, 'I don't know! Oh, I don't know!'

§ XXXII

Rainwater dripping from Cunedda's sodden cloak collected beneath his boots and drained into a missing square of the tessellated flooring. Gwenhwyfar watched the spreading puddle light-headed and distant, as if she were floating with the sensation of over much drink. What was it Da said? Etern dead? Etern was not dead, she had seen him alive and laughing; he had hugged her, kissed her before riding north with Da to fight the Saex. There was no sense in all this! Etern could not be dead!

Morning spread dismal and gloomy beyond the shuttered windows. Rain beat against the patched glass, with squalls of wind squirming through cracks beneath doors and windows, rustling among the hanging tapestries, and flaring the flames of the braziers, everything damp and miserable. At any moment Etern would come swaggering through the door with a cheery wave of his hand, a laugh on his face and a careless tossed greeting as if he had never been away.

One little thought kept ticking and ticking in Gwenhwyfar's mind: It was not Arthur. Thank the gods it was not Arthur! The scream was there, hovering and wheedling closer to the surface. It was not Arthur! It was not Arthur, god damn it, it was her brother, her beloved brother! But she could only think of how it was not Arthur. What was wrong with her?

Cunedda was holding her firmly by the shoulders, saying again all he had just said, for he too could not believe it, needed to speak the words to hear the truth. 'Melwas murdered your brother, my son. He was intending to strike at Arthur, but Etern deflected the thrust, took the blade through his chest.'

Gwenhwyfar wanted to say, 'I know, I saw it,' but it had been her own blood she had seen, blood from her cut hand. The wind had broken the glass, and the glass had gashed her hand. Her blood, not Etern's. Hers. She stood mute, quite still, staring at that incongruous puddle of muddy rainwater beneath Cunedda's boots. Only the water was blood, spreading ghastly red.

Her father felt muddled and dizzy, exhausted. It had been a long, fast ride. No time to stop for rest, for food or drink. Riding fast through the night, with the rain beating in your face, the horses feared of the thunder, the bursts of lightning. Etern, his youngest son! His son, dead! All his children had struggled through the infections and accidents of childhood. Now the sons were grown and at their father's side. To a soldier death followed constant at heel, like an unwelcome shadow; to die in battle could be accepted, expected. Typiaunan had died defending his territory and family – aye, though the killing had come at the hand of murderers. But to be stabbed by a dull blade in some bathhouse brawl? What sense was there in such a wicked death?

Cunedda said something else, had to say it twice over. Gwenhwyfar lifted her eyes, stared at him as though he were talking gibberish. Melwas? Coming for her – why should he do that? What had she to do with Melwas, the man who had killed her brother? She pressed her hands to her ears and turned away, shaking her head, almost losing hold of reality. Cunedda stopped her walking away, his hands on her arms, shaking her.

'Daughter, you must listen to me, must listen well! You are in danger. I want you to remain in this room while I arrange our leaving.'

Gwenhwyfar broke free of his grasp, confused, uncertain. What was happening?

Her father limped to a chair, groaned as he sat. Just a few minutes' rest, just a moment to get his breath, to think. A cold numbness suffused his exhausted body. This day he felt his age, felt the ache of every battle scar. Enniaun was seeing to the horses; he could take a minute to rest. Wearily he pushed himself to his feet. *Na*, he could not, there were things that must be done.

Melwas had fled Camulodunum, could already be here in Londinium, could have dared come for Gwenhwyfar. Ah, but if he were to show his face Cunedda would run him through, strangle him with his bare hands, take a rope and... Talk sense, man! Revenge would come in its own time. For now, Gwenhwyfar must be made safe. If she fell into that murdering bastard's hands there would be little Cunedda could do to stop this abominable marriage – and over the smouldering ruins of Gwynedd's destruction, never would he allow that now! The agreement was finished, ended. The bloodprice of grieving kin demanded it so!

Over and over on that mad ride through swollen rivers, cloying mud and biting wind Cunedda had cursed himself. He should never have agreed to Vortigern's demands, never have come to Londinium!

'Da?' Gwenhwyfar said, standing forlorn and shattered, willing that some form of sense would return. Night had its own terrors, but the coming of day was bringing no comfort. She spread her hands, imploring. 'I do not understand any of this.' She ran her uninjured hand through her hair, clutching at its wild looseness, and stared hopelessly at the sagging man before her with a sudden feeling of standing on the edge of nothing, hovering between the solid and the void. Blackness beckoned, calling, pulling her forward. Gwenhwyfar wanted to scream, to pull back, but the emptiness lured her nearer; it would only need one step more.

Cunedda watched his daughter's spirit staring blind and scared through the dark, empty hollows of her anguished eyes. He should have told her years past, in the security of her own home; not here, not like this. 'I have done you a great wrong, daughter. At the time I had no choice. Happen I ought to have sought harder for an alternative. Can you ever forgive me?'

He took her cold hands and began chafing away the numbness with his own stiffening fingers.

His voice seemed to come from a great distance. She answered flatly, 'Forgive you for what, Da?' Her eyes appealed for help as her mind fought to accept this crazed, whirlpool reality.

Still holding her hand, Cunedda told her in a quick breath of the betrothal with Melwas. Gwenhwyfar listened, the words sounding as unreal as some weird harper's tale. She was shaking her head, backing away. Her safe, comfortable world was being torn apart, ripped to shreds by claws and teeth, fragmenting, dissolving. Etern was dead, and she was to marry with the man who had murdered him? This was surely some waking dream, a wizard's trickery!

She sank to the floor, her knees weak as that blackness brought her nearer the brink of madness. Her father knelt with her and cradled her to him. The cold and wet made his teeth chatter.

'I have done all I could, save murder.' He choked back a sob, abandoned the effort to contain his grief, and let the anguish flood from him, his tears mingling with those of his daughter. 'By all the pity of the Gods!' he cried, 'was there no other way to stop this thing? Did I need to sacrifice my son for my daughter?'

They sat for a while together, holding each other for comfort. Then through the pain came the spear-lunge of sudden anger. Gwenhwyfar recoiled from her father. 'Do you think I would have agreed to this obscenity?' Spirit and pride jerked her back from despair into awareness. 'I would destroy myself rather than go to such a marriage bed!'

'And destroy Gwynedd in doing so?' Cunedda spoke more sharply than he intended.

'It is my right to refuse.' She looked like a wild thing, hair unbound, eyes flashing, her teeth bared in a snarl of defiance. 'It is my right to have a say in my marriage. By British law, my right!'

The reply was harsh, Cunedda's responding anger fuelled by her own. Anger breeds anger. 'You forget – Vortigern rules by Roman law.'

She wanted to hit him, hit something. To draw her dagger from her belt and plunge it into somebody. Vortigern, Melwas; Etern for being dead. Arthur for being alive. Only she had no dagger. The bitch queen had it. The anger vanished as suddenly as it had come, leaving a hollow loss of despair. She tried desperately not to cry.

Cunedda sighed, a drawn-out, helpless sound. 'I had little choice, Gwen,' He limped towards her and enfolded her with his lion paws. 'I am sorry, lass.'

'What can we do?' She buried her face in his chest, refusing to let the tears come. After a while she ventured a look at him.

Though his face usually had a sternness that made even the strongest quail, she knew the tenderness that underlay the necessary façade of a strong leader. But here was a strange expression, never seen before: anxiety and fear.

Cunedda forced a smile. 'Ah, lass.' He moved to a stool and seated himself slowly, his aches progressing into painful stiffness. He looked at his strong, brown hands, the palms callused from reins and weapons. 'Our hands are tied by Vortigern's whims and fancies.' He scowled. 'It's time to return to Gwynedd. My place is in my own land, not dancing at Vortigern's heels. From this time forward, let him see to his own.' He held out his arms, inviting her into his embrace. She responded, hugging him close. Over the years, his daughter had given cause for anger, laughter or shed tears. The most tiresome of children, but held more dear than any fortune in gold or jewels. He stroked her hair back from her forehead, tucked a loose strand behind her ear. 'You are more precious to me than Gwynedd, child.'

She gave a tentative smile. 'Nothing is more precious than Gwynedd, Da. We are mere bystanders in her history. Gwynedd is in her infancy; she will remain great long after our bodies have turned to dust. One day she will breed princes and great kings to be feared and loved throughout all Britain. Gwynedd shall make the laws, fight the battles and keep the peace.' Gwenhwyfar broadened her smile, gaining courage. 'I would like to think we had some small part in the moulding of her proud future.' She tightened her grasp around her father's waist, urgently needing his rock-steady firmness, and was startled to discover how his body shook.

'God's love! You are soaked, you will catch a fever like this!' She plunged into a rush of activity, running to the door, calling for servants to bring another brazier, food and wine, dry clothing. She kissed his cheek, suddenly calm about everything 'You are wiser than that fool Vortigern. You will always outwit him.'

Cunedda laughed, his own tension lifting. 'Then let us pray your faith is strong. Outwitting Vortigern is no easy task!'

Warmed with hot broth and dressed in dry bracae and tunic, Cunedda sat for a while.

Rain still fell outside, the morning brightening to midday and beyond, through the shadow of heavy cloud. Gwenhwyfar, at her father's feet, poked at a glowing brazier. He toyed with her loose hair, so like her mother's. Suddenly, he missed Gwawl. Missed her strength and laughter, her warmth and unswerving love. He wondered if there was indeed an afterworld where life continued on. Was Etern with his mother? How pleased she would be to see him, how proud. He shook the fancy aside. The time would come to grieve, but not here, not now.

He lifted his head as a polite tap sounded at the door. Gwenhwyfar rose to answer it, but Cunedda waved her aside, going himself to the door, sword drawn. Outside stood a young man, his face hidden by the hood of a coarsely woven servant's cloak. A muttered exchange of words, then Cunedda closed the door and returned to the warmth of the brazier. A grim smile twitched beneath his moustache.

'Melwas is not here at the palace – he has taken shelter in a tavern some miles to the north.' He nodded, satisfied. He was right to have made such haste, glad he was where he ought to be – *na*, not quite; he and his family ought to be in Gwynedd, but that would shortly be arranged. 'Vortigern is expected to be returning to Londinium on the morrow. I intend to claim legal blood-right and ride from here in peace.' He sighed. 'I would that we could just go, but I want no Saex riding hard after us, demanding we follow the King's damned formalities. We will do this thing right. Melwas is in the wrong, not us. One cheering thought, Gwen!' Cunedda grinned. 'The King is showing signs of his creeping age. He cannot ride as fast as I!' They laughed together, hiding their true feelings, sharing each other's sorrow as rain pattered steadily beyond the closed window shutters.

'Da?' Gwenhwyfar spoke softly, her voice rousing Cunedda from the pull of sleep. 'Does Arthur know of this arranged betrothal?' It had been a thought hanging with her this past half hour.

'He does.'

She fought back fresh tears. Cunedda slid an arm around her shoulder, pulling her to him as if he would never let her go. 'By all the gods I wish I had ignored this agreement with Vortigern and accepted Arthur when he asked for you, but until this…' He faltered, searching for adequate words. 'Until Melwas provided me with it, I had no escape. Arthur himself pointed out the greatest danger. Were I to let you marry with anyone else your life would be forever endangered.'

One little spark of comfort began to grow in Gwenhwyfar, flaring warmer as she considered it. 'Arthur asked for me?'

'Aye.'

Gwenhwyfar, her head buried deep in her father's lap, let the tears fall. She had cried so much since that vision yesterday evening. Yesterday? Years past, it seemed. Could there be more tears left within her? At least now she understood why Arthur's attitude had changed so abruptly. Why he had danced with Winifred and not with her.

Cunedda's grip on her shoulder slackened and his breathing became low and even. Without disturbing him, Gwenhwyfar found a fur, placed it carefully over him and stood watching him sleep. There were grizzled streaks in his hair, she realised; the red was changing to grey. She had never thought of her father as old. She felt old herself – old and very weary. Her body ached, she was so tired.

Gwenhwyfar stumbled to the bed. She would lie down for a while, close her eyes, let the throbbing pain in her head ease.

She dreamt of muddled images. A glinting knife and red blood, Etern as boy and man, laughing – dying. Melwas with evil leering eyes.

And of Arthur.

§ XXXIII

Late afternoon. Without knocking, Cunedda burst into his daughter's chamber, startling her and Ceridwen.

'Is your packing complete?' he asked curtly.

'Aye, Uncle.' Ceridwen glanced at Gwenhwyfar for confirmation. 'We are ready to leave as soon as you give the order.'

'These here?' Cunedda pointed at two wooden chests standing to one side. Ceridwen nodded.

'Too much.' He strode over to the nearest, heaved up the lid and, rummaging inside, began to throw clothing on the floor. He cursed and left it.

'Sort a few gowns, only what can be carried in saddlebags.' He went over to the window. The shutters were open to let in a little light before night descended and he frowned as the guard patrolling along the water-wall came within view. 'Niece, you leave with Enniaun for Gwynedd within the hour.'

'What of you?' Gwenhwyfar asked, stooping to retrieve the garments strewn about the floor.

'I shall stay to see through your marriage ceremony, arranged for the morrow.'

Gwenhwyfar dropped the clothing. 'But...'

Her father would not listen to protests. Pulling a cloak from the back of a chair, he tossed it at her. 'Use this to bundle what you need for yourself.'

His daughter, clutching the caught cloak, stamped her foot. 'I will not wed that bastard!'

Cunedda's expression darkened. 'Vortigern sends word that you must. He will be here to witness the handfasting, and has personally paid the blood-price for Etern's death. I am given the land along the coast down to the Ystwyth, and the right to the title of prince.'

'You have bargained me away for that!'

'Enough, Gwenhwyfar!'

She bit back a retort, gripping the cloak tighter between her fingers. 'I am to be hostage then?'

'So it seems.'

She bent to pick up a gown, rolled it. Stopped. 'Then why,' she asked, 'do I need to bundle clothing in this cloak?'

Cunedda's agitation changed to a grin. 'Because I am secretly arranging for you to sail tonight to Ygrainne in Less Britain.'

'What!' Gwenhwyfar flung the cloak aside. 'Am I to be forced into exile?'

Drily, 'Would you rather stay in Londinium to wed with Melwas?'

She cried then, caught between the one or the other, felt as she did when as a child she used to play at rolling down a slope. Tumbling down and down, over and over, faster and faster; head spinning, stomach churning. Never knowing when you were going to stop.

Cunedda took her shoulders and drew breath to steady his own racing pulse. 'I have been this past hour with the King's envoy.' His voice was hard. 'Melwas also.'

She gasped. 'Melwas is in the palace?'

'Aye. Vortigern apparently backs his nephew.' Cunedda's mouth drew tight as he held his anger in check. Time enough for that when he had his daughter safe. 'Etern, it seems, drew blade first.' He hushed his daughter's immediate protest. 'I know, it is a lie. But witnesses have spoken for Melwas: money and sweet words can buy anything.' He searched her face. Had she understood his meaning – how important it was to go, and go quickly? 'Vortigern sends word that this marriage is the only way to ensure peace between us.' Vortigern and his poxed kin could rot in their Christian hell for all Cunedda cared He would bow and scrape to the envoy, agree all there was to agree, buy time – and get away. The King could not force Gwenhwyfar to marry if she was not here. And the extra land and title? Ah, well, Cunedda was considering the taking of them anyway. With or without Vortigern's gracious consent.

'I have a man securing a ship at this moment,' he explained. 'You sail at the first opportunity.' He did not add the ifs. *If I can get you safely out of the palace; if you can make sail along the Tamesis before your leaving is discovered.*

'I see.' Gwenhwyfar squared her chin against the churning panic. Given the King's present problems with the economy and the Saex, he would be hard pressed to follow her. She gathered up her belongings, flinging them on to the bed.

Ceridwen plucked up courage, from where she knew not, and stood before her uncle looking him straight in the eye. 'I will not return to Gwynedd, my lord. I will go to Less Britain with my cousin.'

Placing his hands on the girl's shoulders, Cunedda gave her an affectionate shake. 'My dear, she may be gone for...' He paused. For how long? 'Some while.'

'All the more reason to go with her.'

Ceasing her bustle, Gwenhwyfar hugged her. 'Are you sure?'

Ceridwen nodded. 'I am sure.'

'Then I'll be glad of your company.'

Cunedda gave the younger girl a loving embrace. 'I thank you, child, for your loyalty. It will not go unrewarded.'

Ceridwen blushed, stammering, 'I seek no reward, Uncle.'

'Come,' said Gwenhwyfar, pushing Ceridwen forward. 'Put on two of every garment. It will be cold at sea by night and we know not what type of ship to expect.'

'In a while.' Ceridwen was heading for the door, sensible, practical as ever. 'We may be hungry before sunrise. I will see what food I can beg. I have been bringing meals up to you of late – no one will suspect.'

'Go then. Be quick.'

Gwenhwyfar stripped to her undergarments, rummaged among the rumpled clothes and pulled on two layers. Cunedda had taken up her jewel casket and emptied the items into a leather pouch. 'There is extra in here. I shall send more.'

Taking it, Gwenhwyfar hid the pouch within the garments rolled in her cloak. 'Take care of Tan for me, Da.'

Cunedda raised his eyebrows. 'All this, and you take time to think of your damned mare!'

Gwenhwyfar pulled a cord tight around the bundle, remarking lightly, 'If I were to think of more important things, my belly would freeze with fear and I would be unable to set one foot before the other.'

Her father nodded, knowing how she felt. 'I will run her with my best stallion and will breed you a fine colt.'

Gwenhwyfar smiled approval. 'For the Pendragon, my gift to him.'

Choking suddenly, her father held his arms wide, feeling the need to hold his daughter. She ran to him, pressing close to his body.

For a while he held her, stroking her hair, breathing in her perfume. It would be a while and a while afore they met again. Then he set her from him. There was much to do. 'I must wish your brother a safe journey home.' He winked at her. 'He will take Tan with him.'

Forcing a smile until he left the room, Gwenhwyfar slumped on to the bed. Left alone, the blackness edged nearer, bringing fresh fears and pain. She lay down and buried her head in a pillow, hugging its goose-down softness for comfort. The pit was before her again; only one step and she would be in, lost to despair. It was as if a long, silent scream were wailing and wailing inside her head.

Some fifteen minutes she lay there, only roused as Ceridwen ran terrified into the room. She threw a bundle of food on the floor and whirled to slam the door shut behind her, thudding the bolts home. She stood panting, her back pressed against the wood. 'Melwas is coming!'

Gwenhwyfar's hands flew to her mouth, failed to stop the small scream escaping. Think quickly! Turn panic to action. 'He must not suspect anything! Hide these bundles. Quickly!'

They tidied the room, cramming strewn clothing into chests, kicking things under the bed. Would Melwas notice her padded figure? They had never met, he might not.

They were prepared, but the stamp and thud of feet beyond the door made them jump all the same. Ceridwen stuffed her fingers in her mouth, trying to resist the impulse to hide behind her cousin. Melwas bellowed, demanding entry. Calmly Gwenhwyfar walked to the door and spoke through it. 'What means this? I mourn my brother, will accept no visitors.'

'I have urgent matters to discuss. Let me enter.' From his tone, he was not about to go away.

Could she deny him entrance? Gwenhwyfar doubted it. She tried another feint. 'I am alone, my lord, I cannot receive a man in my chamber.' She motioned frantically to Ceridwen and whispered, 'Hide yourself over there,' pointing to the chests. Ceridwen crouched behind them and Gwenhwyfar flung bed furs over her. 'And for the sake of the gods,' she hissed, 'remain still!' Ceridwen giggled nervously. 'Do not let him stay long.'

That,' Gwenhwyfar assured her, 'I promise you.'

Melwas was pounding on the door, but suddenly the noise ceased. Gwenhwyfar's heart beat as loud as his knocking. Had he gone? *Na,* he spoke again, level and explicit. 'Draw the bolts or I shall have my men axe the door.'

Gwenhwyfar waited a few moments, then straightened her shoulders and drew back the bolts. Melwas burst through, almost knocking her aside as he strode into the room, glaring around as if he expected to find some other man there. Gwenhwyfar remained at the door, holding it open. The men, Saex, were standing guard beyond.

Melwas moved to stand within an inch of her. 'If you dare to deny me entrance again I shall order you whipped.' He flung the door shut, challenging her to object.

She stood relaxed but alert. 'To what do I owe this pleasure?'

'I have brought you a gift.' He spoke triumphantly, gloating, knowing he had won out over Cunedda. He took her hand, led her away from the door and slipped a jewelled ring on her finger. 'Tomorrow I shall add a marriage band.' He raised her hand to his lips, his eyes never leaving hers. They were dark green with flashes of tawny gold. Attractive. But Melwas did not know her. Did not realise those sparks and flashes were signs of seething hatred. He turned her hand over to stroke the soft skin of her palm, and placed a kiss at the tip of each finger. Afterwards, Gwenhwyfar marvelled that she had mastered the overwhelming desire to snatch her hand away and spit in his face.

He was a short man, no more than five feet and a few inches, his lack of stature the more obvious because of his bulk. Clean-shaven, he wore his hair cut short in the Roman style, but was dressed like a Saex. His eyes were dark and set too close together, small eyes that darted suspiciously Gwenhwyfar was reminded of a boar. A great ugly stinking boar.

Melwas grinned, a leer that passed beyond pleasantness. 'You are indeed a fine woman. A good catch. Though I would have preferred you to be a trifle shorter.' He let go of her hand.

She wiped his touch away on the back of her skirt, thought '*Would you like me to cut my feet off at the ankles then?*' She smiled placidly.

Melwas enjoyed talking, it seemed – best let him conduct the conversation. 'Circumstances make it imperative that I take you as wife without further delay.' As he spoke, his gaze had dropped to her bosom. She thanked the gods her choice of clothing for this cold weather concealed her body from the neck down!

'I had been told you were a skinny rake.' He laughed lasciviously and moved closer, his body brushing against hers. 'I like to have something to get hold of. Good firm teats and buttocks.' Gwenhwyfar stood her ground. His mouth opened wider to reveal yellow-stained teeth, his breath foul. 'Soon enough we shall have you broader, when I have my son breeding in you!' He bent to kiss her mouth, his lips flabby against hers, his flesh oily. God's truth, he stank!

Gwenhwyfar pulled away, fighting nausea and the desire to wipe his obscene taste from her mouth. 'My lord, this is not seemly. I ought not to be alone with you.'

His laughter shifted to a more malicious sound. 'Why not? We are betrothed, the morrow sees our wedding day!' He smirked at her, drawing her to him, pressing his body tight against hers. 'And after that,' he added, 'our wedding night.'

Gwenhwyfar removed his hand from the lacings of her bodice. If he should discover the layers she wore! He tried again to unfasten her gown, but she wriggled and managed to break free.

'Come, Gwenhwyfar! Need we wait?' He grabbed suddenly at her hair, forestalling any further movement. She fumbled for her dagger, silently cursed.

'I suppose' – he nibbled at her ear, his breath hot on her neck – 'I must express my regrets for your brother's death – though my action was purely in self-defence you understand. A regrettable incident.' His lips sucked at her flesh. 'He and the Pendragon were spoiling for a quarrel with me – in the name of God, I know not why.' His hands moved to her buttocks.

Gwenhwyfar wanted to kill him, gouge his eyes out, rip his testicles from his body, slit his stomach. She managed to step away. 'My brother has always been —' She stopped herself. 'Always was imprudent.' She choked over the words. 'My lord,' she had to have him gone! 'I am flattered you desire me, and I too look forward to our wedding night, but would not haste spoil the excitement of anticipation?'

'I am not one for formality. I take what is mine, when and where I want it.'

Gwenhwyfar walked quickly to the door and opened it. '*I wager you do, you bastard.*' She smiled, forcing all the pleasure she could into that sweet expression. 'Our joyous union must be blessed by the priest, and waiting,' she flicked a flirtatious look at him, 'heightens reward.'

Melwas grinned more broadly and hitched his sword belt arrogantly higher. Gwenhwyfar shuddered but kept her smile firm. 'And your son must be legitimate born.' She spoke with such conviction!

He kissed her again as he ambled past, eyes lingering on her deliciously rounded chest. 'Until the morrow then.'

'I await it eagerly.' She flung the door closed behind him, slamming home the bolts. Leaning back against the door as Ceridwen had done she swore all the most vile and obscene oaths she knew.

Ceridwen scrambled from her hiding place, face red from anger and holding her breath. 'How dare he! What an arrogant spiteful beast!'

Going to the water pitcher, Gwenhwyfar scrubbed at her mouth with fresh, clean tasting water and wiped her face and hands. His taste lingered; again she swilled water in her mouth and spat it from her.

'We must find my father, leave here now. We cannot wait until tonight.'

Her cousin did not argue.

Opening the door, Gwenhwyfar found her way barred by crossed spears. 'What is this outrage?' she demanded, taking hold of each spear, attempting to force them apart.

Saxons, large, fairhaired men – the palace swarmed with the creatures, Hengest's men. Melwas's too, it seemed. But then Melwas always had run with the King's mercenary pack.

Employing others to do the dirty work was no new thing. Rome had often done so, playing off one tribe's squabbles against another. Along the Tamesis and following the line of the Ancient Way, there were third, even fourth generation Saex settlers whose forefathers had fought alongside British auxiliary troops, with land given, according to custom, on retirement from service. Using the English was nothing new – except, unlike Rome, Vortigern had neither money nor land to give in exchange.

One of the guards spoke a few words of guttural British. 'Orders, Lord Melwas. You remain chamber.'

'Am I a prisoner then?'

The man shrugged, holding his spear firm across the doorway. 'No speak British,' he said. Gwenhwyfar had a deep suspicion that he did, and spoke it well.

'Must my cousin also stay?' She resisted the temptation to aim a foot at his shin. The guard shrugged again and threw a brief questioning glance at his companion. 'Gwenhwyfar remain.'

She snorted contempt and slammed the door shut. 'Ceridwen, you must find my father. Hurry!'

Ceridwen bit her lip and reluctantly opened the door to slip unchallenged beneath the crossed spears, blushing slightly at the guards' appraising eyes. She peered along the corridor to make sure Melwas had gone, then hitched up her skirts and fled in the direction of Cunedda's chamber.

§ XXXIV

As she neared her destination Ceridwen slowed her anxious pace, then stopped in dismay. Two Saxon guards stood resolutely before Cunedda's door. She twisted her skirt between her fingers. What to do? Had Enniaun gone? Where were the Gwynedd men? At the barracks or the guardhouse? Could she go there alone, would she have the courage? She must try!

A hand cupped her mouth, another curving round her waist, dragging her backwards kicking and struggling into a dimly lit room. The door banged shut, her assailant slackened his grip and she bit his hand, teeth sinking into flesh. He yelped, but kept firm hold. 'Jesu, girl, I am on your side!'

She kicked out, her foot thudding into his shin. He swore again. 'I am here to help you, for the Christ's sake! Believe me. I am the Pendragon's man.'

She stood still, breathing hard, body rigid, his hand clasped over her mouth.

'If I take my hand away will you be quiet?' He had a soft voice, kind.

Wide eyed, trembling with fear, Ceridwen nodded. Slowly he let go; she instantly whirled round and darted for the door. He caught her and swung her to face him, her small hands flying to his chest, hammering at his body.

'Listen to me, I said I was Arthur's man! Would you rather I let you walk into a viper's nest of Melwas's Saex?'

Her hand slapped his face.

'Fine. Have it your way.' He let her go and flung the door wide, indicating with an extravagant gesture that she was free to leave. 'Go. Melwas will be pleased to see you.'

Doubtful, Ceridwen regarded the young man. Tall, fair haired, aged about twenty summers. His blue eyes glinted in the dim light, a tentative smile forming. Dressed in a simple tunic, weaponless, he appeared to be a servant, yet his stance, bright manner and voice lacked servility.

'Who are you?' she demanded, her head held high and defiant, as she had seen Gwenhwyfar do.

'I am Iawn.' He shut the door.

Ceridwen smiled shyly. 'I apologise. You frightened me.' Iawn laughed, a pleasant sound, rich with humour. 'Remind me not to frighten you too often, it could prove painful!' He inspected the deep teeth marks in his hand, winced then laughed again as she darted forward to inspect the dam age.

'I must get to my lord Cunedda,' she said anxiously. 'Gwenhwyfar is being held prisoner in her chamber.'

'As is Cunedda.'

'His son and the men?'

'Gone. Enniaun slipped the net, thank God.'

'What shall I do? Gwenhwyfar must get away from here!'

Iawn sensed her distress and urgency, was suddenly reminded o his little sister. She would have been the age of this young woman had raiding Saex not butchered her two years past. He experienced an overpowering urge to protect this girl; wanted suddenly to gather her to him, take her to a place of safety.

If he had been at home that day, not out hunting, he might have saved his sister and mother. He bit his lip, forced down the rising nausea. God in Heaven, would the sight of their mutilated bodies never leave him be!

'Do not worry, little bird, we have things under control.' He smiled, hunkered down to look directly into her anxious face, se his haunting nightmare aside. 'There are many of us within the palace who secretly serve the Pendragon – and therefore Cunedda.

Ceridwen brightened, trusting him. 'You are a spy, then I thought you were no servant!' Iawn pouted. 'Damn it, I have worked hard at this disguise It has been no easy thing these past months fetching and carrying, bowing to the likes of them.' He nodded towards the door indicating his contempt for Vortigern and his kindred.

His manner changed, his body becoming more stooped and huddled as he became a man whose only purpose was to serve 'What be your orders, m'lady?' Even his voice changed into uncultured, poor man's speech.

Ceridwen clapped her hands. 'Oh, that is good! You have a talent!'

He bowed modestly. 'I take the character of a servant because they go unnoticed. You would be surprised at how many talk before us, assuming there is no intelligence atween a menial's ears.'

He turned serious then and sat her on a stool, explaining carefully all that was planned, making her repeat her place in things twice over to ensure she had it aright. Satisfied at last, he saw her from the room, catching her hand as she passed through the doorway. He smiled.

'Ceridwen, take care of yourself.'

§ XXXV

Exercising patience, Iawn waited for nightfall. It was an easy matter to organise the escape of Cunedda's few remaining men from close confinement. Before Cunedda's door the silent blades of Iawn's and another of the Pendragon's men dealt with the Saex guard – and they were running unseen down narrow servants' stairs and out through the lengthening shadows of dusk heading for the water gate. Ignoring the soft scuttle of movement, the guard along the wall continued his patrol, obligingly looking the wrong way, turning his back as a shadow slid through the gate. He touched a finger to the pouch at his waist, hanging heavy with gold. So few British were loyal to Vortigern now; so many could no longer tolerate the increasing presence of Saex mercenaries and the dominance of the Queen.

Gwenhwyfar and Ceridwen were ready as gravel rattled against the small squares of unbroken window glass. Ceridwen slid the catch and peeped out, delighted to see Iawn's face staring up from below. He grinned and neatly caught the bundles they tossed down. Heart hammering a battle rhythm, Ceridwen gathered her skirts and climbed nervously out, her toes feeling for the wooden struts of the propped ladder. She felt Iawn's strong hands grasp her waist and swing her safely down. Briefly she clung to him, awkwardly murmuring her thanks. Gwenhwyfar followed quickly, unafraid.

'Your father's waiting beyond the water gate,' Iawn whispered. 'We freed him and the men first lest we should find the need for fighting.' He looked about. No one. Nothing. 'Make use of the shadows. Hurry.'

The night was dark, with no moon, and low clouds covering the stars. It would rain again before dawn. The oars of a small fishing boat dipped steadily in and out of the water, pulling downriver towards the vague, distant shape of a moored ship.

'Iawn has found a fast craft.' Cunedda spoke low, aware that sound carried easily over water. They had expected an alarm from the palace, the raising of the hunt, but nothing had come.

'The crew have been paid well, with the promise of more when I have word of your arrival. Here.' Cunedda pulled a ring from his finger. 'Send this so I may know you are safe.'

Gwenhwyfar took it and slipped it on her own finger, where it hung loose and uncomfortable; nestled it in the pouch at her waist instead. When she looked up, the oarsmen were pulling alongside a timbered hull with a rope ladder snaking down and men leaning over to catch the bundles tossed up to them.

Ceridwen was ushered up the flimsy ladder, followed closely by Iawn, who steadied her feet, talking calmly to her as she nervously climbed. Anxiously she asked him, 'Are you to come with us?'

He nodded.

She slipped her hand into his and held it tight. 'Then the leaving is made that much more bearable.'

In the fishing boat, Gwenhwyfar held her father close. 'Where will you go?'

'Horses are waiting. I ride fast for home.'

No time for more. Hands were pulling her forward, guiding her to the ladder. Before she knew it, she stood beside Ceridwen and Iawn on deck, and the little boat carrying her father was pulling away, out into the darkness. She realised suddenly she had not told him about her mother's dagger, that Rowena had given it to Winifred, and the bitch's brat had taken good care to let her know.

Cunedda called something as the ship slipped her moorings and eased into the strong tidal pull. Gwenhwyfar caught only the words 'safe voyage'. She leant over the bulwark, felt the leap of the ship as the wind took the unfurling sail, sending her racing forward, her bow wave creaming. No use calling out: what could he do about a dagger anyway? She waved, knowing he could not see her through the darkness, finally abandoned the struggle against tears. At least the dark hid those.

It was stupid, childish. Her thoughts were not that she might never see her family or home again, but that Winifred, a thieving, poxed Saex, possessed her mother's dagger!

§ XXXVI

The day after Etern's bloody killing, Arthur went drunk to his marriage ceremony in Camulodunum. The thing had been agreed, arranged, there was no getting out of it. The handfasting had been set for three days hence, but the King, needing to ride urgently back to Londinium, brought the ceremony forward.

Arthur held himself well, despite vomiting profusely in the latrines before summoning the courage to enter Vortigern's quarters. The haze of best barley-brew helped, the only way he knew of getting through this god-damned day. It had helped him sleep too, though not enough to dim the memory of spilt blood and Etern's dead eyes.

The King noticed the way Arthur swayed slightly as he walked slowly into the private chapel. Hengest, standing beside his granddaughter, might have noticed too – happen they all had. Arthur did not particularly care.

It had occurred to him to run, but where was there to run to? Gwynedd? Ah now, Cunedda's mountains would be safe, but he did not want to be safe, he wanted Gwenhwyfar. And he could not have her.

Beside him, Vortigern's daughter spoke her vows in a clear voice, her self-satisfied smile wide with gloating. She was a tall, slender girl, and dressed in a fine silk gown, with flame coloured veil and gold trimmed leather sandals, her beauty was undeniable.

Her perfume, though, was strong, rather sickly. Standing so close, Arthur suddenly realised how much he hated her. And tonight he had to bed her! Or did he? He had taken her already. Vortimer, beside him, gave his elbow a squeeze of encouragement, but did not help matters by whispering, 'Think on the pleasure of an untouched woman in your bed this night!'

A thought came. Arthur whispered back, loud enough for Winifred to hear, 'A bride must be virgin pure, for if she comes to her husband's bed used, then he has the right to strip her naked and whip her through the streets.' He looked at Winifred with loathing, his meaning plain. 'Or accept her for the whore she is to do with as he pleases.'

To her credit Winifred's smile did not waver, but a small doubt began to niggle in her mind. She had the Pendragon. He was hers, but at what price? As the wedding entertainment and festivities gained momentum, the doubt grew. Happen the prize was not worth the winning after all.

Vortigern had left soon after the ceremony. For once, Arthur would have preferred to ride with him.

The Pendragon drank deeper and laughed louder, and eventually, as night fell, he allowed himself to be escorted to the bridal chamber where Winifred waited, the sheets drawn to her chin, her hair unbound. Sweet-scented flower petals were scattered around, the aroma of bees-wax candles. They put him to bed beside her, scattered more petals and blessings and left, laughing, tossing suggestive remarks and lewd advice over their shoulders.

Away to the south, a ship was steering into the flowing ebb current of the Tamesis river, her sails filling, carrying her swiftly for the open sea. Aboard her a passenger freed from an oath of betrothal; but Arthur did not know Cunedda had renounced all allegiance to the King, did not know that from now forward Gwynedd stood defiantly independent.

Tired, Arthur lay back, staring at the ceiling. Winifred had not moved; she sat with knees raised, the covers tucked beneath her chin. 'I recall you were not so modest before.' He took hold of the sheets and pulled them from her. Involuntarily, she made to cover her nakedness with her hands, but turned the reaction aside and let him look full at her rounded breasts and flat stomach.

'No child then?' he sneered. 'No fault of mine. I know of several bastard born daughters.' He threw the covers at her and turned his back saying, 'Cover yourself. I have no need to look at you. I know already the slut I have.'

There was nothing Winifred could say or do as his breathing deepened into sleep.

A face swam through Arthur's dreams, a face framed by wind tossed copper hair. A woman with a laugh as welcome as a waterfall on a hot summer's day. Gwenhwyfar.

Sunlight flooded the room, the morning well underway when Arthur woke, sluiced himself with cold water, dressed and made to leave. Almost as an afterthought he spoke to Winifred. 'The thing is done, you are my wife. Enjoy the title it's all you will ever have from me.' He strode through the door and met with Vortimer waiting outside. Had the man been there all night?

Footsteps from along the corridor. Arthur peered through the dim light, saw Cei approaching and stepped forward to speak with his cousin. They exchanged a few low words, then Arthur laughed, a high mocking sound that almost cracked into despair. He walked slowly back to Vortimer and stood before him, eyes narrowed, finger poking at his shoulder.

'Were you so scared I would wriggle free of this thing that you must stand guard at my door?' He poked again, harder, his face menacingly close. 'Who had the idea to get me so quickly married to that whore in there? Which one, yourself or your poxed father, guessed Cunedda would call blood-right and disclaim all agreements past made?'

He kicked the bedchamber door open, glared at Winifred, sitting as she had last night, knees drawn up, sheets to her chin.

'I am the Pendragon. Remember that.' He slammed the door behind him and stood with his back against it, eyes shut, breath rasping in his throat.

He need not have married her! Gwenhwyfar would by now be on her way to Less Britain so Cunedda's urgent sent messenger said, for temporary safekeeping. She was his, the Pendragon's, with Gwynedd's blessing, should he still want her.

Arthur wondered how a wedding night with Gwenhwyfar would have passed.

What to do? Two choices. Leave, declare Winifred a whore, and take ship for Less Britain to claim Gwenhwyfar as wife? He would need protect her against Melwas, for that bastard would sooner see her dead than with Arthur. Slowly he exhaled. He could live comfortably in Less Britain with Gwenhwyfar.

Or should he stay? Were he to leave Britain and abandon Winifred, Vortigern would never permit his return. Only as War Lord over some great invading army could Arthur then attempt to take the kingdom he so badly wanted. And Cunedda had been right: outside Britain, there was no army for him to command.

Gwenhwyfar or Winifred? Happiness or a kingdom? Choices. *Na,* there was no decision. The thing was done, the shuttle was moving through the loom, with the pattern well cast.

Suddenly, Arthur needed his men. The clash of weapons, the bark of orders and the pounding of hooves. The smell of sweat and blood, a taste of fear and excitement.

Ignoring Vortimer, the Pendragon strode from the building. He wanted Gwenhwyfar but he was determined to be called king. When he had that, he could claim her.

He bellowed for someone to fetch Eira and rode to where, at this moment, the Pendragon belonged. With the army of Britain.

PART TWO

The Weaving

AUGUST 453

§ I

The day had been long and hot. Up here, the ever present hill wind had helped cool the men down, but still they dripped sweat and were short tempered with the string of stubborn pack mules. Arthur called a halt early, although it was only mid-afternoon and they had plenty of light to cover a few more miles.

They made camp quickly and efficiently, securing the mule loads in a guarded tent beside the Pendragon's. Then relaxed a while, taking the opportunity to bathe in the cold waters of the lake, grateful to wash the itch and stink of stale sweat from their skins.

Arthur splashed with them, diving deep into the clear pool, the green depths quiet and mysterious beneath him, stretching down as if to reach the earth's heart. It seemed another dimension of being, amidst this weird light and diffused sound; another place; the other world of Faery, where time had no meaning. He pushed upwards, feet kicking against the pull of water and for a panicked heartbeat it felt as if he were held there, trapped, being enticed down into that magic kingdom where no mortal dwelt. His head broke the surface, dazzling sunlight hitting him smart in the face. Men were laughing and jesting along the shore line, splashing each other, pushing companions into the cool water. Arthur gasped and sucked in sweet, clear air and struck out, relieved, towards them.

From the shore, where he rubbed himself vigorously with his tunic, the pool looked safe enough, but even so he shivered. Superstition! Even in a man of level thinking it was a powerful inheritance.

Cei noticed the shiver and grinned. 'Too cold for you, huh?'

'*Na*,' Arthur confessed, 'too deep!'

Cei nodded understanding, his hand involuntarily making the sign of the Christian cross. 'They say there is an island where the faery folk dwell, on one of these lakes, visible only at Beltaine. An evil place of pagan darkness where God's blessed face would not look.'

'Aye, well, 'tis not Beltaine.'

All the same, Arthur found it difficult to shrug aside that moment of fear when he had fought against the pull of water. How easy would it be to become lost within those silent depths? He shivered again, the memory lying heavy on his shoulder. As Cei had just now made the Christian sign of protection, Arthur's fingers formed the homed sign against the pagan lords of darkness.

Noticing, Cei gave him a sidelong glance of disapproval. He decided against comment, saying instead, 'Should we not take a look at the morrow's ground?'

Arthur grinned back at him, grateful for the chance to turn his thoughts from the unreal to the practical. He strode briskly to the horse lines barking an order at an officer to take command. 'And see to it no one goes near the mule loads while I am gone!'

'Do you not trust us then, sir?' called a soldier sitting outside a tent sorting his gear.

'*Na*, Lucius, I would rather trust a whore to stay virtuous in the men's bathhouse!' Arthur answered brightly, a smile playing on his mouth. The men nearby laughed good-natured, knowing they would not have been picked for this duty were they not trusted. Escorting gold was not a task for the unreliable.

Vaulting into the saddle, Arthur heeled his stallion to canter away across the short, springy turf that in wetter months would be soft and bog bound. He reined in some distance up the hill, Cei bringing his mount round to stay close. They let the horses' heads drop to tear at the grass which held little goodness in this bleak, wind-teased landscape.

Arthur shifted in the saddle and hooked his leg around one of the two forward pommel horns, rested his arm on his crooked knee. Eira grazed, his sensitive muzzle searching for choice eating.

'What are we doing here, Cei?' Arthur asked after watching the lazy swirl of smoke from campfires for a while.

'We are sitting up here thinking of the men down there preparing our supper,' the big man beside him answered jovially. 'And we are bringing a full load of gold from the mines to our bastard of a king. Your action was wrong, you know.'

Arthur glanced sharply across at Cei and frowned. He had known Cei would eventually say something about what had happened.

'The mines must be kept working,' he said.

216

'To fill Vortigern's treasury? Is that worth the killing and maiming of slaves?'

'Is it the death of a few slaves you object to then? Or that we are guarding and carrying gold for the King?' Arthur replied angrily, for Cei's words stung – the more so because he knew him to be right.

He had not wanted to accept these orders, given by the King's eldest son Vortimer, but then he had no desire to be pulled back from the marshlands and return to Londinium either. The Anglian uprising was under control, the British somehow clinging to their supremacy – at least for a while, until the next thrust forward by encroaching settlers who were gaining in courage with every fresh outbreak of war fever. One day the dam would burst.

It had seemed a mundane task to ride westward to investigate rumours of unrest at the mines and to oversee the collection of a long overdue consignment of gold. But it was preferable to sitting idly kicking one's heels. Better than having to play husband to Winifred – mind, even shifting a midden heap was preferable to that.

The rumours had been amply borne out. The slaves were sullen and rebellious, their overseers drunken and slovenly, the mines unworked.

The Pendragon had handled the situation quickly and ruthlessly, hanging the commanding officer for gross negligence, publicly flogging two junior officers and punishing those slaves who refused to work. There had been a brief flair of rebellion from slaves and guards, swiftly and decisively put down.

A handful of dead lay grotesquely bloodied as a result, women and children among the men. Even a handful were too many dead, but the mines were in business again, gold in production under the new, watchful eye of an honest and loyal man. Loyal to the Pendragon, anyway.

'I may not agree with Vortigern on most things, Cei,' said Arthur, toying with the few incongruous black strands in the white mane hanging over Eira's withers.

His thoughts wandered, his sentence left unfinished. Strange how the horse's coat was white all over, save for black tipped ears, black muzzle, knees and hocks. The mane and tail, too, had strands of black, and a broad dark stripe ran from wither to dock. Arthur reflected on some young horses he had seen bred that were almost black at birth, turning to grey then white as they gained height and years. He wondered vaguely if even these few dark markings on Eira would gradually fade.

Cei shifted in his saddle. 'You were saying?'

Arthur patted the horse and looked eye to eye at his friend, cousin and second-in-command. 'If I am to rule one day I shall need to control the economy.' He snorted contemptuously. 'Or lack of it.' He swung his leg back into a riding position. 'Even were I not to rule, I may soon need more than I have at present. Winifred's dowry will pay for the horses Cunedda is breeding for me. But it is not enough.' He gave Eira one last pat, a firm slap on the neck. 'The gold mine and a loyal overseer may come in useful.'

Cei gathered his reins, pulling his chestnut's head away from the grass. He kicked him forward up the rising slope. 'That I appreciate,' he said, flinging the words over his shoulder, 'but why gather the wealth for Vortigern? He is already in financial trouble. Another kick to the backside may just be enough to topple him.' He pushed the horse into a canter.

Eira lifted his head and whinnied, his body shaking with the calling, impatient to catch up. His hooves danced, his head tossed. He needed no urging, bounded forward the moment Arthur relaxed pressure on the bit.

The two men cantered to the summit of the hill, the horses slowing as they reached the steeper incline snorting and blowing.

Arthur could not answer Cei. The same question was in his own mind. He had no answer, save he had seized the opportunity to put as many miles as possible between himself and his Saex-bred wife.

They dismounted on the ridge. Below on one side the camp looked small and distant with ant size men scuttling between the tents. The late afternoon heat had left a haze on the horizon to the south, in the direction of the sea. A mist was rising, promising a cooler day on the morrow. On the far side of the hill, the ground sloped less steeply down to a valley where a river ran and the trackway twisted with the lie of the land, looping outcrops of rock, leaping from one side of the river to the other, avoiding boggy ground.

They hobbled the horses, let them find what nourishment they could, stood studying the route east.

'Do we follow the track?' Cei asked, chewing a blade of grass.

Arthur squatted, then absent-mindedly took two ivory dice from his belt pouch and began idly tossing them in his hand, thinking. He rolled them, throwing a five and a one. He frowned. 'It's a risk whether we take the track or keep to the hills. Either way, we may need to fight if we meet others; Hibernian, Saex or British. Gold is of value to all.' Then again, he could keep it himself; claim they had encountered raiders and lost the lot. But it was a matter of pride really, would he allow raiders to take that which he was guarding?

He spoke quietly, regretfully, an apology in his voice. 'The men need paying, Cei. Vortimer's British men; my men. Were I allowed to bring my full command with us, then happen I might have considered sharing it out among ourselves and heading off into the hills. But what then?' He retrieved the dice and threw again, double two. 'What good would it do us? Could we pitch in with Cunedda in Gwynedd? Buy passage on a ship back to Less Britain? Is that what we want? There would be no goal in mind, no future, save for running like outlaw thieves.'

Cei remained silent, brooding. Arthur was right no doubt, but still something irked him, like an unreachable itch between the shoulder blades. 'I cannot help feeling we are nothing but slaves to Vortigern. We are under his son's direct command, we run at Vortimer's beck and call, but is not the one the same as the other?' Cei hunkered down next to Arthur, tossing his chewed stalk aside. 'I am tired of it, Arthur. Tired of senseless skirmishes that gain us one step forward for every three we take backwards.'

Arthur stared out over the hills, empty of life save for wind bent trees, and birds. There were undoubtedly hares crouching in the grass, deer concealed in the clumps of alder, oak, elm and hazel woodland. Wolves too, lurking in the shadows.

'I had a dream once, Cei. As a boy, I talked of it to,' he paused, remembering the warmth of Gwynedd, 'to good friends. I was to be a great leader and command a king's army – that was before I knew Uthr Pendragon was my father. I thought then, as a boy, men would flock to my side. I expected to scythe through enemies like a farmer cutting wheat.' He stopped. A falcon was hovering nearby, its wings folded, falling down into the grass. 'A child expects the sun always to shine, Cei, thinks the sky is always blue.'

The falcon had missed. It beat upward again in search of alternative supper. 'I still have the dream, but it is so far removed from what it once was. I still want my banner flying higher than any other but the glory has tarnished. Stupid, isn't it? I once lusted after war, all I want now is prosperity and peace; to see people, ordinary people, contended. To see children with full bellies.' Arthur laughed, mocking himself. He stood up and kicked at a tussock of grass, put the dice away. 'I suppose I have grown up.'

Cei stood also, watching something, a disturbance of the air, a faint shimmer of movement. It grew as he watched, shielding his eyes, squinting to see more clearly. A dust cloud was visible some way to the north along the track.

Arthur saw it too. 'Best alert the men,' he said calmly. 'One leisurely traveller does not make such an announcement.'

Cei nodded his agreement. Releasing the hobbles from his horse, he mounted and cantered back, noting with pride the men had seen him coming and were waiting expectantly long before he reached the camp.

Arthur walked his horse to the cover of some bushes. It might have been wiser to return to camp, douse the fires and seek safety in concealment, but curiosity had the better of him. He had a good view up the valley from here, and doubted he would be seen if he remained still.

No one coming from that direction could know of the load the mules carried, should not even know Arthur and his men were in the area. He rubbed at the stubble on his chin. Whoever was coming, was coming fast. He waited.

One horse, stumbling from tiredness was ahead, neck outstretched, legs pounding. Behind, a group of thirty or so riders urging on almost spent mounts. They carried no standard. The animals were small, sturdy hill ponies; not as swift and well bred as Eira and others of his type. The stallion had seen the approaching horses; he neighed a high-pitched welcome.

Too late, Arthur grabbed for his muzzle, cursing. 'Damn you! What has got into your thick skull this day? You are behaving like an unbroken colt.'

Cei appeared, leading his horse quickly over the skylining ridge to join Arthur. 'What do you make of it?'

'Someone is very keen to leave the pack behind.'

'Hunter, or hunted?'

Arthur grinned. 'We will not find out up here!' He ducked his head enquiringly towards the ridge behind them.

Cei replied with a nod. 'I have left some men on the alert in camp; one is concealed up there,' he pointed to the ridge, 'as lookout. The others await your orders.'

Arthur nodded, satisfied. 'Have them form line of battle a little down this slope – near enough the ridge to show we have no hostile intent, but low enough should it be necessary to take action.'

Cei acknowledged the order and turned to mount. Arthur vaulted into Eira's saddle and let the stallion walk forward, picking his own path down the uneven grass of the steep hillside. There was no doubt the riders had seen him. The one in front faltered, reining in his mount so hard the pony almost fell as it staggered to a halt.

Arthur's men came in a steady line over the ridge and took up positions, waiting, the Dragon Banner streaming proud above the bearer's head. The rider saw it and gave a shout and kicked it hard into a canter, heading for the Pendragon.

The animal carried two riders, a man with a smaller, cloaked figure clinging behind. Arthur nudged Eira into a trot, glanced over his shoulder to make sure Cei was following.

Shouting something, the man waved his hand frantically. The pony stumbled, regained its footing, but weariness and the double weight were too much; its head dropped its forelegs buckled and it went down, tipping the two riders to the grass. Instantly, the man was up, sword in hand, running to his companion.

The pursuers were gaining ground, closing in, anger glazing their expressions. Arthur recognised the leader; Brychan, a cross-breed Hibernian settler. Vortigern's man. A spawned cur-son of a fatherless mare! A toad-featured, pig's littered runt!

Arthur frowned darkly as Brychan thundered up to him shouting some abusive comment that, perhaps fortunately, was snatched away by the wind. The other man, coming up to him at a run, he did not know. He indicated Brychan. 'Whoever you are, my friend, I see you have angered the King's sasnach dog.'

Bringing his right hand to his left shoulder in formal salute, the man – a young man – eased his companion behind him a little. 'I have something of his he does not wish me to have.'

His mouth twitching into a smile, Arthur nodded. Aye, so he could see! She was small and slightly built, with dark hair and wide, frightened, brown eyes. Arthur judged her to be about ten and six years. He leant forward in the saddle, resting his arms on Eira's neck, and pointed casually with one finger. 'Brychan's daughter?'

The said Brychan hauled at his frothing mount. He leapt from the saddle before the horse had come to a halt, rushed up the slope, drawing his sword as he ran. 'You will die for this outrage, Gwynllyw!'

Arthur straightened, touched his heel lightly to Eira's flank. The big horse bounded forward, between the enraged Brychan and the young man, Gwynllyw, who shielded the terrified girl.

'There will be no killing without my consent.' Arthur's tone was mellow, with no sense of threat or malice. Those who knew him well, knew Arthur to be at his most dangerous when he seemed relaxed and easy. That good-humoured smile, that sidelong look with narrowed eye and cocked eyebrow.

Brychan's men approached, snarling like wolves. One man impulsively spurred his horse forward and Cei was suddenly before him; smiling, sitting his hose easily, hands light on the rein, a spear tip hovering at the man's throat.

'This is private business, Pendragon!' Brychan growled. 'I order you aside!'

'No business is private before an envoy of the King.' Lazily Arthur shifted his gaze from Brychan to the men. All carried weapons. 'This looks like a war band to me. Does it not to you, Cei?'

'It does.'

'Pah! I say again, this is a private matter!' Brychan stepped aside from Eira and waved his sword menacingly at the shrinking girl. 'Come here this instant, girl! By the gods, I will have your hide flayed from your back for this insult to me!' The girl moved closer to Gwynllyw, clutching at his waist, her head shaking a silent no.

'She is mine, Brychan. I have claimed her – you have no right to deny us!'

'No right! By God she is my daughter and I say who she is to wed! Certainly not some upstart of a petty British chieftain! Gwladys! Come here, now! I order it!'

Arthur shifted his weight in the saddle. 'It seems you are over-free with orders, Brychan.'

The two had crossed swords, figuratively, before, across Vortigern's Council Chamber. Brychan, son of a Hibernian wolf and a British noblewoman, had claimed his maternal grandsire's land, the barren hills between the rivers Usk and Taff, some few years before Uthr's death. Vortigern had welcomed him, a prospective ally, with open arms, granting him favours and friendship.

When Uthr had made his war call there had been few who rallied to him from these parts. Vortigern's gold and Brychan's influence bribed too well. Arthur detested Brychan.

'I say again, Pendragon – withdraw.' Brychan swung round unexpectedly and struck Eira across the muzzle with the flat of his sword. The horse reared, squealing, front hooves raking the air in anger and pain. As the horse went up, Brychan darted forward and buffeted Gwynllyw with his shoulders, sending the man, winded, rolling down the hillside, and grabbed for the girl. Pushing his kicking and screaming daughter before him he attempted to run the short distance back to the safe semi-circle of his men; surprised to find Arthur had moved no less swiftly.

Kicking himself free of the saddle Arthur had dropped quickly, rolling away from Eira's plunging hooves to spring to his feet, sword raised, a yard in front of Brychan. He feinted to one side, dropped, and suddenly his sword was between Brychan and the girl. Arthur took hold of her, drawing her close to him with his left hand, the tip of his blade hovering over Brychan's heart.

He was winded as he spoke, exertion and the surge of blood-heat taking his breath. 'As I said, Brychan, this is my business.'

At an angry movement from Brychan's men, Cei whistled low and threatened them with the spear he held. 'I would not move a hair on your louse-riddled heads if I were you.' He hoisted the spear aloft, waved it in a single circle. The Dragon dipped once in response, and the waiting line of ten riders along the slope above moved forward, coming at a steady walk, spears lowered, swords loose at their sides. 'I have only to signal,' Cei said, 'and they will charge.'

The hill men dropped back reluctantly, looking to their leader who signalled compliance with a curt nod of his head. They lowered their weapons and took a few paces back down the slope.

Arthur grinned. 'Good. Happen now we can talk of this matter like civilised men.' He paused, looked Brychan disdainfully up and down, and added with pointed rudeness. 'At least, I can talk so with young Gwynllyw here.'

Brychan growled and raised his fist, but with a laugh Arthur stepped back to a safer distance, taking the girl with him.

Following little used trackways and lonely hill routes, staying away from settlements where awkward questions could be asked had advantages when escorting a delivery of gold, but there were also disadvantages. The men foraged for food as they marched, at this time of year not a problem. This morning Arthur himself had brought down a fine buck – the butchered carcass would be roasting back at camp at this moment. The tents, good and strong, leather-made, were dry and windproof. There was water aplenty and few worries of raiding parties striking this far inland, which was why they were using this particular route. The one drawback was women; or the lack of them. A soldier welcomes the surfeit of willing girls to share his bed when stationed near town or settlement, grows used to long weeks of campaign or march without so much as a look at a female. But at odd times something occurs during these spells of enforced celibacy to remind the senses of what is being missed. Arthur held the girl close, his arm inside the folds of her cloak, encircling her slim body. As he had dragged her back, away from the proximity of her father his hand had touched the firm, rounded swell of her breast and, suddenly, Arthur wanted her.

Beneath the cloak, Arthur shifted his hand. Her eyes flickered to his, her mouth closing in a bitten off gasp as he squeezed her waist. No woman could mistake his intent at that moment.

Gwynllyw saw it also. The Pendragon personally, he did not know but he had heard stories about his father and those now told of the son, heard enough to shout, 'Gwladys is mine, Pendragon! Leave her be!'

Brychan countered swiftly with, 'God rot you! She is not yours!'

Arthur laughed – he was enjoying this! He covered the few yards to where Eira stood, unconcerned and cropping grass. No trained warhorse moved far once the reins were dropped; such a small thing could save an unseated rider's life in battle. Arthur clicked his tongue and the horse lifted his head, ears pricking. The Pendragon lifted the girl to the horse's withers and vaulted up behind her into the saddle and, wheeling the animal round, cantered the distance between the angry group of Brychan's men and his own waiting line of cavalry. He stopped short just out of their hearing.

The girl sat rigid, back straight, arms still, her lips pressed tight together. She dared not open her mouth for if she did, the scream clamped between her teeth would start and never end.

Arthur bent his head, his mouth close to hers, his lips almost touching that exquisitely pretty mouth. When Eira shifted a hind leg, Arthur felt rather than saw movement to his left. He glanced up into the impassive face of Cei.

'If you kiss her, Arthur, I shall ride up this hill and return to camp with the men, leaving you as dog's meat for Gwynllyw and Brychan to chew between them.'

Arthur forced a good-natured reply. 'A bit of fun, Cei – harmless fun with a pretty girl.'

'What was it someone said to me once? *I want to see contented people, children with full bellies?*' Cei looked Arthur straight in the eye. 'I assumed you were talking of well-being and adequate food, but I must have got it wrong. You were obviously talking of lust and girls' bellies filled with childbearing!' Cei's cheeks were red-blotched with anger, his knuckles white as they clutched the reins. The two horses laid their ears back, sensing the fury. 'Blood of Jesu! What are you doing, Pendragon? Are you determined to kill more men – our men – for the sake of a sea-wolfs daughter?'

Cei had never turned on Arthur before; had never commented on his more indelicate excesses.

'Is the Christian Jesu turning you soft-bellied then, Cei?' Arthur asked, surprised. 'You were never averse to a pretty woman before.'

'In the right place, at the right time, *na.* This is not the place nor the time.'

Arthur regarded the girl cowering away from his holding arm, saw and felt her terror. He gestured defeated to Cei. 'You are right, my friend.'

He took a deep breath, assumed a calm, relaxed smile and eased his hand on the girl's waist. 'So, you do not wish to bed with me?' She said nothing. 'Not with the Pendragon? I possess land and wealth – I could keep a mistress in comfort and jewels for many years.' He sighed, 'I see I am not tempting you.' He brushed a strand of dark hair from her cheek, tucked it behind her ear. She was surprised at how gentle his touch was.

'I apologise, my dear, for all this.' He gestured behind him to the hill men, and then forward to his own soldiers. 'It was necessary, I needed you out of their hearing to talk alone with you. I had no other intention.' He glanced at Cei. Happen the girl believed the lie. Cei certainly did not.

Arthur lifted her down, dismounted beside her, took her by the elbow and walked a few paces.

'So you are not interested in me? Ah well, it was worth the asking!' He grinned suddenly, genuinely regretting his behaviour. He swept her a low bow, then took her hand in his and kissed it lightly.

A faint smile flickered on her pale face. This young man was absurd! For all the fear, she realised that she liked him! Things had happened so fast this day, so many reeling emotions coming tumbling one upon the other.

'It seems, as I cannot have you,' Arthur glanced meaningfully at Cei, 'who can? Your father or Gwynllyw? The choice is yours.'

At the mention of Brychan her heart lurched. 'He will kill me,' she whispered, not daring to look at her father, who stood arms folded, foot tapping.

'I'd not allow him to. I would ensure no harm came to you.'

Gwladys looked up at Arthur, wide-eyed, impressed. 'You could do that for me?'

Arthur knew well he had no jurisdiction over Brychan at all, but still he answered with a swagger of importance. 'Of course.'

Cei snorted.

'I thank you, but I would rather go with Gwynllyw.' She said it decisively, her eyes at last managing to meet his. Arthur was exciting and interesting, but Gwynllyw was steadfast and solid. And she needed a husband, not a lover whose attention could change with the wind.

'We had best sort this matter out then.' With his broad smile Arthur lifted her into Eira's saddle and set her comfortably wedged between the rear and fore saddle horns, walked at the horse's head, leading him by the bridle.

She had never been mounted on such a tall horse before. Her father's ponies stood below fourteen hands, and Gwynllyw's not much taller, but this beautiful creature with arched crest and proud-carried tail stood a full fifteen hands.

She stroked her fingers along the fine muscled neck, marvelling at the silkiness of coat and feeling of strength.

Bracing his shoulder against the animal's chest, Arthur eased the stallion to a halt before Brychan and motioned Gwynllyw forward. 'It seems we have a difference of opinion here. On the one hand Brychan demands his daughter, on the other Gwynllyw demands a wife.' Arthur paused, thrust his thumb through his sword belt, considering the matter. 'Gwynllyw, have you a bride-price to offer?'

'Ten head of cattle and ten of swine. And I ask no dowry.'

'That seems a fair exchange to me – does it not to you, Cei?'

Cei, still mounted, nodded agreement.

Brychan tried to speak, but Arthur motioned him to silence. 'You could fight for her, of course.'

Brychan snarled, 'With pleasure!'

Gwynllyw growled, 'Let me at the chance!'

Arthur just smiled with irritating amusement. 'Brychan has, what, thirty men with him? But then, I have ten ranged behind me and another thirty t'other side of this ridge.' He lifted Gwladys down from the saddle.

Brychan was glancing warily up the hill. He had been considering how many men the Pendragon had with him since the first sighting, and now a figure had been stated was it truth?

Arthur's grin faded. 'Who owns this land we are on?'

'I do,' said Gwynllyw. He gestured behind him. 'We crossed the border stream some half-mile back.'

Arthur slapped the young man's shoulder and grinned again. 'That settles the matter then.' He took hold of Gwladys's hand, placed it in Gwynllyw's and turned to mount Eira.

With a roar, Brychan charged forward, but Arthur's sword came up, stopping him short. 'Brychan, are you so slow to learn? I suggest, and suggest strongly, you get on that ragged hill pony of yours and take your men home.' He thrust his face forward menacing. 'You, Brychan, are on another's land, and to my mind are intent on unrest. By the power invested in me by the King, if you do not get your arse off this land this instant I will have my signaller call the remainder of my men and we will personally escort you off!'

Was it bluff? Brychan considered, considered hard, trying to read Arthur's face. Without success. Brychan despised the Pendragon. Finally, he acknowledged he had no choice, turned on his heel and without a word returned to his men.

'I shall send bride-price for your daughter,' Gwynllyw called.

Brychan mounted his pony and turned it, savagely pulling at the bit. 'For brideprice there must be a daughter. I have but one daughter and she is within my stronghold with the women!'

Gwladys ran forward, distressed. 'Father, please, I did not want it to be like this!'

He spat into the grass by her feet. 'You have lost all right to call me father. You are no longer of my flesh nor of my blood.' He trotted away without a backward glance, his men following silently.

Arthur had mounted, began to ride off, but Gwynllyw caught up with him, placed a hand on the rein.

'How can I thank you? You have done me a great service this day, although I admit to doubting your intentions for a while.' He said it openly,

honest, meant in friendship. Arthur took it as such, proffered his hand for the young man to grasp.

'You must never doubt my intentions, lad! Cei here has conscience enough to look after that side of things.' Arthur winked at his friend. Gwynllyw did not understand, but shrugged aside the question forming in his mind, said instead, 'My priest shall marry Gwladys and myself on the morrow. I would be honoured if you and your men would attend my wedding feast.' He paused, reddened slightly. 'But my stronghold is small. We are somewhat confined for room, a full turma would be difficult to accommodate.'

Arthur roared his laughter, Cei joining in.

'God be praised! Have you not heard of Arthur, Gwynllyw? He is notorious for exaggeration! We have no more than ten and six men, including ourselves and officers!'

Gwynllyw saw the jest, saw Brychan had been made to look the fool, and gladly offered the welcome due all travellers.

§ II

For five days they took advantage of pleasant company, good wine and relaxation. With the gold stored safely in Gwynllyw's own treasure house – a stone-built chamber below ground – Arthur too took advantage of the unexpected holiday. Let Vortigern wait and worry!

Gwladys settled well and quickly into her new household, welcomed by her husband's four sisters and widowed mother. The breeding of her grandmother adequately cleansed the stain of Hibernian blood and her devout Christian faith made her the more readily accepted.

At the wedding feast Arthur made promise of a wedding gift. He had not failed to notice Gwladys's shining eyes as she stroked Eira, had seen also Gwynllyw's appreciative appraisal. He mentioned Cunedda's breeding herds.

'I have heard of them – Gwynedd is well talked of. Is Eira one of Cunedda's then?' Gwynllyw asked, interested. He would be prepared to pay a handsome price, though he could ill afford it, for such an animal.

'Aye, Cei's too. We purchased them from Cunedda when we first came into Vortigern's service, but recently I have taken more. All my officers will soon be so mounted, and the men are to ride part-bred animals, hill ponies crossed with Cunedda's fine stallions.'

It could have been the drink or the congenial company, but Arthur suddenly found himself telling Gwynllyw of his plans for a large cavalry force with all the men, not just the officers, mounted on horses like Eira – drilled, highly trained men and horses.

Gwynllyw was impressed, enthusiastic. 'If I were not committed to my holding, I would gladly join such a company! At least I can give you my backing, for what it is worth.'

'It may be worth a great deal, Gwynllyw. I thank you and...' Arthur stood up abruptly, banged the table with his empty tankard and demanded silence. 'I have not yet granted a gift to the bride and her husband! I shall send to Gwynedd to procure the foundation stock of Gwynllyw's own stables: one stallion and four mares – na,' he winked at Gwynllyw's wife, 'I shall make it five, one entirely for yourself. What say you, Gwladys?'

The girl leapt to her feet and flung her arms around Arthur's neck. 'A mare of my own, like Eira!' She turned to her husband, smiling, delighted; thought, Even my father does not possess such a fine beast!

Seating himself, Arthur touched the place on his cheek where her lips had brushed, felt a twinge of regret that he had heeded Cei's conscience.

Cei, by his side, lightly tapped Arthur's arm, whispered, 'I take it Vortigern's gold will be paying for such a lavish gift?'

'It is in our King's interest to encourage these smaller holdings. We need loyal men.'

'We?' Cei sipped wine. 'Or you?'

Arthur's face broke into a roguish grin, his interest swivelling to assess the serving slave pouring more wine into his tankard. He pinched her buttocks, said to Cei, 'One day I will mean mine, but for now I am intent on more pressing needs.' He fingered the girl's bodice, making a show of inspecting the lacing. She giggled as he whispered something in her ear, her eyes fluttering agreement to his suggestion. Arthur's grin broadened as he leant back in his chair.

'Well, this night is taken care of. As to the future, I think I have assured one man on my side.'

Cei swallowed a mouthful of wine, said with a serious face, 'How fortunate the Fates led Gwladys to be placed under your personal protection from any unwanted advances.'

Arthur scowled and kicked Cei's leg beneath the table. He glanced at her, so obviously happy, the scowl deepening. Mithras, he needed a woman!

The fifth day. Clouds, puffballs of white cumulus billowing like ships in full sail against a blue sky. The heat had become oppressive, thick and clammy. The previous evening Gwynllyw had decided to hunt. The men had gathered at dawn calling the excited hunting dogs to order, had ridden out in joyful groups, singing and swapping tales of victorious battles and women won. The place seemed quiet and subdued without them.

Gwladys wandered through the small Caer, alone for the first time since her arrival. The scatter of buildings here were only one quarter the size of her father's huge complex of Hall, dwelling places, barns and buildings. She preferred her husband's holding; it seemed more comfortable, more relaxed, than the constant buzz of activity at her father's.

She climbed to the top of the defence wall, hoping to find a cool breeze there, saw the ribbon of a river glistening among the trees. Whisking down the stairs she snatched a light cloak from her chamber and calling to a maidservant, announced, 'I am going to the river!'

The water was inviting; cool and deep. She walked for a while, watching ducks swim, a fish rise, a bird dive. No one was around. She was a strong swimmer – oh, why not! She stripped, waded into the water – how cold it was as it reached her thighs! She gasped as she plunged forward, swimming strongly. She felt clean and fresh.

She swam vigorously for a while, letting the coldness bite into her skin, then floated with her arms outstretched, enjoying the pleasurable sensation of water on her nakedness.

'You should not swim alone, it may not be safe.'

She started and rolled over, taking in a mouthful of water as her head went down. Spluttering, she found firm ground beneath her feet, half stood, to hastily bob beneath the river's cover as she saw Arthur standing there on the bank. He was leading Eira, who stood fetlock deep in the current.

'I thought you were hunting!' she gasped, breathless from the ducking and from startled embarrassment.

Arthur patted his horse affectionately. 'He must have picked up a stone, for the sole of his hoof is bruised. I dare not lame him – we ride out on the morrow.' Arthur walked into the water beside the animal, lifted the leg to inspect the minor damage. 'Cold water does wonders for leg injuries.'

Gwladys felt a fool squatting down like this, but her clothes were on the bank, beyond him. How long had he been watching? She blushed, unsure what to do next.

'However beneficial to a horse's legs, river water is not over-kind to a lady's skin,' Arthur remarked.

'My clothes are behind you,' she said, hoping he would move away, dismayed when he did not.

She had been swimming a good while, had not noticed the gather of clouds from the west. The soft fluffed whiteness of morning was dulling rapidly into rain grey. The sun disappeared, leaving the river in dark shade. Gwladys shivered, realised the Pendragon had no intention of moving.

It suddenly occurred to her she did not care. She was a married woman now, beyond his touch. She stood, waded past him and scrambling up the bank began rubbing herself dry with her light summer cloak. She squeaked as she felt his hands on her shoulders.

'You are shivering,' he said, 'let me help you get warm.'

'*Na! Na*, thank you, my lord, I can manage!'

All the same, he took the thing from her, began to rub, gently, at her back, across her shoulders, down her throat.

She grabbed the cloak from him, reached for her clothes, dressed quickly, pulling on her tunic, her fingers fumbling with the lacings.

She trembled as his hands brushed hers, taking the irritating thongs from her to thread them easily, tying a neat bow.

'I am more used to untying these,' he said in a soft, coaxing voice. He was so close. He smelt of horse and leather and male sweat. She stood still, eyes closed, as his lips brushed hers, parting them slowly for his tongue to flick over her white teeth.

She was about to put her arms around him, draw him nearer, when a female voice made her spring away alarmed, red-faced. She pulled her gown over her head, hiding her embarrassment beneath its concealment.

'My mistress sent me to fetch you, lady. She says the clouds are forming rain and you should never come to the river alone.'

'Quite right, girl,' replied Arthur briskly, taking the cloak and placing it around Gwladys's shoulders. 'Exactly what I was saying.' He ushered Gwladys forward, shooed her in the direction of the fortress, almost as if he were marshalling chickens. 'Get yourself back, my lady.'

He turned, smiling pleasantly to the servant girl. 'You, girl, can walk back with me. Wait while I fetch Eira.'

Gwladys, flustered, had trotted a few paces, then she stopped, horrified, and fled back to Arthur's side, grabbing urgently at his arm.

'What if she saw?' she whispered, frightened. 'What if she tells my husband – he is bound not to think well of it! Oh, what shall I do?'

Arthur patted her hand. 'What was there to see? A kiss from one friend to another – do not fret, my sweet, she saw nothing. Go on, get you home. Gwynllyw's mother spoke aright, it is to rain.'

Reassured, Gwladys lifted up the hem of her skirts and ran. She found her mother-by-law waiting concerned and stern within the gates, a lecture on her lips. Chided, Gwladys listened and then burst into tears.

'There, child, I had no wish to upset you but think on it, we are not so far from your father's lands. What if he sent spies to steal you back?'

Gwladys's hand went to her throat. She had not thought of that. 'He would not dare!'

'I doubt he would, but all the same it is worth remembering. Besides, the river can be dangerous. Never go out alone, especially near the water – who knows what devilments lurk beneath its surface?'

Gwladys bit her lip. She thanked the woman for her sound advice, walked with as much dignity as she could summon towards the chapel and spent an hour prostrate before the altar praying to her God for forgiveness. What devilment, indeed!

Arthur squatted on the bank, holding Era's rein loosely as the horse nibbled at the lush grass.

'I have work to do, lord, may I not go?' She was a pretty thing, if you could look below the matted hair and grime. 'Why do servants not bother to wash?' Arthur asked.

'I do!' she replied hotly. 'You'd be mucky if you'd spent a mornin' cleanin' out the bakehouse ovens!'

'You sound keen to get back to the task.'

'I've finished. I were about to clean up when my lady sent me on this errand.'

'So you need to bathe? Your errand is completed, the Lady Gwladys safely gone – now you can wash.' He indicated the river. 'Go ahead.'

At first she hesitated, then, slowly, her fingers went to her bodice; she unlaced the thongs, pulled off her tunic and undergarments. She walked to the water, stepped in, ducked down, as relieved as Gwladys had been to wash away the clinging dirt.

Arthur watched her a while then pulled off his own boots, unbuckled his sword belt and removed the light leather hunting tunic. 'I think I will join you.' He pulled some handfuls of bracken, offered one to her. 'You scrub the sweat from my back, girl; I will scrub yours.'

He unfastened the lacings of his bracae and slid naked into the water, concealing the gasp as its coldness hit his belly.

She stood uncertain, biting a black, chewed fingernail glanced in the direction of the fortress. He was wading towards her, had reached her, caught her arm and tumbled her backwards. She screamed, from the cold more than surprise. He stifled the sound with his mouth, rolling her over in the shallows, holding her close. She responded, giggling.

The first rainfall for two weeks fell from a heavy grey sky. They did not even notice.

After, he paid her well and rode the next day from the stronghold with nothing but a casual memory and a temporary satisfaction.

FEBRUARY 454

§ III

Cei nudged Arthur's arm, indicated the two people entering Vortigern's audience chamber. Arthur frowned, screwing up his eyes to make out the faces through the crush of people and the smoke from the burning torches.

'Who is it?'

Cei gave a deep-throated chuckle. 'A friend. Gwynllyw.'

'Really!' Delighted, Arthur pushed his way through groups of men and women to greet the newcomers, making slow progress across the crowded room. 'Gwynllyw! It is good to see you!' He clasped the man's offered hand. 'Why come you here to Caer Leon through this day's foul weather? And with your wife too!' His look of pleasure turned to one of alarm. Usually the Hibernian sea-wolves did not raid during the winter months, but the weather, save for this day's miserable wetness, had been kind, the seas calm. 'Not bad news, I trust?'

Gwynllyw returned the Pendragon's enthusiastic welcome. 'I had no idea you would be at court – I had heard you were up at Eboracum! No, my friend, no bad tidings, save a summons by the King!' He was a shorter man than Arthur, square-built with broad shoulders and thickset legs, his face blunt-chinned and heavy-jawed. He needed to tilt his head back to look Arthur in the eyes. 'The one disadvantage to building my new stronghold at Caer Dydd is the proximity to this place.'

Laughing, Arthur moved behind Gwynllyw to kiss Gwladys. 'You are even lovelier than I remember!' He stood back and, firmly clasping her hands, observed her state of advanced pregnancy. 'Though somewhat larger!'

Gwladys blushed deep pink and flicked Arthur a glance from beneath lowered lashes. Her husband said with pride, 'I thought it wise to establish full claim to my property so her father could not stir trouble,' adding in an undertone, 'Is Brychan here?'

Arthur tipped his head indicating a group of men seated to the far right. 'Aye, rats smell rotting vegetation from far off.'

Grim, Gwynllyw answered, 'I thought he might be.' But Arthur had no chance to follow the remark, for Gwynllyw added, 'I am receiving dark looks from Vortigern, we had best make our obedience – may we join you after?'

'Of course.'

Arthur returned cheerfully to Cei. 'Gwladys is pretty even in pregnancy,' he remarked. 'Some women run to fat with child.'

'Any girl is pretty to you,' retorted Cei affably.

'Save my wife.'

'Many envy you.'

'Then they must be hard pressed for pleasure.' Arthur accepted dried fruits from a passing slave, chewed thoughtfully. Gwynllyw was presenting Gwladys to Rowena, the Queen making a gushing display of affectionate greeting. 'Who are *they* anyway?'

Cei's reply was offhand. 'No one in particular. Any man who seeks ambition and power would be glad to claw a way up through Winifred.'

Arthur spat out a seed. 'Be clawed by her, more like.' He looked with distaste at his wife, seated beside her mother. They were both animatedly talking to Gwladys, about the child no doubt. Arthur snorted, finding it difficult to believe Winifred could be interested in anything so maternal. Rightly, he ought to have felt slighted by her adamant refusal to be with him, but he had no interest in where she placed her backside. The further away the better.

'Is there a rumour that she has taken a lover, then?' Casually Arthur glanced at Cei, knowing the man would not tattle idle gossip nor hold back truth if asked for a straight answer.

'Not that I have heard. All the same.' Cei spread his hands, 'were she mine, I would have her watched.'

Arthur finished his fruit, wiped sticky hands on the seat of his bracae. Did he care what the bitch got up to? Not particularly. But then, a good excuse to be rid of her could prove useful.

Gwynllyw was approaching, hand outstretched to greet Cei.

Arthur whispered quickly, 'Arrange it. As soon as possible.'

'I'1 do it now. Gwynllyw! How are you?' Cei stayed a few polite moments, then nodded to Arthur and took his leave.

Calling for wine and a stool Arthur attended Gwladys, spoke fiercely to her husband. 'By the Bull man, why drag her to this vipers' pit in her condition?'

Gwynllyw scowled. 'Vortigern expressly asked to meet her. I think he is hatching some plot of reconciliation with Brychan.'

'You have not softened towards each other yet then?'

Shaking his head, Gwynllyw puffed out his cheeks. 'To Brychan, I am a low-born whore-son who ought to be dangling on a rope from the highest tree.' He gave a great bellow of laughter. 'And I suspect, Arthur, he would not object to having you dancing alongside me!' Falling serious again, he went on, 'The pair of them grow anxious because I am not the mild hearth tender my father was. I have taken more land these last three years since his death than he did in an entire lifetime. And I am establishing a good trade with Less Britain and Gaul. The King likes it not that I am becoming a touch powerful in my part of the country.' He glared across the room at Vortigern. 'But if he thinks he can curb my rising position by yoking me under Brychan's rule, then he can damn well think again!'

Alarmed, Arthur looked hastily around. 'Mithras, Gwynllyw! Keep your voice down if you intend to keep your bull head lodged on your neck!'

Gwynllyw compressed his lips, was tempted to make a scathing retort, but seeing sense laughed instead. 'You're right!' He slapped Arthur's shoulder, turned the subject. 'The horses arrived safe. Jesu, but Cunedda breeds fine stock!' Scanning the sea of faces, he asked, 'Is he not here?'

'Gwynedd has cut itself from Vortigern completely since Etern's murder.'

'That was a bad business.'

A surge of bile rose in Arthur's throat. Aye, bad.

Gwynllyw failed to notice Arthur's sudden silence, for he was saying, 'It was good fortune the day I met with you!' He was laughing, at ease, pleased to have met with an old friend and that other men admired his pretty young wife, as large as she was. 'God in his wisdom smiled on us that day!'

Gwladys was not listening. She felt ill. She told herself the unease was due to the bulk of the child, thought the sickness was caused by the heat and noise of this room. When Arthur unexpectedly took her hand in his own, she squeaked and tried to jerk it away.

'I know not if God had a hand in the matter of our coming together,' he was saying, 'but by the Bull, I would not have missed seeing Brychan's face for an empire's fortune!'

Gwladys managed to retrieve her hand, put it in her lap. The fluttering had become a pounding gallop. She felt for the string of glass and jet beads hanging at her waist and, threading them through her fingers, silently recited the litany against the temptations of sin. Arthur's presence caused this turmoil – Arthur, and the thought of that never-forgotten afternoon by the river.

From the dais, Winifred observed the woman seated with the man she called husband, watched his preening attention and joyful laughter. He never laughed or seemed happy and content when in her company. She hated him. Hated his callous disregard of her and his frequent scathing remarks. Hated wanting him so much.

Occasionally, alone in her bed for yet another night, Winifred wondered if she ought to take a lover, but come morning common sense always returned. What if there was a child? What if Arthur were to discover her infidelity? He would divorce her for certain, and was that not what he wanted? Legitimate grounds to be rid of her, to publicly cast her aside and keep all her dowry? Ah no! Divorce would be on her terms or not at all!

Curious, she beckoned her handmaid. 'Find out who that woman with my husband might be.'

The girl glanced across the hall. 'I shall ask the servants, my lady.'

A slave overheard, pricked up her ears. Moving innocently to Winifred's side she poured wine, said, 'Forgive me, lady – she's Gwladys, daughter of Brychan.'

Disregarding the girl's blatant forwardness, Winifred said, 'The daughter stolen from under his nose?' She grasped the girl's wrist. 'How do you know her?'

Masking her fright at the sudden painful hold the girl stammered, 'I was a slave at her husband's stronghold.'

Winifred watched Gwladys smiling at a tale Arthur was elaborately relating.

'She's very beautiful,' the slave announced. 'I remember we all said so when first we saw her. It's a shame she has a temper like a pregnant sow. She had me whipped for no reason and sold. That's how I come to be here.'

Winifred digested the information, though she was not interested in the girl's petulance, beyond an idea it might prove useful. 'Did my lord Arthur also think her beautiful?' she asked casually.

'Oh aye.' The girl poured more wine. Seeing a chance to gain some small revenge, she grabbed at it – there might even be some form of reward! Freedom would taste very nice. She whispered, 'I remember well the time he found her swimming naked in the river.'

A muscle twitched in Winifred's cheek. She said calmly, as if uninterested, 'Indeed? Where is it you work? The kitchens?'

The girl wiped her hands self-consciously on her filthy skirt, her heart racing. 'Usually, lady, but we're all needed out here this night.'

Winifred regarded her shrewdly. A pretty thing beneath the grime. Was it worth taking her spite seriously? 'Would you rather serve as a handmaid?'

The girl's eyes lit up. She nodded eagerly.

Winifred beckoned her personal maid closer. 'Find this wretch some suitable clothing, and make certain she takes a bath.' To the girl, 'We will talk again, later.'

A glow of satisfaction warmed Winifred. Arthur thought he was so clever! Well, she had stumbled on something to turn that cocksure arrogance and, by God's truth, she intended to use it!

§ IV

Wet through, boots and legs plastered with mud, Arthur returned from inspecting the out-wintering horses and went reluctantly straight to Vortigern's private chambers. Each time he was summoned he was forced to listen to a long litany of fresh complaints. At times he felt as though he were a child, being chastised by his tutor for failing yet again to write his Latin verbs correctly on the slate.

He was surprised to find Gwynllyw with the King. Glancing at the young man he was astonished to receive an icy stare of contempt in return. Puzzled, Arthur inclined his head to Vortigern, the only concession of obedience the Pendragon would ever agree to make. 'You sent for me?'

'By the express request of Gwynllyw, I did.' Vortigern appraised Arthur's appearance and the trail of muddy footprints on the tiled floor. Said irritably, 'Could you not change into clean garments before entering here?'

'I was ordered to attend you immediately.'

Vortigern's lips thinned. Insolence!

Arthur added to the hostility by sauntering to a chair, hooking it closer with his toe and sprawling in it, hands hanging over the arms, eye cocked between the King and Gwynllyw.

'You may sit,' Vortigern said coldly. He turned to the other man. 'Would you rather I informed the Pendragon of why he is here?'

Gwynllyw stepped menacingly towards Arthur, drawing his sword. 'Let that pleasure be mine.'

Arthur tilted the chair to its back legs, said with a laugh, 'What in the Bull's name is this? Put your blade up, my friend!'

Gwynllyw's lip curled, hatred pouring from him. The tip of his sword hovered near Arthur's throat. 'I am no friend of yours, Pendragon. Surely you are indeed your father's bastard!'

Vortigern pushed himself from his seat, walked towards Gwynllyw and nudged the blade aside with his arm. 'Put the weapon away, it does not frighten the Pendragon. There will be time enough for bloodshed. Let us talk this thing over.' He sauntered back to his chair.

Arthur let his own chair fall with a thud back to all four feet, stood abruptly. 'Aye, and start talking quickly. I do not take kindly to a sword at my throat for a reason I know nothing of!'

Gwynllyw sheathed the thing, his hand hovering none the less over the hilt. He snarled. 'You have dishonoured my wife Arthur Pendragon!'

For some moments Arthur could not reply. Stupefied, open-mouthed, he looked from one man's face to the other. Of all the reasons to be commanded before the King, threatened with a blade and accused of whatever it was he was accused of he would not have thought it involved Gwladys! Plenty of other women, aye, but not Gwladys!

A string of thoughts came and went. Finally, thrusting his fingers through his sword belt he said, 'I know not how you heard this lie, but lie it certainly is.'

'You deny intercourse with my wife while I hunted?'

If Gwynllyw had not seemed so angry Arthur would have laughed in his face. 'Of course I damn well deny it!'

Gwynllyw raged on, his voice husky with anger. 'You also deny watching her swim? You remember that day, I presume? We left early, soon after sun-up; after a mile or two you said your horse was going lame and you elected to return to the Caer.' His hand clasped tighter around his sword hilt. 'If I had realised then what I know now!' He had the sword half out of the scabbard again, staying the action as Arthur lazily rested his hand on the weapon by his own side.

'Do you accuse me of taking the woman of a friend – and one who had been a bride of only a few days?'

Gwynllyw, almost pleadingly, searched Arthur's face for the truth. The idea of such a betrayal revolted him but Vortigern had insisted his source of information was reliable, and there were the rumours. Only whispers, but whispers murmured over often. Gwladys and Arthur and the river. Then there came the talk concerning the child. It had come quickly. Could he be certain he had the siring of it? And Gwladys? She seemed ill at ease, nervous and restless, turning from him in the intimacy of night. He had assumed it to be the burden of pregnancy but now he doubted. Could it be the guilt of carrying another's child – Arthur's child?

Vortigern had deliberately seated himself, always feeling at a disadvantage standing in Arthur's presence. God take the man, he was so annoyingly tall! Accurately reading the fleeting signs of uncertainty on Gwynllyw's face the King interrupted. 'We hear countless tales of your fondness for women, Arthur. Rumours reach my ears. It seems fathers – and husbands – lock their womenfolk away when your turma is near.'

Vortigern leant forward, rested an elbow on his knee; he was enjoying the Pendragon's discomfort. 'Not,' he added 'from fear of the men – but from their leader. Your reputation, Pendragon, has not done you proud. I would suggest,' he wagged a warning finger, 'I command, you pay less attention to the whore and spend more nights with your wife!'

'Who is the most professional of whores!' Arthur snapped the reply without thinking.

Vortigern was on his feet and across the room in two strides, rage contorting his aged face. 'Retract that or you will face my sword!'

Arthur stood his ground. 'She was not so innocent when she came to me. Who is to say how innocent she is now?'

'You have no proof of this!'

Arthur smiled cynically. 'Neither do you for Winifred's fidelity – or for Gwladys's lack of it.' He turned to Gwynllyw. 'I strongly deny the charge. Whom would you trust, myself or this lying tyrant? Has he said who so generously revealed this absurd lie?'

Vortigern, still angry, reseated himself; said offhandedly, 'You were seen with Gwladys on the river bank.'

'Is that the accusation!' Arthur roared, hands on hips, head back. 'I was seen with her! Of course I was seen with her! Eira was lame, I took him to the river to cool the inflammation; Gwladys was there also, she had been swimming. Know that she was dried, dressed and about to leave for home when I arrived.' A small lie, more a stretching of the truth. 'We talked a while of Eira and the horses. All quite innocent, my friend.' Arthur fixed a pleasant smile, deliberately refused to drop the affable term.

'You were seen holding her.'

Arthur sighed, keeping patience. 'I have already admitted to being with her, Gwynllyw! It clouded over swiftly if I remember correctly, and your wife had suddenly felt the cold. I helped her on with her cloak and sent her back to the Caer. I also seem to remember she was unwell that evening. Did she not say to you she must have caught a chill?'

Gwynllyw frowned. He did remember, quite clearly, for Gwladys had been ill during the night with sickness and sweating. 'The next morning you rode out. She was,' he said, 'far from well. The physician could not say what had caused the malady; he put it down to excitement over our marriage. Of course,' he added in a low hiss, 'it could equally well have been guilt!'

Arthur swung away in exasperation, hit the wall with his clenched fist. 'It is for you to choose, Gwynllyw. There is no truth in this madness, and I shall willingly swear to that by whatever oath you ask.'

Vortigern coughed, drawing their attention. 'The truth may soon be revealed.' His low laugh was a horrid grating sound, as if slate were being dragged over stone. He rose, ambled to a table to fetch wine. A few steps, and he regretted rising as pain spread, the undesired discomforts of old age. With a great effort he forced his body straight, attempted to disregard the searing ache from his hip.

'The child she bears may well resemble its father.' He poured the wine, took a deep draught from the goblet. Wiping the residue from his lips, he turned back to Arthur, a malicious smile creasing his craggy face. 'Unless your wife produces an heir, Arthur – which, given the present lack of intimacy between you, I fail to see occurring – you may be forced to admit Gwladys's child as yours. One of your bastards may have to carry the Dragon when I eventually decide to have you dispatched.'

Arthur flew at the King, sword drawn, ready to strike. Gwynllyw and Vortigern reacted, the elder man more slowly, throwing the contents of the goblet clumsily at Arthur; Gwynllyw grappling Arthur's arm, shouting for him to hold.

Breathing heavily, Arthur backed off, began slowly sheathing his weapon. Vortigern smoothed his rumpled tunic, keeping excess alarm from showing in his face. He walked sedately to his chair, sat, stared unblinking at his son-by-law.

'Should you ever attempt such an action again, Pendragon,' he said slowly, threateningly, 'I shall have you flogged and torn limb from limb. Do you understand me, boy?'

Arthur thudded his sword in the scabbard, nostrils flaring. He returned Vortigern's snake-like stare through slit eyes. For a moment, Vortigern felt his heart lurch, his stomach turn over. He put it down to Arthur's sudden attack, was reluctant to admit fear.

'I understand you, Vortigern,' Arthur said in a low voice. 'I assure you there will be no next time. You have my word: should I have cause to draw my sword on you again, it will be the last action you ever see.' He spun round on one heel. Ignoring the King and Gwynllyw he strode from the room, slamming the door with a resounding crash.

Marching to his own quarters he snarled viciously at servants who crossed his path, sending them scuttling for safety in the shadows. All the while his mind turned over the possibilities. Who had reported his encounter with Gwladys? His men were loyal, not one would willingly betray him. Unwillingly? He paused in mid-stride. He thought highly of Gwynllyw, had known his father, a good, trustworthy man, but had never met the son before last summer. How in the Bull's name could he accept these lies? He snorted scornfully. Easily! Vortigern, damn him, had been partly correct, for some did fear the coming of Arthur's cavalry. They were a wild, fierce lot, apt to get carried away when feeling the need to relax. Was this because the men followed their leader's example?

The Pendragon sighed, rubbing sweating palms over the nape of his neck. Happen they did. Lately he had sought escape in an excess of drink and women.

Gwynllyw must understand – must realise his tally of women did not, except in thought, include Gwladys. So he had made a try for her – happen he ought to admit to that, for the sake of truth. Ironic, he thought, the one time he had not lain with a woman he was accused of it!

Washed and clad in fresh clothing, he strode from his room and made for the one allotted to Gwynllyw. So blind was his desire to talk the matter through he marched straight into the chamber, barely pausing to knock.

He stood motionless, face drained of colour, frozen with embarrassment and incredulity at his own stupidity. It had not occurred to him Gwladys would also be using this same room. He never shared with Winifred.

Gwynllyw's wife stood in her undergarments. The maid squealed, hurrying to cover her mistress. Arthur made some hasty, futile apology; turned to leave, came face to face with Gwynllyw.

There was no sound or movement, then Arthur swallowed, reached a hand forward to explain. The calm shattered.

With a roar Gwynllyw thrust the hand aside, swung forward, driving his fist into Arthur's belly, following through with the other, slamming knuckles into his face. Arthur doubled at the first blow, fell at the second. The ladies screamed. Gwladys, grabbing the hasty covering, darted forward to kneel at Arthur's side.

'Why?' she asked, dabbing at the blood pouring from his nose.

Gwynllyw stared coldly at her. Out of spite, he kicked his boot twice into Arthur's ribs then turned on his heel and strode for the door.

She ran after him, catching at his sleeve, her clutched garment slipping to the floor. 'What is it? What has happened?'

He drew back his hand, made to strike her, stopped himself. 'Now I understand why you wish our first-born to be given to the Church! Because it is not mine! Do you take me for such a blind fool, woman?'

She looked blankly up at his contorted face. 'I do not understand. Please, what has happened?'

'You ask me? Best ask your lover!'

The room reeled; Gwladys slid, legs buckling, to the floor. Her husband stared at her, spat out, 'I have nothing further to say to you.'

242

Arthur stumbled to his feet, clutching at the pain, but Gwynllyw had gone. Wiping away the blood as best he could, he turned to Gwladys. He tucked her fallen covering around her, tried to explain. 'Your husband believes a gross lie. Some vicious tongue has spread a rumour that we were lovers – the child you carry is mine.'

Her eyes flickered up to him, shifted away. He made to touch her, withdrew. Mithras! What to do? 'You have been wronged, Gwladys; I promise all this shall be put to rights.'

She said nothing, just sat staring. It was a punishment this, from God. A punishment for the sin of thought.

Arthur spread his arms wide, then let them drop. His ribs ached; there would be bruising when he stripped off his tunic. He left the room; there was nothing he could do here.

Fitful sleep for him that night encircled by grotesque faces. Gwladys naked before him, heavy with child, screaming. Gwynllyw slashing with bloodied sword; Vortigern watching with those red, snake eyes. Then a bed, a boy lying there frightened, a woman leaning over him, pinning him down, her head back. Laughing.

He woke drenched in sweat. He had not dreamt of Morgause for Mithras knew how long! His hand shook as he reached for wine, feeling sick, disgusted and hopeless.

There had been others in the dream. Women's faces, women's voices, cackling like hags beneath the shadow of the full moon.

Winifred. Gwladys. He groaned, his head in his hands.

And then another. Her face lovely, her smile gentle and kind. Gwenhwyfar. Would he never forget her?

Not until past mid-morning did the answer hit him, as savage as the blows Gwynllyw had given. He was ploughing through ankle-deep mud beyond the stables when he halted, sending Cei bouncing off him.

'God's patience, Arthur!' Cei cursed, peered at him. 'You have turned as white as a sun-bleached sheet! What ails you?'

'May she rot, the bitch!' Arthur said for answer and wading forward, headed for Vortigern's apartments. Cei shrugged, letting his friend and commander go. He knew better than to meddle in Arthur's business. He would find out what it was all about soon enough.

§ V

Arthur burst like a charging bull into Winifred's chamber, sending a scatter of women screaming to their feet.

'Must a husband's attention to his wife be greeted by such hysteria?' he growled. He surveyed them for a few heartbeats, his eyes narrowing as he found what he had suspected.

'Get you all gone – except you.' He grabbed at a red-haired girl, pulling her, none too gently, to his side.

'How dare you enter here in such a manner!' said Winifred, rising from the tapestry frame where she had been sewing. 'My ladies will stay.' The women hovered, unsure which order to obey.

Arthur loosened his sword in its scabbard, saw their eyes flicker from Winifred to the door. 'What I have to say is for your, and her,' he shook the girl, 'hearing only.' He added as a threat, 'I will cut off any ears that hear what they should not. He drew the sword an inch or so. Shrill screams and squawks of alarm as the women hurried away, the last one pulling the door shut behind her. Winifred compressed her lips. The fools – did they think he was serious?

'What is so important you must make a spectacle of yourself before my women?'

Dragging the girl with him Arthur moved to the tapestry, peered close. A Christian scene, almost finished.

'Pretty,' he said, still smiling. 'You are always, I have noticed, surrounded by pretty things, Winifred.' He jerked the girl round to stand before him. 'This one is the prettiest.'

'Take your hand off Tangwen. You are hurting her.'

'Tangwen? Is that your name, my pretty?' He ran his finger over her cheek, down her throat almost to the swell of her breast, his voice soft and sensuous. Then with an unexpected raw edge said, 'I never bothered to ask before, did I?'

He caught a loose strand of her red hair, curling it round his fingers. 'I shall do more than hurt the bloody little liar!' He thrust her from him throwing her to the floor, in the same movement caught up his short-bladed dagger. Tangwen screamed as he knelt over her and gripped her cheeks between the fingers of his left hand. 'Shall I remove that wagging tongue of yours, Tangwen? Bitch! You deserve to have your throat cut!'

The girl squirmed, shook her head, pleading for mercy with her eyes. She shrieked as he dealt her a stinging blow.

'How dare you!' shouted Winifred, darting forward. 'How dare you enter my chamber like a madman and attack my slave!' She clutched up the unfinished tapestry, flew at Arthur and hurled the thing down upon his back. The blow caused no harm, but Arthur released the girl.

Standing slowly, breathing hard, he glared at his wife. 'How dare I?' he asked in a voice low and dangerously level. 'You ask me that? You ask how I dare? Did you force this miserable wretch to tell you of what occurred at Gwynllyw's? Or did she blurt it out without realising how your warped, twisted little mind would use the information? It is unfortunate for you, wife, I recall where I have seen this slut before. I do not often remember the base-born whores I take, but her flame-coloured hair reminded me. That and tattle of a river and a lady swimming there.'

Arthur dragged the snivelling girl to her feet. 'I barely noticed you serving the other night. I suppose you were both counting on that, hoping I was too drunk to remember where and when I had you.'

He thrust the girl at Winifred, causing her to fall against her mistress. Told in graphic detail of how he had coupled with the slave, leaving out no detail and enjoying every word of the telling.

'I have recounted things aright, have I not, Tangwen?' Arthur lunged forward, seized her by the shoulders and shook her until she cried agreement. 'I would hazard a guess she left that particular part out of the telling though, eh, Winifred?'

He struck his forehead with the palm of his hand. 'Fool! Have I not also left a vital part out, Tangwen? What of the reason for you being at the river? What of you seeing me lying with the lady Gwladys?' He spun her round to face him, shaking her again. 'What of it, girl? What of how I lay with the lady? A pretty tale. All of it lies!'

' 'Twas not!' she screamed. ' 'Twas not all lies! I saw you kiss her!'

Winifred pressed her lips tighter together. Stupid girl.

Arthur spat, 'You saw me kiss her. A parting kiss from one friend to another. One chaste kiss was all you saw, was it not? Was it not!' She had not seen more – for if she knew Arthur had stood watching Gwladys bathing, had touched her, then for certain she would have told.

He slapped her again. 'Answer me!'

Tears springing, she nodded.

'Speak up. You saw nothing save a parting kiss of friendship.'

'Aye.'

'Louder!'

'Aye!'

Arthur hurled the girl towards the door. She stumbled and he followed after her, hauled her up by the hair, opened the door and kicked her outside. 'You will wait there.' He pointed to the opposite wall. 'Your mistress has no further use of you, but I do. May your god help you if you dare move so much as an inch!' He slammed the door, turned back to Winifred.

'Well,' she said, applauding mockingly, 'what an excellent performance! You burst in here, order my women out, beat one of them then dismiss her from my service. You must visit me more often, husband, you are quite entertaining!'

Arthur remained silent, watching her through slit eyes, head slightly lowered. 'It was a plausible tale, my dear,' he said; 'how unfortunate it failed. I grant you it almost succeeded, but if you wish to hurt me I suggest you do it direct not by sinking your poisoned fangs into my comrades – or their pregnant wives.'

Winifred laughed, retrieved some of her ladies' sewing that had fallen to the floor. 'Is this also part of the entertainment – riddles?'

Arthur lunged, caught her to him. She gasped as his hand gripped her wrist. 'You push your luck, woman! Luck has a nasty habit of running out when you need it most.'

'I have no idea what you mean. If you are referring to those rumours concerning Gwladys's child, then I would suggest it is I who need the explanation!'

'Who told Vortigern? You? Tangwen would never have had the intelligence or courage to whisper such lies to the King.'

Winifred plucked at his fingers. 'You are hurting me,' she said, pouting. 'It is nothing to do with me – save for the insult of your bedding another woman.' She struggled, kicked once at his shins, then kicked again, her anger overcoming her. She bit his arm, began to fight him with feet, teeth and free hand.

For a while he bore the blows, holding her away from him to stop her causing over-much damage, but soon tired of the senseless game. He smacked his fist into her face.

She staggered, head reeling, the flesh of her cheekbone already swollen and bruised.

'You dare lay hands on me, Arthur Pendragon! You bastard!'

'I will do more than lay hands on you!' He felt no pity or guilt as he beat his wife with his belt across her arms and face. She screamed, huddled down on the floor, trying to protect herself from the flaying leather.

Breathing hard, disgusted with her and himself, Arthur flung the belt aside, turned his back on the sobbing woman.

Humiliated, hurting, Winifred clasped her arms around herself. Her hand touched something cold at her waist. Her fingers curled round the small jewel-studded hilt of a dagger. She drew it cautiously, then, with anger searing as sure as the pain she sprang at Arthur's retreating back, the dagger scything down.

He recognised the death hiss of a blade through air and whirled, grasping her wrist with one hand, prising the light weapon from her clenched fingers with the other.

The jewels, diamonds and rubies, were set within walrus ivory. He had seen such a thing before – long ago. His voice very quiet, very dangerous, he asked, 'Where did you get this?'

'I am not bound to answer your interrogation!'

He gave a sinister laugh. 'Oh but you are. A wife is duty bound to her husband. How came you to be in possession of Gwenhwyfar's blade?'

Winifred looked him full in the eye, unflinching. 'She gave it to me.'

The Pendragon stood silent, memory flooding over him. Gwenhwyfar's hands deftly slitting fresh-caught fish; this blade glinting high, triumphant, as she taunted him and her brother Etern at mock battle. Her dagger, her mother's before that. 'She would never part with such a personal treasure.' Arthur returned Winifred's look, staring her down. 'You stole it, didn't you?'

Winifred snatched at the dagger, screaming coarse abuse. Arthur flung it aside, sending it clattering harmlessly to the floor. She broke free of him and lunged desperately for the blade; his hand grabbed, missed, tore her gown, ripping the bodice. He kicked, sending the dagger spinning out of reach.

She looked wildly around for some means of protection, backing away from his rage.

Arthur remained still, running his eyes over her partially revealed breasts. He leered at her, removing what remained of her clothing with his gaze. 'I know a far more potent way of hurting your evil pride.'

Furious at his implication, Winifred hurled whatever came to hand. Skilfully he knocked aside each missile – a vase, a chamber pot, a stool. Watching his chance, with the ease of a fighting man, he ducked in low and threw her to the ground. She tried to claw his face; he pinned her down, holding her between his knees and with one hand tore the remains of her gown from her. Unlacing his bracae, he entered her quickly, his satisfaction heightened by the burning outrage on her face.

She spat some word of abuse, furious with him, with herself, moaned as a sudden surge of pleasure shot through her body. She pushed herself from him, arching her back, drawing him deeper in as her arms encircled his shoulders, wanting more. Desperately wanting more.

He was kissing her now, his mouth covering hers, his hands on her breasts, stomach, then thighs.

Winifred gasped, twined her legs around him, her body jerking as she climaxed, and again as he came with her. Breathless, her body shuddering, she lay helpless beneath him, limbs spread, head back, panting.

When he moved, it was only to roll from her, spent. He lay there, eyes closed, breathing hard, sweating.

Winifred half sat up, reached a finger to tentatively wipe a drop of perspiration from his shoulder, instead licked it with her tongue. He did not move. Her tongue flicked at his throat, down over his chest, along the line of dark hair running to his navel. She changed to alternating kisses, moved lower.

When he was at last dressed he bent to take up Gwenhwyfar's dagger and pushed it through his sword belt. He sauntered to the door. Winifred remained flat on the floor, her body echoing the crescendo of sensations from their second coupling. Impulsively he strode back to her and seductively kissed her mouth, his tongue probing, lips insistent. His callused soldier's hand briefly fondled her white breast.

Her hand covered his, holding it there. 'Come again to me soon, my lord.'

He kissed her one last time, a light touch to her lips. 'Only if I can find no better place to sheathe my sword.'

She slapped his face with all the strength she could muster.

His laughter echoed along the corridors, mingling with her screamed abuse.

§ VI

Gwynllyw poured himself another large measure of wine, swallowed the whole in one gulp, placed his tankard carefully before him. 'I have been well played for the fool.'

'Are we not all fools where women are concerned?' Arthur said, reaching across the wooden table to help himself to wine.

The tavern was crowded, men sat or stood, drinking, talking and laughing, the place swirling with a variety of noises and smells. It had taken a while for Arthur to find his friend; a longer while, and four jugs of the place's best wine, to convince him of the truth.

Gwynllyw attempted a half-smile. The wine had gone to his head; he felt dizzy and ready for sleep. His speech came slurred. 'What should I do now? How will I explain to Gwladys? Will she ever forgive me this madness?' He groaned and put his head in his hands.

Arthur tossed back his wine; he knew well what he would do, but how to advise Gwynllyw? 'I would go straight to my lady's chamber, order her servants out and bolt the door on them. I would then carry the wronged lady to her bed and make slow, passionate love to her.' A grin broadened. 'After, we would lie close a while, then I would do it all over again. And then...' Arthur paused. What then? He himself would make promises, vow his love and leave her, immediately forgotten and ride back to his men. 'Then, I would order up the horses and go home. Sticking my cock up to Vortigern and Winifred, leaving the pair of them to rot in the dung-heap of their own lies.'

Gwynllyw nodded agreement and stood up, swaying unsteadily. He held out his hand in friendship. 'Sound advice. I will do that then.'

Arthur watched him leave, tripping and stumbling from the tavern, weaving drunkenly through the door and up the street. Turning to a fifth jug, Arthur wondered whether he would make it to Gwladys's chamber, or be found lying drunk in the gutter come dawn's light.

Winifred groaned and pushed her maid aside sending the bowl of bloodied water splashing to the floor. She ached, she hurt. Every part of her body throbbed or screamed with pain.

She hated him, loathed the sight of him! How dare he do this to her? The bastard, the evil, brutal bastard.

Rising from the stool, she shuffled to the bed, winced as her maid again began salving her hurts, buried her head beneath a pillow as the tears came.

She wanted him dead – dead a hundred times over by a hundred sickening methods; but, oh dear God's love, she wanted him back!

Damn him! Damn, damn him! She would let him do it all over again, if only he would come back!

SEPTEMBER 454

§ VII

Eira shifted weight from one hind foot to the other, eyes half shut in semi-sleep, his jaw resting heavy on Arthur's shoulder as his master absently stroked the soft pink velvet part between the horse's nostrils. With a deep sigh, the stallion drowsed in the hot sun.

Arthur was looking up the wooded slope watching the vaguely discernible shape of one of his men, carefully hidden within the dappled foliage. Somewhere behind a horse squealed, kicking out against the bite of a horsefly.

'Damn you!' Arthur hissed, turning towards the unwanted sound. Eira snorted, tossed his head and backed a pace. 'Keep your mount quiet!'

Red-faced, the rider calmed his horse, his eyes, in his deep embarrassment, looking everywhere except ahead and his commander's disapproval.

Then the lookout signalled. With the minimum of noise Arthur's turma of thirty or so men mounted and nudged forward in single file at a slow walk. The horses had come alert, were eager for action.

Arthur reached the end of the hollow and reined Eira back, the horse straining against the curbing bit with impatience. The lookout sat motionless, poised, one hand raised. Not daring to breathe, he willed the band of Saex cur-sons forward, just a few more paces... With a flourish, he dropped his hand.

The waiting was over!

A few of the Angli, to the fore of their band of fifty fighting men, yelled a startled warning as a rushing blur of colour and sound poured from the trees. Fleeting glimpses of pounding hooves, scything swords and thrusting spears. The Dragon, tubular shaped, glinting red and gold writhed and tossed above the heads of yelling horsemen. The wind wailed through its hollow insides and screamed out through its tail of screaming ribbons, turning into a live thing, writhing and twisting and shrieking of death.

The Angli fought bravely while the sudden, swift slaughter lasted; the handful left alive dropped their weapons and fled back along the sun-dappled trackway, their eyes bulging with terror as Arthur's cavalry pursued them, picking off those who fell behind.

Sound drifted from the place of ambush, leaving only quiet. A fox slunk away from the disturbance, wrinkling his snout at the intrusive scent of human blood. Carrion birds gathered, gliding in on silent wings as if summoned by some faery spell; a few began to hop on ungainly legs to peck at the carnage of Anglian bodies strewn about the flattened grass.

With yells of excitement, Arthur encouraged his men forward, the thrill of the chase hot in his blood. Two scared Angli plunged down a weed-grown bank into the river, thrashing through rushing water, attempting to run against the current that pulled at weary legs.

Eira faltered at the crest of the low bank, ears flickering, hooves sensing the weakness of the ground. Arthur kicked him on, intending him to land out in midstream, but the horse's hind legs slipped as he thrust forward, his quarters dropping as he leapt. Somehow he twisted in mid-air, landed awkwardly, forelegs scrabbling for a firm hold. Spray spumed high as he went crashing down taking his rider with him.

The horse panicked, thrashed the turbulent water, ears flat back, eyes rolling. He struggled, kicking with his hind legs, attempting to gain solid ground. Noise all round, shouts, neighing horses. Someone screaming.

A man was at the stallion's head – Cei, taking hold of the bridle, speaking calm words, gentling the trembling, snorting beast. At the sound of a familiar voice, the horse quietened; Cei persuaded him forward. With a heave, Eira lurched free of the water to stand head lowered, flanks heaving.

Cei, his own heart pounding, tossed the reins at someone and plunged back into the muddied water, running against the current, his face white.

Men equally anxious were already lifting Arthur, his blood turning the white river foam a grotesque pink.

Forgotten, the Angli ran on, offering aloud grateful thanks over and over to their own gods.

Merciful darkness had overtaken the Pendragon. He lay still as death as Cei bound the thigh tight, to splint broken bones and stem the bleeding. Men brought forward a hastily fashioned litter, lifted their leader as gently as they could and set their feet, minds numb, for camp.

§ VIII

Cei found himself grinning foolishly with relief as Arthur yelled an oath at the surgeon. 'Mithras' life man!'

'I would not have believed I could be so pleased to hear your cursing!' Cei laughed, folding his arms and leaning against the wall.

'You will be hearing more if this oaf does not take more care!' Arthur grunted his reply, gritting his teeth as a fresh thrust of pain burst from his damaged right thigh.

The surgeon grinned back at Cei. 'I prefer our commander unconscious. At least it made my work easier, and quieter.' He frowned at Arthur. 'If you were to be still, the pain would not be so intense.'

'Be still? Balls, man, how can you expect that with you poking and prodding about as you are! Besides,' he added curtly, 'I have never been still.'

The surgeon straightened, began rinsing his hands in the bowl of clean water Cei fetched from the far side of the small room. 'So you will have something new to try. Horses crashing down upon their riders, then struggling to their feet trampling a man's body as they do so, are apt to leave damage.

You owe it to the blessing of Fortuna you escaped with your life.'

Arthur fought hard to stop the screaming pain from reaching his lips. The past few days of semi-consciousness were a mindless mist of blinding red agony and grey-black drifting muttering sleep. The crashing fall, a distant haze of blurred memory. He recalled the ambush well enough, and the cheer that rang loud in his ears as the few remaining raiders took to their heels. Dimly he remembered urging Eira to jump that bank. The rest was a tangled muddle of choking water and thrashing hooves, shouting voices and screams of agony. His own, presumably.

253

Resigned to inactivity, he sighed. 'How long before I can fight again?' It was a question that had been playing on his mind since morning. Now the incredible pain was showing signs of easing and the surgeon had ceased administering that bitter-tasting drink that always brought back a welcome escape, the questions were coming thick and fast. Some of them were not going to have pleasant answers.

Lovingly packing away the tools of his trade, the surgeon took a while to answer. He glanced at Cei, who raised his eyebrows.

'Fight, you say?' he said, stalling. Fight! By the holy God, all who loved and served the Pendragon had thought, as they dragged him muddied and bloody from that river, he would never walk again, if God in his wisdom granted him life. But fight!

'Well?' Arthur demanded, searching the older man's face. A good surgeon, this one, who had saved many a soldier's life – and wept over the many more he had lost. Arthur put his hand on the man's sleeve, his grip firm despite the weakness that shivered in his body. 'I would prefer to know.' He said it quietly, unsure whether he spoke truth.

Years with the armies had taught Marcus the army surgeon many skills. He could set bones, stitch wounds, pull spears, cut out arrow barbs. He considered himself one of the best in his profession, yet still he found it difficult to break hard news to brave soldiers or their remaining loved ones. It was not easy to tell of death, the losing of a limb or an end to a way of life. How many had he had to tell that nothing lay ahead except bleak years of pain and disabled hardship? He drew in his breath and began to talk dispassionately, detached, telling the truth and telling it quickly.

'With time the bone and muscle should heal well enough to bear your weight. Time, patience and good care should see you walking again. The thigh takes great stress and yours has been badly abused. Fighting needs the agility that comes from strength and stamina.'

'Aye, well, you never were one to mince words!' Arthur said drily, easing himself into a more comfortable position. 'What you are trying to tell me tactfully,' he smiled sardonically, 'is that I may not fight again.'

The man half saluted and made to leave. 'To any other I would say, make plans for another life. But I knew your father, Arthur – I healed enough of his wounds – one near as serious as yours.' His hands tightened on his medical bag. He had loved Uthr. Loved this, his son. 'Battle killed him in the end. I could never expect him to forgo fighting, any more than I could expect him to stop pissing water.' Then curtly, 'You are much like your father.' He saluted. 'I will come again on the morrow.'

Cei stood silent, observing Arthur's grey, stubbled face. At length he asked, 'What do you intend to do?'

'Do?' Arthur replied, shifting slightly and instantly regretting it. 'What would you do? Crawl into a hole somewhere and bury yourself along with your ambitions and plans?'

'Most would. But as the man said, you are Uthr's son. No hole would be deep enough for you. You would sit and fuss and fidget until the earth gave way and spewed you up again.'

Arthur chuckled, then winced. 'Mithras, Cei, when I am eventually in the thick of another skirmish remind me not to be so damned impulsive! Is there a way to fight without being hurt, I wonder?'

'Would there be much point?' Cei said, laughing. 'It is the risk that brings the thrill.'

'As for what I am going to do' – Arthur concentrated his thoughts – 'I am leaving you, my second-in-command, in charge of the men, and I am going to lie here and bellow at all who enter. I am going to be the most tiresome, irritating patient.'

Cei choked back laughter. 'Well, that will certainly be a change of character!'

'And,' Arthur added, rubbing his hand over the itching stubble, 'I am going to have a shave!'

Days passed wearily, the outside thrum of routine barrack life blurring into a haze of time. This day as on any other, Arthur lay dozing, the difference being the rain had stopped and sunlight streamed through the open door of his quarters, lying hot on his face.

Cei entered quietly, but the movement disturbed the sleeper and he woke. Stretching cramped arms, he asked, 'Back so soon? How did it go? A successful raid – I can tell it was!'

'Superb!' Cei walked swiftly to the bed and sat down, his face alight with excitement. 'We swept down from cover as dawn broke – they never knew what hit them! You should have been there – the men fought so well; we have them at their peak. With more men and better horses we will be invincible!'

Arthur shrugged and uttered an explicit oath. 'I ought to have been there. I am their leader, but I lie here doing damn all.'

'Short of following by carried litter, there is not much for you to do about it, is there?' replied Cei, speaking plain. 'It would be better for you if you were to return home to court. These barracks are no place for a restless spirit.'

'Home? At Vortigern's court!' Arthur sneered, snorting with contempt. 'Fight another round of endless bickering with my wife, you mean?' He made a derogatory noise and settled back against the pillows. 'I have no home, save in Less Britain.'

He sighed, his mind wandering to the villa estate where he was born and raised. To the calm, wide river where he swam and fished as a boy, the acres of vineyards stretching as far as the eye could see. He had spent his childhood there, yet it was not home. Home was a place where your woman waited with your children. Where unconditional love welcomed you to the warmth of the hearth.

Home was here. With his men.

'You ought to consider settling Winifred in your own holding, Arthur,' Cei persisted. 'In your own Caer, away from the influence of her mother, things would be better atween you. Especially now, with a child on the way.'

Arthur shook his head, his lips puckered, nose wrinkling with distaste. 'The last time I was with Winifred, a week or so before this,' he pointed to his thigh, 'I felt as though I had entered your Christian Hell. She demands so much of me, and there is nothing I care to give her save hard words. I cannot help it, I despise her. How can you give even a pretence of love when you hate someone enough to want her dead several times over?'

'For all that, she is your taken wife, Arthur.'

'She is a scheming bitch.'

Cei was cleaning his nails with the tip of his dagger. He glanced up at the last words. 'That is not a very kind thing to say.'

'I cannot be kind to her. Besides, kind or unkind, it is the truth.'

Cei inspected his clean hands, stood and sheathed the weapon. 'A wife, my friend, is for producing sons, preparing meals and running your household. God created woman to care for man's need not for intellectual exercise. It is known a woman cannot be as intelligent as a man.'

A disturbance outside stemmed any answer Arthur might have had; a junior officer entered.

'Lord Pendragon, a messenger sent from Llwch.'

'From Llwch in Londinium? Send him straight in!'

Arthur glanced at Cei, his eyebrow rising slightly. Llwch, a well-chosen, well-placed spy in Vortigern's household. His orders, to observe, listen and glean information. A loyal man, Llwch.

A young man, grimed from his journey and with tired black smudges beneath his eyes, entered and saluted. His boots were muddied, even his tunic where the mire had splashed.

Arthur eyed him for a moment as he stood to attention, looking straight ahead. 'You are, if I am not mistaken, Dafydd, son of Idris Ironfist. Have you eaten or taken drink?'

'Na, my lord. I have this minute ridden in.'

'Seat yourself and tell me what news brings you so far so fast.'

Cei crossed to the door and called for food while Dafydd, slightly hesitant, sank to a stool and smiled his thanks as Cei then poured a generous helping of wine. He gulped and wiped his lips, leaving a streak of white skin beneath the dirt.

'It is your wife, lord.'

'What!' Arthur spluttered, spilling his own wine over himself and the bed covers. 'Llwch has orders to send messages of urgent importance. By importance, man, I had matters of state in mind, not the petty grumblings of the sow I am wed to.' Arthur hurled a pillow at the young man, who had come to his feet at his commander's shout and was again standing to attention. The pillow struck him, fell ignored to the floor.

'Her intention of running to Hengest is of no importance, my lord? You are not interested to hear the child she bears, if it be a boy, will be regarded as Saex-born to the people of the queen if it be brought to life at a Saex hearth?'

'Insolent whelp!' Arthur scowled at the messenger, held his hand out for the pillow to be returned. The lad retrieved it, placed it behind the Pendragon's back.

Wriggling himself comfortable, Arthur grumbled to himself. Said louder, 'She would not dare birth a son of mine beneath a Saex roof!' His hand took hold of the pillow, hurled it at the far wall, and he swore as damaged muscles protested at the exertion.

'Can you be certain it is yours, Arthur?' asked Cei.

'She has been close watched. I am certain. Do you know more, lad?'

'Only that there is a smell of smoke in the wind, and growing rumbles of thunder from Hengest's direction. Your wife is taking full advantage of your' – the young man flicked an awkward glance at Arthur's bandaged leg – 'incapacity.'

'Well, let her go. I would be rid of her.'

Dafydd said anxiously, 'Sir, begging your pardon, if your wife sets foot on Saex soil you will lose control of her and the child. Llwch says, if it be a boy, he could one day become a powerful weapon against you – us.'

Arthur waved the lad to silence. 'We had all this talk when Rowena's boy, Vitolinus, was born. A sudden great fear that Hengest was going to sweep out of Tanatus – with fire and sword.'

'Arthur,' Cei broke in, 'a child of yours, brought up in Saex hands, could make a dragon's den of mischief!' He whistled at the unpleasant prospect.

'I shall not acknowledge the boy.'

'My lord,' Dafydd urged, 'forgive me, Saex ways are very different from Roman. Princess Winifred, the mother, can declare her son's fathering. It will be enough for them.'

Cei muffled a groan. 'He is right, Arthur. Once Hengest has the boy, you will never again set eyes on him.'

Arthur ran his fingers through his hair. It had grown longer of late, the ends touching his shoulders. He must have an inch or so trimmed off. 'Oh, I would see him, have no doubt of that. Eventually he and I would meet somewhere across a battlefield.' He glanced meaningfully at Cei, who sat chewing his bottom lip deep in thought.

'She must be diverted then,' Cei said at length.

Sourly Arthur grimaced, not relishing his own coming suggestion. 'Happen it's time she was persuaded into her duty and paid a visit to her wounded husband.'

Cei asked, 'Vortigern has agreed to this visit to her grandsire, I assume, Dafydd?'

'He knows nought of it. This is the Queen and your wife's secret doing. We believe Hengest will soon rise against the King.'

Arthur laughed suddenly, seeing a humorous side. He wagged a finger at Cei. 'If I did not know better, my friend, I would swear this was some carefully hatched plan to rid yourselves of my presence here!'

Cei began to protest his innocence, but Arthur waved him down. 'Na, you shall be rid of me – and my dear wife shall have the pleasure of my company instead. She obviously wishes to bear our child somewhere other than Vortigern's rotting palace in Londinium. Most sensible of her.' He grinned, enjoying himself for the first time in weeks. 'I doubt she will agree to my meddling with her arrangements though!'

§ IX

'Why am I still waiting?' Winifred, her footsteps tapping as she stalked across the tessellated floor, snapped impatiently at a guard. 'Why is my vessel not yet at the water gate? If it is not here soon, I shall forgo the river and ride to my grandsire!'

Her angry words sent her waiting ladies into a twitter of anxious protest. Irritated, she swept an ornamental vase from its pedestal, sending it crashing down to shatter into pieces. 'Will no one discover what is causing this insufferable delay!'

She swung round, ready to vent her anger on her ladies, and found an insolently grinning British officer entering the chamber. He saluted and cheerfully apologised for the inconvenience.

'A merchant ship has shifted its load at the water gate, my lady, it will take hours to clear. We have arranged for a litter to take you to a wharf lower downriver where a ship awaits you.' He pulled absently at the chinstrap of his helmet, added, 'Only I would suggest you do not leave the palace at this moment, better to wait until the dawn tide.'

'What!' Winifred's stare was murderous. 'I have every intention of leaving now, on this coming tide.'

'There is trouble, my lady – a rabble protesting over some minor incident at the palace gates. The King's guard is dealing with the matter, but the mood in Londinium is tinder dry.'

Winifred glowered at him. 'I am not afraid of a petty rabble, centurion.'

He shrugged. '*Na*, my lady, I don't doubt it, but I would not advise venturing through the town in your condition.'

'What does my father pay his guard for – to sit on their backsides all day or to protect the royal household? Are your men not capable of escorting me safely?'

The centurion sighed. 'Quite capable, lady, I only thought…'

'You thought? You ignorant pig's muck, you have no brain to think with!' Winifred strode through the archway, her poise somewhat diminished by her pregnant bulk. She called, 'I am ready to leave with this tide. Either you escort me or I find an alternative guard. Do I make myself clear?'

The centurion saluted and said, 'Perfectly, my lady,' adding under his breath, 'Be glad to get rid of you.'

Winifred was heading for the pillared colonnades which led to the palace main entrance. With a muttered curse the centurion hastily caught her up and barred her way.

'My lady, we must use a side entrance. The mob is dense to the front of the palace. My superior thought, should you still insist on departing, it would be best if you slipped away unnoticed.' He indicated the direction.

She regarded him coldly. 'Can this rabble not be contained? Are our soldier so weak they cannot contend with a few scum?'

'There are pockets of fighting, lady, but the situation is well under control, We merely think of your safety,' he glanced at her bulk, 'and that of the child.'

She nodded curtly, realising the sense of his words, but reluctant to give ground. She walked before him in silence, her ladies trotting and whispering behind.

Guards slammed their spears to attention as the group neared the side entrance and walked through into a narrow alleyway. There was rubbish strewn here, blown by the wind or dropped by unauthorised passers-by taking a short cut alongside the palace wall. A rat disappeared into a hole somewhere at the base of the wall.

The centurion handed Winifred into the waiting litter, made to draw the blinds. Winifred stared at him, her hand itching to wipe the silly insolent grin off his mouth.

'Your face is not familiar to me,' she said peering close, suspicious. Her finger flicked the sash around his waist. 'Yet you wear the colours of the King's guard.'

'I am new to the honour of serving the King, lady, but I assure you I am not new to command. You will be safe under my protection.'

Winifred was contemptuous. 'Then if you are so sure of my safety we shall go directly to the wharf and I shall keep the blinds open. I prefer not to be hidden away.'

'*Na!*' He spoke with authority. 'I am certain of your safe conduct because we are not going direct to the wharf and because your litter shall be closed. The rabble are protesting over the favouring of trade with the Jute kind – given your connection with these people and your destination it would not be wise for you to be seen at this moment.' He took hold of the blinds with a firm hand, 'We shall take a minor detour to ensure no one from the crowd suspects where we go. Then we shall head for your vessel. Best not to cause any undue antagonism.'

'I will not travel so,' Winifred insisted.

'My apologies, lady, but I have been given my orders.'

'Who by?' she demanded, again probing.

The officer shrugged, astonished at her suspicion. 'There is only one alternative to the King's guard,' he said.

Winifred sucked in her breath.

The centurion looked over his shoulder to make sure no one observed or listened. He leant forward, on a pretence of drawing a cover over her and whispered, 'The Queen takes great care in ensuring the right men follow her with loyalty and discretion.'

Winifred's eyes rounded, her mouth forming a silent 'oh!'

If the centurion was her mother's man, then surely he could be trusted? Satisfied, she pulled the blind shut.

Settling herself as the litter jolted forward, she smiled, contented. She was on her way; nothing would now go wrong! With the help of her grandsire she could achieve more with the birth of this babe than ever she had dared dream! She would hold the Pendragon by the throat – no, the nether regions would be more appropriate! You did not love me, husband, did not treat me well, so fear for the future!

She closed her eyes, her thoughts of Arthur. How foolish she had been to be so dazzled by him, to be so taken by his surface charm and appeal! Underneath that seductive smile lay an arrogant, self-opinionated louse. Happen she should have let that girl Gwenhwyfar have him. It would have been she who was now rejected and mistreated, she who had to suffer his whoring and drunkenness, his verbal and physical abuse.

The litter stopped; she heard gates opening and they moved on. She would soon hurl revenge in his face! But not until she felt the swell beneath the Jute ship that would carry her to safety could she breathe easy.

The journey was short and, apart from the distant roar of rioting crowds, uneventful. The litter ceased its lurching and Winifred parted the blinds to look out upon a small wharf some distance downriver away from the town. She stepped out awkwardly. A flicker of alarm crossed her mind as she realised the ship bobbing gently on the slack water was British. That foolishly grinning centurion took hold of her arm and led her firmly towards it.

'I was to travel under Jute sail,' she protested, attempting to shake off his hand.

'British or Saxon,' he hastily corrected himself, 'Jute, it makes little difference, you will reach your destination.'

Winifred looked about her. Luggage was being unloaded from wagon to ship, but there was no sign of her women. She asked their whereabouts.

'They are in safe hands,' the centurion said, then, indicating the vessel, 'Shall we go aboard?'

Winifred frowned, reluctantly allowed herself to be escorted up the narrow gangplank. He left her on deck with a polite excuse that he must see to the loading of her possessions.

The ship's captain, a squat, plump man, hovered at her side and gestured graciously for her to follow him below.

'Welcome aboard, my lady, I trust you will have a pleasant voyage.' He showed her to a small but adequately private cabin situated near the stern.

'Send my women to me right away.' Winifred gave her order as the captain made to leave her. He spoke no word, merely nodded his acquiescence. Winifred prodded at the none too clean or comfortable bed squashed to one side. Her women would have to sleep cramped on the floor; it would be no hardship for them.

There was the expected noise and bustle of a ship about to make sail. She ignored it as she lay silently alone. Her head ached and her ankles were uncomfortably swollen. She would close her eyes a moment. Just a moment.

It was with the first creak of movement that she pushed herself upright and muttered a curse. The fool of a captain had forgotten her orders! She took her cloak and swept up on deck – to see the riverbank dropping behind as the sail began to fill and lift the ship into the ebbing tide.

Waiting for her was that damned centurion, still grinning. 'Where are my women?' she demanded.

'Safe,' was all the reply she received.

Patience snapping, she snarled, 'If you do not remove that inane smirk from your face this instant, my hand will remove it for you!'

'Strike one of my officers, would you?'

Winifred froze, her face contorted with a mixture of rage, disbelief and fear. Involuntarily, her threatening hand, raised to wipe away that grin, went to her own mouth. She pressed her teeth hard into her flesh to stop the scream. Slowly, she turned to face the speaker.

Men were setting down a litter. Arthur lay comfortably sprawled, eyes bright with triumph.

'You bastard!' she spat.

'And I am pleased to see you also, dear heart. You look well.'

'Why are you here? What is this?' She was frightened, but masked it by an outpouring of rage.

'I heard you were anxious for somewhere safe to birth my son. Most commendable.'

Her hand was on her throat; her fingers could feel the thump-thump of the pulse bounding in her neck. Does he know?

'We go to a place where my son will not be contaminated by any Saex disease.'

How much does he know – or guess?

She flung at him, 'I suppose you arranged that convenient uproar in Londinium also!'

He smiled. 'It was not so difficult.'

She raged then, for a while, stamping her foot, demanding the ship put about, return her ashore. Her protests fell on deaf ears. In desperation she ran to the side, stretching her arms imploringly towards the land slipping so fast away. Briefly she considered jumping overboard and swimming for the shore.

Arthur read her thoughts. 'I would not advise it, the distance is deceptive. It would be a tough swim for a man; a pregnant woman would not survive.'

'I demand to know where we are going!'

'To my mother's.'

Glaring, Winifred made to return below. Her husband's presence sickened her; if he saw, he would assume the nausea came from the ship's motion.

'Where are my women?' she asked for the second time, half turning back to him.

'I dismissed them. There are women aplenty to serve you at my mother's. I have arranged for a trusted female to serve you while at sea. I will send her to you.' Arthur held up his hand to attract her attention, his expression ominous as he added, 'I warn you, wife, to treat her well. Save you, she is the only female on board. Treat her badly and I may consider withdrawing her for my own use.'

Her fury drained away and suddenly Winifred felt very tired, very alone. 'Why do you hate me so, Arthur?' She took a faltering step. 'I have done you no harm. I have given you wealth and pleasure in our bed. I have been a good, dutiful wife.' She laid a hand on her swollen abdomen. 'I bear your son, the next Pendragon.'

Arthur's eyes flashed. 'Would this be the same son you intended one day to use against me had Hengest been so foolish as to leave me alive?'

Jesu! He does know!

'No! Oh no, my lord!' Winifred waddled forward, knelt before him, her hands held out, pleading. 'Who told you such a lie!'

'Contrition does not suit you. Suffice to say I know your planning.' He took her chin between his fingers, studied her at close quarters. It occurred to him he had never really looked at her before, never cared to go beneath the facade. 'What were you to gain from this, Winifred?'

Her body slumped, her shoulders dropping, head lolling defeated and dejected. All she could do now was save herself. If he also knew Hengest was preparing to rise and that she had intended to go with him, then it was her end. Lie. Cover yourself with a lie!

'I wanted you, Arthur.' She lifted her eyes. 'I only wanted your love. Was that so very much to ask?'

'So you seek a divorce. That makes sense.' He flicked her chin aside, let her go.

'I love you.'

'What a liar you are.'

That was the whole trouble, the whole topsy-turvy reasoning behind this running away. She did not lie. By some cruel stroke of fate she did love him – loved him and wanted him, but only as her own, her very own, not to share with those others.

Hardness, a feint to hide behind. 'Men and women snigger behind my back that my husband knows the tavern sluts better than his wife. Or that I can only please my husband when he is wine-soaked.' Winifred pleaded again. 'I do not understand. When you bed with me, we are so good together; we make love with an ecstasy that surely even the gods and goddesses of old would not have known. Is it so wrong for me to love you?' Change to defiance, 'I intended to bargain with you, Arthur. Me for our son. For his return, you were to take the both of us. Both or neither.' Challenging. 'Put me where I belong as your respected wife and future queen, or have my son one day take your place.'

He snorted with amusement. 'You do not frighten me. Your father never has and you certainly never will.'

'I will no longer be treated like some common piece of gutter muck! I am your wife; you will treat me with honour or forgo the knowing of your son.'

'I can get other sons. When I overthrow your father I will get other sons.' His narrowed eyes bored into hers, malicious, determined. 'By another wife.' He knew it would hurt, and he saw the involuntary flinch as his barb entered.

She flung a retort. 'My father is old, has nothing left to face but the coming of death, but my grandsire shall never bow his head to you! He shall be king next, then we shall see who is the mightier!'

Arthur laughed. 'Hengest? He could no more beat me in battle than he could piss on a forest fire to put out the flames. He is of small consequence.' He clicked his fingers. 'Escort the lady below. See she remains there.'

'I need no escort.' Winifred turned to make her own way, the bumping in her chest easing. He did not seem to know much beyond the outer fringes; that she was to have gone to Hengest for her well-being, not because of what was soon to come. Of that, relieved, she was certain. Certain enough to threaten, 'You may have other sons, Pendragon, but remember this. Mine shall always be the first-born.'

Arthur pulled a fur tighter about him. The evening chill on the river was becoming more penetrating. 'How disappointed you will be should it be a girl.'

Winifred ducked below, heard him add, 'Or you may prove to be as worthless as your mother, breeding only the dead-born.'

His love? Did she truly believe she wanted that? As of this moment, all she wanted was his death.

OCTOBER 454

§ X

Gwenhwyfar reined in her mare, calling to the boy cantering ahead and pointed with exaggerated movement to the ship making her way upriver. Bedwyr tugged his pony around, studying the vessel with his eyes narrowed against the bright sun.

He was much like his elder brother, Cei: brown-haired, brown-eyed, with the same jutting jawline. Gwenhwyfar assumed the sons favoured their dead mother, for they were nothing like their square-jowled father, Ectha.

'She's no ordinary trading ship!' he observed. 'Where is she from, Gwen?' The glow of childhood shone in his face. Eleven, and all the confidence and enthusiasm of the Empire within him! He allowed Gwenhwyfar no time to answer, plunged on with, 'From Britain, do you think? No Saex ship would dare flaunt such a bold red sail!' He screwed up his eyes, shielding them from the glare with his hand, trying to make out the pennant drooping at the masthead.

The ship was under oar now, coming slow around, but Bedwyr was losing interest. The waterway was always busy with traders and the like. He swung his pony inland, kicked him to a trot and shouted a challenge at Gwenhwyfar to race.

Squeezing Seren forward, Gwenhwyfar trotted a few paces after him, her head swivelling to keep the ship in view. She hauled her mare to an abrupt halt, swung her to face the river, gaze intent. There was something about it – that red sail, or the carriage of her prow as she glided with the incoming tide?

A flurry of wind gathered in mid-channel, catching the lifeless pennant as the craft swung landward. Gwenhwyfar caught her breath. For a heartbeat she forgot the present; glimpsed, like a half-seen shadow, a memory of when she was a girl. She had been riding then, with a boy up on the hills. How long had it been now? How long since her flight into exile and, following her heels like death's shadow, news of Arthur's marriage? A lifetime, it seemed. Was it truly only a little more than a year? One long, lonely year.

Bedwyr was shouting for her to start the race. She waved acknowledgement, and pushed her mare into a canter, looking back over her shoulder just the once, for a final glance at the ship. Tear-blurred vision and the gentle sloping heath had hidden the span of river from view. She forced a brave smile for Bedwyr's benefit. 'We had best get to old Gaius's,' she said, 'before his Juliana finishes her baking!'

Bedwyr whooped and thudded his heels into the pony's ribs, startling it forward into a plunging gallop. Gwenhwyfar let him win.

Gaius's farm was a favourite place to visit. A one-time cavalry officer of Rome settled now on his own few acres, he enjoyed the civilian life with his wife – who baked particularly wholesome barley-cakes. The elderly man greeted them with a friendly wave as they turned into the courtyard. Flinging himself from the pony, Bedwyr darted forward to give his friend a hug of greeting, the man embracing the lad in return. Juliana appeared, dusting flour from her hands. She swept Bedwyr to her, pleased to see him. His eagerness and high spirits eased the ache for her own two sons, killed long ago serving Rome.

She smiled an equally warm greeting at Gwenhwyfar. 'You time your visit well, my dears – I have cakes ready to come from the oven. And a pot of sweet honey to spread on new-baked bread.'

Bedwyr yelped with delight and sped off for the kitchen, his sandaled feet kicking up puffs of dust, Juliana plump and matronly in his wake.

'Do not get under foot!' Gwenhwyfar called.

Handing the horses to a slave, Gaius ushered Gwenhwyfar to the porch and calling for refreshment, seated himself on a couch opposite his guest. He enjoyed a chance to talk and laugh – what better than to spend an afternoon with a pretty young woman who delighted in hearing the prattling of an old fool? Ah, if he were only many years younger, happen he could bring the smile back to her pale cheeks!

Gaius sipped his wine, nibbled his cheese, observing Gwenhwyfar with an indulgent smile. She had first come just over a year ago; walking quiet and ashen-faced beside young Bedwyr, a lad bursting with life and energy. Gaius had been instantly reminded of another such boy – young Arthur had helped to while away many an afternoon with talk of horses and soldiering. On that day, Gwenhwyfar had led her lame mare, seeking help. Gaius had welcomed her, tended the horse and offered to loan a remount.

They had come often after that, at first to inspect the mare's fetlock, later to enjoy the company of two elderly people. Juliana cooed and fussed over her visitors; Gaius, in his calm way, instilled much learning into the energetic young lad; together they brought a small flicker of happiness back to Gwenhwyfar. To Juliana, she was the daughter she had never birthed, a girl in need of a mother's guiding hand and unquestioning love. To Gaius she was a puzzle. Always quiet and soft-spoken, she would sit with Bedwyr listening to the tales Gaius told of his days with the Roman Cavalry, or help eagerly with the chores, never minding hard work. She could chop wood or reap corn as well as any man, was calm and gentle with an injured or frightened horse and had a knack of soothing an irritable nanny goat or petulant ewe to stand a while for milking. She rarely spoke of her home. With the passing of time the old couple came to understand why. The speaking was too painful.

'Riding here,' Gwenhwyfar said, 'I thought of a particular day, years past. I was with my brother on the hills of Gwynedd.' She stopped, remembering so clearly. Etern's grumpiness over her fat old pony, his joy on recognising that pennant. Etern. She would never see Etern again in this life.

Gwenhwyfar was like a tree, Gaius thought, a tree in winter. You knew it was a tree because there was a trunk and spreading branches; but it was not a tree, not until the spring, when leaves burst forth, shining green. Not until then did the thing of beauty come alive.

She looked at him shyly. 'I so miss Gwynedd.'

The man reached out, touched her hand. Her skin was cold.

She continued talking, to ease the choking pressure building in her throat. How to explain the longing for a place? Mountains and streams. Restless sea. Mist, rain; sudden, dazzling sun. 'Being away from Gwynedd is like parting from a lover gone to war. I remember the happy days when we walked and rode together, and hear the whisper of that special voice. I lie at night longing to be close to the one I love. To feel and smell that comforting nearness, warmth and strength enfolding me. But I am alone and my heart knows not when, if ever, we shall meet again.'

Gaius refilled her cup, poured for himself. 'Is it a place or a person you talk of?'

Gwenhwyfar started. 'Oh, a place!' She busied herself with her wine, lifted her eyes with an apologetic smile. She could not lie to Gaius. 'Both.' She sighed. 'The one I cannot go to The other I cannot have.'

'That is indeed love! Love is a piteous condition for which there is no cure!' Gaius said with a laugh.

She laughed with him, and Gaius noted, with the regrets of a man grown too old to do more than think and talk, how pretty she was when

268

she laughed. Unexpectedly, as if it were of no matter, she said, 'A ship has come from Britain.'

'A special ship?' Gaius enquired, something in her offhand manner alerting him. This ship, then, was important.

Gwenhwyfar studied the cup she held. 'Aye.' It was good to talk to Gaius. His legs would no longer carry him far, his teeth were nearly all gone and his hearing not so sharp, but for all that he would listen without a disapproving intake of breath at some private confession, unlike Ygrainne would do. Juliana had too sharp a sense of down-to-earth practicality, and Ceridwen, dear as she was, over-much innocence for the sharing of despair. Besides, Ceridwen was caught in her own web of new-wedded bliss. She saw nought but sun and blue sky since the day Iawn took her as wife.

Gaius could not see so clear, but then Gaius did not see with his eyes alone. He was a man who saw hidden things with his heart, could see the shadowed movement beneath the surface of the pool, or the stars behind the clouds. A friend who cared enough to listen without the need to pass comment or judgement.

Gwenhwyfar said, 'I feel I am the last leaf hanging on a tree at the end of autumn. Dangling there, alive still, but becoming shrivelled and dry. I do not know whether to stay clinging here or let go and get the waiting for death over with.'

Gaius thought how strange that he had compared her to a tree also.

She looked at her hands clasping the pottery cup. Clean, manicured nails, smooth uncallused skin. In Gwynedd, her nails had always been jagged and short, her hands roughened from the continuous handling of horse and weapon. Here, she lived a life of Roman luxury. Pampered, tended like young spring vegetables, noblewomen of Rome did not groom their own mounts, or muck out stables or chop wood for the fire. Or fight. She put the cup slowly, carefully, on the table. 'I can think only of dark times. The mother I never knew. Etern cruelly murdered. The reason why I am here, and the man I love, who is married to another.' Her eyes filled with tears. Memories. So many black and bitter memories.

'Ygrainne talks constantly of God. Her righteous words follow me like a wolf in the night, stalking me, hunting me. I lie awake thinking, trying to sort my thoughts. She talks of the Hell we are condemned to in the next life unless we give our hearts to God in this. This place she talks of, I am already there!' She buried her face in her hands. 'I am empty, I am nothing. I exist in a barren wasteland of endless days and longer nights. When I walk beside the river, I wonder if it would be better to drown quickly there, rather than slowly here.'

Gaius wanted to speak, but held his tongue. To say something now might stop the girl from talking – and she needed to talk, needed someone to listen.

Gwenhwyfar looked up, her face a mask of grief, her eyes shadow-bruised. 'I am frightened,' she whispered. 'Frightened of so many things.'

'We all fear, child,' the old man said, taking her hand between his own and holding it there, unobtrusive but comforting.

'I was managing,' she said, 'living from day to day, never thinking beyond the morrow. I shut out the past. The future also.' She gave a shuddering breath. 'Especially the future.' For a moment she faltered. 'Seeing that ship has brought back all the memories. The longing. The faces. Voices. Much has happened since I was forced to flee from Londinium. My life, the life of ... others. Now,' she looked again at her hands, 'now I am frightened of facing what remains of today. Frightened of tomorrow and the day after. I knew this ship would come. Knew it would bring a day when I had to abandon pretence and face reality.' Her tears fell freely, running down her cheeks. 'I am so alone in this darkness, Gaius. There are people around me, many people, but I am alone. I must face this fear alone, but I cannot! I cannot! I want someone to reach down a hand, and pull me from this depth of despair, from these choking weeds. Anyone! Anyone to say, I am here!'

'Anyone?' Gaius waited.

She said nothing. He had listened well, not only to the words she had spoken; had listened more to those unspoken.

'Anyone, child?' he said again, his voice low and kind. 'Or someone in particular? Someone aboard that ship?'

Through the tears she looked up sharp, startled.

Ah, thought Gaius, I am right! He reflected a while. He must say the correct thing here, wise words of comfort. 'Memories are like battles, and battles can go one way or the other. You can stand and fight, no matter what pain runs from your wounds; or you can turn tail and run, knowing then the enemy will follow and without mercy hunt you down.'

Gwenhwyfar sat silent. Her father's voice came to her, so clear she almost thought that if she were to turn, she would find him standing there behind her. She smiled through her tears. 'It is as you say. I fear this ship, because of who is aboard. But most of all

I fear what may happen because of his coming. I am not sure I can fight the problems he will bring, yet I am tired of running. My Da' – she wiped away the tears with her fingers – 'my Da always said, *Fight fear, and fear will flee like mist before a rising wind.* But how do you fight a dream that has turned sour?'

'As you would any battle, with shield and sword raised, chin and heart high. You fight it, my dear, by looking it straight in the eye.'

Impulsively, she leant forward and placed a quick, light kiss on the old man's cheek. 'Thank you, Gaius. You have given me a small measure of courage.'

Gwenhwyfar stood, gathering her light riding cloak around her. She felt cold, despite the warmth of the day. If she were to ride to battle, she had best go now. She called for Bedwyr, who came reluctantly, cheeks sticky with golden honey. She dabbed at them with the hem of her cloak and smiled indulgently. 'I see you have been enjoying yourself! It is time to return home. Arthur has come.'

§ XI

Before they had ridden more than ten minutes, Gwenhwyfar regretted telling the boy of the ship's passenger. Bedwyr was in a flurry of excitement, all for racing home at a gallop. She could understand his pleasure but could not imitate it. The Pendragon was the boy's hero, his god almost. Gwenhwyfar remembered the excitement she and Etern had felt as they had hurried back to Caer Arfon; the thrill of recognising the Dragon pennant, of realising it was Uthr himself who had come to Gwynedd. Again the stab of pain.

She could not begrudge Bedwyr his pleasure as he rode, always a few paces ahead of her, his laughter echoing the joy remembered from her own childhood. She kept a tight rein on her own emotion, attempted to smile back at the boy as he chattered on.

He repeated once more every detail of the Nativity festival two years past when Arthur and Cei had come home after their first season of service with Vortigern. They had left as boys, and returned for those few brief weeks with feet well set on the road to manhood. Cei had been home since, but not Arthur.

Bedwyr relived those glorious weeks, his child's memory dwelling on the things that had been important to him personally. Presents, games, mock fights. Shared laughter and much happiness.

Gwenhwyfar let him chatter, murmuring occasional agreement at significant points. She had heard the same account many times over – he told his tale of that festival to any who cared listen. It had been hard for him to accept the going of Arthur and his brother when they had followed

Cunedda's advice. Harder still to part with them again after their visit. Bedwyr longed to become a man – would the years never pass? Arthur had promised he could take ship and enter his ala of cavalry when he was older; he would ride his own horse, have his own sword. Would become one of Arthur's men!

Until then, he was left behind in Less Britain: a child anxiously waiting, alone and miserable.

Gwenhwyfar had brightened his dull life. Although quiet and subdued in the presence of his Aunt Ygrainne and his father, Gwenhwyfar had revealed a different side when they rode out alone. She was fun to be with, appreciated the ways of a child – a boy who nursed the wild ambitions of a young warrior. She could tell stories that made your heart soar as high as the clouds, tales of the old gods and brave battles. When he discovered she knew how to handle sword and shield, his worship of her became complete. If his cousin Arthur was his god, then Gwenhwyfar was surely his goddess.

For Gwenhwyfar, Bedwyr provided a welcome release from the behaviour expected of a lady. In the company of adults she conformed, was every inch the young, educated gentlewoman of noble birth but when riding and fishing with Bedwyr, she relaxed and let her natural sparkle – though tarnished at the edges – shine through. And Bedwyr learnt from her. Learnt of Britain, of the Saex; the mountains of Gwynedd. The old ways and the past. He looked forward to his lessons with his fusty tutor after the coming of Gwenhwyfar, eager to surprise her with his own knowledge. They were good for each other, the lonely boy and the lost girl. Companions who supported each other.

As each stride took them nearer home, the feeling of fear gripped harder at Gwenhwyfar's belly, twisting tighter, colder. What should she expect? Was Arthur alone? Ah, was it not that question which stirred this running tide into a hundred, hundred eddies and whirlpools?

As if her thoughts had been spoken aloud, Bedwyr said suddenly, 'I wonder if my cousin Arthur has brought his wife? Aunt Ygrainne was furious when she learnt of his marriage. To wed with the daughter of the man who had slain Uncle Uthr! Remember how she shrieked with rage for days after?' He whistled a short, catchy tune, added, 'I expect Arthur had his reasons. I know he needed gold – he wrote me once he wanted to purchase horses for his men. I expect she was worth the taking for the extra wealth she would bring him. Mind,' he prattled on, unaware of Gwenhwyfar's agonised silence, 'I have heard some men do strange things, fall in love and such, pah!' He spat on the ground, a thing which would earn him a whipping were Ygrainne ever to see. 'That's stuff for girls, not for war lords. Arthur thinks like a soldier, he has no time for soppy things like love!'

He spoke innocently, from a child's perspective. How could he know his words were burning like a red hot brand through Gwenhwyfar's heart?

She stammered out some brief answer. Swallowed the bile rising in her throat.

Arthur's marriage had caused a stir when the news had come, its ripples of gossip spreading wider afield than the villa. The town too had been shocked, speculation circulating for days, the consensus being that Arthur had wed the girl for her handsome dowry. Then the thing had become accepted and forgotten by family, friends and town folk – but not by Gwenhwyfar; she could not accept or forget. She was to have been Arthur's wife, had given her pledge. She loved him and Arthur loved her – she rubbed a stray tear from her cheek – or so she had thought. What was it Bedwyr had just said? Arthur was a soldier, he would not dwell on idle things like love?

They halted on the crest of the vine-covered slope overlooking the villa. The courtyard below was bustling with servants unloading a wagon that sagged from the weight of baggage. The east wing of the building was a hive of activity. Behind wide-flung shutters house servants scurried carrying clean linen and removing covers from furniture. Gwenhwyfar caught sight of Ygrainne hurrying past a first-floor window.

'I expect she is in a right bad humour,' Bedwyr remarked, noticing her also. 'My aunt dislikes unexpected visitors.'

Or anything that upsets the flow of her dull, orderly life. Tactfully, Gwenhwyfar kept the thoughts to herself.

Ygrainne was a woman who was kindly to the sick, generous to the poor, but a woman devoid of warmth. Years of bitterness had deprived her of the glow that once had shone in her eyes. Her life was now devoted to God, leaving no room for anyone else.

Ygrainne never showed affection – not to her nephew Bedwyr, her brother-by-law his father, anyone. She had greeted Gwenhwyfar on the afternoon of her arrival cordially, accepting the girl's urgent need for sanctuary, providing it out of respect for Cunedda. They had kissed briefly, Ygrainne's lips cold and impersonal on Gwenhwyfar's cheek. That had been the first and only physical contact. Used to the warmth and spontaneous affection of brothers and father, Gwenhwyfar ached for the reassurance of fond hugs and sudden whirls of loving laughter.

From Ygrainne's attitude to Bedwyr, Gwenhwyfar could see how distance had grown between the woman and her only son, Arthur. Bedwyr was clothed, fed, educated and disciplined. He had all a boy could wish for, save love. He had loved Arthur above all things. Desperate, both of them, for affection, it was no wonder Bedwyr and Gwenhwyfar became close friends. If Ygrainne noticed the shining love Bedwyr gave to Cunedda's daughter, she gave no sign of it. Gwenhwyfar suspected the woman was relieved. With another to shoulder the responsibility of the boy her conscience was salved.

Yet Ygrainne was a fair woman. Short-tempered and impatient with incompetence, she was nevertheless quick to praise and reward hard work. Towards misdeeds by servants she was fair with punishment, never harsh or unjust. In the worship of her God, however, she was strict regarding rules and obedience, expected the same from her household.

Supervising the opening of the rarely used wing, Ygrainne sighed with intense irritation. She tucked a stray wisp of silvered hair back beneath her veil. How like her son to arrive like this, unannounced and unexpected! Not even an advance warning when the ship docked. He could have sent a messenger, but *na*, not him! He had waited aboard until the baggage was unloaded and travelled with the wagon. Did he do these things from lack of thought, or spite? Herself, she was not a vindictive person, not intentionally, but Arthur? She sighed a second time; somehow, his presence always managed to raise evil thoughts.

Ygrainne compressed her lips. He had generously stated as he entered the villa, it mattered not if his apartments in this wing were not aired. As if she could expect him to sleep on a bed with no linen, in an uncleaned room with stale air! He had waved aside her startled alarm at his arrival, saying to be home was reward enough! He was the bane of her life! Comfort might not matter to him, but he had brought his wife with him, what of her? How degrading to be caught in this state of disorder!

Ygrainne crossed herself, mumbled a short line of holy verse to stifle unbidden words of hatred. During His time on this earth Jesu had said love thine enemy. She fingered the gold crucifix hanging at her waist with the chain of keys dangling there, then closed her eyes in swift prayer. The words of the good Lord were so difficult to put into practice at times!

Ygrainne breathed deeply, turned to watch a servant spreading a sheet upon the bed. With a cry she darted forward and snatched it aside.

'Who laundered this? Look, here, look at this stain!' Pointing, Ygrainne indicated the offending mark, threw the sheet to the floor. 'Fetch a clean one, girl – hurry! Think you Lady Winifred would not have noticed?' Damn her. Damn him!

She marched from the wing, her shoes tapping on the wooden floor. They were waiting in the living quarters, taking light refreshment.

Arthur was laughing as she entered, sharing some jest with Ectha. Ygrainne swept into the room. 'We need more wine, brother-by-law,' she said with stiff politeness. Ectha exchanged a suitably chastened look with Arthur, then fetched a new jug.

Bedwyr whooped loudly as he careered at a gallop down the sloping track. Gwenhwyfar hesitated. Impulsively she shouted, 'I will be along soon! I have an errand!'

He heard; raised an arm, but did not stop. The pony's hooves sent a spray of gravel showering into the air as Bedwyr slithered to a halt and leapt from the saddle. Ygrainne appeared and ushered the boy inside. By the way her hand gripped his dust-encrusted tunic Gwenhwyfar guessed she was scolding him. She glanced at her own clothing. Skirt, cut and sewn to form loose riding bracae, which fell in modest folds when she was not mounted. It was a compromise; Ygrainne would not allow her to wear male gear even for riding. The ill-fitting tunic she wore hung baggy about her top half, and her favourite worn cloak was becoming grubby. The hem, she noted, was torn.

Mastering her mare's reluctance to turn away from stable and feed, she trotted back along the hill track. Gwenhwyfar did not want to return to the villa, but did not want to discard these friendly clothes for formal Roman dress. Nor have her hair bound and styled. Rebelliously she tugged at the braids coiled about her head, let the copper hair tumble loose and free.

She kicked Seren with her heels, lengthening the stride of a reluctant canter into a reckless gallop. The mare, resigned to the change of direction, responded eagerly, stretched her neck and flew. They plunged through a copse, out and up on to the heath, where the wind stung Gwenhwyfar's eyes to tears. Hair and cloak billowed behind, streaming like some giant bird, exultant, escaping, for a brief while at least, the confines of a cage.

Blowing hard, Seren eventually began to slow, dropped to a walk. Gwenhwyfar loosened the reins, let her amble and snatch at mouthfuls of grass. Saliva dribbled green as Seren chewed round the iron bit, snatched for more grass. They had circled, were close by the banks of the Ligre river. The slow water was turning gold as the lowering sun coloured its surface. A few fishermen were beginning to make their way down to the estuary for their night's work. By first light, the market in town would be brimming with fresh-caught seafood. The last swifts darted above hunting insects, their high-pitched cries rising and falling with their whirling, flashing dance.

Gwenhwyfar wondered if the summer birds had left Gwynedd yet. Was the weather mild there also? Ygrainne would be angry with her for not returning with Bedwyr.

Some of her tears were not from the wind alone. She slid from the mare's back, burrowed her head into the black mane. How could she face him? How could she make polite conversation, entertain and dine – sit alongside him? How, knowing all the while he was committed to a wife, and happen a child also by now?

She had thought the anger was gone, the desperate feeling of betrayal eased, but shards of broken dreams remained like shattered pieces of glass dropped on a marble floor. Self-pity had found time enough to weave a snare of despair and hopelessness; time to mix with an ample portion of jealousy, to breathe the sulphur fumes of hatred.

Gwenhwyfar remembered the details a young boy misses. Arthur's eyes. Shining hawk eyes that gleamed when he spoke of things dear to his heart. Eyes that darkened when something displeased him. Eyes that could see uninhibited into your heart and mind. His voice, his hair, his smell. How he bubbled with excitement, hurried to get things done, to get where he was going. Remembered a promise.

What was a promise anyway? Nought but words. Words spoken in childhood.

He must have known Cunedda had annulled that awful arranged marriage with Melwas. Surely he knew? Of course he did! The news would have been all across the country after her flight. There must have been one hell of a row, with Vortigern and Melwas powerless to do anything about it. So why had Arthur still married the bitch?

Even if there were reasons, rational, good reasons why he could not marry with Gwenhwyfar, need he have taken someone else quite so soon?

The sea crossing and those lonely, lost first weeks had been made bearable by her conviction someone would come – Arthur himself – to fetch her home, to promise her Melwas would never have her, that things would be all right. But no one came, save the traders with news of his marriage.

Weeks slid by. Weeks turned to months, months to a year. Now he had come, but now it was too late. A year too late.

The remnants of hope had fluttered, ragged, in a gusting wind of passing time, were crumbled to dust.

She had no way of knowing the tide of events had run too swiftly for Arthur, that he too had been caught in the pull of a fast flooding current and was held there, adrift without any means of steering himself free. For Arthur, there seemed not even a remnant to guide him safe home.

Stroking the white star on the mare's forehead, Gwenhwyfar felt rising anger. How dare he come to taunt her like this! Did he think it amusing? Was he laughing at her? Well, she would soon strike that smile from his face!

Her green eyes had coloured storm dark. She brushed the tears from her cheeks, pinching the skin to hide the blotching. Vaulting into the saddle, she turned Seren for home.

As she crested the rise behind the villa another thought struck her with such force she almost reeled. She hauled Seren to a halt, the mare tossing her head and flattening her ears from the discomfort of a jabbing bit.

There had been no word from Britain for some weeks. Not even wild rumour; for all they knew, Vortigern could be rotting in his grave. Or this Saex bitch Winifred. Could she be dead? Many a woman died in childbirth. Death made no distinction between rich, poor, peasant or princess. Had Arthur come because he had not forgotten; was here to take her home at last!

The seed of an idea was planted and germinated. It flourished and grew.

The mare required no urging with the smell of home in her nostrils. With each long stride of the horse's gallop, the visions increased. Arthur pacing angrily, demanding servants be sent to search for her. He would have banged through all the rooms, bellowing her name, marched to the stables – questioned Bedwyr. She would ride into the courtyard, he would run down the steps from the villa, swing her into his arms!

Gwenhwyfar trotted beneath the archway, through the open gate. Slid, breathless, from Seren her face glowing with anticipation. Where was he? A stable slave appeared. Not Arthur. Ygrainne hurried from the villa, her face creased with suppressed anger. Her words shrill.

'Gwenhwyfar! Where have you been? You are so untrustworthy, girl! My son has arrived with his wife. Make yourself presentable and see Lady Winifred is settled in her rooms. Lord in His Heaven knows what I shall do if the babe she carries comes early!'

For Gwenhwyfar, everything chilled to silence. She saw Ygrainne's lips moving, heard the words but they held no meaning for her. Ygrainne stepped irritably forward, took her arm and began to shake it. Gwenhwyfar stared numbly at Ygrainne's hand, watched it shake, heard her reprimand as if it came from a great distance. She stood unmoving, as if carved from stone.

With the rushing noise of a torrential waterfall sensation returned. Ygrainne's angry voice, the slave waiting to take the mare.

'This is as unexpected for me as it is for you, Gwenhwyfar,'

Ygrainne was saying; 'Must you take all evening to think upon it? Give those reins to the slaves and get yourself cleaned and tidied.' Ygrainne tutted, fingered Gwenhwyfar's straggling loose hair. 'Look at you. You are like some beggar's brat, are not fit to be presented to my son and his wife!'

Habit led Gwenhwyfar to her room, changed her dress, washed her face and combed her hair. The daily routine of washing and dressing. Her hands went through the motions, but her mind was blank, totally void of all thought.

Ceridwen appeared, chattering excitedly; she always looked radiant, Ceridwen. Clicking her tongue she waved a slave forward to take up the task of washing off the dirt and sweat, and to tidy Gwenhwyfar's hair. Gwenhwyfar found herself perfumed and robed in fine garments; her hair styled. Her jewels were fastened in her ears, around her neck and wrists, pinned to her shoulder. Ceridwen talked of Arthur, his wife, the baggage they had brought, the pleasant surprise of their coming.

And all the while, four words crashed and echoed around in Gwenhwyfar's head. Four words heavy with meaning. *The babe she carries.*

Arthur was reclining on a couch with Bedwyr squatting beside him. The boy's face glowed. Eyes sparkling with pleasure, he plied him with one question after another, mostly about men and horses, and the unrest of the Saex; battles, wounds, weapons. A hundred things. He did think to ask about Cei, was satisfied with a statement that his brother was well.

Seated opposite, Winifred sat erect and silent, lips pressed thin. Both she and Arthur looked up as Gwenhwyfar entered the room. Both pairs of eyes widened in naked surprise. For differing reasons.

Gwenhwyfar was obliged to greet them formally. She walked tall and serene to Arthur as Lord, first. He had risen, stood waiting, his face a blank mask. She sank into a deep reverence, dipping her head, refusing to meet his eyes. If he should look into her own eyes, he would know. Would know her body shook, her heart hammered, and he must not know that. He must not discover how easy it was to humiliate her.

'Gwenhwyfar! I did not know you were still here – I assumed you had returned to Gwynedd. When I last heard from your father he indicated he would be sending for you. That was,' Arthur calculated rapidly, *'sa,* in the spring. Oh, get up.' He reached out and took her hands, intending to help her to her feet. She lifted her head, looked at him with a clear challenge of angry defiance. He let her go, as if stung by a bee.

'I have heard of no such wish from Gwynedd.' Gwenhwyfar was surprised, she had expected her voice to creak and squeak, but it came out calm. Quite regal.

'How are you?' he asked, his own voice neutral, formal, without warmth. 'You look well, though thinner than when last I saw you.'

Winifred's guttural accent interrupted. 'Gwenhwyfar carried much puppy fat as I recall.'

With a sweet smile, glad of the excuse to turn away from Arthur, Gwenhwyfar walked over to Winifred, dipped a second reverence. 'Were we not all burdened by indulgence as children? It is for the woman grown to form a pleasing figure.' Gwenhwyfar smiled, her eyes drawn to the bulge of Winifred's pregnancy. She bent forward to place a light kiss of greeting on each of Winifred's cold, artificially coloured cheeks.

Arthur's wife had not missed the barb in the reply. At this late stage of pregnancy she had no figure, did not need reminding of the ungainliness of her condition.

Arthur had seated himself, and indicated for Gwenhwyfar to do the same. She selected a stool placed well away from either of them. There was a moment's uneasy silence, broken as Arthur asked, 'You are comfortable here, at the villa?'

'Thank you, yes. Your mother has made me most welcome.' They spoke in elegant, formal Latin.

Bedwyr, silenced when Gwenhwyfar had entered, began his questioning again. Arthur laughed, rumpled his hair. 'Lad, do you never stop?' Answered, as well as he could.

Gwenhwyfar was grateful for the boy's chatter.

As she had answered Arthur that last time, his eyes had sought hers – those hawk eyes, so hard to read unless you understood the mind that lay behind them. Something she had seen there unnerved her, shook the rigid self-control she was struggling to maintain. She had seen pain there, and a great sadness.

What was this Bedwyr was saying?

'Arthur has been wounded, Gwen. He was nearly killed, nearly lost his leg!' The boy was at her side now. 'He has come home so we can help him grow strong again.'

Arthur laughed, amused at the boy's exaggeration. 'Nonsense! I was never that badly wounded – and I am quite strong already. I cannot ride for a while, that is all. Rather than idle away my days in some stuffy building I thought I would come and see how Ectha here is coping with the estate, and how much deeper my mother has committed herself to the Christ God.'

Ectha laughed uncertainly, unsure whether Arthur jested or not. He felt uncomfortable in the young man's presence. By Roman law Arthur was the head of the family, not Ectha. Uthr had been husband to the eldest daughter, heiress to all her father owned; Uthr had taken the legal responsibility, had passed it to the son at his death. All the same, Uthr had taken little interest in the estate; Arthur even less so – was not even resident. The daily running of the place fell to Ectha.

Wounded? Gwenhwyfar had flicked an anxious glance at Arthur as Bedwyr had told the reason for his being here. Arthur had winced as he had risen to greet her, had put little weight on his leg when standing.

Bedwyr, not at all put out by his cousin's denial, went on to tell Gwenhwyfar the grim details, rather embellished. She listened, thankful she could be occupied with Bedwyr and not seem impolite to others in the room.

Arthur was talking to his mother. She had asked, 'For how long, Arthur, do you intend to stay? You were somewhat vague upon your arrival.'

'A while, Mother, that is all I can say, a while. I expect until the sea lanes reopen in the spring.'

Ygrainne suppressed a groan. That long!

He noted his mother's lack of enthusiasm. 'You wish me gone from here before spring?' His voice was dry as he added sarcastically, 'And I thought you would be so pleased to see me.'

Irritated, she answered churlishly, 'Of course I am. Your visits are rare. I wondered, merely, how long we could enjoy your company.'

Under his breath, 'Liar.'

The room fell silent. Arthur beckoned a servant forward to refill his goblet with wine. He said after a moment, 'I had a desire for my son to be born on my own, unquestionable territory. Pendragon land, not Saex.'

Winifred smiled across at her husband, not missing his sarcasm. Outwardly her look was one of love and respect. 'My husband is most thoughtful in these matters, Lady Ygrainne. We both desire the next Pendragon to be as great as his father and grandsire.'

She accepted honey-sweetened fruit from a slave, said, her voice as sweet as the dish before her, 'My lord husband was most upset his family were not with us to celebrate our wedding feast.' She gazed fondly at Arthur. 'Were you not, my dearest?' She lowered her voice slightly and said to Ygrainne, 'Men can be such boys at times! He will never admit his true reason for bringing me here. Naturally he wishes to show the fruit of our happy union to his own people.' She patted her swollen belly to emphasise her point, smiling all the while at Arthur, daring him to contradict her. 'In Britain,' she added, 'the Pendragon's banner is so eclipsed by that of my father.'

She turned her sickly-sweet smile on Gwenhwyfar. 'It is a pity you left Britain so hurriedly, my dear, for you too missed our wedding feast. It was a grand occasion! My husband was quite overcome with emotion, were you not, love?' She did not miss the flicker of anger in Arthur's eyes, nor the dullness in Gwenhwyfar's. 'Our wedding night was, how shall I say, a fulfilment of joy for both of us. We are blissfully happy together.'

Gwenhwyfar thought, *if she does not stop soon I will slap her*. Said, 'I am pleased you are both content. The child will bring you future joy.'

Winifred had been as startled as Arthur to discover Cunedda's daughter here at Ygrainne's villa. So this was where she had been hiding all these months! If her mother or father knew, they had never said. And Melwas? Vortigern had dismissed Gwenhwyfar's disappearance almost immediately, had more important problems to worry on. The fighting around the Angli settlements had flared again and there were reports of dissent in the north. Sulking, Melwas had taken himself off to his own Summer Land, had not been at court this past year. Did he know Gwenhwyfar was here? She must make sure he did.

More interesting had been Arthur's unguarded reaction as Gwenhwyfar had entered the room. His wife had caught the flicker of alarm and discomposure. That was not like Arthur; he was always in control, always mastered his expression. None could read his veiled thoughts, not through that lazy grin and those impenetrable eyes. But he had let the mask slip for a fleeting second. So, he still wanted Gwenhwyfar then?

Winifred had enticed Arthur, bedded with him; had begged her mother to find a way of securing this marriage – and she had, by some devious method. All that, because she had determined no one else would have Arthur, the best catch in the river. She had thought the past was dead. Gwenhwyfar should have been betrothed to Melwas and then disappeared who knew or cared where. The past should have faded like the memory of yesterday's sunset.

The spark of jealousy, that had kindled when she had first realised Arthur wanted Gwenhwyfar, flared again into life. There was one satisfaction. It had shaken him, finding her here. And Arthur shaken, was a rare sight worth the seeing! For the first time since she had found herself tricked on to his ship, Winifred felt a hint of pleasure. He, her arrogantly perfect husband, had made a mistake!

§ XII

The night was cold. Gwenhwyfar lay curled beneath her sleeping fur listening to the sounds of darkness: an owl hunting; mice rustling; the wind from the distant sea tugging at autumn leaves. She glanced at the empty bed on the other side of the room, wished she still had Ceridwen's bright company during these long nights of loneliness.

Her cousin was happy in her marriage to Iawn, Gwenhwyfar did not begrudge her the contentment – how could she? Ceridwen was a sweet girl though a little too fanciful, oblivious to problems, seeing a good side to everything others thought bad.

Gwenhwyfar's hand touched a wrapped bundle beneath her pillow. The few letters that had come from Gwynedd, from her brothers Enniaun and Ceredig; one from her Da. She lay with her fingers touching the ribbon binding them, willed sleep to come.

Giving in, she pulled the bundle from its place of safety and padded across the floor to sit before the night lamp burning in the corner. She selected one letter at random, began to read. The words were faint in this dim light but she had read them often enough to need little illumination, knew every scrawled word by heart. It was one of Enniaun's. He wrote of a skirmish across the straits from Caer Arfon on the Isle of Mon, said the sea-wolves were having the worst of it. She selected another, this from Ceredig. He told of his first-born son, of his new own-held territory down the coast to the south of Gwynedd's borders. A third, received two weeks since containing word of her own mare's foaling.

She dropped the letters in her lap wishing Etern were alive. He would have written of the mountains, the colours of the trees and the beauty of the horse herds being brought down from summer pasture.

Sitting in the silence of her room, Gwenhwyfar remembered past autumns. The early snows mantling Yr Wyddfa like an old woman's veil. The golds and browns and reds of the trees, leaves clinging like suckling babes to their mothers' breasts. The scent of wood-smoke and damp mountain earth. The kitchens at Caer Arfon alive with the bustle of preserving fruit and salting meat, the making of beer and wine. The cattle, those not to be slaughtered, gathered and, with the warhorses, divided among the outlying steadings for winter quartering. Each head of livestock carried a payment of corn, skins and spun wool for its good care. In this way the lord of Gwynedd saw to it his people were fed and adequately clothed throughout the winter months. For each animal returned fit and healthy, come spring, an extra payment was made. Cunedda's livestock were well tended and his people content.

The seasonal stocking of the storerooms was almost completed in Ygrainne's household also of course, but the excitement was lost here. No sharing of laughter as soft and hard fruits were picked; no giggling of servants and children as the huge vats of bubbling fruits were cooked and poured into storage jars. Here, the slaves and servants carried out their duties efficiently but with a dullness that would erase the brilliance of the sun.

Gwenhwyfar sighed, folded her letters. Samhain was approaching, the night when the dead returned. Despite Christianity the festival survived. The religious ceremony had faded once there were no more Druid priests to officiate, but traditions were hard to break, particularly those linked with joyful festivity – or, as at Samhain, superstitious fear.

Ygrainne had scolded Gwenhwyfar when she mentioned the rite last autumn, impressing upon her that Christians followed Jesu and did not bow to the nonsense of pagan ceremony. Still, Gwenhwyfar had noted, with a smile, Ygrainne devoted herself to deeper prayer on Samhain eve, and Gwenhwyfar's was not the only bowl of milk placed before the threshold as a gift to any wandering spirits.

Bedwyr, with the children of neighbours and freeborn servants, had enjoyed playing the traditional games, although Ygrainne had frowned on those too. This year, remembering the fun, he was eagerly awaiting the close of the month, three weeks away. As a child at Caer Arfon Gwenhwyfar had looked forward with excitement to the festival, when they played and drank and feasted; when tales were told around the Hall fires of people from the past who might, even as the tales were being told, be creeping around the outer walls.

An owl hooted, long and low, an eerie, ghostly sound. Gwenhwyfar shivered, recalling the childhood thrill of being enjoyably terrified by the darkness of Samhain night. No doubt this year, as last, she would be expected to kneel in Ygrainne's cold stone chapel. Oh aye, Ygrainne said she did not believe in the nonsense of Samhain, but she did not rest easy on the night when the dead walked!

Gwenhwyfar caught her breath. Something moved by the shrubs bordering the ornamental garden beyond the window! For a heart-thudding moment she wondered if her thoughts had conjured up a spirit. She fought the panic down. Whatever it was, it had gone.

She relaxed, surprised to feel sweat trickling down her back and laughed at herself. Foolish to let her imagination run away with her. She reached for the small flagon of watered wine standing ready for night use. Half glancing at the gardens, not watching what she was doing, she tipped it over. By chance, Gwenhwyfar caught it before it crashed to the floor but wine gushed in a splashing fountain. She cursed.

Reaching for a shawl Gwenhwyfar covered her shoulders and slid her feet into soft house shoes. Ygrainne would have insisted a house slave be wakened to clear up the mess, but Gwenhwyfar reckoned it quicker to fetch a cloth and do it herself. Why disturb those who slept for such a trivial task?

The kitchens were deserted and silent, a single night lamp casting a dim but adequate light. A lingering smell of the evening's meal pervaded.

Reaching for a beaker Gwenhwyfar poured water for herself, drank thirstily then searched for a cloth to wipe up the spillage in her room. She found something suitable, made her way back along the open colonnaded corridor running the entire length of the villa. Storerooms, kitchens and dining room took up one wing, with servants' sleeping quarters above. The main living quarters formed the central block with the bath-house, Arthur's rooms and extra guest rooms on the third.

Something made her pause before turning to climb the narrow servants' stairs leading to the upper floor. She glanced at the two parallel rows of conifers forming a central aisle through the gravelled courtyard – and gasped. Someone, something, stood there with its back to her, gazing up at the cloud-veiled half-moon.

She must have made an audible noise for the shape turned.

'Who is there?' a voice called, low and wary.

'I could ask the same!' Gwenhwyfar countered, an edge of fear to her words. She stood motionless as a vague shadow walked forward, feet scrunching, oddly unbalanced on the gravel, a third noise clicking with the awkward pace.

The clouds parted and a thin radiance lit up the open space. Gwenhwyfar caught a brief glimpse of unmistakable features before the moon sailed again behind her shielding cover.

'What are you doing out here, Arthur?' she asked lightly, unsuccessfully masking a tremor.

'I could ask the same,' he echoed.

Gwenhwyfar saw the reason for the third sound: he was leaning heavily on a crutch.

Climbing the five steps leading to the raised corridor, Arthur seated himself on the top one, stretching the injured limb before him. He sat quiet for a while, toying with the wooden crutch.

Gwenhwyfar hesitated, undecided between staying or going. She had made up her mind to leave when he said, 'I truly did not expect you to be here, Gwen.'

'As you can see, you expected wrong.' The reply was curt.

He half looked round at her, standing there in her night shift with only a shawl around her shoulders. Her lovely hair tumbled as wild as he remembered; suited her better than that artificial, restricting style she had worn earlier. His initial shock at first sight of her had numbed him; it had taken all his wits and experience to master that sudden leap of panic.

He had known Cunedda had sent her here – it had been his own suggestion, for he knew the people of the town would not gossip and Gwenhwyfar would be safe with his mother. But Mithras, he had not expected her to have remained all this while!

He told himself again she was beyond his reach; he had tried to put her memory from him! Had succeeded, he thought, until she stood there before him, silent and thin and pale – more beautiful than ever he remembered. He had felt his whole being shake as he acknowledged her formal, distant, greeting, stifled the longing to fold her in his arms, kiss her hair and eyes and lips – hold her close and safe.

Then he had glimpsed Winifred, his wife. Saw her hastily veiled gleam of triumph; realised he must never, ever, give way to his feelings before her, because, bitch that she was, she would destroy Gwenhwyfar as easily as crushing a butterfly.

Winifred was only too ready to sharpen her claws at his expense.

His voice cold, Arthur said, 'I am eager to see my son come into the world. A grandchild may bridge the gap between myself and my mother.'

Gwenhwyfar said nothing, looked beyond him to the scudding moon shadows. She had to ask. Had to know. 'Do you love her?'

He groaned, masked the sound by rubbing the persistent ache in his leg. 'My wound is healing all too slowly. Often of a night it pains me. I find walking eases it.' Then, 'She is my wife, Gwenhwyfar.'

The Kingmaking

'She is your wife, aye. Do you love her?' Gwenhwyfar stared at him, her hand clasped at her throat holding her shawl around her, a small protective barricade.

He rose unsteadily to his feet, the pain in his thigh and the grimace on his strained face genuine enough. He said again, 'She is my wife, and Vortigern's daughter.'

'She is the by-blow of a Saex bitch!'

'I repeat,' low, a tinge of menace, 'she is my wife. She carries my son.'

Unable to help herself Gwenhwyfar flung a taunt at him. 'The daughter takes after the mother. All Saex women are scheming whores – are you so sure it is yours?'

Despite his wound, Arthur moved quickly, grabbed her arm in a grasp so tight it hurt. In the morning, Gwenhwyfar would find an ugly bruise where his fingers had gripped.

The anger was genuine, but the direction of it false. He desperately wanted to see the end of the mare he was saddled with, but had no way of doing so save for her death. His pride would not let him show the chains which shackled him to her, so he lashed out in anger at the one he loved.

'I say for the final time, Winifred is my wife! I pleaded her hand,' he snorted in self-disgust, 'took her virginity in my bed. Through her may come an easy way of claiming the kingship. I have added benefits to my ambition – a wealthy woman for my bed to pleasure me, and a son soon to be born.'

Gwenhwyfar laughed scornfully. 'You sound so sincere I almost believe you.'

'I have told no lie.'

'Have you not?' she retorted. 'Have you then forgotten our pledge the day your men cheered you as their lord?' Her eyes flashed in the dim light. 'Have you so easily forgotten you asked me to be your queen, Arthur Pendragon?'

He turned away, limped a few paces, rested his hands on the waist-high railing. His stomach churned, he felt sick. His thigh throbbed abominably, his head also. Aye, he remembered. Remembered all too clearly!

Into the night he said, 'We were children then.'

She answered, 'You asked my Da for my hand. You change allegiance as the tide turns.'

He sucked in his breath and gritting his teeth, cursed silently. She knew then. He almost decided to drop this pretence, almost turned to her to admit all he truly felt, but *na*, how could he endanger her? He loved her too dearly to bring Winifred's spite down on her. Why in the name of Mithras had he come here?

He gripped the railing with his hands. 'I asked for you because our marriage would have brought an unequivocal alliance with Gwynedd and easy access to your father's horses. Cunedda refused me, so I looked elsewhere for my wealth.'

Gwenhwyfar stared at him, stunned. Was this the truth? Could she have been so blindly stupid? Had it all been lies, one long lie after another? She said simply, 'I thought you loved me.'

Arthur shut his eyes, tight, dug his nails into the wood of the railing. 'Then you thought wrong.' He did not want to hurt her; had to hurt her. 'I tell all my women I love them. I suppose for the one night I am with them, I do give love. Come morning, I forget them.'

Once, Gwenhwyfar had been kicked by her father's stallion. She had been eight years old, had foolishly walked behind the animal and paid the price. The blow had sent her spinning across the stable yard to crash into the opposite wall and lie screaming and crying as the pain shot up her leg. There were no bones broken, but she had nursed the bruising for weeks after. Strange, she had completely forgotten the incident until now. It was almost as if, again, she had walked where she ought not and been kicked for her stupidity.

Suddenly, she hated Arthur, hated him more than she would have thought possible. Without further word she turned her back on him and returned to her room. Dropping the cloth she had absently clutched in her hand she crumpled to the floor. Sobs racked her body; great, bitter tears. Her heart, already these past months dangerously cracked, was shattered into a thousand tiny pieces.

DECEMBER 454

§ XIII

Winter was proving bitter and merciless, with a cruel wind that blustered unceasingly, bending vegetation, man and beast before it and whipping the river into flurries of restless agitation. Rain drizzled or soaked alternately; and tempers flared as easily as a spark to dry heath. Gwenhwyfar stayed as much as possible in the seclusion of her room, some days not leaving her bed until near noon. Her hair, if Ceridwen had not fussed, would have been left unwashed and uncombed. She dressed haphazardly, uncaring, for there seemed little point to anything, even life itself.

Iawn had gone with Arthur into Gaul. Ceridwen missed him terribly. She had tried to chirrup brightly at first but Gwenhwyfar's dull depression seemed catching.

Winifred had been left behind. Fortunately for the household, she had taken to her bed after the birthing of a sickly daughter. Quite the ugliest child Winifred had ever seen. It must be some jest, some horrendous joke that Arthur had played upon her, for she had been so certain she carried a son. This mewling and puking girl-child with sallow yellow skin and squinting, crossed eyes was surely not hers? She could not have borne this, this – thing! There was no grief when the creature died. Few expected a child born on the Dark Night of Samhain to live for long.

The days passed, turned to weeks, and they awaited Arthur's return, knew he would return some time before the Nativity.

Winifred waited, relieved the brat was gone. She wanted to go home! She waited for Arthur, hoping he would allow her to go, now there was no son to bind them.

Bedwyr, lonely and bored, awaited his cousin with excitement and expectation; Ygrainne, with the hope that spring would come early and

Arthur would return to his men and take Winifred with him. Gwenhwyfar? She did not want his coming back.

He eventually arrived five days before the day of Christ's birth celebration, his coming throwing the household into renewed upheaval. To Ygrainne's intense annoyance he brought with him the eldest son of Aegidius, King of Gaul. Clutching her rosary of fine carved cedar, she sought the calm company of Father Simon, who tended the villa's small chapel.

'Feelings of alarm and anger are natural, my daughter,' he said, setting a tender hand on her bowed head. 'All God's children say and think careless things which come to mind in moments of weakness.'

For the first and only time Ygrainne felt her belief waver. Did this man truly understand her feelings for this son of hers? She had been tending the hypocaust stokehole when Arthur had arrived. The brickwork had become worn and crumbled, the slaves too ignorant to use sense in the clearing of it, she had needed to supervise the work herself. How like Arthur to arrive at an inconvenient moment! With soot on her face and grime on her hands she had to welcome Syagrius, a prince! Damn Arthur to Hell! He had made no apology, had sat his horse amid the bustle of armed escort and baggage as if everything was normal. Normal! She had met his eyes as he sat there unconcerned – and his look had frightened her.

The words of the priest's muttered blessing drifted past her. She knew those deep, dark eyes, the eyes of a man who had once loved her so. No, not Arthur's eyes, Uthr's. Tears slid down her pinched cheeks as the painful memories came – memories she had long since locked away under the protection of God's shield. She had loved Uthr, loved his tenacity for life, his determination to succeed. Loved him enough to follow him willingly to the edge of the earth. Uncomplaining, unflustered, heavy with child, she had faced those mountainous seas and an uncertain future for him, for Uthr. And Arthur had looked at her this afternoon with those same eyes, Uthr's eyes. But that look he had given her carried no love, no tenderness. Only loathing and contempt.

It had not been her fault! She had seen the sense in hiding her newborn son's identity, understood at the time of his birthing the threat of Vortigern, whose power spread wider in those days. Uthr was safe enough in exile but would he have remained safe if the tyrant had known of an heir? So she had agreed to the pretence of her son's death, sure in the knowledge it would only be for a while, until other sons came. But months stretched to years and there was no other son. She mourned that only one, the son she had never suckled or held; mourned, and accepted he was gone from her, to all purposes dead. Mourned, and turned to God for His wisdom and comfort. And Uthr had turned to Morgause.

Father Simon had fallen silent, his prayer ended. Ygrainne kissed the hem of his gown, left the chapel and walked blindly into the settling night. She seated herself on a bench, pulling her cloak close against the harsh wind, looked towards the rear of the east wing, at the whitened plaster walls peeping through the darkness of the evergreens. Lamps had been lit, their glow filtering through the cracks of closed shutters. Uthr had never discovered that once, long, long ago, she had sat in this very spot and seen him through the open ground-floor window, loving with Morgause.

Sitting here, nursing her memories, Ygrainne realised Uthr had never questioned her turning to God for solace. He had been a demanding man, a man who took what he needed when he needed it. But he had never forced himself on her and, after the girl-children she bore also died, respected her not wanting him in her bed. Arthur hated her for the love she was unable to give, and Uthr had gone to Morgause for the necessities of manhood because he loved her, Ygrainne, so much. Both things so hard, so unbearably hard to accept.

They searched the villa for Ygrainne when she did not appear for the evening meal. Gwenhwyfar found her slumped, jaw slack and dribbling, beside the garden bench. Down Ygrainne's cheek tears glistened in frosted tracks.

§ XIV

Ectha sat numb with disbelief at the shock of Ygrainne's illness. He nursed an untouched goblet of wine between chilled hands, staring vacantly into space. Slave and servant crept about their duties clearing the remains of a barely touched dinner, quietly awaiting further orders.

Gwenhwyfar was seated to the far side of the room, alone with her thoughts.

Syagrius cleared his throat, his voice loud in the stillness as he said, 'I have instructed my servant to seek alternative lodgings in town on the morrow.'

Arthur began to protest but Syagrius silenced him. 'With your mother taken ill it would be inconceivable for me to intrude further.'

Ectha summoned a weak smile. 'The household has been put to no trouble. Gwenhwyfar is more than capable of running things, are you not, my dear?'

She nodded polite agreement, careful not to let her reluctance show. The acceptance of responsibility was as necessary as a warm mantle in winter, but she would wear it as heavy as she wore the weight of exile. Ectha assumed she would step into Ygrainne's place and organise the villa's daily needs with as much efficiency. She had not the heart, or conscience, to refuse him.

She said now, aware of her duties, 'You are most welcome to stay; happen company would be a good diversion at this moment.'

He smiled warmly, stood and formally bowed. 'I thank you, but arrangements are in hand. My business on behalf of my father will take but a short while.' His smile widened as he stepped forward to take Gwenhwyfar's hand in his own, raised it to his lips. 'I accepted Arthur's offer to stay here as an excuse to meet you, Lady Gwenhwyfar.'

She blushed. He was no more than ten and five years, not even a man yet, with barely a need to shave those fine hairs more than once in the week. Yet here he was, with the self-assurance and expectation of full manhood.

His intimate gaze reflected all he implied, and more. Gwenhwyfar pulled tentatively to free her hand, but he held it firm.

'I must state,' he said blithely, 'Arthur did not speak the full truth of you.'

She glanced briefly at Arthur who was sprawled along a couch frowning, interested of a sudden in his fingernails.

Syagrius had seated himself beside her on the couch, moved closer. She could feel his body, young and muscular, very intent, through the fine stuff of her gown. He still had hold of her hand.

'Arthur told me you were fair, but not that you were a Venus. I wished to see for myself the dazzling green eyes and spun copper hair he speaks of.'

'Oh?' Gwenhwyfar was flustered. She tried again to release her hand, moving away as far as Syagrius would allow. 'Has he then mentioned me? He has not spoken over-many bad things about me, I trust?'

'Mentioned you?' Syagrius laughed, his fingers gripping tighter, his eyes never straying from her face. 'He talks of no one else! Atween you and me,' he dropped his voice, but deliberately not too low, 'I believe he has a bit of a problem.'

He looked shrewdly at Arthur who glowered back. 'He has a wife whom he dislikes intensely. Assuredly a mistaken marriage.'

Arthur laughed, the sound striking harsh behind its falsity. He swung his legs to the floor, limped to Syagrius's side and placed a hand on his shoulder.

Gwenhwyfar took the opportunity to reclaim her own hand.

'My dear boy,' Arthur said, forcing amusement. 'How you do exaggerate! I mentioned my mother's guest but once. I doubt our dear Gwenhwyfar will take kindly to such obvious flirtation. By the Bull, how these unwhelped boys expect to shed innocence early these days!'

'I can assure you, friend,' replied Syagrius, addressing Arthur but refusing to look away from Gwenhwyfar, 'I shed my innocence of women many months past.'

Gwenhwyfar, though, was bridling. 'And why, Arthur Pendragon, would I not appreciate a man's flattery? I am a free woman of marriageable age, I have no tie of betrothal.' She smiled radiantly at Syagrius. 'And,' she added pointedly, 'I once said I intended to fly high. Who has a wingspan to rival the future king of Gaul?'

Syagrius raised his eyebrows quizzically, not quite understanding. 'None, lady, even the Legions of the Eagles can no longer soar above my father's power and soon, my own.' He grinned suddenly, aware something in the game had altered here, that Gwenhwyfar was no longer backing away from him, but responding to his courting! God's favour, he could scarcely believe his luck! Could she be interested in him? Well, why not? As she had said, she was a free woman, and he had to seek a suitable wife one day. But Gwenhwyfar? Dare he seriously try for her?

With a forced laugh, Arthur motioned their guest to his feet, steered him for the door. 'We have been travelling since dawn, my lad, and the household seems as weary. It is time we retired to our beds.' He gestured good night to Ectha and Ceridwen.

Syagrius, on the point of protesting, changed his mind as Arthur's elbow jabbed him sharply in the ribs. Sweeping a bow he said to Gwenhwyfar, It seems I am dismissed, Lady. I bid you a fond good night.'

Boldly he returned across the room, tipped up her face with his fingers and brushed her lips lightly with his own. His taste was pleasant, sweet and soft. Lingering.

Stunned, Gwenhwyfar watched him leave, ushering an equally astonished Arthur before him. Heard him say, 'Well do I understand your feeling for her now, Arthur! She is...' She heard no more, for the door had closed.

The room spun; she must see about watering the wine more on the morrow!

Well do I understand your feeling for her now, Arthur! Why had Syagrius said that? What had he meant? Confusion whirled with the dizziness of strong wine and tiredness. Arthur had ignored her, almost to the point of rudeness, and yet his hostility to Syagrius's boyish flirting was acute. Gwenhwyfar sighed – so many snarled tangles! Wearily, she pushed herself to her feet, telling the servants to seek their beds. 'Come, Ectha, you must go to your bed also. A mild sleeping draught would do no harm,' she advised.

Ectha's personal slave nodded his agreement. He noted her reddened, tired eyes. 'I shall see to him, Lady. Such a draught would not come amiss for you also?'

Gwenhwyfar shook her head. '*Na*, but I thank you for your concern. Ectha,' she had to shake the man slightly to gain his attention, 'Father Simon is with Ygrainne, she is well tended.'

Lost in his worry and shock, Ectha seemed dazed and confused. Gwenhwyfar smiled reassurance, said, 'She is a strong woman and will be well in a few days. The physician said it was only a weakness of the spirit; a warning that she must ease on the way she pushes herself.'

The blankness on Ectha's face remained. His slave placed his hands protectively on his master's shoulders. 'He is most fond of his brother's wife. As we all are.'

A shout of alarm followed immediate by a crash echoed through the house, coming from the far end of the open corridor outside. Gwenhwyfar ran, at her heels Ectha's slave and Ceridwen, followed by startled servants.

Arthur lay crumpled in a heap at the foot of the stairway. Syagrius stood at the top.

One hand extended, half afraid to touch, Gwenhwyfar crouched beside Arthur. Was he dead?

Syagrius hurtled down the short but steep flight of stairs, squatted beside her. His face was chalk white. He spoke in short bursts, breath coming fast. 'He was angry. I was teasing him. I meant no harm. He just slipped and fell. I did not touch him, I swear!'

'No one is saying you did,' Gwenhwyfar replied calmly.

A sigh of relief swept through the group of peering servants as Arthur's eyes flickered open. He groaned, swore.

'Be still, do not try to move.' Gwenhwyfar rested a hand on his arm.

He looked up at her, his face contorted with pain. 'I have no bloody intention of moving, woman!' He was sweating profusely. When Gwenhwyfar touched his hand, the skin felt cold and clammy.

Ectha's slave sent someone scurrying for a blanket, another to fetch Cynan, Arthur's own servant. Ceridwen picked up her skirts, and shouting, ran for Iawn who appeared some moments later with three of Arthur's guard. 'What has happened?' he panted.

'Arthur has fallen,' Gwenhwyfar explained, allowing room for Iawn to examine his commander. When the leg was touched Arthur yelled. Iawn straightened, worried, and ran a hand through his fair hair. 'Seems that leg has been damaged again. It has been bad all this while. Best send for the physician, my lady.'

Gwenhwyfar herself groaned, leant back against the wall, closed her eyes a moment to let the world spin by. 'He will not appreciate being sent for twice in one night.'

'I need no physician so urgently he must leave his bed.' Arthur's protest was made with eyes shut and held breath. 'Get me to my room, I shall do well enough 'til morning. He is coming to see Ygrainne again then, is he not?'

Iawn and Gwenhwyfar, echoed by the servants, disagreed with the idea vehemently.

Teeth clamped, Arthur attempted to haul himself upright, pain tearing through the tortured muscles of his damaged thigh. 'See, I am all right,' he gasped. 'I am in no urgent need of the physician.'

'Very well.' Realising his stubbornness would have it no other way, Gwenhwyfar gestured to four of the men to raise him. 'Take him to my chamber – it is the nearest.'

Syagrius watched them climb the stairs slowly. He stood stiffly against the wall, ashen-faced and silent. Gwenhwyfar laid her hand on his arm. 'It was not your fault, accidents happen. Get to bed, there is nothing more you can do this night.'

'What of his wife? Should she not know of this?'

'I doubt she is interested, but I shall send a servant to tell her.'

'Gwenhwyfar.' He caught her arm as she turned to go. 'I know I was teasing earlier, with those things I said, but,' he bit his lip, unsure what to say, 'he thinks the world of you, but is too proud to admit it.'

Gwenhwyfar smiled amicably. What did this boy know of things that had passed between herself and Arthur? 'Get to bed,' she said again, not unkindly.

Ceridwen held the door wide as they manoeuvred Arthur through and laid him on Gwenhwyfar's bed. Father Simon appeared, anxiously enquiring if there was anything he could do. Servants clustered in the doorway twittering with concern.

Tired, irritated by their combined uselessness Gwenhwyfar turned on them all. 'The matter is in hand. I have all the help I require.'

Cynan ran in, alarmed, his face shadowing; he was a trusted, reliable man, and Arthur thought highly of him. Efficiently he ushered spectators away, closed the door on them and hurried to his master's side, where he began gently removing clothing.

'He ought have the physician,' he said as he worked.

'So we all say, save your master,' Gwenhwyfar retorted. 'Ceridwen, can you fetch Livila? She may be old but her healing wisdom is great, Ygrainne has little faith in her, but she does well enough for the servants.'

Cynan nodded his approval. 'I hear she has skilful hands, enough to see us through this night at least.'

Ceridwen touched Gwenhwyfar's arm. 'Is there ought else I can do?' she asked.

'You can help by getting yourself to bed – and looking in or Bedwyr to see he sleeps sound. Go, get yourself to your husband.'

With eight brothers Gwenhwyfar had seen male nakedness often. She had seen Arthur, the boy, undressed many times in Gwynedd; how often had they swum naked in sea or river, or helped clean each other in Cunedda's small apology for a bathhouse? Seeing him lying vulnerable upon her own bed, holding out against the pain of Livila's administrations, Gwenhwyfar saw a different person, saw him for the first time as a man. Male genitalia meant little, no more than a stallion's equipment or a dog's. She had known from an early age what it was for, had seen males of a species mounting females. Watching now, tense, weary, frightened and muddled, she found her eyes drawn repeatedly to his maleness, its significance starkly taunting.

He had a wife. Had lain with her, taken his pleasure with her and given her his child. Why had he reacted to Syagrius? God's truth, but her head ached!

Livila demanded her attention, asking for light to be brought closer; she fetched another lamp and set it on a side table. How thin Arthur was, she realised with a start. Muscles slack against taut flesh, bones gaunt. It had not shown so starkly in his face.

As if reading her thoughts, Cynan said, 'My Lord has lost much weight since the accident. He has fretted to be about his life, but this thigh is stubborn to mend.'

Livila's worn teeth clicked in her slack jaw. 'It be the way. Men will not rest or give damage time to heal. See here where this flesh be bruised? The muscle beneath be torn.' She hissed as Arthur squirmed at her touch, face contorting in a fresh burst of pain. 'Aye, lad, it hurts. You are fortunate, no further bones be broken, just unhealed muscles re-rattled.' She regarded him solemnly through age wrinkled eyes. 'The surgeon who tended you has worked well. The bone has mended clean, it be these muscles we must tend to now. With rest and my salves you will soon fetch as good as new.'

Arthur saw the old woman through a haze of red agony, swore under his breath. Damn them all. Rest – how could he rest?

At some point during the early hours, utter exhaustion made seeing and doing automatic. Obediently Gwenhwyfar had held the lamp higher or lower, fetched, carried, passed bandages as Livila requested, The room and the people within were distant, fogged. Arthur had been given a sleeping draught, commanded by Livila's stern threats to swallow. As dawn approached he slept on. Cynan was curled on a pallet on the other side of the room, snoring gently. Livila had gone to her own given place,

The sky paled from black to the dull grey of a clouded winter's dawn. Numb, cramped and exhausted almost beyond endurance, Gwenhwyfar slept where she had last sat, on a stool with head pillowed on her arms resting on the bed. She stirred, raised her head, found Arthur watching her. His skin glistened with sweat, his eyes burnt bright with fever, but at least he was conscious and aware.

'Did I ever tell you,' he croaked, 'you are so, very, very beautiful?'

'And did I ever tell you, Arthur Pendragon,' she replied, wondering that she had enough energy to speak, 'you are a bastard?'

Arthur smiled weakly and fumbled for her hand. 'Frequently.'

§ XV

Rowena's son was a greedy boy, always suckling at her. Now his first birthday was well behind them and his teeth nearly all formed, she would need to consider his weaning.

Her father handed her a cloth to wipe the boy's mouth, said with a grunt of disapproval, 'Your mother had a wet-nurse to feed the childer.'

Rowena smiled indulgently at her son as she sat him on her lap. Her mother had not lost the babies she had birthed. 'Vitolinus is special, Father. I enjoy feeding him with my milk. Jute milk, not British watered muck.'

Hengest laughed, took his grandson from her and seating himself, began bouncing the child on his lap.

'You will have him vomit, he has a full belly.'

'Ah, but he likes it!' Hengest chuckled as the boy gurgled and demanded more.

'All the same,' Rowena warned.

Reluctantly her father gave ground and, snuggling the boy in his arms, carried him to the cot, laid him down and tenderly covered him. 'Hush, my little son of Woden, go you to sleep so you may grow fine and strong like your grandfather.'

Rowena indicated the slave might clear away the mess of feeding and changing a child, waited until the girl had left and she was alone with her father before saying, 'I had a second letter from Winifred yesterday.'

Hengest turned his head towards her, straightened himself from rocking the cradle. 'Has she found enough sense to tell us of the Pendragon's movements?'

Rowena shook her head, took up her spindle. 'She writes only of her unhappiness. She says the babe was a girl. It died.' Rowena shook her head again sadly. Was death also to follow her grandchildren?

Hengest made no reply. Winifred had been a spoilt child; he had no time for her whining and demanding, nor for her constant changes of mind.

'She says Arthur has her close watched. Ygrainne's Roman priest managed to send this letter, as with the first, in secret,' Rowena said.

Wrinkling his nose beneath the great bush of beard and moustache, Hengest resisted the urge to spit. Christians! Bah, weakling sentimentalists!

He wandered around the room, this semi-resplendent royal room. Bronzes, tapestries, fine furniture; none of it hid cracked ceiling and mould-spotted walls – or stopped the draughts. Woden's breath, but his wattle-built Hall was in better condition than this decaying Londinium palace!

'How much longer will Vortigern be?' he asked impatiently. 'Considering he asked to see me, I am not pleased to wait like this.'

Rowena vaguely flapped a hand. 'I expect he has been delayed.' Her hands had never returned to their former slimness; too many pregnancies had left them puffed and misshapen, the fingers slow to respond. Spinning and needlework were becoming difficult tasks for her lately. She set the spindle down, rubbed the ache in her knuckles. 'He will come soon, Father. You heard, I assume, there was an attempt on his life a few days past?'

Folding his arms, Hengest nodded, frowning. 'The man was caught and tortured, I hear, but would not reveal who hired him.'

'You know nothing of it, I suppose?'

Affronted, Hengest put his hand to his chest. 'I most certainly do not! Until I am strong enough to not give a sow's ear about who rules as king over the British, I prefer to follow the trail I know!' He found himself a seat, calmed his frayed temper. 'Nay, it was not of my doing, daughter.' He spread his hands over his thighs, rubbed them up and down the woollen cloth of his bracae. This place was so cold! 'Aside, a man of mine would have succeeded.'

Walking across the room Rowena poured herself apple juice, added a herbal remedy to keep the pain of joint-ache at bay. Said, as she took a sip, 'My husband is convinced the Pendragon was behind it.'

'That drunken whore-user? He'd not be able to stab a pig on slaughter day!'

Rowena hesitated before answering for her father had a low opinion of Arthur. He had argued savagely against Winifred marrying with him, and took pleasure in reminding Rowena of the objection whenever yet another trouble sent her daughter pleading for help. 'I think you underestimate the Pendragon, Father,' she said carefully.

'He is a boy playing at a man's game.'

Rowena held her tongue. Then why were men clamouring to join his command? She said, 'Winifred wants to come home, she asks me to organise a ship. Do you think if I were to write to Arthur he...'

Hengest erupted to his feet, stamped across to stand before her, fists on hips, legs spread. 'Woden's Breath, Winifred is a woman grown and fully capable of seeing to her own concerns. She sowed the seeds and must now harvest the crop. The fact that only nettles have grown is her problem.'

'But Father!'

'The Pendragon needs her wealth to keep his head from sinking below the stink of his own drunken vomit. He'd never allow her out from behind his shield – and frankly, I don't want her. She's useless. She deserves to belong to that cock-crowing whore-cub. They deserve each other.' He turned away, reached for his cloak, and approaching the door, hand outstretched to open it, stopped surprised as it swung inward to reveal Vortigern standing there.

'A cock-crowing whore-cub?' he said drily, entering the room. 'You can only be talking of the Pendragon. Where he is concerned, Hengest, I try to remember that such creatures have spurs and are bred to fight. They need to be kept secure until needed in the pit.'

Vortigern shut the door and crossed the room to kiss Rowena's cheek, went next to peep at his sleeping son. 'Unfortunately, one sure way to do so for this particular breed is to tether him by marriage to my daughter. I do not like having him so close, but life has a habit of kicking us in the balls, does it not?' He poured wine, sniffing suspiciously at the goblet before drinking.

Hengest said wryly, 'You are wary of poison then?'

Vortigern shrugged, admitted, 'I am even wary of my own shadow these days.'

'Rowena says you think the Pendragon was behind this attempted murder?' Hengest said, accepting wine and resisting the temptation to also smell it for poison before drinking.

Vortigern glanced casually at the woman who had returned to her spinning. She made out she was the dutiful, loving wife, but he knew what she got up to and where her true interests lay! Rowena was her father's daughter first, her son's mother second, queen third and loyal wife last. Vortigern seated himself more comfortably; the day had been long and tiring, and there was still much to do. How angry Rowena would be if she knew it was he who had made sure the Pendragon knew about Winifred fleeing to Hengest! He could not allow his daughter to go, any more than he would ever allow Rowena her freedom. The Pendragon had one good use. He saved Vortigern the bother of keeping an eye on Winifred.

'Do you know,' Vortigern said into the silence, 'how many of the Caesars were murdered by their own guard?'

Hengest shook his head.

Vortigern chuckled. 'Neither do I in precise number, but too many, I am certain!'

Hengest laughed with him, the small moment of cold ice thawing slightly. They warily respected each other, these two men; respected each other's hold on power and authority, had no interest in the petty matter of like or dislike. Personal friendship lacked importance when running alongside survival. 'It is a wise man who chooses his guard personally, and ensures they have reason to stay loyal.'

Vortigern acknowledged the observation by raising his goblet, added, 'Or by choosing those who have the better reason to keep him alive.' He motioned for his guest to sit. 'My eldest sons fight me. My son-by-law will rejoice at my death – the list goes on. My Council disagrees with me as a matter of course – were I pronounced a saint, Council would still disagree with my decisions.' With an exasperated sigh he added, 'It is a qualification for election, to disagree.' He regarded Hengest thoughtfully, this bull-muscled Jute who needed only to sound his war horn to bring keels by the dozen across the sea. As he would, one day soon. 'You have sure reason to keep me king,' Vortigern said, pointing his finger knowingly at the man seated opposite him.

Hengest feigned innocence. 'It is a matter of honour for a jute to serve his lord well!'

'Pig swill! It is a matter of tactics. You know I will grant you all I can in return for loyal service from your men. Few British are willing to remain so loyal to me now; I can turn nowhere but to you, and for that you can ask whatever price you seek. Were either of my two eldest sons to take power, or, God forbid,' Vortigern shuddered, 'the Pendragon, you would be kicked out of Londinium and the Isle of Tanatus as swift as would a dog jumping with fleas.'

'Vortimer may hold sway over Council, I agree, but the others? I fear them not.'

Vortigern leant forward, eyes slit, fierce. 'Then you are not the wise commander I have taken you for all these years! The Pendragon playacts at his drinking and whoring, a leisurely pastime for him when there is nothing better to do. Give him a horse, a sword and a turma of men and he is a different man. Have you seen an adder basking in the sunshine,

Hengest?' He waited for the man to nod. 'Then you know full well how unwise it is to poke a serpent with a stick.'

Hengest was not convinced. He finished his wine, stood. 'This is all very interesting but I have many things to tend to. For what purpose did you ask me here? Surely not to talk of the Pendragon's non-existent virtues!'

'I want your men, and only your men, as my personal and palace guard, at least until the coming of spring.'

Hengest was shocked but held the surprise in check. Things were bad for Vortigern then! 'If I agree, what is there for me?'

Smiling cynically the King answered, 'Enough land to keep you and your people occupied until I am long dead and mouldered to dust. Probably enough to see you through until the coming of age of my youngest son here.'

Hengest's eyebrows rose. 'That is a lot of land.'

'I need a lot of protecting.'

§ XVI

Within Ygrainne's Christian household the Roman Saturnalia was celebrated as the Nativity. In the solemn little chapel Father Simon spoke the words of the Mass with feeling to his small congregation Gwenhwyfar stood beside Ectha, dutifully murmuring her responses and accepting the holy communion of bread and wine.

Christianity had so neatly sidestepped the pagan practices, conveniently encompassing the old festivals, with suitable modification, into its own belief. Saturnalia for instance, a pagan festival of laughter and celebration and for the giving of gifts; reminiscent for the Christians of the gifts given to the infant Jesu.

Saturnalia, with the bringing of evergreens into the house as a reminder of the spring soon to come. Living green, bearing fruit amid the dark days of winter. As Mary bore Her Son during the darkness of sin. The pagan holly became the thorns placed on the head of the crucified Christ, its red berries the drops of blood on His forehead.

Mistletoe, the fruit of fertility adopted as a symbol of His birth. So Gwenhwyfar worshipped the birth of Jesu, and began, like so many, to forget the old ways.

Afterwards Father Simon accompanied the family back along the mud-slushed pathway to the villa, escorting Winifred. She was an unexpected presence. Out of courtesy Gwenhwyfar, as acting headwoman, had invited her to share the family's day, explaining politely they celebrated the birth of Christ in a modest manner. To her surprise, Winifred had accepted eagerly.

Arthur's wife had entered the chapel, sinking into a low reverence before the altar, ostentatiously flourishing a glittering gold crucifix and bejewelled rosary. Father Simon had greeted her enthusiastically, delighted to see her.

Watching them Gwenhwyfar thought the two seemed well acquainted. At the first opportunity she questioned the servants, discovered Father Simon had regularly attended the Lady Winifred while she had been confined with her illness following the birth, and death, of her child. Gwenhwyfar shrugged the matter aside; she cared little about Winifred or, for that matter, Father Simon.

Late afternoon. The sky was darkening with the threat of more sleet. Gwenhwyfar entered Arthur's chamber in search of Bedwyr. She laughed, the amusement spreading from full red lips to sparkling green eyes. He was seated beside Arthur, huddled beneath swathes of bed furs.

Arthur was expounding some greatly embellished tale of battle. 'Is it so cold in here?' she asked, indicating the fur mound.

'It's damn nigh cold enough to freeze my essentials off!' replied Arthur, grinning impishly. 'I sent Bedwyr to find someone to replenish the braziers, but it seems the household is too busy with seasonal festivities to bother about a wounded soldier cursed with the indignity of being bound to his bed.'

Gwenhwyfar prodded at the nearest brazier, ignoring his petulance. 'More charcoal is needed, I shall send someone to see to it. Bedwyr, the meal is all but ready, run along to wash and change.'

He protested loudly.

'Suit yourself, stay with your cousin if you wish.' Gwenhwyfar turned to leave the room, paused. 'Except,' she looked blandly at the two of them nestled cheerfully together, 'if you choose to remain here, you will miss eating.'

Aghast, the boy tumbled from the bed. Normally, he ate in the kitchens only permitted to join the family for special occasions. He had no intention of missing a rare treat!

'Hold!' Arthur bellowed as the boy scuttered across the wooden floor of the first-floor chamber. He pointed to a chest which stood beneath one of the small casement windows. 'Look in there, lad.'

Bedwyr trotted to it, flung the lid wide, dived on two packages rolled in cloth.

'The largest is for you,' Arthur said, added, 'Bring the smallest to me please.'

The boy did as he was asked, cradling his own prize in his arm, slipping the wrapped cloth from the concealed contents as Arthur relieved him of the smaller bundle. With a gasp of delight, Bedwyr brandished a sword, a real soldier's sword save for the blunt edging.

'It will do you for now, lad. When you are a man grown, come to me and I shall replace it with one a little sharper.'

Bedwyr ran to Arthur and hugged him, clamouring his thanks, eyes shining with pride and pleasure. Then he dashed from the room eager to prepare for dinner and a chance to show his gift.

Gwenhwyfar closed the door muffling the sound of his retreating, delighted whoops. 'Your mother will not be pleased at your choice of gift. She has no wish for him to become a fighting man.'

Arthur snorted contemptuously. 'I am well aware she has plans to see him in some holy profession. If that is what he wishes, then that is his choice. But,' he shoved the weight of heavy furs from his leg, 'I may need every fighting man in a few years. I would rather have my cousin serving me, not God.' Drolly, 'And aside, it has harmed no holy man to have knowledge of wielding a sword. I have something for you. Come here.'

She hesitated, a flutter of panic telling her to leave the room - now. Her heart beating fast, she stepped from the door, came to the side of his bed. He took her hand, gently but firmly, enclosing the soft whiteness within his own firm grasp.

'You are trembling?' he asked softly.

'You were right, this chamber is cold.' She kept her eyes downcast, studying the bright pattern of the woven bed cover peeping beneath the furs.

'Are you afraid of me, Gwen?'

She looked up at that, meeting his brown eyes. They watched her intently, cutting through any pretence as easily as looking at the world through clear glass.

She answered truthfully, for few could lie to Arthur. 'I am not afraid of you. I...' She halted, uncertain. She was not afraid, yet why did her heart beat so wildly? Why did the desire to run from the room overwhelm her?

He placed the package in her hand, curled her fingers round it. 'For you.'

She glanced from him to the parcel, frowning curiously, and tentatively unwrapped it. Across her palm lay a slender woman's dagger with carved ivory hilt set with jewels.

'How did you come by this?' she breathed, not daring to believe the happiness swelling within her.

Arthur shrugged carelessly. 'Oh, I came across it.'

'I never thought to see it again!' Her words came faintly, barely audible, so deep was her happiness at having her mother's dagger once again. A lump of emotion caught in her throat. She bit her lip, shook her head, willing herself not to cry like some immature child.

Arthur reached out and squeezed her hand. 'I recognised it, knew it for what it was – I'd seen it often enough in Gwynedd, after all.'

Was he still as she remembered him after all? He was older, battle wise, but, meeting his intense gaze, she recognised and welcomed with joy those qualities of understanding and empathy that had drawn them together as children.

'You do remember, then?' she asked cautiously, scarcely daring to hope for a reply. 'You have not forgotten how it was.'

He relaxed, the skin wrinkling with laughter lines at the corners of his suddenly caring, expressive eyes. Very quietly, he said, 'I shall never forget, *Cymraes fach*. Never.'

Gwenhwyfar had never thought to hear him call her by that name again. Shyly, she leant forward, placed a quick, light kiss on his cheek. A sound came from the door as it opened, followed by the rustle of a gown.

'I see you are recovering well, my husband.'

Gwenhwyfar leapt away from the bed as if stung, her face flushing pink.

'Winifred, how nice of you to take the trouble to come and see me!' Arthur drawled.

'I have left my own bed only these past days, husband, plagued with a fever and other, women's, troubles.' She swept past Gwenhwyfar, ignoring her. 'But I have kept myself constantly informed of your well-being.' Placing a sensuous kiss on her husband's lips, she sat on the bed, took his hand possessively in her own.

'I have been desolate,' she said with convincing sorrow, 'being so weak from the difficult birth and then the distress of the taking of one so young from us. And now this!' She patted his hand fondly, then dabbed at her eyes. 'I so feared I should lose you also.'

She settled herself the better beside him. 'Thank God you are recovering and all my worry was for nought. Our child has gone, but there will be many chances for others.' She bent forward and gave him a second, more lingering kiss.

The door closing broke her from the embrace to call, 'Oh, Gwenhwyfar!'

Reluctant, Gwenhwyfar re-entered the room.

'My dear child.' Winifred shifted slightly so as to look at her. 'I must thank you for your kindness to my injured husband. I understand you have nursed him well.' She clutched Arthur's hand between her own, tight against her breasts. 'You have so many other duties in addition to this, what with Lady Ygrainne ill and the seasonal festivities.' How sickly sweet that false smile of hers could be.

'Now I am well I can take some of the burden from your shoulders.' Winifred turned back to Arthur, stroked hair from his eyes, an action he detested. 'I shall take care of my dear husband now.' A honey-sweet smile. Tainted with spite.

Gwenhwyfar dipped a slight reverence, said 'It will please the household you are well enough to leave your room.'

Arthur called, 'Come back later, Gwen? I would be ...' he paused, searching for the right words with Winifred listening, 'pleased at your company.'

Clutching her dagger between her hands, Gwenhwyfar nodded once, made to leave, heard: 'The blatant cheek of that girl, my dearest! They all talk of how she oversteps her position, you know. I am surprised your mother stood for it.'

Closing the door, Gwenhwyfar did not wait to hear Arthur's reply. If he had one.

JANUARY 455

§ XVII

Sitting by the window of Arthur's chamber, Gwenhwyfar stared out at the black night and the curtain of rain. It fell so thickly she could barely see the courtyard below. 'There will be flooding by morning,' she said as a gust of wind battered heavy drops against the thick glass. She shivered.

'Come away from the window if you are cold,' Arthur remarked, engrossed in the parchment he was reading.

'I am not cold,' she retorted. All the same, she wandered over to a brazier, held her hands out to it.

'It must please you Winifred is now able to nurse you,' she said, added to his derisive snort, 'I had no idea she was so devout a Christian.'

'Nor had I,' he answered drily, letting the parchment roll up on itself. 'It ought not surprise me though – she has wit enough to know where to place a safe footing. And,' bitterly, 'she is clever enough to snare the unsuspecting. Pay no heed to her, Gwen. I choose who I wish to have with me, not her.'

Gwenhwyfar fingered the dagger sheathed safely at her side, its ivory handle proud against the wine red of her gown. She smiled to herself, recalling Winifred's glare of outrage when she had noticed it there.

It had happened while the family was being served with the second course of the celebrational dinner. The first course had been eaten with relish: olives, baked dormice sprinkled with honey and poppy seeds; spiced eggs and honeyed wine. Ygrainne portrayed her home as a humble residence, but when guests were to be entertained her kitchens were found to be well supplied, and her cooks of excellent ability.

The servants had carried in roast sucking pig stuffed with pastry and honey and served with chicken livers, beets and wholemeal bread. Iawn had noticed the dagger, remarked on its craftsmanship and asked whence it had come.

Politely Gwenhwyfar had passed it to him, allowing him to inspect it more closely, saying, 'It has been mine since my mother's death,' adding, looking straight at Winifred, 'And so it always shall be.'

Gwenhwyfar had thought of relating the scene to Arthur in the days between, but decided against. He might think she was prodding to hear how he had come by it.

The Nativity gaiety, such as it had been, was past and a few flurries of snow had given way to incessant rain battered by a north-easterly wind that gusted around the villa and found every crack and gap to scurry through. Spring seemed a long way ahead.

Arthur patted the bed. 'Come sit beside me, I can barely see you in those shadows. It is not easy to hold a decent conversation by bellowing across the width of a room.'

Timidly she came, sat perched on the edge like a bird ready for flight. She had been here in this room on four or five occasions since that evening when Winifred had swept in and underlined her position as Arthur's wife. Had come this evening at Arthur's express request because Winifred was safely tucked up in her apartment nursing another feverish head cold.

'How does your leg feel?' she asked, for want of anything better to say.

'Like a lead weight,' he answered.

'Cynan tells me it heals well at last,' she could not resist teasing, 'now you are resting, as you were first ordered.'

'Cynan talks too much,' Arthur replied.

With no warning, he leant forward and took her wrist holding it firmly, a little too tightly. 'Be wary of Winifred, she has the tongue and bite of a viper.'

Gwenhwyfar made a light-hearted attempt at parrying his sudden concern. 'Then surely I ought not be in your bedchamber alone with you.' She attempted to retrieve her arm, to pull away from him.

To her surprise he said, '*Na*, Cymraes, you ought not.' He let her go, lay back against the pillows, a hand covering his eyes.

The pain of heartache gripped him as he said, 'How can I lie here knowing you are moving around out there where I cannot see you? I want you to stay, talk a while.' He let his hand drop, his face sagging with defeat. His eyes were closed.

For a moment, Gwenhwyfar hovered between staying where she was, perched on the edge of the bed, or leaving. Just as she decided to go, he opened his eyes, held his hand out for hers.

Hesitant, she gave it to him.

With his fingertips he stroked the satin smoothness of her skin, turned her hand over to examine the palm. 'Your hands were rough, with torn nails, in Gwynedd.'

'Horses and weapons are not kind to hands.'

'Nor to men's bones, it seems. Love of Mithras, Gwen, what can I do?'

Withdrawing her hand, folding her fingers together in her lap, she deliberately misunderstood.

'You can read, play board games with Bedwyr or tell him more of your outrageously exaggerated campaigns. There is plenty to amuse you while you rest.' She got to her feet, fastidiously smoothing the place where she had sat.

He plucked irritably at the bed cover beneath his hand. 'I do not want to be amused, Gwenhwyfar. I want you.' There, he had said it.

A few strides would take her to the door. Her fingers could be on the handle, she could be away in two beats of the heart. So why, in all that was wise, did she remain standing here like a fool beside his bed?

She pretended not to have heard, but her voice came too shrill. 'If you are bored, I could sing for you.' It was a fine excuse; without waiting for a reply she whisked away, intending to fetch her harp from her own room, feeling hot colour burning her cheek.

Her chamber was quiet. She lit a single lamp that cast a flicker of shadow over the scant furniture. Gwenhwyfar opened the small chest standing at the foot of her bed, brought out a soft leather bag, slid from it her harp. It was a light instrument suited to a woman's touch. Her Da had thought to send it, knowing her love of the thing.

Kneeling beside the open chest, she laid it on her lap, strummed her fingers over the strings. It needed tuning. Her harp was a link with home. Home. Absently she plucked at the strings, tightening or loosening. Satisfied, she drew her fingers, gently, with a butterfly touch, rippling a whisper that vibrated with velvet sound.

She sang softly her voice low, the words reflecting her despair, and her tears began to fall. Tears of surrender to the loss of hope, the ache stabbing like a war spear, her tears spilling like blood from the wound. Her head sank into her hands, and she sobbed.

Someone took the harp from her. Arms were about her shoulders, drawing her forward, enclosing her in a circle of loving protection. For a moment she clung, unaware, grateful for the solidity and the strength stopping her from sliding further into the cesspit of blackness that insatiably beckoned, that would not, would not leave her be. Her tears at last eased and, cried out, she slumped exhausted, her head against his shoulder. Still he held her tight, not letting go.

Her arms went around him pulling him to her, betraying her violent need to keep him close.

'I thought you had forgotten me, thought you felt nothing for me.'

Arthur stroked the damp hair from her forehead, his hand cool; crooned to her loving and gentling. 'I have never forgotten you, Cymraes. Feel for you more than ever you could imagine.'

She believed him, knew he spoke the truth.

Self-conscious, Gwenhwyfar twitched her shoulders, shrugging herself free of his touch, and drew back from him a little. In the pouch hanging at her waist she found a cloth, blew her nose, rubbed fingers over puffed eyes.

With one finger under her chin he tilted her face up to him. What had he caused her? So much grief, so much pain and hopeless loss. If he stayed here with her in this chamber, how much more grief and pain would streak her beautiful, wonderful face with tears?

'I am in a web, and Winifred with her father sit in the middle like giant black spiders,' he said.

'And you were lured into it like some unsuspecting fly?' The words burst from Gwenhwyfar before she could stop them. Her eyes flashed fire, the inner ring dark green around the gold-flecked iris. She stood, moved away from where he sat awkward on the floor.

With great calm Arthur shut the lid of the chest, used its solidity to haul himself upright. He sat on its closed lid, wincing at the pain coursing from his thigh. Blood of the Bull! Would this thing never stop throbbing? Folding the thin robe he wore tighter round his naked body, he said, 'As you wish. I saw the web. Walked smack into it. Winifred was all you were not. That is why I wed her.' He had his back to Gwenhwyfar. It was easier to talk truth that way, without the need to look at her.

'I agreed to the marriage when I thought you betrothed to Melwas. By the time you fled Britain, it was too late; I was already trapped, with no bolt-hole save for Vortigern to use as an excuse to make an end of me.' He gave a wry smile, ducked his head to watch her over his shoulder. 'And even for you, at that time my lovely, I had no wish to die.' Using his hands as a brace, he sought a more comfortable seated position. 'I had already taken Winifred to my bed, that night of the King's festival. But then, I suppose you knew that.'

Gwenhwyfar shook her head. Wished he had not told her. She had no heart to hear the telling of detail.

'Ah well, no matter, you know now.'

She stood beside the single lamp across the room its feeble light trickling shadows over her face and body, glowing through the unruly copper wisps of hair that always refused to stay bound.

312

Strange, she had never studied a flame before now. The bob and dance of its yellow flicker calmed her chaotically spinning thoughts. How intricate its colours, how perfect its shape.

Keeping, with difficulty, the discomfort from showing, Arthur limped to her side. Standing deliberately close, he drew her to him. His lips closed over hers, a brief touch. She put out her hands, one on each side of his chest, pressed him, unconvincingly, from her.

'I don't want...'

'Are you afraid still?' he said, his voice low, searching. '*Na*, but...'

'No buts, my Cymraes, no more buts, there is a time when it is best not to think, just do.'

He kissed her again, more demanding, his tongue parting her lips, running along her teeth. His hands brushed across the smooth skin of her shoulders, bringing her nearer so that her body touched against his.

Suddenly afraid, the wheel spinning over-fast she pushed him away. 'What of Winifred?'

Arthur released her, stood with head lowered, jaw set, fists clenched. What of Winifred? Ah, if only he knew the answer to that particular riddle! She, his wife, was beneath this same roof, was not some unbidden spirit of the imagination. Come dawn, she would still exist, not vanish with the morning mist. He felt no love for her. Felt nothing for her, not even hatred or contempt.

Why had he accepted her? Because she was everything his Gwenhwyfar was not. Sour against sweet, rough against smooth, loud against quiet. Deceit against truth, and hate against love.

'I care for you, Gwenhwyfar. I love you. Have always loved you.'

Arthur reached for her hand, kissed the palm. There would be dangers, from Melwas, Vortigern and Winifred. Great danger, death even, but what appeal had a safe life if it meant parting?

'At the first opportunity, I shall rid myself of her.'

'Oh, Arthur, do you dwell so deeply in the land of faery dream?' She covered his hand with her own, her fingers curling within his. 'You will never be rid of her.'

They were standing close again; he could feel the contours of her body through his light robe.

'I will.' His hand tightened around hers. Then he acknowledged, 'Even if I cannot rid myself of her, she is nothing to me, a signed contract only. We were pledged with the vows of the Christian ceremony. I put more faith in the Old Ways.'

He glanced at the warming glow of the charcoal brazier and gave a sudden smile. 'This may not be your father's hearth, but it will suffice for our needs.'

Shaking her head bewildered, Gwenhwyfar let him lead her to it, stood where he placed her, opposite himself, the brazier between them, their hands clasped above its heat.

Two ways lay before her. She could step forward on to either path, but having once set foot to it there would be no turning back. One way began rough, with great jagged stones to be clambered over; beyond lay flat land, easy walking, but a country of endless emptiness. The other way was steep, with rocky outcrops and plunging valleys full of uncertainty and storm.

What to do? Which path to take? Her heart would surely break if she made him go, knowing he would never ever come back to her. But if she let him in, took him, what fears lay ahead then?

She knew what he was asking of her. Bid him be gone, or commit herself. To what? This desperate loneliness?

Of a sudden sure of her path she raised her head, said clear and confident the words of the Old Ways, the words spoken across a father's hearth at the binding together of a man and a woman.

'Your life is my life; your death, my death. I will follow where you lead, through water and fire, across earth and stone. My love for you shall burn until the very sun ceases to give us warmth and light; until the moon sinks behind the hills to rise no more. Your dreams are my dreams. Your destiny, my destiny. May the Mother of Earth bless our union.'

He led her three times round the fire in the direction of the sun's path, then took her to him, a little breathless, not believing this was actually happening. *Mithras! Do not let me wake come morning to find this was all a dream!*

Gwenhwyfar stood trembling as he unfastened her shoulder brooches, let her gown fall. Beneath, she wore a tunic of fine linen. She raised her arms and he lifted it over her head, cast it aside. He fumbled slightly with the ties of her breast band, then let that too drop to the floor.

For a moment he stood looking at her, savouring her, his lips parted. She stepped to him, her firm young breasts and curved hips pressing timidly against his own responding body.

His thigh ached abominably, but then so did his need for her. He would have liked to lift her and carry her to the bed, but knew his limitations. Difficult enough to shuffle himself along! Instead, he steered her gently towards it, held his finger poised in the air a moment, went to the door and slid the bolt home.

Winifred was abed, but who knew with Winifred?

A catch of pain escaped as he came beside her, cast quickly aside as his nakedness touched hers. With pain forgotten he took time to claim her for his own, the ache in his thigh subdued by the intensity of need. He wanted to take things slowly, patiently; she was to enjoy this, her first experience of his love.

§ XVIII

The old man stumbled through the great oak doors into Cunedda's Hall as evening was fading into the chill darkness of a winter's night. Tables clattered over, benches and stools scraped or tipped as men leapt to their feet, alarmed or concerned. Several ran to the man, propped his sagging and bloodied body with their arms, then half carried, half dragged him towards Cunedda, who had risen from his seat and was striding down the length of the Hall.

'Who has done this?' he demanded of the old man. 'Who dares attack and injure an elderly and respected man of Gwynedd?'

The wounded man grasped at Cunedda's woollen cloak, his gnarled and bruised fingers clutching tight. 'Sea-raiders,' he gasped, his breath coming in rasping pain from wheezing lungs. 'They burnt our settlement, took the women and children, our cattle.' He coughed, blood frothing with the spittle. 'They left me, a useless old man, for dead, but I came to you, came to get help.'

'When?' Meriaun asked. 'When did they come?'

The old man looked at him, squatting next to his grandsire and offering a cloth to stem the blood. 'Night afore last.' He took the cloth, put it to his bleeding scalp and cast his eyes over the surrounding ring of faces, said to the shaking heads and muttered curses, 'I came as quick as I could.'

Cunedda sympathetically patted the man's shoulder. Old age and aching bones slowed a man so; aye, and that without injuries such as these! 'You did well in the circumstances.' He scanned the warriors gathered in his Hall, questioning with gruff expression their thoughts and reactions.

Nodded satisfied. '*Sa*,' he said. 'All we need do is find the nest-hole of their pitched camp and claim back what is ours.'

The old man tried to laugh, coughed again, his lungs fired from age and injury. '*Na*, I have the knowing of that!'

Men leant closer, intrigued, interested.

'I came across them two, three miles further up the coast from my settlement.' He gathered breath, the sound rasping in his throat. 'I had to circle half a mile to avoid their set watch.'

'Are you certain it was the same party?' Dunaut asked.

'Aye,' Rumaun added, 'There is many a camp this winter. The raiders come and stay. We have a summer ahead of us of nest-clearing.'

'Oh, I'm sure,' the man wheezed. 'I stayed close long enough to recognise the women, and a raider with a great thatch of black hair. It were he who knocked me to the ground, splitting open my skull!'

Meriaun, Dunaut, Rumaun and the other warriors looked at Cunedda. He only needed to say the word and they would be running for horse and spear! Cunedda watched the trail of leisurely blue smoke drifting up from the hearth fire, watched as it curled a while among the carved rafters before slipping away through the smoke hole into the darkness above. His knees pained him these cold winter days, his back ached and his eyes were not so sharp as they used to be. But for all that, the prospect of settling a score with these plagued sea-pirates was not unwelcome. He regarded the waiting men a moment, noted their eagerness, their edge of excitement. Winter was a dreary time, months of sitting around a fire telling tales, preparing for the new-coming season. Aye, it would be good to fetch up the horses. He grinned. 'Let's go!'

The black hour before the coming of dawn lay quiet and still. No moon, but the bright patterns of winter stars glittered against a cold-frosted sky. The breath of the horses came in great clouds of steam, mingled with the heat of their sweating bodies. They were thick-coated this time of year, well protected against the bite of Eryri's sharp frosts and deep snows.

The Hibernian men were sleeping, huddled within oar and sail tents or beneath upturned keels. Their fires had died long since, but a bellyful of roasted ox and stolen ale, coupled with a captured woman, kept the worst of the winter chill away. The first few did not know the death that hit them, muffled by sleep and blankets as they were. The swords of Cunedda and his warriors sliced life and rousing screams with well-placed blows. Others had time to leap awake, fumble for weapons, make some small attempt at defence. None had chance to live, for Cunedda's fury was great and his revenge complete.

The killing was soon over and the several fires that burnt the sea-raiders' ships along with their mangled bodies and bloodied blankets rose thick and black to greet the lightening dawn sky.

Only there came no rejoicing from the sons of Cunedda. No cheering derision as Meriaun had set torch to the first pile of brushwood, flesh and bone. No happiness or carousel at victory. What joy was there in death? What pleasure came in the killing when their beloved Lion Lord, Cunedda, lay slain and growing cold beside the spilt blood of their enemies?

MARCH 455

§ XIX

Winifred watched Arthur and Gwenhwyfar ride out, trotting beneath the arched gateway and kicking their horses into a steady canter beyond. The two sets of hooves left marked tracks through the dew-soaked grass, already tinted a lush green with spring growth. She glowered, knuckles gripping white against the wooden sill.

'To where do they ride?' She spoke the thought aloud, turned startled as a servant answered.

'Most times, to the farmstead of Gaius Justinian Maximus, lady.'

Winifred's eyebrow rose. Gaius? She had heard Arthur talk of him. An old man who farmed his own land beyond the estate's boundary. She turned from the window, casually, as if only half interested. 'How know you this?'

Fidelia blushed crimson, realising her impertinence at speaking out. She busied herself bundling up soiled bedlinen.

'Well?' Leaning against the wall, Winifred tapped her foot, expecting an answer. This girl knew something, and Winifred did not like others knowing things she did not.

If they had not been alone Fidelia would never have spoken, but Winifred's personal maid was elsewhere and the girl had long since discovered that you must seize an opportunity when the gods gave it.

She held the bundle of linen to her, hiding behind it as if it would give her protection. 'I am friendly with a young man.' She lifted her chin. She was no slave but a free woman, and entitled to make the acquaintance of a man of her choosing.

Irritably, Winifred fluttered her hand at her. What cared she for a servant's peasant life? 'Your life is of no interest to me, girl.'

Fidelia lowered her defence, put the bundle down on the bed and walked the few bold steps to stand beside Winifred, eager to exchange gossip. 'My man is a shepherd. He cares for the estate's flock up on the heath. He is often on our high ground, above Gaius's farm.'

'Is he now?' Winifred smiled encouraging. 'And he mentioned your master's presence at this farm of – Gaius, did you say?'

'Aye, my lady. He said he sees him there often, always with Lady Gwenhwyfar, sometimes with young Master Bedwyr also.'

Winifred maintained her friendly smile while digesting the information with cold malice. 'And what, child, do you suppose they do at this farmstead of Gaius Justinian Maximus?'

Fidelia chewed her lip, unsure what else to say, aware too late, she had already tattled over-much. She lifted her shoulders and hands. 'They talk, lady, with the old man and his wife.'

'Talk!' Winifred threw up her hands. 'La, la, la! They ride that distance nigh on every day, to talk!'

The girl stepped back, alarmed at the burst of cynical laughter.

Winifred turned again to stare out the window, her arms folded tight. The two riders had gone. Thoughtfully she fiddled with a ring on her little finger. She turned back to smile at the girl.

'I assume you cannot yet marry with this sheep-herd of yours for lack of money?'

Fidelia inclined her head. He was a good man, kind and thoughtful, with passable features. A moderate lover, though she had been with better. She had lain with Arthur once, her first time that had been, several years past. For all it was before he had left to serve with Vortigern and before he had married Winifred, best not mention it!

Herding sheep was a fair living if you did not mind being poor. Were he to marry, her man would be given permission to build his own dwelling place where he could take his wife and raise his children. But sheep were demanding, silly, smelly creatures. Fidelia had no liking for them. Her man often spent days away with them, especially at lambing. Come spring, she barely saw him unless she cared to make the long walk up to the lambing pens. Once there, he had no time for her beyond a few exchanged words and a quick cuddle. Certainly no time for lovemaking. He had to keep a close eye on those stupid sheep. He would be gone soon now the ewes were heavy with lamb. One week more then he would be off, up to the pens with his lantern, his wolfskin cloak and his tom-eared dog.

Something worried Fidelia about their relationship. Though a good man, he would always be poor, his life always dreary. She did not relish either prospect.

Winifred held out the ring to her. 'Take this as a token for your service, my faithful woman.' She laughed at her play on the girl's given name, added, 'I reward well those who serve me.' She stared meaningfully at the girl who, understanding, took the ring.

Winifred dismissed her and went to her writing table. She must get a third letter to her mother! Her one anxiety now was if Hengest were to move before the coming of summer she would be trapped here with Arthur –and then she would not reckon much to her chances of remaining long on this earth! If only she had borne a living son – or carried another! Hah! What chance of that with the Gwynedd slut taking Arthur's attention!

'Talk!' she snorted, a stylus snapping between her fingers from over-hard pressure. 'Is that the name they give for whoring in this God-cursed place?'

It took five days for Fidelia to discover more. Five days of walking with her man on the hills, of pretending to enjoy helping with those stinking sheep. Steering the conversation, probing and questioning, she found answers as hard to come by as wild strawberries in midwinter.

It was a dreary day. Low grey cloud drizzled rain, accompanied by gusting wind that rattled at the windows and crept through cracks under the doors.

Fidelia was combing Winifred's hair. There had been others around all morning, but at the first opportunity of privacy the girl said in a low voice, 'I met with my man last evening, lady.'

'What is that to me?' Winifred kept her tone indifferent, anxious not to push lest she push too far too soon. She had no intention of spoiling all this delicate work by rushing.

'He told me something of interest.' Fidelia paused, the comb in her hand, eyeing the jewel casket standing on Winifred's table. That small ring the other day had fetched four gold pieces at market.

She had decided not to mention her little gain to her shepherd. Instead, had hidden the coins in a secret hole behind a half-rotten timber in one corner of her bedroom in the servants' quarters.

Casually Winifred pointed to her casket, ordered Fidelia to fetch it and made a pretence of selecting jewellery to wear for the day. 'I swear I do not need all this.' She held a brooch to her shoulder. 'Look at this, I never wear the thing.' She tossed it to the girl. 'You have it.'

Fidelia snatched the brooch up, put it deftly into the pouch at her waist, continued combing Winifred's hair. 'My man said it was a curious thing how, when Lord Arthur and Lady Gwenhwyfar visit Gaius, the old man and his wife do not seem to entertain their company but go about the day as if no one were there.' Her mistress seemed pleased with the information; now she was started on this course she cared little that she was betraying the Pendragon. What had he given her? A quick tumble in the hay, a tossed bronze coin and the need to seek old Livila to have the gotten babe removed. He had not laid eyes on her a second time, though she made it clear she was available. Fidelia would have liked to be mistress to Arthur, as Morgause had been to Uthr. The prospect would have offered a better life than that of a shepherd's wife.

For Gwenhwyfar, she felt a twinge of conscience. Gwenhwyfar had shown kindness, had given her a discarded tunic last summer. But the weight of gold eased the doubt considerably.

'When young Master Bedwyr accompanies them, my man says Gaius takes the boy with him to the fields or to tend the stock.' Fidelia peeped through slant eyes, saving the best until last. 'My lord and lady remain within the house, alone.'

'I see.' Winifred affected a puzzled, innocent face. 'Why do you suppose that might be?'

With deft fingers, Fidelia began braiding Winifred's hair. 'It is not my place to say, except...'

'Except what?'

The girl hesitated. If she said this next thing, she could be opening a box of trouble.

'Speak out, girl!'

The lid was lifted, she might as well open it wide. 'I was about to say, why does any woman in love spend time alone with a man?'

'And you believe Lady Gwenhwyfar to be in love!' Winifred laughed, inwardly seething. How dare that Gwynedd bitch be so blatant! How dare she give the servants cause to gossip and twitter! Arthur was her man. She thought she had made that quite plain to the both of them. She said, incredulous, 'Surely not?'

Fidelia finished the braid, twisted it neatly around Winifred's head, securing it with pins. 'It is obvious, lady! From soon after the celebrations of the Nativity she has been a changed person. Gay and light-hearted, with a look of happiness about her. Why, I have never heard her sing so much. She used to mope about like a laundry day turned wet with sudden rain.'

Winifred sat stone-faced, her hands clenched, nails digging into her palms. Anger threatened to burst from her tight throat. Bitch! This had been going on for some time – she ought to have suspected earlier! Winifred cursed herself; she had suspected, but thought they would not dare become lovers, not while she was in the same building! How could she have been so stupid and blind?

Arthur had come to her two or three times since he had been up and about on that lame leg of his. Said it was paining him still, gave that as the reason for not coming to her more often. She cursed herself inwardly again. Fool! She had mutely accepted his excuse for his apparent lack of appetite, welcomed it even, in view of her preoccupation with her own business. She had taken his word for truth. God's curse, when did Arthur ever speak truth?

So he was tumbling Gwenhwyfar? He would pay for making a fool of his wife; by God's grace, he would pay dearly!

But first she must play this thing through. No use to rave before this servant girl. She must seek to gain support and sympathy.

Winifred slumped forward, slithering off her stool to the floor with a little groan, her face crumpling in anguished disbelief. The effect was very good. Fidelia, with a squeak of alarm, dropped the hairpins and rushed to Winifred's side, placing a comforting arm around her heaving shoulders.

'Oh, my Lady! Do not weep, I beg you! We all know our men are deceitful. The Pendragon is so like his father in that way!'

Winifred clung to the girl, sobbing. Stammered, 'My dear, sweet innocent child, you have no idea how I suffer at his hands!' She had judged her timing perfectly. Through tears, 'I was forced into marriage with him. He took me, you see, took my maidenhood; seduced me with honeyed words and empty promises.' Bitterly, 'He wanted my dowry, my wealth, that was all, not me. What could I do? I wanted to tell my father it was rape, but who would listen to my word against the Pendragon?'

Fidelia was close to weeping also. Oh aye, she knew all about how the Pendragon could seduce a girl with sweet words and gentle hands!

Seating herself upon the stool Winifred patted the girl's hand. 'How I envy you your choice of a simple, kind-hearted sheep-herd!'

Fidelia was caught and bound. She, a serving girl, was sharing intimate confidences with the King of Britain's daughter!

Winifred hurried on; she had her chance, she was not going to miss it. 'He has beaten me, forced me to comply with his depraved ways.' Winifred held the girl's hand tightly. 'What harm have I ever caused him? I have been a loyal, faithful wife, while he has bedded others and openly shamed me! He keeps me here as a prisoner; has forbidden me to ride out, or go to town. I cannot write to my family or friends, am not allowed to communicate with any save those within this household and the good Father Simon. I am watched night and day by his guard.'

Those last were true. Arthur had given specific orders that his wife was not to leave the villa's grounds, she was to be guarded at all times, and no letters written by her hand were to be sent. He did not know of the two already dispatched.

'Why should he do this to you? It is so inhuman!'

Winifred had taken a chance with the cultivation of this particular girl, assuming her to be willing to risk much for a few trinkets. But then Winifred was always shrewd. She pressed on. 'He is inhuman. He is the vile spawn of a monster's loins.' She placed both hands around the girl's. 'All I wanted was to seek a divorce. He does not want me, has no care for me, but would he grant it? No. Instead he brings me, against my will, here. Keeps me as if I were some political hostage or a criminal to be locked away! I lie abed at night wondering whether I shall ever be free, whether I shall ever be allowed to speak with my mother again!' Winifred wept, her head bowed, buried in her hands. Said through great sobs, 'And even whether I shall see the coming of a new day. I fear so much that he may decide to make an end of me!'

'Oh, Lady!' Fidelia tried to comfort her, put her arm around her mistress, held her close, rocking her like a child in need of love.

Winifred, her face hidden, let slip a smile. She had her! Hooked and landed. She grasped Fidelia's arms urgently, holding them tight. 'I must get away! Get to the safety of my grandsire. Arthur cannot touch me there.' She let the girl go and hugged herself, rocking backwards and forwards on the stool. 'But how can I? I am not allowed to communicate with anyone beyond this villa. Arthur has forbidden it:' She shook her head, sorrowful, dejected. 'My parents do not even know whether I bore my child safely. Know not whether I live or die.' Untrue, of course, but Winifred cared little for truth.

'Lady, that is a vile, wicked thing!'

Hooked, landed and gutted.

Fidelia knelt before her mistress. 'What can I do to help? Tell me and I shall do as you ask!'

Scarcely able to contain her delight, Winifred shook her head, pathetic in her self-pity. 'None can help me.' Then a sudden idea. 'Wait, there is something! If I could get a letter to my father! He will know what I must do!' She had decided against her mother this time. Two letters sent and no hint of a response to her pleading.

Crossing quickly to her writing desk, Winifred made a pretence of searching, found a small parchment scroll. 'I wrote this some months past,' she lied. 'Arthur refused to allow its sending, though I openly showed it to him.' She unrolled it. 'It says nothing untoward, speaking only of our child's birth and taking, of my health. Nothing that should not be said. I end by asking the King to arrange for me to come home.'

She thrust the parchment towards the girl and Fidelia made a pretence of scrutinising the neat lettering. It was upside down. As Winifred had expected, the girl could not read.

She was uncertain what she wanted to do, between seeing Arthur and Gwenhwyfar torn to pieces by horses, roasted alive on spits or disembowelled slowly with a blunt-edged knife. Perhaps a taste of all three? Whatever death awaited those two, she must first get home!

She took the letter back, rolled it and secured it. Safer not to place a seal. It was a pity she could not ask Father Simon to send another letter, but no, best to use the girl this time, though she seemed hesitant. Seeing her doubt Winifred opened the jewel casket again, placed a bracelet on the table. 'Of course, such loyal friendship deserves reward.'

Fidelia eyed the wonderful rubies and diamonds. If she sold it, she could ensure a life of considerable comfort; could do better than a sheep-herd for husband. Yet if she should be discovered it would be a whipping and dismissal from service – at the very least.

Casually, Winifred added a pair of earrings, said, coaxing, 'These items are worth much gold, Fidelia. Think what you could do with gold coin!' She took a second bracelet. 'This is to pay for the cost of carrying the letter; its value should exceed what is required. You shall, of course, keep any excess.'

Winifred paused a moment, made to retrieve the items. 'I ask too much of you.'

Fidelia grabbed at Winifred's hand. 'Lady, you do not! I shall see to it your letter is sent.' She stowed the jewellery in her pouch, the parchment safe between her breasts, and scampered from the room.

Winifred went to the window. She smiled at the drizzle-wet hill sloping beyond, drummed her nails on the wood. 'Make a fool of me, Arthur Pendragon? We shall see who laughs the louder!'

Soon, when her letter found its way safe, Vortigern would demand Arthur's recall; they would be going home and his little game of illicit love would be ended!

§ XX

Juliana looked sideways at Gwenhwyfar, who sat with legs swinging on the edge of the kitchen table. Playfully slapped a hand creeping nearer the dough she was kneading. 'You be too old, young miss, for sneaking bits from my baking!'

Gwenhwyfar laughed. 'Never will I be too old!'

There was silence for a while. Gwenhwyfar began to hum a lilting melody; Juliana pounded her wheat bread. The grain had lasted well this winter, stored in the new granary Gaius had built last spring, she was thinking. She said, 'And what will you do when his wife discovers all this?'

Gwenhwyfar ceased her tune.

'She will, you know. You cannot hide from it. One day you will have to face up to the fact he has a legal wife.'

'He is to divorce her.'

'Ah.'

Silence again. Juliana pounded at her dough, flour covering her arms. 'What do you mean, *ah?*'

Patting the dough into shape, Juliana set it aside to rise, dusted her hands, wiped the table clean.

'Do you know why he married her in the first place, my dear?' she asked mildly.

'He was forced into it by Vortimer as a safeguard against her marriage to one of her own kind.'

Juliana nodded. 'I heard that rumour also.'

Gwenhwyfar bridled, jumped from the table. 'Are you suggesting Arthur has lied to me? That he took her willingly?'

'He was not unwilling, was he? He needed funds, child. Needed that fat dowry.' At Gwenhwyfar's scowl, the woman placed her hands flat on the table, leant forward. 'Lass, neither of you has stopped to consider this thing through.'

'We have!'

Shaking her head Juliana measured out fresh flour, began mixing ingredients for honeyed cakes. 'The reasons of then, girl, still exist now. More so.'

Gwenhwyfar snorted.

Juliana wagged a spoon at her. 'Arthur can no more divorce Winifred now than he could refuse to take her as wife then. It made sense for him to marry with her. He must become king, and as Pendragon and husband to Vortigern's Saex born, he could take command of Britain and the Saex in one blow. There are many Saex who are not loyal to Hengest, those who were born and raised in Britain – as were their fathers. They are not loyal to Vortigern either, but the Pendragon? He is different, altogether different. And there are the practicalities. To become king, he needs her wealth; her title and her son to command the Saex. I say again, he cannot, will not divorce her.'

Gwenhwyfar snorted louder. 'What do you know of it?' She hoisted herself once more to sit on the table, folded her arms, sat hunched, hostile.

Juliana was vigorously stirring her mixture. 'It does not take much of a brain to work out the obvious.'

'They detest each other. They have no relationship, no feeling, nothing.'

'Yet, I hear, he still visits her bed.'

Eyes flashing, 'You have good hearing then!'

'I have friends who are servants, child, and servants talk.'

'He has not slept with her!'

'And I say he has!' Juliana beat harder at her mixture. 'He is the Pendragon, girl. He needs a son.'

'I shall give him one.'

In exasperation, Juliana slammed her spoon down on the table. 'You talk like an ignorant peasant! You are his mistress, nothing more.' She took a handful of dough, began shaping round cakes between her plump red hands. 'You will never be the mother of his heir. Winifred, for one, would never allow a bastard born of you to take precedence! La! I wish I had never allowed this thing to happen when it began! I ought have whipped the both of you and sent you away to Father Simon for the confession of your sins!'

'Then why didn't you?' Gwenhwyfar shouted her retort, then slumped, miserable.

Clicking her tongue, Juliana cleaned the sticky mixture from her hands, moved round the table and held her close as if she were a daughter.

'Why did I not? Because I would rather have you where you are safe, not doing this silly thing in some open field or hidden bush where any could watch. Arthur is like a son to me. I have watched him grow from boy to man. I am proud of him. But la,' she cradled Gwenhwyfar to her, 'I am not so proud of this mess.'

Gwenhwyfar pulled a little away, close to tears. 'Juliana, do not say such things! I have been so happy these past weeks.'

'How long can happiness last? If Winifred should find out...'

'She will not.'

'That, my dearest, is where you are wrong.' Arthur stepped into the kitchen.

Dressed in rough-spun tunic and bracae, with a plain bronze buckle fastening the leather sword belt at his waist he looked like any soldier's son, except his air of authority and leadership belied any lesser rank than supreme commander. As Gwenhwyfar went to meet him, he encircled her slim waist with his arms, affectionately kissed the tip of her nose. 'Winifred will find us out – I would wager she has already done so.'

Gwenhwyfar nestled closer to Arthur's strength. 'I am not afraid of her.'

'Then you ought to be! She can cause much trouble should she decide to poke her stick in this ants' nest. And poking where she is not wanted is something my wife excels at.'

Agreeing with him, Juliana added, 'I would think twice, and once again before placing too much trust where that one is concerned.' She slid her cakes into the oven. 'Have you thought what is to happen,' she asked, 'when you return to Britain, Arthur?' She indicated his leg. 'Your wound is well healed, God be praised, and the sea lanes are open again after the winter storms. How long before the army calls you back? What are you to do with your wife and mistress then, eh?'

Gwenhwyfar shuddered as a dark shadow passed over her. When Arthur goes? She had not thought of it, had not stopped to consider much at all beyond the here and now. She looked up with trust at his firm jawline, his long, straight nose and those piercing brown eyes, half concealed by the hair flopping over his face.

With conviction she said, 'I am to go with you.' When he did not reply, she said again, with more of a question, 'I am to go with you?'

He wiped a hand around the previous night's growth of stubble he had not bothered removing that morning, perched his backside on the table where, before, she had sat, and held her at arm's length the better to see her.

'Only Winifred comes with me when I sail on the morrow.' Gwenhwyfar stared at him. Hearing the words, not comprehending.

'I have been meaning to tell you these past few days,' he said, 'but I did not want to spoil your happiness too soon.'

Gwenhwyfar swung away to stand before him, hands clenched to her hips. 'Spoil my happiness too soon? Like thunder out of a blue sky you sit there and calmly tell me you are going, not with me, but with her? I am to be discarded then? Dropped by the wayside like some worn cloak!'

'Cymraes, it is not as you think.'

'Oh, is it not?' She stamped her foot. 'How do you know what I think? I will tell you, shall I? I think you are a lying, deceitful, whoring bastard!' She fled from the kitchen, through the small but comfortable living space and beyond to the privacy of the bedchamber.

Arthur heard the door slam, looked helplessly at Juliana. 'She had to know.'

The woman matched his gaze. 'Aye, she had to know. But not like that.'

He flared up, more angry with himself than with Juliana. 'How then? Tell her days since and destroy what small happiness she has had? Wait, and tell her tonight in front of the entire family?' He slammed the table with his fist, swore. Began again, calmer. 'I apologise. You are, of course, right. I had not meant to tell her like that. I had intended to tell her later.' He hung his head. 'After our last time together.'

Juliana touched his arm, recognising his pain. 'You do love her, then?'

He groaned, swung away from the table, stood facing the wall, his hands resting above his head. 'By all the gods there have ever been or ever will be, I love her.' He leant his forehead against the whitewashed plaster.

His muffled voice did not hide the ache. 'I have been ordered to return by Winifred's father to attend a meeting of Council with Hengest. There is to be a new treaty.' He laughed wryly. 'He mentioned his concern for my wife's welfare.'

'Does he not have cause for such concern?' Juliana asked rather tartly.

Ignoring the sting, Arthur wandered to the table, brought a stool from beneath it and sat down with his chin resting on his hands. 'She is a clever, cunning bitch. I would pay a high price to discover if she did manage to get a letter home, despite all my efforts to prevent it!'

'Father Simon?' said Juliana thoughtfully. 'She has spent many an hour with him these past months. I know he is impressed by her devotion to the faith, and her generosity to the Church as a whole.'

'You seem to know a lot about my estate's goings on, old woman,' Arthur said cynically.

Juliana laughed, removed the cakes from the oven, their tantalising aroma filling the kitchen.

'I go often to town and hear talk, and I am observant at Mass inside your mother's fine chapel on the Lord's day.' She handed him a hot cake which he ate appreciatively. 'Young Bedwyr chatters enough for me to know the inside workings of your villa backwards! Plus,' she added, 'I have heard nothing but praise of Winifred from the good father himself.'

Arthur made a derisory noise. 'Winifred, like her mother, can make a fine show of benevolence when it suits her.'

'The light of God can move in mysterious ways, Arthur.'

'I doubt,' said Arthur, wiping crumbs from his lips, 'even God would welcome that bitch into His kingdom. She is material more suited to the other place.' He pointed downwards. 'Father Simon is a man who sees good in every soul. He has begged and badgered me, these past weeks, to allow her more freedom. What does he know of politics? Does he not realise for the price of a gold ring she could be up and away, running to her Saex kin? I will not let her go where I cannot have her watched. Not while she still bears the title of wife.'

With a quirk of her eyebrow Juliana added, 'And of course, how could you allow her out while you are making so free with that one in there?' She nodded at the door, in the direction Gwenhwyfar had gone.

Arthur grinned, his eyes shining. 'How could I indeed?'

'Has it occurred to you, lad, your wife might not want to be parted from you?'

Arthur coughed, spluttering crumbs. 'What? Winifred? She wants me as much as a boil on the backside!'

Juliana persisted. 'Are you so certain? Wife to the Pendragon is a title worth the having. I have heard she weeps for you at night when you do not go to her.'

'Your ears are hearing the wrong tales.' Arthur pushed himself away from the table and took another cake, Juliana swiping ineffectually at his hand. 'During our short period of marriage I have made it my business to see through all Winifred's tricks and schemes. Her tears do not fool me one drip of rain water.'

'Yet you still answer Vortigern's summons?'

'Until I am in a position to do otherwise I have no choice. If I step over-far out of line, I could find myself in a worse position than my father did. I am biding my time. It will come.'

He walked to the door, munching at the cake, spoke through a full mouth. 'I am going to Gwenhwyfar.'

'Be gentle with her.'

§ XXI

Go away!'
    Arthur ignored Gwenhwyfar's muffled curse, sat on the bed beside her crumpled body. He cautiously rested a hand on her back. She shook it off. 'I said go away.'

'Not without talking first. I am sorry, I did not intend for things to be like this.' He sighed. 'Sorry' was such a hopelessly inadequate word. She remained face down, her arms curled around her head.

'Why?' She rolled over, sat up.

Arthur sighed again. What should he say? What could he say? 'You know why.'

'I do not!' she countered. 'I have no idea why you are sailing for Britain on the morrow with your wife. I have no idea why you are taking her instead of me!' She swung her legs to the floor, moved away from the bed and the man sitting on it. She stormed around the small room, arms animatedly emphasising her words. 'You are the Pendragon, rightful Lord of Dumnonia and the Summer Land; Lord of Less Britain. By all that is right, you ought be seated where Vortigern sits. You ought to be king.' She laughed derisively, stabbed an accusing finger at him. 'You? King? Ha! You cannot run your own life, let alone that of others! Vortigern barks and you jump! The Pendragon? What an empty title! Your father in the other world must be covering his head in shame.' Her voice began to rise, shrill and tense. 'You are nothing but Vortigern's puppet! Are no better than the rest of them who fawn and grovel at his feet!'

'Have you finished?'

'*Na!* All those lies about how you hate her, how she makes your life a misery. How you, you poor, poor man, were forced to marry her. Go on tell me, tell me again how you have no choice but to take her back with you. I dare you!' She spat the last words in his face.

His own anger rising he grasped her wrist. 'You seem to have forgotten I have no power over the lands my father once held. He was exiled, remember? He lost those British rights. He died fighting trying to regain them, or have you forgotten that also? I have no wish to die for a hopeless cause that is lost before it is even begun!'

'So you admit to being a coward!'

Arthur came very close to losing his temper at that moment. He drew breath, swallowed hard, held it in check. 'I value my own life and the lives of my men too highly to spill blood needlessly.'

She still wanted to fight. 'So claiming your rights is no longer necessary?'

'Gwenhwyfar, you are being deliberately obtuse. I have no love for Vortigern, nor his accursed daughter.'

Gwenhwyfar interrupted, 'Yet you share her bed!'

'Blood of Mithras! Once since the Nativity!' Lies came easy to Arthur. 'I get no pleasure from her.'

Gwenhwyfar spluttered with laughter. 'I suppose the begetting of the daughter she bore you was no pleasure either? Or did you play God and produce a second virgin birth?'

'That is blasphemous!'

'My, all of a sudden you are a Christian!'

'Ah, my Cymraes, let us not quarrel,' he said, his hands spread, pleading.

'That is all I am to you, Arthur. How Juliana and her husband must laugh. Arthur the Roman and his Cymraes, his native woman! His British whore!'

Arthur's temper snapped. It seemed such a little thing to push him over the edge but the name had been a special one to him since their childhood, the endearment signifying much more than a name between friends. Why, he could not say, it was just a thing that was. A link with childhood pleasure and vowed love. *Cymraes fach,* 'little British woman' he had called her during those happy, sunny days in Gwynedd. He had dropped the 'fach' unconsciously when he took her as his own.

Arthur's voice was quiet, almost menacing. 'I thought the one I gave that title to was worthy of it.' He added bitterly, 'I thought she was far-sighted enough to realise the tangle of politics is a hard knot to unravel. Someone, I thought, who would be able to understand when my back is up against the wall. One who could share the pain of having to wait, and wait, and wait again until a move sure to win without being butchered can be made. I thought a Cymraes would know this. Obviously she does not. ' He turned to go. Angry at himself for being angry.

'But I am not your woman!' she screamed. 'British born or no, do you not see that? Winifred is!'

With his back to her his hand on the door, he said, '*Na*, Gwenhwyfar, it is you who cannot see.' He left, could not go back.

Juliana watched him ride away. If she saw the tears streaming down his face she made no mention of it to her husband. Nor to the girl who lay across a bed, broken with grief, unaware of the new life growing within her.

§ XXII

Late afternoon, and the drizzle of the past two days had passed, leaving a leaden grey sky with low cloud that threatened more rain to come. Winifred wandered in the direction of the chapel. Father Simon, without seeing her, entered the squat building through the low door as she paused on the far side of the gateway. She glanced at her escort who nodded vaguely and settled himself on the grass growing alongside the wall. It was normal routine. Every afternoon Winifred went there to pray. Every afternoon the guard, a Christian himself, allowed this slight deviation from orders and let her enter the chapel without an escort. Save for the occasional presence of Father Simon, who was near-sighted in faith and vision, it was the only place outside her chamber where Winifred could sit unobserved. She paused in the porch before entering. The letter was to go with the noon tide, Fidelia had said, in trusted hands on a fast ship bound direct for Londinium.

The door was ajar. Winifred, her hand on the latch, was about to step inside when she heard the priest's voice saying, 'Well, a stranger in my domain!'

Who was he talking to? Pushing at the door she stopped short as Arthur's voice answered. What was he doing here? She had watched him ride out again with that slut this morning, was not aware he had returned. She stood silent, ears alert, listening.

'My mother's chapel,' Arthur stressed the ownership, 'has few reasons to draw me here.'

'Yet you come today?'

'Because today I have a reason. My wife comes here, I believe?'

Listening outside Winifred bristled at the disgust in his voice. Had Arthur discovered the sending of her letter? A coldness congealed in the base of her stomach. She knew enough of Arthur to fear him. If he had read that letter she would certainly not see the dawn!

Inside, unaware of the listener beyond the door, the priest in his turn stressed ownership. 'All are welcome in *God's* house.'

Arthur did not miss the point but let it pass. He disliked Father Simon, he knew not why. He was a man who followed the ways of many of his kind, preaching the words of God, unflinching in his duties towards Christ, the sick and the poor. Arthur guessed his dislike stemmed from his mother who worshipped the man almost to the point of blasphemy. He was her friend, mentor, confidant and confessor, and she had thrust his words, God's words, down Arthur's throat so often in his boyhood that he was heartily sick of the three of them. The holy trinity? God, Ygrainne and Father Simon!

As much as anything, it had been the need to escape their combined preaching that had persuaded him to take Cunedda's advice and leave, to gain experience under Vortigern's rein.

'Why does Winifred come here?' Arthur snapped the question, expecting an instant reply. Father Simon stared back at the young man before him. Noted the tired eyes, the sallow, drawn skin. The defiance shielding uncertainty.

Father Simon was given to trusting the promises of his small flock. He believed all could be saved and baptised to the true faith, with patience and understanding. He believed no man, woman or child was wholly bad, merely ignorant of God's way. Some thought him a fool. Happen he was.

'Your wife,' he answered, 'comes here to pray for deliverance from this cruel prison you have immured her in.'

Arthur laughed. 'Is that what she has told you? Your eyes are veiled against deceit, Father.'

'On the contrary my son, they are wide open.' Father Simon seated himself. 'My eyes tell me you are troubled, else why would you be here in Our Lord's house? My ears tell me you do not trust your wife. My heart tells me you are as imprisoned as she, and,' he added, satisfied at knowing he was right, 'my logic tells me all these things are connected.'

'My wife,' Arthur hissed, 'is a liar and a cheat.'

If he had meant to shock the priest, Father Simon showed no sign of it. He answered, 'And are you not?'

Outside, Winifred almost laughed aloud. Well thrust!

The priest grew stern. 'You exchanged the vows of marriage with her willingly.'

'I did not. I was blind drunk.'

'You consummated the marriage; she has since given you a child.'

'She has given me pain and hatred.'

'Which you have returned.' Father Simon, refusing to be drawn placed a hand on the younger man's shoulder. 'My son, can you not see what grief you have caused her? Taking her away from home against her will is distressing enough, but confining her and banning all communication with her family, is that not unreasonable?'

'Not when she plots against me; not when she intended to deprive me of my own child.'

'But the child died. Your argument is invalid. Could it not be you keep your wife under guard because in your heart you do not wish to lose her? Because you have love for her?'

'What?' Arthur exclaimed sardonically. 'Love that bitch!' He stood up and moved away, fingering the carvings along the top of his mother's high-backed chair.

'Then let her go.'

'Are you judging me?' Arthur had the chair between them, hands still now, his stance daring the priest to answer.

Father Simon smiled benevolently, resting his hands on his knees. 'It is our God who judges, not I.'

'Your God, not mine,' Arthur hurled back. 'I follow the soldiers' god, Mithras.'

'Mithras? Can the shed blood of his sacrificial white bull protect you more than the love of Christ?'

This persistent paganism was a constant thorn in the priest's side. The thorn festering with the knowing the son of Lady Ygrainne stubbornly refused to let go of the old and embrace the new. But then, Father Simon knew Arthur well. He had never been one to do as others advised. This Pendragon trod a lonely path.

Arthur backed down, raising his hands in surrender, walked around the chair and sat down, his leg hooked over the arm. 'I have not come here for theological debate. I have come for your help.'

Beyond the door, Winifred raised her eyebrows. Arthur – seeking help!

Inside, Arthur rubbed at sore eyes; he had not slept well these past nights. His thigh pained him often during the hours of darkness, and then there had been Vortigern's summons. He drew his cloak around him; it was chill inside these cold stone walls where no sunlight fell.

Rising from his seat, Father Simon walked to the altar, twitched a corner of the covering cloth straight. It was a beautiful thing of fine linen, stitched with care by Ygrainne.

'This night and the nights to follow Father, I ask for all the help I can get, from whatever God or gods are willing to give it.'

'There is only the one true God. He can offer all the help you need if you would only bow to His will.'

Arthur shook his head, unfolded himself from the discomfort of the hard-seated chair and began prowling around the small building – lightly touching carvings, moving a candle holder set in a niche, slightly to one side. The candle tipped, fell to the floor. 'I am beyond saving. The help I speak of is not for me, not directly.' He retrieved the thing, set it back in its place, said, 'We have had our differences, Father but you are a good man with a kind heart. I ask if you will see to the well-being of Lady Gwenhwyfar. She will be in need of friends after I sail on the morrow.'

Winifred froze, her eyes opening wide, her body tensing. Tomorrow! Leaving on the morrow! He could not possibly be intending to leave her here in this godforsaken place! She willed herself to be still, forced down the sudden urge to storm through the door and demand to be taken with him. To scream and scream. She must listen!

Father Simon sounded equally surprised. 'Is this not rather sudden?'

'I received word of recall some days past.' Arthur was now inspecting an embroidery hung at the back of the chapel. He recognised it as more of his mother's needlework, vaguely remembered her working on it. Aye, that blue bird swooping down – as a boy he had stood watching her fashion it. He remembered her needle flashing, fingers deft, the little bird appearing with each neat stitch like some work of magic. He would have been about five summers old.

Father Simon, clasping his hands together in an attitude of prayer said, 'It may be indelicate of me to say this, but infidelity usually results in one party's extreme hurt.'

Arthur's eyes narrowed. His silent response meaningful.

'And the Lady Winifred?' The priest's calm gaze ignored Arthur's hostility. 'I would not see her the injured party. She is your wife.' Sharp, judging, 'The other woman is not.'

Sidestepping the reprimand Arthur ran his finger along a shelf, inspected the black smear of dust left on his finger. 'Is there anything you need for this place? Salvers, gold plate?'

Father Simon folded his arms. Arthur always had been irritating, was forever ducking issues of importance as if he had not heard.

'Your lady mother is most generous with her gifts. We have all we need.' He would not have the subject turned. 'What of your lawful wife?'

'None the less,' Arthur's hands were open, offering generosity, 'I would be pleased to donate something. A chalice?' He strode towards the altar. A crucifix stood there and two silver candlesticks. 'You do not have one. I shall see what I can obtain.'

The priest inclined his head, his hands burrowing beneath the folds of his loose sleeves. 'That would be most gracious of you. I thank you.'

Almost an afterthought Arthur announced, 'I am returning Winifred to Vortigern. I wish to divorce her and wed Gwenhwyfar.'

Outside, Winifred caught her breath, relieved at first that she was to be taken home, then outraged as his meaning sank in.

Father Simon was slowly shaking his head, his lips pursed. 'It is a sad day when solemn vows are broken.'

Winifred's hands were clenching and unclenching, her eyes bulging. She mouthed silent curses, sending all the poxes and plagues possible to various parts of her husband's anatomy.

'I am to end soldiering.' The Pendragon laughed ironically. 'Who knows, when I am settled here on the estate I may even abandon Mithras. A farmer has small need of a soldier's god.'

Father Simon did not laugh or smile. 'It will be hard for you to give up such a life. Hard for your lady wife to be so cruelly set aside.'

Almost to himself Arthur added, 'Harder still to give up the hope of holding all Britain.' Louder, 'It will be no cruelty for Winifred. For once I am obliging her by giving her what she wants.'

Ah, no! Winifred was thinking. You will not get away with this! You will not discard me like some dried-up milk cow and exchange me for a wide-eyed heifer!

Laying his hand on Arthur's arm, the priest asked with a frown, 'You would renounce all for this one woman?'

'All of it.' Arthur leant his hands on the altar, shoulders drooping. 'Gwenhwyfar does not know of my plans – neither does Winifred.'

Outside, Winifred sneered, mouthed *Ha! Do I not!*

'Gwenhwyfar believes I am deserting her, which is why I came to ask you to watch over her while I am gone. I would rather have my wife safely set aside before giving Gwenhwyfar what she deserves.'

Oh, she will get what she deserves! Have no fear of that, my husband! In a fury Winifred retraced her steps from the chapel, marched back along the narrow path leading to the villa her guard scrambling to his feet, taken unawares. She slammed into her room and threw her cloak on the floor, screaming at scurrying servants to leave her.

So he was to abandon her! Was to take that whore as wife in her stead! Oh no, no, he would not! She would not let him. Forgotten now her desire for a divorce, her plans to be rid of him. Those things were all on her terms. *Her* terms, not his.

What angered her the most, made her teeth clench and her hand sweep phials and bottles from her table, were all those wasted hours. That soft treading and simpering, her forced smiles, her splendid charm. All winter she had striven to win confidences, gain sympathy. Father Simon, Fidelia, others. All that work to gain their trust, and a letter sent this very day to her father, all that and Arthur was leaving with her after all! Damn the man, damn him to hell!

She lifted a wooden box from the chest beneath the window. Inside, a phial, wrapped in soft velvet. As she uncovered it, green sparks gleamed as light caught the rough-made glass.

She lifted it held it up to the window, a malicious smile curving over her lips. 'He will not have her. If he does not have me, he will not have her.' She laughed, head back, mouth open. Laughed.

Reaching for the bowl of dried fruits beside her bed she sprinkled a few drops of the liquid, watched as it seeped through the wrinkled skins of dried dates and figs. Then she stoppered the bottle and returned it safe inside the box, wrapping it again in its protective cocoon of velvet. The lid shut, Winifred washed her hands in a bowl of water, dried them, called for Fidelia. One more task, one final trinket given.

During dinner, Winifred was unnaturally talkative, almost gay. As was Ygrainne, now recovering well from her illness, gaining strength by the day, colour returning to her cheeks.

Their last meal together. Both women were happy, eager for the departure. Both had expressed delight when Arthur informed them of the imminent return to Britain. Winifred had kissed him, holding him close. It gave her a sense of well-being, of gloating power to secretly know his plans.

Ygrainne felt relieved and relaxed now he was at last taking his leave. With God's blessing it would be a while before he returned!

Ectha asked the question Winifred had been burning to ask, but had thought better of. 'Where is Gwenhwyfar this night? Does she know of your departure, my boy?'

Ygrainne answered for Arthur. 'She was taken ill at the farm of Gaius Justinius Maximus. A message was sent. I shall send a litter for her on the morrow; it was too late to do so this evening.' She sniffed. 'Why she rides there so often, I know not. There is as much to do here on the estate as on some poor farm.'

No one answered her.

Ectha took a further helping of roasted pig. 'She is missing an excellently prepared meal.'

Winifred smiled. No matter – one as well prepared awaited her.

Ceridwen sat silent on Gwenhwyfar's empty bed. Iawn, her husband, was staying in Gaul and consequently, was wishing God speed to the men of Arthur's guard – which meant they were emptying many wineskins this night. He would not be abed until late.

She disliked retiring without him; she missed his comforting bulk, his strong arms protective around her. She patted the swelling bulge of her stomach. How proud he had been when she had told him of the coming child!

Her thoughts went to Gwenhwyfar. What a hopeless tangle she had got herself into. She would be so alone and miserable again now Arthur was going.

When the message had arrived from Gaius Ceridwen was all for riding straight to be with her cousin, guessing at the reason for this sudden illness, but Ygrainne forbade it saying it would soon be dark, unsafe to ride. She could go on the morrow, with the litter.

Ceridwen padded on bare feet to the window, peered out at a star-peppered sky. She would away to her own bed. No use waiting for Iawn this night. Absently, she selected a handful of Gwenhwyfar's dried fruit from a table nearby, blew out the single lamp and went to her own chamber, eating as she walked. Some of the fruit tasted bitter, she swallowed quickly, finished the handful, dusted sticky hands on her shawl and went to bed.

Within two days, Ceridwen was dead.

APRIL 455

§ XXIII

Returning, Arthur discovered, was like being thrown into a deep river and being swept along by the current unable to swim for shore or cry out for help. It was incredible so much could alter within so short a space of time.

It had not seemed so from a distance. The smoke from domestic fires drifting over red roofs, the glimpse of taller buildings beyond the solid bastions of the city wall – from this last curve of the river the city had seemed ordered and bustling in the midday sunshine. Ships were moored along the river frontage; the bridge ahead thronged with carts and men and cattle. With it all, the distant thrum of sound: voices, music, animals; donkey, cow, horse. The clatter of hooves, the rumble of wheels. Children shrieking, men and women shouting.

As he drew closer, he saw the smoke trails were less numerous than he had thought, the carts not so laden and the city wall, and beyond it the roof tiles, were cracked and crumbling with great gaping holes here and there. And the ships were all Saex. Dozens of them. Trading ships with sails furled, some with cargo offloaded, others with barrels, baskets and pots still aboard. Moored among them were flat-bottomed oared vessels, the largest Arthur reckoned to measure around sixty feet in length between the high curves of prow and stern. As his own ship slid by one of these great war monsters, lying like the rib-exposed carcass of some huge dead animal, he counted eleven rowing benches; calculated at least sixty men per ship.

He stood on deck, hands pressed against the rail, frowning. Why so many Saex? Where were the British craft and other coastal traders?

He peered astern. She was still there, although now hanging to leeward. The Saex craft had slipped her moorings down by the estuary signal station and had eased into the wake of his own vessel. She had kept her distance, but there was a distinct feeling of being herded like a lost sheep back to the fold. She was flying a banner depicting a white horse. Hengest's emblem.

Hengest. Warrior, leader. Hengest with his brother Horsa and his three keels rowed by fierce, loyal men had come, it seemed, a lifetime ago. Exiled from their Jute homeland they had landed on British soil in search of ale for their horns, meat for their bellies and blood for their swords. Had found all three under Vortigern's employment. Only now, the ale was running sour, the meat turned bad and the blood? Aye, well, there was always plenty of blood for the taking.

By the number of moored ships, those three original keels had somewhat multiplied.

The following ship trailed Arthur almost to the bridge. There, before the current took her, she heeled aside, turning in a wide curve to make fast against the first of the Saex-crowded wharves.

The six oarsmen of Arthur's sailing vessel gave one last stroke, shipped their oars and let the flow and their own momentum take them forward to the bridge and under the towering wooden structure, between two of its many piers. Arthur shut his eyes He was no sailor. Those rising stone pillars seemed to come close! Then they were through, shooting out the other side, the oars again dipping into the churning water that fought to make way between the barricades.

A few British ships were this side, gathered in a protective knot along the wharf at the mouth of the tributary river. His own ship back-paddled and swung in sluggishly, leaving the race of the river, heading for the palace water gate. She bumped against the oak planking. Mooring rope clasped in his hand, a crewman leapt ashore before she ducked outwards again, made her bow fast and ran to catch a second thrown rope astern.

Arthur did not wait for the plank to be lowered, jumped instead to firm ground and climbed the steps up to the palace two at a time, his simmering anger overriding the lurch and sway of sea swell. Two ragged guards at the gate, Saex, stared impassively as he strode past. Had the palace always seemed as shoddy and world-weary? Had it always been so in need of repair, or had he just not noticed?

Spring-grown weeds choked the cobbles, plaster had fallen away in great chunks the exposed brickwork beneath beginning to crumble. His footsteps echoed under the entrance arch, unchallenged. He swung along corridors, up some steps, along more corridors and swept into Vortigern's outer chamber where he came face to face with Melwas, Vortigern's sons Vortimer and Catigern, a British captain and, to his intense relief, Cei.

'What in the name of the Bull is happening here?' he thundered, removing his cloak and tossing it to a slave.

'You may well ask,' Catigern drawled from where he sat sprawled across a couch like a swatted spider.

Cei had sprung forward the instant Arthur entered and greeted his cousin warmly, taking his hand, grasping it firmly. 'You are quite recovered? I see you are, praise be to God – when I think of our fears some months past! Thank God they were proven false.' He released Arthur's hand. 'We expected you days since.' Quietly he added, 'Where in all Hell have you been? I have worried myself sick for your well being!'

'You alone, I presume,' Arthur answered, ducking his head towards the glower of displeasure on Melwas's face.

Louder he said, 'I had business to attend afore I came here.' He steered Cei aside, said hastily, 'I have been seeing to my divorce from Winifred. I have endowed her with the small parcel of land I hold along the south coast. That will suffice for her.' He grinned with a devil-may-care gleam. 'She has promised, with dark threats, to find lawyers to claim back her full dowry.' He clapped a hand on Cei's shoulder. 'I don't think she realises how irritatingly long these lawyers can take over domestic settlements!'

Vortimer crossed the room to clasp Arthur's hand. 'It is as well you delayed no longer. Within a few weeks this place will be no more than an empty shell.'

'It seems little more than that now!' Arthur said derisively. Then with caution asked, 'Why?' There was an odd smell here somewhere. 'What has been happening while I have been away? Why are there no British guards here or manning the signal stations? I saw no sign of life, save for Saex, the entire length of the Tamesis.'

'A thousand whys and a thousand more to follow.' Catigern was very drunk.

Cei poured Arthur some wine and part answered his question. 'Vortigern has used only Hengest's men for some time now, he claims he can no longer trust his own breed.'

Arthur took the wine and laughed. 'It has taken him this long to discover it?'

Cei did not echo the humour. 'Our men are camped a few miles from here.' He pointed out their general direction beyond the north gate. 'The King is withdrawing. Moving west to make Caer Leon his royal capital.'

Arthur, the wine halfway to his lips, lowered the goblet in stunned disbelief.

Vortimer took up the telling from Cei. 'The traders and merchantmen have not come to Londinium this spring. Nor will they the next. They say the Saex are too numerous along this eastern coast for safe trade.'

'And from next month they will be taking over the sea lanes also,' added the army captain, perched on the edge of a table.

When Arthur looked blankly from one to the other it was Melwas, surprisingly, who said, 'My uncle proposes to cede the British Cantii territory to Hengest's overlordship.'

'What?' Arthur spun round to face him, spilling his wine.

Melwas returned the hostile stare, dark eye to dark eye.

The door to Arthur's right was closed. Setting his goblet down with a decisive thud, spilling more of its contents, Arthur strode over to it.

'It is no use,' said Vortimer stepping in his path. 'The King's mind is set. He will bring eternal peace, he says, between our two peoples this way.'

'I thought he was supposed to have done that when he took Rowena as wife.'

'A meeting between Council and Hengest's Eldermen to finalise the treaty is arranged – that is why so many Saex ships are gathering on the river. My father will not back down. There is nothing we can do.'

'Damnation there isn't!'

Arthur thrust Vortimer aside, kicked the door open and burst into Vortigern's private chamber, slamming the door shut behind him.

The King barely glanced up from the parchment he was reading. 'I thought I heard your pleasant tone, son-by-law. Do come in.'

'What do you mean by this?' Arthur shouted, coming to stand before Vortigern's table, his arms folded, his expression thunderous.

'Exactly the question I intended to put to you,' said Vortigern unruffled. He searched among the pile before him on the table and tossed a parchment towards Arthur, who, glancing at it, recognised Winifred's neat hand. 'I am none too happy with the way you have been treating my daughter.'

Momentarily taken aback at the change of subject and with annoyance that the bitch had managed to get a letter through, Arthur stared at him. 'I do not give a dog-turd about your daughter! What has she to do with this foolishness?' Angry, his hand swept the parchment aside, taking with it several other scrolls that rolled and bounced to the floor.

'She has much to do with it – she wrote it.'

Arthur ignored the King's deliberate twisting of his meaning. 'I will not allow you to so casually dispose of British land!'

Vortigern straightened some of the chaos Arthur had caused and laughed sourly. 'You will not allow? Tch, tch, we are coming the high and mighty today!' He sorted a muddle of written accounts into a neat pile. 'Unfortunately for you, boy, I do care about my daughter. And,' he added pointedly, 'it is my kingdom to dispose of as I please, not yours.'

'You will not give it away to Hengest!'

'Not even for an assurance of peace? I suggest you listen to facts before you start belly-aching.'

'And I suggest you listen to sense, old man!' Arthur shouted.

Vortigern rolled another parchment, deliberately taking his time. He set it aside, reached for another. 'Hengest has assured me he will be content to settle his people alongside those British who wish to remain in the Cantii land. They exchange one over-lord for another, that is all. It is no new thing, has been happening for centuries. The farmers care little what lord they pay taxes to, as long as they are left to farm in peace.'

'And in return?' Arthur's voice was cold, hostile.

Vortigern sighed. This really was none of the Pendragon's business. A king did not have to justify himself. 'Naturally he will pay land tenure to me in the form of grain and goods.'

'Naturally,' sarcastically. 'Is that all?'

'What else need I ask for?'

'Hostages.'

Vortigern leant back in his chair. 'Hostages? My dear boy, Hengest is my father-by-law.' Spelling facts out, 'His daughter is my wife. Why would I have need of hostages?'

Arthur's eyes had narrowed to fierce slits. 'You will do this over my dead body, Vortigern.'

'That,' the King replied with a chill smile, 'I can arrange.' His voice hardened. 'I and Council make the decisions. Not you.'

Arthur rested his hands on the table. 'And I can hold the entire British army.'

Vortigern laughed, attempting, unsuccessfully, to hide his unease. 'I will take that as an idle boast, the sort boys crow after the taking of their first woman.' He feigned contempt, well aware Arthur's threat was a distinct possibility. His manner changed, turned dark and ominous. 'I do not like threats, nor do I like those who make them. The matter is closed.'

He pushed his chair away from the table. 'As for my daughter, I intend to ensure she receives a public apology for your disgusting behaviour, adequate financial compensation for her humiliating experience, and that from here on you bestow upon her the full duties of a husband.'

Vortigern over-rode the response of verbal abuse by continuing with, 'I would not like to hear any alternative view, boy. I would take any attempt by you to set aside my only daughter as a personal insult, would regard such an act as treason.' He too leant his hands on the table. 'Do I make myself quite clear, Pendragon?'

Winifred's pleading letter had annoyed Vortigern. He had allowed this marriage for two reasons: to keep a close eye on Arthur and to block him from making any other, more alienable marriage. Now in this sent letter the silly girl was begging him to seek a divorce for her? Ah no, he could not allow the Pendragon that freedom! 'I assume she is disembarking from your ship? I wish to see her at once,' he commanded.

'She is not here.'

From his seat his eyes never leaving Arthur's, Vortigern said, slow and deliberate, 'You had best not have the nerve to inform me she remains a prisoner in Less Britain.'

'She is in this country, safe from your clutches until such time as I see fit to return her to you. After I have completed the dissolving of our marriage, you can do what you want with her.' Arthur was again standing with arms folded. 'I'd send her to Hengest if I were you: her scolding tongue will drive him to fall on his own Saex sword.' His hand shifted to the pommel of his sword. 'You can have her back when I get what I want. All that I want.'

The King linked his fingers across his stomach and tapped his thumbs together. 'Which would be?'

Arthur hesitated, his carefully rehearsed words forgotten. He had intended to exchange Winifred for his freedom but this absurd treaty changed everything. Or was it an opportune excuse not to give up his command and his dreams?

On the voyage from Less Britain he had taken time to think, to sort the tide of fast running emotion from sound sense. Would he survive a life of farming? What did he know of overseeing the estate, or of wine production? Nought! Ectha saw to all that. There would be nothing for Arthur to do save sit and watch a bulging belly gradually flop over his bracae belt. He was born to be a soldier, it was in his blood.

What of Gwenhwyfar? Would she think as well of him if he were to turn tail and abandon all he had dreamed of, worked towards? She had once said she would have only the best. To throw away the chance of securing the kingship would achieve nothing. Would she despise him, as much as he would despise himself? In all truth he did not think their love would hold, given such a bleak future as life on the estate under the shadow of Ygrainne. But there were alternatives. They could go to Gwynedd, he could fight from there. Or he could demand the return of his father's lands in exchange for Winifred's safe release.

On board ship he had tossed the ideas back and forth, regretting his confidence of rash intention with Father Simon. It had all seemed so reasonable there, with the raw wound of Gwenhwyfar's scalding tears stabbing his heart. He had sat morosely nursing one wine flask after another, drinking himself almost senseless as the ship battled her way through a heavy swell, hugging the safety of the coast, unable to put into the wind for fear of being smashed to pieces.

It had been Winifred who had cleared his mind. That first night, after a scant meal shared in the confines of the captain's quarters set aside as their own, she had confronted Arthur.

'Where are you taking me this time, husband?'

'Somewhere I can keep close watch on you while I negotiate our divorce.'

She had not replied for some moments, then, to his surprise, said, 'With my co-operation, you will not need to negotiate.'

What was she up to now? he had wondered.

Winifred had smiled at him then, had taken his arm, kissed him lightly on the cheek. 'I have been as miserable as you in this union,' she had said, so sweetly. 'I too wish it to end. On my terms.'

He had nodded; that came as no surprise. 'Which are?'

'We sort out our differences in private. Let it be seen our journey to Less Britain, the birth and sad death of our child, has united us. All I require is that I do not lose face.' She had played with his hair, twisting the dark strands in her bejewelled fingers. 'I wish to have my own, substantial estate and wealth, and for it to appear we are reconciled. In a few months' time, our divorce can come about as an amicable arrangement.' Fiercer, 'I will not be set aside or shamed, Arthur.'

Winifred had rejoiced at his shrug of acceptance. 'I suggest, husband,' she had said, unlacing the thongs of his leather tunic, 'we make the best of this unfortunate situation.'

Like any male used to regular pleasure he had great need of a woman's body, and strong wine, far from damping his urge, usually heightened it.

Each night of the tedious journey, made longer by the battle against an ill wind, they shared a bed. Gave, and received, pleasure. Holding his sleeping head to her breast through the hours of darkness, Winifred lay calculating the time of the month and praying for her womb to quicken. She had decided against divorce. Would not give him that freedom. It would be more satisfying to keep him chained, bound to her by neck and ankles. More amusing to watch as he grieved over his dead, high-born whore and watched as, week by week, she, Winifred, swelled with child.

Their ship had dropped anchor a short distance west along the coast from the fortified harbour of Portus Adumi. Sending men to obtain horses Arthur had escorted his wife inland to the estate he had acquired the previous summer. She had ridden beside him, head high, smiling and proud. Triumphant.

His memory of Gwenhwyfar had been betrayed by his return to his wife, and Winifred's monthly course had not come! Her bleeding had always come on time before that wretched girl-child was born, and again since. There was no reason, save one, to expect this month to be different.

When this babe came, it would be a son. Within the turn of the month Arthur would know Gwenhwyfar was dead, that his wife was pregnant, and all hope of freedom was lost. She smiled broadly as they rode. Revenge had a taste as sweet as wild honey.

Arthur stood now, facing Vortigern, wondering whether to make his demands or wait. This treaty must be stopped. It would be the end of Southern Britain were so much to be given for so little. He was going to divorce Winifred, he was determined, and he had little doubt Winifred was equally adamant no divorce should take place. For months past she had wanted their parting; now she did not – but then Winifred was always perverse, wanting a thing only because it was her own idea, rejecting it if it was not.

Arthur had not been so blind drunk on board ship to not realise Winifred's submission was all sham, that she was thigh deep in some scheme of her own making.

The King grew tired of waiting for an answer. He said, 'The contents of my daughter's letter proved very interesting. I have no doubt Cunedda's eldest son will be much angered to hear of your, shall we call it indiscretion, with his sister. Especially when he hears of the matter after it has been dragged through the alehouses and taverns. At least Cunedda's death has spared him the knowledge his precious Gwenhwyfar outshines any Messalina.'

'You bastard!' Arthur had never known such overwhelming anger as that which took hold of him at that moment. He was filled with a blinding white rage at the vile comparison with one of Rome's most notorious whores.

He drew his sword. Action slowed to stillness for Vortigern. He had goaded too harshly, too soon, and realised it too late. Like all bullies he had little courage. Quick wits, coupled with a savage ruthlessness had given him the position and reward he required. Blood and guts on the battlefield nauseated him beyond endurance. Facing Arthur's naked blade he remembered suddenly the last time Arthur had drawn sword against him. Remembered Arthur's threat.

Arthur remembered too. It had been no idle threat and nor was this. As the blade whistled down Vortigern felt a warm wetness trickle down the inside of his legs. He closed his eyes. Screamed.

The fatal slash of iron through flesh never came. He felt something touch his cheek, a hiss, a rush of air. Heard a scuffle, hard breathing, a clatter. Tentatively the King opened his eyes, put shaking fingers up to a wet stickiness below his left eye. Looked unbelievingly at the blood daubed on them.

The door stood wide, a group of horrified men gathered there.

Melwas, knowing Arthur's hatred of Vortigern, had deliberately placed himself within hearing on the far side of the door. The unmistakable venom in Arthur's raised voice and Vortigern's scream, took him through to his king's aid, regardless of protocol.

'For once,' Vortigern said drily, masking the fear that made his body tremble, 'I will refrain from chastising you for the rudeness of your entrance, my nephew.'

Melwas grinned, indicated with a jerk of his head for the captain, standing astonished with Vortimer and the others, to call for Jute guards. They came, seized Arthur from Melwas's hold, roughly dragging his arms behind his back. Melwas released his grip, bent to retrieve Arthur's sword from the floor and placed it on the table before Vortigern.

The King shuddered, forced his eyes from the blade smeared with his own blood. He pointed with trembling fingers at the weapon.

'You shall pay for this outrage, Pendragon. The penalty for treason is death.'

Melwas's hand was already drawing his own sword. 'Let me finish him now!'

'Stay your hand!' Vortigern stood up, walked slowly round the edge of the table, stopped before Arthur, who stood mutely defiant between the two Saxons. 'You will die, Pendragon – eventually. When I am ready to let you. When I have you on your knees, begging for me to release you from this life.'

He turned sharply to Melwas. 'I give this whore-son to you, nephew. I must know the whereabouts of my daughter. I am certain Arthur will be only too pleased to tell you.'

Melwas saluted, a triumphant leer stretching his black-toothed mouth. He motioned the guards holding Arthur to follow, and led the way out.

Cei stepped forward, his hand on the hilt of his sword. Arthur shook his head warning his second-in-command to stand down. Muttered, 'I was stupid enough to miss the bastard's throat.'

The guards dragged Arthur away, marched him to the small block of prison cells set beneath the far walls of the palace, where Vortigern enjoyed providing his enemies with a lonely, agonising death.

By evening and the coming of the dark, Melwas took successful word to his uncle. Immediately, a fast jute ship was placed under his command, and by the coming of dawn he was heading for the fortress of Portus Adurni and an estate lying halfway between the port and the ancient Roman town of Venta Bulgarium.

§ XXIV

In considerable discomfort from the beating he had endured, Arthur huddled in the corner of a dank cell. The place was dim although not altogether dark, for light from the distant guard's room crept through a gap under the bolted door. High up in the stone wall a vent of a handspan's width gave on to the outside world. As dusk had settled a small number of bats had descended from the eaves and flittered silently through the opening into the gathering darkness.

The long night passed slowly. His face, swollen and bloody, ached; pain stabbing at his side from fractured and bruised ribs made it difficult to sit or lie comfortably in the scatter of musty straw. More than the pain, he disliked the creeping fear that clawed at his stomach. When they had brought him in here he had tried to ignore the sudden clutch of cold panic that, once it took hold, would not let go. He tried hard to conceal the dryness that came into his throat and the shaking that rattled his body. Melwas had laughed, highly amused at Arthur's ashen face, placing it as fear of what the guards were about to do.

The two of them had carried out their orders with alacrity and enthusiasm, while Melwas watched, leaning against the far wall, arms folded, eyes gleaming and nostrils flaring from the pleasure. Fists and feet battered without mercy, until breathless, in pain, bruised and bloody, Arthur gave in and told of where he had taken Winifred.

Melwas took the surrender of information as a weakness. Arthur thought of it as common sense. Why suffer beyond endurance for something not important? For a while he had held out as a matter of principle, furious at Melwas's gloating, but had soon set principle aside in deference to thudding pain. As a parting gesture Melwas had rammed his boot, twice, into Arthur's groin. He had walked away laughing, leaving Arthur semi-conscious and floating in a haze of red blood and dizzy blackness.

Sunlight streaking through the small vent illuminated swirling particles of dust that danced and spun in an unrehearsed pattern of intricate steps. Through the buzzing in his head Arthur could hear the Saex guards talking, but understood little of their guttural language. He must learn the Saex tongue, he decided. If ever he got out of here, The coming of day had eased the stifling fear of enclosed places a little, but not much. Arthur stared at the wooden door. The single shaft of sunlight ran straight as an arrow, from the vent to that door. He tried to look away, tried to set his mind to thinking on other things, but his eyes would be drawn back to those particles of dust swirling and tumbling down from the outside to the door. The door. The way out. The clutching desire was to run at it, beat on it and kick at it. He would if only he could get up, if only his body did not ache so; if only his head would stop this giddy whirling. If his legs would stop their shaking.

He turned his back on the door, lay in an awkward heap keeping the weight off the side most injured. Inside he was screaming. He sat up, stared again at the door. His mouth would not open; fear had tightened his throat, clamped every muscle rigid. The walls were swaying, bearing down on him, collapsing.

Arthur fell forward, vomited, spewing until his stomach heaved empty. It did not help. Still the walls swam and closed in. He shut his eyes, held them tight closed. Beads of sweat stood out on his forehead, ran down his body, saturating a tunic already stained from sweat and blood. 'Mithras,' he groaned through clenched teeth, 'by the love of the sacrificed Bull, please grant me death!'

§ XXV

While Arthur huddled within his prison of walls and fear of confinement, many miles to the south a storm tossed ship ploughed her way through heaving seas.

Gwenhwyfar raised her head bleakly as Iawn stooped beneath the awning of oiled leather. His face, grey and hollowed from grief and stubbled from days of untended beard growth, bore a greenish tinge they all echoed, save for the hardiest members of the crew. Although even they had muttered prayers for deliverance to the new Christ and the old gods.

Struggling with the single flapping sail and the bucking oars, the Christians among the crew touched carved crucifixes dangling at their necks on leather thongs; pagan worshippers, a variety of talismans. This crossing of the channel between Gaul and Britain, these experienced Breton sailors agreed, was the worst within living memory.

It seemed to Gwenhwyfar, squatting beneath the rigged shelter to the stern of the stout little craft that her misery could not, surely, grow worse: until she looked up and saw the drawn tautness of Iawn's face.

'Tell me,' she said wearily, resigned, knowing he was about to impart further bad news.

'We are apparently some distance off course. The steering board is barely operable and our captain doubts the mast will hold much further strain.' Iawn lurched forward as the ship fell over a side wave, spray cascading across the deck.

'Gwenhwyfar's attempted smile did nothing to hide her despair. 'Aside from that,' she flapped her hand feigning indifference, 'all is well?'

Grim, not echoing her false humour Iawn hunkered down beside her, his broad shoulders hunched in his sodden cloak. 'The captain has no choice but to run before the wind; there is no way of turning and heading back to where we should be making for.'

'We are going in the wrong direction, then!' Gwenhwyfar pounded the sea-drenched deck beneath her with the palm of her hand. 'We go east not west. Oh, Iawn, I want to go home!' She heard the childish whine in her voice, was powerless to prevent it. More than ever in her life Gwenhwyfar felt pushed to the edge of control. The despair of those long months cloistered within Ygrainne's suffocating hospitality, the news of her father's death and the agonising end of her much loved cousin, even the pain of Arthur's sudden departure were nothing to this! She longed for the security of Gwynedd's mountains, her brothers' solid protection. She was running away, running for a bolt-hole, but the holes when she reached them were blocked, so she had to turn around and run again, and keep running. Almost, with the misery of a churning stomach, thudding head and tears that would not cease, Gwenhwyfar had forgotten why she was running. Best to forget. It was all too horrible to remember; but their faces continued to haunt her.

Iawn had not challenged her decision to leave Less Britain. Gwenhwyfar announced her intention the day after his wife had been laid to rest within the little cemetery beside the walls of Father Simon's chapel. Iawn had been numb, feeling nothing beyond disbelief at his loss. Even now, here on this god-forgotten ship, he expected to see his Ceridwen appear, face flushed with excitement over some incident of nature; the first butterfly; the first peep-peeping of fledglings in a nest; an arching rainbow; the wondrous colours of a glowing sunset. Ceridwen had delighted in al things of beauty, instilling the same appreciation in Gwenhwyfar and Iawn. Now she was dead, gone. Committed to the dark of the earth.

Na, Iawn had made no objection to running away.

Gwenhwyfar's grief was deeper, for she had the knowing of the sinister truth behind Ceridwen's death. Only Gwenhwyfar and Livila knew, and one other. The old woman had guessed at poison but who listened to the babbling of a feeble-minded servant? Certainly not the physician, who regarded Livila as a harmful witch and often said so to her face.

Ygrainne would be relieved when the tiresome old woman, the only member of the household who had refused to embrace the love of the Christ, relinquished her stubborn hold on life. Poisoned? What nonsense. Who would wish to poison Ceridwen?

Livila guessed and Gwenhwyfar knew. They had exchanged glances over Ceridwen's deathbed, seeing the truth in each other's eyes, sharing their awful knowledge.

Arthur had warned of Winifred – she could be dangerous, he had said. But she had made one mistake, one vital mistake. By not ensuring the poison reached its intended victim, by killing Ceridwen instead of Gwenhwyfar the Saex bitch had dug herself a grave. Winifred would die; Gwenhwyfar would see to it, one day, no matter how far in the future, when opportunity came. One day, Winifred would pay for Ceridwen in kind. There would be no gentle easing into the next life, a soft sigh of breath, a peaceful departure. Ah no, not for Winifred. She would face the horror of an appalling death.

Iawn did not know of the poison. Seeing his grief, feeling his pain, Gwenhwyfar could not tell him of it, had not the courage to tell him Ceridwen had died in her place. Enough of a wound in her own heart; she could not twist the knife in his. Some things were best left unsaid.

'I must reach Gwynedd!' she moaned now, desperate.

'Lady, we could all drown, assuming the ship were even capable of being turned.' Iawn dropped his gaze, said, 'For myself I have no fear of death, I have no wish to live without her.' He shut his eyes, fighting back tears.

Gwenhwyfar reached for his cold hand, took it in her own, said nothing. What use words?

He struggled to compose himself. 'My duty is to safeguard the Lord of Gwynedd's sister. I cannot risk your death, nor can I risk the ship's crew coming with me to meet my God.'

Gwenhwyfar nodded. Of course he was right. 'Where does our captain hope to put ashore?' she asked with a false bravado.

Iawn shrugged. 'The first port he can reach. He dare not attempt to turn too soon or this storm will flatten us like barley before the scythe. We must run before it until such time as he can ease this floating coffin into a new course.'

Gwenhwyfar smiled again and drew her damp blanket more tightly around her shoulders. 'Then we must leave our fate to the gods.'

Iawn managed an answering smile. 'For all my faith in God, I would rather, at this moment, trust your life to the skill of our captain and his crew.'

As the weather-shrouded southern tip of the Island of Vectis appeared in the distance against the murk of a dark sky, the swirling rain squalls had eased to a steady fall of drizzle and the wind had blown itself out of violent temper. With relief, and a hasty prayer to God, the captain manoeuvred his craft away from the tossing open sea and slid her into the calmer waters running between island and mainland.

As they churned into the sheltering straits, the gusting wind dropped and the crew cheered. Portus Adumi and safety lay ahead!

Huddled in the rain-sodden blanket Gwenhwyfar shed its weight with relief and stepped out on deck, watching with interest as the ship made its way along the waterways, limping, tired and battered, but near enough in one piece. There was much laughter and jesting among the crew.

She was looking west, to the wide stretches of marsh running along the coast so missed another mast and its cross-chequered sail, moving swiftly out of port.

Someone in the crew raised a worried shout, pointed, his arm full out-thrust, head turned in alarm to the captain.

Gwenhwyfar swung round at his shout. She shielded her eyes, peered through the shadows of mist at the ghostly outline.

Another yell and the crew scattered, their relief melting into fear and disbelief as they hauled at the ragged sail and laid to the oars.

Confused, Gwenhwyfar watched their scurrying, listened to their cursing and swearing as they bullied the sluggish ship to respond.

Iawn ran to her, scooped her aside, manhandling her towards the stem hatchway that led to a dark stinking hold below decks. She fought free of him, demanded to know what was happening.

'That ship, lady,'

'I am aware of it.'

'It is Saex.'

'It sails from a British harbour – happen it is one of Vortigern's mercenary fleet.'

Irritated at her unusual stupidity, Iawn snapped a reply. 'British ships do not fly the Saex flag. No merchantman of any nation would run close to such a ship. They are sea-wolves.'

Rubbing her fingers across her forehead, trying to ease the persistent ache behind her temples, Gwenhwyfar struggled to think clearly. The stress of this voyage and the whirling confusion of the past days fogged her mind as deftly as the haze beyond the bows masked the outline of that ship, now altering course and heading fast straight for them.

The captain roared orders but the weary crew, not needing them, had already swung into defensive action. The mate passed close by Iawn, running to take a bow position. He tossed half order, half advice in his clipped accent. 'Get woman below, open deck no place for her.'

He said no more, running to tend his own salvation as best he could. Once that ship closed it would be every man for himself. No matter who she was, few of the crew would put Gwenhwyfar's safety above their own. It was the risk you took with the sea; you faced storm and sickness alone. And Saex sea-wolves.

Iawn was worried. He thought furiously of the best course of action, understanding the almost hopeless situation. This was a merchant ship, a

trader, not a warship, its only weapons his own and the daggers the crew
carried. Against a Saex ship! God, do not think like that! If he could hide
Gwenhwyfar she might be overlooked. He glanced at the land, a good
mile distant. Could she swim if he were to drop her overboard?

Gwenhwyfar read his thoughts. 'I am not that strong a swimmer,
Iawn. I have little desire to drown.'

'It may be a preferable option.' He opened the hatch cover, indicated
she was to climb down.

'And if you are thinking,' she said firmly, 'that I am going to scuttle
into some foul corner and cower like a trapped rat, then you can think
again.'

Iawn opened his mouth to protest, read her determination. He had
seen that same look on Cunedda's face. He nodded, drew his sword, ran
a thumb along its fine double edge. 'Then we had best prepare ourselves
for a fight.'

Gwenhwyfar nodded back at him, one brief nod. All of a sudden her
headache was gone; she felt alive and eager. Throwing her cumbersome
cloak from her shoulders, heedless of the steady rain, she gathered her
skirts and drew the back hem forward between her legs. Tucking it up
through her belt, she pulled the leather tighter about her waist to form a
crude pair of bracae to allow unhampered movement. A sailor scurried by
and she grabbed at his woollen cap, plucking it from his head.

He turned with a snarled curse, biting the scathing words back as
he saw who the thief was; shrugged good-naturedly as Gwenhwyfar
produced a small bronze coin from the pouch at her hip and threw it to
him.

He tossed the coin in the air, caught it, then with his thumb flipped it
over the side of the ship. 'Gods'll be wantin' that. Best t'pay for me way to
the next world now while I 'ave the chance. I'll 'ave little need for money
soon I'm thinking'.' He made to walk off, turned back with a toothless
grin. 'Have no need for me cap either.'

Gwenhwyfar had plaited and bound her hair in Roman fashion before
leaving Less Britain. Most of the pins were lost now, great hanks of hair
straggling loose and unkempt during the rough weather. She curled the
hanging loops on top of her head, pulled the cap tight down, tucked away
a few stray wisps.

'Not so obvious a woman now?' she queried.

Iawn grunted.

The Saex were gaining rapid ground. What chance had they, a lame
deer running against a young wolf? Gwenhwyfar waited, alert, shoulders
back, chin lifted. Beside her, Iawn.

'Stay beside or behind me, whatever happens,' he ordered.

Waiting, watching, as the Saex ship beat relentlessly nearer, her legs braced against the pitch and roll of the wooden deck Gwenhwyfar thought of everything and nothing. Voices, half-forgotten phrases; faces, drifting and passing. Memories and dreams mingling with regrets and hopes.

She could see details of the Saex rigging; see the cross-woven strips running through the sail giving it that chequered pattern. See the dull glint of drawn weapons and the hands clutching grappling hooks held at the ready. Faces, as the two ships came together, the Saex vessel ramming her heavy reinforced bow into the fragile sides of the trader.

Gwenhwyfar stood in the stem flanked by Iawn, a boy, the captain's slave, no older than ten years, and, surprisingly, the mate.

A great cry went up. Attack from the Saex, yells of defiance from the trader. The sea-wolves boarded, leaping the gap between the two ships, others throwing their hooks, bringing the ship around, alongside. As the two hulls crashed together, more leapt, savage in their eagerness to kill and plunder. Two of the crew were dispatched immediate, others putting up a fight as more and more Saex poured aboard.

For a moment, while she still had a brief second in which to think, Gwenhwyfar wished she had obeyed Iawn and hidden herself away down below. She stood trembling a little behind him, feeling the tight knot of fear binding in her belly. She had seen men killed before, knew the flood of blood and choking cry of death, but those had been deaths on her father's orders, executions, punishments. She had seen the wounded return from war with limbs shattered or removed, faces misshapen, bodies hacked, eyes gouged out, noses split. Death hovering, like gulls over a catch of fish. This was different. This was cold, bloody, and happening for real.

Her stomach clamped tighter, a gasp escaping her lips as she looked up and saw. She felt sick. Standing on the Saex deck, legs spread, fists on hips and laughing as he watched the merciless slaughter stood Melwas.

Gwenhwyfar clutched at Iawn, shrinking behind her protector, but Melwas looked directly at her, their eyes meeting across the two decks.

His nostrils flared and he gave a wide, lazy grin. The wind caught his cloak, spreading it like wings behind him. He looked like some bird of prey hovering, waiting the right moment to plunge down and sink its talons into a defenceless victim.

He folded his arms, waited. He had recognised her, knew who she was.

Something made Gwenhwyfar glance up at the low-hanging sky; she caught sight of a ragged fluttering at the masthead.

How stupid of them! There, for all who cared to see, flying alongside the Less Britain pennant, proudly proclaiming the ship's passenger, rain-sodden but clear enough to distinguish, the Lion banner of Gwynedd.

The Saex were upon them now, this valiant little group in the stem. Iawn and the mate struck forward. With his sword, Iawn took off an arm, the mate with his thinner and shorter sailor's blade plunging into the fight, hacked through flesh and bone.

Others came on, relentless. The boy had sunk to the deck, curled himself in a tight ball, moaning in terror. He never saw the blade that slit him almost in two.

An instinct for survival stirred Gwenhwyfar – that and remembered voices of brothers and father, shouting, bullying, never letting up on those days of weapon training. *Go, Gwenhwyfar! Thrust, go for the belly, throw your body weight behind your dagger – light on your feet, girl – light, I said! GO!*

She lunged with her dagger, screaming the Gwynedd war cry, drawing bright blood from an opponent's severed artery as her weapon scythed through a thigh.

The mate went down. He struggled to regain his footing; a blade pierced his throat. It took a while for his life blood and spittle to gurgle from the wound, spouting foul redness over wooden deck and leather boots.

Iawn fought savagely, using sword, shield and body with skill; fighting with strength and wit. It was useless. He pushed Gwenhwyfar with his elbow towards the rail. 'Jump!' he screamed, eyes as ferocious as the order, turning his head for her to catch his words.

A sword, raised high, glimmered bright against the leaden sky some trick of light reflecting off its shining blade. This was no ordinary Saex sword, but a thing of finer work, crafted, surely, by the hands of faery folk? Gwenhwyfar's line of sight flickered to it as Iawn shouted, taking in every detail of its fascinating, deadly beauty. A sword made for a king's hand.

Iawn saw it also, hesitated, caught off guard by the massive brute wielding such a fine weapon. The blade slashed down, whistling as it cut through wet air. It sliced through Iawn's helmet, through scalp, bone and brain. Blood and matter spewing out, drenching everything. Gwenhwyfar screamed. A hand grabbed at the cap on her head and her bright copper hair tumbled free. The huge Saex, lowering his wondrous sword, stared, momentarily astonished at his lucky catch, then said something in his guttural tongue to his companions who laughed.

Gwenhwyfar flew at him, biting, scratching and kicking. All her Da's training clean forgotten. The man guffawed louder, lifted her off her feet with one hand. She saw a blade glint and fall. Blood gushed into her eyes and then came darkness.

§ XXVI

Gwenhwyfar clawed her way to consciousness through a swimming haze of pain. Her arms felt numb, her body cold and drained. It was a battle to open her eyes; when she managed it she looked straight into the bloodied, vacant stare of Iawn's eyeballs, wide in his severed head. She vomited where she lay in her crumpled, bound heap.

Her arms were tethered behind her, ankles roped together. Wriggling, ignoring the protests of aching muscles, Gwenhwyfar managed to turn herself from the gruesome trophy dangling from the mast. A drizzle of rain pattered on her upturned face, its coolness reviving her thrumming senses. The ship was moving fast, running before a lee wind, skimming through troughs of rail-high waves. It would have been a fine ship, had it not been Saex. Sickness swelled in her throat again. She closed her eyes. Still they remained, Iawn's blank, staring eyes and the crunch of metal slicing through bone and sinew, severing head from neck. Her stomach heaved. She fought hard against bile and tears. Failed against both.

Reluctantly she opened her eyes again; the sky moved near then far, rising and falling as the ship breasted the waves. On the edge of her field of vision, woollen bracae tucked into deer-hide boots, braced in a wide stance against the roll of the sea.

'You have not had a pleasant journey.'

Melwas.

'So you attack and slaughter your own kind openly now? Has the hidden sliding of a knife into gut lost its amusement?' She was not looking at him, but knew he shrugged, uncaring.

'My men require payment. If they can claim it themselves from gained plunder, then so much the better.' He squatted then, so she could see his face. 'Aside, I would be a fool to miss the opportunity of claiming what is rightfully mine.'

'You forfeited any rights when you murdered my brother!'

He leered at her, showing blackened, gapped teeth. *Sa,* she still had fight left in her. 'You have not forgotten me, then?'

Gwenhwyfar's hatred was manifest. 'Gwynedd never forgets.'

'Yet your father conveniently forgot our betrothal when he spirited you away.' He grabbed her hair, his hand lashing out, fingers curling in its length. 'I will not be made to look the fool.'

'You make yourself a fool.'

He struck her for that, once, across the cheek. A dribble of blood oozed from her lip, mixing with the trail of dried blood from the wound made by that Saex sword pommel striking her on the temple.

'More of a fool!' she added, refusing to be cowed. 'Only fools threaten Gwynedd.'

He struck her again, harder. 'Gwynedd will bow the knee to me. I intend to make a start with your submission.'

Gwenhwyfar regarded him unflinching. 'I am not afraid of you, Melwas the fool. My brothers are stronger.'

He walked away, tossed over his shoulder, 'But your brothers are not here, are they?'

As the ship rounded the chalk cliffs of Dubris, the wind and rain ceased at last, though a grey sea still rolled beneath oppressive, greyer skies.

Gwenhwyfar recalled little of the horrendous, cramped voyage. Melwas did not bother her again, nor did the Saex, busy about ship's business. They sailed up the coast, darkness well settled long before the crew lowered the mast and took to the oars Rowing steadily, they sent the vessel skimming into the Tamesis estuary, their low-chanted song keeping rhythm, the reflection of steering lamps bobbing on calmer water. The tide would turn soon and carry them forward, up river.

The pitching and rolling eased once they joined the calm of the river, and finally Gwenhwyfar fell asleep. She must have slept for a long while, for dawn was well past when the ship bumped the shore, jolting her awake.

She recognised the wharf of the water gate at Londinium. Two Saex, one the man who had killed and beheaded Iawn, hauled her to her feet, releasing her ankles but not her bound wrists. He wore her dagger, tucked proud beside his wondrous sword. They marched her forward, her numb limbs shaking, and she stumbled as they dragged her down the plank to shore and up worn steps into the palace.

Saex kind were everywhere. She did not see one British guard the whole length of the debris-choked pathways and dusty corridors between the wharf and the chamber to which they took her. But then that was to be expected. Melwas would not risk her meeting with a possible sympathiser.

They cut the rope binding her, threw her to the bed and left, talking in their language which to her ears, sounded as pig-like grunts. A key turned in the lock and the bored scrape of feet indicated men moving to stand easy outside.

So, she was a prisoner then.

Gwenhwyfar looked about her for some vague hope of escape. The room was small, with the bare essentials of furnishings. A bed, a chest, a table. There was one window, narrow and rectangular, unshuttered. Thin though she was, she doubted she would be able to squeeze through. Even if she could, there would be a considerable drop beyond. She attempted to open the casement, but the iron lever was rusted and refused to move. Rubbing away grime and dust with her fingers she peered through a single pane of the thick glass, wondering if it were possible to smash a way through.

She started and whirled around as a woman entered. A British slave bearing water in a jug and a platter of food.

'I am Gwenhwyfar of Gwynedd. Melwas is holding me prisoner.' Gwenhwyfar emphasised her voice to that of command. Slaves were expected to obey. 'I need get word to my brother. There will be a manumission for you if you help me.'

The woman did not even glance up, but placed the items on the table, turned away and left. Gwenhwyfar hurled the platter at the closing door.

She fumed for a while, uttering all the obscenities she knew, cursing the slave and cursing her daughter's daughters. Exhausted of oaths, she realised her hunger and devoured the provisions, sitting cross-legged before the closed door picking crumbs from the wooden floor. She drank some water. Appetite and thirst satisfied, she set about her appearance.

Stripping herself of boots, torn gown and sodden under-garments, all stinking of vomit and blood, she kicked the things away from her and washed as best she could in what water remained in the pitcher.

She stood naked and shivering, reluctant to creep into the bed where it would be warm, although she was tempted. Twitching the top fur covering aside, she discovered coarse linen beneath. She stripped the bedding, fashioned a crude wrap-round linen garment and added the fur as a cloak. Then she sat on the floor at the far side of the room, opposite the door, her back to the wall, and waited.

§ XXVII

Vortigern was a creature of habit. He liked his bed, liked even more the seclusion and peace his bedchamber offered. A place in which to deliberate and plan ahead; a quiet, undisturbed cocoon where he could think upon the day past and the day to come. This morning the evening's Gathering occupied his thoughts. It should prove interesting, amusing even to observe Hengest and his clamour of jute Elders and Thegns sitting opposite a sullen-faced Roman Council. Things looked set fair for a promising event! A few knots to be untangled; whispers to be dropped in ears, promises or threats to be made – ah, that was the irritating thing. Vortigern wriggled his shoulders deeper into the comfort of his pillows. There were those few who were still mumbling their misgivings about this unconditional giving of land to Hengest. He cracked his fingers, delighting in the pleasant nastiness of the sound. They would come to his way of thinking; that, or be subtly reminded of debts or taxes yet to be paid.

A discrete tap on the door interrupted his thoughts. He growled an answer, beamed a smile as Melwas entered. 'Ah, nephew, come in! A good voyage?'

'A very good voyage!' Melwas replied with an expressive sweep of his hands. Seating himself at Vortigern's bidding he took wine from a slave, drank thirstily.

'You found my daughter?' Vortigern asked, motioning for another pillow to be placed behind his shoulders.

The question must be answered, but Melwas hesitated.

Astute, the King caught the pause, frowned suspiciously across the room at his sister's son. 'I trust Winifred is in good health?'

Melwas nodded eagerly. That he could answer. 'She is very well.' He added, 'We encountered a Breton trading ship as we sailed out from Adurni.'

Vortigern grunted as he pummelled at a lump in the stuffing of the pillow, hardly listening.

'We took it.'

Absently the King said, 'Good, good.'

'The haul paid the crew well.'

'Even better.' Vortigern was not to be sidetracked. 'What is it you are not telling me about my daughter?' He snorted in disgust. 'I assume she was disgruntled that I have forbidden her divorce from Arthur. She always was one to want her own way.' He fixed Melwas with his small, sharp eyes. 'Is she still planning to plot against me with Rowena? The pair of them have dangled fingers in the forbidden honeypot for years.'

Melwas's laugh at Vortigern's thin pretence of humour was a little overdone.

'Is there more?' Vortigern had a niggling feeling the pleasing day he was looking forward to was about to turn sour.

Melwas toyed with the remainder of his drink. 'This is an excellent wine. Greek, is it not? Uncle, it is good to be back in your service again!' He looked sheepishly at the floor. 'I was an ass to stay away so long.'

'You are often an ass, nephew. You let anger rule your better sense. Be that as it may, I know you well enough to see there is something you are not telling me.'

The younger man shifted on his stool, fidgeting uneasily. 'As I said, Winifred is well. She sends her devotion to you and is, as you ordered, under escort to Caer Gloui.'

Vortigern was not satisfied; there was something more here. He said, 'It will be easier to keep a close eye on her alongside her mother and young brother, Vitolinus.' Did not add that his villa of Caer Gloui had high, secure walls and a dependable British guard. And that it was many safe miles distant from Hengest.

Melwas raised an eyebrow at the King's revelation. This was unexpected. 'You have sent the Queen and your son west also?'

Vortigern chuckled. 'She was most annoyed. My two clucking hens can sit in their roost and share their impotent scheming! I do not intend to take Hengest's word of fealty unquestioned, Melwas. Rowena is too ambitious, particularly now she has a son to dandle on her knee. She would like to reign as regent in his name, her and her father between them.' He laid a finger on his nose. 'It has been done before, you know: mother kills father for infant son to rule.' He nodded his head slowly, deep in thought, adding, 'This night I finalise my greatest treaty and pay Hengest off into the bargain. I thought it best to have his daughter and grandchilder safe beyond his grasp, just in case there were any bright ideas hatched atween them.' He wagged a solemn finger. 'You do not quieten a chained dog by parading a bitch on heat before him.'

So, Melwas had learned something this day he had not known! 'You do not trust Rowena, then?'

Vortigern laughed. 'Trust her? Trust a woman – a wife? I would as soon trust a starving beggar to ignore a bannock of bread cooling on the kitchen sill!'

'She is a hostage then, against Hengest?'

The King stretched and yawned, threw the bedclothes aside and beckoned his slave forward to dress him. 'She is my dearest wife, Melwas, but also a most convenient weapon to level at Hengest's heart. He dotes upon his daughter and her infant son.' His voice became muffled as his head disappeared beneath a garment. 'All his kind have this close affinity with kindred.' He resurfaced, stood as the slave tied lacings. 'It is the same with these tribal British – owing this, that and the other. Loyalty to kin! Pah, can't see the reasoning of it myself.'

Raising the last of his wine in salute Melwas gestured agreement. The King would not see the loyalty of brother to brother, father to son, would he? To gain wealth and power Vortigern, as a young man had murdered his own elder brother and his father, was often close to doing the same with his grown sons.

Dressed, waving the slave away, Vortigern returned to the subject of his daughter. 'So Winifred is well, but...?'

'But, my Lord?'

'What is amiss?'

Puffing out his cheeks Melwas spread his hands wide. 'She refused to leave the estate where I found her. The Pendragon has apparently signed the land over to her. She demanded to know where he was and, when I told her, insisted he be set free.'

'God's truth!' Vortigern turned to his nephew in amazed surprise. Was the girl totally mad? 'What is she playing at? I receive a letter begging my help in securing an immediate divorce – and now she is pleading for the bloody man's life!' He paced a few steps, then turned to Melwas again. 'What ails her?' He scowled. 'Has she decided to back the Pendragon?' Vortigern kicked at the side of a chair. 'There is some scheme for the Pendragon to ally with Hengest against me, eh?'

Melwas brought a sealed document from his pouch, held it a moment in his hand. It would be betraying the trust of his cousin to pass it over but his loyalty was to the King! 'She paid one of my men to deliver this to

Arthur – she thought her gold was enough to keep the thing secret.' He half grinned. 'My men know better than to go against me.'

Vortigern took it, looked with distaste at the small roll of parchment. 'You know what is in this?'

Melwas spread his hands, affronted. 'My lord King, it is addressed to Arthur!' His grin widened. 'Of course I know what is in it!'

Pursing his lips Vortigern broke the seal, noting with a nod of approval how well Melwas had patched his own breaking of it. He read grimly.

'So, after the agreement of this treaty, Hengest is plotting with Rowena to murder me?' He tossed the parchment aside. 'I knew that months ago.'

'Aye, but do you not find it interesting that Winifred is warning Arthur, and is offering to help him to do away with her mother and brother? With you dead, the country in turmoil and Rowena out of the way – the path would be clear for the Pendragon.'

Vortigern glowered and sat down in his comfortable high-backed chair. 'So my daughter aims to become queen!' His eyes shone wickedly. 'What ambitious kin I have!' The smile snapped off. 'You managed to persuade her to Caer Gloui?'

'Eventually. She agreed when I promised to secure the Pendragon's release.' Melwas grinned. 'Unfortunate that I arrived back too late to stay his execution.'

Vortigern's smile returned, his lips curling over toothless gaps. 'Most unfortunate.'

'In light of this,' Melwas indicated the letter, 'is it wise to have your daughter so near your wife?'

'Oh aye. They will be under close guard. Aside,' Vortigern cackled with amusement, 'happen the one will do away with the other and save me the task.' He regarded Melwas shrewdly, added, 'I assume you would enjoy disposing of Arthur?'

Melwas stood up. 'It would be my pleasure.'

Aye, Melwas took much enjoyment from the suffering of others. He was an evil breed, which was why Vortigern liked him. His nephew had the stomach for these 'unpleasant' duties, unlike his two sons who complained and whined if such-and-such a thing was not right in God's sight.

'The Pendragon is where you left him. I thought a few days to sit and shiver and dwell upon his circumstances would be of use to his over-large sense of cock-sureness.' Vortigern rubbed his hands together, delighted. The day was looking good again!

'The Pendragons have been a boil on my backside over-long. It is time the nuisance was lanced.' He looked at Melwas. 'He is to be dispatched with no undue attention. See to it this night. Minds shall be on this Gathering.'

Melwas agreed, began making to excuse himself but Vortigern lifted a hand to stay his going. 'I would suggest a Saex blade would be best. It may be prudent to lay blame at the hand of our, er, friends.'

A nod of agreement. Melwas walked to the door, stopped, said with a half turn to the King, 'That Breton ship.'

Vortigern had gone to a table, was busying himself with some papers. 'What of it?'

'I took payment for myself also.'

Ah, Vortigern thought, *there is more to tell, then!* 'In what form?'

'A woman.'

The King's eyebrows shot up. 'They use female sailors in Less Britain now, do they?' He warmed to the thought. 'What a superb idea. A sure way to enliven the dullest sea voyage.'

Used to his uncle's lewd humour, Melwas explained further. 'She was a passenger. We had no trouble finishing her bodyguard.'

There it was again, a vinegar-sour threat to darken this sunny day, a sudden feeling his nephew was about to tell him something he was not going to like. 'Go on.'

Uncertain whether it was wise to continue, Melwas was forced to plunge on. The old man was sure to find out sooner rather than later – best say now. 'She was mine anyway, I have simply claimed my own.'

His voice lowering to an unpleasant growl, Vortigern said, 'Go on.'

'The passenger was Gwenhwyfar of Gwynedd.'

The fool! Vortigern took three strides across the room, was before Melwas. 'If a war comes because of this, you fight it alone!'

'Cunedda agreed betrothal!'

'Cunedda is dead. I remind you he claimed the right of blood feud. Until it is settled the claim passes as inheritance from father to son.'

Vortigern laughed suddenly, his mood swinging away from ill-humour. Cunedda's sons would be furious! He slapped Melwas on the shoulder. 'Good luck to you, lad. If you can hold her, then she is yours.' He held a finger up in warning. 'Just remember, this is between you and Gwynedd. I will have nought of it.'

Pleased, relieved, Melwas said, 'Then I have your permission to take her as wife?'

'Wife?' Vortigern was astonished. 'Why do you want her as wife? *Na,* lad, keep her as mistress.' He noticed Melwas's glower of displeasure, slapped his shoulder again. 'Have it as you will! But take my advice, do not bother with formalities, at least not straight away. Take her as your woman now. Once she is in your bed and breeding, Gwynedd will be gagged, unable to shout over-loud.'

His nephew grinned by way of reply. 'Exactly what I had in mind.' He bowed, anxious to put words into action but Vortigern stayed him. 'Your lusting must wait awhile, lad; I have duties for you, details of this evening's work. Let me break my fast – meet me within the hour.'

Melwas saluted, headed whistling for the kitchens to satisfy his growling belly. What a day! The end of the Pendragon and the taking of Gwenhwyfar! He sang a few bars of a Jute war song as he waited for the slaves to serve him.

§ XXVIII

Dusk. Gwenhwyfar heard the stamp of feet and thud of spears as guards stood rapidly to attention. This was it then. He was coming. She stood, clutching the fur around her, stubbornly not allowing the fear to show as Melwas entered. He brought two slaves, the woman who had come earlier, and a boy. Melwas threw a blue gown on the bed, noting the stripped linen. He sat beside the gown, ignoring Gwenhwyfar, allowing the boy to pull off his boots.

The woman shambled about the room lighting the lamps and candles. Melwas stood, the boy removed his leather and iron-studded war gear. 'When I have done with you,' he said, talking to Gwenhwyfar but not looking at her, 'you will dress yourself as befits a woman of mine.'

Standing in undertunic and bracae, Melwas picked up a boot, hurled it at the slave woman, striking her in the small of the back. She spun to face him, afraid. He gestured impatiently for her to leave, kicked at the boy, indicating he should also go. The boy scooped up his master's body armour, retrieved the thrown boot and scuttled out behind the woman.

'A loyal slave, that woman,' Melwas mused, approaching Gwenhwyfar. 'But damned useless at times, on account of her being as deaf as stone.'

Gwenhwyfar was able to master a blank expression. So that was why she had been ignored! The woman had not heard her! Ach, let Melwas taunt, it would get him nowhere.

He stood, arms folded, observing her makeshift robe, then he reached out to finger the untidy hair cascading around her shoulders.

'It is a pity I cannot show you off at the feasting this night. Ah, well. I will savour you for myself.' He wrinkled his nose at the distasteful smell which clung to her. 'Should have had you bathed,' he muttered.

He attempted to kiss her but she pulled away. Melwas let her go a few steps, then lunged forward, grabbing her hair and pulling her back. He kissed her on the mouth, holding her firmly to hi, with a free hand, felt inside the fur, took her breast, fondling the nipple as his mouth bruised hers.

'I have spoken with Vortigern,' Melwas said, his face close to hers; 'he has acknowledged my claim to you.' His hand fondling beneath the fur pulled at the linen sheet; it fell to the floor. Struggling, Gwenhwyfar kicked at him with bare feet. With her hands, she clung to the fur, clasping it around herself.

He held her all the tighter, ignoring her flailing legs. His pawing hand moved down over her stomach, brushed her inner thigh, his fingers groping upwards and she brought her knee up, slammed it into his groin. He slumped, grimacing, let her go.

Gwenhwyfar fled for the door, but he was quicker, catching the trailing end of her covering, pulling it sharply, tripping her. She fell heavily and lay winded.

'As of this day you are my woman.' He stood over her, spoke with dark menace. She did not answer; he did not expect her to.

Slowly, taunting, he removed his woollen shirt, revealing a muscled, hair-covered chest. He unhitched the leather belt at his waist, let the bracae fall, stepped out of them and stood naked. His intention, with his manhood rapidly swelling, obvious. Clasping her wrist, he hauled her upright, held her, crushing her mouth with his.

During the long day Gwenhwyfar had thought and planned. She had intended to fight, if necessary kill herself before submitting, but now it was happening, brave ideals slid away. Was that not what he wanted – for her to scream and beg for mercy?

His broad soldier's hand smashed her cheek, tearing the already bruised and tender skin. He wanted her to cower away, wanted to master and break her.

Gwenhwyfar remained still, silent, staring back at him. He found it unnerving looking into those green eyes that shone with calm defiance. Angered, he knocked her down and tore the fur from her, expecting her to shrink away or fight.

She lay motionless on the floor as he knelt astride her, pushed her legs apart and thrust himself into her, his impatience making him finish quickly and without much satisfaction. He withdrew almost at once, rage reddening his face. Yelling his fury he stood, beating and kicking her, shouting. 'You bitch, you damned, heathen, whoring bitch!'

Gwenhwyfar laughed up at him, aware she had won. She made no attempt to ward off the blows, she just lay there laughing.

'Who took you first?' he bellowed, kicking his foot into her ribs. 'Who claimed your maidenhood? What bastard was it?'

'Arthur,' she mocked, her body shaking, teeth chattering. 'Arthur. He is a fine lover.'

Melwas's hands were at her throat, squeezing, choking her. Panic, already close to the surface almost peaked, but Gwenhwyfar forced herself to think clear and calm. Relax. Let the body go limp, submit to his rage. She placed her hands on his, in a feint to prise the gripping fingers away, then moved quickly and precisely. Raising her hands she slashed at his eyes with a woman's shaped nails. At the same instant she jerked her knee up, ramming home into his genitalia. With her hip, she thrust his pain-doubled body aside and, rolling clear, sprang to her feet. She grabbed for the water jug and smashed it over his head.

Crouching, holding the remaining broken shard before her as a weapon, she waited a long minute, but he lay unmoving.

Snatching up the gown he had brought, Gwenhwyfar ran to the door opened it and, throwing it wide, ducked low into the lithe, swift movement of a forward roll.

The guard, one of Hengest's mercenary Jutes, had been dozing, not expecting Melwas to emerge for some while yet. His momentary hesitation, combined with her unexpected manoeuvre, gave Gwenhwyfar the precious time she needed. She jabbed the jagged, broken edge of the jug at his face, ripping through his eye.

He yelled in pain and surprise and dropped his spear.

Catching it before it touched the floor, Gwenhwyfar drove the iron tip through his chest, paused only to remove a dagger from his belt. She took to her heels, clothing clutched against her nakedness, thankful she had some knowledge of the complexities of the palace corridors.

She almost ran straight into a further group of Jute nobles making their way to join the noise of Vortigern's great Council chamber. Changing direction along a side corridor, Gwenhwyfar found herself by a door leading to the gardens. Creeping into the shadows, she squatted, gaining breath and time to think.

Melwas was not dead, would be after her all too soon. The fine drizzle was soaking her hair and clinging uncomfortably to her naked skin. She shivered, her sweating body rapidly cooling. Tugging the woollen Saxon dress over her head, she found two brooches pinned to secure the shoulders. The jewellery, doubtless valuable, was, to her British eyes vile and repugnant, but would have to suffice for now. She fastened them quickly, then huddled into the shadows to plan her next move.

These gardens formed a square bordered by guest chambers opposite; the King's private apartments to the north and on this east side. Along the fourth ranged the administrative offices. Over them, on the first floor, brooded the council chamber and the banqueting hall where Vortigern held his rare but magnificent feasts. Lights blazed from every window.

The private apartments lay behind her. Beneath the centre of the illuminated first floor of the public rooms lay an archway leading out to the palace, flanked, she could see, by Hengest's men, standing in knots talking and laughing. The torches beneath the archway and glow from the windows lit up their drooping moustaches, rough skins and fierce eyes.

Opposite, through another central arch between the guest apartments, were domestic buildings and, beyond those the lower gardens leading down to the water gate. Would that, too, be guarded? Why so many of these Saex, so many lights and moving shadows beyond the windows? She could hear the distant hum of voices, the bark of male laughter. Melwas had talked of a feast. What was happening?

She eased forward, keeping low, wriggling on her belly where necessary, making full use of the concealing shadows from low walls, shrubs and hedges. Clearing the arch, running for the darker hiding places, she found herself in the domestic quarters. The unmistakable aroma of horses assailed her; urine, dung, hay. Few men were about here. She peered cautiously into the first barn, slid inside and ducking under a rail settled herself beneath the manger at the far end of the stall. The occupant, a wise-eyed bay of good quality, snorted and snuffed suspiciously at her. Losing interest, he returned to his hay.

Warmth, and the steady munch of horses eating was relaxing and soothing. Gwenhwyfar ached, every bone and muscle felt battered. Her right eye was barely open, her eyelid and cheek bruised. She hurt dreadfully where he had so roughly penetrated her.

Gwenhwyfar laid both hands on her belly, wondering. She had thought of this thing often during the long days at sea. Was the sickness all from the swell of the tide? The need to speak with a woman had been desperate, but impossible. But did she need confirmation? Her bleeding had not come, surely she needed no other sign? One thing to be thankful for, she had known before this night that she carried Arthur's child, had known days before Melwas took her.

She trembled again as she remembered him. His grotesque form as he knelt over her, his leer of triumph as he had entered her. Gwenhwyfar closed her eyes, felt the ground beneath her spinning.

She wanted to sleep, to find oblivion, but she could not, she was not safe here. At any moment Melwas and his Saex dogs might come searching. She managed to get to her feet, clung to the horse with his soft warmth and unyielding strength. Friendly, he nuzzled her, welcoming the company. Gently, she pulled one of his brown ears as a parting gesture and slipped back into the night.

From here she had no idea which way to go. Noticing a pile of discarded sacking she selected a suitable length and fastened it around her shoulders, using one of the gaudy Saxon brooches to secure it. She stole in the direction of the kitchens, hoping to blend in with scurrying servants and slaves. No one paid her any attention; she must look as shabby and dirty as any of them if her legs and feet were anything to go by.

A mule cart was making to leave by the narrow service gate. Taking her chance, Gwenhwyfar ran and, resting a hand on the back, walked behind the vehicle for all the world as if she belonged to the carter.

He never noticed her, being busy at the heads of the mules, and the guard at the gate did not glance her way. She was out!

Think quickly! The eastern area of the city, once a wealthy district, she knew to be almost derelict. It had been abandoned during the last plague to sweep through Londinium and no one had come back to claim property – happen they were no longer alive, or had no inclination to return. She ducked down a small side street between palace walls and shops, and ran silently on bare feet keeping to the shadows, ever watchful. Once, at a street intersection, she almost ran into a group of drunken Saex. Gwenhwyfar hid in a doorway, her heart pounding, and let them weave past. She was more careful after that.

The rain fell steadily. She was sodden, cold, and so very tired. With a sob of relief, found a building she remembered. She had walked through this obsolete corner of Londinium one afternoon, attempting to escape the palace confines and Winifred's tedium. How long ago was that? It seemed like centuries past.

This particular house she remembered well. It was large and had obviously belonged to someone of great importance. She had asked various people at the palace but no one seemed to know or care who its owner had been.

Apart from broken windows and its partly fallen roof, it looked habitable from the outside. She squeezed past the door which leaned askew from one hinge, and picked her way carefully through weeds and debris. Something scrunched under her feet, a sharp pain shot through her right sole. She muffled a cry and slumped against the wall, hunkering amongst the scatter of sharp-edged, broken roof tiles.

At least it was sheltered here, and away from the noise of the streets. In the distance she heard drunken men singing, and, further away, shouting. Nothing more.

§ XXIX

Gwenhwyfar must have slept, for a sound startled her awake. She groaned; her body felt as though it were being torn very slowly into pieces. The shouting she had heard earlier, before drifting asleep, was now louder, more persistent and definable. Shouts and cries. Frightened screams. Footsteps ran by, fairly close, nailed boots rapping along the cobbled road leading to the nearest city gate. More followed; a crowd of people panting as they ran, someone among them sobbing; the cry of a baby.

Clinging to the solidity of the wall Gwenhwyfar pulled herself upright, wincing as her cut foot touched the ground. Staying within the shadows she limped cautiously to a broken window and peeped out. As she bent forward, the sacking around her shoulders caught on something sharp and ripped. The brooch tumbled to the floor; she heard the chink as it fell, made no move to retrieve it. Let it lie among the shards of roof tiles for someone else to find! Ugly thing.

She could see nothing beyond the fallen building between herself and the road, except a vague blur of hurried movement. As quietly as she could, given the darkness and the rubble on the floor, Gwenhwyfar crept from the house, curiosity drawing her back in the direction of the palace, from where the confused sounds of distress came.

She reached the main roadway and found herself looking at a panic-stricken crowd flooding past. Men and women, mothers with babies in their arms, others with frightened children clutching at their skirts. Slaves and servants mingled with the free, all of them pushing and clawing their way forward, desperate to reach the gateways out of the city, to get to the open marshes and fields beyond, to head for the distant spread of woodland.

Wild, drunken Saex were herding them, swinging forward into the terrified crush of people, slaughtering any they caught hold of, man, woman or child. Maiming and laughing.

Two came close to Gwenhwyfar's sheltered hiding place, engrossed in kicking some ragged thing before their feet. It struck against the wall a few paces before her, rolled away and was trampled and swept forward by other feet. The Saex, swearing and cursing at the loss of their plaything, reeled drunkenly after it.

Sickness choked Gwenhwyfar as she recognised the thing. A child's open-mouthed severed head.

Trembling, she retraced her steps along the alley, back into the sheltered, quiet darkness of the squalid, mostly untenanted buildings. At a movement to her left she squeezed herself into a doorway, through the door hanging by its rusted hinges. Four Saex reeled from a corner wine shop, its frontage broken down by the industry of their axes. One carried an unstoppered amphora, its contents spilling out; the others, shouting with laughter, dragged a luckless slave girl. She was screaming, pleading for help that would not come. She kicked one of the brutes, who swore and threw her to the ground.

His companions cheered as he unfastened his bracae.

Gwenhwyfar crouched, buried her head, hands pressed tight to her ears. She did not want to see, or hear but she could not blot out the sounds and movement as the four of them took swaggering turns at the girl. Her screams rose with the first two, then faltered. After the fourth, fell silent after one last, shrill sound.

The Saex lurched away, gulping their wine, searching for fresh sport. Eventually they met with a group of British soldiers who dispatched the barbarians as dispassionately as they had slit the girl open.

Gwenhwyfar hesitated, unsure which way to go. To the palace, or back into the derelict quarter?

Footsteps, the sound of boots moving nearer. A group of men, shadows only, at the intersection of alleys slightly to the left. Gwenhwyfar drew back into her safe place, flattening herself against the wall, her breath held.

She had ready the dagger she had stolen from the guard outside Melwas's room. One man stopped, bent over the body of the murdered girl. He swore vehemently. Ripping the helmet off his head, he wiped his hand over an ashen face.

'What in God's name is happening here?' he asked rhetorically.

Gwenhwyfar closed her eyes for a joyous moment of thankful prayer, then ran forward, sobbing with relief, tears pouring down her cheeks. 'Cei! Cei!'

The man swung up, saw the running figure, stood alert with sword raised; glimpsed a face barely recognisable beneath blood and bruise.

'Gwenhwyfar! What are you doing here?' She was in the safety of his arms, leaning against him.

On his barked orders a protective wedge of men formed instantly around their commander and the young woman clinging to him. Cei managed to make a little sense out of her confused torrent of words, and using his brain, added two and two and came up, more or less rightly, with a tally of four.

'Melwas is back?' he asked urgently, holding her from him. When she nodded, he swore a heathen oath. 'Do you know where he is now?'

She shook her head.

One of the men, as grey-faced as his commander, said, 'Let us pray to God we are not too late for Arthur.'

Gwenhwyfar's heart lurched. She put a hand to her mouth. 'Arthur?' she cried. 'He is here?'

'Vortigern has him under arrest,' said Cei. He was looking up and down the alley as he spoke.

Gwenhwyfar felt her legs go weak, and as she crumpled Cei eased her to the ground, wrapped his own cloak around her.

She came round almost immediately in a state of great distress. 'I did not know Arthur was here,' she muttered. 'What have I done?' She clutched at Cei's hand, her nails digging deep into the flesh. 'Melwas – does he know Arthur is here?'

'It was Melwas who escorted him to the cells some days since.'

The soldiers' peering, anxious faces blurred before her. The words of her taunt at Melwas echoed like some evil chant. 'Arthur!' she scrambled to her feet, pushing Cei aside, her pain forgotten. 'He is in danger!' She was desperate to make them understand!

'Aye, we know, that is why we are here, a last attempt to free him.'

'Na, you could not know. Melwas, I told him – I...' Oh, they would not understand!

Cei was holding her arm tight, keeping her close, steering her forward at a trot now as they neared the palace. Her foot stabbed, her legs and arms and ribs screamed with each breath, each movement of muscle, but she did not care, cared for nothing save running with Cei to find Arthur!

They entered through the same service gate she had left by, save there were no guards there now. They could hear screaming and the smell of blood and fear hung heavy in the air.

Cei would have preferred not to be encumbered by a woman, but what choice had he? Leave her – amid this madness of death and destruction?

They waited within the palace walls to assess their next move, then ran to the rear of the kitchens. The screaming was louder here. 'Why leave it so long before helping him?' Gwenhwyfar panted.

Cei glanced at her. 'I have been pleading with Vortigern all this while – tonight I gave up only to find the city crawling with Saex. They are like carrion come to pick over the dead.' He nodded back towards the city. 'Particularly in that direction. I have lost three of my men getting this far.'

They ran behind the height of a woodpile, paused for breath. The noise and stench reminded Gwenhwyfar of animal slaughter pens.

The kitchen door was flung wide casting a beam of light across the courtyard. A woman lurched out, bleeding profusely from a near severed arm. She came close, screamed as one of Cei's soldiers caught her and dragged her into the shadows. They bound her arm, gave her drink from a leather flask; took some while to calm her.

'What is happening?' Cei had to repeat the question over and over.

All he could get at first were the words, 'Saex' and 'killing'. Then, as she calmed, 'The Saex have killed all at the King's Gather! Now they slaughter servants and slaves also!' Cei looked at his men, stunned. But then, was it so hard to believe?

'It had to happen,' one man said.

Another said, 'A mad dog eventually turns to bite his master's hand.'

They left the dying woman, tucking her for her safety deep behind the pile, then made their way slowly forward, dodging between buildings, killing those Saxons who reeled into their path, ignoring bodies strewn at their feet.

Breathless, they reached Vortigern's cells, a stone-built building at the farthest easterly corner of the perimeter walls.

Cei ordered two men to stay outside, told Gwenhwyfar to remain with them.

'I will not stay out here, with this.' She indicated the small rectangular courtyard and three bodies. Two men, one woman with her skirts thrown over her head, blood that had trickled down her thighs, drying.

He did not like it, but said, 'Follow, then. Stay well back.'

She nodded, entering the narrow corridor into the building cautiously behind the men, feeling the comfort of the stolen dagger gripped tight in her hand. Cei motioned for silence. They heard Melwas's voice ahead and his malicious laugh, followed by the sound of blows.

Cei's eyes narrowed and he stepped forward, his sword waving before him. They came to a corner and peered round, Gwenhwyfar shouldering her way through the men.

Two Saex guards stood in an open doorway ahead. From beyond, Melwas's voice.

'I was ordered to kill you, and so I shall. Slowly and with pain, Pendragon. When they find you come morning they will think you were just another victim of these murdering barbarians. Make a fool of me, would you? I think not.' Melwas struck again – then felt, rather than heard, a movement behind him.

He turned, gasped, as he saw two things. The guards falling dead, blood gushing from throats slashed open, and Cei lunging forward.

For all his weight, Melwas moved swiftly, parrying the blow with the handle of his whip. They grappled. Melwas kicked out, sent Cei sprawling.

He raised the whip, intending to strike Cei, but the blow never fell. Melwas slumped forward, blood trickling from his open, surprised mouth.

Gwenhwyfar stared at the dagger in her hand, at the warm slime of blood sliding down the blade, staining her clenched fingers.

One of Cei's men ran forward and slashed through the ropes binding the Pendragon; another knelt over Cei, who lay dazed.

With great effort, gasping from pain and lack of breath, Arthur pulled himself upright, stumbled to Gwenhwyfar.

'You look as I feel,' he croaked.

With a sob she flung the weapon away, and herself into his arms. He let her stay there, let her cry for a while, stroking her hair, murmuring soothing words, wincing as jolts of pain shot through his own hurts.

She tried to speak once, but he shushed her quiet. 'I know what happened, my Cymraes. He bragged of it to me.' The bastard, every detail.

'You do not understand,' she sobbed, catching her breath. 'I told him it was you who first had me; I did not know you were here!'

The full impact of her mocking words to Melwas struck her. 'He was going to kill you because we were lovers!' Her voice rose, hysterical.

Arthur tried to calm her, holding her close, holding her tight, though it hurt; kissing her with difficulty through his own swollen lips. 'He was here to do that anyway. Vortigern had given the order for it to be done this night, while all were occupied with this Gathering of treaty.'

His head jerked up as Cei clambered to his feet, snorting, 'Not treaty: massacre. The Saex have turned, made their move. Hengest picked the time and place well.'

Arthur cursed obscenely. 'There have been some happenings this night which will not be easily forgotten.'

One of the men left on guard outside ran in. He saluted when he saw Arthur, carefully avoiding looking directly at the more obvious hurts on his body.

'Sir, a few of the palace buildings have been fired and Lord Vortimer has at last arrived with soldiers – some of them our lads. They say Hengest's rabble are too far gone with wine and blood-lust to put up much more of a fight. Most are taking to their ships.'

Cei nodded curtly. 'Detail four men to escort Lady Gwenhwyfar and the Pendragon to safety.'

Arthur interrupted. 'Hold that order, soldier! Four men to escort the lady, and someone to find me clothing of whatever sort, and suitable weapons; quickly!'

The soldier saluted smartly and ran off at the double. Cei began to protest. 'You are in no fit state to fight!'

'On the contrary, I have never been fitter!' More gently, 'Anger does wonders for the healing of hurts, Cei.' As he talked, Arthur rubbed at Gwenhwyfar's arms, attempting to ease the trembling chill. Her eyes, hollow in sunken sockets, gazed at the spreading dark patch on Melwas's cloak between the shoulder blades. She shuddered.

'Let us leave here,' Arthur said, indicating the body. 'She has seen enough horror for one day.' He added in lower tones, 'And I'd not be sorry to leave.'

'Like as not to see many more before dawn,' Cei muttered, taking one last look around as they made their way outside.

Arthur gulped mouthfuls of sweet air, grateful that few had seen his conditions of imprisonment or noticed the haunted look in his eyes. Melwas had treated him brutally, but the beatings and floggings had been nothing compared to the enclosing darkness. He swallowed hard, fighting the remnant of his childhood phobia, unsure how he had survived the clutching terror of these past days

But survive it he had. He was here, in the air, living and breathing.

Clothing appeared, a Saxon tunic, bracae and short sword. Arthur made a noise of disgust but dressed without further protest. Even Saex weave was preferable to bare skin.

'Lady Gwenhwyfar must be taken clear, then we will see to our business.' He clapped Cei's shoulder, grinning. Fresh air and freedom coursed through him. He felt little of the swelling or bruising, nor the spiteful pull of lash marks across his back. Tomorrow would be time enough to wince and allow the shakes of fear to run their course.

He beckoned a man to him. 'What is the situation beyond the palace walls?'

'None too good, Sir. Part of the city is burning – what they cannot loot they fire. The river is crammed with their ships. Little hope for the poor beggars who live out there, even with us now here.'

Arthur scowled. The picture, although for a soldier a familiar enough one, saddened him. 'This could be the end of Londinium. Plague; trade diminishing down the years to a dribble, and now this? Love of the Bull, Cei, did he not realise this would happen?'

'Vortigern? I think not. He hoped ceding the Cantii territory would be enough for Hengest.'

Arthur buckled on the sword belt, nodded in the direction of the stables. 'We shall use the horses. I will not let good stock go to waste.'

It took a while to bridle the stabled mounts, for the smell of blood and smoke and the crackle of flames made them uneasy and restless. Five were hastily saddled and four men mounted, leading the reins of the spare mounts. Arthur helped Gwenhwyfar on to the fifth. She winced as she seated herself, and patted the fidgeting horse, feeling a tingle of comfort on realising it was that same bay she had met earlier.

Arthur gripped her thigh, smiled up at her. 'My men will escort you through the city – the Saex are on the run by the sound of it. You should get through safe. Stay within the mass of horses, none shall touch you there. Once clear, go to our camp, rest there. I will join you as soon as I can.' Whenever that would be!

He stepped away and slapped a hand on the horse's rump, sending it springing forward. The others surged round and they set off at a canter, hurtling beneath the archway, through the gates and out into the streets. Drunken groups of remaining Saex sprang aside with cries of alarm as the hooves came trampling. The horses gathered speed, galloping now, ears laid flat, nostrils flaring in a frenzy to escape the smells and sounds of surrounding fear.

The west gate loomed ahead, watch-towers standing empty, unmanned and shrouded in smoke and flame. The great gate stood wide, but a group of Hengest's men stood ground before them, waving their arms and shouting. The leading horses, already terrified, baulked. One reared, throwing his rider. In an instant, the Saex were on them.

§ XXX

Londinium was finished. Not even on a battlefield had Arthur seen such carnage.

Dressed in uniform now, after an hour's snatched sleep and some welcome hot food in his belly, he stalked through the smoking remains of the city. He poked at bodies with his toe, his frown of anger deepening.

They had found Gwenhwyfar's escort, their bodies horribly cut to pieces and hung like dead rats on the city gate. Four men, no woman.

Arthur stopped by a naked female. Her body bulged with pregnancy, her eyes staring, mouth open, her screams frozen in death. He wondered if they had mutilated her before or after they had killed her. How many had taken her? She was little more than Gwenhwyfar's age. He groaned, turned aside and was violently sick.

The three men behind respectfully turned their gaze away from his grey, beard-stubbled face.

Arthur walked on, one of the men stepped to his side said with quiet sympathy, 'We will find her, Sir. We will.'

Arthur looked at him, glanced meaningfully back at the girl's body. 'I am not entirely sure I want to.'

They entered the palace grounds. More bodies, more blood. To the left, the prison cells. Arthur made to turn to the right, thought again, headed left.

'Search over there,' he ordered, pointing away from the cells, 'I have a task of my own to do.'

It took him an eternity to step through the doorway from dull sunlight into musty darkness. Heart hammering, sweat trickling down his back he eased forward along the internal corridor.

Melwas lay there, none having bothered with him. It was a petty thing to do but when he had finished Arthur felt an immense satisfaction of revenge. His only regret, the body was long dead. Punishment for rape should be dealt to the living.

He stood upright, wiped the soiled blade of his dagger on Melwas's cloak and left, hurrying from the oppressive place.

Arthur was not a religious man. Save for his faith in the soldiers' god, Mithras, he used appropriate gods as and when he required them. At this moment, he welcomed the belief of a world beyond, praying that the humiliation he had caused to Melwas's manhood would reach the spirit and plunge it into internal suffering.

The body was discovered some few days later by a Romano-British woman searching for food and safe shelter. She fled at the brief glimpse of a man's mutilated body, his private parts hacked off and stuffed into his mouth. Telling others of the scene, she would add, 'Wicked are these Saex! Barbarian wicked.'

For Arthur, it had been small recompense, but Gwenhwyfar would appreciate the gesture. If he ever got to tell her. He bit his lip. She was not within the city, that much was certain and she had not reached the camp. If Hengest's Saex had her, there was only one way to barter for her return. Exchange her for Rowena or Winifred.

Rejoining them, Arthur growled at his men to follow. Cei was making his way across the bloodied courtyard from the direction of the great hall.

'Leave all this,' Arthur bellowed as the man came closer. 'We ride to Caer Gloui.'

Cei chewed his lip, staring bleakly at the surrounding heaps of bodies. He sighed. So much death, so much more to come. 'Vortimer wishes to speak with you.'

Arthur repeated an oath, ordered his men to get the horses ready.

'Has Vortigern been found?' he asked as he walked with Cei.

'Vortimer has him, I do not give much for his chances of survival should anyone lay hands on him. The British are shouting for his head – and other parts.'

'A shame they did not do so before now. Ah, Vortimer!' Arthur stepped through charred timbers into what remained of the great council hall. The bodies of those murdered had been removed, but the bloodstains pooling the tessellated floor remained. One relief was that many elders and nobles had deliberately stayed away from Vortigern's call to this Gathering of

Council as a protest. Those who sided with the King or sought favour were the unfortunates. Some, Arthur privately mused, they were well rid of!

The King's eldest son, Vortimer, looked up, haggard, from a parchment he was reading. Behind him his brother Catigern stared warily at Arthur. It was no secret that one day the Pendragon would make a bid for the kingship. The brothers, it seemed, were pooling their strength against him. Today the door to power stood wide open, but together they barred entrance with spears crossed. It would not be this day the Pendragon took command.

Arthur perched himself on the edge of a charred bench. 'This was bound to happen eventually. No soldier, Saex or British, will fight unpaid without strong cause. There must be a reward at the end. Our men fight for their homeland, women and children. What is there for the Saex? They fight in Vortigern's army for no quarrel of their own. If they are not given what they ask it must be expected that one day they will take it.' He halted. Neither of the old king's sons answered.

Arthur went on, 'They were hired as mercenaries to swell the army so Vortigern could hold sway over counter claimants to the throne – against men like my father. They are no different from countless other such troops employed by Rome in this country and others.' Silence from Vortimer and Catigern. Arthur finished with a slight shrug of one shoulder. 'They were not paid. Were given nothing, save empty promises. The Saex were never to be content with only the occasional tossed bone.'

He thumped the bench, then lurched to his feet. 'Do not look at me as if it were I who caused all this! As I hear things, Council voted against Vortigern, refused to cede the land as payment. Hengest intended to take what he wanted with or without permission.' He gestured at the mess. Shouting almost, he concluded, 'If I were in Hengest's boots, like as not I would do the same!'

Catigern stepped forward at that. 'A pretty speech, Pendragon. It sounds to my ears almost as though you back Hengest. Are you in league with him, then – you and your bitch wife?'

Arthur refused to take the bait, not wishing to become involved in argument. He needed to be gone. '*Na*, man, grant me more sense than that! I am pointing out Hengest's view. A leader's view.'

About to make some hot reply, Catigern was silenced by his elder brother who asked, 'You deny all knowledge that Hengest was intending to rebel?'

'Beyond personal speculation, aye.' Arthur was becoming suspicious. 'What is all this?'

'You deny plotting to murder our father; that your wife was to help you?'

'Of course I bloody deny it! Blood of Mithras, I have been in the cells facing death myself for the Bull knows how many days!'

Catigern sneered, 'A place of convenient safety.'

Never having liked Catigern much Arthur thought it best to ignore him, to talk instead direct to Vortimer. 'What has my wife to do with this? Ex-wife. I have applied for legal divorce.'

Vortimer tapped the parchment he had been reading on his palm. 'That is not what she says, not in this letter.'

'What letter?' Arthur held out his hand for it.

Vortimer hesitated, then passed it over, saying, 'I found it among my father's papers.'

Arthur scanned the words quickly, tossed the thing back to Vortimer. 'I have not seen it before. What she says is rubbish. I will take the kingdom if I get a chance – you know that – but not with her, not on her plotting. I say again, I am to divorce her and marry with Gwenhwyfar.' He brought his head forward, his eyes narrowing, said menacingly, 'May I remind you both whose idea it was I marry Winifred in the first place? I did not want her then. I do not want her now.'

Catigern growled, 'Yet you were at my father's throat the other day.'

Arthur sneered at him. 'When am I not? I usually have good cause. Come to that, when are you not?'

Vortimer released a long sigh. 'We had to be certain, Arthur – you do see?'

He did not, but again, he let the matter pass.

Vortimer tore the parchment in half and half again, let the pieces fall to the floor. 'Council, for right or wrong, condemned the giving of land as payment for service. Vortigern gambled and lost and the Saex responded with murder. It is in my mind Hengest knew full well he would not get what he wanted so easily and used the occasion as his chance to strike. As you rightly say, Arthur, now he will try to take whatever else he wants. While we are in disarray, he will step in with Rowena and the boy.'

'So what do you intend to do? I assume you have taken command?'

Disliking the tone of Arthur's question, Catigern pushed himself further forward to defend his brother. 'He intends to regroup the army – our army, British men. We will make a stand against Hengest. A wise decision, do you not think, Pendragon? Or is this a chance for you to seize command?'

Arthur laughed, amused at the hostility. 'Aye, it is.' Turning his back on Catigern he stood beside Vortimer.

'I have already said, I know nothing of this plot between my wife or Rowena and their Saex kin. I am not sorry to see Vortigern fall – we share the same sentiment there.' He winced at the stiffness in his limbs. 'If I were foolish enough to dispute leadership with you at this moment, Vortimer, what few fighting men we possess would be obliged to take up arms against each other. Many would rally to my Dragon, but as many would go to your Red Boar. Would that not be playing into Hengest's hands?'

He turned his head, his eyes piercing Catigern. 'Hengest knows Vortigern's fall will re-open the dispute of leadership.' He directed his attention back to Vortimer, held out his hand in friendship. His knuckles and fingers were bloodied, bruised and swollen where Melwas had repeatedly stamped into the flesh.

'For all your brother's taunts, Vortimer, I can wait a short while longer.'

Vortimer visibly relaxed, accepted Arthur's hand. 'I am relieved to hear it. I would not wish to give the order to, er, detain you, should your plans not be, shall we say, beneficial?'

Arthur smiled lazily. 'Yet I noticed neither you nor friend Catigern here attempted to secure my release from your father and cousin's pleasures? It would have suited you to be rid of me at the expense of someone else's conscience.'

Vortimer began to protest, but Arthur lifted a hand to silence him. 'In your position I would have done the same.' *Though,* he thought, *with more efficiency, no wasting time with sadistic pleasures. I would have had them instantly hanged.*

'While you show sense, Vortimer,' Arthur grimaced as he stretched the ache from his shoulders, 'I will buckle myself to your orders.' He paused, regarding Britain's new king. 'For a price.'

'Which is?'

'My father's West Country lands. Dumnonia and the Summer Land must return to my overlordship; and custody of Rowena, her son Vitolinus, and Winifred.'

Vortimer frowned. 'Melwas is lord of the Summer Land, and Meirchion governor of Dumnonia. Were I to say take them, I would have two men up in arms against me.'

'Melwas is dead.'

Vortimer raised an eyebrow. 'You are certain?'

Arthur seated himself again, regretted it as fire shot across his buttocks, up his back and through his shoulders. Riding was going to be an agony. 'I can show you his body.'

A smile formed on Vortimer's lips. 'One less problem to deal with then.'

Arthur said, 'And Meirchion is a worm who slithers from rock to rock. He allied with Vortigern against my father. It is only a matter of time before I kill him also, for all he is cousin to my father.'

'I would rather you delayed in the slaughter of too many men you hold in dislike, Arthur. Enough died here last night; if you add to the tally, I will be hard pressed to form a Council.'

Saying nothing Arthur simply regarded Vortimer, his silence making his intention all the clearer. He would have the West returned. Legally given, or in his own way.

'I freely grant you the Summer Land. But Dumnonia with it? That would make you a powerful man, Pendragon.'

'With or without the land, Vortimer, I am close to being that. If I wanted, I could hold most of the army. With men at my back I can take all I want, without waiting for you to give it.'

This was true. Vortimer puffed out his cheeks. 'May I suggest a compromise? Meirchion has no male heir and is growing old. Persuade him you are to be that heir'

'I have your word you will recognise such an agreement when the man dies?'

'If I in turn have your sworn fealty to me, then *sa*, it shall be so.' Vortimer regarded Arthur sternly. He knew the position. The Pendragon was not yet strong enough to make his claim, but give him a few more men to command, more campaigns and experience under his belt and the situation would change. To hold the entire West Country, as his father once had, would give him command over those needed men and bring in the wealth to attract and finance others. This cavalry idea of his, for instance, would be a viable concern were Arthur to have the finances those territories would bring, and would provide the grazing land for the breeding, rearing and keeping of horses.

'I have already agreed to fight alongside you,' Arthur said, heaving himself upright, stifling a groan. 'In as much as fighting the Saex anyway. More, I cannot guarantee.'

Vortimer walked a few paces, considering.

Catigern had been silent, but now he went to his brother, spoke in a low tone. Arthur caught a few, not over-complimentary words.

Vortimer replied sharply, ushered Catigern aside. Arthur was no fool and he was a good soldier – too good. There was every possibility the bulk of the straggling British army would decide to follow the Pendragon today, would not wait for the morrow.

Arthur said, with a good humour that emphasised his intent, 'I will have the land, Vortimer. It was my father's and his father's before him. It is mine by right. Vortigern stole it. I am taking it back.'

'By agreeing I give away a substantial portion of revenue.'

'Which is why Vortigern took it in the first place to parcel out to his lapdogs. Your father had control over all but Gwynedd and the wild lands to the north.' Arthur shrugged, made as if to leave. 'Keep your legacy whole then, Vortimer. If you can.'

'Hold!' the new king called, raising his hands. 'I do not have the ambitions of Vortigern. I am a soldier, not a king or emperor. As long as we can achieve the same aim – to hold these barbarians from our shores – then I am content. Have your land.'

'But brother...' Catigern blurted disagreement. He had hoped for the same package Arthur was claiming. Vortimer was giving Arthur the position of second-in-command!

'Na, Catigern!' Vortimer rounded on his brother. 'I have no hope of holding this kingdom together. Vortigern tried and failed. Let Arthur have what is his, and good luck to him.'

He clasped Arthur's hand, 'Understand it is yours to see to, though. Do not come bleating to me when you find Meirchion is not willing to submit to you.'

'Oh, he will submit,' Arthur said confidently.

Vortimer had no reason to doubt him, fully expected to receive word the Governor of Dumnonia had met with some 'accidental' death ere many moons waned. So be it – the matter was not his problem.

'The women and the boy?' Arthur asked.

'The boy is too young. I will not have him harmed.'

Catigern, already angry with his brother's decision, burst out, 'You cannot let him remain free! God's truth, why not hang your sword up now!'

'Hold your tongue!' Vortimer roared. 'I am King. I say what is to be! I have no intention of letting the half-Saex boy loose, but nor will I have him harmed. I command you, Pendragon, to see him placed in close custody somewhere safe.'

Arthur nodded. He could accept that, for now. 'And Rowena?'

'Rowena is to be executed on a charge of treason.'

Arthur thought briefly before answering. It would give him great pleasure to comply, but, 'Is that wise? Will it not antagonise Hengest?'

'I care not what Hengest thinks of my decisions. She is evil and I would have an end to her.'

'What of Vortigern?' Arthur queried, letting the subject rest a moment. 'Someone said he was not killed?'

Vortimer's answer was hard as stone. 'They left him alive. Hengest, apparently, would not order the death of his daughter's husband.' He added sarcastically, 'Kin, you see.'

Catigern spat. 'Vortigern ought to hang alongside Rowena!'

His brother indicated a bundle huddled in a far corner. 'I agree, but there is nothing left worth hanging.'

Puzzled, Arthur crossed the hall, tore away a layer of what he had taken to be piled rags. He drew in his breath sharply as he gazed on a crumpled, pathetic old man, slavering at the mouth, whimpering and mumbling feebly.

Vortigern. The translucent skin drawn tight over his bones gave his face the look of a skeleton's mask. He fumbled for the protective covering Arthur had pulled aside and withdrew into its shielding darkness, eyes staring, seeing the red blood gushing, hearing men and women shrieking. His world had collapsed and his mind had fled.

Vortimer stood at Arthur's shoulder, regarding the sorry shell of his father. 'He will not trouble us again. He ought to die, but it would be as pointless as murdering a child.'

Arthur did not agree, but held his council.

Vortimer asked, 'Can I trust you to see to Rowena's end?'

Arthur looked wearily at the man, his king. 'I cannot say. I thought to exchange her for Gwenhwyfar, should she be held captive.'

'Is that likely?' Vortimer placed a sympathetic hand on Arthur's arm, aware of her disappearance. 'When we have defeated these barbarians, when they are on the run, they will not be in any position to bargain. I promise you, Arthur, when Hengest capitulates before me you can demand from him what you will. For now, I must have Rowena dead, if only for my own satisfaction. She defiled the memory of my mother and she must pay for it. I would that I could personally string her up, but I have an army to bring together. I ask again, Arthur – can I trust you?'

Arthur thought on it. Were he to go seeking Rowena he would be conveniently absent from the army. With no Pendragon to rally to, those men who had small liking for Vortigern's progeny would follow Vortimer through lack of choice. He ran a hand through his hair. He would like a bath, but idle luxury must wait. It had been a rash idea, this one of exchange, clutching at frayed rope. Leave it.

Vortimer added, seeing Arthur's doubt, 'You must face the facts, man. If they do have Gwenhwyfar, then what is left of her will not be worth taking back. For you, she is dead, Arthur. Dead.'

'She is alive, of that I am certain.' Arthur held his hand out to seal their agreement. 'Very well, you have my word Rowena will hang for treason. So too, shall Winifred.'

Vortimer shrugged, uncaring. 'Do what you will with her, she is your wife. You know where to find them?'

'Aye, Melwas insisted on informing me. At Vortigern's summer villa outside Caer Gloui.'

After he had gone, Catigern, bitter at his brother's ruling said, 'You are a fool to trust the Pendragon. I am your brother; I should hold the honour of high command, not he.'

Vortimer was standing close to where his bundled father lay. He nudged the heap of rags with his toe and the thing shifted, crabbing across the floor.

'If you think you could hold higher command than the Pendragon, then it is you who are the fool, Catigern.'

MAY 455

§ XXXI

It had rained, on and off, for most of that spring. The rivers were running swollen, crops lay rotten and blackened, and mud oozed thick, clinging and stinking. The low ground between the Hafren and Caer Gloui was continuously soggy underfoot, squelching beneath boots, seeping into dwelling places and old people's bones. The river would burst its banks soon if the rain did not cease. There was little anyone could do, save wait, watch and pray.

Arthur rode into the Caer two days after the beginning of the month. He hated this town – and more, hated its inhabitants.

'They are like those eastern birds Aegidius of Gaul has strutting around his palace grounds,' he said to Cei, riding at his side. 'Peacocks, birds stuffed fat with their own importance.'

'This is a rich area,' Cei answered neutrally.

'What has wealth to do with it?' Arthur snorted his contempt. 'Not all rich men are crinkle-nosed asses!'

Cei laughed. 'Most are! Even you!'

Arthur blustered indignation and Cei laughed the louder. 'You are so sure of your own convictions you will never tolerate other people's views!'

'That is not true!'

'*Na?*'

'*Na*. I listen to some people.'

Cei roared delight. 'Only those who agree with you! Take these townsfolk. You know but a handful of them, yet you judge all by those few. There may be one or two pleasant families living hereabouts.'

Straight-faced Arthur nodded towards a man who was approaching, hitching one trailing end of a worn toga from the mired road. 'Think you this may be one of the two, Cei?'

The man shook his fist. 'You are not thinking to ride through this town with that rabble in attendance!' He was shouting, red-faced, pointing at the sixty mounted men of Arthur's two turmae.

Arthur halted Eira, swung round in his saddle and regarded the men behind him, as if he were surprised to find them there. He scratched the stubbled beard on his face and sniffed loudly. 'I am not thinking of it, old man,' He nudged his horse forward at a walk, his men following.

Cheeks scarlet, the elderly man stepped in front of the stallion, causing Eira to toss his head and lay his ears back. Arthur eased a hand down the rain-soaked neck.

'I will not tolerate unlawful gangs of, of...' the man blustered, seeking an appropriate word, 'of heathen Vandals entering this town!'

Arthur half grinned at Cei. 'Not even one or two.'

Cei chuckled.

'There is nothing amusing about this!' The man's voice was rising. 'You army people are all the same, think you own the place! Unless you have come to help shore the river banks against flood, get you gone!' He waved his arm about, setting the horses dancing.

Arthur had heard enough. 'In the first place, my men are not a rabble. They are a trained, disciplined cavalry unit. Secondly, we have ridden many miles in this incessant rain. We are cold, wet, hungry and tired. My men and their horses require shelter.'

'Then seek it outside the town!'

'There are inns aplenty within. And third,' Arthur leant forward, across his stallion's neck, said emphatically, 'I am not *thinking* of riding through, I *am* riding through.'

He spurred his horse forward, the animal responding to the pressure of heel and leg, shouldering the obstructing man aside.

The two turmae rode solemnly past, not daring to let the laughter inside them show, leaving the man shaking his fist and spluttering apoplectic oaths.

The inns welcomed them with pleasure, grateful for custom. Travellers were few and far between this wet weather.

After seeing men and animals well settled, Cei and Arthur retreated to a quiet corner of their chosen quarters, welcomed the steaming bowls of broth placed before them.

'I rather think you ought not have angered the old man.'

Arthur sucked broth from his bowl. 'Daft old dung-heap.'

'*Na*, you will not be famed for being a leader with tact,' Cei grinned.

'Tactics, not tact, interest me more.' Mopping up the last of his broth with a chunk of bread, Arthur pushed away the empty bowl and reached for wine. 'They annoy me, people like him. First to complain, first to belly-ache and whine. Last to do anything. How many give a toss about what is happening east of here? How many give a damn about Vortigern's failed, blundering policies and this mess we are mired in?'

Cei wiped spillage from his lips. The broth had been good. 'More than we would give credit for. The Hibernian raid heavily along the coasts.' Cei signalled to the innkeeper for a refill. 'These people are as aware as we are of the dangers in losing control.'

'Oh aye, they are aware. As you say, sea-wolves come along the coast looking for land ripe for the taking. *Go fight the Saex, keep them from our doorstep,* they say. Yet when it comes to paying the army or hosting us for a night, Caer Gloui and such towns are of a sudden safe within their walls, have their own militias and weapons. The army is not needed. Not wanted. Go away! Fah!' He spat into the fire, sending up a hiss of sparks.

The innkeeper's daughter brought the broth and a second jug of wine, good quality stuff set aside for men of rank and means. Her liquid dark eyes met with Arthur's. She blushed, lowered her gaze.

'The bathhouse is available should you require its use,' she said shyly, not meeting his eyes. Arthur's line of sight flickered to her rounded bosom; glanced at a figure who sat hunched and dozing, his clothes steaming, before the heat of the fire.

'Gladly would I accept such an offer,' Arthur indicated Cynan, 'but my servant is asleep. He is a faithful lad and I have not the inclination to disturb him.' Rubbish. What were servants for? The girl blushed a second time, said quietly, 'I am sure I can arrange an alternative attendant, my Lord.'

Arthur grinned at that, pushed the bench from him as he stood. 'Then lead on, girl!' He winked at Cei, who stretched, laughing.

'No tact,' Cei said. 'Open and obvious!'

§ XXXII

Shaved, clean, and relaxed from a night of pleasure and sleep, Arthur entered Vortigern's private residence sited beside a curve of the Hafren two miles beyond the west gate of the Caer. It was still raining and the river, Arthur noted absently, was already lapping against the outer wall. He was not surprised to find Winifred and her mother expecting him.

Winifred ran to Arthur as he drew rein, skittering out from under the portico, her veil tossed carelessly over her head, feeble protection against the pouring rain. She embraced him, kissed him, her mouth lingering on his, her fingers delicately touching the remaining bruises on his skin. Letting him know she wanted him, had missed him.

He did not brush her aside, but then neither did he return the embrace and kiss. The opposite of her desire; let her know he did not want her, did not miss her.

Clinging to his arm Winifred walked inside with him, staying close, her body brushing against his, heedless of his wet clothing.

Slaves bustled forward to take wet cloaks, offer wine and remove boots. Arthur shed his cloak, drank down a goblet of wine, kept his boots.

'Did you receive my letter? I had to take great care lest Melwas discover it – or Mother. She was plotting with grandfather. I had to warn you, dearest.' Winifred spoke breathlessly, in a whisper, fearing her mother might discover her betrayal. Rowena was not one to cross, not even for her daughter. 'Thank God you are safe through it!'

Winifred pressed herself against him, resting her head on his chest, her arms tight around his waist. Of all the stupid, pathetic things, she meant it, actually meant it! 'When we heard of,' she swallowed, 'of what happened, I was so afeared you too had been killed.' She smiled up at him, loving him. *God alone knows why*, she thought. 'I was so relieved to hear you were come to Caer Gloui. I have been kept here at my father's command, not allowed to leave. Have you come to take me home?'

Arthur had not answered, had walked away from her into the living quarters to where Rowena was waiting.

Winifred trotted to keep pace with him. 'I risked much to warn you into stopping my father holding that Gathering, or at least for you to act well on it.' She broke into a sudden broad smile. 'But you did! You did act! Oh, Arthur, I knew I could be of help. I knew by betraying Mother and Hengest, I could open the way for you to claim your title!' She linked arms with him, prattled on about Melwas coming for her at the estate, forcing her to leave. 'The brute was so rough and insolent. I managed to bribe one of his men to take the letter – I had fears my father would not let you free, but I thought, as my husband, he would be honour-bound to release you. '

Arthur stopped dead, plucked her hand free of his arm. 'Shut up, you stupid woman.'

For a moment Winifred was taken aback. Her face began to crumple, her lip quiver but he was not watching, had walked on. She took several deep breaths, followed him, excuses formulating. He is tired and wet through; he is king now, has much on his mind. Gleefully, thought, *with Arthur king, I am queen!*

'I have heard rumours.' Rowena reclined along a couch, dressed richly, one hand resting lightly on the head-rest. She inclined her head as Arthur entered, said, 'Are they true?'

'If you are asking is it true that your father's wolf pack has shrugged itself free from the leash, then aye, it is true.'

If she was pleased, her face gave nothing away. 'And my husband?'

'He matters no more. Vortimer has the kingdom now.'

Winifred had entered a little behind Arthur. She ran to his side. 'What? But you are the Pendragon. You are to be king!'

'I am content for Vortimer to rule.'

'No!' Winifred stamped her foot. 'I warned you of this uprising so you could be there to step in!' Too late, her hand covered her mouth, head swivelling towards her mother.

Rowena's eyes had narrowed. What was this! Her daughter turned betrayer? She had no opportunity to question, for Arthur was speaking to his wife.

'You are so fond of me then, Winifred? Yet a few months past you were prepared to flee to the Saex, keep my child from me and make plea for divorce. You must love me well!'

Her arms twined around his waist. 'I do! I was so confused and scared for the child then, I thought you were close to death – and,' she pointed accusingly at her mother, 'and she made me do it!'

Rowena sat composed. 'I? Nonsense, daughter! You begged for my help, said you could not abide the foul-mouthed, slime-trailed man you were forced to call husband.' Only a woman such as Rowena could remain so pleasantly smiling while delivering insults.

Beneath the calm exterior she was furious. So! Winifred had turned against her, was sidling up to this posturing braggart, Pendragon! Was after being queen herself, no doubt. Beyond that, she was angry with Vortigern for sending her to this accursed place. How dare he usher her off like some scolded child! Then, she was angry with her father for taking action while she was unable to reach a place of safety. She had expressly said in her last communication she needed to be there when he struck, to claim the status of king for Vitolinus. And she was angry with Arthur for being who he was.

She talked smoothly, hiding her rage. 'It was you who talked of divorce and of ending your marriage, not I.'

Winifred had always known her mother was a bitch, had seen her tongue lashing a variety of unfortunates. Until now, the sting had never been aimed at her. Well, she was her mother's daughter, had watched and learnt and copied. Winifred could be just as much the bitch!

'Because you put the idea in my mind! You ought not have trusted me, Mother. I know all the details of that planned murder! She forced me to run, Arthur, threatened me and our child – and you. She said she would have you murdered if I did not do her bidding.'

Clinging to him, Winifred implored Arthur to believe her. 'It was God's providence you rescued me. I am your loyal wife, I will serve you well as queen.'

Rowena broke in quickly. 'My son is named heir. If Vortimer is calling himself king I, as regent, shall have him arrested on a charge of treason.'

Arthur smiled, strolled to a couch and seated himself, placing his muddied boots on the fabric coverings. 'Vortimer is the first-born son – and is not tainted by Saex blood. You and your kind are no longer wanted here.'

'Without my father's help, these shores would be harassed tenfold from what they are now!' Rowena's composure was weakening. 'My father's people kept to their side of the bargain; it is you British who have lied and cheated and stolen from us. Add to that, my brother fought well against the northern uprising, or have you forgotten?'

'*Na*, lady, I have not forgotten how your brother, on your husband's orders, murdered Typiaunan, eldest son to Cunedda of Gwynedd.' Arthur spoke quietly, his disgust intense. 'It seems cold blooded murder sits well on Saex shoulders.'

'My father sought just payment. Council has brought this destruction!'

'Have you finished?' Arthur growled. 'It was your Saex who hid their daggers. The British were unarmed. Most were old men. Helpless, defenceless old men. What brave people you are! Thank you, Winifred,' his mocking, pleasant smile lingered on his wife; 'I will have wine.'

She glowered – she was no servant to order about! None the less, she fetched and poured wine.

He drank, belched, wiped his mouth and swung his legs from the couch. 'You talked of treason.' He went to stand before Rowena, one hand resting on his sword. 'You are under arrest. I am here to hang you.'

Rowena turned white, her hand, gold and silver bangles jingling, flying to her throat. 'But I am the Queen.'

'No longer. You are Hengest's daughter and you are to die. Here and now.'

Rowena thought fast. She must gain time. 'What of my son?'

'What of him?' Arthur examined a bowl of dried fruits, took a selected handful, stood chewing. He wondered how long Vortimer would last. The man was too soft, you needed an iron stomach to survive in this game.

He went to the closed door, opened it. Beyond were two of his own guard. 'You have a choice, Rowena. Die now, quietly, or on the morrow after my men have enjoyed you.'

'You have no right!'

Winifred saw a chance. She simpered up to Arthur, took his hand between hers, held it to her breast.

'The Pendragon has every right.'

Arthur patted her holding hands with his free one, smiled down at her. 'You, wife, will be keeping your mother company.'

'What!' Winifred paled, tried to pull away, but he held her fast. Gwenhwyfar had told him of Ceridwen, briefly, a few hurried words as the horses had been saddled. Enough.

'But I sent you warning, I tried to help you I...'

Arthur could be so cold behind that safe, deceptive smile. 'I never received such a letter. I know nothing of it. I have seen the evidence to assume you to be in league with Rowena here, so you are to die also, my sweet.'

With one hand he stroked her cheek, seductively gentle. 'You are no use to me alive. Your death will bring me all your wealth and solve the need for those messy little divorce settlements and such.'

She should have known he would turn on her! Why had she bothered to try and help him? Why had she not, instead, paid Melwas to run him through? 'If you plan to marry with your Gwynedd whore, you will be disappointed, husband. She is dead.'

Arthur stared at her, his smile sudden gone. How did she know?

Winifred saw the anguish course through him, realised, with jealousy, the deep love he felt for Gwenhwyfar. Inside she glowed with triumph. With her gone he would still need her as wife.

Dry mouthed Arthur demanded, 'Who told you this?'

She was still standing close, but he had let her go. She took his hand in hers again, pressed it to her cheek, thinking quickly of a plausible answer. 'From Caer Leon. Messengers are searching for you – they assumed you would be at the King's new seat of administration. When they found you were not there they stopped here, naturally, knowing I was here. I sent them on to Londinium.'

'Messengers?' This smelt like a rotting carcass. 'What messengers?'

Her cheeks were flushed, her breath coming a little too quickly.

'Why,' she said, 'messengers from your mother. That last night, Gwenhwyfar was detained ill with that elderly farming couple, remember? It seems she was more ill than anyone suspected. She died.' In a sympathetic voice, she added, 'I am so sorry. I assumed they had found you, assumed you knew. I know how fond you were of her.'

Arthur swung his hand, his fist smashing into her face. Winifred screamed and fell, blood pouring from a broken nose.

'You lying bitch! I have seen Gwenhwyfar this past week in Londinium!'

Bear's breath, no! Winifred lay crumpled on the floor, blood gushing. What had gone wrong? She had poisoned her. Gwenhwyfar was surely dead!

He was calling for guards. They were coming into the room, spears and swords at the ready.

Rowena, ignoring her daughter, had risen from her couch. 'I am no fool, Arthur.'

'That, I grant, is true,' he hissed.

'I accept I have lost, I am to die. May I take a few moments to bid farewell to my son and make preparations to meet my God in privacy?'

'*Na,* you may not.'

Rowena tried again, polite, calm. Thinking. *Damn you, you bastard, may you rot in Hell!*

'As a Christian, you cannot forbid me my prayers, Pendragon.'

'Has your daughter never informed you? I care little for religion. I find it convenient to change faiths as the whim takes me. As you seem to do.'

'We are true Christians, as well you know!' Winifred retorted through the veil held to her face to stem the blood,

'Do not talk to me, bitch!' Arthur shouted at her. 'You are nothing to me, nothing except a discarded vessel where I once emptied my need.'

She knelt on the floor, fingers bloodied. 'Can I be blamed for loving you?'

'Love? You know not the meaning of the word!'

'Do I not? I have given you love in your bed, I have borne you one child, believe I carry another. I love you, husband – why else would I write you warning? What more can I do to prove myself? Our son, when he is born, will bear witness for me!'

Arthur did not hear, not wanting to listen. He beckoned the guard. 'Take them away.'

'With respect, Sir, many among us are followers of Christ. We acknowledge the need for these ladies to hang, but you must in turn acknowledge their need to make peace with our Lord.'

Arthur roared his anger, came within a handspan of striking the man. 'Are you challenging my authority, you insolent pat of cow dung?'

Cei strolled in almost casually, as if it were only by chance he was passing, whispered in Arthur's ear.

Arthur cursed, kicked at the table sending fruit and bowl clattering to the floor. 'Very well. A few moments only; have them close watched!'

Cei spoke quickly to the guard who saluted and ushered the women from the room, Rowena composed, Winifred weeping. 'You realise she is playing for time, Cei? She will be hatching some means of escape.'

'Your men will follow you to the edge of this earth, Arthur, but not if you deny them our God.'

'I deny them nothing, so long as it does not interfere with me. And this interferes, Cei!'

'Reject Christ if you will, but walk that dark path alone!' Cei flung the words at him and marched from the room, following in the wake of the group heading across the atrium for the private chapel. He called to a servant. 'Summon the priest, and fetch the boy!'

Furious, Arthur stormed to the outer courtyard where some of his men had already flung two ropes over the boughs of a sturdy tree growing close to the perimeter wall. 'Will this be sufficient, lord?'

'It will have to be. Curse this rain – will it never cease?' Arthur kicked at the tree trunk, leapt back in alarm as the thing moved. His eye strayed to the wall and he stood, fascinated, as the cracks, hitherto unnoticed, spread and divided. Water trickled through the brickwork.

A low rumble grew in volume from the far side. Slowly the wall crumpled and water began pouring through. The river, swollen to bursting point by the rain was suddenly gushing into this quiet paved area, sweeping debris, shrubs and men with it.

Arthur and two others grabbed at the dangling ropes, hauling themselves into the branches of the tree, which creaked and swayed, but held.

They watched in disbelief as the flood waters burst through into the villa, ripping timbers and brickwork apart as if they were parchment.

Everywhere was river. There was no wall now, no ordered garden. Trees, dragged up by the roots, clawed grotesquely through its churning waters. A dead sheep swirled by; a cat, yowling, clung arch-backed to what looked like a house-rafter. On the far side of where the wall had once stood the distant town of Caer Gloui seemed like an island within a boiling turmoil. An apple bobbing in a pond.

Arthur could only guess at the panic down there within those fine buildings.

Then he saw something which made him shout out and attempt to leave his safe perch.

Two women, one with a child clutched in her arms, scrambled over the fallen masonry of the villa's small chapel, floundering through knee-deep water. They reached higher ground, ran for the shelter of the woods.

Arthur shouted, waved his arms, trying desperately to alert his men who struggled, dazed and confused, among the debris and could not hear his voice above the roaring waters. Swearing all the oaths he knew, he tried again to let himself down into the swirl of muddied water below. He gasped at its coldness and strength. For a wild moment he struggled to retain his balance, gained a footing, thrust forward against the current to higher ground where the men were gathering.

He scrambled out of the flow of flood water, chest heaving, clothing sodden, muscles aching. Too many hurts had battered his body of late! A soldier put a hand under his arm, hauled him up.

Mithras! Arthur looked at the anxious faces crowding round, at six men, beyond where the wall had once been, clinging to the reins of frightened horses. Thank the gods they had left the animals out there to graze, had not taken them into the stables! Other men were thrashing about in the water. Arthur reached out a helping hand to Cei.

When those who had survived were safe, gaining their breath, stunned and wet through, Arthur peered again to where he had last seen the fleeing women.

There was no sign of Winifred, Rowena, or the boy Vitolinus.

Several explicit oaths flurried through Arthur's mind.

AUGUST 455

§ XXXIII

They sat, cross-legged, nursing sword or bow; or stood leaning on war ribboned spears. Silent, or whispering. No loud sound. Waiting.

On the far side of the ford, another army waited for the order to move forward. Hengest, slightly apart, stood with several of his thegns, his brother and his son. He stood, legs widespread, fists on hips, surveying the wide river crossing that stretched away before him. A dull sky overhead. The sun well risen behind the thick covering of cloud, promised little warmth this day. It would rain before long.

He sucked his lip, scratched at the red beard covering his chin. Ah, it felt good to stand ready before his men, holding them in check, anticipating that tumultuous roar of release.

Men close to him watched their leader, eager and expectant. Those further down the line glancing often at the White Horse banner, waiting for it to dip to signal the advance.

Hengest was resplendently dressed on this, his day of supreme victory. His helmet was decorated at the apex of the skull with a gold effigy of a boar, the whole thing a milky greenish-grey in the misty half light, the colouring coming from plates of split horn placed between the silvered iron frame. His red cloak, covering chainmail shirt, lifted in the wind.

He shifted his right hand to the hilt of his sword, which hung from a baldric fastened across his chest with an ornate gold and garnet buckle. The pommel felt good in his hand, warm, vibrant and alive.

Behind him, his battle slave caressed two spears taller than himself and with them, a huge iron-studded shield.

When victory came there would be reward for all, slave and warrior alike. Men waited. The Jutes, their fair hair braided on each side of their faces and a tail of hair hanging from the crown, stood with oval shields resting on the ground and short swords at the ready, waiting.

One man, dressed as richly as Hengest, stepped forward. He too had a red beard and hair, a stout frame, muscular legs and a warrior's stem face. They were much alike, these two brothers.

'Is it not time?' he asked.

Hengest nodded once, turned and took shield and spears from the slave. '*Ja*, my brother, I think it is time!'

They came like a rush of wind sighing across a field of sun ripe barley. Swift, not silent, an indefinable whisper; a soft shush of distant noise. There were so many of them! The front ranks seemed static at first, barely making headway down the hill flanking the river. Bobbing heads, lifted spears, waving standards, all coming on at a steady walk.

Their voices and war horns, tossed by a following wind, reached the waiting Romano-British. No single words, just a composite sound of nearing death.

Arrows from the British bowmen hissed across the water. Their deadly flight would be seen to blacken the sky, were any man fool enough to look upward.

They were close enough now, the Saex, to show individual faces; mouths open in battle cry, eyes wide, blue, green or brown against white. They came relentlessly down the hill to the bank of the river as if impervious to the hail of spears and arrows sent to main and kill by the British. Where one man fell, another stepped into his place.

The water churned white foam as men began to wade. Mud mixing with blood. Those who fell, dead or still alive, stayed down, trampled underfoot. Men began to fight hand to hand; sword clashing on sword, spears thrusting into soft flesh. Where weapons were dropped or lack of space rendered them useless, they used their hands, teeth and feet. Wrestling, grappling. Battle, and the scream of death.

Seated astride Eira Arthur waited, taut and furious, watching the carnage at the ford spread below his vantage point of this raised ground.

His men, ranged behind him, stroked their horses' sweating necks, curbing them back. The tension for rider and beast as tight as a strung bow.

Vortimer was wrong! His plan sound in theory, but in practice monumentally wrong.

Their infantry stood firm at the ford, refusing to give ground, denying Hengest's Jutes access across the river. But for how long? An hour? Two? Then what? It was not sufficient to hold this crossing, they must push forward, take it in decisive victory and put an end to this thing before it grew into something more.

A half wing of Hengest's Saex broke away, swung along their right-hand bank, moving off at a steady jog trot. Ducking low through scrub, they avoided those few arrows or spears that sailed across the dividing water.

Arthur had been ordered to wait, to hold hard in case the line failed and the enemy managed to break across the Horse Ford. It was the one place wide and firm enough for herded cattle or horses, ridden or driven, to cross. Other places up and down river afforded access to single riders or men on foot, but the Horse Ford was a drovers' way. An essential crossing to hold, for either side.

Cei pointed with his spear at the disappearing Saxons, said, 'If they find a way over downstream and close behind us, we are finished.'

Arthur remained silent: no point in answering the obvious.

'The marshes may hold them back,' Cei added unconvincingly, 'but they are canny with the ways of water, and there are paths of firm ground aplenty for men in single file on foot down that way.'

'Vortimer knows,' Arthur hissed. 'Do you not think I told him of this when I argued against our position? Would he listen? Mithras, what a mess!'

The rain drizzled, puddling underfoot so that in places it was difficult to tell rain-sodden earth from river marsh.

Arthur dared not take the horses too far down river; the ground was too soft, too treacherous. Yet could he allow a free path for these Saex to creep through?

He signalled a rider forward, spoke briefly, sent him galloping to where Vortimer and his brother, with the infantry reserve, watched the battle below. Within moments the rider returned with a second mounted man, Catigern himself.

'My brother the King does not wish you to leave your position, Pendragon.'

'I don't give a fart what he wishes! There is a sizeable force wading across the river down there.' Arthur pointed through the murk. 'It is an even wager they will negotiate that marshland. If they are not stopped they will come up behind us. How else does your brother,' sarcastic, 'the King, intend to block their path if he will not allow my cavalry to see to it?'

'The ground is not firm for horse! Jesu, we had the selfsame argument yester-eve!' Catigern waved an irate hand towards the battle. 'Our men are holding up well, Hengest cannot cross. A bit more of a push and we may be able to thrust them back.'

Patience went. 'Well! Well? Bull's blood, man, another half hour and our men will be done in! Thrust back? Soon they will not be able to stand on their legs! If Vortimer cannot see it is time to bring the cavalry into play and get this thing finished, then he has no right to lead us!'

'Are you challenging my brother?'

It took many deep breaths for Arthur to stop himself bellowing 'Aye!' He managed a controlled 'I want to do something useful with my men, not be left sitting here like brooding hens.'

He gathered the reins, edged Eira forward, smiling at Catigern. 'Tell your brother, the King, in my opinion it is essential we ride to protect our rear.' The smile went. 'If he does not like my opinion, then he can go to his Christian God's Hell!'

Arthur kicked the stallion into a hand canter, his men following without question.

Catigern cursed, shouted impotent orders to hold position, knowing even if Arthur's men heard they would not obey. He wheeled, galloped back to his brother where he spoke brief word, and gathering to him the waiting infantry reserves, took them to join the wavering ranks of weary soldiers at the ford.

The day was a disaster. Mid-afternoon, and Hengest pulled his flagging men back. Too weary to follow, the British let them go, knowing this to be a breathing space only, for men to bind their wounds, clean bloodstained weapons and regain their breath – until another day.

Neither side had won. Both had lost. Neither side held control of the ford; both sides lost many and many a brave warrior.

Hengest took one last look across the rain sodden plain below him before he entered the shelter of the trees. Beside him his son Aesc stood as sober faced as his father. Four thegns carried a dead man, his red beard bloodied from the wound that had split his face open from temple to jaw. Aesc plodded after them into the woodland.

'I will be back for your stinking Weleas blood!' Hengest shouted, holding the stained blade of his sword before him. 'I promise you this, by the name of my dead brother, slain this day at Agealesthrep!'

He followed the bier, his legs and arms as heavy as his heart. There would be another fight, another day, but not yet. Now was the time to bury the dead and to mourn. Now was the time to send for more keels, to grow and gather in strength, ready for that day.

Vortimer and Arthur were arguing. Had they not been so tired they might have come to blows; as it was, their words were bitter enough.

'You disobeyed me, boy!' Vortimer shouted.

'I saved many from certain death!' Arthur yelled back. 'The Saex were well-nigh across those marshes – as I said they would be. What was I to do? Sit astride my horse and welcome them forward?' He swept a hand before him, bowed slightly. 'Feel free, Saex, come up behind, stab us in the back like you did in Londinium! Let the son be as bloody stupid as the father!'

It was then that Vortimer almost struck the Pendragon. Instead, he shouted, 'And how many horses did you lose in that bog? Ten? Twenty? Forty?'

'I lost ten and seven. Compared with losing the whole of the army, a small price to pay.'

Vortimer, stopping himself from thrusting his knuckles into the Pendragon's teeth, said, 'I was about to send the infantry reserve there. Infantry could have handled the situation. Instead, Catigern had to lead them where you ought have gone.'

Arthur exploded into anger. 'Infantry could not have moved fast enough – you left things too late! Catigern did right by moving the reserve to the ford!'

'Where cavalry would have performed a better job – and happen would have left my brother alive!'

'Ah, so that's it?' Arthur thrust his face into Vortimer's with contempt. 'The truth. You hold me responsible for Catigern's death!'

Cei, ill at ease at this quarrelling, interrupted, holding an arm between his king and Arthur. 'No one is to blame for anything. We all know battle decisions have to be made in a hair's breadth of time. Some go well, others do not. That is war. Many a good man has lost his life this day. Many more are with us to fight again.'

Other officers present stood shuffling and feeling embarrassed, hoping not to get involved; the Pendragon's temper was too volatile, this new king untried.

Arthur had heard enough. He strode for the open tent flap and ducked through, tossing out as he went, 'Unless the cavalry is used to its full potential, Vortimer, I am no longer with you.'

Cei, uncertain, made to call him back. Vortimer, sighing heavily, seated himself. God's truth, he was tired! He said, 'Let him go, Cei; he is in a hot temper, but he will cool. He has more need of us than we of him; he will be back tail tucked atween his legs before long.' He managed a weak smile. 'Only do not tell him I said so.'

Cei regarded the man. He liked Vortimer and admired him for his dedication to country and duty. Yet Vortimer was no longer a young man. His face, this evening, looked more like a skeleton's mask than anything human; his hands, Cei noted, were shaking.

The day had gone badly. Had Hengest's brother not fallen and the wind, consequently, been taken out of Saex sails it might have gone worse. Defeat had been uncomfortably close.

Cei saluted, turned from the tent. He respected Vortimer, acknowledged him as king, but he had been wrong in this. Very wrong. And Arthur right.

Vortimer knew it too, knew it for himself and from the expressions of those officers waiting for orders. It was Arthur they needed, Arthur with his knack of knowing what to do and where to do it – and doing it well. Closing his eyes, Vortimer let his head and shoulders sag. He had a sad, but relieved feeling that he was not going to be king for long.

Cei caught Arthur up, touched his arm. 'I was told earlier there is someone you ought to see among the wounded.'

'There are many I ought to see, Cei. My men, those who fought bravely this day; boys, old men who will never fight again. Then I ought to see those few Saex prisoners we took. And the horses.' He put his own hand on Cei's arm. 'Not now, Cei, later.'

Cei was insistent. 'I was told this thing before Vortimer summoned us. You ought to see this one.'

Arthur shook off Cei's restraining arm. 'I am tired and I am hungry. Has Llwch questioned those prisoners?'

'Aye, they know nothing of Gwenhwyfar.' Cei stepped in front of his cousin, blocking his path. 'I say again, you ought to see this man.'

Arthur was not listening. 'I have small hope of finding her after all this while. Easier to seek a thread in a hay meadow.'

Cei again, louder, 'Will you listen to me!'

'Who is it, then? Why the urgency?'

'Osmail.'

'Osmail? Cunedda's Osmail? Gwenhwyfar's eldest brother Osmail?'

'Aye to all three.'

'What in the name of the Bull is he doing here?' A sudden thought: 'Happen he knows of Gwenhwyfar's whereabouts! A ransom demand gone to Gwynedd?' As he spoke Arthur was hurrying to the hospital tent erected on the outskirts of the camp. He ran most of the way.

He thrust back the entrance flap, and stood aside to allow exit for two men removing a corpse. Arthur looked, did not recognise the dead man. A bearer said, 'We will have many like this come morning.'

Osmail lay near the back, what remained of his leg swathed in fresh bandaging, already soaked through. He had no colour, save for a tinge of blue around the lips.

Arthur touched him gently. The man roused briefly, managed a weak smile of pleased recognition. His eyes rolled white, then the life spirit sighed from him. Osmail was dead.

Arthur's head slumped forward. Suddenly he wanted to weep. 'Are none of his brothers here?' he asked, cursing that he had not come earlier.

'None,' Cei replied. 'I asked a few questions; he joined us yester-eve, rode alone. None knew why. None asked.'

Arthur bent to examine the small pile of belongings beside the dead man. Boots, helmet, bloodied cloak. A leather pouch. In it, a scrap of parchment. Eyebrows raised, Arthur read aloud:

'Branwen. Understand why I did this thing. I must make peace with myself before I can do so with my God and my father's spirit. You are safe with the Holy Sisters of the Virgin; the gold I left in your keeping will suffice to keep you in comfort. I write this, knowing you will receive it should death be my path on the morrow. I ask you to forgive me, and pray for my departed soul.' Arthur screwed up his eyes at the scrawled writing. 'What in damnation is this all about?'

Cei took it, reread it. 'No doubt his wife will know.'

'Where did he fight?'

'No idea. Someone pointed him out to me when I was searching for our own wounded, said you would wish to know one of Cunedda's brood was here.'

Arthur rolled the parchment. 'Which someone?'

Cei grinned. 'Someone else I believe you would be interested in meeting.'

'A day for surprises, eh?' Arthur grinned back. 'Well, where is he?'

'I am here!'

Arthur spun round at the voice, saw a man vaguely familiar, a few years his senior.

'You are?'

The man laughed good natured, held his hand out in greeting. 'I am named for your grandfather, Ambrosius Aurelianus. My brother – your father – and my friends call me by my British given name.'

Arthur started forward, delighted, to embrace the man, his uncle. 'Emrys! I ought to have known you! What brings you here?' They clapped each other on the shoulder. 'Are you not needed to defend your own coastland?'

A shadow crept across Emrys's face. 'There is nothing left to defend. We were raided, some months past. My wife and daughter are dead. An all too familiar story.'

'Sea wolves?'

'Saex pirates, aye. They came, took what they could carry, slaughtered what they could not. They left me for dead. With God's protection they missed my son, hidden by the quick thought of a slave.'

'You came alone to fight with Vortimer, then?'

'Your cousin Geraint is here also. He has two sons born, did you know?'

404

Arthur was guiding his uncle from the tent, talking animatedly. A soldier's arm plucked at his tunic as he passed.

'Glewlwyd! What? Wounded?' Arthur hunkered down, concerned, beside one of the bravest of his turmae.

'Nothing serious, my Lord – a sword slash, 'twill heal.' The man nodded a respectful greeting at Cei and the other man he did not know, said to Arthur, 'We did well – could have done much better had we been used right.'

Arthur patted his shoulder affably. 'And we shall be used right the next time we fight, I promise you. I have finished with simpering in the shade alongside those who have not the stamina to stand in the full sun.'

Beaming, Glewlwyd attempted to rise from his bed. Arthur playfully pushed him back. 'Take your time to heal sound first, man. You are no use to me in pieces!'

With his two companions Arthur left the hospital, the idea planted so long ago in his mind ripe at last, ready for the harvesting.

As they walked Emrys talked of everyday things; poor crop yields, raiders, his family. His young son.

Arthur, not listening, deep in thought, suddenly stopped him. 'Vortimer has not the ability to lead us and I will not follow a blind man into darkness. I am going to make the break. Now. I intend to gather men to me, fetch up those horses Gwynedd has ready and gather more from my restored lands to the west. But I need the backing of prominent men. Are you with me, Emrys?'

A man hailed him, coming up behind saying, 'After this day's bungling I am, Pendragon, for certain!'

Arthur spun to greet Geraint, son to one of Uthr's sisters, with warmth and pleasure. They had met on occasion as boys, had liked each other's company. Geraint greeted Cei, but acknowledged Emrys, Arthur noted with interest, with distinct reservation.

The four men strolled to Arthur's tent in search of food and wine as Arthur outlined his ideas. He could barely contain himself at the knowledge that at last his ambition was becoming some solid thing, hovering just beyond his grasp. The years of waiting were almost over.

But where to start that first push to send the stone rolling downhill? It needed one stone only to gather speed, taking up rocks and boulders, shrubs and trees as it went. Rolling faster and faster, becoming an unstoppable landslide. One stone.

While they were eating, huddled around the dim glow of a single brazier, the conversation turned for a while to lighter topics.

Geraint, mentioning his infant twin sons went on to say, 'My wife had a liking to show them off to her family; we were visiting there when we heard of the Londinium massacre. We were on the road home when Vortimer made his call to arms. I had not the time to escort them safe home, so have left them with the Holy Sisters of the Virgin at Yns Witrin.'

Arthur started in surprise, fingers hurriedly feeling for a rolled parchment tucked in his belt. 'Twice today have I heard of these Sisters!'

He slapped a meat-greased hand on his thigh. 'That settles one nagging thought, then! We ride to Dumnonia to persuade Vortigern's placed governor that he is now to swear allegiance to the Dragon, and on the way we call at Yns Witrin to see your lads, Geraint,' he raised his goblet in salute, 'and Osmail's widow.'

Things were looking hopeful. Happen Branwen knew something about Gwenhwyfar.

Geraint yodelled his delight. Cei handed round more meat. Emrys, embarrassed, cleared his throat.

'I will not be with you.'

Silence.

Arthur laughed. 'You do not have to ride if you have no wish for the exercise, Uncle! Go gather your son and meet us at our rallying place in Gwynedd.'

Emrys twiddled a chicken bone between his fingers. 'I meant I will not back you in this fight for a royal torque Arthur.' He looked at his nephew with no trace of embarrassment. 'For the same reason that I would not back your father. I do not hold with kings. We are of Rome, we have an Emperor. We are a province of Rome and should look to her for guidance and protection.'

For a moment Arthur sat silent, astounded. Was the man serious? When Emrys said nothing more, Arthur realised he was.

'Rome cannot help us. We have been abandoned to our own fate,' he said.

'I disagree. We are temporarily left to our own devices but Rome will recover from her trials, you will see. Some few seasons from now the Emperor will gather his armies and come to our aid. He will not be pleased to see another claiming his title.' Emrys placed the bone to burn on the brazier, got to his feet. 'For all that, I wish you well, Arthur.'

With narrowed eyes Arthur observed, 'Yet you fought this day under a king.'

'As, should your bid be successful, I may one day fight under you. I recognise the need for a leader, a man to command while Rome sorts her troubles, though I would wish that leader had not reverted to an abandoned tribal title, but that's as may be. Through temporary need I must recognise a king, whoever he is, but I will not become involved in civil fighting over who is to be that king. Again, I wish you well.' He was gone, stepping from the tent into the wet night.

Geraint and Arthur looked at each other incredulously. Geraint shrugged, poured himself more wine. 'Living in the past, that one,' he said.

Arthur laughed, tore with relish into his meat, reached also for the wine. 'I remember Uthr saying his brother Emrys had an odd way of thinking. They never saw eye to eye on anything. I always put it down to the years between them, but happen it is more than that. Fool of a man! Rome will not be back. Eh, Cei? You are quiet this night. What say you?'

Cei stretched, tossed his sucked bone into the flames, finished his wine and stood. 'I say it is time I checked the men and horses.' He walked from the tent, saying over his shoulder as he left, 'But you ought know, for the most part, I agree with Emrys.'

§ XXXIV

Gwenhwyfar knew something was to happen. Not precisely when, but soon, very soon. It was an odd feeling this, something inside niggling like an image vaguely remembered after a waking dream. For the past week she had climbed the Tor each morning, settled herself close by the largest standing stone on the summit and watched. For what, she did not know, just watched.

It was not a Christian place, this Tor, the Holy Sisters did not like her walking here. Yns Witrin it was called, the Glass Isle. Even in the driest of summers there was always water spread around the foot of this conical hill – sodden places, marsh oozing underfoot, pitted with deeper bog that could trap and drown the unwary. Come winter, or after weeks of rain such as this year had brought, the low flat levels became a plain of dotted lakes and running channels. The brooding height of the Tor reflected in those vast, mirroring waters. An imaged island as delicately translucent and brittle as glass.

Shrouded in morning mist and with its ancient miz-maze path winding back and forth in ritual pattern up the steep slopes, the Tor squatted over a cluster of little hills, like a matriarch presiding over her mixed brood sheltering within the fall of her shadow.

It might not be Christian, but it was a revered and mystical place. A sanctum of the Old Ways, of the Mother Goddess and Avallach, God of the Underworld. She danced on the buttercup-spotted or frost-rimed grass, He slept beneath, in his domain of Avalon within the darkness of the hollow hill, waiting for the souls of the dead to find their way by night down the passages into the Other World.

Once, there had been many who served the Goddess; now the young women went to the Christian Mother. Daughters learnt the litany of the Holy Church, not the ancient learning of a Goddess who was sliding into obscurity. Only three priestesses were left down there at the base of the Tor, their poor dwelling houses built along the shore of the water.

Theirs was an ancient, once elite, clan. The Ladies, they were called, women of the Goddess. With the passing of the three, the Goddess would be gone from the Tor. Forgotten.

Drawn to this richly spiritual place, Christian people had settled their community among the cluster of hills set on the flat of the Summer Land. They had built their little chapel and crude dwellings; set up their market place and expanded as each year more came. The chapel became a church, the dwelling houses merging together into cloistered orders where men and women could live and work alongside God and Christ. Traders arrived. Farmers brought their produce and cattle to the market and prospered; a tavern flourished to provide bed and food for weary travellers who came to worship at the wondrous-built church, or seek healing or learning from the holy men and woman. Under the Christ God the Glass Isle thrived.

It may have been very pagan, this Tor that hovered above the mist of a damp spring or autumn morning, or floated on a flood plain of glistening, sky-bright water, but Yns Witrin possessed a pull of awe and inspiration. A place where it was easy to listen to the voice of your God. Within the spirit of the Tor, you could see through the shaded windows of your own soul.

And the Tor was a place of the Mother. Whether she were the old Goddess or the Virgin Mother of Christ, she was still the Mother. Gwenhwyfar had been safe here under her protective wing, was calmed and becoming healed of fear and the disgrace of an unwanted and uninvited invasion of her body. Rape carried a powerful backlash of wretchedness.

To her, this quiet hill was a patient, contented place away from the dark, crowding shadows of horror. A place for the female. A sanctuary where time drifted with the moon cycle and where the earth beneath your feet understood the pain of labour and the joy of birth.

Have other women stood here, where I stand on this wind teased summit? she wondered. *Watching as I watch, waiting as I wait, for their child to be born or their menfolk to come back from war?*

Probably. The Tor was a guardian shield for women. It was said children were conceived or borne with ease and safety up here. Women's natural troubles were healed. The Tor, a buffer against the harsh reality of life out there in the bad lands.

It seemed so long ago, so far away, that rain-drenched night in Londinium. Yet it haunted her, clinging like stale perfume. Sickly and repulsive.

She had a vague recollection of how she came to be here. She remembered the shouting and a clash of weapons; fearful desperate faces. Pounding hooves, sobbing breath – her own? Frightened horses bolting. Her arms clinging exhausted to a bay horse, muscles locked, unable to let go until he shuddered, eventually, to a halt.

Gwenhwyfar had no idea how far that wild flight had taken her or to where she was taken. Knew only that her body ached and head throbbed. She was unaware of the jagged slash across her forehead, barely recalled the swinging hilt of a sword on a rocking boat that had caused it. The scab had long since peeled itching away, the scar beneath fading white against darker skin.

The Holy Sisters said she had ranted delirious in fever for several days.

Had an inner sense guided her to them? Or had it been the wandering bay horse with a rider slumped across his withers who had trotted to other horses, eager for company? Whatever, the six women making their way to join the Sisters of Yns Witrin had taken her to their wagon, tended and cared for her. Unsure who she was or where she had come from, and unwilling to delay their journey, they had decided to take her with them.

In her dazed state Gwenhwyfar had raised no objection.

The gentle Sisters fluttered round her, enfolding her in the safe seclusion of their nest, clucking and cooing, thanking the wisdom of the Virgin for guiding a daughter to safety. Gwenhwyfar let their attentions wash like healing balm over her muddled mind, having no energy or inclination to contradict them, relieved and thankful that the Goddess – under whatever guise – had brought her here, once strength and sense began to return, to idle among these gentle women of peace.

Once, she had visited the Ladies, going across the spread of the lake to their huddle of meagre dwellings at the base of the Tor. The two she had met had welcomed her, were as kind as the Sisters, but – and this surprised Gwenhwyfar – could offer her no more comfort than the Christian community. Strange, it was the quiet, simple lives of the Holy Sisters that provided the inner peace she craved.

The Ladies were brash and gaudy – their bangles jangling at their wrists, the vivid-bright tunics, the startling blue tattooed in writhing swirls on face and arms. Inside the squat building they took her to a heavy, mind-numbing aroma muddled her mind even more and left her disorientated and distant. They were kind, concerned and eager to help, but Gwenhwyfar sat with them tense and stiff, like a doll carved of wood.

And something else she realised as she punted the little boat back across the lake: they seemed to be living a pretence. A theatre play. Women dressed up as the Goddess's Ladies, raising their hands to the sky and calling with shrieks and cries for the Mother to hear and help. Not that it had been like that; there had been no wailing or moaning, but the intoned prayer had jarred with a stilted rhythm which had grated and pierced the ears instead of relaxing and pacifying the spirit as did the chanting of the Sisters.

Gwenhwyfar would walk on the Tor, but she never went back to the Ladies at the Lake.

The Sisters led a life of rigid routine revolving around daily chores and prayer. Their speech was quiet but not without laughter; indeed, they laughed often, sharing the many pleasures of their God's created world of happiness and beauty. In the Sisters' chapel or about their duties, they would often sing, chanting their praising rhythms to the glory of God. A comforting sound.

One other reason kept Gwenhwyfar away from the Ladies. Morgause was one of them. She was the third Lady.

After leaving the Ladies on that one visit Gwenhwyfar had walked down the sloping path, through the clusters of alder and willow and had met with her, coming up from the lakeside.

They had not exchanged words, merely stood, the one eyeing the other, stone faced, critical. Morgause was dressed as a Lady of the Goddess, her golden hair loose with the blue-painted patterns tattooed on her cheeks, forehead and bare arms. In comparison, Gwenhwyfar, with cloak clutched tight to her breast, was pale, frightened and tired.

This was the Lady they talked of then, down in the market place and in the tavern; the women with clacking disapproval, the men with shared winks and nudging elbows. She had wondered, Gwenhwyfar, meeting with the two Ladies, what there was in them for the men to be so excited over. They were old, shrivel-skinned, claw-fingered women with creased, toothless smiles.

Her Holy Sisters were virtuous, pledged to serve God, not a man's lusting. The Ladies welcomed the pleasure a man could give. Though what pleasures could be shared with those two crones Gwenhwyfar could not imagine. Not until she stood before Morgause. As young and perfectly beautiful as ever.

She had dipped her head and stood aside to allow Gwenhwyfar to pass, honour-bound to a guest of the Goddess. Gwenhwyfar had murmured her thanks and hurried by, barely noticing the child, darker skinned but with the same golden hair, tucked behind Morgause's flame-coloured skirts.

The wind lifted Gwenhwyfar's loose hair; she liked letting it flow unbound up here on the Tor, it added a sense of abandoned freedom. She would have liked to cast aside her clothing too, run naked over the short, springy turf. But that would shock the dear Sisters too much, and besides she did not have the courage to prance about in the open birthclad.

Overhead, a screech of swifts darted, swooping and diving, their calls shrill but wildly exciting. She watched them pass, clapped her hands at their breathtaking aerobatics. As quickly as they had appeared, they were gone, skimming down the side of the Tor and away.

Gwenhwyfar closed her eyes and breathed in deep, holding the heady scent of morning-damp air, releasing it slowly. Thank God today the rain had ceased! Gwenhwyfar smiled, felt the babe within her kick at her belly.

That was one thing she was grateful for. One solid thing that had given her strength to defeat the evil sense of dirt that Melwas's stench had left on her. The child she carried was too large, too well formed, to have been put there by him. She placed her hand on the bulge, felt another hefty kick. 'Ah, babe, you are anxious to see your Da? Soon, will I send for him and he will come for us; soon.'

'Talking to yourself? They oft-times say it is a madness sign.' Gwenhwyfar swivelled, startled. Morgause leant against another of the standing stones, her arms folded, expression mocking. The child was with her again, a pretty girl for all the grubbiness of skin, hair and dress – and the startling sign of fear that surged, naked, in her wide, dark eyes.

Gwenhwyfar had seen similar eyes somewhere before. Where?

'Happen it is best to talk with yourself if you know the answers make sense.' Gwenhwyfar spoke to the woman pleasantly; the Tor did not lend itself to bad moods and sour answers. 'Aside,' she said with a smile, 'I talk to my child.'

'Ah, your child.' Morgause seated herself on the grass a few feet from Gwenhwyfar, querying with her hand and a raised eyebrow whether Gwenhwyfar minded. It was not for Gwenhwyfar to say – the Tor belonged to all.

Morgause leant her head back, letting the warmth of a sudden burst of sun shine on her face. To the grey-blue sky she said, 'Why are you here, Gwenhwyfar of Gwynedd?'

'I could ask the same of you.'

Smiling at the neat answer, Morgause indicated Gwenhwyfar's swollen belly and said, 'Except I can guess your reason. Now the great Cunedda has gone you fear Gwynedd might throw you out for breeding a fatherless bastard?'

She liked hurting, Morgause, enjoyed the pleasure of another's pain, would poke and stab at vulnerable places and watch her victim squirm under her torture. Animals, children, unprotected adults – few were safe from torment at Morgause's hand. If she had intended to hurt Gwenhwyfar with this one, though, she failed. Gwenhwyfar had long accepted her father's death – liked it not, but accepted it. And her brothers would not reject her when she became ready to contact them.

Morgause sat forward, hugging her knees. 'As I recall, Cunedda had a fondness for fatherless bastards.'

Gwenhwyfar did not miss the inference, said with a lifted eyebrow, 'He had a father, though, didn't he – Arthur?'

Several thoughts wandered through Morgause's mind: Uthr, and his son; the love she held for the one, the hatred for the other. The son should have been hers. If she had borne Uthr a son, then... then what? Would Uthr still be alive, would she now be queen? The thread of Fate would never weave so smooth a pattern. Even had she borne a son, Uthr would still be dead, she would still have come here to seek shelter with the Ladies, become one of them. It suited her to be here. For now, until the time came to move on.

'So,' she said to Gwenhwyfar, pleasantly, 'you come to the kingdom of Avallach and the garden of the Goddess to bide your time before dropping your child.'

'I come to share the peace of the Holy Sisters.'

'Hah!' Morgause snorted with amusement. 'That pathetic bunch of nanny-goats! What would they know of bastard brats? It is in my mind you hide away here lest your brothers discover your condition. You ought to have had it aborted.' Morgause ran her hands across her own flat belly. 'We of the Goddess know how to keep a womb empty.' She giggled, a crude sound full of suggestive pleasure. 'Though men try hard to fill it.' Scornfully she added, 'I doubt your Sisters know anything of such matters. Would scream rape should a man dare catch a glimpse of an ankle beneath that drab garb they encase themselves in.'

'The nuns are good, kind women – do not mock them.'

'What, all of them? Even that other one from Gwynedd? Branwen.' Morgause was massaging her toes, wriggling each one between her fingers.

Gwenhwyfar answered affably, 'I see little of her, she has private lodgings.' Thought, *thank all God's goodness!*

The little girl had wandered some way off, was absorbed in picking daisies and threading them into a joined chain.

Gwenhwyfar had no wish to talk to, or of, Branwen. Disagreeable woman! She said instead, 'She is a pretty child, your daughter.'

'What makes you assume she is my daughter?' Morgause laughed.

Cocking her head to one side, Gwenhwyfar watched the little girl. She was dressed in a rough-spun tunic, sleeveless, reaching a little below her knees. A shabby bandage was bound about her right hand. There were bruises, Gwenhwyfar noticed, on her arms and legs. A lot of angry bruises, but then children were always falling and hurting themselves.

'I say it because twice now I have seen her trotting at your heels and because, although she has not your delicate skin, she is very like you.' And someone else?

Lifting her shoulders Morgause made light of it. 'So she is mine. The Goddess smiles that she has another to follow her path.' She gathered up her skirt, folding the cloth back to her thighs, and stretched her bare legs to the sun. She threw Gwenhwyfar a sly sidelong look; eyeing her bulge, assessing how far the babe had grown. 'Who is the father? Or can you not name him for fear of decrying his wife?'

Gwenhwyfar replied, indifferent to the taunting, 'I have no intention of fighting with you, Morgause. It is no business of yours to know. I could as well ask who fathered your girl.' She added with a twist of returned spite, 'Or do you not know?'

Morgause watched the child a moment through slit eyes. A stupid girl who answered questions in a mumble and had downcast eyes, a runny nose, a bottom lip that trembled most of the time and clumsy hands that dropped everything. She still wetted the bedding. Punishment seemed to have no effect, even though it was becoming more severe.

Take this morning. The idiot child had spilt scalding porridge all over Morgause's gown. She had immediately plunged the girl's hand into water boiling in the cooking pot; doubted whether even that punishment would have any effect. The child would be as clumsy some other time, some other way. A tiresome, disappointing weed of a brat.

With a sigh, 'She is nothing like her father.' Morgause scratched at an itch along her inner thigh and lay back, her hands tucked behind her head. 'It is as well he does not know of her. He would be disappointed.'

'I think my man will be pleased with mine.'

Morgause learnt much from that. The father, whoever he was, knew nothing of the coming child. Also, Gwenhwyfar was not certain of him. She took that to mean there had been some passing affair, torrid meetings of a night, a sharing of lust, and now the man had gone. Back to his wife? Probably. It usually went that way.

'That is just as well,' Morgause said, climbing to her feet and straightening her skirt. The sun was becoming blanketed by a thick bank of cloud. It was darkening in the west, more rain coming. It was time she went. She looked north across the flood plain, north to where, somewhere, the Goddess was still held in awe, where this Christian God had trod no lasting footprint. The Ladies were revered in the far north, were welcomed. A gifted Lady could soar high among the Picti people. Could, if canny, fly as high as a queen.

Aye, it was time she went from Yns Witrin.

In passing she said with unexpected good intention, 'The Goddess has a place for girl-children should yours be born female. She does not need to know a father's name, would welcome yours to her bosom.'

'As would the Christian Virgin.'

The kindness disappeared. 'Hah! That is not how I heard it.' Brushing at a grass stain Morgause came to stand before Gwenhwyfar. 'You would fare better under the Goddess, she is in need of new servants.'

So that was why Morgause was being so friendly this day! Gwenhwyfar had wondered. She held her tongue, for Morgause spoke the truth of it. The nuns were kind-hearted, well-meaning and loving, but a few had tutted and mumbled over her condition.

When Gwenhwyfar first came there had been guarded questions, met with a polite silence. They knew her name, that was all, but of her parentage, her home, and the father of the child Gwenhwyfar had said nothing.

All that had changed several days past when Branwen and Osmail arrived. This was a small community where word, especially scandal, spread faster than a winter flood, and Branwen had within a day made it her business to give full detail of Gwenhwyfar's history. But, not even Branwen could discover who had fathered the child.

Was that something moving out there on the plain?

He was dead of course, Osmail. He would never have survived a battle, she knew it as surely as that distant muddle of movement was forming into a turma of horse.

She had entered the community chapel one afternoon and had seen a man sitting there. 'Osmail? Osmail!' She had dropped the gathered flowers intended for the altar and run to him, throwing her arms about him, tears of joy and laughter mingling with his own. He had come, he said, to leave Branwen and his sons with the Sisters while he rode to join Vortimer, driven by some crazed need to prove he was his brothers' equal. Proving nothing, Gwenhwyfar had retorted, except that he was a fool and could die as easily as anyone else. But he had gone all the same, riding out the next morning.

One other part of their conversation came back to her as she sat in the cloud-patched sunshine up here on the wind-whispered Tor. 'They are searching for you,' he had said. 'Our brothers and Arthur.'

She had deliberately not informed anyone of her whereabouts. That they would be suffering pain she realised, but it would be a short, soon mended hurt. Her own hurt, for the time being, came more important. She was not ready for the harassment of the outside world, was not ready for the sympathy and swamping affection that, however well intentioned, would drown her severely cracked spirit. The Sisters gave her those things, but in a distant, impersonal way.

'Soon,' she had promised Osmail, 'I will send a messenger soon. When I am ready to take up my cloak and go out into the world again; but for now I need time for my wounds to heal, here within the peace and privacy of Yns Witrin.'

And suddenly she received the welcome knowing that 'soon' had come. She was ready to turn aside from tranquillity and face reality.

'I must be getting back,' Gwenhwyfar said, rising to her feet. She took a few paces down the slope, stopped to say, 'I shall tell the Pendragon when I see him that you are here, Morgause.'

Morgause laughed, hands on hips, head tossed back. 'So he may avoid the place? Do not bother yourself, I am leaving. I need somewhere more,' She smiled. Wicked, Morgause's smile could be. 'Beneficial.'

She watched Gwenhwyfar go; watched, too, the horsemen for that knot of clouded shapes was definitely horsemen. The girl had come up, was standing a few inches from her mother.

'I met with Gwenhwyfar when I had the Pendragon,' Morgause said to the wind. 'Not this Pendragon, I speak of the father.' She clasped her arms about herself. The wind was growing chill. 'He was a man worth the having.' She looked down at the child who stood wide-eyed with fear, thumb stuck in her mouth. A patch had spread on her skirt where she had wet herself.

'Love of the Mother!' Morgause snarled. 'Uthr was worth the having, but by the pleasure he gave, were you?'

§ XXXV

Tired horses, steaming from a fine spatter of rain on hot coats filled the rutted courtyard of the small tavern built alongside the outer wall of the Holy Sisters' compound. The keeper welcomed the arrivals graciously, if somewhat doubtfully, making rapid calculations for sleeping arrangements.

Cei slapped him on the back, almost toppling the little man. 'No panic, we stay but the one night to rest horse and man.'

Two men had remained mounted, the officer in charge and another man – a civilian, for all he was dressed in war gear. They talked briefly but earnestly out beyond the arched gateway.

It had surprised Arthur that Emrys had joined them after all – although, as he had been quick to explain, only to ride as far as Yns Witrin. 'I have a fancy to reside a while with the holy Brothers.'

Put out by Emrys's rebuff, Arthur had said he could suit himself what he did. They had ridden in silence for the first few miles.

Emrys was saying he did not care to stay at the tavern with Arthur and his men, was all for seeking a more suitable bed within the Brothers' monastery, away to the left of the road.

Arthur took that as another slight. Said, 'Go where you will, Uncle. It is nothing to me where you sleep.' Thought, *We do not need your solemn face casting disapproval on our drinking and whoring this night.*

He swung Eira aside, intending to trot into the courtyard – halted. For a long, long, moment he sat there staring up the muddied lane, unable to take in what he was looking at.

Gwenhwyfar had walked slowly back, taking her time to amble down the slope of the Tor, coming the long way round to avoid the Lady's lake. Then she had stopped to drink from the women's water of the spring. It was good water, red-tinged, bubbling from the ground even in the hottest of summers, so she was told. It was healing water, folk said, and indeed she always felt a surge of energy after drinking there, no matter how tired she had been before.

Then it had started raining; a fine, warm drizzle. She had walked on along the narrow track, stopping to listen to a bird trilling a bursting chorus of glorious sound. Stooped to peer, fascinated, at a webbed nest of new-hatched spiders, the little things weaving their way from the massed clump of siblings, climbing hesitantly out along leaf stems and grass stalks – a minute, busy little world. Further on, a beetle lay in her path, its legs waving frantically in the air as it struggled to right itself.

She flipped it over, watched as it scuttled away, shiny black. She could hear voices ahead, and horses. The rain was falling harder now. She had no wish to meet with riders, not yet, so she ducked her head against the wet and walked a little faster, aiming for the rear door into the Sisters' garden.

Suddenly Arthur was off Eira's back and running up the lane.

She looked up, faltered, her veil slipping back from wet hair.

His arms swept around her, lifted her off her feet, swinging her round and around. Then he put her down, gazed at her, still unbelieving, thinking this was some dream; he would wake any moment and find her gone. Finally, almost choking with happiness and relief, he kissed her.

He was aware, as his breathing calmed and his heart eased its wild hammering, of men gathered down the lane, faces grinning, voices raising a cheer. Cei had come up behind, was saying with a broad grin, 'Can we expect a more amenable mood now, lad?'

Emrys too had wandered up the lane, was regarding the woman in Arthur's arms with interest. He had heard of from sources other than Arthur. Gwenhwyfar ferch Cunedda,

They were very different, Emrys and his brother Uthr. Eldest and youngest, with fifteen years between them. Emrys had been a babe in his mother's womb when their father died, was a child when Uthr fled into exile. He was no soldier, Emrys, had lived a quiet life of learning, of books and study. With his elder siblings gone about their own lives and his father dead, he was left in the care of his mother. A good, pious woman who brought up her last son in the way she had been taught; to honour God and Rome, the one almost blending with the other – but then her father had come from Rome, was the son of a Senator. He had served a while as Duke of Britain, governor of the entire north – until Rome had recalled the legions and he had gone marching away with them. Emrys's mother had stayed in Britain, with her husband.

Emrys had met Cunedda and disliked him for all the reasons his elder brother had liked the man. Cunedda was ambitious, had a liking for war, was brash and lewd and cherished a love for an independent Britain and a return to the Tribe. Uthr and Cunedda were glad to see the back of Rome. Emrys had never trusted Cunedda, nor Uthr. And Arthur was too much his father's son. Did this daughter too take after her father?

He stepped forward to greet her. Recoiled, for as Arthur let her go her cloak flapped open, revealing her swollen figure. 'My God, she carries a child!' The shocked exclamation left Emrys's lips before he could halt it.

No one spoke.

It had not occurred to Gwenhwyfar to wonder how Arthur would react to the discovery. She had always assumed he would be pleased, but seeing Emrys's horrified disapproval she was suddenly afraid.

Arthur must have seen the panic scuttle across her face, for he took her hand in his, said to Cei, 'Settle the men and horses and escort my uncle to his chosen lodging. I have unfinished business to attend.' He slid his arm around Gwenhwyfar, drew her close to his side, clearly dismissing his audience.

To her he said, 'Where can we talk?'

She indicated an open doorway in the convent wall through which herb and vegetable gardens were visible. He led her there, shut the door, looked about. Beneath a drooping willow he saw a crude bench, took her to it and seated her. Standing over her, he gathered his thoughts.

They both spoke at once. 'Gwenhwyfar...'

'Arthur...'

Laughed.

'Let me speak, Cymraes.'

She bent her head, her hands folded in her lap. He was not going to want her now – now she bore a child which only her word said was his.

Arthur had not dared to hope he would find her again, and now he had did not know what to say. This child she carried – he had gone over and over all the things that could have happened to her these past weeks, had not thought of this one possibility. It must be his. Wasn't she too far advanced for it to be Melwas's – or had there been someone else? Mithras, how to ask without giving offence? Ask – he had to. He started clumsily.

'I did not expect you to be with child.'

'I did not expect to be with child. It is a thing that seems to happen when two people lie together.' Her answer came out harsh, too flippant.

'Na, I meant,' He fumbled for words, decided to leave it a moment.

'Winifred has gone. I know not where, nor do I particularly care. She may be drowned or have reached her mother's people – I hope the former. Either way, officially, legally documented, she is no longer my wife.'

He sat beside her, sharing his cloak, covering her shoulders with its ample width. Awkwardly he took her hand in his own, found it cold to the touch. 'I have much to do, Gwenhwyfar. Vortigern is no more and Vortimer is unfit to lead. It is almost time for me to take the kingdom as my own.' He glanced apprehensively into her green eyes, watched, fascinated, the swirl of gold at the centre. 'For the next months, years, I must gather all I can to me, will have to fight those who stand in my way.' He studied her hands. Slender fingers, smooth skin. 'I would that there might be a loving woman at my side.' He brought her hand to his lips, kissed it. 'I have a thousand dreams spinning in my head, Cymraes. I need desperately to share them with a woman who has the heart to see them with me.'

Wistfully she answered, 'We had so many dreams as children. Where do they go when we grow? Are they swallowed up by the mundane things of everyday life? Or do we lose them, leave them behind us in the dust, for new children to find and take up?'

'My dream is still with me, Gwenhwyfar. Unaltered, save that I may have tidied up the ragged edges along the way of growing up. Come with me, as my wife.'

She looked into his eyes. Few could read Arthur's thoughts; few were allowed to see beyond those veiling outer shutters that kept the inner feelings safe hidden. Gwenhwyfar alone could see into his heart, see as clear as if looking into a clear pool. Her free hand went up to his cheek, caressing, a delicate touch. He was unshaven, the prickle of stubble sharp on her palm. He smelt of horse and leather, rain and sweat. His wet hair was stuck against his forehead and hanging limp about his neck.

'I recall you making a promise to me once, Gwenhwyfar, close by Gwynedd's sacred Stone. You vowed your sons to me.'

She smiled at that. 'You remember, then?'

'I would not forget it.'

'This son I bear you shall be the first of many.'

Tentatively Arthur stretched out a hand to touch her bulk. 'It is mine, then?' He asked it hesitant, afraid of hearing the wrong answer.

Gwenhwyfar pressed his hand down firmer. He jumped, astonished as a tremor jerked at his palm.

'Would a babe acknowledge any man other than his Da?' she said for answer.

He stroked a finger lovingly down her cheek. She was thin, pale, needed feeding and loving. There were things he had to ask, had to know.

'I know what...' He paused. He meant to say 'Melwas', but found he could not say that name aloud. 'What he did to you. Cei, others, have guessed it. This child – you are sure it is...?'

She bit back the threatening tears, knew what he was thinking. And if he thought it, what of others? 'Am I sure it is not his? *Na*, it is not, it is yours.' She attempted to swallow her tears.

Arthur was content. Nodded his acceptance, slowly, with deliberation. He held both her hands in his, rubbed their cold fingers. 'Even if it had not been mine, I would still ask you to be my legal wife, Gwenhwyfar.'

'Even though I carried his child?'

Arthur scowled, had to admit, 'I want you for certain. The child? In truth, were I not satisfied it was mine, then *na*, I would not accept it.'

Scarcely breathing she asked, 'And are you satisfied?'

He said simply, truthfully, 'Aye.'

Gwenhwyfar kissed his eyes, his cheek, then his lips, held him to her, savouring his nearness, his firm responding hold. The nightmare had passed; she was awake and it was a beautiful day. The rain dripped through the leaves, pattered on her closed eyelids. Who cared about the rain? For Gwenhwyfar, the sun shone.

A great sigh left her, her head lying on his shoulder, his hand rubbing her back. She said, 'Even the simplest of men can see with their eyes and count on their fingers. This child was begun well before Melwas raped me.'

She lifted her head, surprised at herself. The word had just come out, of its own accord. Not once since that first halting telling to Arthur had she spoken of the thing – not to herself, not to the Sisters or the Ladies. But now she had said it, and suddenly it was not so hideously frightening any more. She laughed, kissed Arthur again, revelled in his return kiss.

She said, smiling radiantly, 'Your son and I have waited so patiently for this day.' She tapped his chin with her finger. 'We do not intend to be parted from you again.'

He laughed, jumped up, lifted her to stand on the seat his arms encircling her broad waist. 'Pregnancy suits you well,' he observed.

'Mud and sweat,' she replied, wrinkling her nose, 'do not do the same for you!'

'Well that, woman, I am afraid, is a thing you need grow used to!' He gathered her to him, holding her weight easily in his arms. 'Which way this church I have heard so much reverent talk about?'

She dipped her head, puzzled, towards the east. 'Over there, why?'

'You will see.' Arthur carried her from the gardens and up the muddied lane, bellowing for Cei, who came running.

'Get you to that church – fetch Emrys and Geraint.' Arthur shifted Gwenhwyfar to a more comfortable position, kept on walking. 'And any other who would care to witness my marriage. Oh, and fetch me someone fitting to hear our vows – no poxed insignificant novice Brother, mind. Find a priest or something.'

There was much shouting and running. Yns Witrin, normally a quiet, sleepy place, was suddenly filled with noise and activity. Sisters came bustling and twittering; Brothers, with less gaiety but as much curiosity. A Bishop came trotting from his quarters, solemn eyed, a little flustered. He did not have much occasion to solemnise marriage vows in a community of nuns and brethren.

'A Christian wedding!' Arthur declared, setting Gwenhwyfar down before the church door. 'So none may doubt or counter my claim on my queen!'

Geraint, with his wife, hurried up and slapped Arthur on the back pleased his cousin had found his lost love. He embraced Gwenhwyfar, kissed her and handed her to his wife who, smiling, welcomed her as kin. Arthur's men, too, were crowding round, delighted. There would be a few days of relaxation now, and some good drinking and enjoyment ahead too if they were lucky! Aside, many knew Gwenhwyfar, remembered her quick wit and knowledge of horses. She was a woman well liked and accepted by Arthur's men.

Then it was Emrys's turn. He had come to the church in a flurry of unease. He took Arthur aside while some of the Sisters and Geraint's wife were twining hastily gathered flowers in Gwenhwyfar's unruly hair.

'My boy, it is my duty as your Uncle, to ask if you are certain of this thing you do.'

Thumbs hooked through his belt Arthur took a step back from his father's brother and regarded him through narrowed eyes, head cocked – for all the world like someone listening intently.

Encouraged, Emrys rested a hand on Arthur's shoulder, meaning to draw him a little away from the crowd. Resolute, Arthur stayed put.

'She is of good birth, I grant, Arthur, but – well, lad, I must be blunt – I think you are acting hastily. This child – it is not seemly for you to marry with her while she carries it. There will be talk, speculation.' Emrys cleared his throat, realising belatedly this was not going well after all. 'Let her have the child and, whether it be boy or girl, give it to some holy house for rearing where it will serve good by being with God but will also be soon forgotten, and then take her as wife. It is my advice, lad. Sound advice.'

Gwenhwyfar had come up behind him. Arthur looked over Emrys's shoulder at her, said, 'What say you to my uncle's advice, Gwenhwyfar?'

Her cloak had been gathered around her against the damp and cold, but now Gwenhwyfar tossed it back and walked proudly to Arthur's side, showing her swollen figure for all to see. She threaded her arm through his.

'I think that to advise our next king to set aside his first-born heir is most unwise. I might almost think, my Lord,' she addressed Arthur but looked with open challenge at Emrys. 'any who would give such advice must have his own reasons. Happen he does not welcome a son born to the Pendragon because he has an eye on a royal torque for himself? There were many who were privately glad when Uthr was slain, not expecting a son to come after him.'

A single, curt incline of his head saw Arthur agree with her. He took Gwenhwyfar's hand, began to walk with her inside the church. He halted on the threshold. 'There are those who, for whatever reason, did not back my father when he took his chance to rid this country of tyranny and greed. There will be those who, for the same reasons, will not back me. I will say this to those men. I give not a damn whether you pledge me your sword or not. I will be king, and my son,' he laid his hand on Gwenhwyfar's stomach, 'my son, will be king after me.'

He looked with challenging defiance at Emrys. Uthr had never liked his younger brother, had said once – and Arthur remembered this from childhood, 'A young man who spends more time with his books and on his knees before God is a man I would trust to hear my confession or to give spiritual guidance. But I would not trust such a man to guard my back with a sword. Book learning can make a man think he knows many things; book learning serves no purpose when you are faced with the blood red death of an enemy.'

'You serve your conscience as best you will, Uncle Emrys. I have already taken Gwenhwyfar as mine in the manner of the Old Way; I now take her in the Christian way. I am happy with that. If you are not, well then, that is for you to grieve over, not I.'

The Pendragon, polite, nodded dismissal to his uncle and took Gwenhwyfar inside the church. Emrys did not follow.

A small girl had wandered unnoticed into the crowded church. She had never seen inside a Christian building before, was awed by its dazzling whiteness and the gleam of gold arrayed on the altar. It was a wonderful place. She watched from a secretive corner, enthralled as Arthur and Gwenhwyfar exchanged their vows. Felt the laughter and happiness that soared in this peaceful little building.

When Arthur led his bride from the church, he saw her and smiled. Impulsively he tossed a small bronze coin at her. She made to catch it, missed, her face puckering at the humiliation of her clumsiness before this great crowd. Arthur stooped, picked it up, placed it in her hand, curling his fingers around hers. 'Do not cry, little one, I will not have tears this day.' Then he was gone, and all the dazzling people with him.

No one had ever smiled or spoken to her in kindness before. She had never known laughter, happiness or love. Her only companions were slaps and bruises, tears, and fear of her mother's temper and violent hatred.

Morgaine was always to remember Arthur for his kindness. Remember and love him for it, although she knew her mother would be angered, and probably beat her were she to know of it. For Morgause hated Arthur, wanted him dead. Morgaine knew that because her mother had said so, not an hour since.

DECEMBER 455

§ XXXVI

Caer Arfon seemed no different. The solid timber palisade rose formidable from the sea wall, the Lion flag of Gwynedd fluttered lazily against a backcloth of bracken-browned, snow-shawled mountains. Gulls wheeled and cried, the sea beat its restless pulse of incoming, outgoing tide. It all seemed much as Gwenhwyfar had left it.

Sliding an arm around her broad waist, Arthur pointed to the nearing wharf. 'We are here. I promised you your son should be born in Gwynedd.'

'Our son,' she corrected amiably, settling her weight against him. She filled her lungs with the sea air of home, closed her eyes, savouring the fresh tang of salt. Her husband's pleasing nearness.

They had been at sea two days; their first chance of private conversation and close contact. The ship boasted one bed, which had become Gwenhwyfar's, and Arthur had curled with his men under blankets on deck, when he had found time for sleep. Most of the journey he had passed in deep discussion with the captain, taking a keen interest in the mysteries of navigation and handling the craft. Never one for idling, he took the opportunity to learn and appreciate new skills, absorbing the ways of the sea with an eagerness matched by the crew's willing patience to explain.

Wind and weather had remained calm, but the sea had been heavy, the small coast-hugging craft wallowing in the swell like a bloated whale. Gwenhwyfar had sailed or paddled boats almost since before she could walk, was used to the sea but perhaps because of her bulk and her anxiety to get home, this journey had been nothing but sickness swamping her belly. She rested the back of her head against Arthur's shoulder. In a little while she would be walking on firm ground – thank the gods!

The babe was causing her discomfort. Its head was low down, pressing on birth canal and bladder, hard in the pit of her womb when she sat or walked. The necessity to relieve herself frequently was irritating. Her only comfort was the ungainliness of advanced pregnancy would soon be over – this voyage home to Gwynedd was left late for peace of mind.

Then, too, the foetid odours of that unpleasant stronghold they had come from still clung. Savouring the fresh air, she said, 'I thought we would be entombed with Meirchion in Dumnonia for ever.'

Arthur laughed. 'He was rather tedious.' Leaning over the rail, he studied the foaming water swirling against the hull. 'A hesitant man,' he said, 'unsure where to lay his wager until the winner becomes a certainty. It took a while for him to decide which way to bend, with me or Vortimer.'

'He knows you for what you are then, husband.'

Arthur looked at her suspiciously. 'What do you mean?'

'That your fingers are itching to bleed each wealthy man dry. Meirchion and my brother to head the list.'

'Certainly not!'

'Certainly so! In Enniaun's case you want every ounce of horseflesh he owns for next to nothing in return.' She relented, her smile twitching into laughter. She twined her arm through his when she realised he had taken her seriously. 'I am teasing!' She sighed, placed a light kiss on his cheek. He was so quick to take offence these days; living on a knife edge, sinking often into a brooding silence.

He did not answer her, was watching the shore coming nearer.

Gwenhwyfar pulled a little away from him, leant her arms on the rail as he did, looked out over the tossing grey sky. The Caer ahead was growing larger – another five, ten minutes and they would be there. Could she never say the right thing to Arthur? If being king meant constant bickering, then she would rather he decided on a more agreeable role. Gods, if she were ever queen, would she have to visit other such places as Meirchion's stink of a stronghold?

She shuddered at the recollection of the place, her features wrinkling into a grimace of distaste. An ordeal was not the whole of it!

'Almost eight days was I cloistered with that odious wife of his!' she said to the sea. 'Phew, God knows when she last bathed!' Gwenhwyfar scratched her head, still feeling the itch of parasites; numerous washings in salt water scooped by the bucketful had seen them gone, she hoped. 'I shall scream if I find any fleas from that place on me!'

Arthur whistled through his teeth, his quick anger forgotten. He held her, the embrace awkward because of her size.

'You are complaining? I had Meirchion himself! Did he ever cease eating? I think I did not see him once without some form of food clasped in his greasy paw. Chewing all the time he ducked and swerved, talking of everything under the sun but the reason why I was there! When I did finally manage to get in a word about the holding of land, he went off on a separate path about the whys and wherefores of his right to possess it because of his service to Vortigern! Service? Fah! Grovelling, I call it. Like a pig at the trough.' Arthur spat over the side.

'Poor Meirchion,' Gwenhwyfar said, finding some little pity. 'After all these years when he thought himself secure, you arrive unannounced, tell him you are now lord and demand his allegiance.' She laughed. 'He did stop eating, Arthur, I saw him. For a full minute he stopped chewing as we entered – his jaw hung open like a hooked fish!'

'I did not demand! And he was not that surprised to see me, knew well I would come one day.'

'We were in danger, Arthur. Had he a named heir, Meirchion would have had us murdered before the sun set on the day we arrived.'

The ship was slowing, the square blue sail flapping as the men hauled it down from the central mast. Others sat waiting, poised to dip oars into the churning sea.

'If he had such an heir I would have approached the matter differently.' Arthur gazed outwards. There were people gathering on the shore. 'I chose the path I took because Meirchion is a superstitious man; he would not harm an unborn child.'

Gwenhwyfar moved away, standing squarely behind him, hands on hips. She had just realised! 'You took me as security, didn't you? Did it not occur to you that you might be goading Meirchion beyond endurance? There are ways of achieving what you need. Openly declaring war if he refused to do as you say is not very diplomatic!'

'What was I to do then?' He turned, rising to her anger. 'Meirchion, I care not whether you side with me or Vortimer now his useless father is destroyed. Please, suit yourself; use my rightful inheritance of land, wealth and men against me! I assumed you had more sense, wife!'

'As I assumed you did!' she shouted back at him.

The ship bucked as the oars dipped and pulled, banking the craft sharply to the steer-board side. Misbalanced, Gwenhwyfar lurched forward, caught by Arthur who lunged swiftly to avert a fall. He held her a moment, then kissed her.

'Remove that pout of displeasure,' he said. 'You are right. As you usually are.'

He braced her weight against his own body, steadying her against the manoeuvring craft. 'I was full aware of the danger to you and the child, but I had to take the gamble. I need Meirchion's willing agreement to back me, and I needed you for protection.'

Gwenhwyfar opened her mouth to protest, but he stopped her words with a second kiss.

'For all his blustering, he understood the position as well as I, Cymraes. Since the day your Da declared me as Uthr's heir, Meirchion has known he could lose all – so could I – if war broke out between us. Yet I could not risk complacency. I had to enforce the threat of aggression, or gain nothing from him.'

'And knowing you were going to threaten, you walked us openly into his lair?'

Arthur grinned, kissed the tip of her nose. 'Guessing Meirchion would chance fighting me, but never your kin. You were my pass to safe keeping.'

'You took a great risk, Arthur.'

'My whole future is a risk, love. Our future.'

Gwenhwyfar looked earnestly up at the man before her. Arthur stood several handspans above her own height – a tall man, as his father had been. Dark-haired with those piercing hawk eyes. 'You will keep the promise you made him?' she asked, suddenly unsure and afraid of this callousness she had not seen in him before.

Vaguely he answered, 'Happen.'

Alarmed, she responded quickly. 'Arthur, you must! You promised he could hold those lands until his death!'

'You are over-protective of Vortigern's former friends all of a sudden? A moment since, you were condemning him as an odious parasite! That is politics: setting one loyalty against another to gain the upper hand. How else am I to gain support? Men must learn to see me as more powerful and more dangerous than Vortimer. How think you your brother Enniaun survives as Prince of Gwynedd?'

She kicked his boot, not hard, but enough to show displeasure. 'Because he keeps promises.'

Arthur's mouth twitched. 'Not many of them, Cymraes – and only the ones that serve his purpose. I pledged Meirchion's security – and I intend to honour that pledge, so long as it suits me and he keeps his word. The winner, love, is the man who can smile and promise the sun and moon, knowing he has only mountain mist to give.'

Placing his hands on her shoulders, he turned her round to face the shore rushing to meet them. 'If Meirchion remains loyal then I shall leave well alone. That I can promise.'

Rich-clad people stood to the forefront of the crowd gathered at the wharfside. Gwenhwyfar sighted two brothers who still remained at the Caer, the twins Rumaun and Dunaut. With them, various nephews, nieces and cousins. The dark-haired young woman beside her brother Enniaun she guessed to be his wife, Teleri, a princess of the northern Picti people.

A wave of unexpected alarm swept through her. She had been away so long. So many things had changed; she had changed. She clung to Arthur's arm, trembling slightly, whether from excitement or fear she could not tell. A little of both?

'How can I face them?' she asked.

Shrewdly Arthur replied, 'As boldly as I face the Lion's son in his den.'

The ship bumped, ropes were flung, caught by eager hands. A plank was run out. Gwenhwyfar found herself engulfed in enthusiastic greetings and tears of welcome. She could not control her own brimming eyes, clung to her eldest living brother smiling, laughing and crying all at once; her emotions tumbling together like fleeting rain showers on a bright sunny day.

Teleri touched Gwenhwyfar's cheek with her own, not quite a kiss, an uncertain greeting, more polite than friendly.

Rumaun pushed forward before the two women could exchange further conversation, swept his sister to him with a yell of delight.

'How round you are, Gwen!' He poked gently at her protruding bulk, added, 'I trust there is only one in there!' He winked at his twin brother and they all laughed, Gwenhwyfar saying, 'One is quite sufficient! Do you not agree, Teleri?'

Off guard, the woman muttered a shy and embarrassed reply.

Enniaun held his wife fondly at his side, smiling down at her.

'You have another niece!' he told Gwenhwyfar. 'A bonny lass. She will be a good playmate for your child as they grow!'

A sharp retort almost left Gwenhwyfar's lips. Her child would play with no daughter of this Picti crab! She bit it back – that was unfair. 'Happen she will,' she said.

Teleri trailed silently behind as they walked up the incline to the Hall. She was a shy person, awkward and often clumsy in her eagerness to please. She tried so hard to do the right thing, aware the Picti were resented here in Gwynedd, usually ended by making herself look a fool. Gwenhwyfar's coming worried her. She had heard so much about her husband's sister – how could she survive beneath such an eclipsing sun?

Seeing Enniaun's easy laughter with Gwenhwyfar, Teleri felt a stab of sharp envy. For all the kindness shown her she still felt like an outsider. Head down, hands clasped tight together she followed at the rear of the crowd of happy people, wishing Gwenhwyfar had not come, would go soon.

At the doorway to the Hall servants and slaves waited, eager to give greetings. Gwenhwyfar embraced some of them, a special hug for Brenna who was as old as the hills and as dependable.

Teleri took up the cup of welcome and carried it in both hands towards the Pendragon.

The confusion and jostling was great. People were pushing forward, reaching out hands in greeting. Hounds milled about, barking, tails wagging. One, a great brindle, a favourite of Enniaun's, launched himself at his master. Annoyed, he kicked him aside and the dog tumbled, yelping to fall awkwardly against Teleri. She was of small height and build, like a sparrow she seemed. The enormous dog knocked her off balance and she stumbled to her knees, spilling red wine over herself and those gathered at the threshold. Some laughed; more grumbled.

Arthur had assessed her at first sight. He always had an eye for a pretty girl, and found this one's slight form and shyness attractive. Had she not been wife to Enniaun, well, who knew how much more he might have decided to learn of her? He stepped forward, gallantly helping her to her feet. He kept hold of her hand, grasping it tightly in his own as he swept his eyes over her, raising a deep flush on her face.

She felt disconcertingly naked before his gaze, knowing his look for what it was, a measuring of the body beneath her gown. The wine, where it clung to her bodice, highlighted the round curve of her breast.

'You need spill only a token gesture to appease the gods.' His voice was as smooth as the rich wine.

Teleri met his eyes and felt her legs begin to shake. He lifted her hand and kissed the white skin. She withdrew it sharply and mopped ineffectually at her sodden dress, attempting to conceal her embarrassment.

Someone hastily refilled the cup and handed it to Arthur to drink first. He gave his blessing on the household then spilt the customary small drop on the floor, adding to the accidental spillage.

Unexpectedly Gwenhwyfar remembered another such cup, when Cunedda had returned after Uthr's death. She could see herself there again, a leggy girl with cherry buds for breasts, scrawny and impatient for the excitement of womanhood. How young she had been!

Arthur handed the golden cup to her. For a moment she held it between both hands, staring into the dark pool of liquid. She had not expected Enniaun's wife to be quite so young and pretty. Nor had she missed that look of keen interest from Arthur. Beside Teleri Gwenhwyfar felt an ungainly lump with swollen feet and puffed ankles, waddling like a land-bound duck.

How does he see me she wondered. *As I was in Less Britain, a girl breathless for his loving, living in the dream days of sunshine? Or as I am now – irritable, often crying for no reason, with sharp words always on my tongue?*

'Welcome home, sister,' her brother was saying, his voice distant among her thoughts. *Home,* Gwenhwyfar thought with a start. She looked about her, at the Hall stretching wide and grand beneath soaring rafters, at the happy faces and welcoming smiles. Family, friends.

Caer Arfon had been the only home she had known. There were other, more modest strongholds scattered throughout this vast territory of Gwynedd, some in which they lived for months at a time, depending on the season, the availability of game and the pressing calls of justice and law. None were 'home', save Caer Arfon.

Gwenhwyfar sipped the wine. For so long had she wanted this, to come back to Caer Arfon. Now she was here, she found the pink glow had faded, leaving only smudged grey edges. With startling clarity she realised the truth. Now her Da was gone, and she had Arthur for her own and a child coming, Caer Arfon was no longer her home.

She swallowed a gulp of wine and its strength burnt her throat with a stinging warmth, sending her head spinning a moment, leaving her thoughts suddenly settled and clear. She had never wanted to be headwoman here; that status belonged to Teleri, the new prince's wife.

Caer Arfon was the place of childhood and those days were gone, for she was a woman grown with a child restless to be born.

Straightening her shoulders Gwenhwyfar tipped the remaining liquid to the floor. A hard lesson to learn, but there could be no going back, only forward.

They were waiting, feet shuffling, some coughing, impatient. Those memories of childhood were distant but there all the same, and the future lay ahead with who knew what changes? Well, so must it be!

Gwenhwyfar looked at Arthur eye to eye, gave him a dazzling smile which he returned from his heart. It shone from him, a radiance, every part of his body smiling his pride in her and love for her. She placed her hand confidently in his and stepped across the pool of wine lying on the threshold.

She was coming to Caer Arfon, not as daughter of Gwynedd but as wife to the Pendragon and mother to his child. She had outfaced the dark dreams and set aside the shadows that lurked among the haunting echoes of fear.

§ XXXVII

Afrosted night, with a crisp scent in the air and a sharp bite to cheeks and fingers. The white touch of winter was beginning to shoulder aside the mellow golds and reds of autumn. Gwenhwyfar stood gazing at the snow-tipped mountains, rising silent-shadowed against a star-scattered sky. Old friends, the mountains.

In the Hall, heat from crowding people and glowing fires had flushed her face, wine and food warming her from within. She shivered, pulled her cloak tighter. The cold had soon chased away that drowsy, complacent glow, filling her nose and lungs with brittle wakefulness. The mountains would always be there, and the stars. The river still ran into the sea, and the tide washed against the shore. Reliable, dependable things.

The Stone stood before her, a black pillar pointing like a finger up towards the four corner stars of Orion and the brilliance that was the eye of his faithful hound following at heel. Gwenhwyfar walked forward, boots crunching on the white, spangled ground. Her hand touched the cold hardness of the Stone her fingers caressing its familiar rough surface. How many other clear nights such as this had she stood here to set free confused thought?

What scenes the spirit of this carved rock must have witnessed! Warriors gathered for a hosting, hopes and hearts edging as high as Yr Wyddfa as they honed an edge to their weapons, talking among themselves, confessing fears or boasting bravado. Daily comings and goings to and from the Hall. Spring lambs, born calves; summer harvest; autumn gather and slaughter; winter cold. The pledging of loyalties and swearing of oaths. Arthur had stood here as a boy, when he became Pendragon. Uthr, before he left to meet his death. Osmail, Etern. Her father.

A step crunched on the frost-hardened ground.

'Gwenhwyfar?'

Without turning she said, 'The mountains are so ageless, Enniaun.'

He came up beside her, his eyes lifting towards the hills. 'With the coming and passing of seasons they wear different cloaks, but it is good to know beneath those mantles of green, brown or white they remain as always. They were here when we were born, will be here when we die. 'Tis a sobering thought.' He seated himself beside the Stone, his back leaning against it. Tipped his head to watch the stars.

'They shone as bright two nights past, for Samhain. We lit a fire to welcome our Da and brothers, should their spirits decide to come,' he said.

'I thought you might.'

'It is a pity you were not here.'

'It is a pity they are dead.'

Enniaun stretched his legs, shuffled himself more comfortable. 'We must all die, sister.'

She rounded on him. 'That we must, but do we need to walk into death's embrace? Da ought not have gone; he was not so young, nor so agile.'

Enniaun lifted his hands, palm open. 'Nor was he in his dotage and crippled. His was the death every warrior seeks, Gwen. Triumphant in battle, not suffering age or the bone ache, not waiting for death to remember you.'

An owl glided silent above the thatch of the Hall, his wings ghost white under the light of the stars. Gwenhwyfar watched his passing, said, 'I thought I had accepted their deaths. But now I am here, where I can see and hear and smell them, the ache of grief has returned.'

'It never leaves, not with someone we love. Their presence burns too vivid in our memories. Happen that is as it should be, for otherwise we would too easy forget.'

Gwenhwyfar squatted beside her brother, shifted herself close for warmth. He draped the swirled length of his cloak around her shoulders.

'So much has changed,' she said.

'Change has to come for life to struggle forward. We none of us can ever stand still.' He smiled, took his sister's hand between his own. 'We are not the mountains or stars, sweetheart. Would we not grow bored waiting for nothing to happen?'

She smiled at that and squeezed his hand. 'Bored, aye, but much safer.'

He thought a moment, rubbing the cold of her hands with his fingers. 'I heard a story once. A man was told by a wise woman in five days he was going to be crushed to death. Well, at first he didn't believe her, but as the fifth day approached he began to get nervous. Come the dawn, he was so frightened he decided to stay all the day in his bed.'

'And so he cheated the wise woman's prediction?'

Enniaun laughed. '*Na*. The roof fell in on top of him.'

Gwenhwyfar swiped at her brother's head with the back of her hand. 'Idiot,' she said, but she was laughing, the black mood lifting.

'Did he die easy, my Da? No one ever wrote me the full details, only that he had been killed.'

'I was not here either. I was away to the north agreeing trade and alliance with old Necthan.' He sighed, clasping his hands together. 'Had I been here, then happen Da would not have gone.' He hung his head, said quietly, 'I mourn him too, sister, for I have had to replace him, and no one can ever fill that vast emptiness left by the Lion Lord Cunedda.'

For a while and a while they sat together, silent, watching the stars tread their endless dance, until Gwenhwyfar at last said, 'It is forgetting that troubles me. So desperately am I trying not to forget Da's face, Etern's laugh or even Osmail's scowl. But they are all slipping away, fading as a rainbow does after its brief shine of glory. And then, the things I so need to wipe from my mind – Melwas, and what he did to me, Ceridwen's death of agony, Iawn... all those horrid things, not one tiny detail, not one, will leave me.'

'They will, Gwen. When your child is born you will have new things to think on. Change, you see.' Enniaun kissed her cheek then stood, stamping his feet and clapping his hands to his sides. 'I tell you one thing that must change – me out here for me in there!' He laughed as he nodded up the hill towards the Hall. 'Are you coming?'

She stood also, stretching an ache from the pit of her back. 'I am tired. I think I will go to my bed.'

Giving his sister an affectionate hug, Enniaun began to walk away, but stopped and faced her again as she called out, 'I believe, brother, that lion cubs are often as strong as their sire, the lion.'

He grinned. 'I have heard that also.' About to resume his walk back to the Hall, he halted again, said into the darkness, 'I can tell you one other thing, Gwen. Our father's death shall be avenged. I have vowed to rid Gwynedd of all the poxed sea raiders who have taken it upon themselves to dirty our soil.' He looked at her across the few feet separating them, his expression so reminiscent of his father's. 'And that vow shall not change until it is completed.'

434

§ XXXVIII

The complex of buildings behind the Hall beckoned cheerfully; servants had lit night torches which burnt in friendly welcome. Caer Arfon had always seemed grand to Gwenhwyfar as a child, but then she had seen nothing else save her Da's other strongholds, all smaller than this one. For the first time she saw it for what it was, a hotch-potch mixture of Brythonic and Roman. Thatched roofs among slate, daub and timber walls running alongside stone built. Round, traditional dwelling places and the family's impressively Roman chambers. All this, ranged around a rectangular chieftain's Hall. Compared to Ygrainne's grand villa the buildings, even those in the Roman style, were primitive.

Gwenhwyfar paused before entering her chamber, aware that never again would she share a room with chattering girls. Her position of wife, especially wife to the Pendragon, afforded her the luxury of privacy, but with that came solitude and loneliness. She swung away from the door, headed instead for the darkness of the walled garden.

So many memories, bad and good. So much truth to be faced. She walked slowly, head bent, lost within her own world of thought. The sound had been there, but remained unnoticed until it ceased abruptly with a stifled exclamation.

Gwenhwyfar's head snapped up. 'Who is there?' Servants up to some mischief? No answer. There was no moon and the stars gave little light here in the shadows. She said again, commanding, 'I know you are there. My Lord Enniaun will not tolerate illicit coupling within his private grounds – get you gone!'

A vague movement, a rustle, like wind rummaging through fallen leaves. Then silence. Angrily Gwenhwyfar strode forward, gasped as a single cowled shape appeared before her. A woman. The star silvered light fell on her face – Teleri.

Gwenhwyfar was about to say something harsh, but compassion stopped her. Instead, 'You are shivering, have you no thicker cloak? Here, take mine.' She unpinned the brooch at her left shoulder and swung the woollen garment from her. Teleri hunched herself into the warmth, stumbled a thank you through chattering teeth.

'Why are you out here?' Gwenhwyfar asked.

'The garden is a good place to be alone,' Teleri answered, with a catch of despair in her voice. Standing so much closer now Gwenhwyfar could see the tracks of tears on her cheeks. She took Teleri's hand impulsively in her own.

'You and I, Teleri, are two lost souls, weeping for everything and nothing!'

Taken aback, all Teleri could think to say was, 'I thank you for the cloak.'

The misjudged dislike Gwenhwyfar had felt for her brother's wife evaporated as she saw her for what she was, a lonely girl far from home. Someone lost and afraid.

Gwenhwyfar could understand that.

'We are strangers you and I, Teleri. We should not be, for we are both women of Gwynedd.'

'You may be, not I. I am an alliance, a surety between a husband and a father.'

Gwenhwyfar was staggered by the desolation in her voice. 'Are you not happy here?' she asked. 'Does my brother not treat you well? Enniaun loves you, he has said so.' Gwenhwyfar was concerned. Her family would treat any deserving woman with respect – especially one brought as wife. Even to Branwen they had shown politeness, however grudgingly. She said confidently, 'My brother would not keep a wife against her will – for all the alliances offered.'

Teleri bit her lip, aching to talk, to free herself of the unbearable loneliness. She must take this chance to speak out, the opportunity might never come again.

'It is not that I am unhappy. My husband treats me well, as do his brothers and their wives.' She added with a show of courage, 'Though I am glad I never had cause to meet with the one they call Branwen.' Staggered at her impertinence she said hastily, 'It was with sorrow that I learnt of Osmail's death. I pray often for his soul.'

Gwenhwyfar smiled and slid her arm through Teleri's, inviting her to walk. 'That is kind – thank you. The whole stronghold was relieved when Branwen passed beneath the gate!'

Teleri's brow creased. 'Then you were not friends with her?'

'Friends! By Heaven I was not! I nearly fainted with horror when I met her again at Yns Witrin!' Gwenhwyfar laughed.

Teleri laughed with her, a strange sound to her own ear, for she had rarely laughed these past months. Suddenly she was talking, with an urgent need to spill her heart. 'I can do no right! Everything I touch I break, every word I say is wrong. I am clumsy in action and tongue. Your brothers think me a fool.'

'They do not! Dunaut told me this very evening of his liking for you, said you were unsure of yourself but you made Enniaun happy.'

A glow of cheerfulness warmed Teleri. She said breathlessly, amazed at her sudden ability to talk, 'I am one of two and twenty daughters produced from five wives. My father made it known he had no hope of arranging good marriages for more than the favoured few. My mother was British, a Christian. When she died I found solace within the small community of holy sisters, where I began learning the language of herbs and healing remedies. My sisters were not the kindest of girls.'

'You did not want to become one of God's women?'

Teleri paused, glanced at the heavy gold and sapphire ring on her finger, her marriage band. 'Somehow that dedicated life seemed so, so...'

'Dreary?'

Teleri smiled shyly. 'I had no choice, you see. I hoped that if my healing proved useful my father would look on me with more favour.' Teleri lifted her hands. 'It did not, but it did unite me with Enniaun. He spent a while with us, negotiating agreements of trade and alliance with my father, and fell badly on a hunting trip. I was summoned to see what I could do. I must have been of use, for within the month I found myself married and on my way south to Gwynedd.'

Gwenhwyfar whistled. 'As quick as that! He was surely taken with you.'

Teleri shrugged, spoke as she saw the truth. 'It was for my healing. He has little love for a fumbling birdbrain.'

'Nonsense. I have seen how he looks at you, heard the fondness in his voice when he speaks of you and his daughter. Which reminds me – I have yet to meet her.'

Impulsively taking the other woman's hand, Gwenhwyfar ran forward – an awkward shuffle rather than a run because of her bulk. 'Come, you shall introduce us now!'

'But she is sleeping.'

'We need not wake her.'

Teleri was running too, laughing, overwhelmed at the pleasure coursing through her. She had dreaded Gwenhwyfar's home coming, dreaded facing such an incredible person. Her own sisters were harsh, vain creatures who constantly sneered and jibed at her, sapping her confidence and courage, and Teleri had expected Gwenhwyfar to be the same. Although the night was dark, it seemed to her the sun had burst from behind storm clouds. Gwenhwyfar was not contemptuous, was not aloof. Apart from the baby daughter she cherished, for the first time in her life Teleri had discovered a friend.

Hand in hand they scudded breathlessly across the gravel courtyard. Abruptly, Gwenhwyfar stopped, pleasure fleeing from her face. Her thighs felt wet, sticky, and a gush of water splashed from her, spreading on the ground at her feet. She cried out in alarm, frightened and embarrassed. Teleri darted to her side, uttering reassuring, calm words.

'It is only the waters of the womb that have broken. It is quite normal – it happened to me. Your bairn wants to come!' The younger girl, confident in her knowledge, guided the elder one forward, calling for assistance. Servants appeared. One ran for old Brenna who came bustling from the kitchens.

Within the security of her own chamber, cleaned and reclothed in her night shift, Gwenhwyfar felt a little foolish. There was no pain, no momentous thing happening to her body; just a dull ache in her lower back, and her thighs were cramped, uncomfortable, but no more than the usual feeling that accompanied the start of her monthly flow. Then it came, a tightening of muscles, like cramp or the urgent need to relieve oneself of a constipated stool. It heightened and Gwenhwyfar bit her lip to stop the trembling. As suddenly, it passed.

Teleri grinned. 'It gets worse!'

'If you are to be a friend,' Gwenhwyfar retorted, 'I would rather you did not tell me such things.'

Mares, bitches, sheep, sows, slaves and servants birthed often enough, she reflected. But all the same, the screams of women who had a difficult time clung obstinately to her mind. 'Is it very bad?' she asked.

Teleri gestured for Brenna to answer. She was ageing now, this old freed slave, but kindness was as much a part of her face as wrinkles and creases. Brenna had made life tolerable for Teleri.

'For some 'tis easy, some hard,' the old woman said, crossing the room to take Gwenhwyfar's hand in her own. 'We are in the hands of God.'

Gwenhwyfar winced. 'I would rather put my faith in Our Lady. What does a male god know of birthing?' She caught her breath. 'That one was stronger.'

'They will get so. By this time on the morrow we shall know if you carry boy or girl.'

'That is exactly as you told me, Brenna!' Teleri exclaimed. Through the shudder of another contraction Gwenhwyfar said, 'I must meet my niece another day, it seems.'

When another pain came, Brenna placed her gnarled hand on Gwenhwyfar's abdomen, counting softly to herself. She peered at the birth canal, probing gently with her fingers, and grunted, satisfied. She snorted as Gwenhwyfar remarked, 'Birth is not over-dignified.'

'For that matter,' the woman replied with a laugh, 'neither is conceiving!' She gestured for Gwenhwyfar to cover herself. ''Twill be some while yet. Babies come in their own time, we can do nothing to hurry them from their bed.'

There was a commotion outside. Arthur burst in, thrusting aside a group of household servants. 'Have you no work to attend!' he barked, slamming the door in their startled faces. He strode over to Gwenhwyfar, saying anxiously, 'I was told you were taken ill!'

Gwenhwyfar shook her head. '*Na*, husband, not ill.'

'Fools!' Brenna snapped, stumping from the room. 'Can I never trust another to take a message correctly?' She was gone, her voice chiding, grumbling. Teleri made to leave also.

Gwenhwyfar said quickly, 'Do not go. Stay with me.'

'If you wish it, I shall be glad to help.' Teleri felt a vast surge of happiness at that. She smoothed the expensive material of her gown, said, 'Let me change into clothing more suited.' She smiled shyly at Arthur. 'Something plain is more appropriate.'

Arthur waited until she had gone. 'My son is coming, then?'

'So it seems.' Gwenhwyfar narrowed her eyes. 'You must not tease Teleri.'

'Tease her? Would I do that?'

'Aye, you would.' She was going to say more, let it drop as a fresh wave of contractions rippled through her.

'Arthur,' she whispered, holding him tight, welcoming the strength of his arms, 'I am frightened.'

'Of what? Birth occurs every day.'

Gwenhwyfar flared at his tactless remark, plunging away from his embrace. 'Does that make it easier or safer? You men desire the pleasure, want the sons – but forget the hardship we endure to provide both!'

'The pleasure is yours also,' he answered. The last thing he wanted was an argument, but, by the Bull, Gwenhwyfar was touchy these days! The slightest innocent remark and she was off, galloping in full stride. It was getting so that he was reluctant to remark on anything, important or trivial.

'Is it?' The words were out before she could swallow them.

Arthur sat silent on the bed, staring at the wall ahead, not at her. 'I assumed it was,' he said after a while. 'I am sorry I do not please you.'

Kneeling on the bed covers, Gwenhwyfar shuffled forward. She touched his shoulder. 'I did not mean it to sound like that.'

'How did you mean it, then?' He shrugged her aside, churlish.

'In Less Britain it was...' She fumbled for the right words. 'Before, I wanted you and needed you. I enjoyed our lovemaking, it was good. It is just that,' she did not know how to say her thoughts. 'You must not expect too much of me too soon! I cannot comfortably give you my body with a child so large within me!'

Gwenhwyfar masked the pain of a contraction, her hand pressing tight against her abdomen. The pains were growing stronger, more frequent. She moved from the bed and walked across the room. Her back ached terribly; her legs felt unsteady. Reaching for the wall, she turned to him, hands spread in appeal. 'I love you. I always have and I always shall. All I ask from you is time to come to terms with what has happened to me. Is that too much for you to give?'

Another strong contraction shuddered through her. She gasped, clutched quickly at the back of a chair.

Arthur sat motionless, watching her. He too was frightened. He loved Gwenhwyfar, but fear dried his throat, numbed his senses, shook his legs. Fear. He knew all too well how many women died giving birth or from complications after. If it should happen to Gwenhwyfar...

He steeled himself, forced himself to stand behind her. He placed his hands on her shoulders, gasped as she jerked away.

'Leave me alone!' she snarled, almost running from him, across the room.

'I cannot do a damn thing right for you lately, can I?' He stood a moment, head drooping, arms slack at his side. 'I love you, Cymraes.'

The contraction passed, but fear of what lay ahead and thoughts of what crowded behind made Gwenhwyfar say, 'Love! Men use women for their own gain. Use and abuse! By the Mother, you shall not misuse me!'

Proud men are reluctant to give ground, and Arthur did not know how to show himself with shield down. For too many years of miserable childhood he had hidden behind a defence of bland indifference where women were concerned. The wall was too strong to breach with one blow, although for Gwenhwyfar, it was crushing, slowly, coming down. But not this night. Fear bound the mortar tight.

He knew he ought to give support and encouragement, desperately wanted to. Why then did he bellow, 'I shall use you as my woman and my wife, in my way!'

Was it so surprising she screamed, 'Get out! Get away from me!' Her shrill voice could be heard clear across the courtyard. Brenna, supervising the moving of the birthing chair and sundry other items, picked up her skirts and trundled at a hobbling run back to the chamber. Reaching the door, she reeled as Arthur swung blindly past her.

Gwenhwyfar was huddled on the floor, the pains coming sharper, lasting longer. Teleri appeared. With a puzzled glance over her shoulder at Arthur's retreating form, she asked, 'Is all well?'

Cradling Gwenhwyfar Brenna persuaded her to rise, to walk, as her labour swept on. She nodded at the door. 'Shut the Caer out, lass. We will manage better without the world peering in.'

§ XXXIX

Rumaun found Arthur in the early morning hours. With a skin of wine, he sat curled in one corner of his stallion's stall, half buried by bracken bedding. Eira snorted as Gwenhwyfar's brother squeezed past his rump. The horse was settled now and eating contentedly, although it had taken some hours for the shivering to cease for Eira disliked the sea. Arthur would have preferred to ride to Gwynedd from the south but Gwenhwyfar had wanted to get home. It was quicker by sea.

Rumaun patted the beast, giving reassurance, called to Arthur. 'Are you sleeping?'

Arthur grunted, opened one eye, shut it again. '*Na.*'

Settling himself with a tired sigh, Rumaun pushed the horse's inquisitive muzzle aside, reached for the wineskin. Tipping it to his lips, enquired, 'Is there any left?' He scowled as only a few drops trickled from it, and threw the empty thing down. 'We have been searching for you. Did you not hear us calling?'

If he had, Arthur gave no indication. He remained hunched, arms clasped around himself, chin tucked low, eyes firmly closed.

Determined, Rumaun continued. 'The babe has come. Mother and son are fine. She had a quick time of it. Like her mother, she births her sons well.' He faltered. What more should he say? As most of the Caer, he was aware of the harsh words exchanged between his sister and her husband. He said,

'Women react in peculiar ways when carrying a child, and Gwenhwyfar has always been one for a sudden storm, though they blow themselves out. You must not take her words to heart.' Rumaun trailed off as a tear trickled from beneath Arthur's closed lashes.

Emotion was rarely suppressed by a warrior. Any man would weep for the death of a lord or a beloved son, wife, brother or friend, and none thought the worse of him for showing honest feelings. Yet this was no death. Where the reason to mourn?

He grasped Arthur's forearm. 'Gwen is well, Arthur, believe me. Tired, Brenna says, but well.'

A great breath of relief juddered from the Pendragon, 'Mithras be praised – thank God!'

Rumaun hid a smile at Arthur's mixture of faiths, but aye, he agreed.

Arthur opened his eyes and stared blankly out of dilated pupils. 'I have let her down.' He drew a hand over the extensive stubble on his chin. 'Not for the first time either. Damn this pride of mine!' He slammed his fist into the wall, causing Eira to snort and toss his head. 'I have to keep proving myself, showing how good I am! All the while knowing I live a lie!' He laughed bitterly. 'And Gwenhwyfar is the only woman with courage enough to tell me the truth to my face.'

Rumaun nodded. 'Aye, she's never been one to mince words.'

A pause, then Rumaun said, 'Problems look their darkest in the early hours, especially with a head pounding from over-much wine.' He stood up, stretched and brushed stable bedding from his bracae. 'Brenna says you can go and see your son and wife.'

Arthur toyed with the edge of his cloak, pulling the hem through his fingers. He did not answer.

Rumaun's patience was running thin; it had been a long night. 'In the name of God, man – put this black mood from you!'

Arthur raised troubled eyes. 'Does Gwenhwyfar wish to see me? Can she forgive me?'

'What is there to forgive?' Rumaun headed for the stable door. 'A quarrel? We all have those. I can understand your anxiety for her safe delivery – but that is past.' He opened the door, pushing Eira, who had walked behind him, back. 'However, I would suggest no woman would forgive a husband for not coming with all haste to take up his son.'

Arthur took his meaning and grinned agreement. 'Aye, you say right.' He stood easing the stiffness from shoulders and back, and shoved Eira's rump aside. He put his hand on his brother-by-law's shoulder. 'I had best make my peace with her, then.'

He strode from the stables whistling, leaving Rumaun standing confused. God's truth, he hoped his sister understood the man better than he did!

The Pendragon found his wife drowsing, a wrapped bundle cradled in her arms. Brenna ceased her tidying and smiled as he crept through the door.

'You have a fine family. A strong wife and a healthy son.'

He took a step within the doorway, saying nothing, fiddling with the gold buckle of the baldric slung across his chest. The hilt of his sword hanging at his left hip chinked against the metalwork on his leather gear as he shifted weight from one foot to the other.

Carrying a bundle of soiled linen, Brenna patted his arm maternally as she passed by him to leave. 'Give her time, lad – and yourself.' Noting the dark shadows beneath bloodshot eyes, added, 'There is more to a marriage than the lust of coupling. Two people can only live as one when each is prepared to give and receive trust and understanding. Above that lies respect. Without respect for how the other feels, no marriage is worthwhile.'

She placed her weathered old hand over his. 'My eyes have seen many a problem come and go 'tween man and woman. My ears hear of plenty more. Put your trust in Gwenhwyfar and believe in yourself.' Her fingers squeezed his and she left.

'Do you intend to stand there 'til dawn breaks?' Gwenhwyfar asked, her eyes closed. She opened them and smiled radiantly at him.

'I thought you were sleeping,' he said in a half-whisper, stepping closer to the bed.

'I was. Brenna's talking roused me.' She tenderly peeled back the baby's wrap, revealing a wrinkled pink face and button nose. Arthur sat carefully beside his wife, staring in amazed pride at the tiny thing in her arms.

'I have never seen so new born a babe,' he admitted.

The bundle hiccupped, opened his eyes, squinted at the vague, blurred shape of his Da. He was warm, his belly was full of his mother's milk and he was content with this world.

Arthur tentatively reached forward. As he touched the small hand, minute fingers curled around one of his own and gripped with astonishing strength. Arthur gasped, impressed. His eyes met Gwenhwyfar's, a grin broadening on his awed face. 'He is perfect.'

'Of course he is!' she laughed. 'Is he not made from us?' She held the child out to him and when he hesitated, placed the bundle firmly in his arms. For a moment, Arthur fumbled, afraid to harm or drop this fragile being. Gwenhwyfar guided his hands beneath the baby's bottom and head, settling a secure but gentle hold.

'He must have a name,' Arthur declared, touching the softness of his son's cheek with a loving finger.

'That he must. A name fitting for a prince and heir to the Pendragon.'

Arthur glanced at Gwenhwyfar. She looked tired. Her hair tumbled loose, uncombed and free, as he liked it best. His son's hair was dark.

'I was thinking of Llacheu,' he offered.

Gwenhwyfar rolled the name round in her mind. "Tis a fine name, a British name for a British prince.' Teasing, 'You have thought some time on it?'

Arthur crimsoned, admitted, 'Aye!' He leant forward, awkward with the child in his arms, to kiss her cheek.

Gwenhwyfar pointed to the reed-woven cradle. 'He shall be safe in there.'

Carefully, mindful of the head, Arthur lowered his son and covered him with the blanket, tucking it firm around the tiny body. He sat silent for a while, unable to take his gaze from the sleeping child. It was a beautiful thing, new life, especially when the new life was your son.

'Ah, Cymraes, I have been a stupid ass. These past hours I have sat alone with my sins, convincing myself everything that could go wrong with the birth would do so.' He bowed his head. 'I thought I was to lose you and I would forever live with the knowledge we had parted with sour words, as enemies.'

Gwenhwyfar, throat tight, held out her arms to him, cradled her husband as lovingly as she had held the child. 'I could never be your enemy. I dislike your ideas sometimes, but beyond that I love you.' She sought for a way to explain it. 'My love for you is like the full moon, sailing high and clear and bright. Only, occasionally a cloud drifts across hiding her from sight. We cannot see her, all light has gone, yet we know for certain she is still there, waiting for the wind to blow the cloud away. My love for you is like that – always there but sometimes hidden. Do not dwell on words spoken in anger.' She laughed. 'Most women hate their menfolk during labour.'

His arms tightened about her waist, clinging urgently. He held her, his head buried against her full breasts. Already a scent of baby clung to her. 'I was afraid. Of what, I am not certain – anything and everything. Afraid of losing you, afraid of not having your love.' He sat up and took her face between his hands, searching her eyes, a soft, muted green, that reflected their love and happiness.

'I use women – as you said. I have twisted myself into the habit of taking what I want before they take from me. Morgause began it, all those years ago.' It was difficult for him to admit the truth, to allow another into the privacy of his well-shielded fears.

Briefly Gwenhwyfar wondered whether to tell him Morgause was with the Ladies at Yns Witrin and had a daughter. To what point? It would open old wounds – best he knew nothing more of her.

'She frightened me.' He shrugged, feigning casualness. 'I shut that fear from me, buried myself behind a rampart and wall determined never to feel shame and terror again.' His voice filled with hatred, as he added, 'I would kill her if ever I met with her again.' No idle threat, he meant it.

As well, Gwenhwyfar thought, *not to have said anything of her.*

Touching his cheek with the tips of her fingers, she traced the drawn lines of fatigue, said softly, 'Do I frighten you?'

Arthur caught her head, brought it up to his lips, kissed each finger, then the palm. 'You more than any. In a different way. Others, I have taken as I willed with no thought save for myself. I needed to dominate them, show I was not scared of their feminine power. Whores care not how they are treated as long as they receive payment, and Winifred, I think, enjoyed it that way. But you,' he placed tender kisses on her eyes, cheeks and lips. 'You frighten me because I am so scared I might lose you.' He faltered, embarrassed at talking of these deep-running feelings. 'I know it is because of what Melwas did that you are unable to respond to my touch, but still I tell myself it might not be the reason. And that one there,' he indicated the sleeping child, 'I was jealous of him. He kept me from your bed.' He stayed the words of protest that were forming with another, longer kiss. 'But I am proud of him now he is here.'

She responded by returning the kiss with a passion she had forgotten existed. 'Do you love me, Arthur?'

'Need you ask that of me?'

'I need.'

'Then aye, I love you. I have never loved any other than you. Nor have I had love in return, for the sake of love alone. I fear the slender thread that binds us will snap. That I have sawn through it.' He added something more. 'You are more than my wife, you are my Cymraes. You are one alone, special, a single bright star shining in the blackness.'

'Then why talk of a slender thread, husband? For myself, I am bound to you by a chain of iron. Unbendable, unbreakable. Even death shall not free my soul from yours.'

He lay back, resting his head on the pillow and snuggled close to her warmth, surrendering to the tiredness that hammered persistently behind his aching forehead.

Gwenhwyfar held him lightly, thinking on his words. 'I know of the conflict within you, dear heart, but I too have such a battle to wage. Happen together we can conquer this war which is tearing at us. Given enough patience.' She tilted her head to see his face more clearly, realised his breathing had slowed, shallowed.

Brenna entered the room some while later. Gwenhwyfar put her finger to her lips, whispered, 'My two men sleep.'

446

APRIL 456

§ XL

Marching was never a very appealing part of army life. Marching with full equipment in the pouring rain, and leading a perfectly rideable horse could bring some men close to mutiny. Except, the Pendragon was putting himself through the same punishing routine, and the men were wanting to become part of his elite Artoriani. Arthur had made things quite clear to them at the outset: 'If you are not fit, if you cannot stand the pace, then get you back to Vortimer's soft-bellied lizards.'

Throughout the winter men had drifted to Gwynedd in groups of three and four, singly, or brother with brother to join Arthur. From Dyfed, fifty young men had braved the first heavy snow to set their spears beneath his banner. The warming of spring saw more coming, the groups larger, the men eager. With those who had left Vortimer with Arthur, they had enough to form a full ala quingenaria. Five hundred enthusiastic men, striving to become the fittest, best-disciplined and most admired troops since the Roman Eagles had lifted the standards for which they were named, and taken sail back to Rome.

Arthur was determined to have them the best. These men, and those who would follow when the name of the Artoriani came familiar to everyone's lips. He saw a day, in the not too distant future, when every young man who could sit a horse would seek to join his cavalry. But that day was not yet here, and until then he had to prove himself – and his men. So they drilled and they marched, they practised their fighting skills. On horseback, on foot. In pairs, as a group, as a turma of thirty men. And together as an ala.

Arthur wiped rain from his nose and hefted the shield slung across his shoulders. As commander he did not need to carry full equipment but the muscles of horses and men had to be tightened and there was no better way than trotting ten miles over rough terrain carrying a full pack. He glanced behind at his men, walking with heads ducked, some with arms resting over their horses' necks. Three miles to home. On the morrow they would practise again with spear throwing. Mounted, dismounted, from a walk, trot and canter. Already he had his men able to do most things at any pace. The jest around the campfires at night was that by the time Arthur had finished with them, they would be able to piss into a bucket at fifty paces while riding at full gallop.

He would let them mount up soon. The horses had not required the rest, but the men needed the additional exercise. Walking in this regular, steady-paced rhythm with his hand resting lightly on Eira's sodden neck, Arthur's mind began to drift – easy in safe territory where there was no need to watch for an enemy's approach.

Several letters had arrived three days back. Most had been routine correspondence that came with any position of command. Two had not.

From Vortimer word that Vortigern was dead. He had fallen, hit his head on a step and never again opened his eyes. Whether he had in truth fallen or was pushed, Arthur had no particular care; the man was gone, leave it at that. With the news, a plea for the Pendragon to return with all possible speed. Arthur would have ignored it, let the fool drown in the ruin of his own making, except Vortimer had not asked, had not ordered, but had begged. *'I will need every able man, Arthur, and you with your following are more able than most. I beg for your help, on your terms, Pendragon. Your terms.'*

It was tempting. Very tempting.

And then there was the second letter. From Winifred.

Arthur halted Eira, signalled for the men to mount. Settling himself in the saddle, his thighs sliding neatly under the curve of the two pommel horns, he waited for the men to make ready, then moved off at a trot. Dusk would be falling soon and he had had enough of this damned rain. Enough of trailing through these mountains, too. Training was all very well, but occasionally there came a need for more. For the real thing.

He would go back to Vortimer, as the man said, on his own terms, and he would sort out this latest problem with his ex-wife. Gwenhwyfar would not like either of his decisions, but then she would not need to know of the second thing, would she?

Plunging his stallion into the foaming race of a river, Arthur gasped as its coldness hit his feet and legs, even through the warmth of grass-stuffed leather boots. After all, he reasoned, Winifred can do no harm now, and this son of hers means nothing to me, or Gwenhwyfar.

But if that was true, why did he feel this chum of dread in the pit of his stomach?

MAY 456

§ XLI

Winifred's son had been born a lusty, healthy boy. With the coming of spring, he reached six months and he was crawling, gurgling and as chubby as a fatted ox.

Winifred adored him.

Sitting across the room, watching the man she insisted on calling husband drink his wine she realised two important things. She loved Arthur and, though he had never seen their son, he detested their child.

'So,' she said breaking the uneasy silence, 'you have gathered almost a quarter of the men loyal to my half-brother to your side.'

'I am as loyal to Vortimer as ever. It is just that some men prefer to ride behind my Dragon rather than his Boar.'

'While awaiting the chance for the dragon to slay the boar, aye, I suppose you would be.'

Arthur drained his goblet and stood up. 'I agreed to see you, Winifred, against my better judgement. I expected to be insulted but not accused of treason. Say what you wanted me to hear and let me be gone.'

Winifred too stood. She lifted the wine jug from the table beside her and crossed to refill Arthur's goblet. 'Sit, husband, let us not quarrel.' She gestured towards the couch, smiled as she perched next to him, her skirts not quite touching his leg.

'I understand Vortimer intends to stand against Hengest some time soon, make a valiant attempt to send him back across the sea.'

Arthur laughed and moved along the couch away from the over close proximity of his ex-wife. 'Did you arrange to meet with me just to discover the intentions of the King? Sorry, Winifred, find yourself another tattle-tale.'

She kept the smile pinned firm to her lips. He was as irritating as ever! 'I asked to talk with you to discuss our son's needs, husband. I am merely attempting to make polite conversation.'

Laughing all the louder, Arthur reclined back, his legs and arms sprawled haphazard. 'I believe you, Winifred, truly I do.' He shook his head, still laughing, and sipped his drink. This wine was strong. He usually took more water with it, but he'd not lose face before this black-clad scheming bitch. All the same, he had best keep a clear head, which would not be easy the way Winifred kept topping up his goblet.

He touched her robe with one finger. 'Why this drab garb? It looks most tragic, but does little to flatter your colouring.'

Her eyes sparked slightly, flattered, she inclined her head. 'I wear it in mourning for my father, and also because the Holy Christian Sisters tend to wear such clothing. However, I thank you for the compliment.'

He grunted. 'It was not meant as one.'

Winifred was not to be rebuffed. She took his hand in her own, replied, 'All the same, it sounded as one.'

Withdrawing from her touch, Arthur plumped a cushion more comfortable behind his back. 'And since when, Winifred, have you been a Holy Sister?'

Not missing the sarcasm she decided to answer truthfully. 'Since the day you abandoned me to widowhood.' Arthur grunted again, unimpressed. 'I have founded a women's cloister on the edge of my estate, they have granted me the honour of conferring me as Abbess.' Ignoring a third snort of derision she continued, 'In fact I am here at Verulamium to meet with Bishop Patricius to discuss where to found another such house.'

'Patricius? Was he not the fat fool who married us?'

Winifred ignored the insult. 'I thought it most fortuitous you were also here.'

Arthur bit back a retort. Nothing about Winifred was ever by chance. She was a schemer, like her mother – too much like her mother. He had never trusted either of them and was not about to alter strong-founded opinions just because Winifred professed to be enshrined in the Christian faith. She could be wailing to Woden on the morrow if it suited her.

In fact, this afternoon's meeting had taken Winifred a lot of arranging. She had to speak with Arthur direct, but had to wade through a mire of past misunderstandings and prejudices to do so. The use of the Church would prove costly but, as she had succeeded in seeing Arthur, it would be worthwhile.

Now all she had to do was convince him of her loyalty and get him to acknowledge his son as his heir. Not that she needed formal acceptance, but why climb over the rocks if there was firm sand to walk upon?

'You knew I had sent letters from Less Britain, didn't you?' she said.

Letters? Arthur carefully controlled his expression, sipped at his wine. One letter he knew of – but letters, plural? 'Naturally,' he lied.

Winifred smiled to herself. So-o he had not known! 'Then, as you also know, I pleaded with my mother to send help, to bring me home. It took a while, Arthur, for me to realise she had no need of me, not since she had a son to take my place.' She put her hand over his. 'A son, Arthur, who may one day become king, can mean so very much to a woman.'

He did not answer, nor, Winifred noted, did he this time remove his hand.

'That time at Caer Gloui, my mother left me struggling against the water swirling around our legs, left me to drown. She cared only to save her son.' Glancing sideways at Arthur: 'You know she and my young brother are with Hengest?'

Arthur nodded. He knew.

Winifred shifted closer, her thigh pressing against his, fingers closing tighter around his hand. 'When you slay Hengest, I ask you to slit Rowena's treacherous throat also.'

Drily Arthur observed, 'This request would have nothing to do with each of you vying for your own son to become king of the British?'

Winifred laughed, playfully squeezed his thigh. 'Nothing at all.'

Deliberately, Arthur retrieved his hand and moved his leg away from hers. He sat forward, twisting his head to look at her. 'I already have a son to follow me. He is named Llacheu ap Arthur and his blood is pure British with no taint of Saex poison.' He rose and tipped the wine on the floor, then opening his fingers he let the goblet fall, trod on the shattered glass.

Placing his hands on the couch on either side of her, he leant close, his lips almost brushing hers. 'You have your entire dowry returned, the estate near Portus Adumi and your freedom to do what you will, within reason. Go raise your son to be a farmer or a priest and keep him well out of my way, Winifred.' He kissed her, a parting touch of mockery that sealed his threatened meaning. 'If you do not, he will be nought but dust mouldering in a grave.'

She did not move away from him, sat completely still, but her voice trembled as she questioned, 'You would not slaughter your own son?'

Arthur walked from her and crossed to the door, lifting his cloak from a stool as he passed. 'I would not advise you to put me to the test.'

For a long while Winifred sat staring at the door he had closed behind him. She had turned from her mother's people to ensure her son became Arthur's heir. That the father would not accept the boy came as no surprise, but she had wanted to try, wanted at least to try. She stood, ignoring the shards of crushed glass crunching beneath her boot among the puddled wine. Cerdic would one day be king, Llacheu or no Llacheu.

Winifred smiled to herself as she left the room by a second door. Preferably no Llacheu.

JULY 456

§ XLII

July. The sun hung against a cloudless blue sky, rivers which ran as torrents in winter had dwindled to the trickle of streams, and even the mountains of Eryri seemed to sag beneath the heat. The coast had become too dry, the hot wind blowing sand into eyes, nose and throat; beaches stank of rotting seaweed and dead fish and birds. Enniaun moved his household to an inland stronghold where the mountains and valleys funnelled a cooling breeze.

Gwenhwyfar was helping to work the horses. She enjoyed the young stock, admired their natural reluctance for discipline, tempered by an eagerness to please. She was lunging a colt, setting him circling her on a long halter rope. His dark mane fell in a cascade from a proud neck and he carried his tail high as was the way with his ancestors, the desert-bred horses. His coat, the smudged charcoal colour of a youngster, would not turn white until maturity. Gwenhwyfar had especial pride in this one, a son of Cunedda's best stallion and her own mare Tan. A big colt, fast and powerful but with the manners and affability of a riding gelding. She called him Hasta, the Latin for Spear.

At the start he had fussed and cavorted, refusing to drop his head, bend his spine and flex his hocks beneath him, but he had soon given in to Gwenhwyfar's insistence on a relaxed swinging stride. His ears flicked at the sound of her encouraging voice as he went through the paces of walk, trot and canter, his head tossing and tail swishing against the irritation of flies.

As he worked she was pleased to observe that already his body was supple and compliant, his muscles strengthening. Soon it would be time to turn him out in the horse runs, to rest and grow into that last strength of maturity. By next spring he would be ready to wear bit and saddle, take a light rider. As he paced round her, she thought on next summer's work. To sit astride him, ease him into leg and hand commands, taking him through each stage of learning gradually and with sympathetic patience. By the time he was a four-year-old he would be ready to start the serious work of becoming a warhorse. It took many years to raise and train mounts for use in battle. There were no short cuts, no making do. When a man's life might depend on his horse's instant response, there could not be.

Other young horses were being put through their lessons at practical distances around the training ground. To one side of Hasta, a three-year-old chestnut was misbehaving, rearing against the restraint of a bit, refusing to go forward.

Gwenhwyfar clucked to her colt, urging him on, talked to him, steadying his extending, excited pace. The chestnut suddenly plunged backwards into Hasta, sending the younger and smaller grey, crashing down. Hooves thrashed for a moment, kicking up dust, then Hasta was on his feet again, his off-hind leg trailing as blood dripped, spotting the dry ground.

Gwenhwyfar swore, hastily wound in the long rein and soothed the frightened young horse as best she could. Men came running, slowing their pace as they neared. Enniaun pushed his way through the gathering crowd. 'I saw what happened,' he said frowning. 'This is the third time this week that chestnut has caused trouble. How is your youngster?' This last to Gwenhwyfar, who was bending over the wounded hind leg.

'Superficial, the blood makes it look worse. He'll be lame some while though.' She cursed inwardly, said aloud, 'He was making fine progress too.'

Peering at the cut hock Enniaun agreed with her diagnosis. Straightening up, he studied the chestnut. 'We will geld that one – he'll make a fine riding horse but he has not the sense for a war mount.' He signalled someone to remove the offender and as the crowd drifted away, walked with Gwenhwyfar, leading Hasta, across the training ring to the stables.

'You have worked hard with this colt.'

Gwenhwyfar patted the horse's neck. 'He is for Arthur. Eira serves well but is ageing. Besides, when Arthur brings his cavalry together he will need more than one reliable mount.'

'Will he be ready?'

For a moment Gwenhwyfar was uncertain whether her brother referred to the horse or Arthur. Either way the answer came the same. 'He will be ready when the time comes.'

They reached the stable yard, dry in this weather, normally squelching in ankle-deep mud. Gwenhwyfar tied the halter rope to an iron ring in the wall and fetched water, calling for a slave to bring linen, taking her time to thoroughly wash and clean the wound. Enniaun stood at the horse's head, playing with ears and forelock, watching his sister's experienced hands.

Arthur would be calling for the rest of his men soon, and those horses that were ready. Rubbing the grey's forehead, Enniaun was suddenly reminded of his father. Cunedda had promised the Pendragon all the horses he needed, but Enniaun was not the horseman his father had been. And there were the coasts that needed cleansing of Hibernian scum and Council to attend and – oh the list was endless!

'I cannot supply all Arthur's needs, Gwen.'

She finished, patted the animal's rump and straightened, pushing sweat damp hair from her forehead with her arm. A smear of blood smudged her cheek. 'He knows that, does not expect you to.' She led the horse to the nearest stable, fetched hay, watched him settle to eat, resting the weight from the injured leg. 'It is not so essential now he has control of the entire West Country and the pick of the horses. All we need is the time to train them, and the men to ride them.'

'Men will come. As for time, there is never enough of that.' Enniaun was squinting through the glare of sunlight towards the gate arch. Riders were coming in. He did not recognise the horses, nor, as they came nearer, the riders themselves. He began to brush the dust off his tunic and step forward. Gwenhwyfar glanced up as he ceased talking, watched the riders with a frown of curiosity. If she hadn't known better she would swear that was... Blood of Mithras, it was! Winifred!

Fortunate that Gwenhwyfar had an excuse to escape, dirty as she was from her own and horse sweat and blood. She exchanged polite greetings and departed as soon as she could for the security of privacy. This stronghold was not so grand as Caer Arfon, smaller and more restricted with not a Roman building in sight, but for all that the wattle-built round-house was comfortable and private.

Gwenhwyfar found she was shaking as she entered Enniaun's Hall as evening descended deliciously cool. A thousand thousand questions skittered through her mind as she made her way through the throng of men pushing to seat themselves for the day's meal. Questions that needed answers. Why was Winifred here? And why was she travelling with Bishop Patricius?

Gwenhwyfar had noticed Winifred's black clothing, the white veil. So she had become a Holy Sister. That at least explained why she rode with the bishop. But why here to Gwynedd? To stir trouble, for sure – there could be no other reason.

It came as a surprise, and rather disconcerting, to see Winifred's polite and demure – almost humble – behaviour. She served the bishop herself with food and drink brought in by the slaves, and served Enniaun, although, Gwenhwyfar realised with amusement the humility did not extend to serving others of the family, notably herself.

In accordance with custom Enniaun could not ask their business until his guests were fed and rested. The waiting passed in an agony of impatience; by the time the slaves at last began to clear away the trestle tables and remains of the meal, Gwenhwyfar was almost squirming in her seat.

The bishop drank his wine slowly, asked for a refill, then excused himself for the latrine. At last he settled himself and the Hall grew quiet.

'Lord Enniaun,' he began, 'I come with the Lady Pendragon' – there came several sharp intakes of breath, that was Gwenhwyfar's title – 'to plead for land to be given to God.'

Enniaun's brows had drawn together, but he answered pleasantly, 'Much of my land is already given to God. We have several chapels here in Gwynedd.'

'Chapels, but no holy house. Dyfed has a cloister, as does your brother's land of Ceredigion. My Lady here' – Patricius indicated Winifred – 'has ridden with me these many weeks past to find a suitable place in her father's Powys.'

Winifred had been sitting silent, head bowed, hands in her lap. At this she looked up and added, 'I needed to create something of God for my father's lost soul. A holy building would come near to providing penance for him, but two such places would ensure he rested in peace.'

Several nodded their heads in agreement.

'And you thought to found somewhere in Gwynedd?' Enniaun asked with curt politeness.

Winifred was about to reply, but the bishop silenced her.

'It was my suggestion, Lord Enniaun, for Gwynedd is the only British-held land that has not fully embraced God. An oversight which saddens my heart. My Lady Pendragon has offered to set the matter straight.'

Gwenhwyfar was saying nothing, staring with growing rage at this pompous fat man and the arrogant scheming woman seated beside him. Enniaun could not agree to this – this absurdity! But to her horror he was nodding his head, offering his hand. No! This must not be! She leapt to her feet, slamming the table with the palm of her hand, the noise bursting like a thunderclap around the confined space of the Hall.

'I will not allow this! A Saex whore's bitch founding a holy house in our Gwynedd – and in Vortigern's name? It was her father who slew Uthr, my husband's father...'

Winifred stared coldly at Gwenhwyfar and interrupted with a shrill cry. 'Under God's law a man can have but one wife. I am the Pendragon's wife, the mother of his son.'

Gwenhwyfar turned pale. She stood a moment, rocking, then sat heavily, the room spinning. Son? She said son. Winifred had a son by Arthur?

'Yes, I have a son, Gwenhwyfar.' Winifred's voice shot like a spear into Gwenhwyfar's numbed mind. 'Born later by a few weeks to yours, but mine was conceived in wedlock to my husband. My husband, Gwenhwyfar, the one I have never accepted the order of divorce from. The one recognised by Holy Church.' She bent low, said into Gwenhwyfar's ear, 'I have made appeal to his grace the Pope, Gwenhwyfar. I am a respected woman of the Church, you a pagan slut. It is my son he will declare legitimate, not yours! My son who will become the next Pendragon, the next king.'

She would have said more, kicked harder while Gwenhwyfar was down, but Meriaun burst forward, stood with hands planted on the table, a snarl of contempt etched on his face. 'I challenge you on this decision, Enniaun. I will have no house, however holy, built by the kin of the man who ordered the brutal murder of my father.'

At his words the Hall erupted in an uproar of assent. Men and women came to their feet and moved towards the high table, growling and muttering. Enniaun was standing, appealing for calm; some heard and faltered, most ignored him, surging round Winifred, Vortigern's daughter.

It was only the bishop, lumbering to his feet and thrusting her behind him, who saved Winifred from the mob. Enniaun leapt forward, physically pushing the angry crowd back. 'I call for peace!' he was yelling. 'Peace! Calm yourselves.'

His urgent words got through. The anger subsided, bubbling beneath the surface – better than the raging torrent of a moment before.

Enniaun patted the air with his spread hands, calming them further. 'Be seated, all of you. Let us talk of this thing in a civilised manner.'

Gwenhwyfar was shaking. Civilised? Winifred, the bitch who had murdered Ceridwen... but then the fight went out of her. There was no proof, only a suspicion. And it was not Winifred who had caused the death of her kin, but her father. Winifred was innocent of the charges. The bishop was talking, she realised, stating the laws of the Holy Church and the Pope in Rome. If Cunedda had been here he would have kicked the man's fat backside from here to Dyfed, but her Da was not here; Enniaun was Prince of Gwynedd, and Enniaun was a devout follower of Christ.

§ XLIII

Six days Gwenhwyfar endured Winifred's presence, six days of her gloating and patronising insults. Six long days of clenched fists and fingers that itched to take up a dagger and cut her accursed throat. And then the messenger from Arthur arrived.

He galloped into the Caer, his mount labouring with lathered neck and frothing mouth. The rider slithered from the saddle, his knees buckling with exhaustion. Someone fetched him water and he drank in great gulps, gasped, 'Urgent word for Lord Enniaun!'

A brief letter, bearing Arthur's seal but written in a strange hand, struck Gwenhwyfar with dread. If it was addressed to her brother, then surely it carried bad news? She watched, fingers clutching her tunic as he broke the Dragon seal, watched with held breath as he read quickly, muttering the written words.

Gwenhwyfar thought, Is Arthur hurt? Dead?

Winifred swished into the Hall, Bishop Patricius puffing like a lapdog at her heels. 'A message from the Pendragon?' she demanded. 'For me? May I have it?'

Enniaun ignored her, read through to the end, though there was little to read. He lifted his head, said to the gathering crowd, 'Hengest has made his move; he has met with Vortimer near the ford of the river Crae, way beyond his designated territory. They outnumbered our British. Three to one.' He gave the communication to Gwenhwyfar, hovering ill at ease at his shoulder, let her read for herself. Absently, she passed it to Winifred, who scanned the writing quickly 'This is not Arthur's hand,' she said.

No one bothered answering her. What mattered if it were Arthur's hand or not? The writing would not alter the facts. Arthur's hurriedly dictated words, written by a clerk in a precise, neat hand, told that he and his men, stationed to the north of Londinium, had ridden swiftly to give Vortimer aid but arrived too late. The stilted words conveyed little of the destruction they had found, the bare facts only, two short paragraphs that could not hope to match the indecent slaughter.

Arthur sent word of the killing and asked for Enniaun to send south those men and horses that were ready. He would await them at Caer Leon.

'I have taken command, Enniaun, and I intend to finish this thing with Hengest. I need to complete my Artoriani.'

The Pendragon had been too sickened to say more. How could words describe the death of good men? When he arrived, too late, at the Crae ford, bodies were strewn across a churned battlefield, the ravens already gathered, gorging on the corpses and flapping around the broken standard of Vortimer's Boar.

Fighting the nausea that heaved within him, Arthur found what remained of the King. Hanging from a cracked and blood-stained banner's shaft, he found Vortimer's head, one eye already gone, the other dangling from pecked sinew. As for the rest of him, there was no way of knowing which stripped and mutilated body had once been a king.

Arthur had sunk to his knees and spewed the revulsion from him. The stench. Men, taken prisoner and grouped together with their hands bound, had been tortured and butchered, their ribs torn open, insides ripped out.

With Vortimer dead, the sons of Vortigern were no more – aside from one Saex-born cur, the boy Vitolinus.

Standing staring bleakly at the grotesque remains of men he had known, Arthur realised that leadership was his for the taking. Why then did he weep? For this waste of men? For the sorrowing wives and fatherless children? It should not have happened. Not like this.

At the edge of the stench and vileness, hearing his men retching and coughing as they gathered the dead, Arthur had dictated his matter-of-fact letter. He spoke the words dull and flat, a toneless, distanced account of fact.

Dismissed, the clerk hurried away to seek a messenger, glad to escape. Arthur stayed watching as his men began to bury the mutilated corpses.

AUGUST 456

§ XLIV

Meriaun, Typiaunan's son, was to take the horses to Arthur. In no uncertain terms he told Enniaun what he thought of his deal to parcel out Gwynedd land to the greed of the Church and the lying daughter of a murdering bastard. Told his dead father's brother he would join with the Pendragon and return no more to Gwynedd. Enniaun let him go, knowing a man's passionate temper often cooled given time.

What Enniaun did not expect, nor Winifred, was that Gwenhwyfar took herself and her son with him. They arranged it secret between them, she and Meriaun. Winifred might have the power of the Church behind her plea for her son, but Gwenhwyfar was now Arthur's wife, and no God-kneeling Saex was going to over-shadow Llacheu! A son may be named heir, may be first-born, second-born, bastard born, if the army did not want him as king when the time came to claim the title then king he would not be. The sure way to get an army to shout loud for their chosen man was for them to know that man. Oh aye, Gwenhwyfar would go to Arthur, and take her son with her! Winifred could claim what she liked, but Llacheu would grow and learn and live with Arthur's men. It was him they would choose when the time came for another Pendragon! Llacheu, not this rat-spawned Cerdic.

They left Caer Arfon, heading south along the coast where safety lay in their own land and Ceredig's adjoining holding. Two women, a young boy, two hundred men and three times as many horses. There came no trouble those first few days, aside from a kicking match between two stallions and another with a bruised sole. The horses settled well after the initial excitement, walking steady, with heads down, ears lopping and tails swishing.

The weather held fine. Warm days with a pleasant breeze. From Ceredig's borders they had turned south-east, making for the welcome of Builth, but those friendly lands were behind them now, with the hostile ranges of plunging valleys and lonely hills rising ahead. The desolate land of the wolf.

At least these open hills gave scant cover for raiders. Trees and thickets hid men only too well – and they knew there were men following them. The Watchers, they called them, for want of a better description. Watchers keeping pace, never showing themselves, two, happen three men.

Little clues and gut feelings told Gwenhwyfar and the men they were keeping pace a steady mile or so behind. That prickling sensation on the back of the neck, the knowing that eyes were on you. The thought that if you turned round quick someone would be there – but when you did, there was nothing save a swaying branch or waving grass and a blurred shadow.

Once at night they heard the whinny of a horse, hastily muffled. Come dawn, Gwenhwyfar sent a scout to ride in a sweeping half-circle behind them. He found the remains of a fire, with flattened grass where men had lain, and horse droppings. A second dawn, a signalling whistle carried clearly.

Shadows unobserved, like midnight wraiths, always following. Their presence unsettling, unnerving. Sometimes dropping further back, never coming nearer, always there. Watching.

When the heavy woodland at last fell behind, Gwenhwyfar and the men breathed relief for this open country. Nowhere now for their unwanted companions to hide. Let them show themselves or be gone!

Around the night-time fires talk of who they might be had taken many meandering turns. The favoured theory was that they were men of Builth, ensuring the travellers came and went in peace. The new-claimed petty kingdom was friendly with Gwynedd, but friendship was too uncertain to trust wholehearted. Horses such as these would be a fine prize indeed for an ambitious young man who had elevated himself to the tribal title of king. But they had passed into the open hills, out beyond Builth's borders, and no attack had come. The tingling along the spine and hair rising along the collar faded under the expanse of blue sky rolling along the hilltops. Men relaxed. The Watchers, whoever they were, seemed to have gone.

Such was life – one problem exchanged for another. Before them lay uncertain territory, the first swelling hills of Brychan's borders over to their right. He was a man who blew with the wind. He could be friendly, but was just as capable of falling into an unexpected rage. Add to that, he had no liking for Arthur; he might take pleasure in stealing his horses.

Not far ahead lay the Usk valley, and from there it was downhill to Caer Leon and Arthur. Easy riding, except for these outlying hills of Brychan's.

Gwenhwyfar, riding loose-limbed relaxed on her mare, ran her hand through the hair falling down her back. She had not bound it, not caring to take time over neatness. It was clean, washed early that morning in the cool waters of a stream – who cared for women's braiding? Not she!

She burst suddenly into song, a jaunty tune with a marching rhythm. Her nephew Meriaun, riding close behind, joined in, his rich baritone blending well with her light soprano. Men began to add their voices – and their own, soldiers' words.

The weather was still holding, and they had not far to go. By tomorrow nightfall Gwenhwyfar would be with Arthur. The day was good. The sun shone, and all was well.

Three worries had been constant. The first was wolves, for though it was mid-summer these hills and valleys were their hunting grounds. Their mournful cries could be heard at night, echoing among the hills. Men turned uneasily in their blankets, one ear cocked for a wolf-bark that sounded over-near. Their rank scent sometimes blew downwind, stirring horses into restless unease. Wolves were always a beast to be minded.

Raiders, too, prowled as skulking packs. Sea-wolves – human kin to the grey-coated kind – were no danger this far inland, but Brychan had come as a raider and settled, claiming land for his own, swallowing more and more, like a voracious cuckoo in a sparrow's nest. And there could be others – these Watchers? Many a man resented Gwynedd's influence and power. Others disliked the Pendragon, remembering Uthr his father. Any petty chief could be tempted, when the gift dangled promisingly enough. The third worry, the threat of bad weather.

The last two, of course, came together.

By late afternoon, clouds lumbered in from the west, a great bulk of grey hanging above the hills like a gathering army. Distant grumbles of thunder warned of a storm, and the air fell sickly hot and sullen, lying heavy on sweating man and beast. Horses flicked their ears uneasily, sensing the change, bunching together, a few kicking or snapping.

Scouts returned with word of a sheltered valley ahead; it was agreed to make early camp, sit the storm out. It was a risk to stay so close to Brychan's land, but risks had to be weighed.

They reached the valley as the first stinging raindrops beat against flesh and hide. The horses eased to a halt, tucked their tails and turned sodden rumps into the wind. One or two younger beasts jumped nervously as the thunder rolled across a black sky but, eager for grazing, they settled soon enough.

Tents were hastily erected. Small hope of a fire this night!

Gwenhwyfar saw Llacheu and his nurse, Enid, into the dryness of their quarters, paused before ducking out beneath the flap. She said, with a proud smile, 'My son has travelled well.'

'Aye, he likes horseback!' Enid replied.

Gwenhwyfar laughed. 'The next night he cuts a tooth and keeps us awake, happen we should cuddle him close on the back of a horse to ease him to sleep!'

Smiling, Gwenhwyfar pulled her cloak tight around her and ducked out into the squalling rain. Head lowered, she ran towards the commanding officer's tent. They would all be eager to complete the evening's discussion of progress and the morrow's plans.

The second watch of the night. Gwenhwyfar rode among the grazing horses, sitting easy in the saddle but alert. She did not need to ride watch, but she enjoyed it, insisted she took her turn. Even in such foul weather.

Head bent against the rain, Gwenhwyfar saw a rider slither from his horse. She cursed aloud and turned the chestnut she rode – Caradog had been drunk over-often this trip! More than his share of the strong barley beer the pack ponies carried had passed down his throat. The decurion had lashed him twice already with thong and tongue. There would not be a third time.

With a caustic remark ready, Gwenhwyfar cantered over to his prone body, expecting him to rise unsteadily, grinning foolishly at her approach, some quick excuse on his tongue.

An arrow lay buried in his chest, the shaft still quivering.

Swinging her horse aside, Gwenhwyfar shouted a warning, her voice snatched by the wind. Another arrow! She heard its hiss, felt the jolt as it thudded into the soft muscles of her left bicep.

She thought fast. Ramming her heels into the horse's ribs, she galloped forward, barging into a group of grazing animals. They tossed their heads, snorting, as she pulled the chestnut round on his hocks and brought him to a slithering halt. Here, amid the cover of other horses, she drew her sword. Raising the blade high, she swung it above her head, screaming the war cry of Gwynedd.

Other men of the watch had already seen and heard the danger; three of their number lay dead. The alarm sounded in camp. Men began to tumble from their tents, cursing, sleep instantly gone, weapons drawn, eager for action.

Those mounted swung into a gallop, streaking to meet the enemy, spears poised, ready to throw at a sighted target.

Gwenhwyfar, galloping hard, shouted for them to pull up, wait for others before attacking. Useless to fight at half-strength in a higgle-piggle of disorder. An officer joined her, an older, experienced soldier. His face contorted with rage, he brought the flat of his sword blade slamming down on the back of any man he could reach, yelling and yelling at them to turn back, wait for the command.

There was no choice – blood was up. Gwenhwyfar rode with them.

Visibility was poor. Rain came in gusting squalls blown by a veering wind. Lightning illuminated the valley, sending dark waiting figures hunched beneath cloaks scurrying into cover. A few let a hail of arrows fly, their hurried aim falling short, blown aside.

Arthur's men, mostly young lads, untried, newly trained, had seen them. Twenty, thirty men? Brychan's? Or had the Watchers at last gathered strength and emerged from hiding? Time enough to discover names and faces later; there was a more urgent need at this moment – staying alive.

The infant Artoriani moved forward, the mounted men well ahead, leaving those on foot to run fast, make their way best they could. Some were still clad only in under-tunics, dragging on leather fighting gear as they ran.

On the hillside, the attackers rose to meet them with an ululation of expected victory. By their dress and weaponry they were Hibernian settlers – Brychan's men. They closed, riders flinging themselves from horseback to fight sword to sword, shield to shield, unable to fight mounted on rain-sodden sloping ground in the dark.

Gwenhwyfar was among the men, furious at their lack of discipline, their 'strike first think later' impulsiveness. Little she could do about it now, but later... She came up with the decurion. His eyes bulged, and he was snarling like a wounded dog-wolf He shouted something to her, and though she did not catch the words she guessed their meaning. What had become of the rigorous training; the day-by-day monotony of drill, drill and more drill? She exchanged blows with one of Brychan's men, striking two-handed with her sword, ripping its blade through his thigh, dodging herself to avoid a similar thrust. Cursed at the stupidity of these raw young men.

A weird dance was stepped in the darkness, men fighting hand to hand, killing or falling wounded beneath lashing rain and rolling thunder. Another man came before Gwenhwyfar, his face leering, lit up ghostly pale by a lightning flash. His foot slipped, the sole of his boot slithering over wet grass. She took advantage, driving her blade up, through his belly. She had to push his body from her sword with her foot, swearing as fluently as any soldier when the blade sucked out, spewing steaming intestines over her feet.

Turning aside, her breath coming in gasps, Gwenhwyfar glanced quickly with another flash of lightning at the horses grazing in the valley below. Only a few, younger colts mostly, were fidgeting, ears flicking, legs stamping. They had been trained with infinite care for Arthur. She snorted – so had the men, but they had so easily forgotten! Just as well the horses had not! The roar and clash of fighting and the scent of blood ought to now come as natural to them as a cock's crow and the smell of dung. Patience had paid off; those hours of mock battles, the quiet calming of nervous horses as cattle were slaughtered before them, the nauseating stench of offal strewn around the paddocks! Gwenhwyfar had time for a quick smile. Her Da had known a thing or two about the training of horses!

The tents away to the left caught her eye. Figures were running, illuminated momentarily, sharp and white against the blackness. Damned fools! Stupid, stupid idiots! They had all turned out, running fit to burst into the attack; not one man left to guard the camp!

A thought hit her like an axe through her skull. She screamed as she ran, slithering on the wet grass of the slope. 'Llacheu!'

The horses had remained where they had been left – another insistence of Cunedda's training. A man must be able to count on his horse to stand when he dismounted, intentionally or otherwise, for an unseated cavalryman could lose his life while blundering around the battlefield in search of his mount.

Slipping for some way on her backside, Gwenhwyfar scrambled to her feet, ran to the nearest horse, seized the reins and vaulted into the saddle. Barely settled, she hauled his head round and raced to her son.

Thunder cracked overhead, smothering Enid's terrified screams as a man dragged her by the hair away from the tent. He was admiring his prize, did not see the single blow that severed his head in a neat stroke, sending it rolling grotesquely down the incline, thick lips still grinning.

Gwenhwyfar pounded on past, her sword red with the man's blood. Enid, released, flung her skirt over her head and crouched shrieking. Gwenhwyfar swung her horse round and came back, heeling him forward, hooves flinging up great clumps of sodden, muddied turf, to meet a second man.

Realising his danger the man dropped his bundle of loot and grabbed at Enid, holding her before him as a shield. He stood ready, half crouched, sword raised, lips parted, watching as Gwenhwyfar galloped closer, his mind registering with amusement it was a woman riding at him.

In Hibernia, the home he had left many years since to settle this new territory with Brychan, some women were known to fight as fearsomely as men. He was surprised at this woman, though. The British men were soft-bellied; the women, Roman spawn, pampered creatures fit only for bedding.

Not this one, it seemed!

Gwenhwyfar's sword whistled down. He thrust it aside with his own; let Enid go with a kick to her buttocks that sent her sprawling on her face, and followed through by reaching up and grabbing Gwenhwyfar's arm, pulling her from the horse.

She rolled, half winded, her hand clasped white-knuckled around the pommel of her weapon. She had forgotten the arrow embedded in her arm. The shaft broke with the fall, but she did not feel the jolt or the sudden spurt of blood.

He saw it though, a dark stain spreading against her tunic. Saw also she was slight, rather on the thin side, not muscled and hardened like the fighting women of his homeland. He grinned. Soft and flabby with fat, or bone-thin wraiths, these British women were nothing more than a husband's lap-pet!

Gwenhwyfar was doubly enraged from the attack and the disobedience of the men, and now this! The strength of a mother protecting her young possessed her. Who dared confront the lioness with cubs nearby? No one in his right mind – but then this man was unaware of the child in the tent. And Gwenhwyfar was unaware of his unknowing.

He taunted her with his sword tip, making mock thrusts, circling around, playing, noticing other things by now. Interesting things, like her pretty face and the promising figure half hidden beneath her leather jerkin. Shapely hips and thighs, a narrow waist. He decided not to kill her but to take her for his own.

Gwenhwyfar saw the intention clear in his eyes. His beard-shadowed chin, square jaw and leer of anticipation reminded her, with a shudder of fear, of another man. Melwas.

They circled, the woman crouching low, her sword ready, body light and balanced, her eyes locked to his; the man amused, eager, willing to play this little game, sure of his superiority.

He moved quickly, spinning as he leapt so that he lunged to the right but attacking to the left towards her wounded arm – and realised his mistake. She had seen it, seen his feint in the flicker of his eyes.

The eyes, her father had taught her. Watch the eyes, they move to where the blade means to pass.

Overconfidence fled from him as his sword, neatly caught by hers, arched through empty air to embed itself in the turf some yards away. He backed off, laughing, masking astonishment, angry at himself for being so easily fooled. A dagger flashed into his hand as he lunged again. Light on her feet, Gwenhwyfar skipped aside, but he had expected her reaction this time. Darting forward, he knocked her off balance with his foot, sending her staggering almost to her knees. She recovered quickly, but not quick enough.

Seizing her right wrist, his grip intentionally painful, he dragged her arm up and back, forcing her to drop her weapon. He shook her arm, the pain ripping along muscles, sending the sword falling into the mud. Triumphant, he held her firm, pulled her body to him.

Gwenhwyfar made herself go limp, struggling against an inner voice of panic telling her to fight and kick, to get away. She breathed slowly, deeply, repeating the rules of defence in her mind: Think. Plan. Fight him and he will fight you. Take him off guard; relax. Play dead.

He laughed again, triumphant, mouth open showing broken teeth. He grasped Gwenhwyfar's copper-gold hair. Forcing her head back, he bent to kiss her.

She gagged at the rank stench of his unwashed body. He said something in his own tongue which Gwenhwyfar did not understand, but could guess at the meaning. As his mouth closed over hers, her fingers encircled the head of the dagger sheathed at her waist.

His chuckle of pleasure was cut short in a vomiting gurgle, blood and froth issuing from his mouth. He staggered, clutching at the weapon driven deep into his lungs, staring bulge-eyed. Gwenhwyfar stood panting, her teeth bared and her eyes narrow slits. The she-wolf and her kill.

A third man had watched from the shelter of the tent opening, his laughter as his companion had bent to kiss the woman fading into open-mouthed astonishment as the man had sunk to his knees and slowly toppled to lie flat-faced and still in the mud.

Furious, he ran at Gwenhwyfar, shouting, an axe raised above his head. Gwenhwyfar whirled to him, aware too late she had no weapons. She lunged for her sword, lying where it had fallen, knew she would not reach it.

Something stopped him. He stumbled a few paces, fell forward, his body inert, blood gushing from his split skull. Enid stood behind him, too afraid to scream. A mallet used to drive the wooden tent-pegs home dangled from her hand, a dark patch, with pieces of clinging white bone and matted hair, staining its solid square head.

Gwenhwyfar snarled, a wild, primitive noise. She had her sword now, used it to hack and chop at the man she had fought, slashing at his face, hands and vitals. Blood was on her clothes and skin, had gutted into the mud, forming a black, stinking pool.

Hands clawed at her, pulling her away. She thrust them aside, striking out with her sword when they refused to leave her be, its blade whistling through the air. Someone swore and let go, then came again, trying to hold her, shouting her name.

'Gwenhwyfar! Gwenhwyfar, leave it! Leave it, he is dead! It's over!'

A voice, a man she knew. His words sank in as she heard what he was saying. Feebly, trembling, she again pushed his hands aside, but her strength had evaporated, leaving behind a sagging weariness.

'Llacheu?' she asked, the need to cry suddenly overwhelming.

They knelt on the ground, the man holding her, his arms strong, so comforting and gentle. She shut her eyes, rested her forehead on his chest.

He looked enquiringly at Enid, who was hovering, uncertain, fingers twisting the folds of her skirt.

'He is safe,' she gasped, still breathless and shaking. 'I bundled him, still sleeping, beneath clothing. They were not here long enough to find him.'

'Hear that? He is unharmed.'

Gwenhwyfar nodded, gulped hot tears.

'Blood of the Bull, Gwenhwyfar!' Arthur roared suddenly, his hands on her shoulders shaking her, his brows creasing into deep furrows of fury. 'If you ever, ever put yourself or my son in such danger again, by Mithras I'll... I'll...' He hauled her forward and held her to him, cradling her head; finished lamely, 'I know not what I would do.'

She was sobbing. 'Meriaun said you would be cross with me for coming without your sending.' She spoke through chattering teeth, her voice muffled against his chest.

'Cross!' Arthur held her away from him, his hands again on her shoulders. She hung her head, afraid to meet his blazing eyes. 'Cross? I am bloody livid!' He shook her with each word, then he was clasping her to him again, rocking her back and forth, smothering her face with kisses, stroking her rain-drenched hair.

'The Bull, Cymraes, but I am also proud of you!' He was laughing, and crying too. Trembling from fear, relief and pleasure. 'Damned proud of you, you foolish, irresponsible, beautiful, beautiful woman!'

§ XLV

She had not wanted to sleep. Her wound, tended and dressed and a bitter-tasting liquid persuaded down her throat, coupled with being tucked warm beneath dry blankets, let drowsiness creep in unbidden She could hear shouted orders, the bustle of more tents being erected and the neighing of horses. She snuggled deeper, content. Slept.

It was quite dark when she drifted awake; the lamps were out. The sound of spattering rain had ceased and all was quiet. What had woken her? An arm slid around her waist, cold feet touched her warm legs. She shivered. 'I did not intend to wake you,' Arthur said.

Gwenhwyfar nestled into his arms, burrowing her head into his shoulder. 'I am glad you did. I tried to stay awake for you. I think,' she smiled up at him, though neither could see in the blackness, 'I think something was put in my drink.'

He cuddled her closer. 'It was.'

'I was tricked!' she protested, tickling his ribs with her fingers, causing him to squirm. As he tickled her back his hand touched the swell of a breast beneath her night shift and he ceased the teasing. His lips brushed hers, half expecting her to stiffen and pull away, the rise of pleasure all the more acute when she did not. He lay back, still holding her, settling his head on the rolled-blanket pillow.

Into the blackness she said, 'Your coming upon us was no accident, was it, Arthur?'

'You have been watched since leaving Ceredig's land.'

Gwenhwyfar caught her breath. 'The Watchers! You?'

469

'Watchers?' Arthur snorted with amusement. 'I sent men to keep a close eye on you.' He chuckled at her start of indignation, laid a finger on her lips to silence her. 'I know what you are about to squawk. They had my orders to stay out of sight.'

She pouted. 'Why? You made us uneasy for no reason.'

'Why?' He jerked half upright. 'Enniaun sent a galloper to tell me you were coming with the horses – Mithras, I was furious! Though whether I was angrier with you, or with him for allowing it, I know not. My wife,' he paused to lean over and kiss her, 'my wife and son are more precious to me than damned horses!'

'I came because of our son!' She too sat up, lying back grudgingly as Arthur pulled her down with him below the warmth of the blankets.

'I know it, Meriaun has told me.'

Gwenhwyfar snuggled closer to Arthur, twining her arms around him, tucking her feet under his legs. Drowsy, she must have dozed a minute, for he was near asleep when she realised he had not answered her question. She kicked him. He only grunted so she kicked him again, harder.

'Arthur! Why did you set men to spy on us?'

Through a yawn he answered, 'Because it occurred to me, once I had calmed down enough to look at the thing rationally, these newly trained men might not need a wet-nurse.' He moved his hand more comfortably around her waist, 'but I was not prepared to entrust raw soldiers with the safety of my wife and son.' He did not add the shambles of this night had proved him right. 'We were riding to meet you when – what did you call my men? Watchers? Warned us a raiding party from Brychan's rat nest was abroad. We came up as fast as we could.' His voice turned cold. 'Just as well we did.' He said no more. The entire valley had cringed at his explosion of rage, once he had been assured his wife slept. One out of every ten men, selected by drawing a short blade of grass, lay buried in shallow graves this night, bludgeoned to death by their disgraced comrades. A serious thing to disobey orders, to take matters into their own hands or desert their post – to leave a camp undefended.

Arthur demanded strict discipline; each man was to work with the other as a team, one welded body. Punishment needed to be severe, for men's lives could be put at risk by those who recklessly disobeyed orders; haphazard enthusiasm left themselves and their comrades open to death. The lesson of Arthur's wrath had sunk in. It was the first and last time men of the Artoriani so disgraced themselves.

To cover his sudden silence, Arthur said to Gwenhwyfar, 'Brychan will think twice about harassing what is mine in future. He will not be pleased at the gift I have sent him.'

Gwenhwyfar made no comment. She guessed his meaning, cared little for details.

He was right. Brychan bellowed and cursed for days after his men found a heap of dismembered bodies flung some yards inside his border.

'How is the arm?' Arthur asked, changing the uneasy subject. 'It aches.' Shyly she added, 'But not as much as I ache for you. We have been apart too long a while.'

Thinking of several pert answers, Arthur cast them aside. Instead he brought her closer to kiss her, savouring the delight of her taste, smell and feel. He stroked the inside of her bare arm, mindful of her wound; moving on to her neck and face, enjoying her softness. He broke away as Gwenhwyfar buried her head in his shoulder and, clasping him tight, said urgently, 'I was so afraid when I learnt of Winifred's son. I still am.'

Holding her with one hand, Arthur stroked her hair with the other.

She lifted her head and said determined, 'I will fight for my son, Arthur. I realise to you they are both sons, but Llacheu is mine and he is a Briton, not some half-Saex —'

He placed his lips over hers, silencing her. 'Winifred was born a bitch and shall die a bitch, Cymraes. I also intend to fight for our son, for I have no illusions about the power a Saex cur may try to wield. Especially not one raised by her hand.'

He spoke so vehemently Gwenhwyfar moved a little away from him. This was a side of him that frightened her. Arthur angered was a man to be avoided. She knew the punishment the men had faced, knew Arthur would have watched its execution dispassionately. She thrust such thoughts aside. Arthur was a soldier; there was no room for soft words and a gentle touch on the battlefield, or from a king who intended to demand discipline and respect.

Taking her hand and kissing the tip of each finger one by one, he whispered, 'For this night, can we forget the harsh realities? I know a place where there is only pleasure and love. I'll take you there, if you want me to. '

'Is that a promise?'

'Aye.'

A rare thing for Arthur, he kept his promise.

APRIL 457

§ XLVI

A mood of guarded anticipation breathed through camp, blending with an unspoken expectancy. Some who were there, sitting around campfires or curling under blankets to snatch a few hours' precious sleep, remembered the carnage they had encountered when Vortimer had been so horribly slain. They nursed mixed feelings of revenge and fear. All of them felt the prickling of fear for the coming of dawn, and battle.

Few of those huddled men denied that by the morrow's setting sun they too could be the victims of Hengest's thirst for British blood.

Only one man instilled courage.

Arthur, son of Uthr Pendragon, toured the camp as dusk fell, pausing to talk or laugh with men who idled away the last remnants of the day. Exchanging a jest with one man, admiring another's new spear, asking after the healed lameness of another's horse. Small things, intimacies, making each man feel as though he were a personal friend. Arthur had made it his business to know the names and characters of all his mounted Artoriani, to know some small thing of each and every one of his nine hundred cavalrymen.

The march from the fortifications at Durobrivae had been an anxious one; the awareness of hidden shadows and the constant edge of alertness had been wearing. They were in hostile territory, pushing resolutely deeper into Hengest's claimed kingdom, advancing along the sweeping heights of the northern downs which commanded a view over thick forest, grassy plain and river meadows that mingled with the salt-crusted coast.

Scouts had routed several set ambushes, vain attempts at harrying Arthur's mounted army. Even so, some ten and three of their cavalry had been seriously wounded from Saex spears.

Three more were dead. Arthur considered the toll a light one, less than he expected. His men knew full well these attacks were designed to slow them down, to annoy and irritate, like flies constantly buzzing. Tactics aimed at goading them further on, to walk into the spider's sticky web. Arthur had complied, had pushed forward with his cavalry, ever watchful, aware the way back could be closing despite the vigilance of a rear guard of infantry.

Before returning to his own tent, Arthur walked to the edge of the rise to stand quiet, surveying the darkening land below. Cei and Gwenhwyfar's nephew Meriaun came up behind and stood flanking him. Three men watching and thinking their own thoughts.

The first few stars were showing, glimmering like diamonds between drifting clouds. A heady smell of damp earth hung in the air. Rain was coming. A man who ate, slept, lived, fought and died under the open sky, interpreted the signs, could read the approaching weather with as much ease as the literate read words written on a parchment.

Cei broke the silence. 'We have ridden many miles for this.'

For answer, Arthur swept his hand across the horizon, to the clearings and farms scattered below. His finger came to a halt, indicated the walled town nestling in the hollow a mile away.

'There are a few people, Romano-British people, left in that town, which was once a thriving centre of trade and wealth. Look at it now. In this light you cannot see clearly, but I know 'tis nothing but shacks and crumbling buildings occupied by a handful of die-hard, stubborn folk who refuse to be intimidated.' He let his arm fall to his side. 'This Cantii territory has always been the first prize. *They came to plunder and make war... and later to settle down to till the soil.*' Caesar, before the birth of the Christ, wrote that. Only he was not describing the Saex kind, he wrote of the people we now defend, people who, even before Rome invaded, came themselves from across the sea and settled here. They called themselves Belgae, a tribe soon to be lost amid the enveloping nationality of Romano-British.' He glanced at his companions, took a slow breath. 'Names and tribes, even loyalties change, but still the land of Cantii is the prize.'

'A prize to be won or lost.'

'Or given.'

Cei frowned at Arthur's soft-spoken reply. 'Given?'

'A prize won must be held. A prize lost must be fought for another time, to save pride. A prize given, exchanged, can be the settling of an amicable arrangement. Vortigern had the right of it there, though he gave for the wrong reasons, to barter time, to save face, and demanded nought in return.'

Meriaun too had been studying the evening sweep of land dotted with homesteads. Good grazing land for cattle, rich soil for crops and fruit orchards. He said, with a curl to his lip, as if he were talking of some unpleasant waste product, 'Many down there are of Saex descent.'

Arthur answered swiftly with heat. 'Their blood may be Saex but their hearts are Roman. As I said, names and tribes change. Those settlers are the children's children of men who fought to defend Rome's empire; men who garrisoned the Shore Forts, who kept pirates from breaching the curtain wall. They have earned their right to our land, earned a right to pledge loyalty to Britain, to be one with us.'

Cei snorted. 'And for how long shall that pledge survive? Already they are welcoming Hengest, allowing him his absurd whim of leadership, paying tribute to him!'

'Do you blame them? They are farmers, the families of veterans, old servicemen no longer active. The grandfathers down there fought for Rome. Not the fathers, not the sons. All they want is to plough and sow and harvest in peace. As long as they have peace they care little who oversees them. It happened before, when the Belgae came from across the sea a handful of years before Caesar. They settled, eventually dominated. Life went on. The Cantii mixed with the Belgae, became one. Then Rome came, settled, dominated. Life went on, the people became one. Romano-British. Romano-Saex.'

'What you are trying to say, my foster brother,' Cei cut in with a hint of irritation, 'is that eventually these Saex swine will dominate?'

Arthur, standing with his weight on his sound leg, considered a reply. His left hand rested against the reassuring feel of his sword. The evening had darkened. The distant outer edges of the great Forest-Where-No-One-Lives was darker still, black against blackening sky. A dog-fox barked, answered by the yip of his vixen. An owl drifted from a tree to their right, flapped its wings once and gave a piercing cry. Arthur's thigh, injured it seemed, aeons past, ached. It always ached when rain was coming.

Into the gathering cloak of darkness he said, 'For the Cantii the Saex will dominate. Who can hold back the tide or command a thunder cloud to roll aside?' He lifted his shoulders, shrugged. "Tis no use scowling, the both of you. 'Tis so. Hengest knows it, I know it.' He jerked his head back at the camp. 'Most of those men know it. I should imagine the settlers on their farms down there know it also, and accept the inevitable.'

'Then why, in God's name,' snapped Cei, exasperated, 'are we here?'

Arthur grinned, his face lighting with a glint of enthusiasm. 'Because, for the prize to be given, it first has to be won!'

Cei flung up his arms. 'Holy Jesu, Arthur, you could ride rings round the Great Henge and not get dizzy!'

474

§ XLVII

Gwenhwyfar propped herself up on one elbow. The pallet was not uncomfortable, but the night air was cold and the flickering lamps denied her sleep. She watched her husband, sitting at the table studying written reports and rough-drawn maps. His face was crinkled with tiredness, eyes hollowed but burning with a brightness of determination that belied the restlessness of his fingers, twitching at the corner of the map he held.

'Come to bed.'

Arthur answered without looking up. '*Na*, sleep would not come.'

'Without trying, how do you know?' she replied simply. She gathered a rough-woven blanket around her and padded barefoot across to stand behind him, regarding the map. She pointed to the marks he had made. 'This is where you intend to make for, before dawn light?'

He nodded. 'I know Hengest waits at Rutupiae. Here.' He pointed to the Shore Fort on the mainland across the narrow channel beside the isle of Tanatus. 'Rutupiae was built by the first Romans to set foot on these shores, Cymraes. Their bridgehead. When the Emperor Claudius came in the wake of the victorious soldiers, he landed there and proclaimed Britain as his.'

Looking thoughtful at the ink marks on the spread parchment, Gwenhwyfar began absently kneading the taut muscles of her husband's shoulders. He arched himself into the feel of her fingers and closed his eyes a moment.

'I have no doubt Hengest is familiar with that knowledge also. The great white monument to Claudius no longer stands, but it is the legend, the spirit of Rutupiae, that counts. It is Britain's gateway. By drawing his army up within sight of those walls Hengest is proclaiming what is his, just as Claudius did.' His eyes snapped open, his hand caught hers and pulled her round to sit across his lap. 'Except when Rome came, they were the mightier power – and we still carry that legacy of Rome. Hengest does not. I wish you had remained at Durobrivae with Llacheu.'

Looping her arms around his neck, Gwenhwyfar kissed the tip of his nose. 'Liar. You wish I had remained with him at Caer Leon.'

Arthur laughed, kissed her with a warmth that betrayed his need. 'Part of me, the sensible part, should have ordered you to stay in safety. The male part of me demands otherwise.'

She nestled closer to him. His hands slid beneath the heavy blanket, feeling the soft excitement of her skin.

'The male part of you, eh?' she said, hiding her amusement. Her hands ran over his back, sending a shiver down his spine. Then she was touching his thigh, her fingers moving to a more intimate area of his body. She giggled; his response had been immediate. 'Do you refer to this part of you, by chance?'

For reply Arthur scooped her up in his arms and carried her over to their bed. Still silent, he stripped with haste, tossing tunic, boots and bracae aside.

Their lovemaking was fervent, leaving them breathless, skin prickling with sweat and hearts pounding. Arthur sought the blankets and cradled his wife close, her head resting on his shoulder, her copper hair tumbling over his chest. He twisted a strand of it about his fingers, toying with its silkiness.

'How do you keep this mane of yours so soft?' he asked.

'By keeping it clean and rinsing it with herbal infusions – camomile, things like that.'

He brought the strand up to his nose, savoured the fresh, clean smell. 'Is that what gives it such a perfume? One of the things I have always remembered about you, Cymraes, is your hair.' He ran his fingers through its lush thickness, tugging gently at a tangle. 'I can remember the sun shining on it when you were a girl, remember seeing it whirl about you as you rode or ran.' He kissed the end of the strand and then kissed her, a bruising possessive kiss which rekindled his desire.

Gwenhwyfar laughed as he began caressing her body with less urgency this time, content to savour her scent and feel. 'And you did not wish to come to bed?'

Arthur lay quiet afterwards, sleep eluding him as he had known it would. Gwenhwyfar, a look of satisfied contentment on her face, slept peacefully, her hand entwined in his. He lay watching her as her lashes flickered and her mouth twitched into a smile. He wondered of what she was dreaming. For all the delights his body had received, he knew he was taking a dreadful risk. Like his men, he was well aware they could be marching into a trap. One that might not hold a bolthole. And he had allowed Gwenhwyfar to enter it with him.

He placed a butterfly's touch of a kiss on her forehead. Her clasping hand tightened and she turned in her sleep to snuggle nearer, her body moulding compatibly with his own. What could he have done? Chained her to the wall at Durobrivae? Ordered the rearguard posted there to confine her in the cells? No other method would have kept her there! Gwenhwyfar had stated she would ride with him. He had begun to realise her statements were not to be taken lightly, were fact.

Cei had argued heatedly against the wisdom of having her with them, yet even he could not deny her determination, and had been forced to admit grudgingly that, contrary to expectation, the men loved her presence.

Gwenhwyfar had felt rather disgusted when she discovered they thought of her almost as a mascot but had wit enough to use their amusement to her advantage, turning it rapidly into respect. Word had spread of her ability to fight and defend herself. Arthur's mounted Artoriani admired her courage. The casual infantry – farmers, traders, men and boys who had responded to Arthur's call to arms – would tell of Gwenhwyfar, riding beautiful at the Pendragon's side.

Arthur had not been slow either to judge the mood of his men. He noted how in subtle ways they paid homage to Gwenhwyfar, saw too they watched over her. The men were like loyal hounds, fiercely protective, and Arthur knew full well there were few men in camp, dozing the light sleep of the alert soldier, who would not willingly lay down their life for him and his lady.

Watching her in the dim light cast by the remaining lamp he was suddenly anxious. She was safe while his men were able to provide a guard, but what of the morrow? What if the years of his planning and scheming should not come to fruition? Who would defend her against Hengest if he and his men lay dead on the battlefield? Was it fair of him to ask these men not only to die for their leader, but for his reckless wife also?

The questions echoed in the night. He did sleep, a restless, haunted sleep where his horsemen thundered across a dark plain, to drown in a river of blood. And a woman stood alone on a windswept hill, a small child huddled at her side while the war drums and horns of the enemy ringed her round, coming ever closer.

§ XLVIII

Arthur was already up and dressing when Gwenhwyfar stirred and opened her eyes.

'Is it time?' she asked, rubbing bleary sleep from her.

'Aye. 'Tis a few hours before dawn rises. We should have plenty of time. With Fortuna on our side we shall catch the whore-sons shitting with their bracae round their ankles!'

Meriaun called out, peered hesitant through the tent flap. Arthur beckoned him in, Cei following at his heels. The two men briefly nodded to Gwenhwyfar, who gathered a blanket close for modesty. Arthur winked at her, receiving a brilliant smile in return. 'Is all well?' he asked Cei.

'Rhys returned half of an hour since. He said the Saex were sleeping like babes.'

'Then let us hope, like children, they sleep sound.'

Outside the tent there was movement. Men rising, hastening to the makeshift latrine ditch to relieve themselves or eating a frugal breakfast. A distant shuffle from horses being lightly watered and fed There was a distant air of solemnity, not the usual bustle and excitement of troops preparing for what could be their last day in this world. It was the manner of death after failure which instilled an influence of mute unease, not the fear of an approaching battle. That, and the awareness this battle was different. It would mark the beginning, or the end, of Arthur's bid to become Britain's Supreme Leader, their unequivocal king.

Gwenhwyfar dressed quickly once the three men had gone. She began to braid her hair but her fingers shook. Until this moment, she had not regretted the decision to leave Enid behind at Durobrivae with the boy. She told herself not to be foolish, to stay calm and not worry – her husband would survive. Sensible advice, which she did not take. Abandoning the braids, she left her hair loose, ducked from the tent.

The air was fresh, washed clean by the rain that had fallen earlier in the night. It had ceased an hour since, leaving the sky vaulted bright with speckled stars. Her boots scuffed the clinging wetness from the grass as she walked to where the men were assembling, beyond the rows of leather tents.

They parted before her. She heard murmurings as she passed, allowed the glint of a smile to break. She guessed how she must look in this dim, flickering torchlight. She had chosen a simple dress of soft green wool, embroidered at neck and hem and cuff, and a darker cloak. She wore few jewels – Arthur's ruby ring on her marriage finger and a gold torque around her neck. Her hair, cascading in rippling copper waves over her shoulders and down her back, provided all the jewels or finery she needed.

Arthur watched her approach, felt his stomach knot with wanting at the sight of her. A cheer, muted, in awareness of possible danger, swelled as he held out his hand to her and brought her to him in an embrace. No soldier watching would deny he would give anything to be in Arthur's position, to feel that lithe, beautiful body against his own; but then, no soldier would ever allow another to take advantage of their lady.

Grinning, Arthur leapt atop a small hillock which raised him about four feet higher than his men. He helped Gwenhwyfar up to stand beside him, his arm encircling her waist.

'You are putting on weight, my lass,' he said cheerfully as they waited for their audience to settle.

Gwenhwyfar made some flippant answer, turned the subject back to the waiting men. Her heart steadied as Arthur began to talk, in a low but carrying voice.

By the Mother! If he should suspect she was carrying another child he would be furious! It had taken all her cunning, all her wits, to accompany him to Durobrivae, let alone this far! As it was, she knew she would have to face his anger when he learnt she had deliberately flouted danger in such a condition. It would make not the slightest difference she was but a few months gone and that the babe was threatened with no more danger than the rest of them. Men were so stubbornly protective in these matters.

Arthur spoke only briefly. He emphasised the necessity for caution, for as little noise as was physically possible.

'We have men posted; we are as sure as we can be that not one of Hengest's scouts will take word to him.' He gestured, and an older, experienced soldier dressed in simple tunic and bracae, but wearing a magnificent wolfskin cloak, stepped forward. He carried something in his hand. 'Mabon brought a trophy back with him when he came in a short while since.'

The man called Mabon, who had fought with Uthr and now served the son, lifted the thing he held. None had doubted Arthur had spoken the truth, but the sight of an enemy scout's head, still dripping fresh blood, well proved the point.

Eira was brought up, stamping and snorting, a light excited sweat darkening his arched neck. Arthur swung easily into the saddle and nudged the horse forward, thought again. He reined the animal back, leant from the saddle and scooped Gwenhwyfar up to his level. She laughed, grabbing hold of Eira's long mane for support. Arthur kissed her and swung her back down to firm ground.

She cried, 'Take care, my Lord! Bring me back a trophy!'

'I will. Hengest.'

§ XLIX

The faint stir of dawn was flaring over a flat, dark sea as Arthur's men spread out in wide formation behind him. Through the previous months they had trained together; tedious hours of endless drill. Practising, always practising, until Arthur was satisfied they knew the movements like the backs of their own hands; recognised each given command; responded immediate and with deadly accuracy.

Arthur's cavalry was a team, a formidable fighting force, their ranks swelled now to nine hundred elite mounted men. The Artoriani. But he needed more. He needed twice nine hundred to maintain his supreme force, and they would come once he had proved his cavalry could be used to mount the main offensive with local militia infantry as rearguard, archers and reserve. Aye, from the morrow they would come.

He looked behind him. Rank upon rank of tossing manes, silvered helmets and waving, bright-coloured banners. Red turma, green, blue and yellow. It was unheard of in Britain, this formation. Normally, the cavalry was placed in reserve or on a wing, never in the centre.

As the sky lightened from slate grey to dusky pink, Arthur ran the tip of his tongue nervously over dry lips. *Sa*, the last report had been true enough. Hengest was no untried fool. If Arthur had not been expected, the Saxon leader had at least anticipated his arrival. A mile distant, straddled before the massive walls of the disused Roman fortress of Rutupiae like a swarming nest of ants, waited Hengest and his Saex army.

Arthur looked towards Meriaun, who commanded the left wing. Meriaun swung his sword in the air, the blade flashing in the strengthening

481

light. Then he looked to the other wing, the right, usually the most important. Often the commander took this wing Men were trained to fight with weapons in the right hand, leaving the left, the shield side, as the defensive one, a fact exploited in battle by pressure from this right wing. Cei held the command.

There was a loud crash as Cei's men brought spears or swords across their shields in a staccato burst of sound. Echoing their example, this declaration for Arthur, came the clash of arms from Meriaun's wing, and from the centre under Arthur. For this day, for this battle, the centre was all important and the Pendragon would have it for his own.

Arthur's grin was a broad beam of triumphant pleasure. The sun was rising, and it was to be a glorious day!

Slowly, so slowly that at first it seemed they barely moved, Arthur led his men forward.

Hengest had chosen the ground and had the advantage. He had the wind behind him, and his back to the dazzling glare of the rising sun. The Saex were advancing too, a mass of swaying bodies, bobbing heads and fluttering banners. The steady thump, thump of spear or sword beating against shields in a regular rhythm. The singsong voice of the war chant whipped forward by the salt scented wind from the sea. Individual calls lost, the sound as one, a wordless moan from a baying beast.

Behind him, Arthur's own men sat their mounts silently, saving their breath for when it would be needed. Disciplined, steady, covering the ground between the two armies at a held walk. He could hear the ripple of hooves swathing through the fetlock high grass; hear the toss and jangle of horses' bridles, the creak of leather and the metallic clink of weapons. It was an eerie sensation, this voiceless progress. Arthur turned, half expecting to see a ghost army ranged behind him, mist figures silent in the rising dawn. He gasped, realised Hengest had made his first mistake.

The sun had risen higher. Its glow lit the sky with a brilliant glare, a blazing flood of gold pouring down upon the morning, the rays striking like bursting flames upon British spear tips and silvered helmets, gold cloak pins, bronze buckles of baldrics and belts and harness. Every metal object on man and horse reflected the sudden burst of brilliant light, emitting a corona of radiance around the entire mass of Arthur's men. To him, at their head, the spectacle was breathtaking, as if the hand of the soldiers' god Mithras was cupping them. How then must it look to Hengest!

Arthur bellowed at the signallers, 'I want enough noise to awaken the dead!' It was not as he had originally ordered. Remain silent until we are closer, he had said, but he had also warned that orders could change rapidly. This was where the drill came in. Obey my orders. Each man listened to the signal notes of the curled bronze trumpets. The instruments blared the command, and were obeyed.

The blast of responding shouts was tumultuous. Arthur yelled a second order, shrewdly gauging the closing distance between the two armies. The bowmen had been expecting it, and at the first sequence of notes from the horns their bows were lifted, aimed and loosed. A thousand, thousand arrows flew, the scream of their flight shrilling through the air. Arthur's army rode steady on, their yells increasing, their arrows falling like a stormy rain of death.

The Saex army wavered, staggered. From a ranked, silent mass, the army before them suddenly took on an ethereal appearance. One minute shaded, a seething, hustled group of darkness, split only by the dim colours of banners and the occasional glint of weapons. The next, a blazing radiance of light with a bestial howl which spat deadly tipped venom. Man after man at the fore of the vast Saex army fell as arrows from the British bowmen found their mark. Hengest saw the doubt, the uncertainty and fear, cursed and swore at his men, bullying, threatening, trying desperately to reinstall lost courage.

Arthur seized his chance. His hand flew up. Bowmen, their arrows spent, dropped back, the space they left instantly occupied by the waiting cavalry.

Like a burst dam, the Saex swarmed forward, daunted by the army ahead but more afeared of their own leader's wrath. With courage renewed they hurtled towards the British. Arthur's two wings increased pace to a jogtrot outpacing the centre, who held back at a steady walk.

The Saex launched their spears, the weapons humming through the air, many finding their mark. Artoriani launched their own volley with the pilum, much favoured by the legionaries of Rome, a well balanced spear with heavy shaft and light iron tip. Some inflicted wounds, but most thudded, seemingly harmless, into Saex shields. The thin, soft neck of the thing bent and caught, so it became impossible to remove and throw back -rendering a shield useless by its dragging weight.

The second volley of spears from the British bit home. Heavier weapons this time, with more intention of maiming. The paced jog increased to a hand canter, one horse's shoulder against another, shields held before the rider, swords ready. When one fell another from behind lengthened pace and took his place. No gaps, no stragglers. Within these last few yards of the enemy Cei and Meriaun took the right and left wing into the charge. Full gallop, plunging into the soft mass of men, shouting the war cry. The wings of both armies came together. Fighting was at close quarters now, mounted men against foot, the discipline of tight formation against the Saex fighting individually, each man for himself.

Hengest's Saex were thrown off balance by this onrush from the two British wings coming in on them from each side. Their centre was left exposed, helpless to aid comrades in desperate situations at the sides, aware Arthur's centre had yet to attack.

Already uncertain and apprehensive, the Saex found themselves suddenly faced with a new, overwhelming onrush of trampling hooves and slashing swords as Arthur yelled the order to move forward, his men responding instant into a gallop. The urge to drop their weapons and run spread rapidly among the faltering Saex. Some, at the rear, hearing the confusion and panic, did run, pushing their way back through the men behind. Within moments, they realised with horror that the British wings, pressing from each side, had driven their own wings inward to tangle with the centre, crippling rear movement and thrusting the Saex forward deeper into Arthur's charge. As space to manoeuvre decreased, their faltering became fear, and the fear became panic.

It was the horses which were so terrifying. Great beasts with bared teeth and trampling hooves. Hengest's men tried their best to fight the riders of these creatures, slashing with short swords and jabbing with spears, but the situation was desperate, hopeless. For each horse or rider that fell another took his place, and another.

Arthur, after the first thrill of exhilaration from the charge, settled to a steady blow-by-blow thrust. The Saex swarmed, many falling and becoming trampled by shod hooves. Faces – nameless, bearded faces with flaxen hair braided and tailed – rose and fell before him. Arthur felt something stab at his thigh, a glancing blow from one of the Saex's short swords which did no damage through the thickness of his padded bracae. He swung Eira round, the horse rising on to his hind legs, thrashing with his forefeet. His nearside hoof struck bone, split a skull wide. The unfortunate man clutched his head as blood spurted, then fell dead. Eira, unsteadied, slipped, righted himself in a flurry of thrashing legs, but not before one of Hengest's personal guard saw and took advantage.

The man was big, built like an ox, with muscled biceps, sturdy torso and thick, bulging thighs. He lunged at Arthur with his shield, the heavy bronze boss slamming into the Pendragon's shoulder. Arthur could not dodge the blow; his left arm suddenly felt numb and his useless fingers dropped his own shield. He reeled and, as Eira scrambled upright, lost his balance and tumbled from the saddle. He squirmed, landed somehow on his feet, facing this formidable giant.

It was as if there was no one else on the battlefield, just himself and this one, massive built Saex. They circled, eyeing each other, assessing the other's worth, taking note of build and balance, of height and sword reach.

Arthur was at a disadvantage through the loss of his shield, but then he was the lighter man, the less blown. And his men were winning, there was no doubt of that. His gaze flickered to the man's sword, no ordinary thing, a weapon of unequalled craftsmanship. The Saex revered their weapons, believing them to possess magical powers. For all their barbarism, Arthur admired their craftsmanship.

The numbness was easing from his shoulder, leaving a dull ache, but he had the use of his fingers again. He shuffled his torso, balancing his weight evenly, light on the balls of his feet. With both hands he gripped his own sword – a well-forged thing with a gilded hilt of bronze and silver, but not comparable with that of his opponent. Arthur suddenly desired that sword. Was going to have it.

The Pendragon's lips parted in a slow smile, widened into a fearsome look of determination, What was it he had said about prizes being won? This was one prize he would enjoy gaining! He watched the Saxon's eyes, narrow slits of brilliant blue, scowling from beneath the headpiece of the warrior's silver etched helmet. Two men, well matched.

As the Saex lunged, Arthur parried with his own sword. Sparks spat from the clash of iron. He followed through with a forceful thrust and they exchanged blows, neither giving ground, neither doing damage.

First blood to the Saex. His sword cut to the side in a feint which Arthur turned, but the Saxon's weapon was superior. It slid the length of the British blade, the honed edge slicing into the padding of the sleeve which covered Arthur's lower arm. The fabric ripped, dark blood welling with the frayed material, staining the white linen. The Saxon plunged forward, taking the advantage.

The ground beneath their feet was slippery from the night's rain and grass churned now into mud, reddening with spilt blood. Arthur swore, attacked with renewed fervour. As he struck forward, the Saxon whirled aside and Arthur spun with him, but his foot tangled with someone fighting behind, sending him tumbling to his knees.

The Saxon lifted his sword high, ready, triumphant, to smash down with the death blow. Arthur squirmed, brought his sword point up, ramming it awkwardly, praying it would make contact with flesh not mail.

With a bellow, the Saxon brought his sword down, the blade thudding into the soil a hair's breadth from Arthur's helmet, the great man toppling forward with it. Arthur kicked out, deflecting the body from falling across his own as it fell face forward, the weight driving the Pendragon's thrust sword deeper through the abdomen.

Breathing hard, Arthur rolled the dead man over, and realised he would have difficulty removing his weapon, so deeply was it embedded. He saw a glint of gold from a small jewelled dagger in the Saex's belt. As his fingers curled round the lightweight hilt, he felt the movement of air behind him. Arthur whirled, striking with the dagger, plunging it into the throat of a Saxon whose axe was plunging downwards.

Sweat trickled down Arthur's back. He swallowed, the clutch of death over-close for comfort. He wiped the blade on his sleeve, started as he recognised the decorative jewelling. He knew this thing, this light, slim-bladed weapon! A woman's dagger, but obviously prized for its quality and beauty. How in the name of Mithras had that ox got hold of Gwenhwyfar's treasured dagger? The riddle must wait. Arthur thrust the weapon into his own belt and bent to retrieve the Saxon sword.

As his hand clasped the hilt, he felt a surge of pleasure course through his body, a tingle of excitement, a sparkle of wonder. This sword was magnificent! Eyes alight, he struck at a Saxon to his left who had a British soldier down, at his mercy. The blade sliced clean through flesh and sinew, severing the warrior's head with a single blow. The reprieved victim scrambled to his feet, gabbling his thanks. Arthur turned to grapple with another of Hengest's sagging army, the sword in his hand seeming to possess a life of its own as it hewed and slashed and killed. A sword for a king. And Arthur would be king!

He saw Eira, wild eyed, close to panic without the reassurance of his rider but, for all that, standing still. Arthur grabbed the reins, ran his hand soothingly down the stallion's neck and mounted quickly. With the familiar guidance from voice and legs, the horse calmed, plunging forward at the given signal towards Hengest's swaying White Horse banner.

Hengest was fighting for his life. He recognised defeat, knew as only a matter of moments before his army threw down their weapons and fled. He looked anxiously around for Aethal, his friend and honoured warrior. Aethal was special, a brave man, husband to one of his daughters. For a while, he had commanded the fool king Vortigern's personal guard of Saex warriors, ostensibly serving alongside the nephew, Melwas, but in truth there to carry word between Hengest and his eldest daughter, Rowena.

Aethal had become separated and Hengest found himself alarmed. If it were known the mighty warrior, Aethal, had fallen, his men would never hold!

A rider was bearing down on them, cleaving his way through the close hand-to-hand fighting. The man wore a scaled hauberk, with a crimson cloak swirling from his shoulders. Hengest could not discern the face beneath the protection of the helmet, but the poise, audacity and charisma were as telling as any recognisable features.

When Hengest saw the sword Arthur wielded, his hopes died. Aethal's sword. The sword forged by the god Weyland near the crystal waters of Freya and endowed, by that same Lady, with powers of strength and endurance. No man who held that sword could be slain, it was said, save by the cunning and strength of a dragon.

Hengest groaned, let his own sword fall slack in his hand. So, the legend was true! Aethal had boasted he could best any fire-tongued beast, dared such a monster to come within range of his blade. They had all laughed, listening to his talk while gathered around Hengest's hearth, proud of Aethal and his strength, amused he had fooled Vortigern and Melwas into believing him their servant. Yet none of them had realised the hidden danger and mocking truth. It was no beast that rose superior, but a man. The Pendragon.

Hengest's Jutes had seen Arthur, recognised that flashing sword. Abandoning their weapons, demoralised, faced with the reality of defeat, they began to flee. As they ran, the cavalry surged after them, cutting them down. The tide had swept out, turning the low land between island and mainland into treacherous mudflats divided by a narrow navigable channel. A few men, weighing the risk of stinking mud or death by British sword, ran out into it, to find their feet stuck, their legs dragged down into its sucking depths. In years to come, the protruding sand bars hastened the silting up of the channel, trapped the land, which as centuries passed became reclaimed, turning Tanatus from island to promontory. A stretch of coast that would, for all time, remember the coming and defeat of Hengest.

§ L

The roar from the elated men echoed over the flat lands of the coast. The great cry was caught by the sea wind and tossed up to the scudding clouds and screaming gulls. As Arthur walked forward, dressed in parade armour with his beautiful wife at his side, the men of Britain let their jubilation explode. Victory was theirs, and they had the right to shout their loudest acclaim!

At Rutupiae all that remained of the splendid monument of triumph dedicated to the Emperor and god Claudius was its battered square base. Guarded well and displayed for all to see, Hengest stood atop its rough surface chained like a common slave. Left weary and thirsty, itching from the dust and sweat of battle, he watched Arthur approach, waited for the order of death that was surely to come. He did not mind the dying, only the manner of its making. It was nothing less than he expected, the losers were to suffer. It could as easily have been the other way around.

One thought occurred to him as he stood, head held proud, giving no sign of fear. It could have been Winifred walking there with the Pendragon. He ought to have tried the harder to secure her place as future queen, but then he had made a grave error the day he misjudged this son of Uthr. Hengest gave a grunt of self-mocking laughter. Had he not been warned to keep a wary eye beneath Arthur's masking cloak of drunken whoring? What was it he had once said of the Pendragon? A boy playing a man's game. The mistake of all men, they forgot to watch the sons growing, realising too late that the young buck had become the antlered stag.

Arthur reached the makeshift dais, leapt up and, taking her hand, helped his wife climb after him. For a moment Gwenhwyfar stared at Hengest, chained there in the centre of the massive block of white stone. She started as his unflinching eyes met with hers.

That haughty gaze, how like Winifred's! Diamond hard eyes, showing nothing beyond the ceaseless plotting and calculation of gain. He was beaten but not deterred, even seemed slightly amused.

Gwenhwyfar clung tight to her husband's arm, directed her attention to the clamouring men. Hengest had shown plainly the thought behind those eyes. I do not fear, for Cerdic, boy of my blood, is yet to come!

Arthur raised his hand for silence, the roar of acclaim fading slowly, reluctantly. Men crowded close, shoulder to shoulder, eager faces lifted to hear the words of the Pendragon. Many had waited a long time for this day's kingmaking.

When he could be heard Arthur took a step forward, cast his wide smile over the sea of faces.

'You have done well, my brothers,' he called. 'Very well! Let none say the men of Arthur lack for courage and strength! From this day, our enemies shall fear our name and tremble before our war cry!' He let them shout and cheer a while before drawing the sword from his side, lifting it so all might see its fine wonder. 'I took this sword from a Saex I killed. I cannot form my tongue around the Saex name it bears, but in our British speech, its calling would be Caliburn.' He let the men have a good, long, admiring look at its perfection. They were listening to him intently, hanging on his every word, barely a sound issuing from their lips.

'It is said by the Saex this sword has qualities of none other and it has a story behind its being. One day a man, a young warrior, was walking beside a lake. He came across a boat and paddled to the centre of that lake. There he waited until the sun and the moon had chased each other twice across the sky. And then, as dawn's finger touched the glass surface of the sleeping lake, the waters parted and a Lady arose from beneath. A beautiful woman, a goddess. She held a sword – a sword that could only have been forged on the anvil of a god. She charged this mortal to take the weapon into the world of men and to wield it until such time as the man it was made for came to take it by trial of strength. A man who was destined to be the greatest of all kings. *"That man,"* this goddess said, *"shall be a king above all kings; a man supreme, who will make the dark light, and turn the blood of war into the calm waters of peace."* '

Arthur laid the blade across his open palms, studied its superb, delicate workmanship, felt the fineness of its being against his skin. He had won his sword now had to win the men, his army, had to use his wits and get them to kneel without question. There would be arguments about the way he intended to do things, bitter disagreement from the Church and men such as his uncle Emrys, who fervently believed that Rome would soon return. He must ensure the support of this army, these ordinary men who would fight unquestioning for what he, the supreme king, decided. With them behind him, the opposition could shout to the four winds, for all the good it would do them.

'That was a story from long past and it was a tale woven by Saxons, yet here I stand before you with this sword in my hand. I fought for it and by greater strength took it for my own. Am I not, then, your King?'

They answered with spears hoisted, swords crashing against shields, and voices proclaiming for Arthur. *'Pendragon! Pendragon! Pendragon!'*

Arthur sheathed the sword, held both his hands high, quietening them.

'Na!' he countered. 'The cry shall not be for me. My cavalry are the Artoriani, but the rest of you, the foot, the militia guard and the medics; all you farriers, scouts and harness makers, shield bearers and grooms. You farmers with your scythes, and tradesmen with club or staff. The hunters with your spears. Professional soldiers or laymen – all of you are from this day of victory the defenders of our country. My army. You need, and shall have, some special name, some special title to wield in battle, a cry that reminds us and our enemies we fight together for our families, for our women and children, those born and those yet to come!'

He paused while a new burst of cheering rang out, then went on, shouting to be heard. 'We need something unique, something that is not just for me, your king, but for us all!'

He took Gwenhwyfar's hand, brought her forward, the evening sunlight flashing against the precious stones of the royal torque at her throat and the circlet of gold crowning her braided hair. Gold twining with copper. 'Many of you know the term of endearment by which I call my woman. *Cymraes.* My Lady Gwenhwyfar can trace her ancestry back to beyond the coming of Rome, to the deeper tribal blood of Britain.' He took breath. Men were listening, nodding. This they knew.

'I speak to you in Latin, the tongue of the Empire because our fathers and fathers' fathers did so. Today, despite our Roman laws and our Roman speech, we think of ourselves not as Roman but as British. Bound together, we are the Cymry, fellow native-born countrymen. This, then, shall be our call, my countrymen. We shall cry *"Cymry"!'*

They took up the challenge eagerly, and swept it straight into their hearts, as he had known they would.

'Cymry!' They shouted it over and over until it drowned the sound of the incoming tide and the shrill cries of the gulls. *'Cymry!'*

The war cry of Arthur Pendragon. The King.

Author's Note

There is very little evidence for what really happened in the hundred years or so between the going of the Romans and the dominance of Britain by the Anglo-Saxons, the English. There is a period of myth and romance, a Dark Age where knowledge has been forgotten and replaced by stories. As time has passed, these tales have become more and more distorted; events and characters exaggerated or invented. We have a few, challengeable facts and even fewer names, the best-known being Arthur and his wife Guinevere or, as I call her, Gwenhwyfar.

Whether Arthur was real or a character of fiction is not certain. We do know fifth century Britain was in turmoil, and that someone had the strength to apply organisation to the chaos. If it was not 'Arthur' there is no other legendary character to fit the gap.

My *Pendragon's Banner* trilogy is my personal view of those Dark Ages. I am not an historian; I speak no Welsh or Latin. I am not expressing fact, merely what might have been. The dates are my own interpretation, gleaned from a hotch-potch of muddled theories and chronologies. They may not tally with those proposed by the professional historian, but as virtually no date of this period can be established as absolute fact, I feel I can justify my theories.

Some few situations and people in my story are indeed fact. Vortigern lived, although this now commonly used name may then have been a title meaning something like 'overlord'. Hengest probably existed, as did Cerdic. Emrys, who fleetingly appears in Book One, is better known by his Roman name, Ambrosius Aurelianus. He did exist. Exactly when and where, is open to question, but possibly in the south. Usually he is placed before Arthur, but to my mind this is not logical, and so in this trilogy he comes after. You will discover how and why in Book Two, *Pendragon's Banner*, and in particular in Book Three, *Shadow of the King*. Cunedda and his sons are acclaimed as the founders of the Gwynedd dynasty, leading down to Llewelyn, Prince of Wales, who died fighting against Edward I of England, who then plundered Wales for his own. It is told Cunedda migrated into Gwynedd from the territory of the Votadini, which ran from modern Edinburgh down into Northumbria. Why and how and when we do not know, except, if it is true, it must have been after Rome had abandoned Britain to look to her own defence and before the firm hold of settled Anglo-Saxons. Some time, therefore, in the early fifth century.

I invented Gwenhwyfar as Cunedda's daughter because I wanted to include him in my story. Imagine my delight when, on searching through some early genealogies (which admittedly are extremely unreliable), I discovered he did have a daughter called Gwen! In all probability she was not Gwenhwyfar, wife to Arthur – but the wonderful thing about this period of history for a writer of fiction is that 'probably' cannot be proven as 'unlikely'! Any writer on these unknown Dark Ages has a free rein of imagination – although I have tried my best to keep that rein curbed within the margin of at least the plausible. For any errors, I apologise, or claim poetic licence!

As for Arthur, no one knows if he was real. A few scattered poems and early Welsh bardic tales were adopted by the twelfth century Normans who were responsible for the stories we know so well today. The knights, chivalrous deeds and the Round Table belong to this later period, as did the fictitious invention of Lancelot, his adultery with Gwenhwyfar, and Merlin the wizard. You will not find them in my tale.

Early references to Arthur do not portray him as a chivalric, benevolent king – the opposite in fact. A down-to-earth, ruthless war leader. This, then, is my Arthur. There are no court niceties in *The Kingmaking*. Legend tells of Gwenhwyfar's abduction and rape by Melwas, and of the pagan women at Glastonbury. I am not the first person to suggest Arthur may have married a daughter of Vortigern and that Cerdic may have been his son.

The tale of Gwynllyw and Gwladys's flight from her father is also an old one, complete with Arthur playing dice and lusting after her, and Cei's outraged reprimand.

For places and personal names I have often had to invent my own, or used a mixture of Latin, Welsh and English. The language my characters use would also have been one of the three tongues. On the whole, I assume Arthur and Gwenhwyfar would be talking in British (Welsh). I have, through necessity, taken one or two liberties with my use of Welsh, for which I apologise. When Arthur first gives Gwenhwyfar her 'nickname' he would probably have said something like *'fy nghymraes fach i'* ('My little Welsh woman'), which is unfortunately too ponderous for those of us who struggle with Welsh pronunciation. I have therefore settled for the more familiar *'Cymraes'*.

Some terms are blatantly out of context with the period but I have used them because they are more familiar in meaning to our modem times. For instance, 'witch'. Correctly, perhaps, I should have used 'hag', but this conjures up a picture of a bent old crone, which is not the description I wanted. It is uncertain how soon after the going of Rome the term 'king' became used. Emerging leaders at this time were perhaps war lords, overlords or supreme commanders, but I have used 'king' because it conveys a consistent meaning in our modem tongue. The terms and traditions surrounding dowries and a man's heir may also, technically, be slightly out of place, but again I stress this is primarily a novel, not a factual record.

The skirmish along the Devil's Dyke in Cambridgeshire is embroidered by my own fancy, for it is not certain when this, and similar earthworks cutting at right angles across the ancient Icknield Way, were first constructed. Some archaeologists and historians place them any time from the Roman period to as late as the seventh century. I feel the Devil's Dyke is neither Saxon nor Roman but an earlier, Celtic boundary. It seems logical that it formed a man-built 'gateway' between the natural defences of the Ouse and the Stour, dense woodland and impassable marsh. The only unprotected area into the ancient kingdom of the Iceni was the 7.5 miles intersected by the ridge along which ran the Way. Iceni artefacts have been found to the north of the Dyke, but few to the south. Therefore I believe the Devil's Dyke would already have been around 400 years old at the time when, in my tale, Arthur was grumbling about Vortigern's incompetence.

The story of Arthur taking his sword from the stone and thus becoming king is a familiar one. It has been suggested however, that during Medieval times there was a translation error of 'from a stone' *(ex saxo)* with 'from a Saxon' *(ex saxone)*. Clerks were occasionally in the habit of dropping the 'n' and putting a stroke above the next letter *(ex saxoe)* which could account for the discrepancy. Alternatively, the stone could be a reference to the sacred stones of the tribal British. Excalibur, the well known sword of legend given to Arthur by the Lady of the Lake is often confused with the one from the stone. In my story, or perhaps in this instance, Arthur's, the two have been combined.

There were indeed battles at Agealesthrep (Aylesford, Kent) and Crecganford (Crayford, Kent), though the dates are not precise. The

Cantii territory does seem to have been settled at an early date. Cantii had become Kent; the name Canterbury still echoes its British inheritance.

I have used the Arabian type horse for Arthur's mounts for no reason except I like the breed. There have been many horse bones found on Roman sites that are very similar to this distinctive horse, so my whim is not entirely fanciful – and no one is certain just how or when the Arabian features were first bred into the sturdy Welsh breed of today's ponies. I like to think this was Cunedda's doing!

It is thought there really was a massacre of Vortigern's Council; Gloucester (Caer Gloui) is renowned for flooding; and archaeologists found a Saxon broach among the broken Roman roof tiles in Londinium…

Helen Hollick
2010

CallioCrest

at the peak of traditional mainstream publishing

CallioPan

eternal youth for master writers

CalliOrum

the gold standard of fiction

CallioViva

histories of exciting lives

CallioSoph

expertise in business and education

CallioClassics

original works with cutting edge analysis

Visit our website at www.calliopress.com

Find out what's new at CallioPress
View extracts from our latest books
Check out our upcoming author events
Learn how we can put your book in to print

CallioCrest   CallioPan   CallioSoph   CallioViva   CallioClassics   CalliOrum

The Callio Press Limited	Entelyx International Inc.
Registered Address	Registered Address
Suite 6 37 Great Russell Street	555 Fifth Avenue N.E. Suite 343
London WC1B 3PP UK	St Petersburg Florida 33701 USA
Company no. 07234475	EIN 20-0766623

www.calliopress.com